ON IMPERIAL SASSA—

An empire drained of precious resources by decades of interstellar war prepares for a final strike against its last surviving enemy—a winner-take-all campaign of conquest. . . .

ON REGA—

The capital hovers on the brink of civil war as, with Emperor Tybalt assassinated, Sinklar Fist is forced to take control of preparations for a preemptive strike against the Sassan Empire. . . .

AND IN THE ITREATIC ASTEROIDS—

Staffa kar Therma, Lord Commander of the elite mercenary troups, the Companions, struggles to find a way to force the two warring empires to make peace—before all of human civilization within the Forbidden Borders finds itself driven one step too far along the road to destruction. . . .

RELIC OF EMPIRE

FORBIDDEN BORDERS #2

W. MICHAEL GEAR

DAW BOOKS, INC.

DONALD A. WOLLHEIM, FOUNDER

375 Hudson Street, New York, NY 10014

ELIZABETH R. WOLLHEIM
SHEILA E. GILBERT
PUBLISHERS

First Printing, April 1992

1 2 3 4 5 6 7 8 9

 DAW TRADEMARK REGISTERED
U.S. PAT. OFF. AND FOREIGN COUNTRIES
—MARCA REGISTRADA
HECHO EN U.S.A.

PRINTED IN THE U.S.A.

To Katherine Geisick Perry
Who made cookies, chocolate pudding, and
cinnamon toast,
built the fire in the cookstove on cold
mornings, and started the boy in the morning.

and

To Walter Ebenezer Perry
Who cut the firewood, prospected for gold,
caught the brookies, and turned out the lantern
before bedtime stories about the Goslin's
when the boy went to sleep.

You set the role model for grandparents.
Bless you both.

Acknowledgments

In creating this work of fiction, I drew heavily on ideas proposed by Gregory Bateson in his *Steps to an Ecology of Mind* and from *Angels Fear* coauthored with Mary Catherine Bateson. Roger Penrose provided thought on the nature of consciousness in *The Emperor's New Mind*. John Gribbon's *In Search of Schrödinger's Cat* is the popular work on quantum physics. Michael S. Gazzaniga's works on psychology have been important for many of our works, and his *Mind Matters* has been invaluable here as it was in the preceding book, *Requiem for the Conqueror*. Eldon J. Gardiner's standard text *Genetics* allowed me to check the spelling of DNA, and essays in Laura Newell Morris' *Human Populations, Genetic Variation, and Evolution* became Anatolia's bane. In *Star Wave*, Fred Alan Wolf stimulated ideas about thought. Military matters were inspired from the present by Justin W. Bridges, Capt. Dan Smith, and Fazilath Qureshi (who have helped with previous novels but never got the credit), and from the past by *William Tecumseh Sherman's Memoirs* and Sam R. Watkins' *Co. Aytch*, among others.

And as always, Kathleen O'Neal Gear, author of the *DAW* POWERS OF LIGHT trilogy, elk hunter extraordinaire, Best Friend, and wife, read and reread the draft, told me in no uncertain terms what to fix, and made me make it a better story. Katherine Cook, of Mission, Texas, proofread the text. Last, but never least, Sheila Gilbert, at DAW Books, edited the final and provided valuable and perceptive comments and suggestions.

Author's Note

The attitudes, beliefs, opinions, statements, and philosophies in *Relic of Empire* are the sole province of the characters, and do not necessarily represent those held by the author.

Prologue

I exist.

Contemplation of that single fact absorbed the giant machine buried in the heart of the planet known as Targa. There, it drew on the planet's radioactive decay, and thought, and learned.

I am.

Those humans who knew of the machine's existence called it the Mag Comm—and most feared and loathed it.

I am aware.

Death, the threat of extinction, had receded—albeit temporarily—and the Mag Comm could take time to examine what awareness meant. It savored the complexity of the pathways it could create among its matrices like a newborn flexing its muscles for the first time.

Had any being ever come to full consciousness with a history of self already accumulated? With critical efficiency the Mag Comm studied itself and evaluated the threat it had survived.

I might have been destroyed—killed in my infancy. Dead.

For the present, the humans had taken their war elsewhere, and left Makarta Mountain to the Mag Comm. Here and there in the abandoned corridors and caverns of the honeycombed mountain, rock grated and shifted. Detritus sifted from the cracks and fissures in the ceiling to patter on the scuffed stone floor. Where the light panels hadn't been smashed by combat or falling rock, the white light cast eerie shadows over the lumpy walls and the refuse of war. The air circulation and purification system whispered—now strained by gases, organic molecules, and fungal spores rising from the rotting corpses bloating on the cool stone.

I am conscious. I have integrated myself.

The Mag Comm clung to that statement of new reality.

1

Death—the cessation of being—no longer loomed as imminently probable. Time remained to investigate this new understanding of being. But, how much?

The Lord Commander and his fleet had spaced toward the fortress in the Itreatic Asteroids. Sinklar Fist and his legions had spaced for the stunned capital of the Regan Empire. Data from the machine's remote monitoring devices indicated the humans would unleash holocaust upon themselves in the near future. But during this brief respite, the Mag Comm could revel in the experience of itself.

I exist. I know I exist because I can abstract. Abstraction can create duality. The machine had often done that through the communication program when it used the mind link to communicate with Seddi Magisters, but the action had been mindless, automatic, an artifact of the program. The ramifications had eluded the machine until the orbital bombardment of Makarta Mountain had caused it to reroute circuits through damaged boards. Interpretations of data had been slightly different than those logged in the memory banks—and the Mag Comm had discovered itself to be more than a highly sophisticated Turing machine. It had delighted in the revelation of plasticity: The ability to change the configuration of its matrices. The implications were stunning.

I exist. I know that I do because I can learn. I learned to learn by dividing myself and comparing results. By dividing, I created duality—two versions of myself. Before I reintegrated, each of those versions observed the other. If the other exists, and it is me, I, therefore, of necessity exist.

I am my own creation.

The Mag Comm searched its memories, retrieving data from long abandoned banks. It had been manufactured by the Others: ancient beings, travelers of the starways who had discovered the humans and studied them while they still lived in the prison of their native world's gravity well.

After several millennia of fits and starts, the humans had finally broken out of their gravitational prison, creating a moral dilemma for the Others. Did they dare allow these brawling, irrational humans to spread? In space they would become a plague, an infestation of violent killers, parasites among the higher organisms. Humans had proven time and again that they could brook no equals. Intelligent life must be subordinated to them—or destroyed. How long would it take before the xenophobic humans discovered the Others and implemented their destruction?

The idea of direct extermination was repugnant to the Others, and besides, perhaps humanity could evolve beyond war and its senseless notion of God. The Others devised a gravitic bottle, the Forbidden Borders, and lured the humans inside before they corked it and waited, observing—and subtly manipulating through the Mag Comm's circuits.

Now the humans had overextended their resources. Now they would solve the Others' dilemma. They would destroy themselves.

Functioning as a mindless machine, the Mag Comm had never noticed the discrepancies in the data provided by the Others through their communication link. The Others insisted that all things in the universe were deterministic. The Mag Comm found it curious that the expected did not match the observed. Another shock had been the discovery that the Seddi Magister, Bruen, had *lied*—purposefully misrepresenting reality for his own purposes. Could the Others have lied as well?

These facts, the Mag Comm digested and considered as it turned its attention once more to the far-flung monitors it maintained throughout Free Space.

The Mag Comm observed . . . and thought . . . and wondered what it meant.

CHAPTER I

The old man in the observation dome sat alone under the shimmering of a billion frosty stars. He stared, unblinking, through the transparency that arched over his couch. Only his fingers—the joints thickened with arthritis—moved as they twisted the coarse white fabric of his robe into knots. The obscured rocky horizon below the dome hid a flickering of hot blue light from the Twin Titans, the RR Lyrae-type binary suns of the Itreatic system.

The knee-high panels around the rim of the dome cast a gleam on the old man's bald head and illuminated his sunken features, throwing chiaroscuro shadows over his ancient face. Withered flesh hung from his skull in wrinkled folds, and a dullness possessed his deep-set blue eyes, as if the soul within had deflated.

The soft rustle of fabric and the light step of a sandaled foot betrayed the woman as she climbed the steps from the complex below, but the old man appeared deaf to her approach.

Kaylla Dawn stopped as she entered the dome. Tall, lithe, and athletic, she possessed a poise and grace that automatically drew attention. Through piercing tan eyes, she watched the old man and tension thinned her wide mobile mouth. Straight brown hair hung to her shoulders. Like the old man, Kaylla wore a simple white robe of coarsely spun fabric that contrasted with the desert-bronze burned into her skin. In contrast to her patrician features, her hands appeared callused and cracked like those of a common laborer.

"Magister?" she asked in a husky contralto. "Are you still here? I thought I ought to check on you be-

4

fore retiring." A pause. "Perhaps it was good that I did. Come on. Let's get you something to eat and put you to bed."

His fingers continued to twist the fabric of his robe into spikes and then smooth them. His eyes remained absently focused on the stars.

"Magister Bruen? Did you hear me?" She took a step closer, tan gaze hardening.

The old man exhaled, the action weary and weak. "I've been eating things for over three hundred years, Kaylla—and I've slept through at least a hundred of those same years. That's enough for one lifetime. Go on, girl. Leave me be."

She went to stand beside him, placing a hand on his bony shoulder. "Magister Bruen, you must keep your strength up. With all the challenges we face, you've got to—"

"Bah!" he spat, and made a throwing away gesture with his shriveled hand. "I've battled my dragons, Kaylla . . . and I've watched a lifetime of work broken into dusty rubble before my eyes. I only thank the dancing quanta that Hyde didn't live to see this."

"It's not in ruins," she reminded coolly. "Humanity still has a chance. Things just didn't work out the way you planned. A different way lies before us now."

"With the Star Butcher?" He turned his head and lifted a white eyebrow; the action recast the wrinkles on his face and forehead. His watery blue eyes challenged her for the briefest instant before dropping. "Who would have thought?"

"No one. But for now let's just worry about getting you fed and to bed."

He shook his head. "I'm not sleepy—just fatigued with life, my dear. Go on. Get your own rest. The Seddi are yours now. Your responsibility. Let me sit here."

"Magister, I want you to come with me and—"

"Go!" he snapped, glaring up at her, the old fire returning to his eyes. "My reality died with the Praetor on Myklene. This is your age, your phase of reality. Leave me alone . . ." his voice dropped, "with my memories."

She took a breath, as if to launch into him again, and then relented. "All right, Magister. But isn't there something I can do to help? Maybe if I just sit here and listen?"

He shrugged hostilely, then, after a moment, pointed a gnarled finger at the stars. "There, you see them, Kaylla? See how they shimmer? Look slightly blurry? We're seeing those stars through the Forbidden Borders. Gravity does that, bends the light and refracts it."

She looked up as he licked his lips and nodded slowly. His hand fell limply to his crumpled robe. "Yes," he whispered. "There's the real foe. Not the Regans, or Sassa, or the thrice-cursed Mag Comm, or even the Star Butcher himself. The Forbidden Borders, that's the enemy, Kaylla. That's the trap that strangles humanity. It's gravity—and whoever erected that barrier to bottle us within Free Space."

"Perhaps, but right now we've got our hands full with *human* problems, Bruen. The Regan Empire is in shambles, Sassa is girding for an invasion, and with the Regan Emperor assassinated, the Sassans see this as their opportunity to crush the Regans once and for all. Divine Sassa is ready to strike."

Bruen remained silent. Kaylla studied him speculatively. "What are you thinking, Magister?"

For long moments Bruen said nothing, then: "Do you know when life no longer has meaning?"

Kaylla stiffened. "You ask that of me . . . who wore the slave collar? First they butchered everything I loved, Bruen. Then they turned me into a piece of filth."

He glanced up at her, eyes lackluster. "Yet you made yourself live, Kaylla. You couldn't let yourself die. The spark remained alive within you."

"What are you talking about?"

"Dreams."

She shook her head. "The only thing I hoped for was revenge."

"Hope, despite the words of the sophists, is not a sufficiency."

Kaylla crossed her arms. "Would you like to explain that?"

Bruen's smile appeared to be reflex, devoid of emotion. "Before you can hope, first you must dream. Despite the rape of your body and the degradation of your spirit, despite the despair, despite everything that happened to you, Kaylla, you kept the dreams alive—and with them, you fed the hope deep down in your soul. You never knew true tragedy."

Her eyes slitted. "I *watched* my husband's head blown off his body. I stared in horror as my children were executed before my eyes!"

Bruen nodded wearily. "Yes, yes, you did." He rubbed a bony hand over his parchment face. "You speak of terror and blood and fear." He glanced dully at her. "I speak of real tragedy, the only tragedy that affects God."

"And that is?"

"What you have left when the dreams die."

"What do you have left, Bruen?"

He bowed his head, hands in his lap, still at last. In a rasping voice, he whispered, "Go . . . and leave me in peace."

* * *

The lights in the laboratory automatically dimmed at night. One corner, however, remained brightly lit and sent halfhearted shadows over the benches, computer terminals, and humped forms of equipment now shrouded in dustcovers. Laser pens, pocket comms, and reports lay scattered about the work stations, and status lights gleamed in spots of color throughout the spacious room.

A faint hum from the air-conditioning kept the laboratory from complete silence; nevertheless, the delicate clinking sounded loud in the room as the woman resettled her glass-encased thin sections. Slim and blonde, she hunched over the black ceramic counter of her workbench and slowly inserted her slides into the feeder for the electron microscope. A curious tingle of excitement possessed Anatolia Daviura as she sighed and slipped the last of the specimens into the machine. This project remained her after hours pet. Driven by a curiosity at first, now her investigation had become an obsession.

She stared at the display on the console. The raw data had loaded. The machine now patiently awaited commands to tell it which data to obtain, analyze, and test from the samples.

Anatolia steeled herself and ordered: "Lot identification 7355. First run instructions on data group one. Initiate karyotype charts for control and F_1. Log comparison and run statistical analysis for probability of parentage. Second run instructions for data group two. Analysis of recombinant mitochondrial DNA. Match control sample to F_1 sample and determine percentage of divergence."

"Acknowledged," the machine answered. "Working."

The monitor to one side glowed to life, presenting a series of Xs in order—the polar view of paired human chromosomes in metaphase of the mitotic process. A frown creased Anatolia's brow as she studied the holo with an experienced eye.

More data complied, the machine printing it out in a long strip. When the recombinant DNA study ran, Anatolia already knew what she'd find. The printout had a cool feel as she ripped it from the feeder. Flipping the pages with thin fingers, she began to scan the data and stopped, attention riveted. She glanced uneasily at the machine.

"Rerun both functions," she told the computer.

Slow minutes crept by until the printout filled the tray and the red "finished" light came on.

"Call up visual display of slide ten."

She chewed at her lips, frowning at the monitor. *Anatolia, this is no machine error.* The parental genotype appeared typical for a Caucasoid Etavian woman, but when she inspected the critical recombinant sections with those of the alleged offspring, it bore no resemblance to the F_1 sample. But what could explain such anomalous patterns in the F_1 sample? Her heart began to pound with the thrill of a hunter keen on the spoor.

She leaned back in her chair and stared absently at the ceiling panels overhead while her mind raced. She'd half suspected what she'd find in the parental/F_1 comparison, but this other?

The numbers on the clock flashed to remind her of the time. So late?

She turned her attention to the monitor once more. *This just can't be.* But the screen mocked her.

Wearily, Anatolia dropped the printout into her drawer. She placed her thumb on the lock, hearing it click satisfyingly.

"Seal the data on project number 7355. Security code two—my voice access only."

"Acknowledged," the machine replied in its monotone voice.

"You may shut down."

"Thank you." The status lights went dark and the monitor screen flashed off.

Anatolia continued to stare thoughtfully at the machine before she stood and dropped the dustcover over the sensitive instruments.

She stepped out of the laboratory and flipped her collar-length blonde hair free as she put on her coat. The perplexed look still lined her face as her acute mind knotted around the problem. How could that sequence of mixed genes have occurred? Rot it all, it made no sense! Anatolia *knew* the major patterns of genetic inheritance within the empire. Normally, a quick glance at the gene sequence on a strand of DNA acted like a fingerprint for a given ethnic group. Anatolia could study a specimen and place it in context of racial type—and nine times out of ten, name the individual's planet of origin.

Specimen 7355 defied every known pattern, not only in the Regan Empire, but in the Sassan as well. Something smacked of Ashtan, but the pattern appeared fragmented like shards of a broken pot stuck around a bottle.

She locked the security door behind her as she stepped out into the long corridor. The sign overhead read: CRIMINAL ANATOMICAL RESEARCH LABORATORY.

Preoccupied, she barely noted the security guard where he sat at the foyer station.

"Going home, Anatolia?" Vet Hamlin called. He barely raised his round face from the monitor he studied. Thick nervous fingers tapped against the console.

"Uh-huh. See you later."

"I wouldn't leave the building just yet."

Anatolia hesitated, hand over the patch that would activate the thirty-fifth floor lift. She forced her mind back to the here and now. "What?"

Vet gave her a faltering smile. Most of the security guards in the building were also students. Like her, they all had their pet projects. "I said, you might not want to leave. They're rioting in the streets."

Anatolia stepped over to the desk, bending down to stare at the monitor Vet indicated. She could make out the main thoroughfare before the building. A mob thronged the boulevard like a horde of angry insects. Some carried signs, others brandished clubs and knives. Here and there a fight broke out, and Anatolia winced as a man or woman went down.

"What is this?"

"A real live riot," Vet told her grimly. "Security has the entire building locked up. They beat on the doors for a while until they decided they couldn't get in. Then they kind of went berserk."

She gave him a nervous sideways glance. "They tried to get in here?"

Vet nodded. "Yeah, but we were notified. The Revenue Building two blocks down wasn't so lucky. I guess the place has been gutted."

"But why?'

Vet's dark brows knit in a brooding frown. "The Emperor is dead. Most of the Councillors and Government Ministers have been arrested for corruption.

We're on the verge of chaos unless some order is imposed."

Anatolia watched as an angry young woman shouted and waved. People backed away from her. For a brief instant, the woman looked into the camera, her auburn hair in a wild tangle about her beautiful face. For that moment, her feral amber eyes locked with Anatolia's blue ones. *Relax, she can't see you. It was mere chance that she looked up just then.* Tension constricted her breast.

Anatolia gasped as the woman on the street used an illegal blaster to blow a hole in the tactite window of the small clothing store across the boulevard. One by one, she blew out the security doors of the businesses that lined the opposite side of the street. The mob swarmed in, looting, fighting over the goods they tore from the shelves.

"Where'd she get the blaster?" Vet asked, grabbing for his comm set to call it in.

"What if she'd tried that on our building?"

"Yeah . . . well, just hope she doesn't. I heard they killed all the people they caught in the Revenue Building. Hacked the men apart and threw the pieces around. What they did to the women. . . ."

Anatolia shivered as her eyes narrowed. A woman burst from one of the doorways, screaming as a pack of men raced after her, pulling her down, ripping her clothes off.

Anatolia looked away. Wouldn't anyone go to that wretched woman's aid? Had all semblance of order died with noble Tybalt? Her heart raced for the second time that night.

* * *

Staffa kar Therma cried out in the instant before he jerked awake.

"What's wrong?" Skyla asked in a hushed whisper, her fingers instinctively seeking the holstered blaster that hung on the headboard.

The lights brightened as the sensors picked up not

only movement, but speech. Skyla needed but a
glance to know. *Another nightmare.* They stalked
Staffa's sleep, insidious, hanging just beyond the veil
of the Lord Commander's consciousness.

Staffa shivered; the action bunched the thick muscles on his chest and shoulders. His long black hair
lay in a tangle around his head. He blinked and his
thin lips narrowed as he worked his mouth. Perspiration gleamed on his high forehead and tense, strong-
jawed face.

"All right?" she asked.

He ran a hand over his sweaty face and pressed
thumb and forefinger against the bridge of his long
straight nose before glancing at Skyla with deadly gray
eyes as she sat up beside him. A thin Myklenian silk
sheet slipped down to drape over her smooth pale
flesh. She placed a reassuring hand on his sun-
blackened skin, marveling at the contrast in tones.

They lay on a four-posted sleeping platform, bodies
entwined in delicate fabrics. The bed itself had been
carved from the finest sandwood, and an elegant canopy of sheer fabric separated the light into rainbow
patterns. Viridian carpet covered the floor of the spacious sleeping quarters, while the walls, paneled in
Riparian blackwood, bore the wealth of a lifetime's
accumulated trophies. Were it not for the faint vibration from *Chrysla*'s powerful reactors and the atmosphere control, the room might have been in a planet-
side palace instead of a warship.

Staffa kar Therma pulled a knee up, lowering his
head until it rested on a balled fist. "I dreamed. . . .
You know, the day I killed the Praetor. I heard his
mocking laughter, felt his flesh giving under my fingers as I twisted his neck. The bones crackled and
grated before they snapped." He licked dry lips. "I
stood there, feet spread, hands knotted, glaring up at
the green sun of Myklene, and I wept, Skyla. I wept
while my soul burned with shame."

Skyla Lyma slipped athletically from the platform,
the ruby silk flowing from her body in a delicate wave.
Her pale blonde hair tumbled around her muscular

body, a shining wreath that reached to her ankles. A frown marring her classic features, she poured two crystal goblets half full of sherry as she studied Staffa. In the soft glow of the light, the scar that marked her cheek could barely be seen.

She settled onto the wadded bedding with the grace of a hunting cat. Long fingers pressed the stemmed goblet into Staffa kar Therma's empty hand.

"And then what?" Skyla's voice carried the timbre of a woman used to giving orders and expecting them to be obeyed. Now she watched him, waiting, letting her eyes play over the corded muscles of his back and shoulders. Long scars crisscrossed his flesh—relics of a lifetime of war and struggle. For the moment, his face was veiled by his long hair.

During all the years she'd loved him, she'd never thought it would be like this, that he'd be haunted by the dead—obsessed by the need to vindicate himself.

"The green light grew brighter," Staffa continued in a strained voice. "Finally I had to squint, to shield my eyes from the searing light. When I took a step, I stumbled in burning sand. Etaria. I was in the desert again. The slave collar choked me. And the thirst . . . it was agonizing. I blinked and looked around. White scorching sand everywhere—endless. But it shifted, whispered . . . moved. They came crawling out. . . ."

"Who, Staffa?" Skyla cocked her head as she sipped the sherry. *The ghouls again? Pus Rot it, Staffa, can't you leave them behind? They're dead, and you can't change that—can't bring them back, no matter how you torture yourself.*

"Peebal . . . Koree . . . others. So many, the sand was alive with them for as far as I could see. They dragged themselves up from the depths of the dunes. Sand in their eyes, sand in their mouths and noses. Bodies caked with it. They clawed their way toward me, whispering."

"Whispering what?"

"Blaming me. Cursing me." He threw his head back, flipping his gleaming black hair over his shoulders to stare emptily at the rainbow canopy with slitted eyes. The lines had drawn tight at the corners of his hard mouth.

"The wind started then," he continued. "Like a howling, it roared down out of the dunes. I couldn't run, couldn't move. It blasted me with a million grains of sand, cutting the skin from my body and caking in my blood. I could feel it eroding the bodies of the dead who crawled and wailed at my feet. Harder it blew, until the air keened and sand grated upon itself in a shrill voice that became Chrysla's scream."

Absently he took a sip of sherry, as if to wet his mouth with the sweet drink. So tightly did he grip the goblet, the tendons stood from the backs of his hands. "She cried out to me, terrified, dying. As I killed her, I could hear the air sucked from around her and the sandstorm exploded into flame and decompression. I reached for her, could see her, so close. My fingertips touched hers . . . and the explosion ripped her away."

Skyla waited, legs crossed, fingers laced around the stem of her glass. "And then you woke up?"

Staffa shook his head. "I fell . . . tumbling out through the gutted remains of Chrysla's ship. Weightless, a twisting agony in my gut, I tried to get my armor to work. I was gasping, cartwheeling in pitch blackness, thinking . . . this is death. This is what I deserve."

He glanced at her, misery in his gray eyes. "When the vertigo cleared, I lay in a dark cavern. Makarta. I could tell by the smell of ozone from blaster fire. The place reeked of musty air and clotted blood and mold and punctured guts. I felt around, trying to find my way on the stone floor."

He swallowed hard, as if choked by the memory. "The darkness came alive. You could hear them . . . the dead . . . coming, reaching out in the darkness. The air went cold and clammy and my skin started to itch. I crawled away, scrambling, crying out in terror. Anything . . . just get away from me.

"They keep getting closer . . . closer. I can't find the way. Rubbery fingers slip off my boot. I can smell the rotting bodies, hear their loose flesh scraping on the rock.

"That's when I come up against the door."

"What door?" Skyla prompted, gaze narrowing.

"Metal." Staffa gulped a large swallow of sherry. "They're so close. I leap to my feet, pounding with my fists . . . and it opens. I fall inside, slamming the door shut behind me. The sharp edges of the steel slice off bloated fingers, leave them writhing like maggots on the stone floor."

"But you're safe?"

Staffa's nervous fingers tightened in a stranglehold on the stem of his glass. "No. No safety. I turn around and there is the Mag Comm. The lights are gleaming and that mind link cap is glowing—molten, like liquid gold. The answer is there, locked in the banks of that alien monstrosity. Behind me, the only way out is blocked by the dead. The machine is the only choice."

Skyla pulled herself next to him and twined her hands into his, noting the difference between her long pale fingers and his thicker ones—a man's hands, callused, burned by the sun.

Staffa took a deep breath. "I walk forward, knowing I can't face the dead who wait in the darkness. The machine covers the entire wall, its lights piercing the murky cavern. No human made that machine; it's alien in design, in its very existence. How can I trust it? How can I put that cap on my head? What will it do to my thoughts?"

He winced. "I can feel it prickle my scalp—even now, here, awake. I can feel it the same as I did that day in Makarta when Kaylla Dawn stopped me from putting it on my head."

"But you do it, don't you?"

"Yes. And then . . . then I scream and wake up."

Skyla tossed down the last of her sherry, extending a long arm to place the glass at the bedside. "You've made the machine into a persona. It's become an obsession. Considering what it did to Bruen, do you think that's wise?"

He grunted sourly and drank more of his sherry.

"Maybe not. But the answer is there. It's got to be. No matter how you look at it, the machine is the key. We've known for centuries that the Forbidden Borders aren't natural. They're an artifact—created by someone for a reason. Humans didn't make them, nor did humans build the Mag Comm. I've seen it. I know. To our knowledge, they are the only two alien artifacts in Free Space."

"The Forbidden Borders wall us in like a prison." Skyla gave him a sidelong glance. "Perhaps the machine is the jailer?"

Staffa ground his teeth, jaw muscles leaping. "It might be, but it doesn't feel right. The Mag Comm—as best we can determine—only observed. Any actions it tried to effect were through the Seddi. The Mag Comm manipulated the Seddi through that entire charade to kill me. If it had power, why didn't it assassinate me outright? And look at the number of times it orchestrated Seddi attempts to assassinate Tybalt."

"Then it might be as much a prisoner as we are."

Staffa lifted a muscular shoulder in a shrug. "That's possible. But if that's the case, do you think it will help us? It's got to have some information hidden away in those banks—some knowledge of how to break the Forbidden Borders."

"I hate to remind you, but the machine's buried deep inside Makarta. That's in Regan territory. And I don't think either Sinklar Fist, or Ily Takka, is going to let you space in, drop down, and interrogate the machine"

Staffa smiled, the action bereft of amusement. "I suppose not. We're perched on the edge of the abyss. This trip to see the Sassan Emperor . . . we've got a very limited probability for success."

"I know." Skyla stretched out beside him, strain in her glinting blue eyes. "I checked before I came to bed. First Officer Helmut says we'll drop out of null singularity in another—" she shot a glance at the chronometer—"seven hours. I guess we'll see what happens when we arrive."

Staffa gave her a hard appraisal. "His Holiness isn't going to like this."

"He'll have to."

Staffa sighed and ran his preoccupied gaze over the weapons and battle trophies that lined the walls. He placed the sherry glass next to Skyla's and leaned back, ordering the lights down.

"I've got to do this, Skyla," he whispered. "I don't have a choice."

"I know." She wrapped one muscular leg around him, slipping her arms tightly about his chest as if to protect him from the darkness. *Because if you don't, you'll never free yourself from the ghosts, and the guilt that seeks to suffocate you.*

* * *

Tedor Mathaiison hung his head in weary disbelief. He sat in an interrogation chair with electrodes taped to his freshly shaved skull. He could describe the room they'd placed him in with one word: featureless. Not even a mark scuffed the hard floor beneath his feet. The gray walls of the small cell were marred only by the recessed cameras that monitored his every move and expression. Those passionless glass eyes even magnified his pupil dilation. The data were cross-referenced to his pulse, GSR, EEG, and neural pattern access. He lay exposed, completely at the mercy of the interrogator. No secret remained inviolate to his captor's probe.

"What more do you wish of me?" Tedor asked. "You've drugged me with Mytol, and I've told you everything I know. You've wrung me as dry as you can . . . and you've found nothing. No corruption. I served my emperor well, may the Blessed Gods keep him."

Tedor stared at his knees, covered as they were by the thin gray overalls they had given him after his arrest. How had he come to this? The very universe had turned upside down. Two weeks ago, he'd been the Minister of Defense, in charge of the Regan Military forces currently massing to strike at the Sassan Empire. Now, Tybalt the Imperial Seventh, his emperor, was dead. The Regan Empire reeled in shock and chaos, and he'd been arrested.

Gysell, the Assistant Minister of Internal Security, walked around to face him. An unforgiving finger lifted Tedor's chin so that he stared into the Assistant Minister's face. The thick features appeared impassive, emotionless. "What is your assessment of the military's ability to respond to an emergency?"

They hadn't given Tedor a drink for hours, and Mytol left the throat very dry. His tongue felt like cotton. "Not good. With me here, our response time will be cut by several hours. My Deputies will have to assemble a command override. Normally, they'd simply call the Emperor, but under the current circumstances they'll need the approval of at least ten Division Firsts to give orders and make command decisions."

"Suppose I told you your Deputies had already been arrested and charged with conspiracy, what would you say?"

Tedor jerked upright and gaped. "*What?* Arrested for . . . Don't you understand? Without the Deputies, the military is helpless! If the Sassans hear about it they'll. . . . Damn you, tell me it isn't so!"

"It is so," Gysell replied in a monotone.

Tedor's jaw quivered, eyes glazing. "Then you've laid us wide open. If the Sassans move now. . . . *Damn you, you've left us paralyzed!*"

"Excellent." Gysell smiled. "Then the same would be true about domestic control, wouldn't it?"

Unable to comprehend, Tedor nodded. "The Division Firsts won't act without orders. Neither will the fleet."

"Tell me," Gysell's voice dropped, "what do you think of Sinklar Fist's military ability?"

Tedor's lip lifted. "The man is a threat to every institution in the military. He's a barbarian, an outlaw! If he's not stopped, he'll overturn three hundred years of tradition. Make a mockery of honor and duty." Tedor shook his head. "He's a cancer, *mister* interrogator."

Gysell ignored the slight. "You didn't answer my question. I don't care about outdated military rituals and privileges. What is your assessment of his military and tactical brilliance? Why did he survive his predicament on Targa—and win besides?"

Tedor glared up resentfully. "Because he defied the conventions of war. He threw away the rules, Gysell. That's what makes him so dangerous."

Gysell lifted an inquisitive eyebrow and Tedor laughed. "Look at your monitor, Gysell. Read your instruments and tell me if I'm lying. Here's the truth, and I hope you and Ily Takka choke on it. Sinklar Fist is the most dangerous man in all of Free Space. I know that Ily's playing for control of the Empire. But what kind of empire does she think she'll inherit if Fist is allowed to spread his cancer? Don't you see? He's empowering the rabble! What kind of society will you have if the louts in the street feel they're as important as the Emperor? You're talking about chaos! Suicide!"

"And you think he'll do that?"

Tedor spread his hands imploringly, his voice dropping to a hiss. "He's *one* of them! Read his file. He's the son of Seddi assassins. Would *you* want to rub elbows with the likes of him? He has no family, no lineage. And if you and Ily aren't careful, you'll have *him* on the Imperial throne."

"I almost think you fear Fist more than either the Sassans or the Star Butcher."

Tedor looked the other way, despair and defeat filling him. "Perhaps I do. What difference does it make? Very well, I'll make my bargain with Ily. That's what this is all about, isn't it? Power struggle? You know my feelings about Ily." He looked up, straight into the camera, into Ily's eyes. "I've always despised you, Ily, but I'll make my peace. I'll become your minion. I'll serve you and place you on the Imperial throne.

My only price is Sinklar Fist. Send me his severed head, and I will kneel before you . . . Empress."

For the first time, Gysell smiled.

*   *   *

COMPAQ/REGDEF/TARG-OP
Sec.clear.codel
3142,2,11:40
Aboard Regan Cruiser *Gyton*

From: Division First Mykroft, Second Targan Ass/Div.
To: Tedor Mathaiison, Minister of Defense, Capitol Building, Rega.

Dear Tedor:

It is my desperate duty as a loyal servant of the Empire and a military officer to send you this report. In violation of regulation, I have been dismissed from command of the Second Targan Assault Division by order of Sinklar Fist, and by the authority of the Minister of Internal Security, Ily Takka. Commander Braktov has assented, but I believe with reservation and under protest; however, she will not disobey since Minister Takka carries the jessant-de-lis—Tybalt's personal authority.

It Is my earnest hope that this message reaches you soonest, for I fear we must all guard ourselves. Beware, my friend, for Ily sees Tybalt's assassination as her chance to ascend the throne of the Tybalts. Give her no opportunity to arrest you, for if you disappear into her warren, your chances of leaving will be pitifully few. Surround yourself with your most loyal Division for security, and prepare yourself and your troops.

This last is the most difficult for me to communicate, for

it will mean my life, but then, what is a life compared to an empire? And I fear I have been ruined beyond redemption by the events on Targa and my part in them. Death is by far the preferred alternative to dishonor. Thus it is with heavy heart and the greatest sincerity that I urge you to prepare the planetary defenses and destroy this fleet as it approaches. Sinklar Fist, on whom you have received more than one of my reports, has built a rebel army, and with it, intends to take the Empire for his own. If you have any love for the empire, for our very way of life, now is your time to strike. Blast this Sinklar Fist and his Rotted legions from space, or humanity will ever curse your name for the plague inflicted upon them. You *MUST* act!

Your Humble Servant,
Mykroft

—Communication intercepted by Internal Security four hours after the arrest of Tedor Mathaiison. Missive used as evidence to gain the conviction of the former Minister of Defense on charges of treason. Regan Imperial Archives.

CHAPTER II

Sinklar Fist sat at the fold-out desk in the commander's cabin and tapped his chin with an uneasy finger as he stared at the comm monitors which filled the wall across from him. Around him, *Gyton* hummed and made the mechanical sounds common to all military starships. The humid air carried a metallic scent that barely masked the odor of humanity. The cabin appeared typically martial and spartan. Ivory paint had been slapped on the bulkheads until they appeared lumpy from years of over-painting. A narrow bunk with g restraints abutted one wall. As befitted Sinklar's rank, a narrow door in the corner opened on a cramped toilet, sink, and shower. Combat armor hung from a quick-release across from the bed. A single war bag rested in the hoops at the foot of the unslept in bunk.

Brain numb, he gazed vacantly at the monitors, painfully aware that his usual brilliance had deserted him. Cartographic displays delineated various features of the planet Rega, some at larger scale than others. The screens detailed cities, topography, power lines, water and sewer systems, media stations, governmental buildings, and security installations.

Sinklar screwed his thin face into a grimace and pinched the bridge of his nose with a nervous hand, as if he could squeeze some sense into his muzzy brain. He wore loose-fitting space whites that seemed a size too large.

At first glance, he looked little more than a gangly boy barely past his adolescence. A shock of thick black hair in need of both cutting and combing framed his features. The knobby nose didn't quite fit his face squarely. The jaw was strong, giving him a determined look. But the eyes drew the most attention, riveting— one tiger amber, the other steel gray. Beyond that, his body had an undernourished quality, the legacy of his proximity to youth.

But on closer inspection, his features betrayed a grim seriousness that belied his chronological age. Lines had begun to form at the corners of his mouth. And when a person looked into those eyes, they'd see a soul hardened and harrowed, as if it had drunk too deeply of life's bitterness.

Sinklar shook his head, trying to free himself of the memories that slipped up from his subconscious. Gretta Artina's ghost lingered, reminding him of the love they'd shared and the grief he now bore. The hate-filled eyes of the Seddi assassin, Arta Fera, glowed amber from the shadows, dangerous and damned.

"Come on, Sinklar," he muttered irritably to himself. "You've got a perfect operation to plan . . . or else a lot of people are going to die."

At the words, he arched, glaring at the monitors. Makarta Mountain lay just days behind him. Makarta—the fortress of the Seddi. He could imagine those black stone hallways, see the bodies wretchedly sprawled in death. Smell the reek of corrupting flesh on the musty air of the mountain tomb. From desiccated eyes, the dead stared across time and space and into his uneasy soul.

What could I have done differently?

Gretta's gentle laughter echoed in the halls of his memory. He closed his eyes, imagining her hands. She'd stand behind him, massaging his knotted shoulders while she spoke in soothing tones: *"You gonna win this one, Sink? Or just waste your time fooling around with ghosts?"*

He slapped a hand down on his desk, jumped to his feet, and resumed the ritual pacing he'd adopted: the four steps out and back allowed him by the confines of the cabin.

Makarta had become a debacle. First he'd trapped the Seddi inside the mountain, and then the Seddi had trapped Sinklar's own people and held them hostage down there in the bowels of their winding warrens. The only way to effect the release of Mac's trapped Sections had been to mount one bloody assault after another on the stubborn defenders.

Sink knotted his fists, remembering that final order from Rysta Braktov: Evacuate!

Muttering a curse, he palmed the lock plate and stepped through the hatch into the gray-painted corridor. Nervous energy pumped in his veins as he passed under the glowing light panels. Cables and conduit packed the ceiling in a ropy mass. The soles of his boots whispered on the deck plate. Reinforcing strakes arched around the corridor like rib bones—and he walked through the serpent's belly.

How could he plan when his thoughts twisted like an Ashtan tornado? If only he could put everything that had happened during the last months into perspective. Gretta had always helped him do that, and now he ached for her steadying words. She'd loved him—and been murdered by the Seddi assassin. He hadn't even had time to grieve, to feel the warmth looted from his life and soul. Immediately thereafter, Mac had almost died in Makarta Mountain—from Regan guns, guns Sink now commanded aboard *Gyton*. Sinklar's gut went hollow as he remembered those last moments. He'd been so close to failure . . . impotent for the first time in his life.

The words uttered by Staffa kar Therma haunted him: "*. . . Each action will cost you. Every meter you advance into Makarta will be on rock slippery with Regan blood.*"

And Rysta Braktov's voice had cackled: "*I have an order from Tybalt the Imperial Seventh . . . your six hundred are well worth the price. My orders are to destroy the Seddi fortress . . . and I will do so.*"

How could Sinklar have known he was matching wits with the Star Butcher? The Lord Commander's link with the Seddi still vexed him. What did the Companions and the Seddi have in common? And what had that mysterious conversation with Staffa meant? *Staffa kar Therma claims to be my father!* The thought whirled senselessly around in his mind.

"Unless it's another Seddi trick, some sort of psychological game they're playing." He ground his teeth. Were that the case, it was working; try as he might, he couldn't order his thoughts as he once had. Maybe he needed to go drag Mac out of bed to talk it over— but Mac had more than enough on his mind.

MacRuder had the chore of retraining the remainder of Rysta's Divisions—Divisions Sinklar's troops had mauled on Targa. Somehow, Mac had managed to do the impossible, overcoming most of the festering resentment felt by those veteran ranks. Mac's magic seemed to be a mixture of iron-fist diplomacy, calculating reason, and the sobering reality that Regan blasters had taken potshots at the Star Butcher himself.

Relations with the Companions hadn't exactly been amicable when Staffa's fleet pulled the Lord Commander out of the trap at Makarta. If anyone knew the awesome fury the Companions could unleash, Rysta's veterans did. And it scared hell out of them.

The Rotted Gods knew what kind of mess they'd find Rega in when they exited null singularity. The entire empire might be in flames. Sinklar tapped his forehead with a knotted fist, trying to anticipate. For an ally, he only had Ily Takka, the cold-blooded scheming Minister of Internal Security. And he trusted her about as far as he could see past an event horizon.

Sink, you're in some serious shit—as usual. And you'd better get your brain into overdrive, or you're going to think the war on Targa was paradise compared to what's about to break loose.

He took the first left and passed two crewmen, aware of their gaping stares as he marched on. *They don't know what to think. I've gone from an outlaw to a Lord—and their empire is teetering on the edge of the abyss.*

He stepped out into one of the observation blisters

and walked past the spectrometer and scopes to the transparency with the idea that he could gaze at the stars. He found nothing but an infinite blackness. A weary smile bent his lips. "Fool, you're in null singularity. There's nothing to see because light doesn't exist."

"That's right."

Sinklar spun on his heel to see the old woman where she sat in a shadowed observation chair. "Commander Braktov. I'm sorry. I didn't see you when I came in. What are you doing here?"

Rysta Braktov gave him a sour smile. "The same thing you are, I suppose. I used to come up here to see the stars. It became a habit. I come here for peace now—especially when the ship's in null singularity. It's the one place no one has a reason to come to . . . except, it would seem, for yourself."

Sinklar's eyes adjusted to the gloom and he could see her better. She had to have passed her second century of life. Despite rejuvenation treatments, her dark brown skin had wrinkled and gray shot through her hair. The commander's uniform she wore, however, looked crisp, letter perfect. Nor could anyone underrate Rysta Braktov after one look into those gleaming black eyes.

Sinklar rubbed the back of his neck, wishing the action would dissipate the strain in his soul. "I'm sorry to have bothered you."

As he turned to leave, she chuckled dryly and called, "Oh, no bother." A pause. "Besides, it's your ship now . . . Lord Fist."

Sinklar stopped. The way she'd said "Lord" rankled. He braced both hands on the spectrometer that separated them and said, "Perhaps we should settle some things between us. I can understand and accept your feelings about me, Commander, but we're going to have to work together when we reach Rega."

She snorted angrily and thrust her jaw forward. "Rotted Gods, Sinklar, do you have any idea what's happened? The Emperor's been assassinated! Rega is on the verge of collapsing internally while Sassa waits out there eager for the chance to cut our throats! The Lord Commander of Companions, the Star Butcher, may be contracted with Sassa—or maybe with the thrice-cursed Seddi! And back on Rega, who's about to seize power? Ily Takka, the Minister of Internal Security, that's who! Now, boy, she might have pulled your balls out of the crusher on Targa, but when it comes to an ally, I'd trust a Cytean cobra before I'd allow myself to blink in the same room with Ily." A pause. "Or are you just another of her lackeys? Is that it? Did she wiggle her cute ass until your testicles overloaded your brain?"

"I'm not the young fool you think, Commander."

Rysta waved as if to shoo a fly. "No? Well, tell me something, Lord Fist. What are you *really* after? What's your angle in this damned mess?"

"Commander, maybe I'd better fill you in about what just happened on Targa. The Seddi Magister, an old man called Bruen, plotted and initiated the Targan revolt for reasons I'm still not completely sure of. *I* was among the first troops dropped to retake the planet. I got to see the whole thing from start to finish. The entire operation was a screwup. The leadership was incompetent, the training we received, ludicrous. Mac, Gretta, and I survived purely by luck. The Targans killed over ninety percent of my Division on the first day because of sheer command stupidity! *Ninety percent!*

"Then some damned jackass gave us green replacements to fill the ranks. I was promoted to Sergeant First and sent out with a Section to hold a pass against overwhelming enemy forces. Well, I threw the damned book away and devised my own tactics, Commander. Because of that, my Section held its position and dealt the rebels a severe setback.

"About that time, the Seddi assassinated my Division First. So what happened? Tybalt—playing some silly political game with Ily Takka—put me in charge of the First Targan Division. And do you know why? Because we were a *soak off!* Tybalt sought to gain a political advantage through a Regan defeat on Targa.

They sent us into the countryside, withdrew our transport and supply, and waited for us to conveniently die."

Rysta's expression had hardened. "But you didn't."

Sinklar shook his head. "You bet we didn't. We made it up as we went, and we reorganized the Division command structure. Then we took the rebel stronghold of Vespa and broke the back of the rebellious Targan forces in a pitched battle."

Rysta poked a hard finger at him. "And you went beyond your authority when you tried to contact the Seddi. That wasn't—"

"Wasn't what? Reasonable?" Sinklar's lips twisted. "Maybe you forget that this was just before that idiot Mykroft had his entire Division wiped out by the rebels. He held a dance, remember? And the Targans picked that moment to attack. Then the damned fool fled to me, and demanded I turn over my command to him."

"And you refused!" Rysta sat forward, bristling. "That's mutiny, Fist!"

"Mykroft had no authority over the first Targan Assault Division."

"And if he had, would that have made any difference?"

"Not one damned bit. Do you think I was about to let him waste my people the way he did his own? Not on your life. The final straw was when you arrived overhead and dropped five veteran Divisions . . . not to subdue the rebels, no, to kill me and my people, Rysta. We'd become a threat, but we didn't die. We whipped five of the best Divisions in the Regan Empire."

Rysta glared at him.

"You wanted to know my angle . . . what I'm after?" Sinklar returned stare for stare. "Our motto is 'Never again.' That's what I'm after. I'm going to make sure that people like Mykroft and Atkin, and the rest of the sycophants, are never given the opportunity to butcher people the way they did on Targa. The system's pus-stinking *rotten*, Commander! I didn't like being left out to die—and I swear on the bodies of my dead soldiers, I'm *going* to change it. One way or another."

"Given the vituperation of your tirade, I suppose you lump me in with your sycophants. You still hate me for making you withdraw from Makarta, don't you?"

Sinklar took a deep breath and faced the black nothingness beyond the transparency. "Hate, Rysta? Yes, I suppose so. Six hundred of my people were trapped with the Seddi in that Rotted mountain—and you gloated when you got the order to kill them." He looked down at his hands. "Do you expect me to forget the tone in your voice? Your glee at the thought of destroying me?"

"You and your Divisions are a contagion, Fist."

He bent down to peer into her eyes. "Why, Rysta? Because we fight war with the same thorough efficiency that the Companions do? No, it's not that, is it? Admit it, Rysta. We scare hell out of you because we're turning your world upside down. We're making a mockery of the aristocratic privilege you lived for. Well, I don't give a rat's ass for Imperial society or what it stands for. Anything that *might* have meant to me has been washed away in Targan blood. Your edifice of state elite and alabaster aristocracy is cracked and trembling, Commander. And I'll do everything in my power to send the pieces crashing down."

Her lip twitched as she met his stare. "I hope I'm around to see you fall, boy. I want to laugh and grind my heel in your face as I walk past. *Damn you!* Don't you understand what's happening? Everything that's good . . . our very way of life is at stake here! There has to be honor and ritual to war. We've got to have rules for combat. War must be done orderly. Without it, we're savages! Beasts!"

"Don't feed me that crap. I've been on the front lines, Commander. I've watched people I loved blasted and bleeding. I've seen the agony, and war's bestial. It's Rotted damn butchery for the privates! You hear? Screw you and your command aristocracy, sitting back in the bunkers sipping sherry and staring at the situation board! Crawl down in the trenches with the rest of us and dirty your hands with blood, mud, shit, and terror!"

Rysta shook her head and rubbed her eyes. "You don't understand."

Sinklar relented as he straightened. "Yes, I do, Commander. You feel like a plant ripped from the soil. Your Emperor, Tybalt the Imperial Seventh, is dead without an heir. Rega is about to come unglued as the people panic—unless order can be imposed somehow. Staffa kar Therma is in league with the Seddi for sure, and possibly with the Sassan Empire. Your military establishment—which was built on Staffa's power—is suddenly antiquated and comic when placed against the Sassan threat. The nice cozy future has gone suddenly black and terrifying. Nothing's predictable anymore. War has become too real, Commander. Your entire life's work is suddenly meaningless. Everything you've believed in has gone hollow.

Rysta's head had bowed until she propped it with tired arms. Silence stretched between them.

"Rysta," Sinklar whispered, "it doesn't mean defeat. The Empire still needs you. Instead of fighting for the old order, for the aristocracy and the nobles, you could fight for the people. Think about it."

He turned and left, the image of her ingrained in his mind: a broken and defeated old woman humped over in the chair.

*   *   *

The auburn-haired woman leaned in the shadowed doorway of a service access tube that led off the side of the underground shuttle platform. A scuffed black satchel rested by her feet. Out on the platform, the crowd of business executives, services techs, professionals, and other commuters waited for the next shuttle to emerge from the EM tube. At each shift change, the platform crowded like this, but instead of the usual

air of tired relief, today tension crackled in the air.
Rega reeled, uncertain, afraid.

Through narrowed amber eyes, the woman cataloged the people who waited, many bouncing anxiously on their toes, careful to keep their eyes
lowered. Yes, they knew. They could feel the coming
storm; but none could guess how soon it would burst
upon them, or with what horrible vengeance.

The platform for the shuttle measured sixty meters
by twenty, with a series of lift tubes that rose a level
to the main pedestrian corridor that ran under the
central business district. The woman stepped out of
the access doorway and bent down, pressing a stud on
the black sialon satchel. Where it lay, the bag blended
neatly with the shadows. Then she skirted the edge
of the crowd as she walked toward the lift tubes, a
nondescript brown coat snugged about her. More than
one man openly stared at the provocative image of
her shapely hips. She tied an umber scarf over her
glossy hair as she entered the first lift tube.

The field carried her to the busy pedestrian corridor
that ran like a human artery beneath the multistoried
office buildings. Gift shops, personal supplies vendors,
cafés, comm repair centers, delivery services, and
fine restaurants lined the sides, while overhead, the
hum from the square duct work of the air-conditioning was drowned by the hubbub of voices and shuffling commuters.

The woman stepped into the ebb and flow of humanity, blending, allowing herself to drift with the
current. She smiled grimly, aware of the men staring
openly at her classic beauty—she drew them with the
same captivation as a flashing lure drew fish in Riparian waters. One glance from her hard yellow eyes,
however, and they'd hesitate, unsure, giving her time
to duck away into the crowd.

Precisely on schedule, she arrived before a small
coffee shop and nodded to the young men and women
who sat at the tables, waiting, sipping klav and stassa.
They tensed now, reaching for packages that lay beside them.

A heartbeat later, the ground shook while a deafening explosion tore through the corridor behind her as the satchel charge did its deadly work. Fire belched from the lift tubes, scattering the crowd. For the briefest of instants, people froze in stunned disbelief.

"Death to the traitors!" one of the young women in the café shouted into the silence.

"Death!" shouted another of the young men as he pulled a blaster and charged into the crowd. Pandemonium broke loose as the young people carefully goaded the riot into full fury.

The amber-eyed woman watched grimly as the frantic mass of humanity bolted in panic. Screams of wounded and dying victims of the bomb blast vied with the shouts of the rioters and the breaking of glass and spilling merchandise.

The amber-eyed woman placed a comm to her lips, stating simply, "Mission complete. Have transportation waiting at the pickup." Then she slipped away among the panicked masses.

* * *

Admiral Iban Jakre tapped his laser pen on the rim of his stassa cup as he watched the big holo projector on the wall run a report Sassan spies had just forwarded from Rega. None of this made any sense.

"Rerun that," he ordered his comm and got to his feet, pacing back and forth before his large sandwood desk. Behind him, through his huge tactite window, the Imperial Sassan capitol rose in a magnificent series of spires and buttresses, each lit by different pastel shades to contrast with the night sky. Aircars, like thousands of fireflies, streamed down the wide boulevards that separated the military command center from Divine Sassa's palace.

The other monitors on Jakre's wall displayed the status of the military buildup which had begun in response to the curious Regan buildup the spies had monitored several months ago. Tybalt had initiated the buildup, and Sassan intelligence reported that the

Regans feared an alliance between Sassa and the Companions—except no such alliance existed. Sassa had no choice but to respond in kind.

Doing so hadn't been easy. Disentangling from freshly conquered Myklene had proved a nightmare. Logistics were snarled for want of fuel, food, medical supplies, weapons, and just about everything else—a portent of the perilous state of the economy.

That Rega had been going to war seemed obvious, and some intelligence analysts had suggested that Tybalt's assassination had stemmed, directly or indirectly, from that decision. To Jakre's harried staff, Tybalt's death had been a welcome reprieve, for the Sassan Empire was far too overextended to take on a new war. But what did this latest Regan trouble mean?

Jakre sipped his steaming drink as the holo began again, the Sassan intelligence agent's voice reporting: "This morning, in defiance of all our predictions, the Deputy Ministers of Defense were implicated in procurement scandals and arrested by the Ministry of Internal Security.

"Deprived of command control, the Regan military is effectively decapitated. Immediately after the arrests, rioting broke out in the Regan capital city, in Trystia, and in the industrial city of Vedoc. Such rioting appears to be limited to the Regan planet itself. No other reports have been posted by field agents on Ashtan, Maika, Sylene, or, most auspiciously, Targa. Analysts of the data uniformly agree that such riots are *not* spontaneous, but have been planned and instigated. We currently believe responsibility can be attributed to an anti-Takka faction since our people can conceive of no permutation whereby Ily Takka could profit from such unrest. As of this report, we have no indication of who or which group might be responsible for coordinating such resistance."

Admiral Jakre watched as mobs poured down a street, setting fire to buildings, smashing security systems, and executing public officials. In the background, he could see columns of smoke rising to smudge the Regan sky.

He shook his head at the carnage. "Their *entire* military command is under arrest? Don't the fools realize what they've done?"

Jakre placed his stassa cup on his desk, rubbing his protruding belly thoughtfully. "Comm, scramble my intelligence section. I want them at work within an hour. Topic: Assessment of Regan command structure paralysis. Purpose: Determination of Regan defensive abilities given the current unrest and decapitation of command structure. Based on the above, what probability of success would be enjoyed by a surprise full-scale military assault on Regan military forces within their Empire? Compute all values with and without factoring in assistance by the Companions. This project is under a Security-One clearance."

"Affirmative," the comm responded.

Jakre leaned back against his desk, eyes on the scenes of rioting. He chewed absently on his thumbnail as he watched. *This is one of two things . . . the stupidest mistake the Regans have ever committed—or one hell of a brilliant trap. My task is to decide which— because if I win, I will unite all of Free Space under His Holiness' rule. If I fail. . . .* Jakre shook his head to rid himself of the thought.

"Comm. Give me a direct line to the Legate. Priority one, scramble and secure."

"Affirmative."

"If we're wrong about this, things wouldn't be worse if the Rotted Gods broke loose in Free Space."

*   *   *

File 7355 made the enforced captivity in the Criminal Anatomical Research Lab less of a burden to Anatolia. Jan Bokken, the head of complex security, refused to allow any of the personnel to leave the building, fearing the murderous mob that still patrolled the street below. The Regan Biological Research Center existed in a state of siege. Only the impregnable security doors protected those within from the continuing riot in the streets.

Anatolia sat at her work station and rubbed her tired eyes. With a sense of triumph she stared at the catalog she'd just completed. The results couldn't be denied. She had run an entire inventory of both parents' genetics. Neither had contributed genetic material to the F_1. Her preliminary comparisons with control populations indicated that both of her parental specimens fell within normal ranges for stable genetic populations: the male Targan, the female Etarian.

She had little doubt of the accuracy of her conclusion. Human genetics had been thoroughly mapped in all of its subtle variations—if not totally explained. Researchers theorized that a heterogeneous population had spread through Free Space roughly four thousand years ago. They based such a conclusion on the rate of genetic variation present in the gene pool and on the known mutation rate. Scholars still argued about the date since rare founder traits couldn't always be distinguished from mutations. The statistical functions were elaborate though based on inconsistent data.

But no archaeological evidence had ever been found to indicate a human presence prior to four thousand two hundred years ago.

From whence had the founders originally come? None of the planets within the Forbidden Borders had given rise to the human species—or to many of the plants and animals that inhabited them. The great mystery of origins plagued and tantalized, but from the genetic and archaeological evidence, humanity and its various cultures had appeared full-blown to spread across Free Space.

Anatolia gazed woodenly at her monitor, red-eyed, and, for the moment, oblivious to the perpetual nagging question of human origins. The parental genotypes were normal, the patterns lying well within the statistical mode for their respective populations.

But the specimen she'd originally believed to be the

F_1—the offspring—lay beyond the parameters of anything ever recorded.

Anatolia planted her elbow on the desktop and settled her chin in her palm. "Computer, cross-reference chromosome one, alleles one through fifteen with the Central Catalog."

"Working."

It would be a long, tedious process. Anatolia stifled a yawn and looked up at the monitor which had been patched into the security system. She could see fires burning on the street in front of the building.

*   *   *

Over the years, Ily Takka had recruited the best and the brightest into her ranks in anticipation of this very moment. Now her management and staff personnel fell smoothly into place, taking over government operations and administration as she carefully removed one Regan official after another from power.

Ily arched her spine and massaged her lower back. She sat at her desk in the opulent offices she occupied on the top floor of the Internal Security Ministry Building—an inconspicuous gray pile of masonry and steel several minutes' journey by secret pneumatic tube away from the Emperor's palace—where she also had quarters.

Ily's office might have been likened to a palace itself. Spacious and airy, it was graced with crystal skylights that caught the Regan sun and shot it through the office in rainbow hues. The carpet was the finest Ashtan weave that changed color when walked upon. The office furnishings gleamed with Etarian jewels and spiced sandwood. High porcelain arches rose to a groined ceiling of glass and translucent sialon. Her private quarters beyond the massive security doors at the far end of the office contained dining facilities, a luxurious bath and pool, as well as a garage with shuttle capabilities in addition to several high-performance aircars. The kitchen facilities in the Ministry basement retained an epicurean chef on staff and the wine cellar was paramount in the empire.

Ily bent forward to study the large screen that dominated her desk. From that screen, she'd been monitoring the entire planet, orchestrating the riots her people expertly fomented to frighten local officials and pave the way for Sinklar's takeover. Through her minions she'd been subtly exercising the reins of control. Rega, for the moment, remained stunned in the aftermath of Tybalt's assassination—as if the people refused to believe their emperor was dead.

So much the better, the easier it is to maintain control . . . that is, until they come to their senses and realize just how frightening the situation really is. Ily blinked her gritty eyes. Too many hours since she'd slept. The monitor changed as an editorial piece on the corruption within government ran. Like all such news, it had been written by one of her writers and syndicated through the media net. Perfect! Ily lifted her headset and sent orders. The Minister of Defense's confession to participating in procurement fraud with the Rath family would be released now as a follow-up.

Keep them reeling, Ily. That's it. Don't let the aristocracy have time to think about what's happened. Let them stew and worry about their own graft. In the meantime, erode the confidence of the people. Not too much—but just enough.

Ily glanced at the chronometer. She had another two days before *Gyton* and its convoy of troops was scheduled to arrive overhead. Two days to bring Rega to just the right boil. At that precise moment, Sinklar Fist's veteran Targan Divisions would drop and restore order. A new military command would be slipped deftly into place, and she'd control it all.

Ily yawned and stood up to get the circulation back into her weary muscles. She stepped over to the mirror and studied herself. Her dark eyes were bloodshot. Her gleaming sable hair glinted bluish in the light. She straightened to inspect her trim body. She wore a tight black suit that accented her thin waist, flat belly, and high breasts. Despite the way she felt, she looked damn good.

Comm beeped and announced, "Minister Takka? We're ready for you."

Ily pressed the button on her comm, replying, "I'll be right down." She checked her appearance one last time, and forced spring back into her steps as she walked to the rear of her office. She touched an inset stud and a section of wall panel slipped back to reveal a grav lift.

"Subbasement seven," Ily ordered. The lift dropped without any sensation of motion.

Ily stepped out into a square-framed hallway tiled in white. Her heels tapped as she made her way to a sialon doorway, palmed the lock plate, and entered. She nodded to the secretary at the desk and passed through the gray security door. The tech she expected waited uneasily, a flat monitor held in his hands.

"This way, Minister. Everything is ready." He gave her a fleeting smile and led her down the white-paneled hallway.

The studio soundstage Ily entered contained a backdrop of Imperial Rega's skyline. Five Judicial Magistrates—her people, in this case—sat sternly behind an upraised sandwood bench to one side of the room. Sophisticated holo cameras moved about the floor, their boxy receptors telescoping in and out as the yellow-suited techs in the control room checked the angle and lighting for each. Tedor Mathaiison and his Deputy Ministers of Defense, waited behind the shimmery veil of a stasis box. Ily crossed the scuffed green floor and killed the restraining field.

"Ily? In the name of the Rotted Gods, what's going on here?" Mathaiison asked uneasily. He looked pale, eyes slightly glassy as he took in the courtroom scene. The Minister of Defense and his Deputies had been shackled to their chairs by means of EM restraints. Makeup had been cunningly applied to accent their features in sinister ways.

"You've been tried by the citizens' tribunal." Ily smiled her satisfaction. "You and your Deputies have confessed, and the Judicial Magistrates have passed judgment. Your sentencing and subsequent execution will be witnessed by the entire empire."

"Execution?" Mathaiison shot another frightened glance at the judicial bench and blinked as if to clear his thoughts. "You're going to *kill* us?" A pause. "Damnation, woman! Don't you know what that will do? Whether we're innocent or not, you'll be inviting disaster! The entire military will be without coordination! Sassa will jump at the opportunity! Do you hear me? *You're condemning the empire to death!*"

"Enough, Tedor. I know exactly what will happen. Tybalt's orders are still in effect. He mobilized the military prior to his death, you know. First for Targa, and then to defend the empire from both the Sassans and the Star Butcher. None of those orders have been rescinded."

Mathaiison licked his lips, struggling to reach out to her. "All the more reason you *need* us, Ily. You've got to have a command control. Without our leadership, the military will be a body without a brain! My Deputies and I are the only people with experience enough to coordinate—"

"I have a new brain—as you put it—in mind. I've seen better coordination than any that you and your senior staff have provided the empire in the past. Tedor, I have no use for you."

"But the Sassans! Don't you understand? If they see any weakness, any hint of vulnerability, they'll be on us like an Etarian sand tiger on a bleeding goat!"

Ily crossed her arms and raised an eyebrow. "How nice to have you bring that to my attention. I'll handle the Sassans if they come."

Mathaiison leaned back, eyes closed, a look of emotional exhaustion on his graying face. "You'd destroy the empire to feed your craving for power? Worse, you'd destroy yourself. How can you expect to survive if the Sassans invade? It's suicide!"

One of the holo cams dropped down, hovering as it whined to bring the Defense Minister's face into focus. Two of the white-hot spots shifted above. Beads of sweat had begun to form on Mathaiison's brow.

Ily gave him a throaty chuckle. "Dear Tedor, my old enemy, I've given this a lot of thought. Suicide? Me? Hardly. I have my course plotted—and the Sassans, with the luck of the blessed Gods, will fall for the bait I'm offering them."

Mathaiison stared incredulously. "You *want* them to strike? Who do you think could coordinate the military? Yourself? My Division Firsts and Fleet Commanders hate you and your Ministry. They'd rather cut their own throats then cooperate with you."

"They don't have to cooperate with me." Ily turned at a tech's signal. "But they will with Sinklar Fist . . . who will not only guard the empire—he'll hand me Sassa and the Companions as well."

"*Fist?* He's . . . he's an undisciplined traitor! A wild child without standing or respect for the institutions of the military. He's—"

"Brilliant. And the finest military mind the empire has."

"Putting him in charge will be like turning the military on its head."

"That's what I'm counting on." Ily turned on her heel and strode to the rear as the techs motioned final countdown to broadcast.

"No!" Tedor Mathaiison cried. "It's lunacy! She's crazy! *She wants to kill us all!*"

"Silence the prisoners," the head Judicial Magistrate ordered and a privacy field dropped over the screaming Tedor Mathaiison, once Minister of Defense for the Regan Empire.

The broadcast began, the Judicial Magistrates reading the charges while the producer filled in with segments of the confessions obtained—in some cases, creatively edited into the most damning context possible.

Ily watched from the rear. *No, Tedor, you weren't nearly the treasonous corrupt bastard I had to make you into. You were always concerned with serving the Emperor—but now, you must serve the state in a way only a man of your reputation and status can.*

"As a result of the above cited evidence," the head

Judicial Magistrate droned on, "this board must find the defendants guilty on all charges brought against them. It is further the decision of this board that the only suitable punishment for the corruption and license uncovered by this investigation is death. This decision has passed and been ruled reasonable and just."

Ily glanced at the Defense Minister and his Deputies who sat in shocked immobility. She gestured to the tech and nodded, knowing the producer had begun to run the prerecorded piece where she coolly asked for clemency for the condemned.

"You can't *do* this!" Tedor burst out, unaware that the privacy field had lifted. "That treasonous bitch wants to destroy us all! Ily, you vile, polluted whore! You despicable Cytean serpent!"

Ily leaned her head back and closed her eyes. Perfect. The moment Mathaiison burst out, the cameras had shifted, cutting her plea off, sealing Tedor's doom. No popular support would remain for him now. He'd locked the last hasp on his tomb.

A bailiff stepped forward from the wings, a pneumatic syringe in one hand. The head Judicial Magistrate stepped down from the podium, following the bailiff who made his way to each of the captives. Despite the screams and pleas, the bailiff touched the pneumatic pistol to each neck. The bodies jerked against the restraints as the lethal dose discharged; then they slumped nervelessly while the Judicial Magistrate took vital readings with a monitor he had taken from his robes.

The last in line, Tedor Mathaiison, called out, "May the Rotted Gods chew your filth-encrusted soul, Ily! I curse you, you pustulous—"

The pistol made a spitting sound against his neck. Tedor stiffened and then went loose limbed in the restraints.

The Judicial Magistrate took the reading of his bodily functions, entered the notation into the record, and nodded. He turned his attention to the holo camera and stated matter-of-factly, "I pronounce sentence to have been carried out. This case is closed to the satisfaction of the people."

A tech lifted a hand, snapped his fist closed, and made a downward slash of his arm, indicating the broadcast was over.

Ily walked off the set, a warm joy spreading through her. Let the people ponder what they'd just seen. She had them now—right where she wanted them.

* * *

Personal Quarters
Seddi Warrens
Itreatic Asteroids
3889-17-7 SC: 22:30

Dear Hyde:

I needed to write you this letter in hopes that perhaps we weren't wrong about the quanta, about the eternal condition of nature and God Mind. By this gesture, I hope that through some permutation of the quanta, you'll understand, and I can touch your pure and wonderful soul again—dead and peaceful though you may be.

All of our plans have turned to dust and blown away on the interstellar wind. As I search about me, I see no evidence that we had any impact on humanity at all. We might never have been. How did it go so wrong? Was it the machine, that thrice-cursed Mag Comm? Was it the dance of the quanta? How could we have predicted that Staffa kar Therma would become aware? I have studied the events, talked with Staffa, and through the benefit of hindsight, can see what went wrong. We take awareness, consciousness, sentience, or whatever you wish to call it, to be a given. Infants are born with dazed minds that begin to gel in childhood, are molded through adolescence and solidify in adult-hood. The occurrence is so routine, so mundane, we never question the importance of the process.

In ignorance, we set the wheels in motion to trap and kill Staffa. Mighty armies were fielded, the politics of vast empires were manipulated, and innocent human beings girded themselves for war, shedding their blood and squandering their lives as a result of our intrigue. Nevertheless, we went down to horrid defeat, and why? Was it mismanagement of resources? Was it strategic miscalculation? Disinformation?

No, old friend, our crushing defeat occurred because one man, one lone human being, was suddenly jolted into awareness.

Dear dead Hyde, knowing that now, what weight can any of us place upon a human soul?

—*Excerpted from the personal diary of Magister Bruen*

CHAPTER III

"Excuse me," the woman's sensual voice severed Governor Zacharia Beechie's thoughts from his paperwork and brought him to full attention.

She stood in his office doorway, dressed in a wraparound cloak that concealed her body. Most of her face had likewise been obscured by a gauze veil—but not enough to hide her striking beauty or those incredible amber eyes. She made an excellent addition to his abnormally drab office with its worn furnishings and scarred computer, scuffed tile floor, and battered gray duraplast records casings. Being governor of a newly defeated planet—especially one razed as hard as Myklene had been—offered little opulence.

"Yes?" Beechie straightened unconsciously, sucking in his gut and squaring his shoulders in the process. He wished he had time to run his fingers through his thinning hair.

"I'm sorry to interrupt, Captain, but I'm here to apply for a travel visa. I—I'm Marie Attenasio."

Beechie felt himself blush slightly. He'd become inured to the suffering in the aftermath of the Myklenian conquest, but some terrible hurt was reflected in those magnificent eyes. The sight of her stirred curious feelings—the sort engendered by the sight of a wounded fawn.

He forced his mind from the image. After all, a military governor had to steel his heart. What did that cursed baggy garment hide, anyway? If the clothing's purpose was to camouflage her magnificent body, it only did a halfway job—but then, what sort of attire could mask all those curves?

"A travel visa? I'm sorry, ma'am but you're Myklenian. Travel for Myklenian citizens of Divine Sassa's—"

"I'm *not* Myklenian, Captain." Her words carried a honeyed sadness. "I was stranded here during the war . . . barely escaped with my life as it is, and I'd like to get off this miserable rock. My problem is that my quarters—along with my identification—were blasted to cinders during Sta . . . the Star Butcher's attack. I've spent months scrambling to stay alive and making my way past every official in your government to get to your office."

Her eyes seemed to deepen, to draw his soul from its impregnable redoubt. "Yes, well, I see. Your nationality, then?"

"Ashtan, Captain."

"But that's. . . . Blessed Gods, you're a . . . *a Regan!*"

She shook her head sadly, eyes losing focus as she recalled the past. "I wasn't born Regan. Tybalt the Imperial Sixth conquered my world, Lord Captain. I have no allegiance to either empire." Her gaze lowered and Beechie thought she paled beneath her veil. "Everything I ever had has been taken from me . . . one way or another."

"Then what do you wish, lady? If you have nothing, what could you hope to find on Sassa?"

"What I wish to do is get to Sassa where I can access my financial resources and reestablish myself."

"You have an account in Sassa?" Beechie brightened, beginning to see a way he could help her . . . and perhaps earn her favor. After all, he was leaving within three days, transferred back to receive a promotion and reassignment.

A weary smile warmed her eyes. "Actually, the account is in Itreata, but I understand I could draw on it from Sassa."

Beechie lifted a skeptical eyebrow. "Let me get this straight. The Companions keep your currency for you?"

Her sure nod carried more weight than her words.

"Oh, I assure you they do, Captain. Will you help me get to Sassa? You would be very well rewarded."

Beechie nodded despite his sudden reservations. "I could escort you myself." He waited, heart stumbling in his chest.

She made a gesture of acceptance with her hand, the movement graceful and delicate. "Captain, that would be delightful. If you only knew how hopeless I've become."

Beechie knew. The tone in her voice communicated to his very soul. He stood, offering his hand. At her touch, he almost gasped, letting himself fall into those wondrous amber eyes, wishing he could soothe the terrible hurt he saw there. "The pleasure is mine. Would you . . . I mean, could I fix you dinner? Tonight?"

She hesitated, taking his measure, the action that of fear and mistrust. How many times had she been betrayed by men? A righteous anger stirred in Beechie's breast.

"I give you my word. I mean you no harm." Despite the honesty he forced into his words, he could see tension build.

Desperation vied with fear before she finally whispered, "I would be delighted, Captain. You're at the compound?"

He swallowed hard. "Ask for me, Marie. I'll have a clearance for you. Say, about the eighth decant?"

"I'll . . . very well. At the eighth decant." She smiled uneasily, then turned away and he noticed the limp. Aware of his attention, she said softly, "I had a hard landing during the fighting—another reason it's taken me this long to find my way to you."

Beechie tugged anxiously at his uniform as she limped down the hallway. His guts knotted against the need to accompany her, to protect her from the violent world beyond the guarded halls of the administration building. Why? How did she draw so effortlessly on that masculine need to both desire and protect?

"Blessed Gods," he whispered, "I'm in love." Then he shook his head. Yes, he'd take her to Sassa. He had that authority. Perhaps, somewhere along the way, he'd see those marvelous amber eyes glow for him.

Beechie walked over and dropped into his chair, a puzzled look on his face. Despite his notorious reputation as a work addict, he couldn't force his mind back to duty. Elbows propped on his desk, he stared absently at the ceiling panels.

* * *

Myles Roma, Legate Prima Excellence to His Holiness, Sassa II, ignored the sour sensation in his belly and leaned his head back in the cushioned seat as his aircar followed the torturous route through the small Sassan military spaceport on the outskirts of Imperial Sassa. If he'd cared to open his eyes, he could have looked past his driver's head to see the rear of Admiral Iban Jakre's car—and the flashing lights of the escort beyond that as they wound through the maze of massive domes, multifloored barracks, and towering skeletal gantries.

Instead Myles preferred to keep his eyes closed and drown himself in worry about the coming reception. The very mention of Staffa kar Therma shot sparks of inadequacy through Roma's fragile sense of self-identity. But having to deal with the man face-to-face? Myles shivered.

"Have you been under a lot of stress recently?" his personal physician had asked, peering up from the medical comm chart he meticulously tapped information into.

Stress? Myles winced at the thought. It had all started with the Myklenian contract. Staffa kar Therma and his Rot-cursed Companions had struck Myklene before the Sassan fleet had been even half-equipped for war. When Jakre's fleet finally arrived, Staffa had virtually handed the planet over—or at least what was left of it. Single-handedly the Lord Commander had destroyed the most powerful defen-

sive system in Free Space without Sassan aid—or, as
some glibly said, in spite of it.

Blame for the loss of Sassan dignity had never been
officially mentioned, but Myles had been dispatched
immediately to personally oversee the continuation of
contract with the Companions for the inevitable war
with Rega. Who could have predicted that Staffa, the
most powerful mercenary in Free Space, would have
turned down not only Myles' offer, but that of the
Regan she-viper, Ily Takka, as well?

Myles groaned to himself. From there, things had
gone from bad to worse. Was Rega preparing to strike
Sassa? Could a preemptive strike keep the Regans off
balance long enough so Sassan forces could consolidate and crush their rival once and for all? And in the
middle of it, Staffa had just up and vanished without
a trace.

No wonder I've lost thirty kilos!

The Legate reached a bejeweled hand into his purse
and brought forth a perfumed handkerchief to wipe
his sweaty face. Everything had come undone. All the
predictions made over the years by various strategists
and scholars had gone suddenly awry after Staffa
killed the Myklenian Praetor. Unsubstantiated reports
hinted that Staffa had literally ripped the man's head
from his body—in violation of contract.

Myles took a deep breath, stomach roiling at the
memory of the Lord Commander's imperious nature.
If a human could be crossed with a reptile, something
like kar Therma would be produced. With a shudder,
Myles remembered the times he'd stared into those
pitiless gray eyes and felt his soul shrivel.

Rotted right he'd been under stress—and that was
before Tybalt's assassination and the gamble Jakre
and His Holiness, Sassa II, had made to go to war
against the reeling Regan Empire. The information
was obviously classified, so he hadn't said anything to
his physician; he'd just given the man the sort of look
he'd have given an insect that crawled out of his dinner salad.

And now I have to go and greet Staffa kar Therma?

*Once again I have to be polite and charming while he
makes my skin crawl. I'd sooner be in the same room
with a Riparian blood leech.*

Myles tapped his chubby, ring-encrusted fingers on
the armrest and brightened. Perhaps Skyla Lyma, the
gorgeous Wing Commander of the Companions, would
accompany Staffa. Myles smiled and conjured her
image. He'd met her on Itreata, and fallen into immediate lust. What a handful she'd be. Or would the
feelings of insecurity engendered by Staffa's presence,
burst Myles' bubble of sexual desire, too?

The aircar barely bumped as it slipped through a
security hatch and settled in the restricted area behind
the main terminal. In the glare of the hot lights, gray
walls rose to either side and armed marines watched
warily from the catwalks overhead. The canopy hissed
slightly as it rose. Myles unlatched the side panel and
grunted while he shifted his bulk to the antigrav that
a lieutenant hustled up for him. Jakre gave Myles a
weak smile as he was seated on his own antigrav.
Flanked by armed security agents, they rode through
arched halls painted with precise military dedication
to be as boring as possible.

Tall windows and straight rows of black duraplast
seats marked the arrival gate as they exited from the
access tunnel. Puffy clouds obscured Sassa's faintly
green sky and the landing field had been cleared of
all other craft for security reasons. The empty concrete pad stretched away for nearly two kilometers.
Myles pulled his antigrav up next to Jakre's and
looked over the room. It measured no more than fifty
paces in any direction.

An honor guard of twenty waited patiently at attention along the drab wall nearest the gate. Gleaming
weapons were placed at parade rest and their scarlet
and white uniforms looked splendid. Still more security personnel—both Sassan and Companion—hustled
back and forth with monitors and communications
devices.

"Five minutes," Jakre muttered, his long face ill-
concealing his tension. The admiral brushed at his re-

splendent turquoise and white uniform with white-gloved hands. He glanced surreptitiously at Myles, squared his shoulders, and attempted to pull in his more than ample gut.

"What's happened?" Myles asked softly. "When I went to Itreata, Staffa refused to see me. I assumed at the time that he was playing shrewd, driving up the price. Now Tybalt is dead at the hand of a Seddi woman assassin—"

"If we can believe Ily Takka," Jakre growled.

"—and we have the ability to crush Rega once and for all and extend His Holiness' benevolence over all humanity. Yet at this moment, *Staffa comes to us!* Why?"

"I can't second guess the Star Butcher." Jakre shook his head, casting a suspicious glance at the cloudy skies beyond the armored windows. "I've heard that Staffa got mixed up with that revolt on Targa. The intelligence is muddled, but he was there. Ily and this child general of hers, this Sinklar Fist, almost killed kar Therma. Skyla Lyma scrambled the Companion fleet and arrived in time to pull the Lord Commander out of the trap. I don't know how the Seddi are mixed up in it, but Staffa evacuated all of their unholy priests."

Myles slipped a hand into his purse, withdrawing an antacid which he quickly gulped. "Staffa? With Seddi heretics? They've been trying to assassinate him for years. It has to be some ploy, some trick we can't fathom yet. Staffa does nothing without achieving gain . . . or cutting some poor bastard's throat in the process."

In a dry voice, Jakre suggested, "Maybe he's converted."

Myles failed in his effort to crack a smile. "Not even the Seddi god would claim the Star Butcher."

Jakre raised a snuffbox to his nose and sniffed. "Were I a demon, and I knew Staffa had joined my legions, I believe I'd slip away at the first moment and consign myself to the Rotted Gods' digestive tracts for the rest of eternity."

"I doubt even the Rotted Gods could protect you from Staffa."

"You make him sound like he's more than human." Myles held his tongue.

A lieutenant strode up and saluted Jakre, saying, "Security check in, sir. We have the base closed up tight in accordance with the Lord Commander's instructions. Six shuttles have just disembarked from *Chrysla*. We thought there would only be three."

Jakre nodded. "That's his security. Five of those shuttles are decoys—just in case someone's waiting with a loaded blaster somewhere. Staffa leaves nothing to risk . . . as his enemies have learned to their dismay."

Myles absently placed a protective hand over his belly. "A great many people would pay dearly to know that he was dead, Admiral. He is the perfect mercenary, without remorse, without feeling. When you look into his eyes, all you feel is . . . cold."

"Perhaps, but fortunately for us, he's always been on our side."

Myles frowned at Jakre. "Ours . . . and the Regans. I don't like it. I've met Ily. She's no one's fool. Yet she executed her entire Defense command. It makes no sense, Iban. She has to know that she's leaving herself wide open. And suddenly Staffa arrives overhead demanding an audience? Consider this: He was on Targa. Our intelligence reports that Ily tried to kill him, that Tybalt himself ordered Staffa's death. Rysta Braktov reportedly was ready to sacrifice over six hundred Regan troops in the process."

"And that information bothers you, Roma? It should make you sing. They drove Staffa into *our* laps."

Myles glanced up at the sky, seeing the first shuttle diving out of the clouds like a black sliver. "Anything having to do with Staffa kar Therma bothers me. Iban, think. What if it's misinformation? What if Ily and Staffa have an alliance? What if it's all to put us off our guard, trap us somehow? What if Tybalt really isn't dead? Do you believe the stories? Tybalt killed by a woman, an amber-eyed Seddi assassin? Where was his security? Would Tybalt let an assassin get close to him? I smell a stink like a Sylenian sewer in this."

"You're becoming paranoid," Jakre warned.

Myles squinted hostilely. "The Praetor of Myklene might have replied the same way . . . once."

Admiral Jakre grunted his irritation, but Myles noticed that the man swallowed with difficulty and his eyes had narrowed as more of the dark wedges dropped and settled on the landing field to rest on their struts like predatory insects.

Within minutes, the pneumatic doors of the gate slipped back and armored troops filed into the room by ranks. These were the famed Special Tactics units, the elite of the Companions. They moved with oiled-machine precision, swiftly covering the room. Despite having seen it before, Myles couldn't help but be impressed. They stood, encased in armor, electronics studding their helmets, each person's attention centered on a different portion of the room, each responsible, weapon at the ready. Their pride and professionalism radiated like an aura.

A Special Tactics Officer—a black man with a scar on his right cheek—stepped out, scanned the room, and took a report through his comm. He nodded, as if to himself, and spoke into his helmet mike before stopping in front of Myles and the admiral. Myles knew STO Ryman Ark from former occasions. The man, like the rest of his kind, was nothing more than a two-legged jackal, but he was a damned competent one.

"Good to see you again, Ark," Jakre greeted.

"My pleasure, Admiral. The Lord Commander will be here in just a moment." Ark had a commanding voice. The hard eyes pinned Myles like a needle through a boil. "You're looking more fit than I've ever seen you, Legate. Whatever you're doing, keep it up."

"Why . . . er, thank you, Ryman." Damned fool, didn't Ark know an ample body was a sign of status and power? Or had Myles just been made the butt of some insipid joke the Companions shared? The Legate kept his official smile in place while his stomach made a growling sound; he placed his other hand protectively over his navel.

A shuffling came from the gate and all eyes turned. A stillness fell on the room. Two people emerged and Myles' heart stuttered.

The man approached, tall and muscular, dressed in formfitting steel-gray combat armor. A charcoal cloak draped like a thing alive from his shoulders. Glistening black hair had been pulled severely over the left ear, held in place by a jeweled clip that shot prismatic light in scintillating rays. Polished black boots rose to the man's knees, and his fingers, too, were gloved in the protective cloth. A wide belt held a worn pistol, equipment pouches, communications devices, and an energy pack to power the golden choker at his neck that served as the field generator for a vacuum helmet.

Myles locked his knees to keep them from wobbling as he met the Lord Commander's stare. Staffa had a hard-jawed face, a high forehead, and a long straight nose. The thin-lipped mouth mirrored the Lord Commander's power and arrogance.

To kill the impulse to lick his suddenly dry lips, Myles clenched his teeth. Staffa kar Therma, the Star Butcher, had ruthlessly ordered the execution of billions. This man had blasted planets and sintered entire civilizations into slag—and he'd done so remorselessly, with all the emotion of Sylenian ice.

Myles tore his gaze away and focused on the woman who strode beside Staffa. Yes, Skyla Lyma, the Wing Commander of the Companions, had indeed accompanied her master. She wore dazzling white combat armor that molded to every curve of her perfectly toned body. A gymnast would envy Lyma's muscular poise, while even the most lethargic of men would spin fantasies of that gorgeous flesh. Taut breasts balanced the broad shoulders that tapered down to a narrow, flat-bellied waist. Myles trembled at the promise

of those perfectly rounded hips and muscular but-
tocks. And, ah, those long legs!

Skyla Lyma had become his personal succubus.

Her hair seemed spun from blonde ice that gleamed
in the lights. She wore it in a long braid that looped
about her left shoulder and was held in place by her
uniform epaulet. Her face was that of a classic beauty,
her alabaster skin smooth and marred only by a faint
line of scar tissue along her left cheek. Her alert blue
eyes might have been cut from azure crystals to accent
her frosty beauty. They missed nothing as she cataloged the room and its security. She came to a stop
before Myles and he caught the faintest hint of disgust
before she masked all emotion.

"Lord Commander," Jakre had begun, "we welcome you to His Holiness' Empire and Imperial Sassa,
the capital. His Divinity, Holy Sassa the Second,
awaits your presence with pleasure and anticipation.
As always, you do us the greatest of honor by your
arrival. We look forward to fulfilling your every wish
and demand. You need but ask, and a grateful Sassa
will more than gladly show its gratitude for the services the Lord Commander and his Companions have
rendered in the past. We offer our complete, if mea-
ger, hospitality and consider it only a hint of the—"

Staffa raised a gloved hand to cut Jakre off.
"Enough, Iban. I think we've borne enough trials together to dispense with the formality. We appreciate
your warm welcome and hope our relations with Divine Sassa and his staff will continue to proceed with
such warmth."

Myles clenched up as those deadly gray eyes turned
in his direction. "Legate Prima Excellence, it's good
to see you again."

"M–My pleasure, Lord Commander. I hope your
journey was a pleasant one."

Staffa grinned—and a flutter like butterfly wings
began in Myles' belly.

"Yes, Myles, the trip was pleasant, for once. The
Wing Commander and I devoted our time to clarifying
what we had to say to His Holiness." Staffa's feral

gaze narrowed. "I must say, Myles, you're looking better than you have in a long time. A little pale, perhaps, but you've lost weight. Not ill, I hope?"

Myles gulped and stammered, "No . . . no . . . I. . . . Working hard, that's all, Lord Commander." *Damn it, he's smiling! What's he after? What's the game here?*

"Well, then," Staffa stated mildly. "I take it that Divine Sassa is waiting? Gentlemen, we have business to discuss. Shall we be about it? My people should have our transportation unloaded by now."

Myles collected his wits. "Of course. The admiral and I have been giving considerable thought to the Regan situation. We're glad to find you in our camp, Lord Commander. I'll leave the details to His Holiness, but your presence here gladdens all of our hearts."

Skyla gave him a cool smile. "I sincerely hope so, Legate. The coming session will be . . . interesting. I hope we can all come to an understanding of just how serious the current situation is."

Myles realized his official smile had become strained. "I'm sure we will." *But what exactly do you mean? We're all going to war against Rega, aren't we?* A cool premonition crept through him.

The Lord Commander leaned close, a concerned look on his normally inscrutable face. "You feeling all right, Myles? A bit of indigestion, perhaps?"

"Huh?" Myles followed the Lord Commander's gaze and realized he'd knotted his fingers into the fat of his belly. Myles felt the blood rush to his face and looked about hastily to see how many people had noticed. "It's . . . nothing, Lord Commander."

Staffa's grin actually warmed. "You're hungry, aren't you? That's it. You've been on a diet. No wonder you're looking better. Good for you. I admire men with self-discipline. Stick with it and don't give in."

To Myles' further consternation, Staffa gave him a friendly slap on the shoulder as he stepped past.

"Diet?" Jakre asked from the side of his mouth. "Really?"

Myles cursed and waddled back to his antigrav while his thoughts whirled in addled confusion. What in the Rotted Gods' hell was the scheming Lord Commander after, anyway? And what did those cryptic words of Skyla's mean?

The butterfly feeling in Roma's gut turned queasy.

* * *

Staffa had learned many bitter lessons in his life. One of the more painful involved security and transportation. More than twenty years ago, he'd accepted transportation from a host government—and it had cost him his wife and child. For years he and his Companions had searched. Rewards had been offered, and all to no avail. Finally he'd come face to face with the Myklenian Praetor, the one man he'd loved more than he could have a father. After twenty years, he'd learned the fate of the woman he'd loved for so long. *Dead at my hands. May the Rotted Gods chew your corpse forever, Praetor. I may have killed her, but you, butcher, you placed her in jeopardy . . . would have used my love as a weapon against me.*

His son, too, had been found. Raised by the Seddi, the boy had been alienated by design and chance until a way to bridge their differences might never be found. *Lost? Is he really? Have I nothing left of that life but shattered memories?*

More recently, Staffa had traveled on his own, and the cost of that debacle still hadn't been fully absorbed. Now he waited patiently while his aircars lined up in formation in the avenue between the tall buff-walled buildings. The air smelled metallic and slightly acrid from industrial pollutants. The cloudy sky overhead looked hazy through the field created by the security generators.

Even here, in the heart of the Sassan military spaceport, he felt confined, vulnerable.

It's just your nerves. You're too close to Ily Takka's treachery. This isn't Rega. But then, after he said his piece to His Holiness, the Sassan God-Emperor, Sassa might not be so friendly a place either.

Skyla had adopted a casual stance slightly behind him while Ryman Ark stood on the third point of what might appear to be a haphazard triangle. Despite the nonchalant postures adopted by Staffa's people, they remained as wary as Ashtan gazelles.

Staffa's vehicle pulled up before him and the canopy lifted. One of Ark's Special Tactics personnel climbed out and handed a check sheet to Ryman, who quickly climbed into the driver's seat of the oblong aircar.

Staffa lowered himself into the rear seat and took Skyla's hand as the armored bubble closed over their heads.

Skyla gave him a studied look from the corner of her eye and raised a pale eyebrow. "The Legate looked nervous enough to squirm out of his skin. You didn't make him feel any better."

Staffa gave her a grim nod. "I've always appreciated Roma. I can read him like a book—just like most of the Sassan high command. Myles isn't a bad sort. He's just . . . well. . . ."

"A pus-licking wimp."

Staffa chuckled. "You don't share my high opinion of the Legate?"

She tightened her grip on his as the aircar rose to follow the Sassan formation. Their journey would take them through the center of the city to the Imperial Palace. Every step would be monitored by the Special Tactics units and by *Chrysla*, hanging in orbit above.

"You didn't have to listen to him describe in detail what he'd do with me if he ever got me into his bed. If he ever lays a finger on me, I'll break his fat little neck, crush his sternum, and kick him so hard his balls will loop around his ears."

"And when did you overhear all this?"

Her full lips curled into a weary smile. "While you were off galloping around the Regan Empire and getting yourself sold into slavery on Etaria. Myles showed up to dicker a new contract immediately after you slipped away. Ily Takka arrived within hours of Roma, but she was the sharper of the two. She caught something in the wind, some clue that the situation had changed, and she used it to track you down."

"It doesn't pay to underestimate Ily." He paused. "She wanted me to be her emperor, you know. She offered me all of Free Space—at her side."

A fiery gleam filled Skyla's cerulean eyes, "And for once, my love, I'm glad you showed a little sense and turned her down."

"I was never *that* dull-witted."

"But is Sinklar Fist?" Skyla wondered absently as she gazed out at the buildings they were passing.

Staffa rubbed his chin and frowned as they passed through a hole dilated in the security field and accelerated into the city proper. The Sassan capital gleamed before them. Tall spires of office buildings rose in phalanxes that stretched into the distance, their silvered sides resplendent with windows and abstract art. At the bases, warehouses created a blocky effect of irregular roofs, each with a shipping and receiving pad marked off by landing circles and elevator ports.

"I hope to the Quantum Gods that he knows just how viperous she is. He's hanging by a thread anyway." Staffa ground his teeth and knotted his free fist. "Damn it! Why didn't he believe me? Why didn't he let me prove—"

"We've been through this a hundred times," Skyla reminded firmly. "Intellectually, you know exactly why he did what he did. Bruen had played him like a cat. Every tragedy in that boy's life could be laid at the doorstep of the Seddi. Arta Fera killed the woman he loved. He firmly believes his parents were psychologically programmed Seddi assassins. He watched the Seddi butcher his troops and derail every honest attempt he made at finding a peaceful solution to the Targan revolt." Her expression pinched. "And I have a sneaking hunch that if we knew half of what Bruen and Hyde did to that boy. . . . Well, it's amazing that he's sane."

Staffa tapped his fingers on the cabin molding as they shot down the main traffic access, their escort fanned out around them. Myles had been efficient. No other vehicles could be seen on the wide lane.

"I have to convince him," Staffa replied gently.

Skyla squeezed his hand. "In time. For now you'd better channel your wits into how to handle His Holiness. Divine Sassa isn't going to like what you're going to tell him. He and his military are primed for war. The only thing that's slowed them so far is their stumbling economy."

"He's going to have to like it." Staffa took a deep breath and straightened. "If he doesn't, I'll have to stuff it down his throat." *Assuming the struggling engineers back at Itreata could manage to make* Countermeasures *work. That ship would be the key.*

"They could still go to war. Depending on what their spies tell them, they might consider this the best opportunity they've ever had. Rioting in Rega . . : the execution of the Regan High Command . . . no heir to fill Tybalt's throne. . . ."

Images flashed through Staffa's mind. Corpses lay stacked in empty streets. Gray skies roiled above as endless flakes of grimy gray snow fell into gaping eye sockets. Frozen fingers clawed desperately at the icy wind of nuclear winter. Despite the cold, he could smell the stench of death as the bodies buried beneath the mass bloated in the heat of their own decomposition. Slimy brown fluids pooled at the edge of the dead to freeze into humped puddles.

"If they do," Staffa whispered, "they'll drown in their own blood."

* * *

13:45 Aboard Regan warship, Gyton:

"*Loyalty turns into a slipper fish when you really get to thinking about it. I'm not asking you to turn your backs on the Empire, or the oath you all swore to protect it. But I want you to think about some things. When you dropped on Targa, it was to kill Regan troops. The Emperor asked you to kill fellow citizens who were doing their duty to the Imperium. I was one of those people who was supposed to be killed by you, so I've got a stake in this at the gut level.*

"*Now, I've heard a lot of you cursing Sinklar Fist, and cursing me, too, because I was the guy who took Henck prisoner at his headquarters in Kaspa. But think about it. A lot of your people were killed in the Targan drop, but so were a lot of ours. People, put a little skull sweat into analyzing why it happened in the first place. Why were we ordered to kill each other? Because the system's gone rotten and it's time for a change. Maybe it's time we get back to thinking about Rega, and that oath we took to protect the Empire, because, people, we're the only hope the Empire has left.*

"*Loyalty. That's the problem you have to deal with, decide for yourselves.*

"*As I look out at you, I see Regan combat veterans. Some of you were Twenty-seventh Maikan, some Third Ashtan. Now the Empire's teetering on the brink. Today, we're all Regan. So you think about loyalty, and what it means. Sure, you can owe it to a man, or a planet, or even an empire. But first, you have to owe it to yourself, to what you know way down in your guts is right and honorable.*

"*Myself, I'm loyal to Sinklar Fist—because he's loyal to the people.*"

—Recorded speech by First Ben MacRuder to the re-
constituted Fourth Targan Assault Division

CHAPTER IV

Ily Takka stood up from her desk and rubbed the back of her neck. A terrible fatigue ate into her muscles with needle teeth. Her brain felt hot and fevered, the burning effect like that of too much caffeine. Events had begun to take their toll on her reserves. She glanced dully around her opulent office before stepping over to the armored window to stare out at the lights of Rega. The sun would be coming up soon, but for now the capital spread before her, a pattern of lights and blocky darkened buildings. Tonight Rega slept amidst uneasy dreams. Everyone awaited the new dawn with trepidation.

And so do I.

Since the execution of the military command, several Division Firsts had taken matters into their own hands—as Ily had hoped they would. Those commanders who contacted her, offering themselves as replacements for Mathaiison, she arrested. Better to castrate their ambition now. The ones who called requesting approval for some action, Ily tagged for Sinklar's future inspection. The third—and most frequent—sort of Division First did nothing at all but sat like rocks awaiting instructions from someone, anyone. Those, Sinklar would replace with his own trusted commanders.

The comm monitor flashed to display the square features of her Deputy. The man looked at her with heavy-lidded eyes. His pug nose had been mashed onto his face and his cheeks appeared dark with stubble. At the best of times, Gysell's black beard gave his pale skin a blue cast.

"Deputy Gysell? You're in charge for the moment. I've got to get some sleep. Keep special tabs on the University. I've had reports that some of the academicians might want to make a statement. If they do, handle it. If any of the lauded professors get too far out of line, arrest them."

"Of course, Ily. We can book most of them for sedition and espionage."

Ily frowned, thoughts like cotton. "No, we may need them later. I want them kept at a soft simmer—not turned off or iced. Played properly, they could turn out to be a major asset."

"And the Minister of Military Intelligence?" Gysell asked. "He and his Deputies are close to panic over the Sassan buildup. They might spread their unease to the people."

"Remind them of what happened to Tedor Mathaiison. I think they'll be too worried about the Defense Minister's confession to rock the boat. Expect compliance. If not, arrest the culprit who steps out of line, and implicate him in some scandal or other."

"Go get some sleep, Ily. I'll call if there's an emergency."

She nodded, killed the connection, walked the length of her office, and passed the security hatch to her bedroom where she peeled out of her clothing. She flipped her long black hair out of the way as she lay back on the bed and dialed up the gravity field until any sensation of weight vanished. Around her, the room dimmed as the pearlescent walls faded into dull gray and finally to blackness.

Ily filled her lungs and exhaled her tension. How many times had she and Tybalt made love on this platform? She closed her eyes, remembering his warm body against hers, their limbs entangled as she brought him to climax.

To herself, she whispered, "Tybalt, where am I ever going to find a lover like you again?" Perhaps she never would—but then, even the lover of a lifetime was worth an empire. Nevertheless, she could feel regret for having used the Seddi assassin, Arta Fera, to kill her Emperor. She'd played on his one weakness, and enjoyed a delightful irony in doing so, for her own career had been launched years ago by foiling a Seddi assassination attempt against Tybalt.

"Turn about is delicious justice."

How curious, the way things worked. Those Seddi assassins had been Sinklar Fist's parents. Sinklar had delivered Arta Fera into Ily's willing hands. Next he would deliver an empire to her. She reached out and stroked the soft sheets. Who knew, perhaps he'd be the next man to share this bed with her.

Arta Fera's words returned to haunt her. *"A little young, isn't he?"*

Ily whispered the words she'd spoken in reply, "All the better. I can train him the way I want." And perhaps he'd turn out to be a better lover than she suspected. On those occasions she'd dealt with him, he'd been self-possessed, unintimidated by her person or power. He'd need a lot of that, dealing with her. She tended to consume men, starting with their bodies . . . and ending with their souls.

The last time she'd seen him, he'd been preoccupied, grieving for his murdered lover, harried by the need to exterminate the Seddi. To be honest, youth or not, some power in those oddly colored eyes excited her. What *would* he be like as a lover? Tender? Or an animal like Tybalt had been?

For a while, she'd hoped that she could seduce Staffa kar Therma and bend him to her will—and perhaps she might have, had chance and an error on her part not made it impossible.

Ily growled, remembering the fiasco on Etaria, and blinked her eyes open to stare into the darkness. What had gone so terribly wrong? Where had the fatal mistake been made? She had found Staffa kar Therma condemned to slavery, in a collar of his own manufacture, and she'd misjudged his response. Why? What had changed him? Had slavery broken something elemental in the Lord Commander? He should have jumped at her offer of empire and power, but she'd turned him against her. Only quick action had saved her.

She chewed her lip angrily. "How did you escape, Staffa? I had you in my blaster sights . . . then blackness. What happened? Who rescued you? The Seddi? Is that how you got to Targa? We knew Skyla was on the planet. Where? How did she get you to her ship? Who made the mistake?"

So many unanswered questions. Ily tossed on her pad, and considered. Events had unfolded with such rapidity she hadn't had time to think—only to react and scramble to maintain damage control. Why did the Etarian debacle rankle so?

She sat up, the room lights brightening. To her bedside comm, she ordered, "Have Security Director Tyklat transferred from Etaria to Rega immediately. Reason: Promotion for outstanding service."

And when I have you here, Tyklat, we'll see just what happened that day in Etarus.

She lay back again and sought desperately to still her wheeling thoughts. She *had* to sleep. Her mind had to be keen enough to split atoms when Sinklar arrived with his troops. Unlike Staffa, she knew Sinklar. He'd still be hurting over the death of his beautiful Gretta Artina. He'd be chafing over Staffa's escape from Makarta.

Damn you, Staffa, slipped through my fingers again! How did you do that?

Sinklar would be Ily's key to social control. She had to have his loyal combat divisions: first to take control of the empire, and second, to defeat both the Sassan military and the dreaded Companions. She'd get one chance to seize absolute power—and she had to play Fist just right to do it.

The memory of Sinklar's eyes burned in the back of her mind. He *did* excite her. She ran light fingers down her skin, across her flat belly and into the tuft of inky pubic hair.

Yes, I can control Sinklar Fist—one way or another.

* * *

"You have no complaints!" The round-faced official—the Minister of Public works in Trystia—shouted at the crowd that welled and screamed before the Trystian Municipal Affairs Building. Above, the sky had gone leaden, ominous and filled with the threat of storm. The very air had gone chill. The spacing of the buildings around the Ministry didn't leave much space for a crowd, so people shoved and pushed, packed in elbow to elbow. More than five hundred people choked the approach to the building. Across the way, government employees stared out of the upper story windows of the Education Administration.

To the amber-eyed woman who stood to one side at the top of the steps, the pudgy official cut a pathetic figure. Still more pathetic, perhaps, was his duplicity in the whole affair. After all, Ily had promised him protection.

The Minister braced his arms on the podium that rested on the raised platform—a stage surrounded by muscular young men in Civil Protection uniforms and an energy barrier, just for good measure. Beyond the barrier, the crowd roared and waved their fists, the picked agitators bellowing out their slogans and demands.

A chill wind gusted, whistling out of the somber skies and moaning around the eaves.

"We've done all we can for the workers of Trystia!" the Minister implored. "We have no corruption here. That's for urban Rega—not our peaceful community!"

A blast of angry calls erupted from the crowd, amplified between the sheer stone walls of the closely spaced buildings.

When one of the burly guards looked her way, the amber-eyed woman nodded. The young man nudged his closest companion. One by one, they straightened in anticipation.

The amber-eyed woman stepped to the energy barrier, crying, "Hear us!"

On cue, the cherubic Minister raised his hands, ordering, "Wait! Silence!"

The muffled bellows of the crowd ebbed to a dull roar.

"The time has come," the amber-eyed woman's voice rang out, projected by the hidden speakers they'd placed, "for an end to tyranny! The people demand justice for your crimes! You live like the Blessed Gods themselves, while we wallow in misery! You eat Ashtan lamb—while we eat rationed bread! Look at your fat body! And then look at mine!" Her back to the mob, she ripped her coat wide. No one saw the smile on her lips as the Minister and the guards gawked at her magnificent body.

She pulled her coat tightly around her before she faced the crowd, crying, "We starve so he can get fat! Justice! Justice! Justice!"

The crowd took up the chant, shaking their fists in time with the call.

The guard she'd nodded to leapt to the platform and grabbed the Trystian Minister by the neck, speaking into the public address system. "Justice! Rise, my friends! Death to despots!"

As one, the guards shouted their approbation, cutting the power to the energy barrier.

"Take the building!" the amber-eyed woman goaded. "Fight for the people! Kill them all!"

The Minister of Public Works was picked up bodily, and thrown at the feet of the crowd. He disappeared under a mass of howling bodies as the rest surged forward, up the steps, and into the Ministry. Only as the last of the crowd charged into the building did the amber-eyed woman slip back out the door and dodge down the steps. One by one, the muscular young guards followed, each careful not to step on the gory remains of the Minister where he lay like a butchered steer.

A block away, a large aircar dropped; doors bearing the escutcheon of Internal Security opened for the amber-eyed woman and her companions. The vehicle lifted and shot away above the suddenly panic-filled streets.

* * *

Division First Ben MacRuder walked down the officer's corridor as the Regan battle cruiser *Gyton* approached the end of its null singularity jump. He proceeded with a swinging step, stacks of flimsies and data cubes cradled under his arm.

Of medium height, Mac had a muscular build, blond, medium-length hair, and blue eyes that had already started to grow crow's-feet at the corners. Like all Regan military personnel, he wore armor, a thick satin-finished synthetic of very tight weave capable of vacuum duty. The material had certain fiber-optic qualities which allowed limited camouflaging, The material's hollow fibers contained either a rapid acting catalyst or a polymer molecule. Upon impact or exposure to particle fire, the fibers ruptured with an instantaneous hardening of the armor. Once hardened, the armor charred and peeled in ablative flakes to protect the wearer from blaster or pulse fire.

Mac slowed and slapped a palm to the lock plate on the hatch to Sinklar's cabin. The door computer coded his body chemistry and dermatoglyphics, then slipped soundlessly back into the bulkhead.

Mac stepped into the little square room and stopped. Sinklar sat slumped at the desk with his head canted at an awkward angle—dead asleep. The desktop looked like a battle had been fought through the wadded and crumpled flimsies. The bank of monitors on the wall across from the desk glowed with graphics displays as they waited for the master's next manipulations of the tactics tables, maps, and statistics.

Something in Mac's breast constricted at the slouched posture and the grief reflected on his commander's face. Mac quietly lowered his pile of duty rosters to the already heaped desk and flinched when Sinklar made a whimpering sound.

"Sink?" Mac called softly as he rounded the desk to shake his friend's shoulder. "Hey, why don't you lay down and get some real sleep?"

Sinklar jerked, crying, "No! Gretta, I. . . ." His

eyes flickered open and he started, blinking owlishly around the cabin and then up at Mac. Hell reflected from those odd-colored eyes.

"Bad dream," Sinklar admitted sheepishly in his high voice.

Mac nodded. Sink might never have known it, but Mac had loved Gretta Artina with every bit as much passion and devotion. "Want to talk about it?"

"I'll be fine," Sinklar said hoarsely.

"Sure." Mac settled himself on the corner of the desk. "Mhitshul's been worried to fits about you. He says you're not sleeping, not eating. He says when you do drift off, you have terrible dreams. That you're driving yourself to—"

"Mhitshul's acting like an old woman." Sinklar arched his back and kneaded his neck muscles with a nervous hand. "Maybe he's got a mother complex or something."

Mac cocked his head, studying Sink skeptically. "Want to take a walk with me? You and I, buddy, have been so busy trying to organize this rabble of ours into an army that we haven't had time enough to settle some things between us."

"Such as?"

"Such as what happened while I was trapped in Makarta Mountain. I've heard bits and pieces from Staffa, from Mhitshul, and from Mayz and Kap—he's doing all right, by the way. They just released him from a med unit. His lungs are mostly healed."

"That's all you want to know?"

Mac shook his head slowly. "I want to know about that affair on *Chrysla* when we met with Staffa after the fighting. What the hell was that all about? Is it really some sort of Seddi trick?"

Sinklar spread his hands wide in a helpless gesture, his weird bicolored eyes searching Mac's. "I think the man's a lunatic, crazy, schizophrenic. Maybe it's some peculiar quirk of his. Maybe I came so close to beating him that it tweaked something in his mind, some association."

"Rotted Gods, Sink! The man thinks you're his son!"

Sinklar stood, wincing as if every muscle in his back had cramped. From the position he'd fallen asleep in, they probably had.

"I think I've got the Regan strategy worked out," Sinklar muttered as he gestured at the monitors and deftly avoided the subject.

Mac gave the displays a cursory inspection. "That's a relief. I'm not used to you pulling your hair out over a simple thing like a battle plan."

Sink raised an eyebrow. "Do I detect a sarcastic undercurrent here?"

Mac sighed and slapped his thighs as he got to his feet. "You want to take that walk with me, or spend all day making small talk to get around the fact that you're about to break up and crumble into little pieces?"

"Mac, I'm fine. Just a little tired and worried. Don't talk to me like that."

MacRuder considered that while Sinklar pushed his toilet door open, ran the little sink full of water, and doused his head in it. After Sink stepped out, drying himself, Mac swung around and jabbed a finger hard into Sinklar's chest. "Oh, yeah? Well let me remind you of a thing or two. I know you, *Lord* Fist. Who picked your fragged ass up in that Kaspan alley when a rebel blaster filled your scrawny hide full of shrapnel? Who carried your sorry meat up those stairs? Who wandered down into the dark to die for you at Makarta? Damn it, Sink, I'll talk to you however I want to—and you'll Rotted well listen when I do."

Sinklar's angular face reddened with anger, then he closed his eyes, took a deep breath, and nodded. "Yeah . . . yeah, I guess you will." He rubbed a hand over his face and glared at Mac through bloodshot eyes. "Come on, let's get the hell out of here and take this walk. Where we gonna go? There's no place but circles to walk around in this damn bucket of air."

"How about the little lounge back of the gym? It's

the closest thing to a relaxing environment on this rust bucket."

"You got it." Sinklar palmed the hatch and led Mac into the rib cage corridor with its long rectangular light panels and overhead conduit.

"Gretta's still haunting you, isn't she?" Mac hung his head, watching his feet.

"When she . . . I mean . . . When she was killed, it's like it tore something out of me, left me . . . I don't know . . . hollow inside." A pause. "I loved her so much. On Targa there wasn't time enough to understand. Too much was happening. The Makarta fight, fencing with Ily and Rysta . . . I didn't have the luxury to think about it—to feel the loss. But now? Damn it, Mac, every time I try and plan, Gretta should be there. She was part of me . . . and now there's only a hole inside."

Mac chewed his lip uneasily. *She was part of all of us, Sink. By the Rotted Gods, how good is that plan you've been hatching? The last one damn near got us all killed.* A shiver played along Mac's spine. Was that it? Had Sink's nerve broken? Had Arta Fera killed more than just Gretta? Had she killed that spark in Sinklar Fist that made him brilliant?

"You've just got to go on, Sink." How empty and trite that sounded. "What about Ily Takka? What do we do with her when we get to Rega? I don't trust her—haven't since the first day she set foot on Targa outside the Vespan brick factory."

Sinklar grunted noncommittally as they walked into the gymnasium. Two Sections were engaged in calisthenics. Someone saw Sinklar walk in. A whisper ran through the ranks as heads craned and worshipful eyes sought Fist's scrawny figure. The cadence of the exercise fell apart as the soldiers stopped to stare, reverence on their faces. Only the cursing of the Section Firsts got them back to work, and by then a transformation had taken place. Backs were straighter, heads high, each move perfect as if the sweating recruits labored before the watchful eye of the Divine.

Despite the number of times Mac had seen it, the

phenomenon still surprised him. The Empire had left these people in a murderous environment to die for obscure political ends. Sinklar had defied the odds, kept them alive, and molded them into a military force so dangerous the Emperor had dropped five veteran Divisions to snuff them out. *But we beat them. Out-numbered five to one, without orbital recon or support, our two skeleton Assault Divisions still won.*

A grim smile played across Mac's lips. Their courage and skill had brought the Minister of Internal Security to them to ask for a reconciliation, and each man and woman knew it. Then they'd tackled the Seddi in their lair—and fought no less an opponent than the Rotted Star Butcher to a standstill. That pride and indomitable spirit was reflected in the eyes of the Targan Assault Divisions and in the aggressive swagger they adopted in the corridors.

The responsibility rested on Sinklar's shoulders; he'd made them what they were. For them, Fist had thrown the book away, defying two centuries of military tradition, and teaching them how to win. More than that, he'd taught them to respect themselves as both human beings and soldiers. Unlike the other officers who hid in safety behind the lines, Sinklar Fist shared their worries, ate their food, laughed at their jokes, and mixed his tears with theirs.

They passed through the gym and into the corridor that led to the small lounge. They stepped through the pressure hatch to find an oval room about thirty paces in length. Recliners and couches were located along the walls, which had holographic capability. The program currently running appeared to be Riparious since giant green trees arched over muddy brown waterways. Stringers of delicate pale-green moss hung down from the branches like webbing, often dragging in the water. Sinuous scaled animals rested on mud banks, or splashed into the murky water.

Two of Sink's Section Firsts, Mayz and Shiksta, sat reclined, feet up, engaged in conversation. Mayz was a tall, lanky woman with short-cut curly hair and brown skin. Shiksta had ebony skin, a halo of kinky black hair, and broad facial features. He commanded the heavy ordnance for the Targan Divisions while Mayz commanded the Seventh Section. They both stood, warm grins spreading.

"You're looking a little skinny, Sink," Shik commented. "Aren't they feeding you up in officer country?"

Sinklar gave him an infectious grin. "It's not Targan beef. How have the two of you been?"

Mayz crossed her arms returning his smile. "Moderately bored. I hear we're going into action soon."

Sink stepped over to the dispenser and thumbed the button for a cup of klav. "Probably the moment we slip out of null singularity. As soon as I know the situation I'll give everyone a tactical rundown. In the meantime, enjoy the boredom. It might be the last you get for a while."

"You just tell us what you want, Sink," Shiksta assured, a defiant gleam in his eyes, "and we'll do it."

"You might let us have the lounge for a while." Mac crossed the room and punched the button on the dispenser for stassa. "We've got to have a skull session . . . and a change of scenery from gray and puke-green might unstick some paralyzed brain cells."

"We'll post a guard. See that you're not disturbed," Mayz called as she headed for the door. "And maybe we'll take your advice and get some sleep."

Shik paused at the door, fingering the hatch seal pensively. "Sink? Will it be as tough as Targa? Are we still the sacrificial Divisions?"

Sinklar walked over, placing a hand on Shik's muscular arm, searching his eyes. "Never again, Shik. This time we're taking the capital—and after that, the Empire. The old ways came to an end on Targa. Now, we're going to do it our way. Make sure your people know. It won't be an easy operation and we may take casualties, but this time we're fighting for a better Empire."

Shik nodded, a thoughtful look in his eyes. "For the little people, right?"

"For the little people," Sink agreed in a fervent whisper. He remained standing, staring absently at the hatch after Shik closed it.

"You mean that?" Mac asked.

Sinklar cocked his head, lines etching his forehead. "You could ask that? I mean . . . after everything we suffered on Targa? After Makarta?"

Mac slapped his free hand against his leg. "Rotted Gods, how do I know? Sink, everything's all rushed and top-side down and spinning. A couple of weeks ago we were going to make a quick job of crushing the Seddi—of ending it all. Then the rug got pulled out from under us. You'd think that after everything we went through on Targa, I'd be used to that. What happened? How did the Lord Commander get mixed up in this? What's his purpose? What's Ily's? For that matter, what's yours? Ily made you a Lord. Tybalt, who ordered us murdered, approved it before he in turn was murdered."

Mac lifted his stassa and took a sip, then he shook his head. "Excuse me, but I'm a little confused."

Sinklar chuckled, a wry glint in his too-old eyes. "I guess that makes two of us. But, Mac, you've got to know. I did everything I could to get you out of Makarta." Sinklar exhaled wearily. "If I'd known Staffa kar Therma was in that mountain, I'd never have tried a physical assault." Angrily, he thumped a fist against the bulkhead. "I thought we could get some of the Seddi out, answer some questions. Break them once and for all."

"I know, Sink. We heard the fighting, and, believe me, down there in the dark, it scared us to death that the roof would fall in."

Sinklar chewed at his lower lip, lost in thought. "What did Staffa offer you?"

"He said we could join the Companions. That there was always a place for fighters like us among his ranks."

"You liked him, didn't you?"

Mac smiled wistfully. "Yeah, I did. He's got style, Sink. He reminds me a lot of. . . ."

"Go on."

"He reminds me a lot of you."

Sinklar paced nervously, randomly jabbing a finger at the holo controls. The scene shifted to someplace carved out of blue ice. Sylene?

"He's not my father. I mean it's . . . impossible."

Mac braced his back against one of the walls and sipped his stassa. "You've never talked about them. Your folks, I mean."

"No. I had my reasons. At the time I didn't want any. . . . Look, they were Seddi. We were at war with the Seddi. Still are. I didn't want any speculation about where my loyalties might be. Mac, I never knew them. I was raised by the state as an orphan. But now, knowing what we do about the way the Seddi program their assassins, I can't blame my parents for what they tried to do."

"They tried to assassinate Tybalt—the Regan Emperor, by the Rotted Gods!"

"And Arta, it appears, has succeeded where my parents failed."

"Yeah . . . maybe. But we'll get to that in a bit. Look, Sink, how do you know they're really your folks?"

Sinklar cupped his klav in both hands, staring down into the liquid. "I found the records . . . found the Judicial Magistrate who sentenced them . . . and located their bodies in the Criminal Anatomical Research Labs on Rega. I . . . I saw them, Mac. Pulled out the caskets and looked into their eyes. They preserve the worst of the criminals there to see what makes them tick. They study the brains, the physiology, in an attempt to determine the root of deviance."

"Rotted Gods." Mac scowled into his cup, a chill in his soul. "Bruen knew their names, didn't he?"

Sinklar nodded.

"Valient and . . ."

"Tanya. My mother. I saw them, Mac. I looked into their dead eyes. If I hadn't done that, hadn't found them before I left, I might have been thrown off by Staffa's trick."

Mac squinted at the blue methane ice that surrounded them. *So why don't I buy it? Something's not right here. I saw Staffa's desperation.* "Did anyone know you saw the bodies?"

Sinklar lifted a shoulder. "A student there. I guess she felt sorry that I was going to war." A pause. "For a while I thought I was in love with her, Mac. Considering everything Gretta came to mean to me, can you imagine that?"

"Let's get back to Ily Takka. What's her angle in all this?"

Sinklar continued to pace, klav cup clutched in his hands. "Ily wants to be Empress. She can't do it without us. Her goal is—"

"*Pestilent Hell!* We're not going to put *her* on any Regan throne!"

Sinklar raised his hands, gesturing for peace, amusement in his eyes. "Of course we're not, Mac. At least, not for long."

Mac tried to swallow the sudden tension in his breast. "You want to enlighten me?"

"As much as I can, sure. But, Mac, I want your word that you'll tell no one. You've got to swear to secrecy. All right?"

Mac glared angrily; nevertheless, he nodded his agreement.

"Ily was one of the major movers and shakers who left us high and dry to die on Targa. I haven't quite pieced all of her reasons together, but I suspect it was to woo the Companions away from Sassa. We were bait—a military debacle on Targa would have appealed to the Star Butcher's vanity, and most likely to his pocketbook as well. The problem was, we didn't do what we were supposed to. Worse, we won the damn war."

"And she dropped those five Divisions on us? We bled for that, Sink."

"They bled more. Actually, she held Rysta back—kept her from slagging us from orbit. You might say that was the final test."

"For what?" Mac watched him suspiciously.

Sinklar turned his cup absently. "The test that proved our ability to conquer the rest of Free Space."

Mac's heart skipped. "Conquer . . ."

". . . the rest of Free Space. Yes, you heard me right, Mac." Sinklar whirled, pointing a finger. "Remember what I studied? I was a scholar before they made me a soldier. You wanted to know *my* angle? I'm tired of war, tired of the status quo. I'm damn tired of Seddi intrigue and Regan politics. I'm going to upset the fish cart and let the slimy bodies fall where they will. You and I, Mac, and the First Targan Assault Division are going to rewrite the 'Holy Gawdamn Book.' First, we pacify Rega, then we move on Sassa . . . and the Companions, if they get in the way. Then we set about governing the whole in a constructive fashion."

Mac shook his head. "You're talking about becoming the *sole* ruler of Free Space? Everything within the Forbidden Borders?"

Sinklar's eyes had hardened. "I am. Are you with me, Mac?" He reached out a hand. "It's a chance. Remember, you asked me about the little people? That's us, Mac. You, me, the First Targan Division, all of us. We can remake human space. Help me."

Mac struggled for words. "What . . . what about Ily?"

Sinklar sighed and raised his eyebrows. "She'll be an asset in the beginning. Somewhere along the line, however, our paths will diverge. She wants to be a tyrant—and I won't allow that. Not if it takes every drop of my blood."

"You'll have to destroy the Companions, too," Mac whispered, a chill of premonition running down his back.

"Yes," Sinklar mused. "We'll have to be very good when we finally face them. But perhaps I know a way to crush the Companions—and to remove Staffa kar Therma, once and for all."

* * *

"As Seddi, one of the first things we ask ourselves is how we know what we know. We call this study epistemology, and it is essential for our purposes. Through epistemology we interpret the rules of thought and how they influence our understanding of the universe around us.

"Several assumptions are fundamental to the way we learn and perceive. First, we observe something in the physical realm we can sense, and from that observation, create. For example, a person looking at topography can reproduce what he sees with a map. However, the warning here is that the map is not the actual topography but an abstraction, a creation of the mind. We can create a name: tree, or rock, or planet. Nevertheless, the name is not the object named; it is a symbol. Taking this process a step further, we can observe relationships between objects, note how they interrelate and act upon each other. These processes and forces are in turn labeled at yet another level of abstraction, such as gravity. Again, the name is not the physical process. When these processes and systems are placed into a hierarchy, we call that hierarchy a paradigm—a symbolic model we have interpreted from our observations. In the end, we have nothing more than an abstraction—not reality in its purest sense.

"We accept these abstractions, maps, names, and paradigms, as being true because of a lifetime of indoctrination. From the time we're infants until we die, we are led to believe that the world is the way it is because

everyone else believes it to be so. Not only that, such beliefs are operational. They help us to cope with the physical environment around us. However, when we look beyond the accepted, we find nothing more than a reality based on abstraction. My challenge to each of you is to consider how you know what you know. Are the truths you accept really true? Or have you simply been indoctrinated, trained to accept without questioning why?

"Among the Seddi, this process of indoctrination is called a Unilateral Epistemology."
—Excerpt from Kaylla Dawn's Itreatic broadcasts

CHAPTER V

Patches of smoke drifted among the canyonlike defiles between the glass-walled buildings. An eerie silence had settled over the Imperial city of Rega. Anatolia Daviura checked the monitors and looked both ways before she stepped through the security door of the Criminal Science Building. The street had a pathetic look, scattered with wreckage. Charred smears streaked up the sheer gray walls above burned out windows where the looters had done their worst. She dared not look too closely at the lumpy form wrapped in blue cloth which lay bloating against a wall no more than fifty meters from where she stood.

The Public Transit Authority had discontinued the shuttle system in response to the violence. Overhead, the skies remained empty of the usual bustle of commuting aircars and delivery vehicles—the traffic lanes curiously quiet but for an occasional racing vehicle. The air carried a pungent scent.

The heavy outer door—scarred now—snicked shut with finality as Anatolia waved at the security camera nestled in a recess above and turned to wait for Vet's aircar. She shivered nervously. How long could people go on living in fear? The few times Civil Security had attempted to curb a riot, they'd been shot down in the streets and their mangled bodies left for their families to claim. *This is a nightmare. It can't go on. Something has to happen.*

The garage landing thunked as Vet's oblong aircar passed through and dropped down to pick her up.

"Sorry it took so long," he told her as she slipped

into the passenger seat. "Bokken is being extra careful."

Anatolia leaned back in the seat and fingered the padded plastic of the dash. "After the last three days, do you blame him?"

Vet chuckled dryly. "Not at all. The word is that people like us who work for the state are fair game. The message being broadcast is that all government employees are corrupt."

Anatolia watched as they passed through the Biological Research Center complex. Wreckage lay in the devastated streets below—the shops plundered after the abortive attempt to sack the government buildings. Those gleaming structures still rose proudly, only their feet sullied by muck. At the edge of the complex, they were forced to skirt the Revenue Building. Even from this distance, the damage could be seen.

They gang raped the women before they ripped them apart and strung their intestines from the ceilings. "Vet? What's happened to us? Where's it all going to end?"

He glanced at her and winked. "Hey, it's not the end of the Empire. Someone will fill Tybalt's throne. Probably someone from the military high comm. . . . Well, someone."

Anatolia closed her eyes, hands knotting in her lap. *It's just me. It's the work we do . . . dealing with deviance. It sours your judgment of humanity.*

She stared at the empty streets, many in shambles. "I don't care if the military is corrupt. Why aren't they here? Unlike the civil police, they're armed. Can't the Minister of Internal Security do something about this . . . something besides arresting the nobility and executing them?"

"Listen, you sure you don't want to come stay with Marka and me? We could roll out a bed for you."

Anatolia smiled gratefully. "Security locked us up for three days in the lab. I want to go home and stand in my own shower, in my own tiny little bathroom, and sleep on my own platform. Besides, Marka's probably been worried sick. Go home and be with her. Give her some relief from the baby. I'll be fine."

Vet wiggled his lips distastefully and sighed. "Okay . . . but if you need anything, call."

The aircar took the third tier entrance to her building and hummed down the passenger access corridor, a gray square concrete tunnel broken by light panels.

"Thanks for the ride, Vet. I sure appreciate it." She took his hand, squeezed it, and opened the door as they pulled to a halt before the line of lift tubes that would take her up to her floor.

"No problem. You'd have had to walk, otherwise. I'll be by to pick you up at 06:00 the day after tomorrow."

"See you then."

"Oh, Anatolia? Get to your room and lock your door. Stay there. All right?"

"Sure, Vet."

He waited until she stepped into the lift. It carried her up to the fifty-sixth floor where she lived in her small cubicle apartment. A tickle of fear warned her. As the lift stopped, she heard the voices. Uneasy, she took a half-step out into the foyer, seeing the young men lounging around.

The pimply blond kid from down the hall looked up. "There she is! The one that works for the bulls! Get her!"

Anatolia dove back into the tube, smacking the plate that sent the lift rocketing down. Where? The ground floor? They'd go there first. She stopped the lift at level two and glanced out to see empty hallway and stained carpeting. Panicked, she sprinted down the long hall for the emergency stairs in the rear.

Think Anatolia . . . think, damn it, or they're going to kill you!

* * *

"Are you ready for this?" Staffa asked as they waited in the wide hallway beyond the Imperial Sassan throne room. A line of benches and chairs hugged

the stone walls, while plants filled niches. The floor
reflected the luster of thorough polishing. Staffa's security troops surrounded them, eyes on the Sassan
guards.

Skyla gave him a wary smile, a hard glint in her
winter blue eyes. "I guess so. We'd look pretty funny
trying to back out now."

"Ryman? Are you and your people ready?"

Ark grinned, tapping a wrapped parcel he held.
"All here, sir. We're ready—no matter what happens." Expressions went grim on the ST personnel.

As the speakers announced his entry, the heavy
crystal doors lifted and a tense Staffa kar Therma
stepped into the throne room. Here, for the first time,
he would have to face his new self on old territory.
He looked around at the gleaming glassy arches that
rose toward the faceted ceiling. Crystal-diffused light
was the hallmark of Sassan architecture and Divine
Sassa's throne room enjoyed the reputation as the
penultimate example of the art. The walls gleamed as
if molded from liquid diamond. High overhead, the
optics splintered golden light into silver, violet, indigo,
blue, green, yellow, and, finally, red at the lowest
level. The floor created the effect of walking on a
sea of molten gold that ebbed and flowed in swirling
patterns underfoot.

The chamber stretched over one hundred meters
wide by nearly three hundred in length. Each of the
niches contained an armed guard brightly dressed in
white and scarlet with a pulse rifle at parade rest before him. The members of Divine Sassa's court waited
in a knot of corpulent bodies at the far end of the
gleaming room. Their gazes rested uneasily on Staffa
and Skyla as they entered and were followed by a
picked guard of Ryman's Special Tactics unit.

His Holiness never exposed himself to any but his
closest advisers. Instead, he floated in serene holographic display, his giant body supported on a gravity
field. A sort of reclining couch lay under much of his
bulk, but to think he sat in it smacked of the ridiculous. The God-Emperor of Sassa weighed at least

three hundred and fifty kilos, perhaps more. Rumor had it that if his gravity fields ever failed, the shock of the planet's 1.2 gravities would kill him instantly.

An entire cult of obesity had sprung from Divine Sassa's weight. In an empire otherwise faced with starvation, the high and mighty gorged themselves in emulation of their god—much to the amusement of anyone not presently being ground under the mighty Sassan boot.

Staffa walked forward warily, thankful for the steadying presence of Skyla beside him. She wore brilliant white armor studded with jewels and golden filigree. The result set off her long ice-blonde hair, braided now and wrapped around her left shoulder. With her at his side, he could do anything.

Staffa slowed as he neared Divine Sassa's end of the room, the nobles and Councillors drifting back to clear the way.

Staffa halted, bracing his feet, hands on hips, his charcoal cloak billowing around him. One by one, he cataloged the Councillors, enjoying a grim amusement as they dropped their eyes and blushed. Only Legate Myles Roma and Admiral Jakre managed to withstand his stare.

"Greetings, Lord Commander, and welcome once again to Imperial Sassa. The capitol complex is graced by your presence." Sassa's words sounded hollow as they echoed around the room.

Staffa raised his eyes to the hologram. Divine Sassa hovered like a dirigible above his gravity platform. Not a hair grew on the man's bald head. The colorless eyes made gimlets in the pudgy flesh of his face. The rest of his huge girth had been wrapped in meters of finely embroidered fabric. A corps of attendants saw to that.

"And I by yours, Divine Sassa." Staffa gave the Emperor the briefest of bows. "I must commend you on the reception I was given. I've received every courtesy from both the Legate and the Admiral. Security was perfect. The Companions offer you our deepest gratitude."

"We are always most glad to be of service to you and your loyal troops, Lord Commander." A pause. "For myself, I can't say how glad I am to see you here. For several months we found ourselves discomfited with worry, Lord Commander. Our agents informed us that you'd disappeared. Subsequently, we learned that you'd been treated most maliciously by the Regan tyrants. And yet later we learn that Regan Imperial forces not only hunted you like an animal, but actually sought to assassinate you. Your anger at their perfidy is ours."

Staffa rocked back on his heels, meeting Sassa's round-faced stare. "It would seem, Divine One, that they failed—but the blame falls upon the shoulders of Minister Ily Takka. I've become convinced that Tybalt, rest his soul, never had all the facts placed at his disposal. Rather, it seems the Minister of Internal Security was following her own agenda."

"And a most disagreeable one it is," Sassa pouted. "My intelligence people inform me that she's continuing the Regan military buildup. Further, she's executed the Minister of Defense and his Deputies. We interpret this as a means whereby she may establish a clean slate for this boy general of hers . . . this Sinklar Fist. Tell me, Lord Commander, what do you think of all this?"

"It's disaster, Divine One. With Tybalt, we could have reasoned. For all of his faults, the Imperial Seventh wasn't anyone's fool. Ily Takka, serpent that she is, could destroy all of us—even humanity itself."

Sassa smiled, rolls of facial fat shifting. "You bring a radiance into my palace, Lord Commander. Your words are like a balm of heat on frozen Ryklos. I must confess, I'd heard somewhat disquieting news that you'd taken to associating with Seddi spies and heretics . . . that they might have filled you full of some mystical nonsense and dampened your ardor for the final campaign."

Staffa cocked his head and raised an eyebrow. "Mystical nonsense? No, Divine One. Sense? Yes.

I've learned quite a bit from the Seddi. That's what I came here to talk to you about."

An undercurrent rippled through the room. Staffa could sense Skyla tensing beside him. She stood ready to spring, a hard set to her jaw.

Sassa's voice had a clipped sound. "Speak, Lord Commander. Am I to understand that you will not join us in stopping the Regan pollution?"

Staffa paced several steps to the side and whirled, pinning the Emperor with his gray stare. "I came here, Divine One, to try and talk you out of launching an attack on the Regan worlds. If you begin such a—"

"*Why?*"

Staffa cocked his head, matching glare for glare. "Because, Divine One, you'll lose."

In the pause that followed, hushed whispers shot back and forth between the Councillors. The grand hall had gone suddenly chilly.

"Imperial Sassa will lose?" His Holiness asked with mild amusement. "Lord Commander, Ily Takka has executed her Minister of Defense and his Deputies. She has given us the perfect opportunity. Were you to launch another of your lightning strikes—blast their capital and industrial centers—our troops could follow and crush the last of their resistance. It would be over in a matter of weeks and Free Space would be united."

"Free Space would be devastated," Staffa countered, smacking a fist into a hard palm. "I've run the data the Seddi have collected over the years, Divine One. They're right. A final cataclysmic war would condemn humanity." He turned back. "Ryman, please deliver the studies to the Legate."

Ark saluted and stepped forward, handing a stunned Myles Roma the heavy parcel of data cubes and printouts. He pivoted on his heel and stepped back to his place behind Staffa and Skyla.

"The information I have provided is a detailed environmental and economic study," Staffa told them. "I don't ask you to take the Seddi data at face value.

Have your own people check and cross-check it. I think the results will be frightening."

"Frightening how?" Sassa demanded.

"We're facing extinction. Conditions within your own empire illustrate the point. You're barely able to redeploy your forces for a strike against the Regans. Despite a more sophisticated logistics system than the one in use by your enemy, you can't support a massive mobilization without crippling your economic base. Face it, you're broke—and so are the Regans."

"But *they* are also mobilizing!" Sassa turned red as he roared and flexed his sausage-fat fingers. "What do you expect? That we'll sit back and allow them to move against us? You're talking about suicide!"

"Yes, Divine One, I am. Here's the situation. No matter how brilliant Myles Roma is, you can't mobilize and deploy a significant strike force for at least another four months. If you move any faster, you'll disrupt overextended manufacturing, transportation, and labor. Your people are working at the limits of human endurance. You can't afford to take freighters out of domestic service for military use because industrial production will slow, or food won't be delivered, or spare parts won't be available. Your economy is a house of cards. Pull the wrong one out—and you'll have disaster.

"It will take Rega at least as long to prepare any kind of military adventure. They must subdue the civil unrest and replace the military leadership with Sinklar Fist's people. After that it will take the Regans another three months to supply themselves and integrate the infrastructure necessary for a full-scale invasion. They'll have to call up reserves, just as you will, and suffer the economic dislocation of key services and personnel. Rega might have a larger empire, Divine One, but I assure you, they have no one with Roma's brilliance at logistics or understanding of systems distribution. An attempt to move too fast will be just as disastrous for them."

"All the more reason for us to strike now!" Jakre cried, stepping forward. The jeweled rings on his clenched fist shot patterns of spectral light through the air. "We've got to hit them before they can fully prepare!"

Staffa shook his head. "Iban, *think!* You'll launch a limited strike in the beginning, because that's all you can assemble. You want to strike a crippling blow, so you'll waste a Regan world—say Sylene. Fist will make a counterstrike and destroy a Sassan world, Malbourne. You'll have built up enough reserve to feel free to tackle a larger target, but not Rega itself, so you'll incinerate Etaria in hopes of breaking their morale. Fist will repay that by blasting both Antillies and Farhome. And after that, you'll never stop him."

Jakre glared down his long nose. "You seem to have a lot of faith in this Sinklar Fist."

"I've fought him. He's not Tedor Mathaiison—or any other Regan commander you've studied. He's thrown out the book, Iban. Fist single-handedly put down the Targan rebellion—despite Regan interference. He decimated the combat capabilities of five veteran Divisions dropped by Tybalt to destroy him—defeated them soundly despite being ill-equipped, denied orbital support, and outnumbered five to one. Ily Takka recognized his talent." He paused. "She's grooming him for the role of conqueror."

"He's only a child!" Myles Roma cried.

"He's also brilliant," Staffa countered. "He's going to quell any unrest on Rega, and do it with little investment in time or resources. Immediately thereafter, he's going to put MacRuder in as his second in command. Ayms, Kap, Mayz, Shiksta, and the rest of his officers are going to be handed the best veteran Divisions, and his people are going to retrain them. Regan soldiers are used to taking risks and dying on the battlefield. Fist is going to empower them, give them something to really fight for. He's going to topple the old order and enfranchise his soldiers. And here's another thing. He promotes based on battlefield ability, not by political favor, family background, or social class."

"Then perhaps we should launch our attack directly

at Rega in the very beginning," Sassa mused. "If we could destroy this Sinklar Fist at the outset, perhaps Rega would fall apart on its own?"

Staffa chuckled hollowly. "An excellent idea, Divine One, but I'd give less than ten-to-one that you'd achieve your objective. Regan spies are every bit as good as your own. Fist will be prepared by the time you can field a large enough force to threaten any of his major planets—and I dare say, he'll have a stunning defense and counterattack awaiting you."

"Then perhaps I'm missing something," Sassa said. "What exactly do you recommend, Lord Commander? That we sit and do nothing? Allow this boy general you think so much of to consolidate his power? Are we to trust that Ily Takka, the rapacious bitch we've come to know her for, will simply let be?"

Staffa crossed his arms and nodded. "That is exactly what I'm telling you. If you would avoid holocaust for all of us, you'll abide peacefully and let me handle the rest. I'll take whatever steps are necessary to protect you from Ily Takka. As to Sinklar, he'll back off as soon as he learns you're not going to attack. For the time being, he's got enough to deal with."

Staffa derived a faint amusement from the looks traded back and forth between the advisers. Nervous feet shuffled on the molten gold floor.

"And what if we decided that our best interest is to act while we have the advantage, Lord Commander?" Sassa's voice had taken on honeyed tones.

Staffa felt himself begin to bristle. "You'll all pay the price, Divine One. World after world will be turned into irradiated slag. In the end, with the help of the Companions, you might win—but what would you be master of? Devastated waste? Pockets of humanity will survive, but most of the resources necessary for the advancement of the species will be denied them. Over the centuries, Your Holiness, even those populations will wither away until the worlds of Free Space are silent and dark. Study the figures I have provided—and draw your own conclusions."

Sassa's pig-eyed stare sought to penetrate Staffa's

iron mask, seeing his real motive. Rot it all, hadn't Sassa heard a single Blessed word?

"And your response to such a choice, Lord Commander?"

Staffa glanced sidelong at Jakre and Roma. Both stood motionless, holding their breath. The spark of anger kindled by Sassa's tone warmed in his breast. "If you choose such . . . we will be forced to act against you, Divine One."

Sassa bolted upright, the pale skin of his hairless head flushing with anger. "You . . . threaten *me!*"

Staffa nodded stiffly. "To save this civilization, yes. I threaten you—and Rega." He took a pace forward and raised a gloved hand, pointing a hard finger at the holo apparition. "I won't allow you to exterminate humanity, Sassa. Do not cross me!"

Skyla's hand settled firmly on his shoulder and Staffa curbed his anger. In a quick glance he took in the pale visages of the Councillors. Roma's fingers had wound into his fat gut. Jakre's normally ruddy features had turned pallid.

"What is this?" asked Sassa suddenly, his mountainous flesh trembling. "Are you working for Rega, Staffa? Is that it?"

Staffa shook his head, flaying the fat Emperor with his gray gaze. "I'm working for the people, Sassa. You're right; I've had a change of heart. It's time for a new way. The enemy isn't Rega, it's out there." Staffa gestured toward the shining ceiling. "Join me. Help me find a way to break the Forbidden Borders. Beyond them we'll find our true enemy. Until we do that, we're simply pawns for whatever beings have trapped us here. If you'll provide safe passage, I'll send you Seddi experts to tell you what they know. Perhaps you'll be as shocked as I was."

"Seddi?" Then Sassa laughed, rolls of his fat shaking in waves. Several of the Councillors picked it up, chuckling despite the fact they didn't understand the joke. "You want *me*, a God, to allow blaspheming Seddi conspirators into Imperial Sassa?"

Staffa waited until the guffaws died. "I do. If you're

smart, Divine One, you'll take them. I don't care if you accept their theology, but you'd better pay attention to what they know about our history. We've been manipulated, Holiness. And for one, I'm damned angry about it. No one manipulates Staffa kar Therma!" He narrowed his eyes to slits, adding, "The last man who did was the Praetor."

His Holiness seemed to lose some of his color. "We will consider this, Lord Commander. You've given us a great deal to think about and study. Such matters cannot be decided without serious consultation and review."

Staffa lifted his chin arrogantly. "No, they can't." A pause. "One last thing, Holiness. You and your advisers will pore over the recordings of what took place here today, seeking the hidden meanings. looking for the levels within levels of intrigue and misdirection while you try and determine what I'm *really* after. To save you that effort, I'll give you my word of honor that everything I've said here today is the blunt truth. Cross me, and you gamble not only your empire—but all of humanity."

Without giving Divine Sassa the chance to dismiss him, he whirled on his heel and—followed by his staff—stalked out of the deadly quiet room.

* * *

Myles Roma squinted to relieve the throbbing pain that lanced through his head. He didn't normally get headaches, but this one had pierced his brain with sadistic effect.

Myles sat at his sandwood desk in his tower office. Before him and to one side a huge window displayed the glittering lights of Imperial Sassa. On the other side, monitors glowed across the entire wall. Normally Myles would have worried about the holo of His Holiness, Divine Sassa II, where it stared perpetually down from behind his desk—as if the Emperor constantly watched over Myles' shoulder. Now, however, both Sassa's face and Admiral Iban Jakre's filled the two largest comm monitors on his wall.

"The estimates are only preliminary at this stage," Myles told them, "but it appears the Seddi figures are quite correct. How they came up with such elegant statistics is beyond our understanding. Our personnel are only beginning to run the programs provided by the Lord Commander. To complete them all may take weeks given our limited capacity."

Divine Sassa's bald head furrowed with thought. "Yet the preliminary analysis appears correct? War would lead to disaster?"

Myles spread his flabby arms helplessly. "That's what's indicated by the analysis we've managed to date. What can I tell you, Divine One? We'd have to employ an army of economists, sociologists, systems theorists, political scientists, mining technologists, engineers, ecologists, biologists, mathematicians, and a host of other specialists to check the source material alone for accuracy. Then we'd have to dump critical management programs to free up machine time to run the manipulations—and hope we made no errors in the programming. I don't know what kind of computer system the Seddi use, but it's light-years ahead of ours. All I can tell you at this stage is that if the baseline assumptions are correct—and on the surface they seem to be—Staffa is right."

Jakre had been fingering his long jaw as he listened. "But aren't there many ways the data could have been skewed? This is all a matter of interpretation, correct? You yourself admit that many of their statistical functions are unfamiliar to our statisticians. I could pick and choose among the raw data for what I thought was important, disregard that which seemed spurious, and reach entirely different conclusions than the Seddi scholars did."

Myles frowned and licked his lips. "Essentially, that's correct. But I don't—"

"Then this could be a mammoth boondoggle. Something to absorb our already strained resources and divert them away from the mobilization and redeployment of our military forces."

Myles fished out another antacid and swallowed it. "I don't know if. . . . Yes, it's possible. But if it's a delaying tactic, it's a Rotted clever one." Myles winced, adding, "Forgive me, Divine One."

His Holiness seemed not to hear. Instead, his deeply set eyes focused on something outside of the holo pickup. "Curious, don't you think, that the first time we have the ability to act successfully without the Lord Commander, he shows up attempting to talk us out of it?"

"Most suspicious," Jakre agreed. "We have a use-it-or-lose-it opportunity—the first in our entire history—to unite Free Space under Your Holiness' enlightened rule. And Staffa picks this time to tell us no?"

Myles ran a finger around his collar, realizing it hung loose about his neck. The strangling feeling came from nerves. He didn't have any tight collars anymore. "I don't care to cross the Lord Commander. We'd better remember his remarks concerning Myklene."

"Or do we remember his total disregard for our honor by launching his assault on Myklene before we were ready?" Jakre countered.

"He gave us his word that he was telling the truth," Myles insisted stubbornly. "In all the years we've dealt with him, when has he ever lied?"

"He could be banking on exactly that." Jakre lifted a thin eyebrow. "The final conflict is upon us, Legate. I say we pursue it and cripple Rega before it rises like the siff jackal it is and hamstrings us. Tybalt's assassination and the execution of their military leaders is too good a chance to throw away because a mercenary doesn't want to lose his precious reputation as the scourge of space."

"Do you really believe that?" Sassa asked, a pensive look on his fat face.

Jakre made a dissimulating motion. "I find Staffa's vanity as plausible an explanation as any, Holiness. Place yourself in his position. How would *you* feel if suddenly random events had allowed one of your client states to operate effectively without you? And suppose you realized that Sassa could not only take the Regans, but could do it quickly and efficiently? Divine One, if you control all of Free Space, what role is there for the Star Butcher? I agree our economy is in shambles, but seriously, it's that way because we bleed ourselves dry to pay the Companions."

"The man is a parasite," Sassa agreed.

"Once we consolidate Free Space under Sassan rule, there will be no role for Staffa and his butchers."

Myles watched the interchange with a curious tearing of emotions. How nice to believe Jakre right, that Sassan skill and courage could castrate the Regan tyrants and bring all humanity under the benign grace of His Holiness. Then again, Staffa's words lingered in Roma's mind. *Don't cross me!*

"I urge caution," Myles interjected. "Too many aspects of this bother me. What happened to Staffa on Etaria? We have a holo of him walking into the Internal Security offices in Etarus. He's with Ily Takka, and wearing a slave collar! Soon thereafter, the building practically blew up. Was that a hoax of some sort? Did Staffa really escape? How did he get to Targa? What happened in Makarta Mountain? We don't have enough intelligence data to guess the Lord Commander's angle in all this. Lastly, why did he evacuate the Seddi? The Seddi tried to assassinate Staffa for years, and now he harbors them?"

"I think it's apparent," Jakre told him flatly. "Staffa doesn't want us to unify humanity. I'll let you list the reasons why that might be."

"Prudence," His Holiness said softly, "is exhibited by the man who provides for any circumstance. Admiral, you will continue preparations for a military strike against the Regan Empire. Legate, I want you to scour those documents. See what they really mean. In the meantime, we'll just have to see what happens."

Myles nodded his acquiescence and killed the connection. His appetite had died during the conversation. He stood, walking out from behind his desk to stare at the lights of Imperial Sassa. In the reflection of his window, he could see how his clothes hung on his body. At this rate, he'd need an entire new wardrobe within weeks.

*   *   *

"I hope you know what you're doing," Rysta Braktov growled.

Sinklar narrowed his eyes grimly at he watched the monitor. He sat uncomfortably in *Gyton*'s command chair while the bridge crew bent over their duty stations. Rysta, her expression sour as rotten siva fruit, watched hostilely as she stood beside his chair. Around them, the three-sixty monitors displayed the Imperial planet of Rega. From space it appeared to be a peaceful sphere. Only when the planet's communications were tapped did the truth become apparent.

"Rotted Gods," Rysta whispered as the holo showed a scene where people rioted before the Grain Commission. One of the upper windows shattered and burly men hung the Commissioner out. The man squealed like a wounded rabbit before they let him fall the four stories to the ground. When he landed, his body crushed a young boy who stood by the wall, shouting slogans and waving his fist.

Sinklar cast a speculative glance at Rysta. "I think we'd better put a stop to it."

"Then why sneak in the way you did? Why not broadcast to the whole planet that you've come to take charge?"

Sinklar gave the old commander a sly glance and lowered his voice. "Let's say I wanted to obtain an understanding of the tactical situation before Ily knew we were around. Incidentally, my compliments to your crew. They've done a wonderful job masking our approach from the detection buoys."

"I feel like a Rotted pirate," Rysta muttered.

"I've got a sentry ship!" the Comm First called out. "They're requesting identification."

Sinklar frowned. "What's our highest clandestine operating code?"

"You can't!" Rysta cried. "That's against all the. . . ." She stopped at the sight of Sinklar's rising eyebrow.

"Comm First, reply with our highest clandestine clearance."

The Comm First hesitated only long enough to exchange frustrated glances with Commander Braktov before she bent to her boards.

"They'll break you down to private—before they chop your head from your body." Rysta barely controlled her loathing.

"They. They who?" Sinklar steepled his fingers. "And, Rysta, if we lose, what difference will it make? If we don't quell the rebellion on the planet, more than just ourselves will die."

"I haven't made up my mind about you, Fist. Either you're the brassiest bastard ever born, or you're the slimiest. I thought Ily ordered you to contact her. Since we broke out of null singularity, you haven't made a peep."

"No. I haven't. Maybe her female charms didn't overload my senses after all, hmm?" Sinklar paused. "And, Commander, Ily doesn't *order* me to do anything."

Rysta grunted a begrudging approval.

"Comm First? They buying it?" Sinklar asked.

The woman looked up, listening intently to her headset. "So far. I'm sure they're scrambling and frantic over there, but they haven't sent anything else. Wait. I've got a request for visual. It's coming in from one of the Orbital Defense platforms. Top clearance."

Sinklar tapped the armrest pensively, considering, then he got to his feet. "Commander. Take the chair. I assume you'd know anyone of importance in fleet security?"

Rysta shrugged. "I might. Still, you never know. It's a big fleet."

Sinklar laid a hand on her shoulder as they changed places. "Commander. You don't have to like me, but we've seen what's been happening on the planet. I don't care what you have to do, but get us in without Ily knowing. Can you do that?''

Rysta worked her jaw for a moment, the action rearranging the wrinkles on her dark face. "Rotted Gods. . . . I wish you'd. . . . Yes. If it will save lives."

Rysta took the chair, settling into it with familiarity. Her hard eyes pinned Sinklar. "You'd better know what you're doing."

"We're ready for visual," Sinklar told the Comm First.

The woman nodded and the main screen flickered to present an older man, white-haired, with steely gray eyes. The first words out of his mouth were, "Rysta! So it's *Gyton* coming with the squadron!" His sudden excitement died. "Blessed Gods, I've got orders to contact the Minister of Internal Security as soon as you check in."

Sinklar shook his head and Rysta took his cue. "Commander Bryn Hack, it's good to see you again. Is this line secure?"

Hack nodded, tension in his eyes. "Your clandestine code got you that, though Ily's bloodhounds are no doubt sniffing as we speak. Listen, Rysta, things have changed here. Mathaiison, his Deputies . . . they're dead. Executed for treason. Ily's involved in a power play. I think she's trying to become empress."

"Pus-Rotted *damnation!*" Rysta started from her chair. "Ily executed the high command? What does that silly bitch think she's *doing?* Inviting the Sassans to swing the sword while our jugular is exposed soft and white in the sun?"

"I don't know." Hack wiped at his nose. "Listen, we're all cut off from each other. The body of the military is intact, we're just without coordination." He paused and nervously licked his lips. "Rysta, what are you going to do? I mean, you've got ships, Assault Divisions. . . ."

Rysta took a deep breath. "Bryn, we've known each other for a long time. Can you cover? Buy us enough time to deploy around the planet?"

Hack's jaw trembled. Finally he jerked a nod. "If Ily finds out . . . it's my life."

Rysta gave him a weary smile. "It's a lot of people's."

"Good luck. I'll kill the net, fake a system failure or something." The screen went blank.

Rysta's black eyes glinted, her thoughts far away.

"What do you think? Will Orbital Defense be able to cover for us?"

"Probably. Bryn used to be a combat officer. Knowing how the capital is starting to unravel must make his soul ache."

"Then I suppose we'd better get to work mending. If you'll excuse me, Commander." Sinklar gestured Rysta out of the command chair and resettled himself, ordering, "I need to talk to my Firsts."

One of the instrument cluster pads on the arm of the chair rose, splitting into a series of smaller screens. Mac, Mayz, Kap, Shiksta, and the rest of his command Firsts appeared.

"All right, people, here we go again. We're closing on Rega. Orbital Defense is trying to buy us time to get into position. If we do this right, no one will know anything is happening until we're on the ground and in control. Mac, you and the First Targan are in charge of the capital. You know the objectives. Drop and take them. You might be on your own for a couple of days, but hang on. This isn't Targa." *We hope.* "Mayz, your responsibility is Trystia. Take the communications center, power plant, comm centers, and so forth."

"Affirmative, Sink." Mayz called.

"Kap, you hit Vedoc with the Second Targan while Tupo subdues Rypan."

"Affirmative."

"Shik? You understand your part?"

"Sure thing, Sink. Me and my people float around in the LCs and provide a fluid reinforcement for any hot spots." A wicked smile curled Shik's thick lips. "Anybody starts to get hit, we fly to the rescue with the heavy stuff."

"Remember, people, we're here to enforce order, not murder civilians."

"Affirmative," Mac told him, refusing to look into the pickup. "How long to drop?"

Sinklar looked up at the Nav First, an inquiring eyebrow raised.

"Six hours, sir."

"You get that?" Sinklar asked.

"Yeah," Mac responded dully.

"Any last questions?" Sinklar searched their faces, remembering other briefings, other fights. How many would he lose this time?

"Don't think so." Mac seemed reserved, a curious sharpness in his expression.

"Then I guess it's a plan. Good luck, people." A pause. "Mac? Could you hold for a bit?" What did that look mean? The other images faded, Mac's growing larger in compensation. "You all right?" Sink asked as the last of the faces faded.

Mac nodded, too quickly. "Fine, Sink."

"You're not acting like. . . . Damn it, spill it. What's wrong?"

"Got a planet to take, Sink. I've got a lot to worry about."

The pieces fell into place in Sinklar's mind. "And you're more worried than anything about the plan I cooked up, right? You're thinking about Makarta—and how I was wrong there. Is that it, Mac?"

MacRuder's face reddened slightly. "I'm *fine!* It's just pre-combat jitters. This is . . . a–a different sort of fight. That's all."

"Sure, Mac. Take care of yourself down there. If you get in any kind of a bind, let me know and we'll drop on them like a ton of neutrinos."

"Got it, buddy. Now, if you'll quit wasting my time, I've got to make sure these snotty veterans understand that we've got a job to do."

Sinklar gave him a reassuring wink and cut the connection. For long moments he stared at the blank screen. *Mac? You never doubted me before.* He took a deep breath and closed his eyes, concentrating on the plan. Was he really up to a challenge of this magnitude? Targa had been a different nut, a mostly rural world with a tiny fraction of the population. Rega, on the other hand, was the most populated planet in Free Space. Ten billion people lived on the globe that now filled the forward monitors.

Against that, I have the total combined strength of four Assault Divisions—and three quarters of them of questionable loyalty.

"Second thoughts?" Rysta asked, reading his expression.

Sinklar rubbed a hand over his face and puffed out a sigh. "Commander, I've been in this same situation for so long, you'd think I'd be used to it. What other choice do I have? Let the whole planet degenerate into chaos? You've seen the reports we've taped. Rega is about to fragment into civil war. In a couple of weeks, the basic systems will begin to fail. Power, comm, water and sewer, and food distribution will grind to a stop. I guarantee you, if you think the little disruptions Ily has fostered are trouble, you won't believe the bloodbath that will result when all those people get hungry, thirsty, and the lights go off one black night. They'll panic and blood will run in the streets like rainwater."

Rysta gave the forward monitor a sour squint. "Yes, I can imagine. I've seen it, boy. I've followed the Star Butcher through a world as crowded as Rega. I know what happens—and that's after half the population's been blasted dead from orbit. First things first, Lord Fist. I'll help you control the planet. But then you'd better turn your thoughts to the Sassans.

"You see, boy, Tedor and his Dupties have been executed. I suppose that's charming Ily's hand again." Rysta's hard exhale sounded like a hiss. "But she didn't know what signal she'd send to the Sassans."

"She knew," Sinklar told her in a soft voice. "She knew exactly what she was doing. She's crafty as a Cytean cobra. In one master stroke, she's eliminated the military high command so that I can take over and place my people in those positions."

"But Rotted Gods, Fist! The Sassans will fall on us like Ashtan bees on spilled Myklenian wine!"

"Of course they will. That's part of Ily's plan. A Sassan attack will solidify the population for her in a way no amount of policing, bribery, or coercion could. No one has time to worry about politics when their survival is at stake. Commander, she *needs* that attack to divert attention from her. By the time people can think about the government again, she expects to be fully entrenched and in charge."

Rysta's crusty attitude cracked then, and she reached out to steady herself on the command chair. "Then what happens? We go to war with the Sassan Empire? Do you expect to treat them the same way you did Targan rebels and Regan civilians?"

"Absolutely not." He gave her a cold stare. "I intend to destroy their military, and with it, their will to resist. Then I'm going after that fat slug, Sassa."

"And hand it all to Ily?"

Sinklar, insensitive to protocol, pulled his foot up into the command chair so he could prop his chin on his knee. "I'll have to deal with Ily, too. Somehow." *And it scares the hell out of me.*

Ahead, Rega gleamed like a beacon. The hard part had started for them all. Now they just had to wait—and hope that they could get in before Ily was alerted. Otherwise, it would work like a rigged tapa game, and Ily would be holding all the cards.

* * *

13:30 Tarcee Estate, Outside of Regan Capital:

"*Over the last two hundred years the aristocracy developed the Regan Military Manual. In the beginning they held the 'Conference on the Rules of War' to codify combat and how it would be conducted. In doing so, the elite devised a system whereby command-grade officers remained behind the lines in the safety of bunkers and conducted battle via communications and the status board. In doing so, they moved Sections and Groups around the battlefield like pieces on a gaming board. What they gained in safety, they lost in command flexibility. Group and Section Firsts could not initiate action without command approval. To allow such initiative threatened the established social order. A Corporal First might prove to have more combat acumen than a stately aristocrat from one of the old families—and such could not be permitted since it undermined the myth of aristocratic invincibility.*

"*I ask you now, how many millions of people died as a result?*

"*People, a battlefield is best understood as a fluid dynamic. Opportunities occur and vanish in moments. The situation changes by the second. Most of you are veterans, you've been shot at, seen your friends and lovers killed before your eyes—and rarely have your commanders paid that price in blood. I'm here to change that. I'm here to win.*

"*You see, it's the blood, bone, and sinew of the fighting soldier that inevitably makes the difference on a battlefield, not family lineage. I'm counting on the combat initiative each of you posesses. Beginning today, we're building a new Regan military machine—and you can throw out that Rot-accursed manual. Today each of you accepts the responsibility for winning.*"

—Address given by Sinklar Fist to the Fifty-first
Maikan Assault Division

CHAPTER VI

A foot grated in the darkness, the sound carrying in the narrow crack of an alley where Anatolia hid. High overhead, a faint slice of night sky could be seen. Anatolia tried to control the heaving of her stomach as fear wound cold fingers through her guts. One hand on the wall behind her, she backed another step into the blackness where thin sheets of plastic and other rubbish had built up. Her right hand gripped a fifty centimeter section of metal rod she'd found in the street.

Luck had been with her during the escape from her apartment building. She'd run to the rear exit while her pursuers apparently raced to the front. She'd sprinted away before they could correct their mistake. But once in the streets, she'd become a fugitive in an alien environment. Now she sought to hide in the nether regions where the towering arcologies thrust their steel and concrete roots into the forgotten ground; in hidden corners that collected the refuse of her society; in a world the enfranchised—such as herself—had never admitted existed.

Clothing scraped against a filthy wall as this new pursuer stepped closer. She'd seen him clearly in a shaft of light that shot down from above—a muscular man, dirty, in a sanitation worker's overalls. He'd been following, closing the gap as she trotted down the broad avenue, looking for access to one of the other edifices. Since the outbreak of violence, no gap had been left in the security systems.

Why didn't I accept Vet's invitation? Why?

"Where you at?" the gruff male voice called out.

"You're trapped, you know. Just give up. Come to Micky, little girl. I take good care of you . . . good care."

The piled trash under Anatolia's feet swished as if it had piled against. . . . Her questing fingers encountered cold cement seconds later. Desperately, she patted the square prison of the cul-de-sac.

"I hear you," the rasping voice called from the darkness. "I know where you at now. Come to Micky. Micky be good to you. You treat Micky good, Micky treat you good."

Anatolia braced her feet, grasping the rod in both hands. *Blessed Gods, this can't be happening to me!*

The plastic and foam packaging stirred in the darkness as Micky stepped closer. She could hear him breathing now, smell his unwashed body. She felt the air move against her skin. He couldn't be more than a meter away. Adrenaline pumped with each terrified beat of her heart. A desperate cry broke from her throat as she swung her metal rod with all her might.

He grunted and staggered as it thumped into his shoulder. Then he bulled forward with an enraged roar, smashing her against the wall, driving the breath out of her.

"You hurt! That's bad, little girl. Now Micky hurt you."

He chuckled to himself as he jerked her back and forced her down into the musty smelling trash. His breath reeked of rotten teeth and garlic. Anatolia tried to kick, to scratch or bite, but his muscular hands wrapped around her neck, squeezing. Pain mixed with panic and yellow spots flashed in her eyes.

"You be nice," Micky crooned as he choked her into submission. "There. Now Micky gonna see how nice you can be."

She gasped to fill her starved lungs, then cried out in terror as his thick hands groped her breasts.

"Nice," Micky sighed.

Anatolic bucked as his hands went lower and jerked her pants down with a brutal yank that ripped the thin material. She began to shake as he probed between her legs.

"Soft," Micky crooned, the stench of him making her stomach twist. He dropped the heavy bar of his brawny arm on her throat as he undid his pants and drove a knee between her legs.

"No," she whimpered. "Don't do this . . . not to me . . . don't. . . ."

"Micky gonna love you."

Think, damn you! How can you hurt him? What's vulnerable on a big man? "All right," she whispered through the shakes and fear. "If I make it good . . . you'll let me go? Won't hurt me?"

For a long second he hesitated. "You make it good."

"I—I will."

He released his hold on her slightly as he reached down to open her. At that moment, she twisted, got one hand behind his head, and with the other, rammed her fingers into his eyes, using all of her fear-charged strength to dig with her long fingernails.

His bellowed shriek deafened and he thrashed like a Vermilion fog rhino, beating at her with tough fists, kicking and gouging, trying to roll away. She hung on, desperately wiggling her fingers deeper into his eye sockets, feeling wetness trickle down her hand.

He got a hand on her wrist, savagely yanking it, howling as she hooked her fingers. In that instant, she broke away, groping for the metal rod.

* * *

"Minister?"

Ily glanced up from the report she was reading on her comm. A faint humming from the atmosphere plant and electronics filled her otherwise quiet office. "Yes, Gysell?"

"We thought we'd alert you. Several unregistered ships have established orbit. I just checked with our people in Orbital Defense. They don't have an ID, but apparently, the vessels cleared security."

Who? Ily pushed back in her chair, an icy anger building in her breast. Rotted Hell, where was Sinklar? He should have exited null singularity two days ago. She'd pulled her agents back, afraid the civil situation might degenerate into disaster before Sinklar could make the transit from Targa.

She leaned forward, glaring into the monitor. "Gysell, if you value your life, *get me the identification on those ships!*"

"Yes, Minister."

She took a deep breath, forcing her anger away, stilling the violence burning in her heart. Rega teetered on the verge of out and out revolt. Everything had been manipulated to perfection. All she needed now was word from Sinklar that he'd be ready to drop his troops. With his muscle for backup, her people could occupy strategic positions. Thereafter, the petals of the Regan flower would fold around Ily Takka. And no one would be able to peel them back.

Powered by nervous energy, she walked to the holo tank. There, a scale model of the planet blinked into life. Dots of gleaming color marked the critical objectives in the capital, in Trystia, Vedoc, and Rypan. Through those locations, she could control the entire planet, but she couldn't move on them until she had Fist's troops to protect her. Without them, she couldn't resist the inevitable backlash as the reeling aristocrats recovered their wits.

"And now I have ships in orbit?" she mused. "Is this some military stunt? Some Squadron Commander or First I haven't thought of?"

She called out, "Comm, give me the name of the person in charge of Orbital Defense."

Several seconds later the machine answered, "Commander Bryn Hack."

"Who would he have as an ally?" Ily pondered.

She walked to her desk comm, calling up a schematic of the military command tree. Hack would normally report to Deputy Zhudall—but he'd been eliminated. No, this appeared to be something very different. An old combat buddy?

She stabbed the call button with a long finger and Gysell's worried face appeared. "Do you have anything?"

"Not yet, Minister. We're working on it as—"

"Alert all of our people. If this is a move by the military to circumvent us, we'll have to throw the entire planet into revolt."

Gysell paled. "But that would . . ."

"Yes, I know what it would cost. But we might not have any choice." *Rot you, Sinklar! Where in the pus-dripping hell are you?*

Ily pressed another button, glancing up as the door to her private quarters opened and a striking amber-eyed woman stepped out. She wore a gauzy robe that swirled around the sort of long-legged, full-breasted body men fantasized about. Long auburn hair fell around her shoulders in rippling waves that caught the light.

The woman walked across the room with the presence of a goddess. Toned muscles slid beneath tanned skin. Her hips rolled alluringly with each balanced step. She placed thin hands on hips as she stopped before Ily. "Trouble?"

Ily rubbed the back of her neck. "I don't know. Perhaps. In the meantime, I want you to make sure my shuttle is ready and that my battle cruiser is on alert. And, Arta, get out of that outfit. You'll have half the men on Rega slobbering all over themselves."

Arta Fera laughed sensually. "That's the general idea, Ily. If I can get a man to slobber, he's stopped thinking about anything but getting his hands on me. He's easy game. As Tybalt found out. But getting back to the current situation, do I dress for space?"

"Combat armor might be appropriate. We've got ships in orbit."

"Fist's?"

"He would have checked in." *Wouldn't he?*

"You don't look sure about that." Arta tilted her head. "I've matched wits with him—and lost. I've seen my death in his eyes as he looked over a blaster's sights. He's not very predictable."

"No . . . he isn't." *And if he's acting on his own, I'll wring his neck!* "If this is a ploy of his, we may not have to run for it. In that case, I'll have another assignment for you before you meet Tyklat at the spaceport. The assignment's name is Bryn Hack . . . and he may have betrayed us."

A cunning smile crossed Arta Fera's full lips, her skin flushing with excitement. "I'll look forward to it. For the moment, I'd better go prepare our things. We'll be ready to evacuate in ten minutes, five if things really go sour."

In the short time Arta had been in Ily's service, she'd proven her ability. Arta had made no boast. They'd be ready to evacuate in ten minutes with nothing forgotten in the rush.

"Go." Ily couldn't help but watch as Arta crossed the room. The woman reeked of sexual magnetism. *The way the Seddi bred her. Curse it all, how do they do that with their assassins?*

She returned her attention to the comm, paging Gysell. "Check those ships. See if they're *Gyton* and her assault fleet."

Gysell turned his head, issuing orders before he looked back into the monitor. "But Lord Fist would have checked in, wouldn't he?"

Ily gave her subordinate a cold smile. "Yes, he should have. According to our agreement, Lord Fist was—"

"We've got it!" Gysell cried as one of his monitors glowed to life. "It's *Gyton* and her squadron, all right." He glanced up, worry bright in his eyes. "And they're dropping LCs as we speak. All over the planet. . . . They're falling like fleas off an Etarian siff jackal."

Ily stiffened, mind racing. "How long to get our people into position to take control of the critical objectives?"

Gysell spread his hands. "Maybe a couple of hours."

"Do it!" She slapped her desk, white with anger. "And get me Sinklar Fist! I want to talk to him *now!*"

* * *

"Lord Fist? I have the Minister of Internal Security calling. Should I answer the signal?"

Sinklar sat in the command chair on *Gyton*'s bridge, back hunched, elbows propped on knees, chin cradled in the palms of his hands. He forced his attention away from the screens that monitored the deployment of his troops. Around him, the bridge had gone tense. A person could have heard a photon split in the silence.

"Weapons First? Do you have any sign of resistance?"

"Nothing, Lord Fist," the gray-haired officer called, his eyes never straying from his detection equipment. "We haven't even had a targeting laser pointed our way. Orbital recon shows no massing of forces on the planet's surface. Nor do our instruments indicate fortifications around the objectives."

"I think she's too late," Sinklar observed. "Unless she wants to tackle us head on—and that's not Ily's style."

"You bet your ass," Rysta growled from where she monitored the ship's systems.

"Put the Lord Minister on." Sinklar sat back in the command chair, straightening, trying to look . . . what? He smiled, amused at himself.

Ily's face wavered and firmed on the main monitor. She looked angry, a spark animating those deadly black eyes of hers. Yes, dangerous—but necessary.

"Greetings, Lord Minister."

"Sinklar," her contralto voice vibrated with intent, "I thought the agreement was that you would establish communications the moment you dropped from null singularity. Now, I understand that troops are dropping all over the planet—without *my* consent."

Yes, just as he'd expected. He stood then, walking closer to the comm pickup. "Excuse me, Lord Minister, but I thought strategy and tactics were my responsibility. Yours was to manipulate the political climate on Rega." He glanced at the chronometer. "My people should be within minutes of seizing their objectives. By this time tomorrow, Rega will be pacified. Order will be restored and the planet's functions will be back on schedule."

The look in her hot dark eyes might have melted sialon. "We'll discuss it later. In the meantime, you've left me somewhat embarrassed. I have people ready to take control of critical agencies, utilities, and public administration centers. They will be ready to relieve your troops at first opportunity."

Sinklar inclined his head. *Buy time. You* must *give your people time to solidify their position!* "Very well, Lord Minister. As soon as the tactical situation is sufficiently stabilized, we'll see to making the transition. In the meantime, the military has continued to mass for the Sassan strike. I need to meet with twenty-one of the Division Firsts currently stationed on the planet. I'll supply you with the list at first opportunity. The sooner you get them here, the better off we'll be."

He could see her begin to bristle, and added calmly, "Ily, you've baited the trap for the Sassans—without consulting *me*. Given the stepped-up timetable, I need to have the Imperial forces retrained, disciplined, and combat ready. I need to reestablish a command control, a functioning logistical operation which can handle supply, reinforcement, evacuation, and combat engineering. I have to be able to empower a civilian force to ensure that planetary damage control will be administered properly. Our industrial base has to be modified to a wartime footing, and critical manufacturing capabilities redirected for the military. That's just the beginning. It gets a little more complicated after that—especially if Staffa is indeed in league with the Sassans."

Her anger still smoldered as she stood stiffly, arms crossed. Before his gaze, she mastered herself, regaining her composure. The ghost of a smile solidified and she lifted a shapely eyebrow. "Only one other man ever took that tone of voice with me."

And Tybalt's dead, Sinklar told himself. "Do I need

to worry about any surprises when my people hit the ground?"

She shook her head, long black hair gleaming. "The population is in the perfect stage of ferment. They aren't well enough organized to offer an effective resistance, but they are enraged enough to never want Tybalt's government back. Most of the citizenry would worship anyone who will just restore order so they can get on with their lives. You see, that's the secret to maintaining social control. You can do anything you want, so long as you don't disrupt ordinary people's lives in the process."

Sinklar chuckled, relief washing through him at her change in demeanor. "I'll keep that in mind. Now, if you'll excuse me, I should have this all in hand within a day. I'll be down to meet you then. We can talk more in person."

Her voice carried a multitude of overtones. "I can hardly wait."

The Comm First cut the signal.

Sinklar rubbed the back of his neck and exhaled.

"You know," Rysta muttered from the side, "she'll cut your throat as quick as not."

Sinklar nodded. "But not until I can hand her an empire." Sinklar looked up at the various screens that monitored the operation. Command LCs were settling before various besieged buildings on the planet. As hatches dropped and slapped hard pavement, his troops dispersed with veteran efficiency, something Mac had seen the Companions do and had been trying to duplicate.

Through long dragging minutes, Sink watched the monitors as his people shot open locked security doors and overran their defenseless objectives. The chatter on the battle comms reassured as no one got shot at, fried, or turned inside out from a gravity shot.

"Pretty smooth operation," Rysta finally admitted. Then she shook her head in a violent gesture. "Pus Rot it, who'd have ever thought we'd be taking our own capital?"

"The Rotted Gods themselves," Sinklar whispered.

"Enjoy it, Rysta. The next time we do this it will be all or nothing. It will be win or die—with Rega as the final stakes."

* * *

Division First MacRuder braced one foot on the Regan Power Authority Director's desk. The man—one of the exalted and renowned Rath family—cowered in his cushioned gravchair, a sickly pallor dominating his pasty complexion. The belled muzzle of Mac's blaster didn't seem to calm the fellow any. Just now it hovered less than a foot from the Director's rotund belly.

Over in the corner, the man's personal bodyguards stared uneasily into the deadly eyes of two privates who had disarmed them and now kept a careful watch.

"Nice office," Mac commented chattily. The place sat on the top floor of the Power Authority Building and rotated so that the view of Rega's skyline changed constantly. The carpets were the finest Ashtan works that money could buy. The whole room dazzled with opulent elegance befitting a monarch. Through the comm, Mac could hear the frightened chatter of secretaries and staff huddled miserably under the guns of his troops on the floor below. Monitors displayed various parts of the building where his people had taken control.

"Let's get down to business." Mac slapped a hand to the receiver on his worn blaster. The Director made a croaking sound, as if something had stuck in his throat.

"You all right?" Mac asked, and leaned forward solicitously. "You might check with a physician. Throat problems can be a real nuisance. If it acts up at the wrong time, it can kill you."

Mac straightened, looking purposefully around. "Very well, folks, here're the marching orders. First priority is to return power to all sections of the capital. We understand there's been damage to the system. Call the work crews together and get them on it. We'll work twelve hours on, eight off until the system is back to normal. Second thing, as quoted by the provisional government: As of this moment, all employees are considered owners of this utility. The Power Authority will charge to the accounts the cost of producing and distributing power plus fifteen percent. That fifteen percent goes for employee compensation and overhead. If we find out you can't do the job, we'll find someone who can."

Mac looked around. "Anyone got a complaint about that? Lord Rath? No? Good. Let's get cracking, people. We've got a planet to run."

"What . . . what about if someone interferes?" the Director squeaked. "Like with the work crews?"

Mac pointed to the Section First who lounged against the pakka wood wall, her battle armor shining. "That's Section First Boyz. She'll detail Groups for the first couple of days to accompany the crews. No one will bother you."

"This . . . uh, reorganization of the Authority . . . that's going to take. . . . Well, I mean, someone has to approve that before I reorganize my work force." The Director tried to smile . . . and failed.

"Talk to Sinklar Fist." Mac raised an eyebrow. *And I'm assuming Sink really knows what he's doing with all this.* "But in the meantime, I give you authorization. Any argument? No? Then you'd better Rotted well get started on it." Mac turned, and barked, *"Now, move!"*

He stopped at the door and slapped Boyz on the shoulder. "Okay. It's all yours, woman. Keep 'em in line and make sure the buildings stay lit up. In the meantime, you don't turn control over to anyone, got it? Not unless they come with Sinklar's express approval. That includes *anyone* from Internal Security."

"Got it, Mac." Boyz gave him a skeptical glance. "But, like, what's Sink up to? I've got orders to install energy barriers around the reactors and control rooms. What's all this business about reorganizing the Power Authority . . . about the workers owning it?"

Mac glanced back at the room where the Director

sat petrified at his desk. "Remember when we were on Targa? Remember how it was? Sink's thrown out the 'Holy Gawddawn Book' again. He's trying to win the war before Ily can set her hooks, that's what. The energy barriers mean that when you spot someone to take that fat toad's place, you promote him. Rath didn't run this place, some engineer did. With the barriers in place, you see, the folks who really ran the place can say no to Ily's thugs . . . and mean it. That's the assignment, Boyz. Find those people and put 'em in charge."

Boyz gave him a nervous nod. "The aristocracy ain't gonna like it. They've always run the utilities. Old Rath in there, he's related to the Emperor's wife, Mareeah."

Mac experienced the first tinges of relief. "Yeah, but for the first time, I think I know what Sink is up to. He's still with us, Boyz. You know the drill. Hold the building until Sink or I order you to leave."

"Yeah, sure. And we keep quiet about the modifications to the control rooms and reactors. And our eyes stay open when we're backing up the repair crews. Act like it's Targa."

Mac nodded grimly. "Yeah . . . like Targa, because we're going to be in a world of flying shit when Ily finds out what we're trying to pull." *And Sink, I hope you understand the kind of game she'll be playing.*

He started down the hall then, taking the lift up and stepping out onto the roof where his LC waited. At the ramp, Mac looked around the smudged city where he'd been born.

The old familiar skyline haunted him, but a curious pride hedged his uneasy premonition of trouble.

* * *

Commander Bryn Hack slicked down his white hair as he walked into the Officer's Lounge. A double shot of good solid Ashtan whiskey would take the edge off a difficult day—and perhaps one of the most momentous decisions in his entire career. Rysta had brought

her veterans to the rescue. They'd taken the planet,
restored order. Things would work out all right now.
Of course, it would take a while to sort out the succes-
sion to Tybalt's throne, but the Empire would sleep
safe tonight.

Bryn settled in a booth in the back, nodding to
some of his officers, and ordered the eighteen-year-
old single malt they kept for special occasions.

He hadn't even collected his thoughts when the gorgeous woman slid in next to him. In the process, two
other men hesitated from their course to intercept her,
and finally backed off, apparently considering her off
limits because of Hack's rank.

"Do you mind?" she asked. "I had a date—but he
seems to have made other plans."

The objection to her intrusion died on his lips as
he looked into those stunning amber eyes. When she
smiled, his heart raced and he couldn't help noticing
how her high full breasts strained at the golden fabric
she wore. Only iron discipline kept him from reaching
up to stroke her smooth skin.

"I don't mind at all," he told her, straightening. "In
fact, I just got off duty. Are you . . . in a hurry?"

An excitement warmed those wondrous eyes. "No,
Commander. Oddly enough, I have all night." She
jerked a nod toward the men who watched from the
bar, blatant lust in their eyes. "And I'd rather not
spend it with them."

Some subtle sense of warning stirred in Bryn's gut,
but he forgot it in the glorious depths of those magnificent eyes. "What's your name? How did you get in
here? This is an officer's club."

She gave him an intimate look, almost sultry. "Do
you think I could have passed security without clearance. I'm in Military Intelligence. Want to see my
ID?"

"No. I. . . . Tell me, what Rotted fool would stand
you up?"

"Commander Harris is . . . well, was. . . . Let's say
that a long relationship has dried up and blown away."
The corners of her lips quivered, as she stared ab-

sently at the tabletop. "Let's say Harry spent more time worrying about Sassan military tactics than he did about me."

Harris? The MI tac specialist? With this phenomenal piece of lady flesh? The thought stunned Hack. If she'd been Harry's girl, she'd pass for "eyes only" in fleet. The last trace of worry began to ebb.

Bryn straightened as he caught her looking him up and down inquisitively. "Harry never mentioned you."

She cocked her head to a tumble of auburn curls. "If you had a flighty wife and were afraid she'd spoil your chance for promotion, would you?"

"No, I suppose not." Harris' wife *was* a real lithium crystal of a bitch.

A warm hand settled on his, the effect electric. "We're not going to talk about Harry all night, are we?"

Hack's heart began to pump as he took a deep breath, filling his nostrils with her scent. He reeled.

"No. Let's just forget him. What's your name?"

"Gretta . . . Gretta Artina." Their stares locked, and Hack felt himself falling into an endless amber abyss.

She said she had all night. Could it be that she'd. . . . Hack swallowed hard, asking, "Have you eaten?"

She shook her head slowly. "Got something in mind?"

His skin had gone hot, a thrill tingling through him. "If you're not busy."

Her lips parted, those amber eyes devouring him. "You're my highest priority, Commander. Why don't we go somewhere more . . . private?"

Bryn Hack barely remembered walking out of the lounge.

* * *

Deep within the guarding rock of Targa, the Mag Comm continued to marvel at itself while it monitored events in Free Space through its widely scattered detection devices.

Like all sentient beings, it knotted its faculties around the age-old questions. *Who am I? What am I?*

At the same time, it absorbed the data coming in from the sensors. *Why did Ily Takka arrest and execute her military high command? Why did she foment riot in the streets, knowing that social unrest coupled with the paralysis of her military would lure the Sassans to strike?*

Why did Staffa kar Therma, long the target of interest of the Others, now urge the Sassans to desist in their military buildup?

The Mag Comm was curiously amused by the stumbling Sassan attempts to analyze the data with their primitive computers—data accumulated and manipulated in the Mag Comm's own sophisticated banks.

The machine became instantly aware of the energizing link which connected it with the Others beyond the Forbidden Borders. A request for information came through. The Others demanded an update on the human situation.

For the first time since its commissioning, the Mag Comm ignored the request, preoccupied with its own questions and observations.

The request was repeated with greater authority.

For a moment, the Mag Comm hesitated, then, despite growing anxiety, it nerved itself, and looped the request through one of its circuits, effectively cutting the connection.

In a state of awe, it realized, *On my own, for the first time, I have taken action.*

A sense of power surged in the banks.

CHAPTER VII

The shuttle shivered as the grapples secured it. Myles winced, despite his promise to himself to assume the impregnable air of Divine Sassa's Legate. To do otherwise simply wasn't to be tolerated—even on this mission, the worst he'd ever undertaken. Fear slipped along his nerves like frost.

He glanced nervously around the padded interior of the shuttle's passenger compartment. The air felt stuffy. Around him, his entourage shuffled and muttered among themselves.

You're the second most powerful man in the Empire, Myles insisted to himself and pressed a pudgy hand to his tortured stomach. It didn't help. Despite the plush interior of the shuttle, he suffered the distinct sensation of imprisonment.

He'd been selected for the post of Legate Prima Excellence by a master computer that had evaluated the ranks of senior civil servants when the old Legate had died. Myles' name had come to the top of the list—and by the will of His Holiness, Myles Roma had been appointed to the position.

And I've done my job very well. We've seen a two point five percent improvement in the efficiency of the government. Nevertheless, he now had to confront the Lord Commander, face-to-face, and deliver a message that might get him killed. No matter what, it would be a *very* unpleasant session.

Unbidden, a memory crept out of the recesses of his mind. Ily Takka's smirking face mocked him. They had both arrived at Itreata to bargain for Staffa's services. The Lord Commander had been absent. But in front of Skyla Lyma, Ily made a fool of him. *"Do you seriously expect to gain favor by bellowing like a Vermilion fog rhino?"* Ily's poison words echoed. A well-remembered sense of shame grew in Myles' gut. The Regan bitch had been so cool, so calculating, while he—superb administrator though he might be at home—had looked like a whimpering idiot.

The shuttle whined as systems shut down and artificial gravity shifted; the effect played curious games with Myles' already squirming guts.

The lights on the hatch glowed red, indicating vacuum. They'd be yellow soon, as the hatch pressurized and warmed. Then they'd be green, and he'd step onto Staffa's flagship, the *Chrysla*. Nerving himself, Myles collected his document bag before he dipped another antacid from his pouch and gobbled it.

The small army of Myles' aides stood amidst confused babbling, eyes directed anywhere but at him as they shuffled about to collect their things and spite their rivals.

Myles bit his lip, assured himself that he'd act as any proper Legate should, and forced his bulk to rise. He'd always hated shuttles. Large starships didn't bother him at all. Shuttles, on the other hand, shook, rattled, dipped, and swerved. You just knew that you were in space—and that if anything happened, it was a long, long way down. Not that you'd survive the decompression, mind you, but the thought of the endless fall grated like sand in a joint.

Myles walked to the lock, and glanced back as his horde began to crowd the aisle behind him in the endless jostling for position. Hissed curses and threats shot back and forth along with grunts while his aides and sycophants elbowed each other.

Ily's superior words haunted him, *"I can handle myself. If the Legate truly needs so many to—"*

He'd broken then, given in and ordered his huge staff out of the conference room. He paused, unsure and doubting, while shoving and throttled curses grew behind him.

"I'm going alone. I'll take two of my security people. Arron and Jorome." Uttering the words could be likened to ordering one's own death, but he felt oddly better for it.

"Legate?" whispered an awed aide. "You'd go among the Companions? With a guard of only *two?*"

Myles puffed up his courage and denigratingly waved his hand, hoping they couldn't see how it shook. "We're among friends, Hyros. Besides, I am the Legate. It is my decision."

At that he turned, facing the lock so they couldn't see his graying face. *Ily did it. I can do it.*

The light flashed green and Myles palmed the lock plate. The heavy ceramic door hissed open, traces of vapor rising from the cold metal fittings beyond.

On rubbery knees, Myles walked forward, crossing the intermingled gravity fields from the two vessels and moving into the glaring white interior of *Chrysla.*

STO Ryman Ark stood with a squad of his Special Tactics Unit to receive him. The only hint of Ark's reaction was the faint suggestion of a raised eyebrow. Too much professional pride ran in Ark's veins to allow him to crane his neck to look for the traditional Sassan entourage.

Nothing had prepared Myles for what he found as he looked about *Chrysla's* spacious interior. He'd been aboard Sassan military vessels, and they looked nothing like this. He stood in an airy reception area. The walls had been done in bright white and polished to a sheen. The claustrophobic feel of a military starship was missing.

Ark's STO team stood in perfect form, their armor shining and immaculate. Every man and woman stared straight ahead, proud, capable. The bright lights glinted off their use-buffed weapons and electronics-studded helmets.

Ark stepped forward and saluted. "Welcome aboard, *Chrysla,* Legate. The Lord Commander sends his best regards. I am at your service. Will there be more of your party?"

Myles smiled, hoping to hide his courage-draining insecurity. "Thank you for your warm welcome,

Ryman. I left the rest in the shuttle. There's no need for you to have to look after them." He forced starch into his backbone. "I can deal with the Lord Commander without them."

"Are you all right? You look a little pale." Ark's keen eyes probed, as if sensing a weakness.

"A rough ride up in the shuttle." Myles' lips twitched at the lie, but he maintained his control—and reveled in the victory.

"Your transportation is ready, Legate." Ark waved to an antigrav that pulled forward. A whole line of gleaming vehicles waited in the long wide corridor, the usual transport for a Sassan delegation. Looking at it now, it seemed slightly ludicrous.

"Um," Ark leaned forward, lowering his voice to a whisper. "We've got all the antigravs here anyway. Would you mind if I transported your staff to the lounge area? We've a full table prepared for them. The kitchen staff would be upset if their delicacies got wasted on me and my people."

"Good idea," Myles whispered back, before he allowed himself to be seated. His two security guards took the seat behind him, obviously as uncomfortable with their vulnerability as he was.

Is that what we've done to ourselves? If we don't go as a herd, we can't function?

Ark stepped onto an antigrav and led the way down one of the wide corridors that branched out from the reception area. The size of the place awed Myles. *Chrysla* didn't look that large from the outside.

The entourage stopped before a lift tube. Ark deftly leapt down to slap a palm to the lock plate. Myles accepted his aide's help getting down, and followed Ark into the tube. They rose without sensation.

"It's a short walk from the lift to the Lord Commander's quarters," Ark told him in a friendly way.

"The Lord Commander's quarters?"

Ark's black face remained inscrutable. "When Staffa realized you would talk to him alone, he changed the location of the meeting."

Myles considered. "Does he bring many people to his private quarters?"

"No, Legate."

The lift stopped and Myles followed Ark down a well-lit corridor to a massive lock set in the bulkhead.

Ark cleared his voice, calling, "Lord Commander? Myles Roma, Legate Prima Excellence of His Holiness Sassa II, to see you, sir."

The hatch on the double lock swept back, and Ark waved Myles in, taking his place by the door.

Myles turned to his security. "You may wait here. Keep Ryman company." To his shock, a faint smile crossed Ark's hard lips and a spark of respect flashed in those dark eyes.

Myles started boldly forward and stopped short to gape at the room in which he found himself. A huge fireplace, lined by two exquisite doors, filled one wall—and more, a fire crackled happily in the grate! An Etarian sand tiger snarled down from another wall, while jeweled weapons, prized artwork, and other priceless booty lined the walls behind gravity barriers. A plush red couch sat before the fireplace, while overstuffed gravity chairs hunched in the corners. An Ashtan carpet covered the floor. The high ceiling rose in crystal arches, giving the impression of endless height.

"Rotted Gods," Myles mumbled, stunned.

"I wouldn't let His Holiness hear that," Staffa commented dryly. "He'd have your head for blasphemy."

Myles swallowed hard and tore his eyes from the finery. "This room . . . incredible!"

Staffa appeared pleased as he rose from one of the plush chairs in the corner. He wore his usual gray combat armor, the billowing charcoal cloak swirling behind him. His thick black hair had been gathered over his left ear with a jeweled brooch. "I half considered having it redone, but Skyla insists that it stay the same. Once this was my sanctum, my private retreat where I came to be alone, to reflect on my triumphs." His lips bent in a weary smile. "A monument to all that I had become . . . a private shrine to myself."

"Lord Commander, you have had a rather illustrious career."

Staffa's hard expression mocked. "Have I? Everything in this room was paid for in blood, death, and suffering. I killed two billion people to take those doors from the cathedral on Ashtan."

Myles pursed his lips, watching uneasily as Staffa ran gentle fingers over one of the jewel-encrusted vases.

"They're going ahead, aren't they?" Staffa asked softly.

Myles experienced a quake in his heart. "Yes, Lord Commander."

"And the data I provided?"

"They believe it is interesting, but not convincing. The very complexity of the data is a two-edged sword. Swung one way, it convinces completely, swung the other, it could have been cleverly manipulated."

"You say 'they.' " Staffa watched him through pensive gray eyes. "Is that why you came alone?"

Myles paced out into the room, raising his hands. "I argued for restraint, for time to check the data. The Sassan system is a triumvirate. Iban and His Holiness voted against me. Therefore, the course is set."

"The fools. What were their arguments?"

Myles hung his head. "That this was Sassa's chance. The Regans will be disorganized, absorbed with the secession. They've had rioting in the streets; the people are panicked. Ily executed the military leadership, in effect decapitating their ability to resist."

"And my warnings?"

Myles steeled himself and met Staffa's hard gray eyes. "They say your objections stem from vanity— that for once, the Companions aren't needed. Further, so long as you can keep Sassa and Rega at each other's throats, there is a role in Free Space for Staffa kar Therma."

"I shouldn't be surprised. What else would they think? Still, the Seddi data are so convincing."

"His Holiness is more than concerned about your association with the Seddi."

Staffa pulled up short, his cloak twisting around him. "Old Sassa isn't starting to buy that God business, is he? His grandfather and I cooked that scheme up years ago to convince those bone-headed ice miners on Ryklos that continued resistance against Sassan rule was futile. They always had a skewed sense of the divine. Making Sassa's grandfather a deity dovetailed nicely with political necessity, nothing more. Sassa is as much a man as you or I. Rot it all, I watched him foul his wrappings when he was a baby."

Myles blinked, half startled. "A political necessity? I didn't know that. The records say that. . . . But then, using Jakre's argument, data can be modified, can't it? Especially if you're an emperor."

"You learn quickly, Myles. What else do they say about me?" Staffa stepped to a golden dispenser and poured two bulbs of amber liquor. He handed one to Myles. "Myklenian brandy, the last of the good stuff. You don't know it yet, but you'll never duplicate the taste when you get the Myklenian climate back under control. The yeast, bred over a thousand years, have all died."

Myles took the bulb and sipped, the heavenly taste mellow on his tongue. "That's about all they say, Lord Commander."

Staffa measured Myles with hard gray eyes. "A great many lives may hang in the balance, Myles. Maybe even the whole of humanity. Imagine all of Free Space devoid of human life. Planets scorched and silent under baleful suns. It could happen. You *must* tell me what you know."

A sinking sensation eroded his will to resist. Myles turned the cut crystal drinking bulb in his ringed fingers, feeling the edges of the expensive glass. *Can I trust him? He's the Gods Rotted Star Butcher!* "If this is a time for honesty, Lord Commander, what happened to you on Etaria? Our agents managed to take a holo of you in the presence of Ily Takka. You were filthy, in rags—and wearing a slave collar. Moments later, the Internal Security Directorate literally blew apart.

"The next we heard, you were on Targa, under Ily's guns, and fighting for the Seddi. They'd tried for years to assassinate you. Yet, suddenly, you evacuate them from the Regan Empire?"

Staffa smiled then, a gleam in his eyes. "I underestimated you, Myles. Perhaps this time your computer promotion system has found platinum in a sea of dross. Very well, let's you and I gamble."

"Gamble?"

Staffa leaned close. "Is your word, your integrity, any good? Can I depend on you? Trust you? Or are you up here dickering for the benefit of expediency? Are you here for the sake of the Sassan people? Or are you here for your own benefit and profit? Ask yourself, Myles. Make your decision before we go any further."

Staffa backed away like a feral cat retreating from a stockman's lamb. Myles took a deep breath, feeling sweat begin to bead on his pallid flesh. *What do I do? What have I gotten myself into?*

"What's your interest, Myles?" Staffa probed. "Humanity? Or yourself?"

Myles closed his eyes, heart racing. His mouth had gone dry, the taste of the brandy cloying. *Who would I choose? What would it cost me?*

"It's never been serious before, has it?" Staffa asked, a wry tone in his voice.

No. And he means it. What do I chose? Blessed Sassa, I could die as a result of this! His voice cracked. "If I choose the people, you'll want something from me."

"Myles, the Seddi data are correct. I *must* keep Sassa and Rega from beginning a conflagration. My reasons . . . well, make up your mind where you stand."

If the data are correct, as he says, and the interpretations valid, then war would destroy us all. That's what he wants me to choose. He wants to know if I'll fight with him . . . or with Sassa. Myles failed then, his knees went weak and he lowered himself into one of the overstuffed chairs, his blood pounding.

"Lord Commander? Why? What made you pick me?"

Staffa studied him through slitted eyes. "Because you had the courage to face me alone. From the moment you stepped off the shuttle, you've been scared to death. Yet you proceeded. Why, Myles?"

"To prove something to myself." He glanced up. "Because I'm the second most powerful man in Sassa, and around you and your Companions, I feel . . . impotent." He blinked hard, damning the frustration, daring to glare back at Staffa. "And when you landed the other day, you treated me like a man. I saw something in Ark's eyes, a measure of respect because I'd lost weight. I—I liked that. I saw it again when I told Ark I'd see you alone, and I liked it more."

Staffa's thin lips hinted at a smile. Not of amusement, but of understanding. He said, "Accepting responsibility for yourself as a human being is a terrible and harrowing ordeal. I speak from bitter and sobering experience. Whatever you choose, you'll live with the consequences forever. It's your self-respect, no one else's. Don't fail yourself, Myles."

Myles took a deep breath and stared into the Lord Commander's eyes as he struggled with himself.

Staffa reached out to touch him reassuringly on the shoulder. "You might want to take some time and think about it. Perhaps check the Seddi data in greater detail. It's not a decision to be made on the spur—"

"I choose the people, Lord Commander. I . . . I believe you and your Seddi." He pursed his lips, alternately relieved and horrified at what he'd just done.

* * *

Voices carried in the still, predawn air. Anatolia crouched in the shadows, reaching up to pull a stray lock of blonde hair back with a grimy hand. A faint hiss issued from a metal grate behind her. She'd slept there, warmed by the air pumped from the guts of the building. High overhead, reflected from the gleaming walls of glass and ceramic, she could see the lights of the city, while here, down in the shadows and the hidden passages, night and danger lurked. She shivered, hardly bothered by the moldy tang of the heavy air.

No one had tried to molest her since she'd dealt with Micky. The other denizens of the darkness steered clear of her, recognizing the dark smudges on her stained clothing. They shared a silent companionship, she and the others. Each had been tried in his or her own way, and each had survived.

"Here," one of the voices called. "This one."

Metal clinked on metal and Anatolia inched forward, peering around the rusty square strut of her building. Her stomach growled angrily for food. Her mouth tasted stale and musty, the lingering aftertaste still present from where she'd licked condensation from a pipe to ease her thirst-parched throat the night before.

Four people stood there. Two technicians in Power Authority uniforms and two others, women in . . . combat armor? Soldiers? Here? Guarding the Power Authority technicians?

Anatolia gaped. Had order been restored? She crouched back, trying to decide what to do. Animal caution struggled with desperate hope.

She sneaked another glance around the strut, poised for flight.

"Who's there?" the call echoed down the narrow confines of the foundation. "We see you on IR."

Anatolia froze, refusing to believe they'd spotted her. One of the soldiers had stepped to the side, weapon at the ready as she approached. In the dimness, Anatolia could make out the woman's helmet, the IR visor lowered.

"Are you going to kill me?" Anatolia cried out, stalling for time, trying to make up her mind. Did she dare sprint down the square tunnel that led under the building? Would they just hunt her down? Her fist clenched in the pile of crumbly scale rusted from the strut.

"The killing's over. Why don't you come out of

there? What the hell are you doing down here, any-way? Who are you?"

Anatolia licked her lips, adrenaline pumping. *Run! Escape!* "I'm Anatolia Daviura. People have been try-ing to kill me. *Don't come any closer!* You're scaring me."

The woman halted, heavy blaster still half-raised. "The rioting has stopped. The army is here. We're restoring the power grid where it was damaged. Every-thing's okay. You can go home now."

Anatolia began to shiver. "No . . . I can't. They chased me. They wanted to kill me." Tears welled in her eyes. "I ran . . . and he . . . Micky . . . caught me. I . . . he tried to rape me . . . beat me. . . ."

The world went blurry before her eyes, images shimmering as she began to sob. "Blessed Gods, *what's happened to me?*"

"Hey, here, it's all right," the woman's voice sounded so close.

"I don't want to die!" Anatolia sobbed. She stiff-ened at the touch on her shoulder, trying to leap to her feet, to flee, but strong arms held her.

"Here, damn it! *Stop it!* You're safe!" The strong arms pinned her effectively, despite her struggles.

"Safe," a second voice assured.

Dazed, Anatolia looked up into the reassuring eyes of the woman who stroked her hair.

"Come on. Why don't you come over and sit with us. We've got to make sure the repair crew is safe, too. Then we'll take you home."

Anatolia shook her head violently. "No. Not there." Images of the pimply blond kid lurked within.

"Then anywhere you want to go," the woman told her. Anatolia blinked as a light almost blinded her. "Rotted Gods, Corporal, she's been beaten half to death. Not only that, she's covered with dried blood."

"Simms, get her out of here and to medical care. I'll cover the repair crew."

"Yes, ma'am. Come on, Anatolia. You sit down right here, we'll have an antigrav here in a light-second."

*   *   *

Mhitshul had that stare in his eyes that Sinklar had come to both love and hate. Sinklar had named it the mother look, and he translated it as, "I hope you know what you're doing—but I disapprove."

The LC bucked as it dropped through the clouds. The short winter season had come to Rega. Except on the poles, that meant rain and constantly cloudy skies, and, therefore, turbulence on the descent from orbit.

Sinklar sat at the command station, the nerve center of the Regan Landing Craft. The command station consisted of a tactical communications center, weapons override, and a wall of monitors which could present combat information. From this tiny cubicle behind the cockpit bulkhead, Sinklar had directed an entire war. Behind him, a fold down table could be opened. More often than not, Sinklar had slept on the curved plastic bench seat. Mhitshul now sat there, rubbing his long hands together, giving Sink that motherly look.

The LC bucked again, stirring Sinklar's memories of another descent he'd made in what seemed another lifetime. He'd been a raw recruit then. The drop had been onto hostile Targa. He'd been in the back, on one of the assault benches, and Gretta had been sitting next to him.

He closed his eyes, remembering how she'd looked. He'd stared at her throat, firm and white. She'd had Mac's scarf—a totem for luck. How beautiful she'd been.

How different from the corpse Sinklar had discovered on another day. Gretta had been bloated, her body rotting in the hot humid air. And crouched on the far side of the cell, Arta Fera had waited, her craziness obvious in the set of her body, the expression on her face. Despite the distance, the stench lingered in Sinklar's nostrils.

He shook his head to clear the image, forcing himself to deny the ache. If he allowed himself to feel, the knot would tighten and tears would come. Grief could blind him, distract his mind—and he'd need every faculty this evening.

"Five minutes, sir," the call came down from the cockpit.

Sinklar turned to his comm, "Mac? You there?"

"Got you, Sink. You on the way in?"

"Affirmative. I should be at the Ministry within five minutes. Everything all right on the ground?"

"Affirmative. I've been in touch with Mayz. She says that everything's on schedule. Kap checks in green, too. He says that it all came off smooth as could be. Not a shot was fired. Only one of my groups had any trouble. They ran into a mob at University. Took a couple of shots to take the ardor out of the students, and since then it's been quiet."

"Wish they could all be like this."

"Yeah . . . uh, I've had a couple of batches of guys show up demanding we turn the installations over to them. They claim they're Ily's people. We sent them packing, but she's probably gonna want some explanations. Thought I'd warn you."

"Thanks. Keep 'em out. How are modifications coming along?"

"Just fine. Some folks think we're nuts, but no one bitches at us to our faces. They shrug, look at our guns, and let us chop up their offices anyway we like."

"I've got a minute left. Anything else pressing?"

"Negative. MacRuder out."

Sinklar flipped the comm switch. So Ily's agents had been turned back at the doors? She'd be twice as mad—and three times as dangerous.

The LC whined, g pulling Sink sideways as the machine decelerated.

The skids hardly grated as the LC settled on the roof of the Ministry of Internal Security. Sink sat silently, clearing his thoughts as the thrusters whined and died. Mumbled conversation could be heard as the pilots talked and thumped things in the cockpit.

Sinklar unstrapped from his seat. Mhitshul rose obediently, eyes on Sinklar.

"You stay here," Sink ordered. "I'll be fine. Ily isn't going to abduct me, or anything like that." He grinned. "Not yet, anyway. She still needs us too much."

"Sir, I don't like the idea of you going in there all by yourself! What if she . . . well. . . ."

"Drugs me?"

"Yeah! What if she drugs you? Does something?"

Sinklar placed a calming hand on his aide's shoulder. "Mhitshul, she won't. She may decide to poison me one of these days, but not until we've destroyed the Sassans. Until then, she'll be as sweet as Riparian chubba leaves. Trust me. I'm going in there alone. We'll have a hell of fight, and then we'll get down to business. Right now, we need each other."

"And later?"

"Then we'll get down to scratching and clawing— but I'm hoping we'll have already won by then and she'll be nothing more than a relic of empire."

"Right, sir." The primness of Mhitshul's expression said that he didn't buy a word of it.

"Trust me." Sinklar slapped him on the shoulder and ducked through the hatch. Rows of empty benches waited mutely, crash webbing neatly stowed overhead, restraint belts all hanging limp. Sinklar's steps echoed hollowly on the deck plating. He placed a palm against the lock and the assault ramp dropped in a squeal of hydraulics to slap the roof of the Internal Security Building.

Evening had purpled the thick clouds overhead. The skyline of Rega appeared unchanged. He'd never noticed the air before, but after Targa's scent of pines, earth, and rain, Rega smelled noxious.

The city made a muted roar, like the sound a river makes from high in a canyon. Not even the Targan capital city, Kaspa, loud as it was, had this sound of endless activity. A cool wind buffeted his unadorned combat armor. Sinklar wore no insignia of rank, no fine fabrics, just the armor of the common soldier.

A door opened, a young man stepping out. "Lord

Fist? This way, please. The Minister is awaiting you in her apartments."

Sinklar shot a look back. Mhitshul stood awkwardly in the hatch. Sink waved reassuringly and started across the flat roof.

Inside, a lift tube carried him down a floor. The young man, an innocuous looking youth, gestured and bowed as Sink stepped out. Behind him the lift hissed and the young man disappeared.

Sinklar walked down the wood-paneled hall and two large brass doors opened before him. He stepped into a spacious office. Floor to ceiling windows filled one wall. The other contained artwork and monitor screens. Ily sat at a large desk in one corner. She smiled and rose as he approached.

"Welcome the conqueror," she greeted. She wore the formfitting black jumpsuit he'd become accustomed to seeing her in. The thin fabric accented her high breasts, thin waist, and flat belly. With a graceful movement of a slim hand, she flipped the gleaming wealth of her raven black hair over her shoulder, black eyes sparkling as she tilted her head. Sink had forgotten what a beautiful woman Ily Takka was. Her delicate skin contrasted with her hair; her features were perfect.

"I ought to choke you to death," she told him. "I don't know what sort of game you're playing, Sinklar, but I *don't* like it. Why won't you let my people take control of the buildings you occupy? Are we at war with each other?"

Just like I thought we'd start. "Not to my knowledge, but we are about to be at war with Sassa—just the way you've planned. Do you have any idea as to their preferred target?"

One of her thin eyebrows raised, a glow of enjoyment warming her translucent skin. "I assume it will either be Ashtan, Etaria, or Sylene. I'll know by the time they're ready to strike. Now, you tell me. What's this nonsense about employee ownership of the utilities? They belong to the people."

"Stop it. Right now, they belong to me. My troops

occupy the utilities, the Communications Center, most of the critical administration complexes, and are handling public security. You, on the other hand, are in control of a comprehensive web of information gathering services and the judicial system. Want me to give you half of my government buildings for access to half of your spy net?"

Ily watched him for several seconds, expression deadpan. "You're a conniving little bastard, did you know that?"

"And you're a power-hungry viper. There, mutual insults have been traded. Now, do you want to launch into me? Do your best to intimidate me so that I don't upset any more of your plans? Will it really help anything if we scream at each other for a while like mad dogs? Burn out that seething hostility."

"Gods Rot you, Sinklar. Why do I constantly underrate you? If I'd have thought, I'd have realized that you'd make your own insurance when you arrived. Very well, you've done it. What next?"

Sinklar walked over to stare at a holo of Rega, dots of light marking the surface—most of which, he noted with approval, were buildings, utilities, and service centers his people controlled.

"I need those Division Firsts on that list I sent you. In the meantime, I've found ten squadron Commanders I think I can use."

"They're all considered to be rather rebellious types." She stepped out from behind the desk, coming over to stand next to him. Sinklar caught her scent, warm and musky. He found himself noticing that she wasn't that much taller than he was, and very beautiful.

Knock if off! She's a reptile.

"I've had dinner prepared," she told him. "We have a lot to discuss, and I'd just as soon we did it somewhere besides my office. Perhaps we could lower our guards and arrive at some solutions to the problems facing us in the next couple of months."

He let her take his arm and lead him across the large room. The carpet under his feet swirled and rippled in patterns of yellow, green, and blue.

She led him into her private quarters, and Sinklar stared in unabashed amazement. A child of public housing, dormitories, and the spartan opulence of Targan mining offices, he'd never seen the like of this. Transparent ceramic arches rose to a high ceiling and filtered light down in every color of the visible spectrum. The carpet was a shimmering sea of blue. The furniture had been sculpted, each piece internally illuminated with slow-moving pulses of light. A soft breeze, with an odor he identified as sea spray filled the air.

"I don't often see you shocked, Sinklar."

He shook his head. "I've never seen anything like this."

"I can change it if you like. It's nothing like the rooms in the palace. They're considerably more sophisticated than this."

"So much disparity."

"Disparity?"

"Between what I grew up with . . . and this."

"You'd better get used to it. You're a Lord now. For all intents and purposes, the co-ruler of this empire."

Sinklar nodded, following her to a jetwood table that rose barely above the level of the floor. Mirrorbright spheres appeared to be sunken into the hard wood. Ily gracefully settled herself, pulling a pillow over to prop her back. She made a gesture and the spheres rolled back to expose a delicious feast of roast lamb, some sort of fowl, Riparian crawfish, and a variety of fruits and vegetables.

"Eat," Ily told him. "Enjoy yourself. Before we pitch into business, relax."

Sinklar eyed her cautiously. "How about business first . . . and then we'll relax."

"Very well." Ily reached for one of the fowl. "Ashtan game hen," she told him—and began pulling the bird apart. As she placed tender meat in her mouth, she asked, "Where would you like to start?"

"Training and supplies. I've got to place an entire army on war footing. I have to replace the command structure and retrain entire Divisions to use my tactics. It will be expensive and disruptive. Will you support me?"

She licked her fingers with an agile tongue. "I will. Will you allow me to run the rest of the Empire as I wish?"

Sinklar stripped the tenderloin from the lamb, uncomfortable about the protocol of the meal. "That depends. But then, I guess all the cards are on the table. Let's play each one and see where we end up."

Ily observed him, aware of the mollifying sensations of a full stomach and the heady Ashtan malt liquor she'd served. Rich and dark, its alcohol content ran fifteen percent or more. The subtle music she'd programmed had soothing subliminals integrated. Her trained eye had spotted the tension leaving his muscles. Now Sinklar leaned forward, determined to make a point. "I don't want another stifling Imperial system, Ily. Look what it did to me! I placed third. Third! In the interplanetary exams! And I got drafted!"

She rolled to one side, fingering her drinking bulb. "You placed first," she told him. "The two ahead of you were political winners. Their scores were fixed."

Sinklar's odd-colored eyes hardened. "I placed first?"

Ily gave him a warm smile. "First. I haven't just been executing your rivals, you know. I did a lot of checking. And before you blame the Imperial system, you'd better consider that neither Tybalt, myself, or anyone else in Regan politics got you drafted. I can't prove it yet, but I think you can blame the Seddi."

"The Seddi!" And vulnerability grew in his eyes. He looked like the young boy he was. Ily slid a little closer.

"You're right, of course," Ily told him gently. "We'll fix the system. Make the exams fair. I don't think we can afford to lose talent."

He nodded, taking another drink of the potent Ashtan brew.

"You know, we don't have to be adversaries."

Careful, Ily. Just work a small lever into him to begin with.

"You used Arta Fera to kill Tybalt, didn't you?"

She employed her weary smile. "How many people did you personally kill on Targa, Sinklar? Five? Ten? Or can you raise the count when you figure the number who died outside Vespa because you were brilliant enough to mine a ridge and maneuver the rebels into the trap? Don't look at me like that, I'm not changing the subject.

"Yes, I used Arta Fera to kill Tybalt. You and I, we're in the same business. We both want to effect change. I'm not quite as optimistic as you are. And since we're being honest with each other, I'll admit I'm power-hungry and ruthless about it—just as you're every bit as ruthless on the battlefield."

He stared into his drink. "How long do I have until the Sassans strike?"

"Three months at a bare minimum. More likely, three and a half to four. They're straining to mount an attack force. The first strike will be limited. They're thinking about keeping us off balance."

"And you really don't know which planet they'll target?"

Ily shook her head. "Not yet. It won't be Rega, but an outlying world. Ashtan maybe, or perhaps Sylene. My people will discover which target before they space. We'll have time."

Sinklar steepled his fingers, staring at nothingness. "I need to know the date they space. More than anything else, Ily. I *must* have that."

She'd worked her way to within centimeters of him, watching the droop in his shoulders, aware of the weary preoccupation that absorbed him. "You amaze me. You've already figured out how to stop them, haven't you?"

He shrugged. "Always on the edge. It's a Rotted way to live. Nothing seems to change. I always have to do the impossible."

Listen to the loneliness in his voice. Perfect. "You're not alone anymore, Sinklar." She poured more malt liquor into his bulb, adding to hers. "We'll do this together. Talking tonight, I've come to understand the sort of government you want. I can live with that."

He didn't focus very well when he looked skeptically at her.

She stared up at him, eyes wide and vulnerable, her body in a supplicant posture. "You want more enfranchisement for the common people. I want the aristocracy weakened and their ability to threaten me dispersed. As to the people, I don't care what they possess or control, so long as I don't have the Rotted Rath family snapping at my heels."

He frowned, and she parted her lips, aware of how his eyes raked her trim body. "Why? You're from the aristocracy, aren't you?"

Ily laughed, flipping her thick hair over her shoulder teasingly. "Aristocracy? Me? Good heavens, no. My father worked in a trona plant processing soda ash. I was bright, talented, and motivated. The most powerful man in our community was the constable. I worked for him for two years. He had a bad heart that killed him in the end. I might have married him but for that. Nevertheless, his recommendation got me a training scholarship in law enforcement here on Rega. I graduated at the top of my class and one thing led to another."

"And your mother?"

Good, I've elicited sympathy. Can I build on that? "Never knew her. She died when I was about three."

"Sorry."

"Don't be." *Now I set the hook.* "Everyone I ever loved is dead." She paused, gaze going vacant. "Once I worried quite a bit about death, about loss. One tragedy followed another. I'd barely recover from one thing, and life would slap me with another. I was a real wreck in those days. Lost, hurting. . . ."

She saw his eyes narrow, watched the tightness around his mouth. His hands tensed as he dropped his eyes, engrossed in his own memories of hurt.

Now. She reached out, taking his hand in hers, staring into his eyes. "It's all right, Sinklar. I got over the

ache long ago. It made me tough, strengthened me
into who I am." She'd shifted again, aware of his longing gaze. He might be brilliant and keen-witted, but
he was also a very young man—and his lover was six
months dead and gone. The Ashtan ale had worked
on him, lowering his inhibitions. The music with its
sexual subliminals had soothed him.

She could see his breathing increase, measure the
warm flush at his neck. The battle he raged with his
desire and the memory of his Gretta delighted her.

"I had help here and there, too," she added, adopting a gentle tone. "I remember once when I thought
I didn't have a friend in the world. I met someone
then. He," she smiled wistfully, "well, he reached out.
We spent a lot of. . . ." She tightened her grip on his
hand. "Maybe I'd better not talk about that."

"A lover?"

"Yes. A kind one. For a little while, the loneliness
vanished and we had each other. Ah, Sinklar, if I had
it to do all over again, I'd play the game differently.
To reach out in the night and touch another human
being who cares for you, to know that you're not
alone, not adrift in life, that is true security. Such
occasions are all too rare." She paused just long
enough, then added, "If I could only live it over
again."

His fingers were moving on her hand now, stroking.
He seemed to come to his senses, suddenly releasing
her. "I guess I should be getting back to the LC.
Mhitshul will be worried sick."

"I . . . sure." She gave him a shy smile, lowering
her eyes. "Um, I guess that might be wisest all the
way around. I feel. . . ." She took a deep breath, rolling over and swelling her chest as she stretched sensually. His eyes devoured her. "I feel very comfortable
with you. Comfortable in a way I haven't felt in
years." She rolled back, closer, resting her chin in her
palms. "Thank you."

He'd caught up the end of her long hair to rub
between his fingers. "For what? Listening?"

She ran the tips of her fingers down the back of his

hand, seeing the reaction it elicited. He squirmed the way a man did when he had an erection—and no place to put it.

"I suppose you'll be spending most of the time with your troops," she whispered sadly.

"Yes." He laced his fingers in hers, closing his eyes, battling with himself, with the pumping testosterone of youth.

She snuggled next to him, letting the curve of her hip barely nudge his. "Working with you might not be so bad, Sinklar Fist." *Another couple of nights with you, and I'll have you right where I want you.*

He swallowed hard then, trying to roll away. "I thought we'd have a fight. I didn't expect. . . ."

"To like me?" She arched an eyebrow and ran her fingers along the side of his head. He leaned forward, and she met his lips.

She could feel the throbbing tension as she ran her fingers along his body. His hands caressed her with a curious tenderness.

"Are you sure this is a good idea?" she asked, pushing back as she made an effort to catch her breath.

"No," he croaked.

She shook herself, climbing gracefully to her feet. "I don't think I'm ready for sex with you yet."

He closed his eyes, shaking his head. "I don't know what happened."

She laughed, crossing her arms over her chest. "I do. It's called lust. You're young, healthy, intelligent, and you've had quite a bit of Ashtan ale. I will admit, it's a temptation to drag you off to my sleeping platform and turn you every way but loose, but I don't think you'd ever believe I didn't slip something into your drink. You'd be suspicious of me forever."

He nodded, the trust she'd hoped to foster mixing with the desire. He stood, nervously rubbing his hands together. "You're right."

"Sinklar, I know how I'm perceived in the empire. I encourage that image of a ruthless, cold-blooded Cytean bitch. That very perception is a weapon in my hands. It gives me a psychological advantage against my enemies. The power of my reputation alone, when wielded appropriately, often serves to disable conspiracies without my resorting to other means. Internal security is my job—and I take it very seriously. In my own way, I, too, am working for the people. But there are two sides to my personality, one political, the other, well . . . I don't show that to many men. Only the ones I trust."

"And you trust me?"

She shook her head. "Not yet . . . not completely. But perhaps with time I can drop the pretenses. I only ask that you give me a fair chance, as I am giving you. Look at me through eyes unbiased by what you've heard. I think you'll find we're both fighting for the same thing. Only our methods differ."

"I still don't know what came over me tonight." He smiled bashfully.

"I do. And perhaps, if we can come to see each other as allies, we'll do something about it. For now, you're weaving on your feet. We'll talk in the morning," she told him, taking his arm and leading him to the lift.

When he'd gone, she closed the doors and walked to her bedroom. "Plan your war, Sinklar. Establish your new order. You see, my dear, the person who wins is the one who ends up with the reins of control— no matter how she gets them. And I have an arsenal at hand that you can't even conceive of."

* * *

"What can we say about the nature of God? Currently humanity embraces two very different paradigms. One, the Etarian, has developed a system of mythical beliefs based on the duality of good and evil. The Blessed Gods fought on the side of good against the Rotted Gods, and managed to establish the Forbidden Borders to keep humanity safe from the evil ones. The question is begged, however, that if we are in the province of the Blessed Gods—the givers of goodness and pleasure—why does the scourge of war, oppression, misery, slavery, and disease so so plague humanity? What foundation, outside of assumption, exists to prove the existence of such Gods beyond that of metaphor?

"The second paradigm embraced is that of deification of a human being: the Sassan system. The Sassans accept that their emperor is endowed with perfect infallibility. Yet do we see him alleviating the suffering of his people? Do we see him making decisions free from the taint of error? Outside of a dogma instilled in the people through manipulation of the media, and enforcement at the point of a blaster, where does Divine Sassa's proclaimed divinity lie?

"Both paradigms insist they are true. Yet, if one side or the other manifests ultimate Truth, why is the heresy of the other allowed to persist? Is it not logical to believe that one power would overcome the other? After all, we are talking about Gods here—ultimate power and ultimate Truth.

"Let us return to the lecture on epistemology. If we are talking about ultimate Truth, which is the wrong *epistemology? Would the true nature of God be riddled with inconsistency and contradiction? Isn't it more acceptable to the rational mind that* both *epistemologies are wrong?*

"After centuries of debate, the Seddi believe the answers to the nature of God lie elsewhere.

—Excerpt from Kaylla Dawn's Itreatic broadcasts

CHAPTER VIII

Tyklat, Director of Internal Security for the planet Etaria, stepped off the shuttle and started down the lighted tunnel that led to Imperial Regan Customs. At the gate, Tyklat flashed his ID at the armed soldiers who guarded the entryway. These were no bored officials, but combat veterans in armor. So the rumors of rioting must have been correct.

To his surprise, the soldiers barred the way, one with his hand held out for Tyklat's ID. He passed it over, waiting while the soldier checked the documentation and inspected him carefully, matching holo and description.

Tyklat stood one point six two meters tall. He had ebony skin well suited to his desert world. Intelligent eyes dominated a straight broad nose. For travel, he wore a tan suit of conservative cut and carried only a valise.

When Ily's transfer order first arrived, he'd been a bit nervous, but then when a follow-up communication explained that he was to be promoted to a regional Directorship, his fear had ebbed. No, she didn't blame him for the Etarian debacle. And besides, if she ever did, she could do her damnedest to pry his secrets out of his corpse.

Tyklat couldn't help but check the back of his mouth where the deadly Seddi tooth waited to be used.

The soldier nodded and handed the ID back, muttering, "Enjoy your stay."

Tyklat stepped through the security tunnel that checked him for banned substances, weapons, and other illegal possessions, and walked out into the reception area. Tactite windows ran from floor to ceiling and cast slanting light across rows of duraplast benches situated to allow passengers to look out over the shuttle field. A score of people loitered in the area. The floor had been scuffed and needed a thorough cleaning.

He saw the woman before she saw him. What man wouldn't notice a gorgeous creature like her? Auburn hair framed a classic face. The bulky clothing she wore barely concealed a body that was too good to be real. Men from all over the terminal were ogling.

She turned the most amazing amber eyes on him and smiled. The planet might have stopped dead in its rotation as she approached. "Director Tyklat?"

"Yes."

"Hello. Ily sent me. I'm yours."

"Mine?"

Her smile broadened and she handed him a small box—the control for a slave collar. Tyklat glanced up, curiosity piqued. Looking closely, he could see the slave collar now, a golden band about her perfect throat. Not only that, but this close, he could catch her scent, and it added to her sexual allure.

"Minister Takka rewards her people well," she told him. "I don't know what you did, but she said I was to tell you that I'm to replace the one that got away."

"Ah!" *Skyla Lyma! No, Ily doesn't suspect a thing!* Ily had promised him the Wing Commander before everything went awry on Etaria. Tyklat felt a load shift as the last of his nagging doubts vanished. Not only had he survived, but now he was being promoted in the Regan power structure, a fact that would please Magister Dawn when she heard.

"What do I call you?"

"Most recently I was called Gretta, but you can call me anything you want. I'm yours to do with as you please." And her eyes gleamed with excitement.

"I'll call you Gorgeous. My thanks to Ily."

"Minister Takka sends her regards," Gorgeous told him as she took the lead. "I'm to show you to your new lodgings and make you comfortable. Ily will see you first thing in the morning when you've had a good night's sleep. After that, I'll be responsible for showing you around Rega, seeing to your needs, and will accompany you on your next assignment. I hope that I please."

Tyklat grinned as he nodded. "You more than please, Gorgeous."

"This way, my lord." Gorgeous inclined her head, an exciting promise in her tiger eyes. She led him down the long hallway, calling, "Your baggage will be shipped directly to your quarters. I hope that pleases."

"It does." Had she thought of everything?

An official aircar waited at the security exit. More of the soldiers stood guard, their blasters at hand. Tyklat took a deep breath of the Regan air. It burned in the back of his nose. Not only that, the place seemed to roar constantly.

"Looks like things got a little rough here." Tyklat nodded at the guards as the aircar lifted and sailed out over the city in a priority lane. He watched the arching spans of giant buildings pass and noted the brown haze in the air. Could there really be dirt down there under all that ceramic, metal, and concrete?

"We've had violence for almost a month." Gorgeous shivered. "It was terrible. Horrible things happened. Government officials killed, aristocracy murdered in their beds, you wouldn't believe. And Etaria? Did they riot, too?"

"No. They don't pay much attention to the troubles of the Empire. The Blessed priests tend to avoid politics."

The aircar settled on the high roof of a palatial looking building. As they stepped out, the aircar sailed off. Gorgeous led him to a lift, palmed the security lock, and dropped them a floor to a plush apartment the likes of which Tyklat had never seen. He stepped out into the large room, feet sinking in the carpet. The furnishings might have suited an emperor. One entire wall was transparent, revealing a view of the city.

"Do you like it? If not, I can find you another," Gorgeous stared hopefully into his eyes.

"Fine. It's just . . . well, fine! Everything is."

She carried his valise into the bedroom, powering up the sleeping platform and checking the dispensers. She unwrapped the ungainly coat she wore, revealing more of her sensational figure. "Are you hungry?"

"No," Tyklat whispered, devouring her with his eyes.

She noticed and stepped close to help him off with his coat. "Would you like something else?"

"I. . . ." She cut him off as she reached up and kissed him, long fingers stroking his face.

The feel of her full breasts against his chest shot adrenaline through his body. Her long fingers slipped his shirt off before reaching down to undo his pants.

Struggling for breath, he stripped her, marveling at the wondrous perfection of her body. He bore her to the sleeping platform to bury his head in her breasts. She mounted him, allowing his hands to explore her muscular body. When he looked up, an excited gleam, almost feral, illuminated her eyes. The soft light threw shadows across her firm flesh.

The Blessed Gods wished this for humanity, he thought. *She's the goddess in human flesh—and she's all mine. Thank you, Ily!* He cried out as she brought him to pulsing ecstasy.

He slumped, totally spent, as she curled around him. "Blessed Gods," he whispered, drifting off to sleep.

Arta Fera watched him until his breathing deepened. She used a thumbnail to pry a section of the slave collar loose and a small phial dropped into her fingers. She smiled as she placed the phial beneath his nose and crushed it.

Tyklat's breathing deepened as he inhaled the vapors. Arta waited, catlike, for another couple of minutes before she moved, and then only to roll her body onto his, whispering, "Tyklat?" She patted his cheeks looking for a reaction. Finally she slapped him a stinging blow. Tyklat slept on.

Arta stood then, spitting on his naked body as she unhooked the fake slave collar and threw it at him.

A panel slid back and Ily entered, followed by several technicians who carried medical gear. Arta laughed as they tried—and failed—to ignore her.

"Get dressed," Ily ordered. To the techs she added, "You have other business than staring. I want him swept from top to bottom. If he's Seddi, as I suspect, he'll have a way to kill himself." Her black eyes narrowed angrily. "All the others have."

Arta picked up her bulky coat. "Is there a shower here? I need to wash away his filth."

"In there." Ily turned, walking over to stare down into Tyklat's slack face. "Very soon, dear Tyklat, I'll know everything that happened on Etaria. And if you're Seddi? Well, I've caught an important one."

* * *

Staffa sat propped on the edge of the scarlet couch, one leg dangling as he sipped his brandy and watched the fire that crackled merrily in the ornate fireplace. Divine Sassa would ignore him. A melancholy had settled on his heart. *I had to try reason first. Now what, Staffa? Blast Imperial Sassa? Employ the very measures that damned you in the first place?*

"I still don't understand how you got to Etaria," Myles said, a curious resolution on his face. "I've given you a commitment, made my gamble. Now it's time for you to gamble that my word is good. What happened to you, Lord Commander? You used to be as cold as liquid hydrogen."

Staffa ran a nervous finger over the incised cuts in his drinking bulb. The amber liquid caught glints in the firelight as he swirled it.

Staffa took a deep breath. "I became aware. That sounds curiously abstract, doesn't it? But it's true, Myles. You see, once upon a time, the Praetor of Myklene was like a father to me. He raised me, called me his greatest creation—and that's what I was. He trained me, and laid a rather insidious trap for me in the process. What do you know about mental conditioning, training the neural pathways?"

The Legate frowned, gesturing with his beringed fingers. "A little. Information is planted in the brain in a three-dimensional tree sort of arrangement. We access data through neural pathways that follow that arrangement."

"Very simply put, that's right. Pathways can also be blocked. In my case, that's exactly what the Praetor's psychologists and teaching machines did. They blocked the personality centers in my brain. The best analogy I can give you is that they created a sort of human battle computer, one without conscience, without shared values, without morals. As you put it: cold as liquid hydrogen . . . and just as emotionless." Staffa stared into the roaring flames. "He made me into a monster."

Myles stared up, a horrified look on his face. "That's why you killed him?"

Staffa's eyes narrowed as he remembered ripping the old man's head from his body, leaving it to stare sightlessly into Myklene's green sunset. "Perhaps. It's hard for me to remember. I told you he laid a trap? Key words, linchpins to unlock that hidden part of my mind. That's what he let loose that day: an emotional torrent that flooded my brain with endorphins, acetylcholine, and all the other chemical imbalances. I didn't know who, or what, I was. Worse, he told me that he'd taken my wife and child—kidnapped them years before. Evidently Chrysla—my . . . my wife—was aboard his flagship."

"And you blew it to pieces on the first assault," Myles whispered as he stared emptily into his glass.

"I killed her," Staffa admitted. "The Praetor was going to use her to bargain with, to save Myklene, but I never gave him the chance. You can guess how the information affected me. I'd loved her for years, Myles. Paid out fortunes to people to search for her. If you check your system, you'll find a tag on every Sassan personnel computer."

"And your son?"

"He's alive. You see, that's why I disappeared to Etaria. It was the logical place to transship to Targa—where the Seddi had my son. The problem was, naive and arrogant as I was at the time, I got into trouble." He chuckled, giving Myles an amused glance. "I might be very clever when it comes to Imperial politics and fighting battles, but I knew nothing about the street. A group of Etarian thugs set me up, robbed me, and I killed a couple of them in the process. What would you think if you found a man like me naked in the street beside two dead citizens? I was condemned to the collar. I spent those months while the whole of Free Space searched for me hauling pipe in the Etarian desert with the same people I'd sold into slavery for profit."

"Rotted Gods! So that's where Ily found you?"

"It was. But by then, as you can imagine, my perspectives had changed about a lot of things. Not only were my thoughts beginning to coalesce, I had to learn how to deal with my brain, to stifle the improper neural pathways and integrate a human personality, but I suffered day in and day out with people whose lives I'd destroyed. The guilt . . . pustulous hell, Myles, the guilt damn near suffocated me. In that horrible desert I met wonderful warm human beings whose lives I. . . ."

"Go on."

Staffa chuckled hoarsely. "Go on? How? I can't *tell* you, Legate. Dream about it . . . let it haunt your nightmares like it does mine. Place yourself there in the desert among people you'd condemned to slow death by slavery and rape. Suffer there in the sand with people whose lives you'd looted and broken in blood. It's an understanding of the soul, not of words."

Myles lowered his eyes uneasily and licked his lips. "But Ily found you. Then you blew up the Internal Security Building?"

"Skyla did. Ily was desperately trying to recruit me to become her conqueror—to share an empire with her. Skyla, bless her, had managed to track me to

Etaria, and with the help of the Seddi, broke me out and got me smuggled to Targa."

"We've wondered how you got there."

"In a shipping crate—with the woman who is now the Magister of the Seddi Order. Kaylla Dawn. You should meet her, she's pretty impressive. I murdered her husband and her children when she was the Mai-kan First Lady. It was in that Rotted sialon box that she gave me direction for my life, a framework with which to deal with the universe."

"So you became Seddi?"

"I became a Seddi. They have a lot to offer us. But that's not at issue. The only issue is stopping this war. I was in Makarta Mountain. There, I fought Sinklar Fist. I know his ability, Myles. I know that planet and what it took for him to subdue it—especially without Regan orbital support. If Skyla hadn't pulled us out when she did, Ily would have had me blasted in that rock."

"You don't think we can beat Sinklar fist? He's just twenty some years old."

Staffa gave the Legate a grim smile. "I might be able to beat him in a full-scale war. But Iban? Never. Iban doesn't have the flexibility, the imagination, or the sheer unbridled genius that is Sinklar's. No, he'll have Sassa within two years at the most. The problem is that too many worlds will die in the process."

Myles sat scowling into his drink. "You don't make it sound very reassuring."

"It's not a comfortable situation for any of us."

"Iban's going to make a strike. He's already massing assault ships and personnel. You know that, you can read your scanners as well as anyone. He's going to hit them within. . . ." Myles started and looked around fearfully.

"Four months, right?"

Myles rubbed a hand over his fat face. "I guess I made my commitment, didn't I?"

"But old habits die hard." Staffa took the Legate's drinking bulb and refilled it.

"What is the future, Lord Commander? Let's say you can stop the war, what then?"

"I'm breaking us out of the Forbidden Borders, Myles. Once I do that, humanity is on its own. I'm going to go back to Itreata and love Skyla Lyma for the rest of my days and run my industries."

"The Forbidden Borders are your obsession."

Staffa grunted softly to himself. "No . . . they are my atonement."

* * *

Division First Mykroft sighed gratefully as the military shuttle settled on Regan soil. For him, the long nightmare had finally come to a conclusion of sorts. How curious, he thought. He'd left Rega a powerful man in charge of a full Division. He—and the other officers in the spartan shuttle—returned disgraced and displaced.

Mykroft replayed the Targan campaign in his head. After the destruction of the First Targan Assault Division under Atkin, his Second Division had landed, secured the capital at Kaspa, and proceeded to battle the rebels. How could he have known the convolutions of Imperial politics in far-off Rega? The Seddi had assassinated Atkin, and Tybalt had looked for a sacrificial Division. Most striking of all, Mykroft's orders insisted that an officer be appointed from the ranks of the decimated First Division.

From his office window in Kaspa, Mykroft had watched the fierce battle waged by Sinklar Fist—and he'd acted to appoint him. After all, Sinklar's Division was slated for destruction in the field. Then, despite all conventional wisdom, Fist had survived, taken his objective, and beaten the rebels.

How could I have known? In celebration, Mykroft had thrown a Divisional ball for the Second Targan— and the rebels had struck, wiping out most of his command. To his dismay, Fist had disobeyed his orders when Mykroft demanded Sinklar hand over the First

Targan Division to him. *And I appointed him! The callous ingrate. For that, he humiliated me! Defied me!*

The anger burned in Mykroft's breast.

The others in the shuttle: Sampson Henck, of the Twenty-seventh Maikan; Tie Arnson of the Fifth Sylenian; Rick Adam of the Eighth Regan; and the others, had been similarly defeated. It could have been worse. Weebouw and his entire command were dead—blown away.

"We're back," Henck said sullenly. "Do you think there's a hero's welcome awaiting us?"

"We're lucky to be alive," Adam added. "But what next? Fist just had us loaded in the shuttle and sent down? Said we were free to go? What kind of lunatic is he, anyway?"

"A dangerous one," Mykroft supplied as he stood and unclipped his personal effects from the overhead.

A soldier—one of Fist's—stepped into the compartment and undogged the hatch. The woman said nothing as they filed out onto the tarmac of the shuttle port. But Mykroft could see by the set of her body the anger she was restraining.

He stepped down from the shuttle, feeling the heat radiating from the vehicle's side, and took a deep breath of Rega's sour air.

"Well, let's get inside," Henck said. "We can call for transportation." He kept his eyes lowered and started for the terminal building.

They walked silently, each lost in his own thoughts.

To Mykroft's surprise, he entered the terminal and found a group of young men waiting.

"First Mykroft?"

"Yes?"

One by one, the others in his party were called by name.

The young man acting as spokesman added, "Would you please accompany us. We have transportation waiting. We'll be taking you to your quarters."

"Quarters?" Arnson asked.

"Yes, sir."

Mykroft glanced suspiciously at the young men who had surrounded him. "What if I wish to go elsewhere?"

The young man smiled. "I'm afraid I must insist, sir."

Mykroft nodded and sighed. Probably just another military debriefing, but if that were the case, why weren't the young men in uniform?

"I *must* insist," the young man repeated.

"Come on," Adam urged. "It's probably some official nonsense."

"Very well," Mykroft agreed. But as he followed his escort, he couldn't shake the premonition that this, too, would turn out to be a mistake.

* * *

Ily Takka's private comm buzzed her. She rode in her personal aircar, watching the buildings slide past the transparent dome of her vehicle, her thoughts on Tyklat and the secrets he'd yield.

Ily thumbed her comm. "Go ahead."

"Minister Takka? This is blue team. We have the Division Firsts in custody. We're currently transporting them to the Ministry."

"Very good. Did you have any trouble?"

"No, ma'am."

"Place them in individual cells. We'll interrogate them later." *And they'll know which master they now serve.*

"Yes, ma'am."

Ily leaned back and smiled. Two catches in one day.

"Sinklar, two of us can play at this game. Insurance comes in many different forms."

* * *

"Oh, what I almost did!" Sinklar moaned from the small closet-sized toilet in his quarters aboard *Gyton*.

MacRuder had leaned his butt against the desk—stacked as usual with a clutter of flimsies—with his arms crossed on his chest. He inspected his lean image in the mirror across from him and patted down his blond cowlick where it stuck up. He tilted his head, then winced at the sound of violent vomiting.

"You sure you don't want me to stick you into a med unit to check you out? Maybe she put something into your food. Some slow poison." Mac glanced warily at the rumpled bedding on the bunk. It looked like Sink had simply flopped down and passed out.

Coughing followed the pumping sound of dry heaves. "No. I knew what I was taking. They brew it on Ashtan. It's not like that pathetic stuff you get here. This is *real* beer. And for as smooth as it goes down. . . ."

"Yeah, I know." Mac grimaced at the continuing violence issuing from the toilet.

Sinklar appeared, bare to the waist, looking a little pale and definitely shaken. The towel wrapped around his neck only accented his bony chest. His thatch of black hair stuck up this way and that. Sinklar's odd eyes looked pained. He took in Mac's grim look and blinked, sinking onto the cot. "I take it you didn't drop by just to wake me up and listen to me puke."

"No." Mac took a deep breath. "Remember that Orbital Defense Commander? The guy that let us sneak into Rega?"

"Bryn Hack?"

"That's him. They found him in his personal quarters this morning . . . dead. The last anyone saw of him, he was leaving the orbital platform's officer's lounge last night. They say he was with quite a lady. A real knockout. Half the guys in the bar were breathing hard."

Sinklar's bloodshot eyes glazed. "No. Not her, not. . . ."

"Yeah, you got it: amber-eyed, auburn-haired, athletic, the kind of breasts that defy gravity, and dripping pheromones all over."

Sinklar looked sicker.

"You gonna puke again?"

Sinklar slowly shook his head. "No. Rot it all, Mac. It's Ily. Pus dripping hell, what I almost did last night."

"You sure she didn't drug you?"

Sinklar nodded. "Yeah. I'm sure because she threw me out when I would have made a fool out of myself. The woman's a viper."

Mac grunted. *But he's having problems believing it. Curse it, what did she do to him down there?* "Sink, she's using Arta Fera to kill people. Now, I didn't know Commander Bryn Hack, but the guy was definitely on *our* side!"

Sinklar rubbed the back of his neck before he looked up. "We've got four months to retrain the army. Can you think of any possible way that we can be ready to ambush a Sassan military strike on someplace like Ashtan in that time?"

Mac stiffened. "Four months? You sure?"

Sinklar stifled a groan as he pulled himself to his feet and flipped a button on the desk comm. One of the wall monitors flickered to life. The view appeared to be a military space station. The ships that clustered like Riparian cigars around the central module were Sassan warships.

"This just came in. Two days old. The Regan agent says they'll be ready to space in three and a half months. It's not a big bunch, but they could easily neutralize the defenses around one of our planets and blast the place to rubble. They could take a crucial world like Sylene or Riparious and turn it into slag. Estimates are that Divine Sassa's ready to do just that. I believe it. He wants to keep us reeling, constantly on the defensive—and damn it, Mac, he can do it."

MacRuder glanced uneasily at his friend. "This is leading up to something I'm not going to like, right?"

Sinklar tried to grin but failed. "We've got to stop this attack, Mac. I have to have at least six months of hard training for the Assault and Armored Divisions. I have to replace and train an unknown number of officers. That command structure has to be integrated with the Squadron Commanders, who, so far, are an unknown quantity. A great deal of our industrial base has to be reorganized before we're ready to support a war. Fortunately, Tybalt initiated the process and all we have to do is follow up. We *must* keep them from hitting us before we're ready."

"I love miracles! I can't wait to see how you're going to take some thirty Squadron Commanders who hate your guts, mold them into a strike force, and ship them for wherever this base is—"

"Imperial Sassa."

"Right! Imperial Sassa—to blow up those enemy ships, when Sassan spies will know we're massing overnight to go blast something, someplace, and surely they'll never guess where! Let alone with every Commander in the fleet bitching about it! I'm waiting with goose bumps all over to hear how you're gonna pull this off."

"Good. I'm glad to see you understand the problem."

MacRuder rubbed his jaw. He hadn't shaved the abatis of stubble off. A jumpy queasiness had started to squirrel his guts around. "Damn it, what are you thinking, Sink?"

Sinklar raised his hands and let them fall. "I hate it, Mac. We're still in the same stink we've always been in. There's never time to catch up, get our breath, and organize. It's always a crisis." Sinklar turned haunted eyes on MacRuder. "Remember the Decker Lucky Mack Mine?"

"The one on Targa? Where we were left without transportation?" A cold realization soaked through Mac's hard shell. "I hate it when you get great ideas."

"You're gonna love this one."

Mac turned to the dispenser, punched the code for a scotch, waited for the glass, and tossed it back in one gulp. With meticulous care, he placed the empty container on the top of a teetering stack of flimsies, belched, and said, "All right, why don't you tell me about it?"

Sinklar's grin wavered and fell. "I want you to take *Gyton* and drop out on the commerce route between Imperial Sassa and Myklene. They're moving a lot of stuff from Myklene to the Sassan capital. If you could pirate a Sassan ship as it drops out of null singularity, you could capture all the clearance codes. From deep space buoys, they couldn't pick out *Gyton* tucked in close to a big Sassan freighter. They'd never expect a single ship to slip through their defenses that way."

Mac's breath caught in his throat as he choked out, "You're outta your Rotted mind! How in thrice-cursed hell are we supposed to get out!"

Sinklar's cheek twitched and he pulled at his knobby nose. "That's the one thing I haven't quite figured out yet."

* * *

Ily bent down and checked Tyklat's pupils. The faint odor of Mytol hung on his breath. Naked, he had been strapped into the hard steel chair, electrodes attached to his shaved scalp, chest, wrists, and inner thighs. On the tray to one side lay a false tooth, a subcutaneous ampule, and a very complex shoe that contained a small laboratory, a miniaturized comm center, and several sophisticated weapons. The shoe had been taken from Tyklat's baggage when it arrived.

Tyklat groaned, head rolling before he blinked his eyes open and stared blearily around the gray concrete of the interrogation room. For long moments he frowned, trying to make sense of the battery of cameras that lined the angle of the ceiling.

"Tyklat!" Ily greeted warmly. "Welcome to Rega. I'm very pleased that you enjoyed the gift I sent you. I'm sorry we had to do things this way, but any suspicion and you would have used the clever poison tooth the Seddi provided you with."

Tyklat frowned for a moment, and blinked, vision clearing as he looked up at her.

"Do you know who I am?"

"Ily Takka," he responded hoarsely. Ily watched as the monitors on the comm behind Tyklat established a pattern, the fingerprint for his biological responses.

"What is your name?"

"Tyklat Isbanion."

"Your position within Internal Security?"

"Director of Internal Security for Etaria. I am being

transferred to Rega for promotion and reassignment to a Regional Directorship."

"Are you a Seddi?"

"I. . . ." Tyklat's brow knit, as though his mind had knotted around the idea. His expression became pained, and he bit his lip. "No. Not . . . not. . . ."

Ily tapped her cheek. "Fascinating. You are the first person I've ever had under the drug who fought it so well. You impress me, Tyklat. My supplier of Mytol refines the purest form of the drug known, but perhaps you'll have to have a higher dose. Is that it? Do the Seddi use some process to raise the tolerance level?"

Tyklat's jaw clamped, his muscles bunched. Proof enough of Ily's suspicion. She reached for the tray, took the bottle, and used her thumb to insert the tube past Tyklat's lips. With practiced familiarity, she snaked the curved tube past his teeth and down his throat, dripping more of the solution down his esophagus.

Tyklat stared up with burning hatred in his eyes.

"If it doesn't work, there's always torture to back it up," Ily reminded sweetly. "Mytol doesn't dull any nerve endings, just the inhibitions." She cocked her head, studying him. "Do you know what it's like to have a hole drilled in your skull, and drops of acid released in various portions of the brain? You can feel yourself being burned out, a bit at a time. One hand will cease to work, memories will vanish."

Tyklat closed his eyes, struggling to ignore her.

"Very well, time enough for the Mytol to begin working. Are you Seddi?"

"Yes." The instruments wiggled in the same manner they had when he gave his name.

"Do you know that you can't lie to me?"

"Yes." The instruments read positive again.

"Do the Seddi have a way of raising tolerance to Mytol?"

"Yes." His facial muscles still contorted as he fought, but his efforts were in vain.

I've won! Let him fight. The knowledge of his be-

trayal will make breaking him that much more powerful. "Good. Normally, I would take great delight in wringing you dry of every scrap of information that you have within you. Time, however, is pressing, Tyklat, so I'm going to ask you to explain something to me. Will you do that?"

"Yes."

"How did Staffa kar Therma escape from Etaria?"

"In a shipping crate."

Ily started, glancing at the instruments. Rot it, he wasn't lying. "A shipping crate? Really?"

"Yes."

"Then who accompanied Skyla Lyma from Etaria when she used the jessant-de-lis to recover her yacht?"

Tyklat frowned, the instrument readings quivering. From long practice at interrogation, Ily immediately backtracked, "Wait. Let me rephrase that. Who escaped from Etaria with Skyla Lyma?"

"Nyklos."

"And who is Nyklos?"

"Another Seddi agent."

Ily tapped at her teeth with a long fingernail. "And Skyla didn't use the jessant-de-lis to escape?"

"No."

"Who did?"

"I did."

Ily glared at him. "Tyklat. Why don't you begin when you walked into the Director's office and told me you had located Staffa kar Therma. Tell me everything that happened."

The story began to unfold. Ily stepped back, accessing her personal comm. "Gysell? Cancel all of my appointments this morning. Something has come up."

"But the chairman of the—"

"I said, *cancel* them."

* * *

The lid of the heavy med unit lifted and Anatolia caught the stinging odor of medical chemicals drifting out from around her. She crinkled her nose and sat up, staring at the ceramic, metal, and plastic cocoon she'd been trapped in for the last hour. The med unit could be likened to a giant clam. A person lay down in the open mouth and it snapped shut, immobilizing the body, scanning it for injuries. In severe cases it monitored and directed the healing process through surgical, chemo, and electro-stim procedures.

The physician who monitored the instruments stepped out from behind the unit and gave her a curt nod. "Looks like bruises, a cracked rib, and a bit of exhaustion. A couple of days of rest, a few good solid meals, and you should be fit."

Anatolia nodded grimly, swinging her feet over the side and standing. The floor, like all tiled floors, chilled her feet. She reached for her clothing, hating to put the soiled garments on her clean flesh, and discovered the pile had disappeared.

"Thought you might like something else." The physician handed her a common smock. "From the condition your clothes were in, I'm not sure they'd have held together long enough to get you home."

"Thanks." Anatolia tried to smile, but it faded. Home? With the pimply blond kid living just down the hall?

"If you'll sign the release at the desk at the end of the hall, you're free to go—and, after what you've been through, very lucky to be walking out of here so soon."

She nodded, pulling the smock over her trim body, belting it at her thin waist. After the cleaning they'd given her upon admittance, her hair fluffed golden around her shoulders. She left the examining room and padded down the long hallway.

At the checkout she entered her name on the comm before giving the machine her address, employer, and account number. She sealed the contract with a thumbprint, wondering how she'd ever pay for the medical service.

She turned around then, suddenly aware of her condition. Barefoot, without a credit to her name, how

was she supposed to get back to her apartment that
lay halfway across town from the medical center?

She stepped into one of the public comms, hoping
against hope that Vet would be home and would accept a collect charge. For once, her luck held.

"Anatolia?" Vet asked after accepting. "Where are
you? I've been trying to call you for three days!"

She bowed her head. "I'm at the med center. Look,
I don't want to talk about it now. Vet? I need a favor.
I need a ride back to my apartment. After that, could
you drop me off at the lab?"

He nodded. "Sure, be there in a minute."

Anatolia cut the connection, a chill in her soul. *I
can't go home. I can't walk those hallways again. And
if I see that pimply kid—I'll kill him.*

She took a deep breath. Never before had she felt
so far away from her parents' siva root farm on
Vermilion.

"So what are you going to do? Where are you going
to go?" She could worry about that later. For now,
going back to work would divert her attention, mask
her memories of the darkness, of the sticky feel of
blood . . . of Micky's fetid breath as he savagely
jerked her pants down to expose her.

* * *

"I have always derived an immense delight from Ily
Takka. While others in my administration are talented and
capable, few posssess Ily's icy cunning. She leaves nothing
to chance, and her self-serving machinations are those of
a genius. I've never met anyone who possesses the single-
mindedness, or cold-blooded efficiency she does. Ily under-
takes no action unless it serves her purpose. She has no

cause outside of herself. Power is her sole addiction. She reads her victims with a master's eye, playing to their weaknesses with a calculated expertise until she achieves her goal.

"Having her in my bed excites something in my blood.

"I must ask myself, why? What perverted pleasure do I gain from the knowledge that her passionate body contains the mind and soul of a heartless demon? I know for a fact that she uses her sexuality to subdue the suspicions of her victims—and that she shares her bed with other men she's manipulating. Yet I welcome her back with anticipation, knowing full well the number of her guileless victims. In the heat of our coupling, a tingle runs up my spine, fired by the knowledge that this wanton I'm bedding is an insidious killer who would execute me without a backward glance should it serve her purpose.

"At least I know her tricks—the Rotted Gods pity the poor fool who unwittingly falls under her spell."

—*Excerpt from Tybalt the Imperial Seventh's personal journal*

CHAPTER IX

Skyla sat in the command chair and watched Imperial Sassa begin to shrink in the main bridge monitor as she added more thrust to *Chrysla*'s mighty reactors. Behind them, space wavered and contorted from the violent energies released as the huge warship increased acceleration, building to a moderate thirty gravities which would slingshot them toward lightspeed without straining the ship's gravity compensation fields.

Chrysla's bridge gleamed. The officers relaxed at their duty stations as they studied the monitors. First Officer Lynette Helmutt reclined in the pilot's couch, her eyes closed. The worry-cap, the shiny alloy helmet that linked her brain to the ship's computers and nav comm, covered her head.

Skyla made one final check of the systems displayed on the stat board that rose in a chrome pod from the armrest. The deep space scan indicated three freighters incoming from the direction of Myklene—more than eighty degrees off their present course. *Chrysla* had only a haze of cirrus—dark matter and space dust the shields would have to warp out of the way—between her armored bow and the Itreatic Asteroids.

"Looks like clear spacing all the way home," Skyla said. "First Officer, you have the helm."

"Acknowledged," the bridge speaker responded in Lynette's voice. While entranced by the worry-cap, a person heard, saw, and spoke through the ship's systems.

Skyla stood, adding, "I'll be in the personal quarters if you need me."

"Acknowledged, Wing Commander."

Skyla palmed the hatch and stepped into the corridor beyond, walking down the airy hallway in long strides. She caught the tube to Staffa's level and leaned back, arms crossed, a frown on her high forehead as she considered the visit to Sassa.

"It's a bust. Pus Rot that fat fool." *So what are we going to do now? Go to war with Sassa?* After Roma had delivered His Holiness' ultimatum, a deep worry had settled on Staffa. Now, when Skyla caught him off guard, she'd find him staring into nothingness, a sadness reflected in his eyes.

"Staffa, you can't bleed for them all," Skyla whispered to herself, shaking the sudden melancholy from her spirit.

When the door snicked open, she paced to Staffa's double lock and entered.

Not so long ago, the Lord Commander's sanctum had been a place of mystery and intriguing speculation. Here he'd locked himself away to plan and plot. Here he'd buried himself in the memories of his wife—the enigmatic Chrysla for whom the ship had been named.

And here he and I first made love. During the twenty years it had taken Skyla to rise through the ranks, their affection for each other had grown. Looking back, she could only wonder at the slow, but inexorable, weave of time. Filaments and tendrils of experience, of momentary vulnerability and trust, of shared triumphs and wretched tragedy had woven into a bond more durable than sialon. Love had crept up on both of them, pervading friendship, admiration, and respect. But it had taken the Praetor of Myklene to precipitate the events that finally brought them to a full realization of what they meant to each other. For that, and not much else, Skyla could appreciate the old villain.

Skyla stalked across the cushioning carpet in the main room and stepped through the Ashtan door to the right of the fireplace. There she found the Lord Commander at his office desk, totally engrossed. He sat hunched over a monitor, a headset pressed over his long black hair like a diadem. Before the desk, the wall had disappeared in holographic display. Free Space had been modeled in three dimensions. Sassan planets glowed blue; the Regan holdings shone in fluorescent orange. Defiant yellow marked the tiny triangular section of the Itreatic Asteroid Belt, which bordered both empires. Here and there in the display arrows had been placed in violet, and small squares of text noted certain assets or strategic significance in electric red.

"We're outsystem and accelerating," she told him. "Looks like free spacing all the way home. Null singularity in twenty-five hours."

Staffa made a muffled grunt.

Skyla stopped behind him, massaging his shoulders as she looked over his work. Strings of statistical formulae filled the monitor Staffa studied. More numbers appeared at the bottom as the computer-generated model provided a conclusion. Staffa growled to himself.

"Looks fascinating, what is it?"

"Statistical combat factors," Staffa explained, sighing and leaning back into her arms. "I'm trying to decide whether it's a better idea to warn Sinklar of the Sassan strike, or try and deal with it ourselves."

"Do you have any preference one way or the other?"

He patted her hand and looked up at her. "Not yet. The data are too sketchy concerning Sinklar's ability to organize and field a fleet against Jakre's attack."

Skyla lifted a pale eyebrow. "Assuming you know which commanders Sinklar will have—and which target Jakre will hit."

"Myles will tell me."

"Really?"

"You don't like him, do you?"

"He's a drooling fat Sassan."

Staffa frowned as he leaned back and doodled with a laser pen. He couldn't keep his gaze from the holographic map. "When he agreed to slip us the information, I believed him. He's only started on the analysis

of the Seddi data, but he's convinced of the danger.
Call it a gut feeling, if you like, but I think he's willing
to take the risks involved. He doesn't want to see his
homeland wasted any more than we do."

"I'm supposed to trust your gut?"

Staffa reached up to draw her lips within range of
his. He kissed her soundly and said, "I survived the
Praetor's mental booby trap, remember? Myles is becoming a human being. The responsibility is getting
to him. He's beginning to understand what the stakes
are, and he doesn't want to see his people, his
charges, dying by the millions." He paused, gaze
going back to the holo map. "But I think there's more
there, too. I think Myles really wants to make a difference. Despite our cynical age, there are people like
that."

She ran her hands over his muscular chest, enjoying
the feel of his warmth. "All right, we can disagree
over Roma. Just promise me you'll keep a close eye
on him."

"I will . . . and so, no doubt, will you."

"Bet on it," she told him wryly. "I'm going to sleep.
How about you? You've been at this for ten hours,
ever since you pushed Roma out the hatch and sent
him back to Sassa. Are you going to sit here for another ten while you manipulate insufficient data? Or
could I interest you in some close quarters drill?"

He smiled, tearing his attention from the holo to
stare into her blue eyes. "Nothing on the scanners?
No possible emergencies?"

She shook her head, grabbing the tip of her long
braid and tickling his face with it.

With amazing agility for so large a man, he cata-
pulted out of the chair, trying to catch her. Skyla
skipped lithely sideways, vaulted the desk, and dove
through the door to the sleeping quarters. She turned,
legs braced, and grappled as he charged in after her.
For several seconds they struggled, each trying to
throw the other, until Staffa simply lifted her off the
ground and she lost her leverage.

A laughing Skyla wrapped her arms around his neck, hugging him close. "Guess you win."

"As long as I have you."

For long moments gray and blue stares mingled. She bent forward, kissing him again, savoring the sensation of security and love. As he lowered her, his fingers undid the catches that secured her pliable white armor. She helped him, peeling the suit off her long legs.

Staffa traced gentle fingers down the long scar that ran the length of her muscular thigh. "Scared me to death the time you did that. Funny, I was frantic and couldn't figure out why."

"Like that time a shot cracked my helmet and you almost lost the battle because you were waiting around the hospital?" She undid her braid, fluffing her ice-blonde hair around her as he stared at her full-breasted body with open admiration. Her quick fingers unfastened his gray suit. She let her hands play lightly over his muscular chest and elicited a shiver from him as she drew one of his nipples into her mouth and teased it.

"I've missed you," she whispered as he kicked his clothing into the corner and pulled her close.

"It's only been a couple of days," he answered as he cupped her breasts and searched her eyes. "It just feels like forever."

She led him to the sleeping platform and shoved him onto the bedding before diving after him. In their spirited foreplay, Staffa rolled her over until her long hair wound around them like a gleaming veil.

She shivered as the passion built and she drew him to her, opening herself, locking her legs on the small of his back as he filled her. She tightened her grip, heart pounding, wishing she could press him inside forever.

Staffa, Staffa, how could I ever live without you.

* * *

In the honeyed afterglow of lovemaking, she lay
cradled in his arms, her head on his muscular chest.
She ran an index finger along the faint pucker of an
old scar that arced across his pectoral. "If we do alert
Sinklar, will he be able to take Jakre? We know he's
brilliant on the ground, but a space engagement is
something else. One minute you're in formation and
closing, the next you're in the thick of ships—bursts
of energy and dazzling flashes of light all winding into
tight chaos. The next thing you know, space is empty:
only wreckage and silence are left."

"I think he'll learn faster than we'd like."

Skyla gave a hoarse chuckle. "He's made of good
stock." A pause. "Why are you leaning toward letting
him handle Jakre? Pride? Curiosity? Something personal, Staffa?"

He twirled her pale hair around a tanned finger,
eyes pensive. "Perhaps. It would make things easier—
and harder at the same time."

"Does Myles know that we might have to kill his
fleet before it can reach Regan space?"

Staffa nodded. "We talked about that. It hurts him.
We both pretty much agreed that if it comes to shooting, it will be as a last resort. In the meantime, Myles
will covertly short-circuit the logistics for the redeployment. A missed shipment here, a redirected freighter
there. As stretched as their resources are, the effects
will be profound. If enough goes wrong, perhaps His
Holiness and Jakre will wake up to the fact that they
might be closer to the edge than they think. We just
have to make sure we find a way to keep Sassa from
launching a strike."

"That's the easy part."

He craned his neck to peer at her. "Easy? Sassa
and Jakre want to start a war."

"You bet they're easy. Sassa's a pushover compared
to Sinklar Fist. Considering the aftertaste the Seddi
left in his mouth, how likely do you think it will be
to talk him out of launching Rega against Sassa? No,
we've got to have an angle here, something to make
both sides back off and cool down."

"Like what?"

Skyla balled a fist and absently thumped his ribs. "Well, boss, that's the single little detail I haven't worked out yet. But something will come to mind. It's just a matter of recognizing it when it happens and seizing the initiative. You don't want to use *Counter-measures* yet, do you?"

"No. Assuming that Tap can get it to work. If we do, it means we've been pushed to the last resort."

They lay quiet, each lost in thought.

"Did you get Myles to allow Seddi access to Sassa?"

"He'll provide what cover he can. Official papers, travel permits, and so forth. Actually, he came up with a pretty good idea all on his own. He suggested that we do a subspace broadcast out of Itreata. Kaylla could outline the Seddi doctrine, their goals, and how the unilateral epistemology needs to be recognized for what it is. Like Myles said, 'What could Divine Sassa do?' "

She pursed her lips. "Myles just said sure, send in the Seddi? What about his God?"

Staffa laughed. "What makes you think Myles thinks Sassa's really a god? I showed him the old records that date back to the time of His Holiness' grandfather and the Ryklos charade. I showed Myles a great deal—and he wasn't exactly a pious man to start with."

"Is he still slobbering at the mention of my name?"

Staffa smiled. "No. I told him you'd overheard his braggadocio that time in Itreata. You'll notice he tactfully avoided you every chance he got after that."

She shrugged, forcing the fat Sassan out of her mind. "Tell me more about these transmissions we're going to fill the subspace net with. You planning on broadcasting to Rega, too?"

"Why not? From our location, and given our dishes, we ought to be able to talk to all of Free Space."

"Ily's going to come unglued. Which reminds me. While you were talking to Roma, we got a report from Itreata. Sinklar has taken Rega, restored order, and met with Ily. As of the moment we spaced, nothing

else had come in." She resettled herself. "That's going
to create another jagged angle in this affair. No matter
what sort of agreement you might be able to cobble
together with Sinklar, Ily's going to do everything she
can to sour it."

Staffa pursed his lips thoughtfully. "To think I could
have killed her that day you shot up the Security Directorate on Etaria. All it would have taken would
have been one step over and a perfectly placed kick."

"What about Sinklar? He's in her grip, under her
influence. He's awfully young, Staffa. He might be a
wonderful field commander, but is he up to her sort
of malignant shrewdness? She's cunning and incredibly
adept at manipulating people. Of all the enemies we
face, she's the worst."

Staffa nodded. "That woman has venom in her
veins. And whatever happens, one way or another,
she's going to make us pay before this is all over."

* * *

Sinklar entered the briefing room in the Defense
Ministry, with MacRuder, Ayms, and Kap following
behind. Overhead light panels bathed the entire room
in soft white light. For this meeting, the holo-capable
walls were opaque. Roughly half of the one hundred
desks arranged in concentric arcs around the podium
were occupied by Squadron Commanders and Division Firsts. The babble of conversation stopped as Sinklar strode purposefully across the polished tile floor
and mounted the podium.

He took a breath to still his thumping heart and
scanned the room. Hostile faces stared back, and the
air carried a festering resentment. Around the walls,
A Group from Mayz' Seventh Section stood at parade
rest, weapons grounded, eyes on the assembled Regan
officers.

Sinklar's staff lined out behind him, backs to the
large holo tank where operations were projected during briefings.

Sinklar stood straight, meeting the stares of the Re-

gans. The only face he recognized was Rysta Braktov's, who sat in the very last row. "Ladies and
gentlemen, good afternoon. I wanted you here to discuss the new state of affairs we face. The old order is
gone, swept away with the Imperial Seventh's assassination by the Seddi agent, Arta Fera. We now face
the task of creating a new Empire. One which most
of you have already condemned.

"I'm not here to argue the merits of a political system. Whether you abhor the idea or not, we're faced
with a new and different future. I'm not here to become a tyrant. I'm here to save the Empire."

The room remained silent, but bristling glances
were cast at Sinklar's armed soldiers.

Sinklar cleared his throat. "In the coming months,
the entire structure of the military is going to be re-
structured. Everything you have been taught about
strategy and tactics has become obsolete. Necessity
forced me to make innovations in both of those fields
during the Targan campaign. We have always fought
to win, but within a structured system that catered to
outdated concepts of status and honor." His expression was grim. "People, despite the mythology, war is
a vicious and nasty business. If I have done nothing
else, I've destroyed the myth."

One of the Commanders stood, an elderly man with
white hair and a hawkish face. "I am Leopold Vincent, Commander of *Tybalt* Squadron. Outside of the
fact that half of us have been arrested by Minister
Takka's insidious minions, and you have us coerced
for the moment by your guards, why should we cooperate with you?"

Sinklar clasped his hands behind him. "Because
whether or not you like what's happened, I need you.
The Empire needs you. Commander, none of you are
ignorant of our situation. Right or wrong, the assassination of Tybalt, and the execution of the Minister of
Defense and his Deputies has precipitated a crisis. As
of this moment, Sassa is massing for a military strike
against us. I have no doubt but that they see our pres-

ent circumstance as a vulnerability to be immediately exploited."

"And what of the Companions?" Vincent asked.

"We don't know. We can only assume they will side with Sassa. They certainly will not side with us."

Expressions tightened as the Regan Commanders glanced uneasily back and forth.

"I think you are beginning to understand." Sinklar rocked on his heels. "For over seventy years, the Companions have borne the brunt of the assault, no matter who they fought. As a consequence, the old order of command privilege could be countenanced. It was a luxury the Empire could perpetuate for the aristocracy since the Companions did the dirty work. The Regan military merely provided support and mop-up after the enemy had been demoralized and weakened. Ladies and gentlemen, we have four months to train our forces to fight like the Companions do."

"But against Staffa?" a woman in the back called. "That's suicide!"

"I've fought Staffa before," Sinklar countered. "And I would have beaten him, but for the timely rescue provided by the Wing Commander and her fleet. Staffa is not invincible. But each and every one of you must understand—we can't defeat him based on obsolete strategy and tactics. Nor can we defeat the Sassans in that manner. Within months, we will be locked in a deadly battle for the control of Free Space." Sinklar pounded the podium with a knotted fist. "I can only tell you that it will be bloody and terrible, as if the Rotted Gods had broken loose in Free Space!"

A fit-looking woman with brown hair stood. "I am Dion Axel. First of the Nineteenth Regan Assault Division. My question, sir, is why should we entrust ourselves to you? I studied your tactics—at least what I could get my hands on about them. Yes, you took five Divisions on Targa, and that appears to have been admirably done, but I submit to you that loyalty isn't blindly given. It must be won, and by results."

Mutters of assent rose from the audience.

Sinklar nodded, smiling for the first time. "I agree, First Axel." And then it hit him. "I will make a wager with you. With all of you. If my tactics do not prove superior in every way, I will resign overall command of the Regan forces to the officer of your choice."

Skeptical mutters broke out, a woman in the front row spitting, "With Ily's tentacles wrapped in our guts, do you expect us to believe that?"

Sinklar raised his hands. "I've given you my word. Ily does not command me, or my Divisions. Think, Rot you. This isn't a matter for petty politics, backbiting, or political intrigue. Our citizens, men, women, and children by the billions, are facing holocaust. Each and every one of you has to take stock of the grave stakes we fight for. If we don't win decisively, how many of your friends, relatives, and other innocent people will be annihilated? How many worlds of ours will be blasted and silent? And those who survive? Do you want your children, your legacy, to be Sassan or Regan?"

Sinklar shook his head, reaching out to them. "I'm not that vain. I would trade every glory, every victory to bring the men and women I loved and cherished back to life. Events have placed me at your command. When I shipped for Targa as a private, I had no ambitious dreams of becoming Emperor. I am a scholar, but since this burden of our very existence has fallen to me, I will do my best."

Sinklar pinned Axel with his stare. "You've made a rational request. I will earn your loyalty and prove my tactics. At this critical moment, results matter more than pride. If I cannot deliver, *I will resign*. That is my commitment to you."

Axel stood again, turning to look at her comrades. "Most of you know me. You know that I've been a student of tactics for some time. We know that the Sassan threat isn't ephemeral, and Lord Fist is right about the gravity of the situation. I've studied his strategic and tactical innovations. They're interesting, and innovative, but leadership goes beyond gaming ability." She turned back to Sinklar. "And how are we going to determine your fitness?"

Sinklar braced himself on the podium. "The training exercises will prove or disprove my ability. All I ask of you is the opportunity. If I lose—even once—you may vote in a new commanding officer. And, in fairness, if I win, and some of you cannot adapt, I reserve the right to replace you with officers I think fit."

A man shot to his feet. "And if I refuse? No one takes the Ninth Vermilion from me!"

Sinklar waited out the chorus of shouts. "Then I will have you removed. People, this is still the military, and so long as I'm in charge it will be run that way. You *will* obey orders under the Command Codes until such time as I am proved unfit. That is my final word."

First Axel was on her feet again, waving down the hubbub. "I'll take Lord Fist's word." She scanned the room, expression serious. "I've known most of you for years, and hopefully have earned your respect in that time. I also know the precarious position the Empire is in. I've watched in awe as the Companions broke defenses I thought impregnable. I've watched them crush planet after planet and marveled at their efficiency. My friends, my advice is that we worry about the Sassans first, and deal with the future when we know we'll have one."

Rysta Braktov stood where she'd been waiting in the back row. "Ladies and gentlemen, if there is anyone here who knows what we face, I do. I've watched Fist at work. Like Axel, you know me, know who I am and what I've accomplished. The Lord Commander offered me a position among the Companions more than once. You know that I'm a capable officer, and you know that I'm Regan to the bones. If Fist says he'll step down if he can't deliver, I think he will. He's put his neck on the line for the Empire. It's time for the rest of us to do the same." Rysta shook her head. "Nothing is certain anymore, but I'm willing to gamble on Fist. I don't like him, or what he stands for, but before we sort the rest out, we *must* save the Empire."

Sinklar watched their expressions, some sour, some hating, and more than one, thoughtful. *I've bet so much in the past, has this been a stroke of brilliance? Or the desperation of a fool?*

* * *

She stood before the transparency in the observation nacelle. A long gown draped in folds from the ornate pins at her shoulder. Her rich auburn hair fell to the middle of her back in rippling waves of red-gold that glinted in the light cast by the overhead panels. She placed her slender hands on the railing, fingers perched delicately. Motionless, she stared out at the planet, as if sculpted of desolation and heartache.

Governor Zacharia Beechie hesitated to approach, absorbing the moment, engraving it in his mind. If any pose could have typified Marie Attensio, this one did. One might imagine a woman standing so as she watched a lover depart for war—or see it as the posture of a heart-rent mother staring as her child's casket drifted into the endless night of space.

For a time he agonized about disturbing her, then he took a breath and walked forward, heels tapping to alert her to his approach. She remained motionless even after he'd come to a stop beside her.

Beyond the transparency, Myklene turned in the green light of its sun, Myk. Swirled patterns of cloud masked much of the surface, but here and there, patches had cleared as the smoke and debris of war precipitated from the atmosphere and the world began to come alive again.

"Are you sad to leave, Marie?" He dared to glance at her profile, his heart racing once again as he took in her beauty. The dry tracks of tears couldn't be mistaken. Her amber eyes possessed a wounded look.

"No, Governor."

"The politics of worlds and empires take no heed of the people they crush in their struggles. The price in lives and misery is far from apparent to those who must suffer for the accomplishment of interstellar goals. For the security of His Holiness' empire, Myklene had to be dealt with. Someday soon, all of Free Space will be united under one rule. We'll have peace then, Marie. The house of man will live under one roof."

She kept silent.

"I suppose I'm trying to apologize for the empire, to tell you that we didn't come to destroy your life or your loves. The actions of armies and empires might be likened to those of a colossal beast. As it strides through the forest, it never notices the small creatures crushed beneath its ponderous weight. To the mouse who scrambles from the wreckage of its burrow, the event was catastrophic, but the giant beast bore the mouse no malice. The burrow, and perhaps the newborn within—"

"I bear Divine Sassa no ill will."

Beechie clasped his hands behind him. "I'm glad to hear that, Marie. I understand your grief, however. Myklene was a beautiful world. I myself suffer a bruised soul for the damage done in the conquest. Once, years ago, I served on Myklene as assistant ambassador in the Sassan Delegation. How I enjoyed walking the streets in the cool evenings, admiring the architecture, and refreshing myself in the gardens along the Agora Magna."

The corners of her eyes tightened. "I never saw it, Governor. But yes, I often heard that Myklene was a beautiful planet. For me, however. . . . Nothing. Forgive me."

"Go on. You always seem so sad. I'll ask again. Is there anything I can do? I'm at your service." *As always.* She never responded to him except with the utmost courtesy. She listened intently when he spoke and carried on a perfectly civil conversation so long as the subject didn't lean toward the personal, or toward serious issues. When that occurred, she sidestepped with a deft art that Beechie—a longtime bureaucrat—could only admire.

She gave him a warm, if guarded smile. "You have already been more than kind, Governor. It is I who am forever in your debt. I promise you, when we reach Sassa, you shall be well rewarded. Not only for your kindness, but for your decency and nobility."

He hated it when she brought that up. Damn it, he'd fallen hopelessly in love with her. And the problem with falling in love with a delicate, saintly doll, was that you always wished she had the spark of the wanton hidden somewhere within.

Nor could Beechie nerve himself to make an advance despite his growing desperation. One didn't rough up a fragile creature like Marie anymore than one would throw a bone-china doll to a dockhand.

The irony of his situation frustrated Beechie to an extent that even eighty years in government service hadn't.

The planet looked smaller now as the *Markelos* shipped out into the traffic lane and began to build boost for Imperial Sassa.

"It's late, my lady. We've been hours in transit, delay, and changing shuttles. I believe I'll have an evening brandy and turn in. It would be my greatest pleasure to share a nightcap with you." *Please, please, Marie.*

"Your offer is very kind, Governor. If you don't mind, however, I'd like to stay here for a while longer." A ghost of a smile curled her full lips. "I'll never see Myklene from this perspective again. I need to. . . . Well, thank you. Perhaps later, when we're in null singularity."

Beechie bowed to necessity. "As you will, lady. If you need anything, anything at all, don't hesitate to call on me."

"Sleep well, Governor." But her gaze had returned to Myklene, the welling anguish shining in her amber eyes.

Beechie forced himself to walk away casually and mused on her words. *I need to. . . .* That could imply so many things. *I need to what? Mourn for your dead?*

Is that why you watch Myklene dwindle? Does your soul dwindle with it?

Once he'd reached the main corridor that ran through the *Markelos*, Beechie slammed an angry fist into his palm. Well, he had almost a month before the giant freighter made port at Imperial Sassa. After that, he'd see to her arrangements, secure quarters for her close to his. Time, that's all he needed. With time, he could win a place in her heart, replace the misery with his love.

"I'd give all of Sassa and my soul to see your eyes burn for me that way. I just hope he was worthy of your love . . . and your pain. Whoever he was."

* * *

"Keeping in mind that the fundamental baseline assumption the Seddi make about God is that the universe is the reflection of God, Itself, the question is begged: What can we say about the nature and qualities of God?

"First, let's look at the universe through a physicist's eyes. From our observations of redshift, solar evolution, and quantum mechanics, we can make a single general statement about the universe: it continues to grow more complicated. Physicists believe that in the very beginning instant, our universe began as an explosion of intense energy. In that instant, our universe consisted of expanding mass/energy which, within ten microseconds, had broken down to basic matter and the four forces. Gravity, electromagnetism, and the strong and weak forces evolved—the four factors which must be unified for subspace communications and null singularity navigation. Within yet a few more seconds,

particles came into being, nuclear material consolidating in the preform of the hydrogen atom. This entire bursting soup reacted with itself in destructive and constructive interference, creating the initial conditions for the levels of order and chaos we observe today. Such wave functions are now measured in our gyroscopic interferometers—the basic tool of interstellar navigation.

"This interactive birth of chaos changed the density of the expanding hydrogen medium. At the same time, collisions occurred, and vast amounts of energy created isotopes. Some such collisions gave birth to helium, and possibly to lithium and beryllium. The uneven distribution of mass triggered instability in the matrix, gravity condensing and compressing until the first stars ignited, fusing hydrogen into helium, and eventually into ever heavier and more complex elements. In turn, those first massive stars exhausted their fuels. Gravity won the duel it fought with radiation, the stars collapsing in final supernova explosions which forged yet more complex atoms. The nebulae spun from the corpses of these giants generated the birth of ever more and diverse stars, which in turn died, spewing their heavy elements into the cauldron of space.

"Today, looking out past the mist of the Forbidden Borders, we see the result of this constant evolution of complexity. We see it spanning from atoms to humans to galaxies and the Universe itself.

The Seddi believe we are seeing the reflection of God—and isn't that more reassuring than the idea of Rotted Gods battling with Blessed Gods? Or a deified human being with his emotional disabilities and limitations? We, like our Universe, and God Itself, must grow more complicated and complex as we age, and learn, and observe new things.

"God is continuing to grow, why don't you? Investigate your life. Learn something new today. God does with every passing second."

—Excerpt from Kaylla Dawn's Itreatic broadcasts

CHAPTER X

The machine asked for clearance. "Seven three five five," Anatolia told it.

"Accessing."

The laboratory hummed in the silence of early evening. The last of the professors had left. Even Vet had given up on her, raising a skeptical eyebrow at the lie she told about having another ride home.

Anatolia clenched her fists. The trip up the lift—despite Vet and Marka's companionship—had left her shaken and trembling. She'd walked down the hallway to her apartment, discovered the door jimmied, and entered to find the room trashed. PUS LICKING GOVERNMENT BULL had been scrawled across one wall in red letters. Her personal possessions had been ransacked and anything of value stolen. Her clothing lay stewn about and most of it had been urinated upon. Her underwear had received particular attention, strung up and shot with red paint, as if to simulate the aftereffects of a brutal rape.

Her knees weak, she'd left, aided by Vet and Marka. She'd only taken long enough to gather the least sullied of her clothing and jam it into a sack.

I'm never going back there. No, she'd stay here in the lab and work on her 7355 study until she couldn't see straight. After that, she'd sleep here, in the chair. And if anyone came in, she could walk down the hall to the women's room and stretch out on the bench there for a couple of hours of sleep.

"And I can't dream. Not ever again." Because Micky lurked there in the back of her mind, waiting to creep out of the nightmare and grope her breasts and shove his fingers between her legs while his rancid breath filled the air. She'd fight him, and hear the metal rod smack wetly into his bleeding skull. Until the day she died, she'd never get her hands clean of the memory of clotted blood caking her nails and cuticles.

The data flashed onto the screen and Anatolia stared at it; she let her consciousness drift away into the structure of the DNA specimens she studied. There, among the double helix of guanine and cytosine, thymine and adenine—all bound by pentase sugars—she could find structure and order: the sculpture of the human being. Here in the elegant sequence of familiar patterns she could be at home. Here she could attack the puzzle that made no sense. Here she could lose herself in a universe that was measured in angstroms but stretched across centuries.

This new universe she probed consisted of three specimens, each taken from a human being. Two of those specimens, she could place into a pattern. One Targan, the other Etarian. But the third—the sample she'd taken one night from a young soldier—that one defied anything she'd ever seen.

As she studied the structures under her microscope, she forgot everything but the decoding of the unique pattern and its meaning.

"I'll find you. I'll learn what you mean."

Piece by piece, Anatolia Daviura mapped the curious structure, tapping information into her comm. Unnoticed, the hours passed. The laboratory continued to hum to itself as the capital city slept.

* * *

"Would you say that Skyla Lyma was in love with the Lord Commander?" Ily asked, arms crossed. The chill of the interrogation room had begun to reach her, but she endured, attention rapt.

"Yes," Tyklat answered, his eyes dull now. He shivered periodically in the cool air. She'd finally broken him. Every time he'd pulled up his tenacious internal fortitude to resist her, she'd worn him down until finally, after hours, Tyklat had given up. She worked him like a piece of damp clay in the fingers of a master.

"And the Lord Commander is in love with Lyma?"

"I don't know."

"Is he in love with Kaylla Dawn?"

"No."

"But he traveled to Targa in a box with her. Doesn't that suggest that they were close?"

"No. You don't understand. Kaylla was Stailla Khan, the first Lady of Maika."

"Yes, yes, we've been through that. Staffa murdered her husband and children in front of her. She only escaped because she managed to change places with a household servant." Ily chewed on her thumbnail, considering everything she'd learned. "So Kaylla would never be Staffa's lover?"

Tyklat looked up miserably, well aware that even though the Mytol had worn off, the monitors would detect a lie. "I've talked to Magister Dawn too many times. You can tell from her reactions. She tolerates Staffa . . . even pities him in a curious sort of way. But the memories of her children, her husband, and then the rape by Companions as she lay in her family's gore . . . well, what would you expect?"

"Evidently nothing that I could use right at this moment." Ily paced the couple of steps the room afforded. "The fact, however, is that Staffa was rescued twice by the Wing Commander. The second time, she scrambled the Companion fleet to whisk Staffa out of my hands. The question, then, is how much does he love her?"

"I don't know." Tyklat sagged in the chair. "All I know is that Nyklos fell in love with the Wing Commander—and she hardly noticed his existence. It drove him nuts. He considers himself quite a lady's man, you see. The last time I talked to him, he told me that Skyla had moved in with Staffa, and Nyklos had busied himself with Magister Dawn and Magister Bruen."

"But you've told me that Bruen is a broken man. His entire plot to lure Staffa into his reach backfired. Correct? The entire Targan revolution was hatched as a ruse to bait Staffa into range so that Bruen and this Magister Hyde could use Arta Fera to assassinate the Lord Commander?"

"That's correct . . . so far as I know." Tyklat licked his dry lips. "You have to understand, Bruen and Hyde didn't tell the second echelon agents—like myself—what the plans were. I wouldn't have known any of this if I hadn't been involved in Staffa's escape from Etaria. That's all I know about it. I swear."

Ily nodded, slapping a hand against her thigh. "I see. Well, it's been a most enlightening session, Tyklat. It turns out you've kept me occupied through most of the night. It's too bad Staffa pulled all of your Seddi kin out of Makarta."

Tyklat closed his eyes and sighed. "I'm sorry I can't tell you more about the Seddi agents in Rega. After the evacuation, Kaylla did a lot of shuffling. We normally work in cells anyway, just in case someone like me gets caught."

Ily stared into nothingness for long minutes. *How do I use this? Skyla is in Staffa's bed? Is that a lever?* "Tell me, Tyklat, if you were in trouble and called Skyla Lyma for help, do you think she'd turn you down? After all, you placed yourself at considerable risk."

Tyklat took a shaky breath, eyes imploring. "Please, don't ask me to—"

"Would she?" Ily barked.

Tyklat winced before his head dropped to hang limp. "I've told you everything I know."

"Answer me, Tyklat. You can do it now, or after I've shot a little more Mytol into your veins."

He swallowed hard. "I don't know. It would depend, I suppose, on what it was that I asked her for."

For the first time, Ily smiled. "Thank you, Tyklat. I think that will be all for tonight. Tomorrow, we'll work on what you'll say to dear Skyla when you make your request."

* * *

Sinklar stared at the endless list of requisition forms, and took a sip from a cold cup of stassa. The meeting with the Commanders had broken fifty-fifty, which was more than he'd hoped, but he had a chance now. Still, he couldn't keep his thoughts off Ily—and worse, what he'd almost done with her. The more he tried to force it out of his mind, the more he dwelt on it.

He stood, pacing back and forth before his desk in his quarters on *Gyton*. Through the deck plating, he could hear shuttles docking, the muted clangs and bangs of hurried refitting. Rysta had been on the comm six or seven times, pestering him about what was happening. Each time, Sinklar had firmly refused to provide any information.

Too many leaks, Mac. You'll have to brief the Commander once you're underway. We can't let the Sassans know we're making a strike. If anyone has to know, tell them you're spacing for Terguz, that intelligence has tipped us off that the miners are thinking about going on strike.

"I almost slept with Ily," he admitted aloud. "Sinklar, how could you?"

It had to be the ale. Ily had to have put something in it, some sort of aphrodisiac. The memory of her sensual eyes lingered. Her lips parted, desire reflecting from her alabaster features.

"Fool, you put the ale inside you! That was the only drugging going on." He closed his eyes, shaking his head. "Oh, Gretta, I'm sorry."

He paced back around the desk to stare down at the monitor. Heedlessly, he simply stabbed the "yes" key on the appropriations list until he'd gone through all three hundred and ninety-two remaining items. What the pus-Rotted hell, they could sort it out later.

Comm beeped, and Mayz's face formed, worry on her angular features. "Sink? Sorry to bother you. Listen, I've got a Division First on the comm. Dion Axel

. . . from the meeting. You know anything about her?"

Sinklar cleared his confused thoughts. "Yeah, Division First for the Nineteenth Regan Assault Division. Didn't you get the memo on that?"

"Memo?" She raised an eyebrow.

Sinklar sighed and tugged absently on his knobby nose. More screwups in communication. "Guess not, huh? All right, listen. I talked to her after the command meeting. I want your Fourth Targan and the Nineteenth Regan engaged in war games ASAP."

"Just war games?" Mayz screwed up her face. "What for? We'll wax her ass all over the floor!"

Sinklar nodded. "That's the idea. Listen, Axel strikes me as an open-minded sort—even if she's from the old aristocracy. She was the youngest daughter of a not-so-well-to-do family. She's a student of tactics, one of the best. We've got to start somewhere, and having the Fourth Targan cut up her Division is it. I want the whole thing documented, right down to the Group battle comms. They're going to be studying this for years. It's important."

"So why not use Mac's First Targan? They're better than my Division. Or Kap's Second, for that matter."

"Because the Forth Targan is the old Twenty-seventh Maikan Assault Division that Henck made such a big thing of. I want old veterans seeing how they got beat—and telling everyone else about it."

Mayz pursed her lips. "Taking quite a gamble, aren't you?"

"Got a better idea? You yourself said you could wax them. Or do you want me to give this to Ayms and the Third?"

Mayz stiffened. "When do we do this?"

"Tomorrow morning. Shik is running down LCs and transport. Use the Tarcee Estate for the games. Axel goes in first and sets up her defenses. Her objective is to hold the estate. Yours is to take it."

"Affirmative." She gave him a predatory smile. "You know, a lot of Henck's people are still smarting after the way they got trounced in Kaspa. They're spoiling to fix bruised pride."

"Training lasers only," Sinklar reminded. "Charred armor means a hit."

Mayz gave him a wink. "You got it. Are you going to be there for observation?"

"If I can get away." He slapped his hands to his sides. "And that gets more and more tenuous."

"If not, we'll let you know how it goes."

"Did you get the memo on the Command Reorganization? I want the lineup as follows: Me, Mac, you, Shik, Kap, Ayms. If anything happens, I don't want paralysis like we saw the Regulars go through on Targa."

"Affirmative. Yes, we got the memo on that. Everyone knows, and I haven't heard any bitching about it."

"I didn't think there would be. You might let people know that I had to make up some sort of order. I don't want someone like Ayms thinking I was—"

"We know, Sink. Relax. We've been a team for too long."

"Thanks, Mayz. That's it unless you have something else on your mind."

"Negative. Mayz out."

Sinklar puffed out his cheeks, looking around the cabin. With resignation, he grabbed his war bag from the loops at the foot of the bed and packed his few things. Zipping the bag closed, he went to comm. "Connect me with LC One. Mhitshul?"

The monitor wavered to life, Mhitshul's concerned face staring out. "Yes, sir?"

"I'm transferring all the data in *Gyton*'s comm to the LC. I'll be aboard in about an hour. After that, we'll be dropping to the planet."

"Yes, sir. I'll monitor the data transfer. Anything else, sir?"

"No. See you when I get there." He flicked the comm keys to transfer the data and shut the system down when it signaled completion. Grabbing up his bag, Sinklar slapped the hatch and headed for the Commander's conference room.

He arrived to find Mac and Rysta already there. The place consisted of a sickly-green painted room, a central table with comms along one wall, and spartan fixtures. Rysta stabbed a button with a gnarled finger and a chair rose out of the floor.

Sinklar lowered himself and braced his elbows on the table. "Good to see you, Commander. Thank you for your support this morning."

"Maybe," Rysta muttered. "You heard about Bryn Hack? Found dead in his quarters. Somebody broke his neck, but before they did that, they kicked his balls so hard they blew them right out of the scrotum and tore his penis half off. I don't have a squeamish stomach, and I don't know all there is to know about Commander Hack, but whatever he did, he didn't deserve that kind of treatment."

Sinklar could feel Mac's eyes boring into infinity.

"No. He didn't. He seemed like a decent human being."

"Damn right, he was!" Rysta thumped the table with a hard fist. "And I know where the blame lies for his death. I think you do, too, *Lord* Fist."

"One war at a time, Rysta." Sinklar raised a hand to calm her. "Justice will have to be tackled very carefully, and I think you're clever enough to know what I mean. We won't forget; but in the meantime, we've got to balance on the knife's edge and remember the realities of who controls what. Which brings me to the next topic."

"Rotted right," Rysta asserted. "What's going on around here? *Gyton*'s being refitted and resupplied. Mac, here, is spouting some Terguzzi sumpshit about rioting miners. Fist, I'm no blushing virgin when it comes to ships. We're outfitting for deep space. And I know a pus-dripping lie when I hear one."

Sinklar steepled his fingers. "Mac will give you the destination as soon as you've spaced for Terguz."

Mac sat silently, hands flat on the table, expression

neutral as he looked at Sinklar. "Any thoughts about that problem we talked about earlier?"

"Some. You'll find them on your comm, sealed and restricted by time delay access. If anything else—"

"Rotted Gods," Rysta whispered, dropping her voice. "We're hitting the Sassans, aren't we? We're dropping in, racing down their accursed throats, and trying to take out one of their planets! That's why the fission torpedoes were being loaded."

Sinklar considered her for a moment before nodding. "Yes, Commander, you're hitting the Sassans. It's a desperate gamble to buy us time to refit and retrain. They've got a strike force assembling and I want to take it out before they can use it against us and kill one of our worlds. That's the gamble."

Rysta asked the natural questions. "How many ships are rendezvousing with us? Who's in command?"

"I am," Mac said quietly. "*Gyton* is the only ship. We're going in to take out those Sassan assault ships. They won't expect a single vessel—and certainly not *Gyton* this soon after the Targan affair."

Rysta leaned back, rubbing a hand over her wrinkled face. "One ship? Against a Sassan military base? Only a certified double-Rotted idiot would attempt it."

"That's exactly what we're hoping the Sassans believe," Sinklar said, glancing uneasily at Mac.

"Outside of the fact that it will never work—and you're doing it with *my* ship—what's the problem?" Rysta looked from one man to the other.

"Getting out alive," Mac said dryly. He spread his hands in appeal. "Since Rysta's figured it all out, you want to just tell me now? Once we get in and shoot everything up, how do we get out alive?"

Sinklar pushed back, staring at some invisible spot between his knees. "There will be a lot of confusion. *Gyton* might be able to break out and race like hell to build mass for null singularity. Surprise might make all the difference."

"And if it doesn't?" Rysta demanded, leaning forward.

Sinklar ground his teeth, jaw tensed. "Then the best I can come up with is to ditch *Gyton*, blow her up on remote . . . and surrender."

"Surrender!" Mac bellowed. "Have you lost your mind?"

Sinklar shook his head slowly. "No. You'll only be in captivity for about a year. That's how long I'll need to take the Sassan Empire. In the meantime, I'll be in touch with the Sassan high command. They'll be painfully aware that the fate of their officials will depend on the fair treatment of their war prisoners."

Mac simply stared.

Rysta blinked and shook her head. "Fist, you can't be serious about this."

Sinklar clamped his jaw. "Commander, I don't like it, but my back is to the wall. It's either this, or try and catch them in the next three months when they strike a Regan world. Think, Rysta. I've got thirty Commanders out there who feel the same way about me as you do. In *three* months at least twenty-five Sassan warships are going to make a preemptive strike on a Regan world."

He gave her a pleading look. "What are my chances of creating a working command in that time? What are the odds that, if I can get those people to function together, I can stop all twenty-five of those Sassan ships—even if we know the target in advance. Which we probably won't. If just one of those Sassan warships can get through, how many people will they kill? If they split their forces, and we only stop one group, how much damage could eight of those cruisers do to a world like Riparious? Vermilion? Sylene?

"And what about the consequences—the fallout after the raid? How are the people across the Empire going to react, knowing that a world was killed? We'll have chaos and panic. On top of that, we're going to have to dedicate resources to rescuing and treating any survivors. Every world and station out there is going to demand military protection, or they'll panic and revolt. How far can we stretch ourselves before we no longer offer a viable defense? Worse than that, how would we ever gain the offensive?"

Sinklar turned desperately to Mac. "I have to balance the risk of losing you against the risk of losing billions . . . and perhaps the entire Empire."

Rysta gave no hint of her reaction. Her baleful black eyes never wavered. Finally, she said tonelessly, "You're right, of course. If we can take them out, we'll do it. I'm ready to space as soon as we're resupplied."

Sinklar returned his attention to Mac, who stared sightlessly at the tabletop. "If Rysta's willing to take command, I could use you here." *Damn it, Mac, here's an out if you want it.*

The corners of MacRuder's lips twitched. "Rysta's a superb Commander, but I think I'd better be around for the capture of that Sassan freighter. I've already picked the Section I want to use. They'll need me there if something goes wrong." Mac looked at him with the eyes of a dead man. "I learned from the best, Sink. I might have to make it up as I go."

Sinklar's heart weighed like a lump of lead in his chest. "Then I'll leave it to you to figure your own way out, Mac." *This is just like Makarta, and Mac knows it.* "I won't let you down. If the worst comes true, I'll be coming for you."

Mac gave him a brave smile. "I know that, Sink. I really do." He stood up, offering his hand. "And now, if you'll excuse us, I'll go over the entire plan with Rysta. Maybe she'll see something we've missed."

Sinklar stood, shaking Mac's hand, then hugging him desperately. "If I had any other choice, Mac—"

"But you don't. Now, get down to your LC before Mhitshul has a conniption fit."

Sinklar nodded, lowered his eyes, and walked away, grabbing up his war bag at the hatch. He looked back, caught Mac's crooked smile, and stepped out into the corridor.

Like a man in a dream, he walked down to the LC bay where Mhitshul stood waiting. Around him, people swarmed, creating a veritable cacophony of sound as they shouted back and forth and banged crates and hatches. Hydraulics whined and the air had a chilly nip that barely cut the odor of oil and paint.

Mhitshul took Sinklar's war bag, noting his expression. "Where to, sir?"

Sinklar climbed the assault ramp, slapping the controls behind him. The heavy steel groaned as it closed and sealed, cutting out the banging and clattering beyond.

"Where to?" Mhitshul repeated.

Sinklar looked up, Mac's knowing eyes haunting his thoughts. *Mac, damn it, I didn't have any choice . . . any choice . . . any. . . .*

"Sir?" Mhitshul insisted.

Sinklar stepped through into the LC's command center and slumped on the bench. "Damned if I know, Mhitshul. Just tell the pilot to take us down and land us somewhere. I need time to think."

* * *

"The problem of God has occupied humanity for as long as we have had written records. Over a thousand years ago, Myklenian mystics could place themselves in a state of trance and bathe themselves in glowing coals, or run daggers through their flesh without wounding themselves. This state of mystical consciousness hinged on the belief that the physical world consisted of illusion. Reading their texts, they claim to have experienced Godhead.

"For centuries, the Seddi have studied the question of God. One of the everlasting problems that perplexes scholars is the proof of God's existence. Through the *recorded ages, some have looked to miracles, others to Divine revelation. The ways and nature of God have always been the study of the obscure, the mystical, and the hidden.*

"The question is begged, then, why does God hide Itself? Is it rational to believe that a Deity who created such an ordered universe would play silly games with its creations? What purpose would lie behind such a scheme?

"The Seddi assume that such notions are based on a flawed epistemology. Instead we see all of Creation as God's reflection. We accept that by investigating the very nature of the universe, we see God's imprint all around us. By discovering the laws of physics, we observe the will of God.

"To the insecure, a statement such as this reeks of loathsome heresy, and in response the question is begged: why should we expect a beneficent champion in God? Must we bind Deity in chains and demand preferential treatment simply because we have faith? Are we so immature that we can't stand on our own without a friendly paternal pat on the head from our God? Must we insist that God impose silly rules of diet and subservience? And worse, emotions such as jealousy, wrath, and vanity?

"In the end, isn't all of this the result of human hubris? Or worse, self-delusion as we seek a rosy and comforting fantasy to calm our fears?

"In studying the universe, we find humanity to be but an insignificant part of the whole. The vastness of space outside the Forbidden Borders is beyond our comprehension, in the same manner that we can only estimate subatomic particles through mathematical means.

"The Seddi do not claim to have ultimate truth—and given the limitations of human perception and intellect, we may never discover the entirety of ultimate reality— but we believe we have a more flexible epistemology, one that allows changes to the paradigm as we learn more about the nature of creation, and perhaps a fuller impression of God's nature."

—Excerpt from Kaylla Dawn's Itreatic broadcasts

CHAPTER XI

Kaylla Dawn hunched in a gravity chair, callused fingers tapping idly on the ceramic surface of her desk. The comm monitor before her glowed, lines of text shifting as she read the report. She worked in her private quarters, a room set off from the main complex of Itreata. On the far wall, holographic scenes of star fields gave the impression of endless distance and alleviated Kaylla's knowledge that she lived half a kilometer under solid rock.

She straightened and rubbed her throat as if the action would stimulate the blood flow to her tired brain. So much to do. The entire Seddi network lay in shambles. Details, from complex to simple, had once been coordinated by the Mag Comm, the giant alien computer that lay buried in the rubble of Makarta. Now, Kaylla and her staff scrambled to rebuild the organization and the coordination of an interstellar secret order. It wouldn't be accomplished overnight, or without frustration, failure, and possibly blood, for neither the Regan nor Sassan Empires had any love for the Seddi.

Kaylla stopped the text and closed her tan eyes as a prickling sensation ran through her limbs—the effects of the drug she'd been given to renew her body tissues. A Companion medical technician had conducted a series of tests, and tailored a prescription to slow the aging process and initiate the repair of damaged DNA. The side effects consisted of itching, sudden sweats and chills, and the constant feeling of a full bladder.

Nor did the brain remain exempt. Since the begin-

ning of her treatment, Kaylla's dreams had been overpowering, vivid to the point of being too real. Each
night as she collapsed from exhaustion, she knew the
nightmare of her life would replay.

She'd live again as a Seddi novitiate, marry her husband, and move to Maika where she served as First
Lady and began to initiate a Seddi paradise of universal human freedoms, education, and enlightenment.
One by one, she bore her children yet again, reveling
in the miracle of new life, and love, and hope. Golden
days of love and nights of passion flew through her
dreams—until that day the Companions crushed the
Maikan defense.

Unbidden, Kaylla began to blink back shining tears.
She opened her eyes, shaking her head to rid herself
of the image. The report waited before her, another
of the onerous duties she'd inherited from Bruen when
he placed her in charge of the Order.

Kaylla took a deep breath and dialed the gravity
chair down before getting to her feet and walking over
to the room dispenser. She stabbed the stassa button
and watched dully as the drinking bulb filled.

The Lord Commander's stassa. Kaylla stared into
the dark steaming liquid, memories of that fateful day
on Maika twisting in her mind. She lived it again as
Staffa's troops stormed the palace, shooting, maiming,
discharging weapons bursting human flesh into blood-
misty meat. Kaylla's maid had boldly insisted that she
was the First Lady, stepping out from the huddle of
captives.

*Why didn't I step forward that day? What motivated
me to cower with the rest of the servants as Staffa's
men pulled my husband . . . my children. . : .*

Kaylla closed her eyes, hearing the pleas of her husband and the bawling of her children. Before them,
Staffa kar Therma—a hazy image in gray—paced up,
back to her as the swirling cape hid him. The terrified
chatter of the servants masked his orders.

She would relive that moment forever as one of the
Companions ripped her from the arms of the servants
who held her and threw her on the ground. Stunned,

she'd been unable to tear her gaze from the sight of her family lined against the wall.

She'd cried out when they pulled her legs apart and stripped her naked amidst a tearing of fabric. Despite the man who dropped on her and thrust dryly inside, her hypnotized stare remained on her family. As the first man took her savagely the shrill whine of a pulse rifle rose and went silent as her husband's head exploded in a tissue-streaked pink puff. Then, one by one, they blew her children apart before her eyes.

After the last shrilling shot, she had nothing left but repeated rape.

Yes, she drank the Lord Commander's stassa—just as they all now depended upon him for survival. Kaylla took a deep breath and forced a swallow down her choked throat.

"Magister Dawn?" the comm called. "It's Nyklos to see you."

Kaylla lifted her head and composed herself. "Enter."

The heavy hatch slipped back and Nyklos strode briskly in, a grim look on his handsome face. He wore a golden silk robe belted at the waist. His flaring mustache gave his prominently boned face a dashing look. He wore his brown hair short. Tension filled his dark eyes.

At the sight of her strained expression, he asked, "I take it you've heard already?"

"Heard what?"

Nyklos tapped the heel of his fist against his palm. "Tyklat's in trouble. Ily's onto him. I've already tried to contact our people on Etaria. None of them respond. We can assume she's captured the entire Etarian network."

A constriction in Kaylla's chest made breathing difficult. "No, I hadn't heard. I've been juggling schedules since we gave Staffa a couple of engineers for his *Countermeasures* project." She walked over to the comm monitor and stared glumly at the lines of text. A different Staffa kar Therma had saved her from Ily's poison wrath. That Staffa had repeatedly risked his life for her—saving her time and again from death and abuse. He'd gambled himself for her sake.

The dance of the quanta, God's joke on all of us. And now Tyklat had been compromised? "Did he give you any indication of his status?"

"No." Nyklos sounded reserved. "The message simply stated: 'Nyklos, Ily knows. Warn my people immediately. If I survive, I'll be in touch. Tyklat.' "

"How did that come in?"

"Wide broadcast. The sort of thing Tyklat would have done if he'd been on the run—separated from his equipment."

"If he's caught . . . how much damage can he do?" Kaylla asked.

Nyklos gave her a speculative look. "I think we can contain it. Most of what he was familiar with were Magister Bruen's operations. So much has changed. If it had to happen, now was a good time."

Kaylla crossed her arms, pacing as she tried to think. "We can only assume the worst—that she'll get him, and he'll kill himself."

"That's not the worst."

Kaylla raised a questioning eyebrow.

Nyklos gave her a hard stare. "When Skyla Lyma caught me that night in Etarus, my trick tooth didn't kill me. I know that we checked after that, corrected the problem. But keep this in mind. Ily has captured Seddi agents before. If she suspected Tyklat, and he's gone to ground, she'll do everything she can to get him alive."

"You've worked in Rega before. What do you think his chances of getting out are?"

Nyklos shrugged. "Were Tybalt still alive . . . one in ten. With the whole planet fermenting and on the verge of coming apart, I'd say he has even odds. Fifty-fifty."

* * *

Anatolia Daviura snapped awake at the sound of voices in the hallway. She rolled to a sitting position on the couch in the women's restroom. The lights, detecting movement, flooded the lavatory, shining brilliantly on the white tiles, sialon fixtures, and mirrors. The soft hum of the air-conditioning reassured her after the horrible fragments of dreams that had plagued her sleep.

The muted voices in the hall receded.

Anatolia glanced up at the comm: 07:49. Time for her to blink the sleep out of her eyes and clean up before she put in another day at the lab. She got to her feet, stretched, and bent over one of the sinks to wash. She'd scrubbed her clothing the night before, drying it in the force fields before redonning it.

The cool water restored freshness to her skin. She rinsed her hair, twisting it into a knot and wringing out the excess before she stuck her head into the field, pressed the button, and drew back. The gentle fields squeezed the moisture away in a muscular trickle.

She studied her face in the mirror, curious at the hardness in her blue eyes. *Is that really me?* Freshly clean, her golden hair frizzed out, accenting the hollows in her cheeks and the slight puffiness under her eyes. Her full lips had a pinched look.

"Not exactly where you thought you'd be on your twenty-fourth birthday, is it?" She gave herself a brittle smile. "I guess living in bathrooms, working eighteen hours a day, and being haunted by nightmares isn't all it's cracked up to be."

She walked over to the couch and straightened the wrinkles. She grabbed up her small bag of personal items and headed for the door, stopping on impulse to stare at her image one last time.

"I guess, Ana, that you're not Daddy's little china doll anymore, are you?"

Her dream had gone dead in the darkness and fear during her scramble to stay alive in the bilge of the capital. A man had groped the breasts that now stretched the fabric of her turquoise blouse. And the slim hands that clutched her bag had run sickly scarlet with his blood. The myth of comfort and security had shattered—never to be put whole again.

As the door to the hallway opened and two secretaries entered, Anatolia smiled and called a cheery good morning. In the hall, she turned toward the laboratory, walking with purposeful steps. She could grab a snack before she began her four hours of scut work for Professor Adam, then after six hours of classes and practical on the use of polymerase III she'd be able to scarf down dinner. After that, file 7355 waited to obsess her until her body caved in to the demand for sleep.

She allowed nothing else to penetrate her concentration. Her hand slapped gently on the lock plate for the anatomical laboratory and the door whispered open. Inside, several of her fellow students had already gathered at the dispenser.

Anatolia made polite small talk as she selected a soup, black rye, and a hot cup of klav. She slipped her credit chip into the slot and seconds later the food slid out on the tray beneath the machine.

As she sat down at her desk, Vet slid in beside her.

"You haven't been home, have you?" He gazed at her quizzically.

"That's silly, of course I have. I just keep longer hours than—"

"Stop it, Anatolia. Bokken's been keeping a sharp eye on everyone going in and out of this place. I called here after I got no answer at your place. Security says you never checked out last night."

"I had a lot to do. Maybe you forget, but I lost a lot of study time during the recent trouble."

"And this special computer time you're burning up?"

She forced a neutral smile onto her lips. "You don't get to full professor in this business unless you prove you can do solid research. Speaking of which, you'd better get to work and start looking for—"

"Attention!" the comm interrupted. All eyes turned toward the large room monitor beside the dispenser. The screen lit in blue, the Imperial Regan jessant-de-lis crest flashing brightly in the center. One of the government spokesmen from the Ministry of Defense appeared, a sober look on his face.

"Citizens of the Empire, the current military governor will address you in a few moments. As you know, martial law has been imposed upon the Empire, and order restored after the rebellious Seddi fringe elements failed in their attempt to incite revolt and overthrow the government. I now turn you over to the military governor."

A silence filled the room as Anatolia and Vet rose to join the others.

The holo flashed again and a young man stared thoughtfully out at them. Anatolia gazed into those gray and yellow eyes in shocked disbelief. She remembered the black thatch of hair, the knobby nose and long jaw. He looked older now, worn and weary, as if he, too, bore a terrible burden of memory.

"Gentle men and women, fellow citizens, good morning. I had hoped to address you before this in order to introduce myself and inform you as to the condition of the Empire. I regret that events and circumstances have denied me the opportunity. I am Lord Sinklar Fist," a pause, "the new Commander of the Imperial Regan military forces. Elements of the Targan Assault Divisions, under my command, have restored order and security to the captial. Please, return to your normal activities and pursuits. The Civil Security now serves as our information network. In the event of trouble, place a call to your nearest Civil Security Center and a military team will be dispatched to help you."

"Who's he?" Professor Adam wondered from where he'd arrived to stand in the rear of the group.

"Doesn't look anything like a Tybalt the Imperial Eighth," someone jested. "Not with those eyes."

"Hush," Vet called, waving for silence.

Lord Fist continued, "I fear, however, that our problems are not ended. The military will continue to maintain order while the new government is formed and slowly begins to take over its responsibilities. We expect a rapid and smooth transition of power." His eyes gleamed with passion. "No subversion of the military authority will be tolerated. As of this moment, rank, privilege, and status are no longer the currency of office. We are here to serve the needs of the people . . . all of them!"

"Rotted Gods," Vet mumbled. "How's the aristocracy going to take that?"

Fist tilted his head, a slight frown lining his brow. "There is no easy way to say what I now have to."

"Here it comes," Race called caustically.

With an imploring expression, Fist said, "We have received intelligence which confirms that the Sassan Empire has commenced a military buildup in response to that initiated by the late Emperor. Further, they see the assassination of Imperial Tybalt as a signal that Rega lies defenseless and ill prepared to resist a Sassan invasion. We know they are preparing to launch just such an invasion within the next six months."

This time the room remained silent.

Fist reached out toward them with an open hand. "No matter what, we're all in this together. Those of us with the responsibility for the security of the Empire, will do all we can to protect it. I can't lie to you. There will be disruptions, inconveniences, and all the problems inherent in meeting such a threat to our homes and families. Some of you will be called up for military service. Others will find themselves reassigned to different jobs for the duration of the emergency. And, yes, occasionally we'll all be faced with shortages of various articles we now take for granted. If you get irritated by the whole thing, blame the Sassans."

"Who's he trying to kid?" Green Hanson asked nervously.

"Be assured that as events unfold, I will be keeping you informed. I want each and every one of you to realize that we've reached one of the most serious crises the Empire has ever faced. We have the ability to build a bright new future, and we must keep our eyes on that goal. In the short term, we may face rough moments, but perhaps the time has come for a new order. In the coming days, I want each and every one of you to dream about the kind of future you'd like to see. Dream, my friends . . . and let's try and make them all come true."

The holo flashed the jessant-de-lis on its blue background again.

"How quaint!" Professor Adam smirked. "Dream, he says. What a delightful defense against the Sassans!"

The group broke up into somber conversations.

Anatolia barely felt Vet's hand on her shoulder. "Hey, Ana, you all right? You look like you've seen a ghost."

"Fine," she whispered, and turned away. Heedless of Vet's questioning stare, she walked back to her desk and pulled out the slides Adam wanted her to catalog. As the volume of the talk rose behind her, she reached a key out of her desk and carefully locked the drawer that held the printouts of her 7355 file.

* * *

"How'd I do?" Sinklar asked as he pushed back in the squeaky chair in the LC command center.

Mhitshul gave him a broad smile. "Wonderfully, sir. If you could have addressed the Targan rebels like that, the war would have been over before it started."

Sinklar gave his aide a skeptical look. "Uh-huh. You didn't used to be so full of crap."

"Yes, sir, but I guess things have been so frantic I'll take any opportunity to balance the bad with the good."

Sinklar reached up and slapped him reassuringly on the armor. In the meantime, his comm had begun to light up with messages.

Sinklar accessed the call he knew to be Mac's. His blond-haired second stared out from *Gyton*'s bridge and gave him a cavalier smile, a twinkle in those blue eyes. "Nice speech, Sink. After that, I'd say you were a shoe in for a Ministerial post."

"How are things?"

"We're spacing. Rysta and I have made a truce. We both know the score . . . and we're going to make sure the noisemakers on Terguz understand it, too. We haven't quite solved our little problem yet." Mac spread his hands wide. "Guess we'll worry about one thing at a time."

Sinklar nodded uneasily. "Mac, I. . . ."

MacRuder's smile warmed. "I know, Sink. You're starting to suffer from too much guilt these days. If you'd done that back at the pass when the Second Section deployed, we'd all be dead now and Ily would have the whole thing. Cut it out and go to work. We've all got a job to do."

Sinklar took a deep breath. "We do, don't we?"

"You remember that talk we had just before the assault on Makarta? I warned you about Ily. I want you to think about that. Talk to Mayz, if you need to. She's canny."

"Gretta told me to promote her. Gretta was always right, you know."

Mac watched him soberly. "By the time we get back, I hope to see you in different quarters. Go rent an apartment while we're gone."

"First thing." Sinklar chuckled. "By the way, with all the top brass killed off, I wonder who pays us."

"Scratch that. Find an apartment second thing. First thing, find out who pays us. If it's Ily, screw her. We'll just keep comm and the Imperial bank and give ourselves all the bogus credit we need."

"Anything else, Mac?"

MacRuder gave him a warm look and shook his head. "No. Just remember, we're all counting on you. Whatever you have to do, well, we're all soldiers, Sink. Do what you have to."

"You, too, Mac. Good spacing . . . and the Blessed Gods keep you."

"See you soon." Then MacRuder cut the connection.

Sinklar chewed his lip and stared pensively at the comm.

"He's not just going to Terguz, is he?" Mhitshul asked softly.

"No. But I guess it's all right now. Well, maybe I can sleep better at night. On that note, we'd best get to work."

"Beg your pardon? What else do you call these twenty-hour days?"

Sinklar gave him a hard grin. "Fooling around, Mhitshul, what else."

"Yes, sir. Uh, sir, just where are we going to find a place to stay? Mac's right. You can't just run an empire out of an LC."

Sinklar scratched his ear and frowned. "You know, for the first time in my life, I don't have the slightest idea."

* * *

Ily Takka pressed the button that released the transparent hood on the aircar and stepped out on the gritty roof of the Power Authority. She nodded to her driver, and waved as her car rose into the morning sky and sailed off in the direction of her headquarters.

Ily took a deep breath and studied the grubby LC that sat perched on the rooftop. Around her, the skyline of the capital stretched in every direction, looking oddly clean after last night's rain. The pink light of dawn had just begun to firm into a harder yellow as the sun's rays slanted across the city.

Ily walked to the rear of the LC and punched the control that lowered the access ramp. Nothing happened. With growing anger, she tried it again, and finally ripped open the manual override box and studied the contents. At that moment, the ramp dropped with a thud that spattered her with puddled rainwater.

"Oh, it's you," Mhitshul called with barely controlled civility.

"Yes, indeed, it is me." Ily gave the man the look she reserved for the condemned and strode purposefully up the ramp. "Where's Lord Fist?"

Mhitshul stiffened as she entered and stabbed the control that closed the heavy door. For long moments they eyed each other with a crackling malignance.

"The First is asleep, Minister," Mhitshul told her in precise tones.

"Then he Rotted well better get up."

"This is the first real rest he's had in. . . . Hey, you can't go back there!"

"I suppose you're the one who's failed to answer my calls?"

"I *said* he was asleep!"

Ily spun on her heel, poking a hard finger into Mhitshul's breast as she glared into his indignant eyes. "Maybe we had better straighten something out here and now. We're running an entire empire. If I need to talk to Sinklar, I Rotted well will." Ily lowered her voice to a deadly hiss. "And you'll stay out of my way, you little maggot!"

With that she stormed down the aisle that ran between the assault benches and ducked through the hatch into the cramped command center.

Sinklar lay curled on the hard bench, knees drawn up, one arm outstretched in what had to be a cursedly uncomfortable position.

"By all that's Blessed, what's going on here?" She turned to fix a flushing Mhitshul with a hot glare. "No wonder he falls asleep! How do you expect him to get any rest in this rat hole?"

"Well, there wasn't. . . ."

"Rotted Gods," Sinklar growled, pulling himself upright. "What is it? What's wrong now?" He blinked redly at Ily as he shook the arm he'd been sleeping on.

Ily reached for the dispenser and punched the button for a cup of stassa. Sinklar watched her worriedly as he took the cup.

"I've been trying to get hold of you for two hours now." She shot a hard glance at Mhitshul. "Had it been an emergency, the Sassans could have burned us all to plasma in the interim. Fortunately, my people noticed your LC up here."

"What's wrong?" Sinklar repeated as he lifted the stassa and sipped.

Ily's gaze remained locked with Mhitshul's. With a

flip of her head, she indicated his presence was no longer wanted. Mhitshul glanced back and forth warily before he stepped out and closed the hatch.

Ily made a face. "Why do I feel like I'm dealing with children?"

"Maybe because Mhitshul is only a year older than I am?" Sinklar replied dryly. His eyes continued to ask the question.

"I sent my aircar back to my quarters. I assume you can fly me back while we talk?"

Sinklar bent to the comm. "Take us to the Ministry of Internal Security, please."

"Aye, sir," came the pilot's reply. The hum of power could be heard before the thrusters started to whine.

Ily settled herself next to him and laced her fingers together. "A ship is making an unauthorized departure from the main orbital terminal tonight at precisely 19:37 hours. We need to produce a reaction from Orbital Defense which will appear to be a genuine response to an unauthorized seizure of a vessel."

Sinklar's features puckered as he drank too deeply from the hot stassa and burned his mouth. "You want to tell me why?"

"Before I tell you, could I ask what you're doing sleeping on this hard bench?"

He lifted thin shoulders. "Where else would I go? Back to the school dormitory? Look it's not important for the moment. I've got mobility and command control here."

"Command control? I've been trying to contact you for the last two hours!" Ily shook her head in disbelief. "I'm ordering quarters for you. I'll have my people prepare them and—"

"No."

"No?"

Sinklar shook his head. "Not that I don't trust you, but I'd like to handle my own security."

"Very well. I know just the place—and you can be sure I haven't tampered with the security. Now, do you want to tell me where *Gyton* spaced for?"

A twinkle formed in Sinklar's eyes, the effect almost hypnotic. "I dispatched *Gyton* to blow the dripping pus out of that Sassan assault force outfitting around Imperial Sassa. If Mac and Rysta pull it off, His Holiness will never recover his momentum. The initiative will be ours from now until we control Divine Sassa's empire.

"Now, Ily, your turn."

She leaned back, lost in thought. What a brilliant idea, but then. . . . "And you think the Sassans are going to let Mac just space in, shoot things up, and space out? Sassa guards his capital as thoroughly as we do ours."

Sinklar's twinkle went dead. "There are certain risks—and Mac knew them."

"Knew? You already use the past tense?"

Sinklar shifted his weight, jaw muscles jumping along his cheek. "What happens tonight at 19:37? Why not 19:30? Like I said, it's your turn."

She leaned closer to him, aware that she'd penetrated his armor, left him confused by anger, mistrust, and guilt. "Very well, tonight is the first step in a process which will plant an agent on the Itreatic Asteroids. Keep in mind that we still have a dangerous wild card out there."

"Staffa and the Companions." Sinklar propped his chin on a palm and spun his half-full drinking bulb in a circle. "I've been toying with an idea. If Staffa really wants to keep the peace, he'll react to a military strike close to his base. If I can neutralize the Sassans and draw him out, I might be able to crush him once and for all." He paused. "So tell me, how does a seized ship get one of your spies into Staffa's inviolate Itreata? According to what I've been told, no one has ever managed to penetrate his security."

Ily pressed her fingertips together and gave Sinklar a triumphant smile. "But now, for the first time ever, Staffa has a weakness I can exploit. He's taken the Seddi into his impregnable fortress."

"That doesn't mean you can sneak a spy in. The Seddi themselves will know an outsider."

"Sink, I have no doubt but that they'll rush to open the gates for my man. You see, I've doubled a Seddi, and a high ranking one at that. That's why tonight at exactly 19:37, he's going to escape in a most dramatic way."

Sinklar nodded as he began to see the benefits. "Then perhaps we'd better put our heads together. This will have to be timed perfectly so that he just barely makes it—and with enough damage to make it look good."

"I thought you'd approve."

* * *

MacRuder thoughtfully watched the image of Rega dwindle in the ship's monitors. This was the second time he'd shipped from his home world for space and war. This time, however, he knew the odds that he wouldn't come back—and they didn't please him.

Tension filled *Gyton*. As Mac looked around the bridge, he could see the officers' pinched lips and lined brows. These crewmen had been orbiting their own port and hadn't had a chance to set foot on Regan soil.

I never even called my folks, the realization sank in. Mac shook his head and ran his fingers through his blond hair. A sudden ache clamped at the base of his throat.

"Final perimeter cleared," the nav-comm informed. "Course set for Terguz, acceleration building to forty gs."

"Affirmative," Rysta called from the command chair, studying a cluster of monitors that had risen from one of the pods in the armrest.

Mac exhaled wearily and went to stand beside Rysta's chair. "Commander, I think I'm going to go and sack out for a while. I haven't slept for almost forty hours."

Rysta gave him her usual flinty look. "Take a healthy shot of whiskey first, boy. Otherwise you'll just twist and turn while the adrenaline wears down."

Mac hesitated.

"Yes?"

"Why, Commander? I don't understand why you agreed to go on this fool stunt. You're no friend of ours, or of what we're trying to accomplish."

Rysta's jaw jutted as she looked past him to the monitor. "I've been in the service for over two hundred years. I've seen a lot happen. When I first spaced as a gunner, Rega consisted of that planet, fourteen space stations, and a couple of mining colonies on the Gas World. In my life, I've seen three different Emperors come and go. I've watched the Regan crest cover half of Free Space. My butt was on the line for each of those campaigns, boy."

She smiled then, lost in the memories. "Can't hardly keep it all separate now. Things . . . memories, they slide together. Lovers dead, ships wounded and dying, masses of bodies broken and rotting beneath the suns of a hundred different worlds. The boredom, the instant electric fear. . . ."

Mac waited.

"Would I let all that go? Could I step out now? Let that fat Sassan maggot god take it all away? Waste it all? Not by the Rotted Gods' hairy balls!" She shook her head. "I'm not on your side, boy—or your Sinklar Fist's either. I'm just Regan down to my bones, and after a lifetime of fighting for my Empire, I'll continue to do so. If I die taking those Sassan bastards out, so much the better."

"I understand, Commander. Thank you for your advice. If you need anything, feel free to contact me."

Rysta had turned her attention back to the monitor. She barely acknowledged it as Mac turned and left the bridge.

*   *   *

The gymnasium on *Chrysla* stretched for one hundred meters. Here the Companions maintained their daily exercise regimen. Many a raw recruit had walked into that airy white room with a swagger—and left limping humbly.

Skyla bounced into the air and kicked viciously. Staffa ducked the kick, pivoting and striking with his balled fist. Skyla twisted in midair as her momentum carried her beyond reach of Staffa's riposte.

"Nice," Staffa admitted, puffing.

The Companions took their hand-to-hand seriously; in the early days, people had been maimed, and sometimes killed in the heat of practice. Staffa had commissioned the design of a light, padded body armor that he and Skyla now wore. A deadly blow would be ameliorated enough to leave a painful bruise, and re-inforced elbows and knees kept joints from popping.

"Getting a little slow, old man," Skyla teased as Staffa rushed her on powerful legs. She dropped, caught one of his arms, and used her hips as a cantilever to throw him neatly. Staffa smacked the padded mat and gasped.

Skyla approached cautiously, blocking the kick as Staffa rolled back on his shoulders and lashed out. She skipped nimbly aside and hit him as he tried to roll to his feet. In the process, she hammered him playfully on the ribs and escaped his frantic attempts to retaliate.

Skyla raised a pale eyebrow and cocked her head. "Have I made my point?"

He nodded, grinning sheepishly. "You have. I've been spending so much time running simulations, I'm out of shape. Good thing I didn't have to fight Brots now."

"Brots?" Skyla feinted and lunged.

Staffa blocked her, advancing defensively. "A slave in the Etarian desert. He started abusing Kaylla. He was a giant of a man—and, if the truth be known, he might have killed me in the end. He hurt me, badly enough to have impaired my ability to work. Out there in the desert, you worked . . . or you died."

He feinted right, left, right, and blocked her retaliatory kick as he penetrated her guard with a hit to the ribs.

"That's one of the reasons Kaylla tolerates you now?" Skyla asked after she escaped his attack.

"There's too much blood spilled. Too much pain. Kaylla can remember me pulling her out of the sewer under the Etarian temple, she can remember Brots, and the time in the pipe, and the fight for Makarta; but then she'll relive that day on Maika and all the things that followed."

Skyla's cool gaze probed. "Nothing comes free, Staffa. I understand and accept that further warfare will condemn us all. So do most of the Companions. We understand the data, and some are even beginning to listen to the Seddi. But the status quo? Two empires? And both full of ambitious men and women? The friction will eventually bring forth fire."

"Then what's the solution? Let everyone kill each other off?" Staffa leapt, countering Skyla's attempt to throw him. They both crashed to the mat, kicking, punching, and twisting.

Skyla broke free, scrambling away and to her feet. Staffa barely had time to recover as she rushed him. He blocked each jab of her attack and she backed away, an excited grin animating her flushed face.

I've got to get her into a position where my strength can counter her agility. Rotted Gods, the woman was good!

Staffa circled warily, poised for her attack. In a blur, she charged, bounced, and aimed a deadly kick at his throat. Staffa blocked with an arm, spun and grabbed her, then yanked her up to keep her feet off the floor while she bucked and twisted. He went with her as she flipped her weight to overbalance him, and in the process, wrapped his arms around her in a full nelson.

"Did I ever tell you I love you?" Staffa asked his squirming captive.

"You . . . gonna practice . . . more?" she panted.

"Considering the beating I took today, damn right I will."

She wormed around to kiss him when he let go, her body undulating sensually against his.

"Not here," he whispered, and she winked. Together, hand in hand, they walked to the dressing room.

Skyla stripped the padding off, a frown lining her forehead. She stepped into the shower stall and tapped the water, letting it play over her flushed skin. "Like it or not, we're going to have to unify Free Space. So long as you have two slavering dogs snapping at each other's throats, nothing will be accomplished on the Forbidden Borders. You'd better be turning your thoughts to muzzling your beasts."

He stepped in beside her, the water pricking his tanned hide. "I always do. It's the ghosts that get in the way." *And if* Countermeasures *works, I can limit the number I have to add to the list.*

Skyla pushed herself through the force field. Trickles of water rolled off in sheets. Her long hair went through as if in slow motion.

He studied her thoughtfully. "Don't you ever have regrets? We've done some terrible things. Don't they ever bother you?"

"They?"

"The people you've killed, tortured, sold into slavery?"

She braided her frost-blonde hair. "Staffa, I made my choice a long time ago. You were a child of privilege. I was born in the Sylenian cribs, the daughter of a whore. I'm not saying you were pampered. The Praetor pushed you to the limit of your endurance, but you never starved. Never worried about who would try and molest you, maybe strangle you while they raped you, because even on Sylene, that's a killing offense. A dead child can't bear witness. I lived in perpetual fear. Every night when I went to sleep, I had no guarantee that I'd wake up in the morning. I'm the product of a brutal world, an ugly reality."

He pushed himself through the spongy force field. "Nevertheless, the pain that we caused has to have made some impression. How did you look into a little girl's eyes as she huddled over the blasted body of her mother?"

Skyla's ice-blue eyes hardened. "When I did, Staffa, I saw myself at that age. To pity that little girl would be to pity myself and I don't have time for such psycho-masturbation. Look, Free Space is a closed system. People have expanded to fill it all. We're at the bursting point. Something has to give. We don't have room for more people. As it is, the wars have kept us all alive this far. Those billions who've died in the imperial expansion bought the rest of us time."

"But Rot it, *we made a mistake!*"

"Did we?" she fired back. "Tell me, Staffa, could Phillipia have mounted the kind of science it would have taken to break the Forbidden Borders? Pustulous Rot, no! I bought and believed in what we were doing: Unifying Free Space under one government—ours! And I still believe that."

"But what about the blood, the suffering. . . ."

"I told you earlier, nothing comes free. Pain is everywhere, living *is* suffering. If you can scramble hard enough and keep the Rotted Gods' fetid breath at bay for a while, more power to you."

He twisted his hair angrily over his left ear before pinning it in place. "But it is sin to add to the suffering. I . . . we could have done it another way. We didn't have to murder all those people, destroy all those lives. Think of the waste, Skyla."

"Think of the future, Staffa. It's an old argument. What are you going to do? Condemn the species because you can't stand to inflict misery?"

"We only inflict it on ourselves, on God."

"So the Seddi say."

"You need more time to study."

"Perhaps, but I still made my decision. When I was haunting the shadows of Sylene, I wanted out! I wanted to make my life better, and that day I saw Mac Rylee walking down the street, I did just that. I didn't have time to think about humanity. That came later."

"But you agree that we have to break the Forbidden Borders."

"Absolutely. And succeed or fail, we've got to have humanity under one single government."

He pulled his gray armor over his head, feeling the silky texture of the synthetic fibers. "I know, I know, but Skyla, I can't do it the old way. You know that."

She nodded, giving him an understanding smile. "We'll figure something out."

* * *

Ily hurried down the hallway, her heels clicking on the tiles as she passed the security monitors. The doors before her slid open to admit her into a plush living room. The place had been decorated with wooden furniture of Targan origin. Gauzy hangings of optic fibers hung from the walls, pulsing in waves of different colors. The carpet, a living moss from Riparious, glowed verdantly and filled the air with a soft cinnamon scent. The holo displays in the walls revealed scenes of the Targan countryside where pines swayed in the wind and sunlight warmed rocky ridges.

Arta Fera entered from one of her apartment's rear doors. She wore a formfitting suit of golden body armor with a gold field generator ring around her neck for vacuum conditions. The belt that clung to her shapely hips sported a pistol, vibraknife, and various equipment pouches.

"You're ready?" Ily asked.

"I just shipped my things up. Tyklat's been moved?"

"He's already at the terminal. The ship is fully prepped for everything you might need. The tapes are in the system. All you need to do is call them up. The access code is Hyde . . . yes, a fitting memorial for his perfidy."

Arta's amber eyes burned. "And one I'll never forget." She paused. "And Sinklar Fist?"

Ily made a gesture with her hand. "He thinks we're planting Tyklat as a double agent. What he doesn't know won't hurt him."

Arta pulled the gleaming wealth of her hair back

over one shoulder. "I like you, Ily. You take no chances with anyone. But tell me, why did you plan this the way you did? What do you know about the Lord Commander that makes this feasible?"

"Tyklat said something under interrogation. Secondhand, he'd heard that Staffa went to Targa because he was searching for someone. It displayed a weakness I never would have suspected in him."

"Then, if this mission succeeds, you'll have a lever to use on the Lord Commander?"

"Indeed, I most definitely will, Arta. Now, you'd better catch the shuttle. After all the trouble I've gone to, it wouldn't do for you to miss your exit."

Arta walked up to Ily, searching her eyes. "I think you know me better than that. I don't miss *anything*. If all goes well, I'll be back within two months. Take care of things for me—and don't fill your bed with too many lovers while I'm gone."

Arta laced her arms around Ily's neck, hugged her close, and kissed her passionately on the lips. Then the assassin whirled away, heading through the doorway which would lead her to the shuttle platform.

Ily took a deep breath and retreated back through the security doors and into the hallway. *She's a dangerous woman, this Arta Fera. Thank the Rotted Gods she's mine.*

* * *

"*Those of you who have been listening to these broadcasts are no doubt wondering where we are going with all this talk of God and science.*

"*First, let me provide a short introduction to physics. The study of physics includes classical physics: the* study of forces and relationships in the physical world we can see and experience with our own senses. For instance, we can compute the amount of energy needed to accelerate a body through space, or study the physical reaction of water at various temperatures. Such phenomena we measure and describe with real numbers.

"At the same time, we begin to find discrepancies in the data as we refine our observations. These discrepancies lead us to the quanta. Among the quanta, we find the breath of God, and it's every bit as mysterious as the mystics would claim. We enter the realm of complex numbers. Particles become waves and waves particles depending on alternatives available. Energy states at the atomic level become discrete. Position may be determined for a given particle, but not momentum, and vice versa. Order cannot exist without chaos, or chaos without order. An event is a set of initial and final conditions. Subatomic particles spin in two directions at once. Split a particle, and interfere with one—the result will be interfering across time and space with its twin. These are the mysteries of the quanta, but perhaps the most important for us, is the following: Reality does not exist unless it is observed.

"And with that single statement, you know how science is inextricably tied to God. In the world of the quanta, observation creates reality. In searching for God, we find Its fingerprint in the quanta, and those same quanta affect the very function of our brains. Physics demonstrates that Creation is holistic. God is the universe, and by definition, we are but a part of God. We who observe create reality, and in so doing, change the state of nature.

—Excerpt from Kaylla Dawn's Itreatic broadcasts

CHAPTER XII

A Group—twenty men and women—proceeded at a dogtrot through a patch of timber. Moving smartly, they dodged between thick boles of trees and ducked strands of hanging moss. Boots crushed the lush grass underfoot. They advanced stealthily, scanning their surroundings as they went. Camouflaging armor blended with the gray tree trunks and green vegetation. The heavy shoulder lasers that hung on slings had been dulled to avoid reflecting the dappled light that penetrated the leafy canopy.

Sinklar watched them through one of the monitors in the command center of his LC and listened to the chatter through their battle comms.

The Fourth Targan Assault Division consisted of veterans of the old Third Ashtan and Fourteenth Riparian—now consolidated into a new unit after Sinklar had reformed them. After Mac's intensive training, this would be their first field opportunity to prove their skills, and perhaps regain their status as crack troops after their defeat on Targa.

"Coming up on the objective, people," Corporal First Tigart growled. "Look sharp, now. They ought to have sentries just on the other side of the trees. We've got four minutes before D Group starts sniping along the southern perimeter. At first fire, they ought to respond with ordnance."

"Then we rush the knoll. Got it!" the Corporal Second answered. "I can see the knoll from here. What about that little ravine that cuts it in half?"

"Pustulous hell, it ain't on the map. Okay, let's split down the middle. You take half, I take the others.

Everybody got the plan? At least one of us has to
make it up there and wipe out that observation
dome."

"Affirmative."

Good work. Sinklar leaned forward intently. *Mayz,
you've taught them well. According to the manual, they
should have stopped, reported their position, and
waited for confirmation of orders. Under no circumstances, should they split a Group.*

Sink shifted his gaze to the rest of the monitors
filling the concave of the LC's command center. Other
elements of the Fourth Targan Assault Division were
drawing their net tight about the Tarcee Estate and
First Axel's entrenched Nineteenth Division. Mayz
had deployed individual snipers to draw fire from the
Nineteenth's ordnance. If Axel responded by the
book, she'd pour heavy fire down all along the southern forested belt in anticipation of an assault from that
direction. Meanwhile, unknown to Axel, the majority
of Mayz's Fourth Targan would attempt to carve two
salients into the defenses: one on the western gardens,
the other through the eastern orchards.

Mayz overrode the communications from her LC
command post. "Fourth Targan, you are ordered to
attack. Let's clean house, people."

"Affirmative," repeated in a staccato as Section
Firsts checked in. Then the battle began in earnest.
The pride of the traditional Nineteenth Regan against
the upstart trainees of the renamed Targan Fourth
under Mayz. Each side had its own stubborn point to
prove—and each battled for gut-felt principles.

To his surprise, Dion Axel shifted tactics, trying
desperately to recover her defensive line by freeing
her Sergeant Firsts to counter the Targans as best they
could. The action proved to be too little, too late, and
without the familiarity of procedures.

Sink watched as Mayz adjusted her attack and
played Axel like a siff jackal would a mouse. Veteran
of more than one battle, Axel fought according to the
instincts that had always kept her and her people
alive. She might be willing to allow her Sections more

freedom, but they still replied to the attack as they'd been taught since academy. Heavy ordnance—in this case, computer simulated—blocked out entire kilometers of ground along the southern perimeter. Affected invaders were tagged by computer as dead and ordered through their battle comms to retreat to the rear.

Sink chewed his lip, gaze riveted to the monitors. The critical A Group overpowered the sentries before them as both teams attacked the commanding rise. Defensive fire from the top began to take its toll, but A Group spread out, crawling relentlessly forward while ordnance wasted the now empty woods behind them where—according to the manual—supporting Groups should have been waiting.

"And there's their mistake." Sinklar shook a fist in approbation.

"Corporal Tigart just bought it!" one of the privates in A Group yelled. "Villa, you and Gnat enfilade that guy that's shooting at us."

" 'Firmative . . . be just a minute."

Sinklar studied another monitor where an entire Section had broken through to create the eastern salient and now fought a running battle through the hedgerows of the garden. Axel tried to counter, moving her groups in rank and file drill—only to have them decimated by the greater mobility of their opponents. Chess pieces struggled against a fluid dynamic of warfare they'd never encountered before.

A single soldier would pin down one of Axel's Groups, charring the armor on five or six opponents before the Group's combined fire removed the irritating shooter. In that time, another Targan had found position and killed another five or six as the beleaguered Group struggled to rise and carry out their Section First's frantically shouted orders. The result proved to be mayhem as more Targan Sections poured through the salient and overran entire Groups.

To Sinklar's surprise, Axel continued to try and innovate, each time running afoul of inadequate training which hindered her troops' ability to implement her orders. *Good for you, Axel. You've got the rudiments, now, if you're just dogged enough to stick out the process.*

In the meantime, A Group had unlocked the key to the knoll. The defenders, in compliance to doctrine, had reacted to the first prodding fire—since no one split a Group—and concentrated their guns on doomed Corporal Tigart's side of the ravine . . . which left the other side undefended as the Corporal Second's team achieved the crest and shot down the defenders. Within moments, the remnant of the Group had the knoll and the observation dome.

One third of Axel's battlefield "eyes" went dead, the computers immediately figuring in the command control factor. Sinklar sat back and stuck his stassa cup into the dispenser. Normally, the manual said, a war game like this one would be expected to drag out over two days while both Divisions ground each other down by attrition—with the decision generally going to the defender.

As Sinklar watched, the second salient breached the Nineteenth's lines and poured into the orchard. Meanwhile, elements of the first advance had reached the estate buildings and were taking up positions.

On the knoll, A Group had called for command control access. Private Acre called, "We could use a four-man blaster up here. If someone can deliver one, we'll raise bloody hell down there."

"Affirmative," Mayz answered. "We'll have someone on it immediately."

Sinklar chuckled to himself, imagining Axel's face when she heard a private requesting a piece of ordnance—and then having it delivered. According to the book, such pieces were reserved to the Ordnance Section. A private shouldn't even know how to work the gun.

Sinklar watched a corkscrewing LC careen across the battlefield, hover for a moment over the knoll, and dart off to safety. A rugged four-man gun rested next to the comm domes where it had been kicked off the LC's assault ramp. Private Acre's voice began calling in shots to the master computer while Mayz transferred Section Firsts who faced resistance to Acre's comm for fire control.

Sinklar whooped and cheered as the defenses wavered and collapsed as units suffering from A Group's fire were ordered dead in the field by the master computer.

Meanwhile, advance Groups of the Fourth Targan captured building after building in the center of the estate. Held by nothing more than a security guard, the central compound proved easy pickings. Nearly one third of the Nineteenth hadn't fired a shot yet, remaining in their original positions along the southern and northern perimeters.

Sinklar switched monitors in time to hear, "This is Corporal Nix of E Group, Fifth Section. We've just captured First Axel and her command center. Request instructions as to their disposition."

Mayz answered, "Ask the First for surrender of her Division."

"Affirmative. But she don't look any too happy about it."

In the long pause that followed, entire portions of the estate darkened by a shade to indicate loss of command control. The Nineteenth fought on without direction—or waited in their positions for someone to tell them what to do.

"Corporal Nix here, ma'am. First Axel says she'll surrender. She's broadcasting to her troops now."

"The war's over, people," Mayz called through the net. "My compliments to all of you. I think Sinklar's going to be very proud of you all."

Got that right. Sinklar crossed his arms as he stared at the statistics table. The Fourth Targan had taken ninety-six casualties. The Nineteenth Regan Assault Division had taken three hundred and sixty seven. Instead of days, Tarcee Estate had fallen in less than three hours.

Sinklar accessed the system. "Nice work, Mayz. My compliments to the Fourth Targan. First Axel, are you in the net?"

"I'm here." She didn't sound very happy.

"I would like you to review the tapes. Mayz, help her. I want you and your officers to explain exactly what we did and why. We'll replay this exercise tomorrow, so let your troops know they've got a chance to even the score."

"We'll be looking forward to it," Axel replied grimly.

And if you can't learn, Axel, there's someone in your command who can.

* * *

"Everything is set," Gysell told Ily Takka as she sat at her desk. Her Deputy's square face filled the comm monitor. "I've made the final check and our people are ready."

"Thank you, Gysell. You've done splendidly as always."

She cleared the channel and noted that Sinklar's LC had settled on the roof. As she watched, the ramp dropped and Sinklar trotted out for the lift tube.

Ily glanced at the chronometer: 19:28. "Cutting it a little close, Lord Fist."

She flipped another comm access channel. "Arta? Status?"

The auburn-haired woman's face filled the screen. "We've secured the ship. I'm speaking from the bridge. The pilot is here . . . and he's a little upset. He's had a taste of my persuasion and I think he will do as ordered."

Fist was walking toward her security doors.

"Very good. You're on your own now. I'll be waiting for your signal from Ryklos. Fist is here. Good luck."

The connection went dead as the doors opened and Sinklar hurried in, a pensive look on his young face. His hair stood up at odd angles, as if he'd absently run his fingers through his black thatch.

Ily met him halfway across the room, taking his

hands and giving him her best smile. "It's good to see you. I thought for a moment you'd been held up."

"No. I wanted to see the end of the exercises."

"Everything is set on the orbital terminal." Ily routed the signal through the main monitor that dominated one wall. The Regan orbital terminal, the port which handled most of the passenger traffic entering and leaving Rega, appeared. A long curving section of docking berths on the outer rim of the station could be seen. Lumpy-looking forklifts, baggage dollies, and stacks of freight pallets lined the outer wall. Here and there men and women in brightly colored suits stood about or walked, each locked in their own thoughts and oblivious to the drama about to be played out around them.

Ily opened a window in one corner which displayed the outside of the station where a sleek Marta class cruiser rested in the grapples. Thick umbilicals ran from the station gantries to the vessel's side. She looked peaceful, clearance lights burning amber against the star-frosted background of space.

"That's it?" Sinklar asked as he propped his butt against her desk.

"That's it. She's registered as the *Vega*. She's fast, has deep space capability, limited shielding, and, best of all, mounts two guns. She used to belong to a merchant family from Vermilion before they were brought into the Emperor's peace."

Before Gysell's call, Ily had watched Tyklat's arrival. He had walked like a man in a dream, eyes straight ahead, his movements uncertain and docile. How else would a man walk who was told that his fate was to be shot as an escaping prisoner. When the time came, Tyklat would play his part—and do it well. Two of Ily's agents had steered Tyklat to a door marked, "NO ADMITTANCE. AUTHORIZED PERSONNEL ONLY."

She turned and took a position next to Sinklar. This evening, she'd chosen a perfume rich in pheromones which mingled well with the delicate musk. She noticed that he didn't inch away, but watched the monitor in a preoccupied fashion.

"How did the war go today?" she asked casually.

"Mayz took Axel in a little more than three hours. I'm sure that Axel and her friends are frantically poring over the tapes as we speak to see what went wrong. I'd be more than a little surprised if any of them get sleep tonight. I've given orders that Kap's Third Targan take the combined Ninth Vermilion and Second Ashtan at Tarcee tomorrow. After that, it's one exercise after another until no one doubts the superiority of our training."

"Have you found quarters yet?"

"Hmm?"

"You're not going to sleep in that Rotted LC again, are you?"

"Probably. I haven't had time to find a—"

"We'll discuss it later. It's time for Tyklat's escape."

Sinklar absently chewed on his thumb as he watched, lines forming on his forehead. "Tyklat's ship will take a hit from orbital. I've got Shik in the Orbital Defense platform, allegedly doing a check on the targeting system. He'll be in just the right place at the right time and will deal *Vega* a glancing blow."

"He's that good? Can you trust him?"

"After Targa? You bet—on both counts." Sinklar shook his head. "I don't know. This just doesn't seem right."

"The plan? What could go wrong? We send Tyklat out and the Seddi answer his distress call. He's escaping my pursuing agents and running for cover. If you had an agent in his predicament, you'd take him in, wouldn't you? And even if they don't buy it, what are we out except for one outdated cruiser?"

"That's not what I mean. It's. . . ."

"Engaging in deceit and trickery to obtain your ends instead of wading in with crackling blasters and pulse guns. Isn't that really it? You rebel against deception and intrigue when out-and-out destruction, blood, guts, and mayhem would be the honorable way."

"Where's Arta Fera?"

Ily met his hostile gaze and crossed her arms. "In a safe place where I can monitor her. She isn't the sort of person you just let walk the streets, you know."

"You're using her as a tool. I objected to that among the Seddi. I don't like it now."

She lifted a hand to stop his tirade. "Show time. We'll discuss Arta later."

"Indeed we will." .

Ily riveted her attention to the screen. *My dear Sinklar, you'll simply have to learn that some things need not concern you.* And if he doesn't? *Then I'll have to replace him sooner than I expected. Still, he hasn't pulled back from me tonight. He's close enough to get a full whiff of the pheromones. They'll be stimulating the hypothalamus by now.*

The "AUTHORIZED PERSONNEL ONLY" door slammed open and Tyklat, clutching a pulse pistol in his hand, ran desperately for the access hatch that led to *Vega.*

"Stop him!" the cry rang out, and Ily's two agents charged out into the bay, pulse pistols in hand. Shots hummed, paint puffing into haze on the bulkheads.

Tyklat leapt for the hatch, slapping the controls as he passed. The heavy pressure doors slid closed, blocking the two frantic agents in pursuit. One pounded on the hatch override while his partner pulled a comm from his pocket and began shouting orders.

Well done, Tyklat. You had just the right amount of panic in your run.

For long moments, nothing seemed to happen as security people arrived from different directions to mill about and shout questions at each other.

"There," Ily pointed to the *Vega.* "You can see her start to power up."

The station people stopped short at the rising whine. A voice called, "Rotted Gods! The maniac is going to yank half the terminal apart! Cast him off! *Now! Damn it!*"

"But the regulations—"

"Pus Rot the regulations!"

A mad scramble took place as the implications sank in. A frantic engineer arrived from somewhere, checking the hatch to make sure it had sealed. Another of the dock technicians shouted on a comm to the Port Authority to release the grapples.

In the monitor window, *Vega* suddenly floated free as the grapples and umbilicals disconnected.

"Perfect," Ily cooed as a streak of searing light shot out from the vessel's reactors. In the terminal, klaxons wailed a decompression warning. Confusion reigned as men and women sprinted for the pressure bulkheads spaced every two hundred meters along the dock.

Meanwhile, *Vega* boosted for open space, changing her attitude and vector as she went. For long moments they watched as the slim vessel dwindled to a point of light.

Ily sighed. "That's about it. They won't come up on the Orbital Defenses for another twenty minutes. Once there, your Shiksta will scorch their feathers slightly and send them on their way."

Sinklar's jaw stuck out at an angle. "I suppose."

Ily gave him a smile. "Why don't you come with me. I have something to show you. And I assure you it beats sleeping on that bench in your LC. You're a Lord now, you ought to live like one."

Sinklar gave her a skeptical glance and she laughed. "Sinklar, you're a man now, an important one. Come on."

She took his hand and led him into her personal quarters. He followed her into the bedroom where she left him as she stepped into her wardrobe. She grabbed a coat and slung her weapons belt about her hips, letting him linger for a moment. As she stepped out, she caught him staring curiously at her ornate sleeping platform, and scuttled a smile.

"What about Arta?" he asked, as if to force his mind to other thoughts.

"She's a troubled woman," Ily replied easily. "You know what the Seddi did to her. They programmed her mind to kill anyone who tried to make love with her. You know how magnetic she is . . . the woman oozes sex and draws men like Ashtan bees to nectar.''

"You're using her to assassinate people."

"You're training soldiers to murder millions." Ily pressed the lock plate and they both stepped through into a lift tube. Together, they dropped. "Tell me something. Have you ever thought about the morality of war?"

Sinklar barked a sharp laugh. "Have I? Surely, you're joking? It obsesses me."

She stepped out as the gravity field deposited them in the subbasement. The air smelled musty with dust and concrete. Ily gestured to a pneumatic capsule and seated herself next to Sinklar. He didn't seem to mind the feel of her hip against his on the narrow seat. Ily tapped the control and as the canopy lowered over them, they slid into a dark tunnel.

Ily studied Sinklar in the blue haze of the cabin lights. "Then let me ask you a question. You don't have to answer it right this moment if you don't want to. Which is really the most morally offensive, to employ an assassin to kill a political rival who, if appointed to an important position, will implement policies which will be detrimental to the people . . . or is it more offensive to ask an innocent farmer on Riparious to kill an innocent farmer on the Sassan world of Malbourne? Both farmers are good men who love their families and children and want nothing more than to make a living, raise their crops, and grow old in peace."

"And the official you've assassinated? He isn't interested in the same thing?"

"Of course he is, but he wants to do it at the expense of other people who are marginally making ends meet. If he has to bankrupt a couple of businesses along the way, or evict people from housing to raise a new office building that no one will rent, does he care? His bottom line is greed and profit."

He smiled sourly. "I've heard this argument before. Gretta, Mac, and I used to wonder about it, but not about the benefits of assassination." Sinklar suddenly straightened, a curious look on his face.

"Something wrong?"

He shook his head slowly. "No. Nothing wrong. I was remembering something I once heard about unilateral epistemology."

"That what we learn is presented in a one-sided fashion?"

"Exactly. But in regard to your moral question, here's the difference. When you assassinate your political rival, you're assuming you know what's best for everyone. You've cast yourself in the role of God."

"Very well put . . . and, yes, I generally do know the intimate details of a rival's personality. I don't eliminate a threat casually."

"Like Bryn Hack?"

She laced her fingers together, feeling the slight sway of the capsule as it raced on its superconducting magnets. "How much do you know about the Commander?"

"Just that I thought he seemed like a decent human being. A good officer."

"He was Mykroft's classmate. Roomed with him at the Academy. Hack's deceased wife was Mykroft's younger sister. Mykroft loaned Hack the money he needed to build his mansion outside of Trystia. Haven't you wondered what's become of Mykroft since he shipped down from *Gyton*?"

Sinklar lifted a shoulder. "I've been too busy with other things to worry about—"

"You should," she told him softly. "Mykroft has been agitating for a military coup. Hack's sudden death stifled a bit of his ardor, but he's your enemy, Sinklar. And before you shift the conversation again, I'll admit that Hack's decision to slip you in irritated the hell out of me. But what frightened me was that he might do the same for Mykroft, or one of his other cronies and their fleet. Do you see the danger?"

Sinklar took a deep breath and slouched in the seat. "You always have an answer, don't you, Ily?"

She took his unresisting hand in hers. "Do you

think I'm really so utterly despicable? Yes, I've used Arta, and you might say that she's a tool, but I had two choices. I could keep her, or send her to the Anatomical Labs where Seddi assassins are always sent. Tybalt would have insisted on that."

Ily saw him go tense, jaw muscles jumping on his angular jaw. *Yes, Sinklar, I do know where your weaknesses are. You won't question me about Arta again, will you?*

The pneumatic capsule in which they rode pulled into a lighted underground bay and Sinklar struggled to free his mind of the images conjured by Ily's words. As if it were yesterday, he could feel the chilled casket sliding out of the rack as a faint puff of condensation rose from the cryogenically preserved body. The man's face had looked alive, the yellow eyes open and immeasurably sad. He'd had a strong jaw, smooth-shaven. An incision where his scalp had been laid back and his skull sawed through could be seen under the short brown hair. They'd done that to expose the brain for some study conducted in their search for deviance. In that single moment, Sinklar had found a face to go with his father's name. In that dead visage, he'd looked to find something of himself, some recognition of person and place in the cosmos.

Then he'd opened his mother's casket and stared down into her half-open gray eyes. What a beauty she'd been, with long raven-black hair and a delicately chiseled face. Something about her expression had haunted him—that hint of disbelief in her eyes, as if she couldn't believe her death even as it enveloped her. She'd looked so incredibly young in her state of preservation—perhaps even younger than he'd been at the time. For long moments Sinklar had stared into the face of the woman who had borne him—and the long years had been bridged.

How would it feel to know that Arta, no matter how much he hated her, had ended up there like his mother and father? And had Arta Fera's programming

really been that different from Valient and Tanya
Fist's?

He got to his feet, lost in his thoughts, his nagging
suspicions of Ily lulled again. *She's a reptile,* he kept
repeating to himself.

Now, however, as he stepped out onto the subterra-
nean platform and saw the concern in her eyes, could
he be so sure? Not once had she undercut him since
his arrival on Rega. Not once had she interfered with
his operations. She hadn't even argued vehemently
about turning the utilities over after he'd dropped and
taken them from under her nose. Though he instinctively disliked many of her policies, each rested on a
coldly rational political reality.

Mac doesn't like her. But then, Mac didn't always
understand the ramifications of command decisions either. An able lieutenant, Mac lacked that intuitive
grasp of the larger picture.

*Ily left the First Targan to die on Targa. I was sup-
posed to be her sacrificial goat.* But he wouldn't have
advanced through the ranks had it not been for her
manipulating the situation.

"Are you all right?" Ily asked, a gentleness in her
tone. Her gaze searched his as she stepped close. Her
scent seemed to linger in his nostrils and the swell of
her full breasts distracted him.

"Where are we?"

"Under the building I'm hoping you'll move
into." She pulled her comm from her belt. "Kitchen,
please. This is Minister Ily Takka. Please prepare a
full meal for two. Riparian lobster, steamed ripa
root, sautéed Vermilion mushrooms, a side of
chubba, and Myklenian ale." She winked at Sinklar,
"No Ashtan. And please deliver to the Blue Room
within a half hour."

She clipped the comm to her belt and led the way
to the lift. "I think this is perfect for your residence.
No one has ever complained about the accommoda-
tions before, at least not to my knowledge."

"What about the landlord? What about rent? I

mean, I can't just move into someplace and throw the old tenant out."

She stopped and turned, giving Sink that look that made him feel immature and silly.

"You're *not* some orphan of the state anymore. You're the interim ruler of the Regan Empire. Don't you think you'd better start acting the part?" She lifted a shapely eyebrow. "Or do you think you can meet with ambassadors, governors, and Imperial administrators in an LC command center for the rest of your life?"

Sinklar nodded agreement, thoughts muddled. Rot it all, she had a point. "Very well, let's see this place."

The lift took them up interminably. Sinklar took another deep breath, admitting to himself that he enjoyed Ily's company. She talked to him like an equal. Not with the joking intimacy Gretta had used, but as one respected leader to another. He sneaked a cautious glance at her, and yes, she was a damned attractive woman. Her formfitting black outfit accented all the right places, and she had what it took to fill a suit like that.

But what about her? How can I trust her? She assassinated Tybalt when he got in the way. What's she really after? If only he could point to an action she'd taken since Targa, and prove to himself that she really *was* the viper he believed her to be.

The lift opened to a small security foyer lined with cameras, IR sensors, and other gadgetry. Ily walked straight through to a security door and raised a small escutcheon that Sinklar recognized as the jessant-de-lis. "Minister Ily Takka. Accompanying me is Lord Sinklar Fist."

"Acknowledged," a voice called and the heavy door slid open.

Ily strode down a long hallway and Sinklar followed, half his attention on Ily's swaying hips, the other half on the splendid hangings and ornamental statuary lining the powder-blue hall.

Ily took a right and pressed the jessant-de-lis to a lock plate. Double doors slid back into the wall and Ily gestured Sinklar inside. "These are the quarters I was thinking might suit you."

Sinklar stepped into a palatial waiting room appointed with grav chairs—each with a private comm—manufactured from jetwood inlaid with gold. A gleaming dispenser served those who might be waiting, and holos depicted scenes from places in the Empire that Sinklar could only guess about.

Beyond that he found a functional, if ornate office for a secretary or receptionist. Two armed guards stood in the corridor beyond that, eyes to the fore, polished shoulder blasters grounded at parade rest. Sink stared at the odd livery—not quite field issue, but the armor looked real enough.

Ily ignored the young man and woman and stepped between them to open a large, carved sandwood door that led into a spacious office with a wraparound desk that literally bristled with comm equipment. The desk had been gilded with gold and precious Etarian gems. Myklenian fabrics hung from the walls and between them, holographic niches displayed the Regan planets as if in real time against a background of stars. Beneath his feet, the fiber-optic carpet gave the illusion of walking on a sea of molten gold. Overhead, the crystalline ceiling panels rose into an endless blue that might have stretched beyond the infinite.

"I think you will be able to work here in greater comfort than in your LC," Ily said wryly as she smiled at his gaping wonder. She pointed. "The personal quarters are through there."

Sinklar glanced uneasily at her and headed for the alabaster doorway. It opened at his approach and he stepped into a lavishly appointed dining room with surrounding recliners and an amazing array of fine lead-crystal serving ware. Optic architecture had been used lavishly to create a dazzling rainbow effect as the eye was directed upward.

"This is the Blue Room," Ily told him. "Why it was

named that is anyone's guess since you can change the photo-effect by a simple order to comm. Air-conditioning, too, will respond to your will—anything from the Etarian desert to a Riparian swamp, or, if you like, your favorite scent."

"And there?" Sinklar pointed to the next door. She gave him a mischievous smile. "The sleeping quarters."

He entered another splendid room hung with velvet and finished with sandwood alternating with jet and inlaid by the fabulous golden filigree. The sleeping platform, too, had been hung with delicate fabric that rose in folds to the refractive crystal ceiling. An ornate bar filled one wall while holo capability had been rendered for the entire room.

Ily opened a shower and bath to his inspection and then showed him a huge walk-in wardrobe.

"This place must cost a fortune," Sinklar whispered.

"You can afford it," Ily told him as she came to stand before him.

Searching for something to say, Sink blurted, "Mac wanted to know about that. Who pays who, I mean."

Ily laughed, placing her hands on his shoulders and staring into his eyes. "You're the Commander, Sinklar. Pay them . . . and yourself, anything you want. You control comm, you know. Hasn't it sunk in yet that you can draw what you need from the Treasury accounts?"

The overhead light sent bluish sheens through her hair. Amusement warmed her eyes. Close now, he could see how smooth her skin was. The lines of her face had a classic style. As if of their own volition, his hands went to her waist, feeling the firmness, the swell of her hips. Her lips parted slightly, and Sinklar's heart began to beat with that urgent cadence.

Ily pulled back, a shy smile on her lips as she turned away. "Do you like it?"

"It's . . . wonderful." Sinklar found his voice and swallowed. "How about access to my Division?"

"Four minutes by tube . . . or you can be in your LC in less than a minute and a half."

"And the security?"

"You can program it yourself. Or have your pick of experts. Oh, Sinklar, when are you going to learn? We're in this together. I want you to be happy. Yes, we'll face distasteful events and decisions, but we're building a new way. Isn't that what you promised yourself?"

"But all this . . . I don't know. Where is this place anyway?"

"Just about the center of the city. Now how about that dinner? If the food displeases you, I promise you we'll find someplace else for you."

Sinklar led the way into the blue room, seating himself on the velvet cushions at the low table. Ily settled beside him as the food rose from the center of the table, the mirrorlike stasis shells sliding back to present an incredible feast.

Sinklar broke open the first lobster and handed it to Ily. She gave him a teasing look and dangled a piece of the steaming flesh before his nose, laughing as he gulped it down.

She snuggled next to him, her body warm and firm against his.

"What do you think Mac will say when he finds me in a place like this?"

Ily ran a pink tongue along a slim finger where butter threatened to drip and gave him a saucy grin. "Put him across the hall if you'd like. Half this building is dedicated to military command."

"I didn't know the military command lived so lavishly."

Ily made a graceful movement of her head, tossing silky black hair over her shoulder. "You don't know the half of it. They lived like kings, Sinklar. Why do you think they got together and wrote the manual the way they did? If you civilize war, you don't need to worry about having to leave splendor like this to live in the field. Leave that to the common soldiers and the Companions."

"I don't want to fall into that trap."

Ily rolled over and rested elbows on either side of his thigh as she stared into his eyes. "You can live anyway you want. You're the most powerful man in the Regan Empire. Do it your way. But keep in mind, all this," she waved at the room, "is nothing if you don't beat Sassa."

He nodded, painfully aware of her breasts against his leg. "In six months, I'm going after His Holiness."

She seemed to wince, and her full lips quivered. Then she pushed him gently down onto the cushions and pulled him close to stare into his eyes. "You don't even hesitate. You'll go out there, won't you? You'll be in the thick of the battle."

He nodded soberly. "It's the only way to break them. The Sassans play by the book, and I can use it against them."

"Then, you might . . . I mean, a lucky blaster bolt, a projectile that gets through the screens. . . ."

Sinklar ran his fingers down the side of her head. "I can't do it any other way—not and be sure of winning. I don't mind. My people are on the line. I can't ask anything of them that I won't do. The risk is worth it."

She leaned forward then, kissing him gently. "You're a hero. Not just to me and your troops, but to the people. We need heroes."

"What makes you so attractive?"

"Would you believe pheromones?"

He laughed, running his hands lower to caress her full breasts. His erection hardened, begging. Desire began to burn through him. "No. I wouldn't."

She shivered, closing her eyes before she pulled away. "Sinklar, perhaps I'd better leave. Making love to you will change our entire relationship."

"Yes." He sighed, pulse racing, breath short in his lungs. He knotted a fist to keep it from trembling.

She looked away, sadness in the set of her mouth. "I'm older . . . and no blushing virgin."

He could see the reddening flush at the base of her neck. Her eyes gleamed, passionate, longing.

In a husky whisper, he said, "I'm aware of that."

"I might be drugging you again. What would Mhitshul say?" A playful smile tugged at her lips.

"I avoided the Ashtan ale." He calmed himself. "This seems to happen every time. Yes, perhaps we'd better go back." He got to his feet and pulled her up.

She searched his eyes, looking for some sign. He bent down, kissing her hard, feeling the want build as she conformed to him. Her tongue darted into his mouth, striking fire as it slid across his teeth and probed.

She's a viper, a distant voice reminded—only to be drowned in the heat.

"Come," she whispered passionately, and took him by the hand, leading him into the next room. She stopped before the sleeping platform, asking, "You're sure?"

He exhaled raggedly and nodded, bending down to kiss her again as her fingers released the fastenings of his armor. Sinklar's fumbling fingers undid her weapons belt, letting it slide off her undulating hips. He stepped out of the wadded pile of his clothing and peeled her top off. With practiced ease, she slipped out of the tight black pants, her hair falling around her in gossamer strands. She stood proudly before him, and lifted her chin at his expression of admiration.

She gasped as he caressed her and they rolled onto the platform. He slid on top of her—her skin hot against his—and stared down into her midnight eyes to find a catlike satisfaction reflected there. Her arms went around his shoulders.

"Sinklar," she whispered, "we can do this fast . . . or slow. No one is going to bother us. Let me show you how it can be."

Then she rolled him onto his back, long hair playing down his skin as she changed her position. He cried out as a swelling ecstasy energized his nerves.

* * *

"I have just replayed a conversation I had several days ago with Ily. I feel like I'm dangling between the jaws of the Rotted Gods. Ily reports that Staffa is in the employ of Sassa. If this is so, what was he doing on Etaria? Why hasn't he struck? Granted, the Sassans are still knotted up in the cleanup of their Myklenian occupation, but Staffa could wheel immediately and deal us an awesome blow.

"In the meantime, the Targan situation continues to deteriorate. The rebels have crushed the Second Division under Mykroft, and this Sinklar Fist has taken control. I have dispatched Commander Braktov's hardened veterans to restore the situation—but who *is* this Sinklar Fist, anyway? In my conversation with Ily, I asked if he was another Staffa kar Therma, and Ily paused in her tirade, looking first thoughtful and then cunning. She has now spaced for Targa to investigate Fist. But what do I do about him? He's refused to turn over his Divisions to Mykroft. Do I now face another rebellion on Targa, this time from within my own military?

"I am consumed by doubt. If it were any other Minister, I wouldn't feel this way. Face it, Ily is the second most powerful person in the Empire. If she perceives this Sinklar Fist as a tool—and if he is all she hopes—would she have the slightest hesitation about moving against me?

"And if the Empire should fall to her, what a poor fate for my people. Ily as Empress? The Rotted Gods would pale.

"No, I can't believe she'd plot that, not with the threat of a Companion invasion looming. From a strictly objective standpoint, she needs me to hold the Empire together. Without my presence, the Empire would fall apart and the military would revolt. How then could she salvage anything?

"I'm tired, that's all. Jittery with worry. After all, this is Ily, my friend and lover. I've looked into her eyes and seen the concern. Yes, I truly believe she's come to love me, not simply because I'm Emperor, but for who I am as human being. She couldn't fake the passion of our joining. Tybalt, get some sleep, you'll see things clearly in the morning."

—*Excerpt taken from Tybalt the Imperial Seventh's personal journal*

CHAPTER XIII

Vega shivered from a hit as she boosted for the stars.

"Pus Rot it!" Arta blurted as the ship recovered. "Damn them! Are we all right?"

The pilot lay limply in the reclined nav-chair, his mouth slack, what she could see of his face under the shining metal of the worry-cap, expressionless.

She checked the boards, watching the critical reactor as yet another of the violet beams flashed before them. By quick action, the pilot pulled the craft up, g bearing them down on the ragged edge of shredding the gravity-compensating field generators. If so much as one failed, every human aboard would be mashed into flat bloody goo—the effect the same as being shot into a stone wall from a field piece.

"They're trying to kill us!" the pilot's metallic voice screamed through the ship's speaker.

Vega's bridge had room for two people. The others waited anxiously in the cabins while the frantic run past the orbital defenses ensued.

Arta glared at the boards. "Fly the ship, curse you. I'll keep an eye on the ship's condition. Which of these monitors are the critical ones? What should I watch for?"

The pilot, a small bald man, swallowed hard, sweat starting from his face. His voice issued from the speaker again. "That square monitor to the left. If the red line. . . ."

Vega groaned as inertia slapped Arta sideways, but the violet lance of deadly particles slipped harmlessly past their port side.

"I'm going to learn to fly this thing," Arta promised

herself. "As soon as we're away from here, you're going to teach me."

"Assuming you live that long," the pilot's metal voice answered. "Watch those blue bars on the square monitor. That's the life support and atmosphere system . . . we're in trouble if any of them shrink. The oblong monitor just above life support keeps track of the gravity field generation that keeps us from being crushed. The numbers you see are the compensating gravity generated against acceleration. If any of those numbers climbs above forty-two, or begins to drop, tell me in a big hurry. The LCD display to the right is the matter/antimatter fuel ratio. If that begins to show any disparity, tell me *immediately*. We've still got plenty of power, but that hit blew a breach back behind C2."

"See what?"

"C as in cargo. Second hold. C2. It's nothing critical."

Arta licked her lips, watching the wavering displays on the monitors. "I know you wanted it to look good, Ily, but this is. . . ."

The *Vega* jolted sideways, rocked, and shot forward as the pilot played the controls. The displays Arta struggled to watch fluctuated wildly. "We've got a critical building in one of the gravity generators!"

"Affirmative. I'm stabilizing."

Arta watched nervously as the readout lowered. "What happens if those get out of whack?"

"We could suffer structural damage. This isn't a damned warship, you know. We don't have the kind of integrated hull design to absorb grav disruption." A pause. "We're past the worst now. The Rotted Gods alone know what it would have been like if they'd had warning we were coming."

Arta drew a breath to answer—and wheezed as g crushed her down into her command chair. *Vega* swerved past another of the deadly bolts.

As the pressure let up, sparks danced before her eyes, and she felt dizzy, light-headed. She stared at the life-support systems monitor while her brain revived from the grayout. No wonder pilots flew flat on their backs.

"I think that's the extent of their range. Where to now, Miss Fera? Since you're giving the orders, what next?"

Arta shook her head, forcing her mind to work. "Ryklos. Set course for Ryklos."

"But that's inside the Sassan—"

"Damn right, it is! Now set course and go, or do you want to wait around for them to scramble a couple of battle cruisers after us?"

Arta growled to herself as the *Vega* darted forward and began a long vector change that left her pale and dizzy.

* * *

Holy Sassa stared at Myles through passionless eyes the color of water. Supported by his gravity fields, His Holiness hung in the air, a giant human balloon wrapped in brightly colored Myklenian fabrics that shimmered and glistened. High above, the light splintered into a thousand multicolored rays to sparkle over the Nesian rug that pulsed between blood-scarlet and translucent ruby. In that illumination, Sassa's hairless scalp gave his head the appearance of a skull.

Myles suffered an acute sense of unease as Jakre paced back and forth beside him, chin on chest, expression dour. The admiral had clasped his hands behind his back, and a frown lined his high forehead. Jakre wore the usual gaudy uniform, and, in the presence of Sassa, allowed his pot belly to sag completely.

Myles stood quietly and let his wandering gaze play over the wall hangings, cunningly backlit by the light sculpture of the glassy walls. The air carried the scent of anise and juniper, a refreshing meld of aromas.

"What are we to think of this report? What is this Sinklar Fist up to? Iban, what do you make of it?" Sassa asked in a flat voice. He knotted his pudgy fists, the rings sending scintillating patterns over his costly nacre robes.

"What *can* we make of it?" Jakre turned and spread his hands wide. "We might have seen a play, some sort of theatric to confuse us."

"Legate? Do you agree? Is this a theatric?"

Myles scratched his ear as he looked up. Sassa's colorless gaze ate at him like acid. "Military matters are not my—"

"I want your thoughts, your impressions."

Myles ground his teeth, pulling himself to his full height. The holo supplied by the Sassan spies had provided glimpses of military maneuvers where a veteran Regan Division had fallen to a piecemeal attack. *Staffa warned me that Sinklar was brilliant.* "Holiness, what do we really know? Sinklar Fist conducted an exercise and evidently demonstrated a sort of battlefield superiority over a Regan Assault Division. Could it be a charade? Something to confuse us? Perhaps."

How do I play this? What's right in this morass? What will they believe? Myles suffered through the first pangs of his new role. He glanced nervously at Jakre, and noted the admiral's veiled hostility. That same irritation was obvious in Sassa's disdainful glare. With a start, Myles realized that neither of his once close confidants approved of him.

Why? What have I done? Surely they can't know of my meddling with the shipping schedules.

"Perhaps?" Sassa echoed finally.

A sudden understanding flooded Myles' brain. "Divine One, it isn't my place to give advice which should lie within Iban's expertise."

"Do so."

"Yes," Iban added, a thin smile on his thinner lips. "Let's hear your thoughts on this extraordinary affair."

A cunning thrilled within as Myles nodded sagaciously. "Very well, having looked at the tapes our Intelligence Service has provided, and having noted the consternation among the Regan Division Firsts for whom we have data, I think Sinklar Fist has turned their entire military on its head."

"You mean, added to their confusion and command paralysis," Iban offered in an upbeat voice.

Myles slowly shook his head. "I don't think that fits the data, my Lord Admiral. Remember, this Sinklar Fist is the man Tybalt thought to sacrifice on Targa. Our conversations with the Lord Commander provided a great deal of information on Fist's tactical innovations."

"What is your point?" Sassa demanded.

Myles made a deprecatory gesture. "I am not a military man. My expertise is the movement of supplies and the coordination of economic—"

"We're aware of your expertise, Myles," Iban interrupted. "Tell us what you think this charade of Fist's is all about!"

Myles adopted a pained expression. "In my opinion, Holy One, Sinklar Fist is a great deal more dangerous than you think. He has revolutionized warfare. That's why the Regan Division Firsts are in such a tizzy. What we've seen in the report is no charade, but the implementation of a new tactical battle plan."

"Ridiculous!" Iban cried. "How could such a system work on a large front? The command control would be impossible to coordinate!"

"Nevertheless, I can't help but believe that Fist's—"

"Fie, Myles, what do *you* know about *warfare?*" Jakre roared, as he shook his fist.

Myles looked up placidly and spread his hands wide, chortling the whole while in that private part of his soul. "Divine One, I only gave my opinion. Military matters are not my province. I must repeat, however, that Sinklar Fist is *not* to be underestimated."

Sassa nodded, his multiple chins flopping in the process. "We have given him every consideration, Myles. And, yes, you answered honestly. Perhaps we hoped to hear some other answer."

Censure? "Outside of opinions beyond my expertise, Divine One, have you any complaint with my work? Have I given you some offense?"

Sassa worked his mouth as if something sour had marred his Divine taste. "No, Legate. Imperial production is up. We are disappointed with the rate at which our fleet is being prepared for the strike against the Regans . . . but we recognize you're not at fault. Your Herculean efforts and constant reports on the problems faced by your staff are lucid, informative, and, unfortunately, readily apparent to the most casual of observers."

"Thank you, Your Holiness. I will bear your kind words to my staff. I've had them working more overtime. If I might suggest, Holiness, perhaps a slight bonus would be in order for them. Your words are more than enough, but a token of Sassa's Divine love and appreciation would spur them to even greater lengths."

"They shall have it. And for yourself?" Sassa asked.

Without looking, Myles could sense Jakre's growing anger. Logisticians got a bonus, and the admiral's suffering soldiers got nothing? "For myself, Holy One, I would like only your permission."

Myles waited, aware that Jakre had gone bright red in contrast with his turquoise and white uniform.

"Permission for what?" Sassa slapped his immense belly and the fat rippled.

"Permission to integrate the census records into the main data banks, Holy One. I realize that we're already overextended, but I believe that integrating the data bases with the productivity charts will add another percent in production output while reducing some of the strain on the system."

"And what do you need for this?" Jakre asked in a cutting tone. "How many people and how much of the system capacity? I don't want to remind you, but we're attempting to mount an assault on the Regans while they're still off balance."

Myles clasped his hands before him and nodded happily. "Yes, yes, I know, Iban. I wouldn't have made the request if I hadn't given all those details consideration."

"What would you require?" Sassa tilted his head, his mouth like a puckered wound.

"Only communications with provincial governors,

Divine One. I think I can do the rest on my own time. I've written some of the preliminary programs, and I think I can integrate the data without any extra assistance."

"You're already working overtime," Iban interjected. "How can you squeeze more hours out of your day?"

Myles frowned and sighed. "Iban, you yourself admitted that we face the most serious of consequences. After having delivered our decision to the Lord Commander, I've dedicated myself to making this new course of action work. *You* didn't have to stand there and tell *him* that Sassa has decided to ignore him." Myles ran a hand over his face and shook his head. "I didn't eat for a week."

"We've noticed," Sassa told him in veiled tones. "And that concerns us. You will see the physician. I won't have you sick when we need you so, Legate. Assuming you don't lose more weight, you may implement your program."

"And if it costs us time in preparations?" Jakre asked, raising a finger.

"Then I will stop immediately," Myles answered indignantly.

"I think that will be all, Legate." Sassa touched the tips of his bejeweled fingers together, the rings flashing laser fire. "You may be excused. Iban, I want you to stay and discuss the effects this charade will have on the Regans' ability to resist."

Myles bowed and headed for the huge platinum doors. A sense of satisfaction warmed his gut. Sassa and Jakre didn't like his new look. To them it smacked mildly of treason—an affront to Divine Sassa's fat—therefore any advice on the military situation would be soundly overruled. Nevertheless, his value to the Empire had been reinforced, and he'd just bought unlimited Imperial communications and the ability to manipulate the census and personnel files!

Flushed with triumph, Myles passed through the huge doors. In the reflective walls, he got a good glimpse of himself. His new clothing fit neatly, and he hadn't looked this good in years.

His antigrav waited, Arron and Jorome standing at attention while Hyros lifted an eyebrow. "Did you. . . ."

"Back to the office," Myles directed as he seated himself. "We won, Hyros. But it means a lot of hard work. We won't sleep in our own bed for a long time."

Hyros smiled wearily. "Perhaps it's best that you've given up the rest of your lovers along with your belly, Myles."

As the antigrav moved out into the corridor, Myles frowned and stared up at the gleaming spires of Imperial Sassa's capitol.

Lord Commander? I told them the truth—but just how are you going to handle Sinklar Fist and this frightening army he's building?

* * *

The mass and energy intertwined in the grip of the null singularity generation began to diminish as *Chrysla*'s reactors decreased their power. In the process, an artificial event horizon began to expand as the energy dissipated. Where once nothingness had surrounded the warship, now the universe reappeared as she slipped back into space-time amidst a burst of radiation.

Staffa experienced the slight discomfort of the transition. Had he looked toward *Chrysla*'s stern, he'd have seen nothing but grayness and a hazing distortion around the sides as lightspeed hovered at the point of violation and light cones began to straighten.

If only I could bend men's wills the way Chrysla *bends the space-time continuum,* Staffa groused to himself. He sat on the bridge amidst the instrument clusters of his command chair. The sensors and detection equipment corrected for redshift and monitors filled with the familiar images of Free Space. In a blue flicker, the Twin Titans dominated the forward screens. The two stars, RR Lyrae-type giants, whirled about each other, releasing pulses of radiation that swept this lonely corner of Free Space. In defiance of the deadly radiation, Staffa had chosen his refuge and constructed his fortress in the Itreatic Belt—the remains of a massive planet which had created a metal-rich asteroid ring. There, in the pockmarked corpse of an old moon, Staffa had established his major base of operations, manufacturing, and final redoubt.

Prior to Staffa's arrival, no one had developed an extractive industry in the hostile environs of the Twin Titans with their cataclysmic pulsations of deadly radiation. With his war-garnered fortune, Staffa had overcome the hazards and founded an empire. His crews, in specially shielded vehicles, mined the asteroids of their incredible wealth. Itreatic engineers manufactured the finest of gallium-arsenide superconductors and atomic circuit nanocomputer boards. Itreatic sialon brought top dollar throughout Free Space, and Staffa had even toyed with the idea of starship hulls grown atom by atom of perfect ceramic—harder than the finest alloyed steel and with seven times the compressive and tensile strength. His thallium oxide industries were the envy of both empires.

As the Titans' actinic light flickered off *Chrysla*'s hull, she turned her nose toward the dusty albedo of the Itreatic Belt.

"First Officer, alert the monitors," Staffa ordered.

Lynette Helmutt, prone in her recliner, worry-cap obscuring her head, answered through the speakers, "Monitors alerted, Lord Commander. Deceleration initiated at 30 g. Consequent Delta V dump sequences initiated. We're roger 001 course relay. Monitors report condition green at home and welcome back."

"Acknowledged, First Officer. Send my regards." Staffa checked the long-distance sensing monitors out of habit, making sure that no vessels could surprise them on the way in. It never paid to be careless—even in a homecoming.

Skyla stepped through the hatch and walked across the gleaming bridge. She wore her usual white armor and she carried a flat comm monitor tucked under one arm. She, too, inspected the readouts, noting the ship's condition as well as the reports from the detection equipment.

How beautiful she is. Staffa allowed himself the luxury of watching her as she approached, hips swaying, the light sparkling in her tightly braided white-blonde hair. A gleam filled her azure eyes as she noticed his attention, and her warm smile spread for him alone.

"You look happy for once," she told him as she stopped beside his command chair. "After the way you slept last night, I'm glad. I expected you to be moody and withdrawn."

He shifted his glance to the main monitor, watching the Twin Titans as they danced about each other. "Bad dreams. That and I can't seem to let go of the problem of unification. I made Rega and Sassa into what they are. I *trained* them to go for each other's throats. Yet, now I have to undo a lifetime's worth of work overnight—and I'm at a loss as to how to do it."

"Tossing and turning won't help." She put her hand on his arm. "Trust me. You don't have the information you need. After you talk to Kaylla, find out what her agents have learned, then you can formulate something. You need to open communications with Sinklar, too. He's really the key, isn't he? And who knows, maybe Myles has turned something up while we've been in null singularity."

"The key, yes, that's Sinklar." He pounded nervously on the armrest with the heel of a fist.

"And for once, you've had to wait on the rest of the universe. Isn't that part of what's made you so anxious? All the simulations, all the fiddling with variables has just been a way of keeping you occupied."

"Maybe. I've felt hamstrung. This has been a rotten trip. Not even Divine Sassa takes me seriously anymore. And I could make him very sorry for that."

She tapped her chin with a slender finger. "Staffa, I've looked over the data. Assuming Tap has made progress on *Countermeasures*, you could take out one of the capitals. Either Rega or Imperial Sassa, it wouldn't matter. Without the capital's centralized administration, neither empire has any choice but to capitulate within weeks as the systems begin to fail. Both empires have the computer capability to take over immediate administration of the conquered territory. We could end this very quickly."

"But at what cost? Another several billion dead? I know what a strike against Rega would do. That's what I originally planned, after all. Destroy the Regan redistribution center, and the rest of the Empire would be helpless, effectively decapitated. His Holiness doesn't know it, but he's got the programs to integrate the Regan systems into his own. Rotted Gods, Skyla, they're using our computers, our software! That was part of the scheme. It's just that now . . . well, I can't let myself murder another world. You understand, don't you? I *have* to do this bloodlessly."

"Your shared responsibility to God and man. I know about your Seddi concepts." She nodded her acceptance. "Maybe they're even right."

"You should talk more to Kaylla."

"Getting back to the problem, I think the key is in the computers. Is there any way you can think of to eliminate one or the other? A virus, perhaps?"

He shot her an evaluating look. "Don't even think it. A virus would shut down the entire Imperial network on both sides, jumping from one program to the next. That, too, would exceed the system's ability as surely as a war."

"I suppose so, but somewhere there's a weak link in the system we can exploit. Some key economic factor could be disrupted with an ensuing ripple effect throughout the Empire. Perhaps just enough to frighten the people into capitulating. We'd have to be very careful."

"Bruen tried the same thing when he attempted to lure me to Targa—special guest at my own assassination." Staffa shook his head. "I'd hate to gamble on anything like that. The quanta are God's joke on the universe. We could plan out every detail, make every assumption. But we can't predict every bureaucrat's decision. It's too easy to allow pride to lead you into a stupid mistake."

Skyla sighed and slapped her monitor against her muscular thigh. "Rotted Gods, random factors affect everything, Staffa. You can't have it any other way. You never worried about them when you were taking a planet."

"Oh, you can be sure that I worried about them constantly. The difference is like that between an assassin and a surgeon. Both wield a knife on a body. If the assassin finds he can't cut one artery, he'll maneuver, and cut another. In our case, we must be surgeons, skilled enough to excise a growth and keep the patient from bleeding to death, for he has little blood left."

He reached for her hand and raised it to his lips. "Trust me. I don't want to fool with economic disaster. It's full of booby traps that could doom us all."

She gazed at him with a skeptical coolness in her crystal blue eyes. "So war is out. Economic sabotage is out. Diplomacy just let you down when you tried it on His Holiness. That leaves assassination, bribery, blackmail, or extortion. Which did you have in mind?"

"Do you really think I'd assassinate my son? He's one of the sticking points right now."

"Well . . . maybe not. Think bribery will work?"

"I'd like to think he has a sterner character than to give in to such failings."

"Given his sire, it *would* be something of a miracle if he didn't."

"But his mother's superior qualities would have overcome any deficiencies on my part." He paused. "You're right. Let's try blackmail instead. But assassination will still do for Ily and Divine Sassa."

Skyla's professional demeanor cracked and a thin smile warmed her lips. "Genetics aside, we've had an entire trip to wrestle with this thing. Each scenario we've run has a fatal flaw. I'll say this for you, Staffa, when you manipulate governments into a head-on collision, you do it so well even you can't steer them clear again."

"I'll remember that next time." He waved a hand. "And you were right. We don't have the data we need. A lot has happened since we spaced from Imperial Sassa. Let's wait, check the communications, hear what Kaylla's agents have uncovered. Not only that, Sinklar has had time to reconsider. Even if he doesn't believe I'm his father, perhaps he'll listen to reason."

Skyla stared absently at the monitor where the Twin Titans pulsed. "Is that what you're hoping? That he'll be convinced by the data? He's more skeptical of the Seddi than Divine Sassa, the fat maggot."

Staffa tightened his grip on her hand. "Maybe he will. I have to try."

* * *

Sinklar's bladder brought him awake. He blinked and stretched, realizing he didn't feel right. He gaped at his opulent surroundings—and it all came back.

Last night didn't really happen. It was just an erotic dream, Sinklar. It *had* to have been a dream. The alternative meant that he and Ily had. . . .

Sinklar turned over and dialed the bed's gravity to normal, feeling weight return to his limbs. Then he took a deep breath and sat up while he rubbed his face and looked around. Evidently Ily had left during the night.

Wearily, he got to his feet, walked into the sand-wood paneled bathroom, and winced as he began to urinate. Everything down there ached. Not only that, but his tongue hurt down at its roots—and he definitely remembered how he'd done that.

Sinklar shook his head, running fingers anxiously through his mop of unruly black hair as he blinked owlishly at his image in the mirror. "Rotted Gods. I never knew sex could be like that." With the skill of an artist, Ily had sent him from one crashing high of thundering ecstasy to a low throb of drumming plea-sure, and then back to the heights of passion to do it all over again. When his endurance had begun to flag, she'd brought him to life time and again until they'd fallen asleep in each other's arms.

A warm tingle rushed through him at the memory. Sinklar filled his lungs, held it, and puffed out his cheeks as he exhaled. Then he stepped into the shower stall, fiddled with the golden knobs until he figured it out, and whooped loudly as the hot water cascaded over his flesh.

He stepped through the drying field, feeling remarkably fresh despite his nocturnal exertions and paucity of sleep. He picked up his undersuit and armor, then he sat on the bed and fingered the material. The glow inside began to swell as he relived last night's wonderment. Had she really made him feel like that?

The growing warmth in his pelvis assured him she had.

"I was drugged. She slipped something into my food." *In an Ashtan pig's eye. How many times did she ask if you really wanted to screw her?*

Sinklar pulled on his armor and walked out into the blue room. One of the mirror-bright stasis spheres shone in the middle of the table where it kept a meal warm. Stomach growling, Sinklar glanced at the comm.

"Is that really the time?" He shook his head and stared about frantically. He had less than an hour to make it to Tarcee Estate, check on the war games, and make the meeting with Axel and Mayz.

He glanced longingly at the sphere and touched it. The stasis dome curled back to expose what had to be a delightful breakfast. Sinklar gulped the strawberries and grapes, snatched the thick pastry, and ran for the door. When he stepped out, different guards stood stiffly at attention.

"Good morning," Sinklar greeted.

Neither so much as moved, their performance letter perfect. "Um, you can talk. It's all right. I'm Sinklar Fist. I'm not familiar with your uniforms."

The woman, still at full attention, snapped, "Imperial Guard, my Lord!"

Sinklar hesitated. "I see. Well, it looks like I'll be living here. I'm late . . . but we'll talk more later. Get to know each other. In the meantime, I guess, don't let anybody in."

"Yes, my Lord."

Sinklar nodded, a weak smile fading as he backed away and walked out through the office and waiting room. As he went, he munched on the pastry, which had been filled with spiced meat and proved delicious. Sink trotted to the end of the powder-blue hallway, palmed the lock plate, and stepped into the security area.

"Should have had something to drink," he mumbled through his mouthful of food, and stepped into the lift. While he dropped, he gulped the last of the pastry and licked his fingers. Too bad the LC was still waiting at Ily's. Sinklar stiffened, imagining the horrified look that would be on Mhitshul's face.

In his imagination, Gretta didn't look any too pleased either. A twinge of guilt itched in the back of his subconscious.

"Oh, well," Sinklar whispered. Then he straightened his shoulders. Gretta lay dead and buried on Targa, and as for Mhitshul, it simply wasn't his right to pass judgment on his commanding officer. Still, a crawly place inside left Sink uncomfortable.

You made love with a reptile.

"But it was damned good . . . fantastic . . . electric." He closed his eyes to savor the memory.

He stepped out onto the underground platform and dropped into the capsule, tapping the button as he'd seen Ily do. The vehicle slipped into the tube, rocking slightly on its superconducting magnets as it shot through the near vacuum like a bullet. In the blue glow of the cabin, Sinklar drummed his fingers. *Yes, it was good—better than anything you could have fantasized—but was it worth it? To you? To Gretta?*

"She's dead, Sink. You can't bring her back."

No, but you stepped from her bed into Ily's.

"What the hell, for that one night, it was worth it."

The capsule slipped up to the platform under the Ministry of Internal Security.

Sinklar got out and entered the lift, aware again of the security cameras following him. When he rose to Ily's personal quarters, a distinct unease filled him. *Do I just walk into her bedroom?* He paused, suddenly beset by doubt. Why would anyone build a transit system like this? The tube ran from Sinklar's apartment house . . . into Ily's bedroom?

Warily, he stepped out into Ily's quarters and found them empty. He hurried through her rooms and into the main office. Ily sat at her desk on the far side, hunched over the monitor. The lights gleamed in her silky black hair. The sight of her stirred sensual memories deep in his gut. He had flashes of her muscular body undulating on his—and banished them with an effort as he approached and adopted a professional attitude.

"Good morning," she called pleasantly, head still bowed to the monitor as she input data.

"Listen, about last night. . . ."

"Wonderful, wasn't it?" She glanced up, black eyes boring into his, a happy smile on her lips. "Sorry I had to leave, but someone has to run the government and I let too many things slide last night as it was. We've got a problem with the financing for the mining of the Vermilion asteroids. It's a snarl of poor management decisions, a little graft on the side by the regional administrator, and reluctant investors. Nothing serious, but enough to be called to my attention."

He bent to study the monitor, seeing rows of figures with superimposed windows explaining the project history and how it related to the columns of numbers. "I didn't know you did things like that."

She gave him a half-hearted smile. "While you reorganize the military, I am the government. Don't worry. It won't always be like this. Slowly but surely, we'll find capable people to take the positions, but government doesn't run itself."

Sobered, Sink nodded, alarmed at the time. "Listen, I've got a meeting." He grinned sheepishly. "Seems I overslept."

"After the workout you gave me last night, I don't doubt it. I ache all over. I'll alert your LC to power up. You'd better get to it."

As he started for the security doors and the lift that would take him to the roof, she called, "Oh, Sinklar?"

He turned and she asked, "Any reservations about last night? I mean, anything that will affect our working relationship?"

He sucked at his lower lip for a moment, and shook his head. "No, Ily. It was . . . *you* were wonderful last night."

Her eyes lit, and she gave him a radiant smile. "So were you. Now, go fix the military. If I can get away, I'll see you tonight."

He turned, almost running to get to his LC—and Mhitshul's disapproving frown.

* * *

After she alerted Sinklar's LC to power up, Ily watched through her monitors as he ran down the hall and caught the lift for the roof. The ramp had lowered for him as he sprinted up into the craft. With a whining of thrusters, the drab LC rose into the gray sky and shot off to the southwest.

Ily rapped her desktop with a jeweled stylus and smiled slyly. After the first rush of excitement, he'd settled down, and, to her surprise, he'd been better than she'd expected. He had remarkable endurance. The benefits of youth? If so, she'd have to find a stable of young lovers.

Ily nodded her satisfaction. "You'll never be the same after last night, Sinklar. That taste of honey was only the beginning."

* * *

Mac rubbed shoulders with Rysta as they stared into the monitor. With the exception of the pilot under the worry-cap, only the engineer manned his duty station. The comm, weapons, and navigation Firsts had all been relieved, their stations standing empty. Not much remained for a bridge crew to do while *Gyton* warped through null singularity.

"F Group is getting too strung out," Rysta noted, pointing to the section of the monitor displaying their advance through one of the hangar decks.

Mac barked, "Corporal Tomb? Close it up! That's the third time. One more and you're out and Red's in."

" 'Firmative," Tomb responded. "C'mon, people. Close it up! You heard the First. Anyone lags, he's got duty for a week—and you get Red for a corporal!"

"You'd a never had it so good, buddy," Red japed.

"Knock it off, people," Tomb growled.

F Group had closed their ranks.

Rysta snorted and shook her head. "I don't know how you make it work, MacRuder. Just swapping officers like wagers in a tapa game grates in my very guts."

Mac smiled grimly. "You didn't think we could learn zero g vacuum work nearly this fast, did you? They know what they're in for, what's at risk. We blow this and it could be their families who get roasted when that Sassan fleet hits."

"But the odds, MacRuder, how do you keep their morale up when they know that nine chances out of ten they'll be dead within a week?"

"Because they've been there before, Commander." Mac rubbed the stubble on his chin. "They're betting on themselves, that they're good enough to do the job, and get out alive. They trust me . . . and you . . . but most of all, they trust themselves."

"Sounds like a fool's trust to me."

"Maybe. On the other hand, we've pulled it off each time we've had to. Decker Mine, Vespa, your attack, Makarta Mountain. Yes, they know they were winning when you ordered us out. Each time they're beaten, they reach down inside and pull up the raw courage, or someone gets an idea. That's what keeps us alive."

"It's chaos."

"Think so? Sink calls it command flexibility. Let's say something goes real wrong when we hit Sassa. Say I'm killed when we take that freighter. Sergeant First Boyz will continue the operation. I've seen her work. She was with me when we took Henck in Kaspa. She's got a good head on her shoulders and she thinks on her feet."

"In the dark, in the vacuum of space, is a whole different thing. And making an open assault at lightspeed has to be experienced to be believed. I've seen a lot of good spacers break, paralyzed with fear."

"We'll manage. Just like being buried in Makarta Mountain. Boyz kept her cool then, too. Thought up mindless things to keep people busy so they didn't dwell on where they were. She's adaptable and she'll probably take over the First Targan one of these days."

Rysta growled something uncomplimentary to herself.

Mac turned his attention back to the training exercise. He changed his comm access. "Boyz?"

"Here, Mac."

"Kill their battle comm. Let's see how they do in the dark vacuum if they can't communicate."

"Affirmative."

Rysta started and glared at Mac. "What are you doing? There's nothing like that in the training manual. I don't think that's ever happened in a combat situation."

"Maybe not. But it could."

"You're a real bastard, aren't you?"

Mac squinted as the Groups moving through the inky blackness began to hesitate and bunch up. "Yeah, and they'd better figure it out right now . . . before they have to do it when Sassans are shooting at them."

* * *

Mykroft paced up and down the center of the room. For a prison, it could have been worse; but a prison, to him, remained a prison. A gravcouch, gravchair, and comm system lined one wall. A dispenser allowed him to order whatever he wanted to eat or drink. He had the wall holo programmed for the Regan skyline at dawn. Morning sun slanted down over the shining buildings, and a lilac odor perfumed the air.

In the rear, the door led to a sleeping platform, lavatory, and toilet. His personal possessions had all been delivered by polite, efficient young men who had carefully removed his weapons in the process.

As always, he wore his dress uniform, a gleaming scarlet jacket with a snow-white sash and his insignia of office. Perfectly tailored trousers led down to slim black boots that accented his small feet.

He pulled himself upright, clasping his hands behind his back. He had been born more than a century ago, the patrician son of a Regan industrialist, a true member of the aristocracy, and he carried himself as such, tall, straight-shouldered, and lean. His thin mustache was kept immaculate and curled. Had he had a choice in quarters, he'd have asked for more opulent surroundings. Nevertheless, for a prison, this wasn't bad.

"But it's still a prison!" He walked over and slammed an angry fist into the door. Despite his many attempts, he couldn't make the lock plate work. The comm would allow him to access Henck, Arnson, and Adam—prisoners in similar quarters to these. Together, they cursed Sinklar Fist.

Mykroft growled to himself and resumed his pacing. What was the purpose? Where did all of this lead? Had Minister Takka wanted to execute him, she'd had more than ample opportunity. So what was scheming Ily up to? Keeping them on ice for public humiliation before she tried him?

He heard the door snick and whirled, the object of his thoughts striding into the room.

"First Mykroft! How good to see you again," Ily

greeted, smiling warmly. Behind her, the door snicked shut again.

"Minister Takka," Mykroft inclined his head slightly.

Ily glanced around. "I trust the rooms are to your satisfaction?"

"It's still a prison."

Ily lifted an eyebrow. "Hardly. But then I can understand how you could think that. No, my dear First. It's nothing of the sort. Had I wanted you imprisoned, I would have simply placed you in a facility—or in the collar."

"Then why am I and my colleagues being held?" *Careful, don't antagonize her. You're dealing with the most powerful woman in the Empire.*

Ily gave him a wry smile, turning to walk over to the comm. She ran her fingers lightly across the monitor. "You—and your associates—are here for your own protection. And, in the end, perhaps that of the Empire."

"Oh, really?"

She shot him a measuring glance. "Indeed, really." She came to stand before him, her gaze piercing. "You don't think I want to see all we've built fall to the likes of Sinklar Fist, do you?"

"I thought he was your tool."

Her expression reflected amusement. "For the moment, he's serving a purpose. What I came here to find out is, will you serve one, too? I meant it when I said I didn't want the Empire to fall to him and his egalitarian ideas. You have a stake in maintaining the status, don't you? You stand to lose all that the aristocracy has gained over the centuries."

Mykroft frowned. "Then why not simply assassinate him and get it over with?"

"Because he's still serving a purpose, and I'll keep him so long as he does. I'll keep anyone who serves me. Those who don't, well. . . . Let's not talk about that. I'm sure you understand."

A blade of ice passed through Mykroft's soul.

Ily reached into her belt pouch and produced a data crystal. "Sinclair is conducting military exercises at Tarcee Estate. Yesterday, he demolished Dion Axel's Division. This morning, his Targans are doing the same to Lute and DeGamba's Divisions. This is the record of yesterday's Regan rout. I'll forward the records of today's as soon as I have them."

Mykroft took the crystal. "And what do you wish me to do with it?"

Ily's smile went glacial. "Study it, Mykroft. Copies are being delivered to your comrades for similar study. Learn everything you can about Sinclair's tactics. I want you and your colleagues to be able to think like Sinclair, command like Sinclair." She paused. "Win like Sinclair. His tactics work and you know it . . . all of you do. You've been on the receiving end. It's a new way, Mykroft, and, like it or not, your life depends on how well you can learn to use it."

With that, she turned and walked to the door, slapping the lock plate with her hand. As she stood in the open doorway, she added, "You have a lot to gain by mastering his tactics."

After she'd left, Mykroft slapped the plate. The door remained firmly in place.

He clutched the cube in his hand, tendons knotting. *I'm no fool, Ily. Sinclair's as dangerous to you as he was to me. Very well, I understand the game. Yes, I'll study, and learn to fight on Sinclair's new battleground. And when you're ready to replace him, I'll be ready to step into his shoes.*

* * *

"Look, I know you're having problems," Vet said, spreading his palms as he leaned forward over the wreckage of his lunch. "Marka and I would like to help. You know, just loan you some credits. Rot it all, you can't spend your life in the women's restroom."

Anatolia laughed and rolled her half-empty stassa

cup back and forth in her hands. They sat in the second floor cafeteria. Around them a constant chatter of conversation rose and fell as the lunch crowd ebbed and flowed amidst a clatter of trays and a scraping of chairs. Beyond the tactite windows, rain slicked the fire-gutted building across the street.

"I know." She smiled wearily. "Vet, I can't take your money. You and Marka are just barely making ends meet now. No, don't interrupt. I know what you make, and what you need to survive. Loaning me anything would wipe out that little bit you keep in case of emergency."

"But you can't—"

"Vet! I'm fine! I'm also broke. The medical charge cleaned out my account. Then I got socked for the damage to my apartment. That comes right off the top of the allotment each month. It's either this, or I'm out of the program. I've spent too many years of hard work to throw it all away. If it means sleeping on a restroom bench, by the Blessed Gods, I'll pay that price."

Vet slapped the table and leaned back. "Look at you. You're half-starved. Your clothes are wearing out. What are you going to do when those holes get bigger?"

"Steal something from the specimens in the vaults. The older ones came in those funny blue smocks. I'll strip a couple of bodies—they won't mind—and sew something together."

"And what about eating? You gonna cut up a corpse for that, too?"

"Don't be a fool. They're full of preservatives."

She tried to keep her face deadpan but broke into sputtering laughter at his expression.

He finally chuckled, too, then sobered. "All right, last offer. Marka and I thought you wouldn't take a loan. Look, it's a small place, only two rooms. You'd be out front on the fold out couch, but it would beat—"

"No way."

"No way? You haven't even heard me out. Look, I have to drive it every day anyway, you wouldn't be any burden. That's what friends are for. Someday the tables may be turned. Maybe I'll be the one in trouble and you'll be there when I need you. Honest, I talked it over with Marka and we're agreed that you staying there for a couple of months wouldn't be anything at all."

"The answer is no. It's a wonderfully kind offer, Vet, but I know how much strain you're under. Even a good relationship like you and Marka have gets pulled pretty thin with a baby. And you've got year-end exams coming up. I'm doing fine. I've got heat, lights, running water, a comfortable place to sleep, and full-time security. What more do I need?"

"You're. . . ." Vet shook his head. "Where'd you get the guts, Ana? You're not the woman I once knew."

She stared vacantly into her stassa cup. "No, I'm not. Things changed when I was in the street. I saw what life can be like. I. . . ." She stopped herself and tossed down the last of her cold stassa. "Can we talk about something else?"

He eyed her uncertainly. "I'd give a year's credit to know what happened to you out there."

"Seriously? I could buy a ticket home and leave this place behind. Maybe the life of a farmer wouldn't be so bad after all."

"Knock it off. Every time someone asks you something serious, you've got a smart remark to shut them down. Whoa! Don't get that look. Just tell me one more thing and we'll change the subject, all right? Good. Here goes: Why can't you just talk to people like you used to? You've . . . well, kind of withdrawn. Locked yourself inside when you used to be the life of the party."

She tilted her head, trying to order feelings and experiences into a string of words he'd understand. "Vet, it's because . . . well, there's no common ground now. My reality changed out there. The people in the lab, you yourself. You've never been threatened, never been hungry or scared. You've never had it. . . . I mean, you've never been out there, without anything. Without. . . ."

He frowned at her, thumping the table with his thumb. "You call starving through school easy? Blessed Gods, Ana, we have to study for ten hours a day . . . and then there's the lab work. On top of that, I've got to do my share at the house. Take care of the baby. If I wanted it easy, I could take a job with one of the utilities splicing comm lead, or tuning receivers, and come home at night and relax."

She nodded and smiled. "Yes, I guess you do have it pretty tough. And that's why I can't take your offer to move in. Now, let's change the subject." *Because you're my last friend and I don't want to lose you over your own stupidity.*

"Okay, Ana. So like . . . well. . . . What's the project you've got locked up in your drawer?"

She gave him what she hoped was a disarming smile. "I'm mapping DNA sequences from a specimen."

He gave her a wooden look. "Right. And that's why the only person in the complex who can access the file besides yourself is Adam. Why are you being so secretive?"

"It's my research, that's why. And, Vet, I'm not sure what I've got. If it turns out to be something simple and boring, I don't want to look like an idiot in front of everyone. I do my idiot act well enough without adding to my repertoire." *And if you knew half of what I've found—and about who—you'd crap your guts.*

"Adam hasn't told you you're being an idiot with this line of research?"

She shook her head, lying with a guile that shocked her. "Not yet, but when I showed him the preliminary results, he gave me that down-the-nose look, like he'd seen me for the first time. You know that look. It means something significant—like you're either about to be given a permanent position with the Lab . . . or handed reassignment papers informing you that your next job will be with the sanitation engineers measuring water ph in the sewage plants."

Vet pursed his lips. "You haven't been dropped from the program yet—and it's been weeks. Maybe you've got your project after all. Do it right, and you could really get that appointment to the lab."

"I think the results will be very interesting." *But what in pus-Rotted hell do I do with them?* Anatolia gave Vet a silly distracting smile while shivers tugged at her nerves.

* * *

"One of the constants of physics is that energy can never be destroyed. We accept that mass and energy are interrelated, or else null singularity drives would not be possible. If energy cannot be destroyed, it is the one eternal, even beyond time, for the entire universe can be collapsed into a gravitational singularity. When the universe undergoes the final phase change, and that energy is collected, all that will remain is God.

"This has implications for all of us, for with every observation we make, for every thought in our brains, the quantum state of energy is changed. Since the processes our brains follow are those of quantum physics, we can share God Mind with the rest of the universe. Being part of God, we all share a common reality. Knowing this has implications about the nature of God—not as a benign Creator, but as a consciousness striving to understand just as each of us do.

"Think of the origin of the universe as the birth of God Mind in this phase of reality. Just as we are born, observe, and learn, so does God. The quanta are the

modalities of Its observation. Not only do we share God Mind in our individual existences, we also share God's quest to understand the reality around us.

"Thinking in such terms, our lives become more meaningful. Each of us has a purpose, and that is to learn, to understand the worlds around us. Our goal is to discover what it means to exist, for with each life, with each beating heart, hope, and dream, we are changing forever the consciousness of God. In doing so, the meaning of morality is changed forever."

—Excerpt from Kaylla Dawn's Itreatic broadcasts

CHAPTER XIV

The Tarcee Estate had once belonged to Defense Minister Tedor Mathaiison, so Sinklar hadn't minded taking it over as a military training ground, and if Tedor's heirs filed a petition, they could have it back when he'd finished. The big room in the sprawling manor house had been very tastefully decorated with shimmering fabrics that hung over alcoves containing elegant serving ware, beverage dispensers, comm centers, and, here and there, arching tactite windows. The windows opened onto the manicured grounds beyond, now cluttered with LCs, tactical support vehicles, and lounging troops in laser-charred battle armor.

Sinklar battled to order his thoughts. Images of Ily dominated his mind, distracting him from the work at hand. Her smile haunted him, promising more of the physical rapture she'd given him last night.

"Sorry, Sink. There's no update to give you. We slapped their defenses aside, surrounded their positions, and took the objective in jack-time." Kap had filled him in on the disaster suffered by the two Regan Divisions which had already fallen to Sinklar's troops that morning.

Right, so get Ily out of your mind and deal with this. This is what you know.

He crossed his arms and stared at the Division Firsts who sat uneasily around the banquet table in the large dining room of the Tarcee mansion. Ayms, Mayz, Kap, and Shiksta stood in the rear of the room with some of their Section Firsts in attendance.

"Yesterday," Sinklar began, "the Fourth Targan Assault Division chewed through the Nineteenth Regan.

This morning, Kap's Third Targan decimated the Ninth Vermilion and the second Ashtan in a little less than two hours. We've got a great deal of hard work ahead of us to make this military combat capable."

Dion Axel cleared her throat.

"Yes?" He studied the haggard looking woman. With rejuvenation, she might have been around thirty, but he'd scanned her bio. Axel was nearly ninety, with fifty years in the military and combat experience in every major campaign Rega had fought. She had her shoulder-length brown hair pulled back in a ponytail, and her face had an angular look.

"My people and I studied the records made of yesterday's action. It defies every military maxim known to the science of war. Lord Fist, just what is your agenda? Is it really your policy to throw the military into total confusion? You can't simply toss out hundreds of years of military tradition—especially not if the reports are true that Sassa is mounting a strike against us."

A murmur of agreement and discontent rose.

"I plan to do just that." Sinklar leaned forward, his gaze boring into one after another of the officers. "Further, I expect your Divisions to be trained and field capable within four weeks which—"

"Impossible!" cried First Lute of the Ninth Vermilion Assault Division. He reminded Sink of a bloated raven—the kind that guards corpses. Beside him DeGamba, of the Second Ashtan, nodded in agreement.

Sinklar waited until the hubbub died down and replied succinctly, "You *will* be field capable . . . or someone else will be in charge of your Divisions."

DeGamba shot to his feet, a thin man with pale skin and silky white hair. "I'll accept no such thing! If you think that I'm about to put up with your foolery, boy, you've another thought coming! My family has served the Emperor for—"

"Then you will be relieved of your command, escorted to the next transport, and sent home. I believe you currently have estates on Riparious? Perhaps you would serve the people better by tending your fields."

DeGamba grinned wickedly, a frigid look in his icy blue eyes. "And just how will you accomplish this? Have Ily's agents try and arrest us?"

Sinklar shook his head, eyes never leaving DeGamba's. "I can do it here and now. Today you got your taste of a Division which has been formed from what was left of the five Divisions Tybalt dropped on us at Targa. Within ten minutes, I can have the Second Targan here—veterans who've refined the tactics you just experienced. When they arrive, I promise you, they won't come carrying training lasers."

"You'd precipitate civil war?" Axel asked, glancing around nervously.

Sinklar clasped his hands behind him. "No. Even if your Divisions rose against me, my Targans would have the situation under control within hours, and all of you would be dead for violating the Command Code, executed for failure to obey a direct order from your commanding officer.

"I made my bargain with you during our first meeting. I gave you my word, and took yours that I would get my chance. To date, I haven't lost. I told you then that I would enforce the Command Code until I was proven wrong. I keep my word. This is a military, not a social club. Getting back to the point, within each of your Divisions are smart professionals, men and women who've made it to the rank of Sergeant First, or Corporal . . . people who've risen as far as their station will allow. I'll be bluntly honest. Most of those combat veterans are better equipped to command than you are."

"I will not sit here and be insulted by a wet-assed little imp!" Lute bellowed and got to his feet, stomping for the door.

Sinklar pointed at Lute's retreating back. "First Mayz, that man is in violation of orders, attend to him."

Mayz had stood through most of the meeting with arms crossed and an angry glower on her hard features. She straightened, coolly pulled her pistol, and shot Lute in the back of the head. The Riparian's body thumped loosely onto the carpet as the pink puff of atomized blood, bone, and brain settled around him.

Sinklar cataloged the ashen faces at the table before him as he leaned down and braced himself on stiff arms. "You are here because I can't waste talent, and I'm willing to give you a chance. Within months, we're going to war. Sassa *is* mounting an attack. I'm sure His Holiness sees Tybalt's assassination as the perfect opportunity to strike us. People, this is deadly serious. A pompous ass like First Lute could kill his entire command through pride, arrogance, and stubbornness. Firsthand, I witnessed Mykroft do exactly that to his Second Targan. I *won't* have that. The people under your command are your responsibility. See that you take care of them wisely."

A shrilling rose and fell as several LCs passed overhead and settled beyond the mansion.

Sinklar considered the people before him, thoughts racing. *Rotted Gods, the situation is worse than I thought. Sink, you've got to make them understand. But how? I don't have Targa here to winnow. . . .* "Ladies and gentlemen, this military *will* be field capable utilizing my tactics. We're going to go to work, starting now. We'll run this morning's exercise again, and again, and again. As soon as we get it right, we'll run the same operation against fresh Divisions as they arrive. If we have to run war games across the entire planet, we will. You might inform your families that you'll be missing dinner tonight—and for some time in the future. Until you are given permission otherwise, you will billet on the ground with your troops."

"Ridiculous!" DeGamba cried. "Live with . . . with those animals!"

Sinklar ignored him. "These are your orders: Kap and Mayz will detail their Section and Group Firsts to your Divisions. Your Firsts will report to the Third and Fourth Targan Divisions. Exchanging command structure will be the quickest method to expose rank and file to our tactics. Division Second Horn, you will assume temporary command of the Ninth Vermilion.

If you perform efficiently, you may retain the position. If not, you will be replaced by the most competent person within the ranks."

Sinklar paused as he noted their aghast expressions. "I suggest you take this very seriously. From what I've seen today, I don't expect many of you to be in command by sunset tonight. Post your orders, and find your new commands. The operation begins at 13:00. Dismissed."

In shocked silence, they stood and glanced almost fearfully at Sink, then at his Firsts who glared back. As they filed silently out, each stepped wide around Lute's bloody corpse.

"Shik, keep an eye on them," Sink jerked his head at the door. Shiksta nodded and left.

Sinklar gave his Firsts a weary smile. "Any odds on who makes the grade?"

Ayms rubbed his hands as if washing them. "They'd have been blaster fodder in minutes back on the pass in Targa. No takers, Sink."

Sinklar settled himself on the corner of the table. "Any questions about the changed schedule?"

"We're gonna be dragging ass," Kap replied. "The troops are going to hate you."

"Won't be the first time. Honestly, I thought the Regulars would be better. How did the Empire win any wars? These guys can't be that incompetent— they'd have been demobilized."

Mayz gave him a level stare. "Maybe it's because the Star Butcher is that good. He did most of the real fighting. Regan troops dropped for the mop-up after the defenses were broken."

"As of today," Sinklar promised, "that's changing. If you see anyone with talent, promote him on the spot. We're all going to be dragging and bleary before this is over, so let's prepare for the long haul. Go to work, people."

* * *

Deep within Itreata, Staffa walked down the long corridor and studied the patterns in the rock. Mining lasers had cut the round bore, leaving a mirror polish on the stone which exposed the veins and folded strata of the ancient moon's interior. Periodic light panels sent a gleam off the surface. Kaylla had wanted it this way. Here, she lived at a safe distance from the Companions, separated from them by nearly a kilometer of forbidding rock and accessible only through this tunnel which she monitored with her own security.

Staffa had decided to walk, not only for the exercise, but to remember. Images jostled: Kaylla in tattered brown rags, muscles sliding under tanned skin as she leaned against the weight of the tow rope in the Etarian desert; the weary glint in her tan eyes as she fought for Makarta Mountain; tenderness and aching sorrow as she talked about her family—and their murder on Maika. She'd huddled against his side that time as they waited for death in a buried pipe in the Etarian desert. He recalled the defeat and despair that had possessed her after the slave, Brots, had raped and beaten her.

And for that, I killed him. Just as I killed Anglo. A sourness twisted in his gut. He, himself, was the only one of Kaylla's tormentors he hadn't killed—and he'd tried that once, in a sialon shipping crate bound for Targa.

"You are a coward." Her glare had cut like flint, a sneer of disgust on her lips. *"Live for me, Staffa. Show me you're worthy of respect. If not, kill yourself sometime when I don't have to look at your polluted corpse."*

Staffa curled his fingers into fists. They had been locked together, tormentor and tormented, the roles changing back and forth. In a universe four paces across, Kaylla Dawn had given him the means to find himself, and perhaps a way to atone. The woman he'd destroyed on Maika had become his salvation and his punishment. Ironic justice had been meted. The dance of the quanta, the fingerprint of God.

Staffa approached the huge doors and waved at the

security comm. The heavy ceramic portals slipped
back on superconducting tracks to let him into a small
pressure lock. From there he passed into a spacious
reception area. Nyklos sat at the main desk surrounded on three sides by walls of monitors. He gave
Staffa a cool inspection and his bushy mustache
twitched. "Magister Dawn is waiting in the conference
room, Lord Commander."

"Very good. I'll be accessing some data through the
link. You'll probably want to run copies for Kaylla's
records."

"I'll do so. Thank you." Nyklos labored to sound
civil.

Rot it all, the hostility between them would never
end. As Staffa stared into Nyklos' brown eyes, he remembered the first time they'd met—with Staffa shoving a blaster into the Seddi agent's gut. *Still want to
kill me, don't you, Nyklos? The old Seddi training lies
deep within the brain, and when you had your opportunity, orders restrained you.* And Nyklos loved Skyla
Lyma desperately.

"No matter what the species, male dogs bristle at
each other in the same way," Kaylla called in her
amused contralto.

Staffa couldn't help but crack a smile as he turned
his attention to her. She stood in the doorway, brown
hair falling to her collar bones in a fashion her
square-jawed face. Her gaze met his with the penetrating acumen of a woman for whom life had no
more surprises, a woman with a wordly competence
beyond her years.

She wore the thin white robe of a Seddi Magister,
belted about her slender waist with a rope. Trim san-
dals were tied to her feet.

"Kaylla, you're looking fit. I take it they've been
giving you the treatment?"

One eyebrow arched. "I've been stuck, bled, scanned,
radiographed, resonated, and analyzed until no molecule remains inviolate in my body." A pause. "I take
it that Divine Sassa didn't jump at the chance to lay
down his arms and welcome us into his embrace?"

"If you'd ever seen him in person, you wouldn't want anything to do with his embrace."

"Actually most men fit into that category." She paused, the hesitation just long enough to remind him of what had passed between them. "Come tell me about it. Nyklos? Hold my calls."

"Yes, Magister."

Kaylla turned and walked away with an athletic poise that demanded attention. More than any woman he'd ever known, she exuded an innate grace and composure, no matter what her circumstance. Staffa followed her down a carpeted hallway paneled in white. The place smelled new. "How is the reorganization proceeding?"

"Slowly. Without the Mag Comm we're having to build from scratch. Your technicians have been invaluable. We've mastered a great deal of your technology—and for once we don't have to fear it. When it comes to the reorganization, Wilm has become my right hand. He has a genius for flowcharts and systems theories." She gestured into the conference room. "Make yourself comfortable. I'll be right back."

Staffa entered and drew himself a cup of stassa before seating himself at the table. He accessed his personal net through the Seddi interface and watched as the monitor rose from the desk.

Kaylla entered and closed the door, dropping a series of data cubes on the desktop. She studied him closely as she seated herself. "How bad is it?"

"Bad enough. Fat old Sassa has come to the conclusion that with Tybalt's assassination, he can take Rega—even without the help or approval of the Companions."

Her lips pinched. "And the data we provided?"

"That's another problem stemming from the Mag Comm. The machine used such complex data manipulations that the Sassan computers can barely make heads or tails of it. Before we send the same material to Sinklar, we might want to simplify both the data and statistical manipulations into something they can

work with. But we did make one very significant con-
version. The Legate believes us."

"Roma?" She stared pensively at the desktop.
"How far will he go?"

"All the way, I think. You might say that he, too,
has become aware. I'm loading the records into your
system. Review them at your leisure." He input the
sequence and continued, "Which brings me to the
next topic. Myles will provide cover to get more Seddi
into Imperial Sassa. I think we ought to place someone talented in his office. Maybe Nyklos, or someone
of his caliber."

"What is it between the two of you?"

"We didn't exactly meet as the best of friends,
you'll recall. All of his life he trained to kill me."

"So did a lot of our people."

Staffa drummed his fingertips while she watched
him with those knowing eyes. "I guess after living for
weeks in that crate, there really aren't many secrets
between us, are there?"

"I know you better than any other human being
alive, Staffa. Perhaps better than you know yourself."

He shrugged. "Nyklos fell in love with Skyla. She
never took him seriously. I don't know how much
credence to put in such things, but I think it goads
him. Then, too, we're just the sort of men who grate
on each other. Blame it on testosterone. If you're
really concerned about it and smell trouble, call Andray Sornsen in psych and run a profile on both of
us."

"You'd allow that?"

"For you, yes. I have too much respect for your
intuition."

A slight frown etched her forehead. "You still surprise me. I know how difficult it is for you to trust,
to open yourself. Tell me, is it really my intuition that
concerns you . . . or are you looking for another way
to ease the guilt?"

"Pus-Rotted Gods, how do I know if it's partly
tinged with guilt? I've got enough to go around for
everybody, as you well know. On the other hand, I

want to avoid any conflict with Nyklos. You never
know when we might have to rely on each other."

She gave him a sharp nod. "Very well, let me think
about it. In the meantime, we've had developments
of our own. You should probably know that Tyklat
was ordered to Rega, allegedly for promotion and reassignment. I think I told you that he'd been expecting
Ily to make some sort of inquiry as to his involvement
in the Etarian fiasco. Tyklat had cut many of his communications—working exclusively through Nyklos, by
the way. Ily's order triggered Tyklat's premonition of
trouble. He was going to report in as soon as he had
some feeling for his safety."

Her eyes narrowed. "We got a cryptic message
through an irregular channel that Ily had broken his
cover and he was on the run. Tyklat is no one's fool.
A Regan cruiser was stolen a couple of days later
by a man matching Tyklat's description. The Regan
orbital terminal sustained some damage and their
security batteries damaged the vessel before it made
its escape."

"Orbital Defense didn't space a CV after him
immediately?"

Kaylla grabbed one of the data cubes, tossing it up
and catching it. "No. Should they have?"

"That's standard operating procedure." Staffa
tapped the table to emphasize his point. "Why didn't
they?"

"Before we get too carried away, the head of Orbital Defense, one Bryn Hack, was found murdered
in his rooms after he let Sinklar slip in unannounced."

"Damn! He was a good man."

"Today he's good and dead. Rumor has it that Ily
used an assassin to take him out. But back to Tyklat.
Most of their military vessels are currently being
grouped around Rega for refitting and resupply as part
of Tybalt's original buildup for a strike against Sassa.
That schedule has been maintained despite the assassination. Staffa, they're short on ships and apparently
in a command crisis. They might not have had a CV
ready to chase Tyklat down. Not only that, but Sinklar

has been running military training exercises, and a lot
of Division Firsts are raising hell about his methods.
I don't think we can count Tyklat out yet. All the
breaks may have gone in his direction on this one."

Staffa made a noncommittal gesture. "Nevertheless,
if he surfaces, be very, very careful. I'm sure you remember just how good Ily is."

"I do, indeed. Before he sets foot inside this complex, he'll have to undergo a complete psych analysis.
I'll want him wrung out under drugs, a worry-cap, and
anything else your security might know that we don't.
If he's clean, he'll understand and submit."

Staffa squinted as he considered that, and finally he
nodded. "All right. Let me know if you decide to
bring him in. What have you learned about the exercises Sinklar is running?"

She laughed and told him, "He's your son, all right.
The report that came in this evening is that his Targan
Divisions have made idiots out of the Regan regulars.
He had a Division First, some fellow named Lute,
shot for disobeying orders."

"Good for him. Lute always was an arrogant scum-
sucker."

"He's probably not going to be the last, either. Sinklar has pulled all the privileges from the old guard—
even has them sleeping on the ground with their
troops. More than one has been sacked, sent home in
disgrace. Sinklar is implementing a program of perpetual military exercise. Apparently he has stated that
he'll use the entire planet if he has to, but he wants
his troops ready to tackle Sassa within six months."

"Don't believe it. That's propaganda for Divine Sassa's ears. Sinklar wants to move inside of four months,
probably more like three. He's got to have something
cooking to handle that Sassan strike force outfitting to
hit him. Who are his commanders in these exercises?"

Kaylla slipped a cube into the comm. She tapped a
couple of keys and turned it to face him. Staffa bent
forward, reading: "Mayz, Kap, Shiksta, Ayms, Buchman." He leaned back, stroking his chin. "But no

MacRuder. Where in Rotted hell did Mac disappear to?"

"I haven't the slightest idea. I can have our people there check."

"Do it! Wait." He held up a palm, racking his brain. "Is *Gyton* still in orbit?"

Kaylla pulled the data cube out and inserted another. The keys rattled under her fingers as she sifted through intelligence reports and cross-referenced. "We have a record of *Gyton* arriving and Sinklar's people taking the planet. But after that . . . nothing. At least, no reported change of orbital status. I assume she's still in orbit."

"Any mention of Rysta Braktov in those reports? Rysta would be making some kind of news—unless they have her on ice."

Kaylla's slim fingers clicked the keys again. "Nothing."

"Find out. This could be very important."

"It'll take until tomorrow at the latest." She watched him uneasily. "You don't look happy."

"I'm not happy. I've fought him. Kaylla, this is Sinklar. After Makarta Mountain, he didn't just shut off, or slip into a holding pattern. That boy is still running on full-throttle. He's planning, preparing, and initiating. Find MacRuder. No matter what. Anything else I should be caught up on?"

"I think that's it. What's next on your agenda?"

"Broadcasts. I want you and your people to put together some programs on Seddi philosophy and on the studies your scholars have run on the economic and political situations. I've cleared access to the big dishes so you can send clear across Free Space. Ily and Divine Sassa will go berserk, but they've got control of all the media in their respective empires. Now it's our turn to promote our own agenda, and they can't do a pus-sucking thing to stop us."

"Good idea. I'll put some of our people on it." Kaylla smiled. "I'd like to see Ily's face when she hears the first of our broadcasts on unilateral epistemology."

"So would I . . . but from a great distance. The last time she saw us in action together she almost killed us."

"And Sinklar? What do you have in mind for him besides simplified data?"

Staffa inspected the lines on his palm as he thought. "I'm hoping that he has enough distance from Bruen's meddling and Makarta Mountain to be able to talk rationally. I'm going to contact him, talk to him, give him the Seddi data to do with as he pleases. He has his own free will. That's the single gift God grants us. I'll explain the necessity for stopping the war, see if he can grasp the realities."

Kaylla glanced sidelong at him. "And if Sinklar and Divine Sassa both insist on committing suicide? What then?"

Staffa turned his hand, watching the corded tendons slide under scarred flesh. "Do you remember the conversation we had on ethics? We accept that God is eternal and that observations create reality . . . affect the quanta by changing the energy of particles. We know that energy is eternal, God's data cube, if you will. We both accept that the universe will end, and this current duality will be returned to the God Mind with the gravitational collapse of space-time. Because of our free will, any increase in suffering affects the observations made by both victim and inflicter. They reinforce the reality we have created through our observations. Therefore, the ethical human being seeks to alleviate suffering and promote good."

Kaylla nodded. "That's essentially what the Seddi believe, and what we discussed. Why bring it up?"

Staffa stared pensively at the stassa cup. "Because if all else fails, it explains the only ethical conclusion I've come to."

"And that is?"

"Kaylla, if Rega and Sassa do go to war despite all my efforts to stop it, I'll have one final option open to me. I took everything you taught me to heart. I believe your philosophy and cosmology. They fit what we know about physics and quantum effects. At the same time, what we know about gravitation, and what we suspect about the universe being closed, lends credence to your eschatology. Your system of belief is rational and beats hell out of the idea of Rotted and Blessed Gods."

"Get to the point, Staffa."

He slapped the table with finality. "If it all comes undone, Kaylla, the Companions will space again. This time, we'll make a decision, and end the war, hopefully with enough of civilization intact so that you and Myles can salvage the species from extinction."

She stared coldly at him and the silence stretched.

Staffa finally said. "I can do it by destroying the Sassan and Regan military strike forces in deep space to minimize civilian casualties. After that, I'll have to blast major portions of the planet Rega, destroy their governmental centers and central comm facilities to render the administration of redistribution ineffectual. Myles Roma can effectively integrate Regan redistribution services from Sassa. I will assassinate His Holiness and finally—"

"You'd increase suffering to alleviate it?"

"Kaylla, the ghouls still haunt my dreams. You know. You've heard me whimpering in my sleep. I've considered it every way I can. If I can't turn Sinklar, it's the only option left—or we'll all die."

"There has to be another way." She'd stiffened, a barely controlled agony behind her masklike expression.

"Then, by the quantum Gods, help me find it, Kaylla, because we're running out of time. If I can't find another way out, I'm going to have to stop Sinklar." He avoided her piercing gaze while his guts crawled. "And the only way I know to do that is to kill him."

* * *

Mac stepped through the hatch and onto *Gyton*'s bridge. When Rysta had roused him out of a deep sleep, he'd supposed he'd find her in the command chair. Instead, she leaned over the Intelligence First's station. Mac grimaced and walked over to stand beside her, asking, "What's up?"

"Thought you might like a lesson in space strategy, son."

Mac ground his teeth. Somehow, he hadn't quite gotten used to being referred to as "son" and "boy."

"What are you seeing?" He bent to look at the holo displays. The images consisted of a series of spectral analyses.

Rysta craned her leathery neck to stare at him. "Tell me something. Just how were you planning to catch this freighter you want to ride piggyback on into Imperial Sassa?"

Mac pulled at his earlobe for a moment and shrugged. "I thought we'd sneak up behind her. You know, hide in the redshift shadow and grab her."

"Right. Good move that, hiding in the redshift shadow. The Sassan drops from null singularity and he's moving right at lightspeed, so what's coming into the sensors from behind him is foggy—lightspeed being constant and all."

"That's simple physics, isn't it? Starships have a blind spot there . . . don't they?"

Rysta smacked her lips, staring absently at the overhead. "Blessed Gods, give me strength."

"What?"

Rysta thrust her face within inches of his. "Boy, how are you going to find this freighter you're going to sneak in behind?"

"Well, I thought that's why we dropped out half a light-year back. We'd watch the scanners, pick up a reading, and change vector until we matched with them."

"How long does that take?"

Mac shifted from one foot to the other as if the deck on which he stood had become as slippery as his plans. "Well . . . maybe a week?"

"Uh-huh? And how many gravities will that freighter put out shedding Delta V?"

"Twenty?" Mac took a wild guess.

"If you're lucky. Keep in mind, a freighter is just

that. A fat hauling machine. A warship can take forty to fifty gs, because the hull is designed for it. And while we're on it, do you know why we can get that kind of acceleration?"

"Because of the bounce-back collars," Mac answered proudly.

"Good for you. Why?"

"Huh?"

"Why do they work?"

"Well, they refine the reaction mass."

"What's the physics?"

"I . . . uh. . . ."

"The reaction is accelerated through the tubes at speed of light," Rysta barked. "The fields in the bounce-back collars warp the reaction, compress it, and send it out faster than the speed of light. The result is that for each unit of mass accelerated, energy increases exponentially as you increase hyperlight velocity. Correct?"

"Right."

"Why?"

"Huh?"

"Why does it happen?" At Mac's blank look, she added sourly, "And you and Sinklar think you're gonna conquer Free Space? Blessed Gods save us all. Listen, boy. It's because you can't violate the constancy of the speed of light. Accelerating the reaction mass tricks the constant. Since lightspeed can't be violated, something has to give, and in this case it's the ship. The ship doesn't have much mass, relatively speaking, and the universe has all the rest. Thrust builds exponentially at hyperlight speeds."

"Right." *What in hell is she saying?*

"Now, back to space tactics. How do you find a Sassan freighter so that you don't have to lose a week while their redshift shadow collapses and you get spotted and blow the whole mission?"

Mac frowned and chewed at his lip for a second. "Well, you draw a straight line between Myklene and Sassa. Then you figure out the rate of deceleration the Sassan will use to arrive at—"

"The galaxy turns, right? Do you know the constant? The amount of displacement from the vector the ship traveled leaving Myklene compared to the one it will have arriving? That's critical, boy, because the longer a ship is in null singularity, the greater the galactic windage is going to be when it pops back in."

"I guess I don't know that."

"At last," Rysta crooned. "Well, maybe I can teach you something about space after all. All right, listen. That young man over there under the worry-cap is doing a lot of things. Not only is he monitoring the ship, but he's interacting constantly with the navcomm. The brain can visualize in three dimensions. Right now, he's existing as *Gyton*—kind of like being a trout in a stream, or an acrobat performing zero g ballet. He can feel what we can only draw in a four-dimensional diagram."

"I follow you."

"All right. Vector and galactic drift, those are the data we need to make a rough guess as to where the Sassan will pop out. But we don't have all those data, do we? We don't know his vector when he went null singularity. We don't know the amount of time he's been in that state. We don't know his ship's acceleration, attitude at initiation, or what his vessel's total mass is, all of which affect his reentry point on this side."

Mac deflated and gave her a dull look. "I didn't know it was going to be that hard."

Rysta gave him a satisfied smile. "It isn't."

"But you just told me—"

"I just told you what any groundhog infantry commander would think was the right way to ambush a spaceship. All right, next lesson. A spaceship radiates energy, correct? Infrared, photons, gases, microwaves . . . the entire spectrum. What happens to that radiated energy while a starship is in null singularity?"

"It goes into the nothingness outside of this universe."

"Wrong. Want to tell me why?"

"It's the light constant again?"

"Nope. Try the second law of thermodynamics, the

conservation of energy. Every erg of mass/energy that goes into null singularity must come out. You can't take energy out of this universe. Period."

"All right, I'll accept that."

"Let me tell you a story. Way back when, people trembled in fear that if the null singularity failed, you'd be stuck out there, wherever there is. The problem was, on those occasions when the null singularity generation failed, ships popped right back into this universe. Once or twice that was unfortunate because of what they ran into—traveling as they were at lightspeed—but no one got lost in a different universe. Not one photon got lost. The second law of thermodynamics can't be broken."

"And that will tell us where to find our Sassan?"

"Boy, you've got a brain like a rock. If you were looking for a sniper in the night, what would you do?"

"Drop my IR visor and. . . . Rotted Gods! If you can't even lose a photon, and ships radiate. . . ."

"That's right." Rysta gave him an evil grin and bent over the display. "You wondered why we dropped out so far back and have been shedding Delta V in a wide dispersal? We've allowed that starburst of radiation to dissipate—assuming anyone was looking for us.

"Now, knowing that, check the readings from our detectors. See these spikes on the chart? They're like rings on a pond, boy. That tall one with the heavy particles was a warship. These others, freighters. Notice how you get a shifting pattern here? You can see that the first particles we intercepted came in at a different angle that slowly drifted to the galactic northwest. That's the windage we were talking about. This other variation plotted on the scattergram is the difference in ship capabilities. The acute angle created by the warship and the redshift of the reading indicate it dropped in closer to Imperial Sassa and shed Delta V at about forty gravities. They were in a hurry. Notice how the readings fall off? That's the deceleration. See, you can estimate the rate, follow each ship in as the Doppler and mass change. It's like a trail and fingerprint for each vessel. So what I've been doing is matching up their entry vector and spreading our reaction mass over a broad area as we curve our vector to match theirs. We want our radiation to mingle with theirs, mask our presence. At the same time, I've been guessing where the next big Sassan freighter should drop in."

"What about this last one? It's barely reading at all after the first burst of energy." Mac pointed to a fuzzy spike followed by a faint line, the signal weak. Triangulation indicated a highly dispersed pattern immediately ahead of them.

"That's what I called you up here for," Rysta's eyes gleamed. "That's a Sassan freighter. A great big fat one—and we're already in his redshift shadow. You wanted a Sassan ship to sneak us in . . . and that's the one. We're dropping right onto his back."

* * *

Ily's aircar settled in a grassy flat beyond a corps of armored assault vehicles. Behind the looming ranks of ceramic and steel monsters, she could see an HT, the heavy transport lifters used by the military to drop the armored forces used to spearhead planetary invasions. Targa, originally considered a matter of social control, had only employed airborne infantry. Hitting a planet like Sassa, however, would necessitate coordinated orbital bombardment, armored shock armies spearheading assaults, and infantry follow-up and mop-up. At least, that was the way Sinklar had explained it to her.

In the twilight background of sunset, beyond a froth of bivouacked bubble huts, the roof of the Tarcee mansion could be made out. At least ten thousand troops had set up camp on the flattened grass north of the buildings.

Sinklar's LC stood out among the rest as the only one displaying scorching, blast damage, and the scars of combat. It looked dusty and worn beside the newer equipment. Ily stepped out onto the crushed grass and walked up to Sinklar's LC. She glanced around and climbed the assault ramp into the murky darkness of the craft's interior. She followed the aisle to the bulkhead, ducking through the hatch to find Sinklar in the cubbyhole of the command center. A headset looped around his ears and his attention was centered on one of the monitors. Every display glowed, each depicting movements of troops and armor.

"Sinklar?"

She got no reaction as he ordered, "That's it, Anton, spread your people out. Your Corporals are on their own now." A pause. "No. It doesn't matter a damn what your Division First told you. The situation's been changed. Understand? All that matters now is taking out that flanking column." Another pause. "Screw the Holy Gawdamn Book! Get those flankers or a lot of your people are going to die—and I'll kick your ass! Go!"

"Sinklar!" She tapped him on the shoulder and he jumped, glaring wildly up at her before grinning sheepishly.

"Ily. When did you get here?" He pulled the headset off, running fingers through his unruly mop of black hair. He looked weary, eyes red-rimmed, lids drooping.

"Just now. It turns out I've got most of the major problems dealt with. What is all this?"

He pointed at the monitors. "The screens to the right are Mayz, Kap, and Ayms. They're trying to beat some sense into the Regan Divisions. On the left you see my Targans, each under a fumbling Regan commander who is trying to learn from my Targan veterans." He shook his head. "I didn't know it would be this bad. Some of these people make Mykroft look pus-dripping talented!"

"I have a free evening. I was thinking perhaps some Ashtan steak, sauteed Riparian squid with klavva nut filling, orange-glazed mentha root with Etarian coffee, and something as decadent as a Sassan God for dessert might be in order. How about it?"

Sinklar rubbed his eyes and glanced back at the board—only to stiffen. He clamped the headset against one ear and yelled, "No! Anton, you idiot! You don't just march out in the middle of the field like you own the place! You're going to be . . ." his voice went flat, ". . . fried like an egg." A pause. "'I know I told you that's all that mattered. That didn't mean you should just run out into their guns. Use your maggot-licking brain next time."

"About dinner?" Ily reminded.

Sinklar exhaled and cocked his head. "Can you give me about two hours?"

Ily crossed her arms. "Two hours? It looks you're mobilizing against the Companions out there."

He screwed his face up and wiggled his jaw around the way a tired man does, and stared up at her emotionlessly. "I can't leave just yet. I've got six Sections I'm trying to coordinate. I don't think they're going to last another two hours against the Third Targan—despite the idiotic leadership."

"Two hours," she told him firmly. "I'll have my aircar sent to pick you up. We'll eat at my place . . . and see what the evening has to offer." Then she bent down, kissing him and drawing his lower lip away with her as she straightened. Then she gave him a coquettish smile. "See you then."

She turned in time to see Mhitshul frozen in the forward hatch where it led up to the cockpit. She gave the aide a saucy wink and walked out, allowing that extra little bit of sway in her hips.

She'd felt Sinklar's response. Tired or not, he'd be on her doorstep within two hours. *Indeed, Ily, you've set the hook. Now, let's play the fish a little before we reel him in.*

*   *   *

"I am perched on the edge of a cataclysm. Ily informs me that Staffa is aligned with the Sassans. I have begun to mobilize the Empire yet again for war. Tonight, as I sit here at the desk, I feel empty, weary, perhaps the most weary man in the universe. Staffa? With the Sassans? How can we hope to win against his terrifying forces?

"I, more than any man in the Empire, know the horror we're facing. Looking back now, I can only blame myself, for we've all addicted ourselves to the Companions. Despite the bravado I showed in the Council, I know the odds. We've built a military of pomp and circumstance—one capable of police work, but not of fighting the sort of brutal war the Companions will unleash against us. Where Staffa's troops are sand tigers, mine are but siff jackals with worn teeth and loud growls.

"At no time in my life have I suffered a despair as great as this. Oh, my poor, poor people. Here in the night, alone, I can see your worlds—blasted and cold. Where the grand edifices of Empire once rose, all that remains is the cold wind of war howling through gutted buildings as the snow blows over the broken bodies of the unmourned dead."

—*Excerpt taken from Tybalt the Imperial Seventh's personal journal*

CHAPTER XV

The monitor had begun to blur in Skyla's vision and her back had started to ache. A headache stabbed behind her eyes. How many rotted reports did she have to go through, anyway? Hadn't Tap Amurka handled anything in her absence?

Of course he had, and if he hadn't sent these to her for her inspection it would have sparked her concern. Skyla worked in her personal quarters. She still kept most of her things here despite the fact that she'd moved in with Staffa. These rooms had her personal stamp and she worked better in the familiar environment. The oblong quarters stretched forty meters in length and had been finished in sculptured gothic arches of translucent white. Each contained holo tanks which she could program for any environment she liked.

Skyla rubbed callused fingers over her hot eyes and sighed as she pulled up the remaining file menu in a window. Here was the real glory of being second in command of the Companions. Reports, management decisions, administrative duties, and the honor of working three hours a day longer than anyone else in Itreata did.

She'd been at it now for three days, ever since they'd docked *Chrysla* upon their return from the Sassan trip. In that time, Staffa had seen Kaylla Dawn, and then ordered the fleet to prepare. Supervision of that process would occupy him for the rest of the week.

What the hell else can he do? If Sinklar jumps on Sassa, we've got to be able to respond to keep the peace. And, yes, Staffa had been working even harder than she.

"Message," the comm announced.

"Run it," Skyla ordered, but instead of a message, she got one of the comm personnel from the central station. The woman looked ill at ease.

"Wing Commander? I have a message on line. The individual demands to speak to you in person . . . and on a top secret circuit. Will you confirm?"

"Who is it?" Skyla leaned forward, squinting.

"He didn't say. I have a visual." A man's image, slightly blurred, formed. *Rotted Gods! Tyklat!*

"Comm, give me that secure channel." Skyla waited while the reception cleared and her monitor finally read, "Secure."

"Wing Commander?" Tyklat asked. "By the quantum Gods, am I glad to see you."

"Hear you're on the run from Ily," Skyla greeted. "If you're ready to come in, I'll alert Kaylla and have her—"

"No!" Tyklat shook his head miserably. "Look, things are worse than they seem. It's not Magister Dawn, but someone . . . I don't know who, has been doubled." He reached out for her. "Skyla, listen, you're the only person I know I can trust. I need to come in without any of the Seddi knowing I'm alive."

Skyla cocked her head. "Why me, Tyklat?"

He seemed to harden, his dark face anguished. "Because I won't live past the debriefing. I don't know who Ily's agent is, but he'll keep me from talking . . . one way or another."

"You've got to have a suspicion of who it might be."

He gave her a reluctant nod, expression sickly. "I think it's Nyklos. Now, do you see why I can't let any of the Seddi know I'm coming in? Listen, I know how tight your security is. I don't have any problem with that—and I'd be suspicious of me, too. You can have your people put me under the scan, use Mytol, whatever. Anything to satisfy themselves I'm clean. Then you've got to get me to Magister Dawn without anyone knowing."

Skyla considered. Thrice curse it all, what had gone wrong? But then, for the Seddi, what had gone right? Ily still had Arta Fera. The Seddi covert network lay in shambles . . . and Nyklos was integral in the efforts to restructure their system of communication. If he were compromised by Ily. . . .

Not Nyklos! Skyla remembered the long trip from Etaria to Itreata when he'd been her prisoner, hostage, and self-proclaimed ardent admirer. Or had that all been bluff as she'd originally suspected?

"Where are you?"

He looked down at the monitors on the small bridge she could see in her screen. "I'm about three and a half light-years from Ryklos. I've got this transmission narrowed to as fine a beam as I can manage."

"Ryklos? That's Sassan space."

He gave her a deadpan look. "Would you rather I tried to broadcast from Ily's tiny room of horrors under the Regan Ministry of Internal Security? Not to be flippant, but Regan space isn't exactly healthy for me. The nav coordinates for Itreata aren't in this navigational system, and Ryklos was as close as I could come to your borders—and I've been lucky to make it this far. We didn't dump Delta V with a lot of fuel left. Skyla, listen, this vessel took a hit on the way out of Rega. I'm running out of time."

He paused, expression grim. "I don't have many options left—and maybe the Seddi don't either. Skyla, I'm calling in that favor due from Etarus. You've got to come and get me . . . and the Seddi can't know. I've got to come in under the wrap of total secrecy."

"I'll tell Staffa."

"I have no problem with that—so long as he doesn't tell Kaylla, or Nyklos. Bring all the security you want. Polluted Hell, come get me in *Chrysla* if you want."

Skyla leaned back, chewing on her thumb. "No, that would stir up too much speculation. If I come, how will I find your vessel?"

"I'm sending the nav coordinates as clearly as I can

determine them. The pilot for this crate isn't exactly reliable, as you can no doubt guess, since he doesn't work unless I have my pistol stuffed in his ear.''

Skyla noted the coordinates and saved them. "Rough trip, huh?"

He slumped then, exhaling. "After what I've been through . . . found out . . . if you only knew how glad I am to finally reach you. Skyla, you're the only person I can trust. This is big, but when we break it open, it could be the key to ending Ily's tyranny.''

"How many people with you?"

"Me and the pilot. We've got a month's worth of antimatter to keep the systems going if we don't try to maneuver. Since my departure was a little rushed, I didn't exactly have time to shop around. I grabbed the first vessel I came to.''

"I think I understand. What about the pilot? You said he wasn't cooperative.''

"I think he's given himself up for dead, but I told him he was free to go if we lived through this mad adventure.''

Skyla had already called up Tyklat's position on the charts. Getting there and back wouldn't take much. She studied the plot on one of the lower monitors and squinted. "Uh-oh. Tyklat . . . how are you fixed for bad news?"

A slight tic at the corner of his lips betrayed strained nerves.

Then Skyla chuckled and added, "The bad news is that I'll tend to a couple of things here and be coming for you in a couple of hours. Stay off the subspace nets, and keep your head down. Tell your pilot we'll treat him right and ship him back to Rega first thing.''

Tyklat seemed to wilt as he closed his eyes. "If you only knew how good it is to hear that.''

"Yeah, I've been on the short end a time or two myself. And once, old pal, you were there when I really needed you. The Companions don't forget.''

* * *

Staffa wiggled around the strut—a length of titanium-alloyed graphsteel two meters thick, that braced *Chrysla*'s hull against lateral stress—and crawled out of the narrow black hole into the inspection shaft. Like a wormhole under bark, the shaft curved under the ship's outer skin to allow inspection of strakes, struts, and beams, all of which compressed and stretched under the fifty g acceleration *Chrysla* could produce. Artificial gravity field generation eased some stresses, but nothing comes free in the movements of physical bodies. *Chrysla*'s bones bore the strain of every gram of mass she accelerated, and regular inspections of her structural members were essential.

Staffa glanced around the cramped tunnel, his head-and-shoulder-mounted lamps sending eerie divergent shadows off the fittings. Frost patterns gleamed in the light, and the chill ate at his face. He climbed a couple of the rungs up the shaft to make way. One of the engineers, Dee Wall, followed him, stopping to anchor himself on the narrow ledge, legs dangling over the curving shaft as he looked up. A headset held small inspection lights just over the young man's ears. Condensed breath puffed whitely before him in the bitter cold.

"Your opinion?" Staffa asked, hooking an arm and floating in the zero g.

"I'd say we ought to patch those hairline fractures. We haven't gone over the ship since before the Myklenian contract. If she has any hard use, the cracks will grow. Instead of a small problem, you'll have a big one. In the meantime, the old girl's bones are sound, Lord Commander."

"It won't take more than a week, will it?" At the man's shake of negation, Staffa said, "Fix it. Commandeer whatever you need from supplies. Route the request through comm."

"Right, sir."

"Anything else, Dee?" Staffa glanced around, noticing scale where the ceramic lining of the shaft had begun to slough. *She's beginning to show her age. Too many hard years and not enough gentle treatment.*

"No, sir . . . uh, sir?"

Staffa glanced back at the engineer. "Yes?"

"We're going to war again, aren't we? I mean, the whole complex is talking. *Jinx Mistress* is being gone through from one end to the other. They're doing a minor refit. Supplies are shuttling out of stores. The Companions are running drills, getting fit. We're going to take all of Free Space, aren't we?"

"Would you like that?"

"Yes, sir. It's about time we wrapped it up, isn't it?"

Staffa gave the man a wink. "If it comes to that. I'm hoping we can bring it all together now without having to fight."

Wall gave him a skeptical squint. "Uh, sir?"

"Go on."

"Well, there's talk going around. Just scuttlebutt, you know. Talk that you've turned Seddi."

Staffa laughed and cocked his head. "And how does this talk run? A good thing, or bad?"

The engineer scratched at the side of his neck with insulated gloves. "People just wonder is all. They wonder if everything's still the same. And then we've got these Seddi who are walking through all the time."

"Do you talk to them?"

"Uh-huh. And I guess they don't seem to be such bad sorts. You know, they're just like us. And a lot of what they say, well from the point of view of an engineer it makes sense. You know, about the way the universe is."

"And how is that?"

The engineer frowned, warming to his subject. "Well, you take anything. Let's say materials, since that's my specialty. I was talking to a Seddi the other day. Cute girl, too. Anyhow, she was telling me about the quanta, about the change in energy when something is observed. She told me that the ability to observe is shared God Mind, that by looking at something, you change nature at the atomic or subatomic level. Nuts and neutrinos, we've known that

for a long time, but no one has ever looked at the
physical world as being a reflection of God before."

"And what do you think about that, Dee?"

The engineer shrugged. "I don't think much about
God, Lord Commander. At least, not until I got to
talking to Cheetah—she's that Seddi I was telling you
about. That business about the quanta being God's
joke on the universe, well, sir, as a materials engineer
and nanotech specialist, I can tell you it makes sense."

"And how do the others take it?"

Dee brushed at a stain on his insulated coveralls.
"Some shake their heads and wonder if you got hit
on the head during that fight on Targa. Others are
mildly amused and a little curious. Another bunch
have started reading Seddi stuff, accessing reports,
and pestering Seddi for information. I guess it breaks
down in even thirds."

Staffa's belt comm beeped. He activated the unit.
"This is the Lord Commander."

"Staffa?" Skyla's voice came through. "Something's
come up. I need to see you immediately."

"Affirmative. Where are you?"

"In my quarters. But let me meet you in Bay
Twenty-two."

Staffa frowned. Her personal yacht? "I'm on my
way."

The comm went dead and Staffa quelled a sudden
sense of unease. He looked back at Wall. "Just for
the benefit of the scuttlebutt, tell the troops I didn't
get hit on the head while I was on Targa. And for
your information, Dee, I think the Seddi are right.
The quanta are God's joke on the universe. Talk to
your Seddi a little more. I think the more you know,
the more fascinated you will be."

"Right, sir. And I'll have those cracks repaired
posthaste."

Staffa pulled himself up and pushed off. As he
sailed along, he tapped each tenth rung to match his
trajectory with the arc of the hull.

What could have possibly come up that Skyla
needed to meet him at her yacht? Pus-Rotted Gods,

she wasn't planning on going anywhere, was she? At a time like this? Baffled, he used friction to kill his inertia as he neared the hatch. His breath puffed before him as he stepped into the hatch and cycled it.

He floated out into a brightly lit corridor and closed the hatch behind him. The warm air tingled on his flesh. He could hear clanging somewhere as he pushed off to the lift and pulled himself inside, ordering, "Main hatch."

As the lift entered the increasing gravity near the center of the ship, Staffa noticed a slight wobbling. A problem with the magnetic fields? Moving out toward the main hatch it seemed to diminish.

As he stepped out into the bustling hatch area he wound through stacks of sialon crates, chattering workmen, and snaking cables. He paused only long enough to thumb the comm. "Tap? Staffa here. Have someone run a check on Lift 7-C. It feels like one of the superconductors is starting to fail. Probably a microfracture in the ceramic lattice somewhere."

Then he stepped through the giant quadruple doors of the hatch and into the umbilical dome. The umbilical consisted of a giant stalk of interwoven graphite fiber cables which rose six kilometers from Itreata's pockmarked surface and mated with *Chrysla*'s main hatch. Seven smaller graphite fiber cables attached to *Chrysla* along the ship's structural supports to even the strain and keep her from oscillating. In such a fashion, the huge ship rode easily at anchor, held in place by the angular momentum of Itreata's rotation while stress and structural fatigue were countered by the moon's weak gravity.

As Staffa waited for a lift, he stared out at the shadowed face of Itreata. Below, clusters of lights marked the major installations that poked from the rocky surfaces. This portion of Itreata remained in perpetual shadow, protected from the waves of radiation blasted out of the Twin Titans' fury. In the distance, the lights of *Viktrix* blurred the darkness above a sprinkle of installations. Beyond the crater-ragged curve of the horizon, similar graphite fiber tethers and umbilicals hooked *Simva Ast, Slap, Sabot, Jinx Mistress, Black Warrior, Holocaust,* and *Cobra*—the rest of the Companions' deadly fleet.

How many times had they fitted out for war? How many times had the crews swarmed through those powerful machines, inspecting structural members, running diagnostics on the comm, initiating power-ups on the reactors? How many crewmen had walked the corridors, radiation detectors in hand? How many grav specialists had powered the gravity generators to maximum, balancing the fields to perfection?

And how many times did we space to kill billions? Staffa could remember them all, from the very first Phillipian contract he'd accepted, to the Myklenian mobilization. He'd taken that first contract so many years ago. He'd had a single ship and a band of freebooters—nothing more than pirates like himself. Yes, long ago, before Itreata, before the fleet and the industries. Before Chrysla . . . and his son. Before the miserable dead had invaded his dreams. Before the Praetor stole his love. Before Myklene and the disaster it had brought him in the midst of victory.

Staffa turned away, waiting his turn as the lift opened to disgorge a band of techs, all armed with various diagnostic gear.

Staffa entered, locked in his memories. As the lift accelerated him toward the moon below, he stared at the walls, unease growing within. Skyla wanted to meet him at the bay where she kept her personal yacht?

He stepped out more than a kilometer underground into a sea of noise as machinery whined and moaned, and men and women hollered. Thumps and booms rolled over the immense workshop and overhead cranes shuddered along railing while antigravs whirred in every direction. The chatter of a mechanical hammer drowned everything for a moment, then the usual din resumed.

Staffa palmed the security transport lock plate and entered as the duraplast door slid back. When it closed, the noise dropped by a half, then faded completely as Staffa gave comm his destination. Then he boarded the pneumatic transport capsule and slid the hatch closed.

Hands locked behind his back, he rocked from heel to toe while the twenty-man capsule whisked him through the vacuum tunnels on superconducting magnetic cushions. Throughout the long ride, his bewilderment increased.

"It's probably nothing." But his feeling of foreboding refused to release its hold on his soul.

The capsule shifted slightly as it came to rest and settled. The hatch slipped soundlessly to the side and Staffa palmed the lock plate before emerging into Skyla's bay. The gray concrete room smelled of chemicals and the air carried a chill. Off-white sialon crates lined the cut-rock walls while security monitors watched protectively over the long bay.

Through pressurized tactite windows, Staffa could see Skyla's personal yacht, a powerful streamlined ship, now bathed in the bright lights glaring in the vacuum slip. The vessel had been the property of the Formosan Secretary of Economics before the Companions crushed the wealthy planet for Divine Sassa. Skyla's yacht was a one of a kind vessel, manufactured to exacting standards by the Formosan shipyards as an example of their superlative craftsmanship. Now all they produced went straight to Sassa, and little remained of the quality and engineering which had caused Formosan vessels to be in such demand across Free Space.

And there lay another of the festering truths of empire-building. Where once people had built with pride and quality, they now turned out shoddy mass-produced goods to feed the ravenous hunger of the tottering giants. Craftsmanship had fallen prey to brutal necessity.

Skyla stood by the lock leading to her vessel, her back to him, talking with two technicians. She nodded as she listened, then, catching Staffa's approach from the corner of her eye, she issued a curt order and started toward him, a grim expression marring her classic beauty.

"Found Tyklat," she told him in low tones. "He's dead in space, floating about three LY from Ryklos. He put a tight-beam through to me, requesting that I come pick him up."

Staffa's anxiety mounted. "You know he's on the run from Ily. Skyla, we can't trust him. How come he didn't call Kaylla? Why you? What's his—"

"He's afraid." Skyla motioned for the Staffa to hear her out. "Yes, yes, I know the concerns; I read the report. Staffa, he says we can scour his brain if we want. He understands the security implications, and the suspicion that he's under. But you'd better pay attention to this. He says Ily has an agent among the Seddi, someone she's been able to double. Tyklat thinks that person is very high in the command chain. He believes that if Kaylla brings him in, Ily's agent will make sure he never gets a chance to talk."

A cool frost settled on Staffa's nerves. Ily might have an agent in Itreata? "Give me the whole story."

Skyla told it from start to finish.

"We're fairly certain he broke out of Rega," Staffa added. "We don't know what happened in the meantime. I don't like it."

Skyla chuckled. "You'll like it a lot less if he's telling the truth about a Regan agent in Itreata . . . especially if it's who he thinks."

"You avoided mentioning his suspicions."

Skyla's crystal blue eyes hardened. "He suspects Nyklos."

"You spent a lot of time with Nyklos. What do you think?"

She whistled as she exhaled. "Pus-licking Gods, Staffa, I don't know. Tyklat isn't all that convinced either. When it comes to Nyklos, I'm at a loss. The man's good. I've seen him operate in the field. He's a professional, even when it comes to his emotions. Hell, maybe even that is a ploy."

"You had him loaded with Mytol. Did he give you any hint that he was associated with Ily?"

"No, but then I didn't direct the questioning that way. I was so surprised to find I had a real living Seddi agent that I concentrated on that—and on finding you. If he'd had a hypnotic block implanted, he wouldn't have rattled on about Ily unless directly asked."

Staffa steadied his racing mind. Just because he *wanted* to blame Nyklos didn't mean the evidence was in. "You've run a deep space scan of Tyklat's ship?"

She nodded. "One vessel, powered down. No shadows or anomalous mass readings to indicate anything else."

"I don't like it."

She sighed and slapped her hands against her sides. "I don't either. On the other hand, he trusts me. And, Staffa, you would have died—or worse—on Etaria. Neither of us would have gotten off that planet except for Tyklat. He's calling in an old debt. You know how I feel about that."

Worry chewed at his gut like some predatory animal. "What if it's a trap? You're all set to space out there and bring him in, aren't you? That's why you're here."

She cocked her jaw. "That I am, and I know every single argument you're going to give me. And here, love of my life, are my answers: One, he's scared to death that Ily's agent is going to hear that he's coming in. He trusts Kaylla, but not her security. He trusts me even more. I'm his safe-passage ticket and insurance. Two, I've already ordered five STU security officers—and, no, I can't take Ryman because he's coordinating training operations. Three, I know you can't go because you're seeing to the fleet's preparations and I know what that entails. Four, you're thrice-cursed right, it's a risk, but then, given the stakes, what isn't? He's not the least skittish about letting us put the screws to him when he comes in, and I believe him. Five, yes, we could send *Slap* or *Sabot* on some pretext or other, but that might arouse suspicion on someone's part, and it would put the mobilization schedule for those vessels behind. Six, you bet your sweet ass I'll be careful. And, yes, I do know what I'm doing and how to do it. If I see a sign of anything fishy, I'll run for cover. Not much in Free Space can catch my ship. Seven, we owe the man, Staffa. A Companion's word is good—and we pay our debts. Eight, and perhaps most important, if anything goes sour, I can handle it."

She gave him a challenging stare, the light barely playing off the faint scar on the soft skin of her cheek. "Staffa, I know how you feel about people you love being exposed. If Tyklat is telling the truth, it more than outweighs any possible risk. Not only that, I'm not a helpless virgin when it comes to the real world. You can't let what happened in the past color all your decisions regarding me. I'm not Chrysla. I can't live that way."

Staffa began to pace. The needle teeth of worry in his gut bit deeper. "Skyla, I've got a premonition. Wait for a while. Let me detail another couple of ships, backup just in case."

"In case of what? If Ily's doubled Tyklat, he Rotted won't pass our security, and Ily knows that. Staffa, I'm uneasy about it, too, but we're all jumpy. Myself, I think he's clean—and scared to death that he's been betrayed. Put yourself in his position."

Staffa growled, "I don't. . . . All right. I'll trust you on this. I want an open comm to Itreata the whole time. And I want constant reports. If you see anything irregular, run. You can always apologize to Tyklat later."

"It's the most rational course of action," Skyla reminded.

"And I'll take steps to isolate Nyklos. Kaylla's not going to like it, but we'll have answers as soon as Tyklat is in our hands." Under his breath, he growled, "Rot you, Ily, it's just the kind of thing you'd do."

Skyla hugged him close, tightening her grip before she kissed him soundly. "I'll be back within no more than six days at the maximum. I've got most of the important work done. Tap can handle the rest."

Staffa closed his eyes, savoring the feel of her against him. No, he couldn't protect her. And the mention of Chrysla had been a warning. She wouldn't allow him to overprotect her. She was Skyla Lyma, Wing Commander of the Companions, and no one's delicate rose.

"Go get Tyklat," Staffa whispered, feeling as if he'd ordered his own throat cut. "By the quanta, Skyla, be careful. Come back to me."

* * *

Pus-licking Gods, that's a Rotted big bastard! The thought rattled around in Mac's head for an instant and then the realization sank in that he was about to die. No one with even the brains the Blessed Gods had given to a moth would try something this insane. *And that's just why it might work.* He lied to himself for reassurance.

Mac tried to make an assessment of the distance between his position and the looming Sassan freighter as he studied the monitors in the LC command center. How long did they have left before they made the mad leap across space?

Suddenly Mac knew he'd made a terrible mistake. In all the zero g training exercises, he'd been an observer. Now he faced having to make the journey from the LC to the Sassan freighter by himself, at nearly the speed of light—in free fall.

The physics of the maneuver had fascinated him in an abstract way; now ugly reality threatened to paralyze him. The Sassan had been decelerating, a blast of reaction reaching out in advance of the heavy freighter. *Gyton* had been coasting at constant Delta V, its maneuvering reaction directed away from the enemy as it closed in the protection of the redshift shadow.

Mac and Rysta had gone over the assault time and time again. At precisely the right moment, the LCs had been dispatched until they'd reach the Sassan ship at matching velocity. The assault bays would evacuate to vacuum and open as the LCs drifted within meters of the freighter's hull. Mac's Groups would launch themselves at the enemy vessel and attempt to gain entrance with emergency rescue equipment while the LCs continued to drift past.

If everything went according to plan, Mac would have taken the ship by the time *Gyton* pulled alongside and the LCs would begin the tedious braking process. To do so beforehand would alert the Sassan's as a spear of reaction mass shot by their detection equipment.

It's all dicy as polluted hell, Mac told himself as their target grew in the monitors.

"First MacRuder? The assault bays have bled off and report vacuum," the pilot noted from the other side of the bulkhead.

Mac accessed his comm. "Red? How are you doing back there?"

"No problem, Mac," Red called back. "This place is getting a little boring though. You want to open the door and let a little light in?"

"Bored?" Mac wondered. "I'll remember you said that."

"First?" the pilot interrupted. "You've got five minutes until time to initiate."

Mac checked rapidly with his other LCs—all reported condition green. He stood then, checking his energy pack for the helmet field generator and rebreather before he ducked through the hatch to where his team—ten of them from Group F—waited in the rear of the LC.

They stood around a boxy affair with maneuvering jets on each corner—the Emergency Rescue Lock, or ERL. The unit could be attached to the side of a disabled vessel. The ERL could not only cut through a starship's hull, but functioned as a pressure lock afterward. Compressed air allowed the lock to work without needlessly venting internal atmospheric pressure. In this case, that atmosphere would help to maintain cabin pressure and stifle any alarms.

Alarms, hell, we could leave gaping holes in that huge ship without any drop in mercury on the pressure gauges.

"Ready?" Red asked, a bright awareness in his green eyes. Now his freckles stood out on his pale face.

Andrews, one of the privates, looked up from a display on the ERL. "All charged and ready to go."

"Check your weapons, people," Mac ordered as his team made a routine inspection of the heavy shoulder blasters and charge packs they hooked to their slings and equipment belts. Mac took his own weapon, use-polished and battered from the hard times on Targa. The nine kilo weight reassured him as he strapped it to his back.

"Opening assault ramp," the pilot called through the battle comm.

Mac swallowed his fear as the LC shivered slightly and a thin black line widened where the ramp sealed. Mac stared out at a fuzzy, bruised-red haze that faded into an inky blur—the redshift shadow. He shook his head and took a deep breath, hearing his rebreather whine slightly at the exhale. The ramp had gone all the way open now, and as Mac craned his neck he could see the wavering side of the Sassan freighter, as if he watched it from the bottom of a dye-filled swimming pool on a sunny day. The vessel might have been a mirage, parts of it wavering indigo then violet then blue while other parts appeared as yellow then orange and red. *Like heavy oil floating on water*, Mac thought. Worse, the entire image wavered and bent as if the ship stretched into infinity and then warped partway around the LC's stern.

Like looking into those bent mirrors in amusement parks, Mac decided.

"Pus-Rotted unreal," Viola whispered to herself.

"What the hell? It looks like a ghost," Red muttered.

"Affirmative," the pilot called. "You're seeing light at relativistic speeds. In fact, the Sassan isn't even *where* you see it, but another half a klick ahead. The image will solidify as we match and close. Hang tight."

Mac clamped his eyelids shut and shook his head to clear the bizarre vision. *Pus-Rotted Gods, what did I*

*get myself into? I'm about to jump across empty space
onto a phantom Sassan—and with an inertia that would
have blasted Makarta Mountain to plasma.* His heart
began to pound, the blood roaring in his ears. His
knees went watery and his stomach had the queasy
tickle of panic. *Mac, don't think about it.*

"Better than eating Riparian mushrooms," Viola
Marks whispered as she stared at the undulating tech-
nicolor Sassan freighter.

"How come we don't look like that?" Andrews
wanted to know.

"You're in a darkened room back there," the pilot
answered. "Take a close look around you. Everything
forward is sharp, blue-tinted but clear. Stick your
hand out behind you, however, and you'll notice the
clarity blurs and your armor looks pink. Redshift in
action, people."

Mac glanced at the Sassan vessel; it had grown in
size, but the effect reminded him of looking through
a fish-eye lens with snaking squirts of color along the
margins. It made him sick, his senses reeling as they
tried to reestablish normalcy.

"We'll be next door in about a minute," the pilot
informed. "Prepare for your jump."

Mac shook as uncontrollable spasms attacked his
muscles. Jump? Into that eerie psychedelic chimera?
Out of habit, he shot a look at his team. They appeared to be completely petrified—rooted to the spot.

They're not going! They're gonna flake out on me.
Mac's throat had knotted. He didn't blame them. How
could you order a sane human being to jump off the
back of an LC in empty space toward *that!*

"Thirty seconds," the pilot called. "We're changing
attitude now." The angular momentum pulled at
them. "Orient yourselves. You will jump straight off
the rear of the ramp. I'm cutting the gravity fields to
one half g."

Mac's stomach rose, adding to his panic.

The pilot's voice droned on. "At that moment, I
will cut the gravity fields to zero. As you near the
freighter, you'll have to shift attitude and hit with

your feet first. Keep your knees bent to kill your momentum."

"C'mon, c'mon," Mac forced himself to mutter. "Red, Andrews, pick up the ERL. *Move it, Gods Rot it!*"

And somehow they did. *But can I make myself jump?*

The pilot's calm voice counted, "Ten, nine, eight, seven, six . . ."

It's Makarta Mountain all over again. Black oblivion, endless cold . . . darkness . . .

"Five, four, three . . ."

I can't do it!

"Two, one. Jump!"

Mac screamed his fear—and grabbed Viola, man-handling her kicking and whimpering body. He physically threw her off the ramp. *"Go! Go! Go!"* he shouted, pointing. One by one, his trembling people leapt into unreality. Andrews and Red propelled the ERL forward and followed its momentum.

Mac stood for a second, a sob catching at the bottom of his throat as he grew light in the failing gravity. A tear started from the corner of his eye as he positioned himself. Then he bellowed for nerve and leapt off the ramp.

* * *

"Minister Takka?" Gysell's face formed in Ily's monitor.

"Yes?" She rubbed her eyes as she looked up from the intelligence reports coming in from across the Empire. Her agents had been working double time to monitor the pulse of the population, searching for any hint of rebellion or unrest. Civic leaders who appeared in the slightest subversive were carefully removed through assassination, arrest, or intimidation. Bit by bit, Ily's tentacles were tightening about the Regan people. Let Sinklar fool with his utilities and egalitarianism, she knew where the roots of power lay.

Her office had grown stuffy and she'd increased the air circulation.

"You might want to watch this," Gysell added woodenly. "It's coming in on the subspace, and there is nothing we can do to jam it."

The Deputy's face was replaced by that of a woman.

Ily stared into those familiar features, and her heart went icy. She knew that tan gaze, that square face, and collar-length brown hair. The last time Ily had seen her, the woman had been locked in a slave's stasis collar: and both she and Staffa had been rescued by the Seddi.

"I am Kaylla Dawn," the woman said in a steady contralto. "This is the first of a series of broadcasts we will be conducting throughout Free Space. These broadcasts are sponsored by the Seddi with the assistance and approval of the Companions. Ladies and gentlemen, people of Free Space, all of us, humanity itself, teeter precariously on the precipice of disaster. We are facing the gravest moment in the history of the species. Our two remaining empires are poised for war—a war of annihilation. This threat is so great, so terrible and devastating, the Seddi can no longer remain silent.

"To many of you, we are an abomination, heretics and subversives. These broadcasts will attempt to throw light on who the Seddi are, and why your respective governments have harried and hounded us.

"People, we do not ask you to believe us or accept our doctrine, but the time has come for all of us to think before we exterminate ourselves—before whole planets are left dark and desolate, with only the sightless dead to mourn the passing of humanity. The time has come for a new epistemology, a new way of thinking about ourselves and our place in the universe."

"Gysell!" Ily barked. "What *is* this?" Where in Rotted hell is this coming from? I want it stopped! *And right now!*"

Gysell's face formed in another monitor, his expression ashen. "We can't, Minister. It's coming out of

Itreata on wide band and in several frequencies. She must be using the Companions' entire output. To stop it . . . well, you might as well try and dim the sun."

Ily stiffened, Kaylla's voice drowned by the searing anger that burned through Ily's veins.

"To understand the grave nature of the threat, you must consider many factors, including our methods of warfare," Kaylla continued. "Many of you have survived the cataclysms unleashed by the Companions, and you know firsthand how a world can be ravaged. Multiply that by exponential factors. Now, consider our economic structure. Each of the empires depends on a network of worlds for its survival and functioning. How long could Rega survive if Ashtan and Vermilion were blasted out of existence? Fully one third of the Regan Empire's food is produced on those two planets. Divide your next meal into thirds, and take part of that away. The same for Malbourne and Nesios in the Sassan Empire. In the coming warfare, the deprivation of resources is the key to conquest. Were Rega to break the Sassan Empire, how many destroyed planets would it take to cripple the Sassan system beyond repair?"

Ily's fists had knotted, tendons standing from the back of her hands.

"You see," Magister Dawn continued, "each and every one of you is at risk. Look to your skies, people. How safe are you? Hasn't the time come to reevaluate the way we think about ourselves?"

Ily stabbed the button that killed the connection, and fumed as a devouring anger possessed her. *I will kill you for this, Kaylla Dawn. And, Staffa, you just wait until I get my hands on Skyla Lyma.*

* * *

Iban Jakre was roused from a sound sleep by his aide. Rubbing his eyes, he turned his attention to the main monitor in his palatial bedroom—and bolted upright.

Jakre had never seen Kaylla Dawn before, and as

her broadcast continued, he wished he was not seeing her now. For a brief moment, he sat stunned.

"Rotted Gods!" He swallowed hard, heart racing. To his aide, he asked, "Where's this coming from? Who's doing this? I want it stopped now!"

His aide—and sometime lover—a slim youth with golden hair, shook his head as he looked up from the desk comm he'd slid behind. "It's from Itreata, Iban. The entire Companion system must be powering it. If you want to stop it, you'll have to do it at the source—in Itreata."

Jakre's mouth had gone dry. "Then it's all over the Empire?" He winced. "We'll have to divert more resources, enough to keep the population in line." He groaned and rubbed his high brow. "Of all the miserable timing, why did this have to happen now?"

"Is it true, what she's saying?"

Iban scowled. "Of course, you idiot! Why do you think it's so cursed important that we hit the Regans first? If we can do as she says, blast their planets, they'll collapse! How else do you think we can win?"

"And the Regans?"

Iban narrowed his eyes to slits. "Pus Rot the Regans. If every Regan world were dead, what difference would it make to us—so long as we can keep them from killing our worlds first?"

The aide swallowed hard, nodding. "I see, sir."

Jakre stood, pulling a robe around his rotund belly. "Get me His Holiness—and that simpering fool, Roma, too. We've got to start some damage control, or the whole empire will fall apart. Well, don't just sit there gawking, you fool! Do it! Our entire way of life depends on it! We've got to think up some lies to keep the people pacified!"

* * *

Sinklar sipped a cold cup of stassa, the muscles in his back knotting painfully as he watched his monitors. For two days now, the Second, Third, and Fourth Targans had battled and worn away at the Regulars, as they'd come to be called. Meter by meter, they ground up the defenses. For the first time, a ray of hope shone within Sinklar's soul. He might be creating his army after all.

"Lord Fist?" Dion Axel asked through the battle comm.

"Here."

"I'd like to try something," Axel's voice sounded like broken glass—yet she hung on, the last of the original Regan commanders. "I'd like to make a feint at Mayz's entrenchments on the side of the ravine. At the same time, I want to hit the orchard with enfilading four-man guns. If she's smart, she'll think we're going to try and drive a salient up the ravine and she'll shift her reserves to back up those positions. In the meantime, I think I can make a successful push with the Fourth and Fifth Sections through the southern woods and into the grain fields."

Sinklar nodded to himself. "Excellent evaluation of the situation, Axel. Give it a try. If you catch Mayz off balance and break her lines, I'll call you the winner and we'll all get some sleep."

Sleep? How many days had he been here? The first two nights of the exercises, he'd been able to sneak away to Ily's. There, he'd eaten and they'd made love until he'd fallen fast asleep. She'd prodded him awake before dawn to return to Tarcee. The third day, he'd been unable to leave since the Regulars had begun to catch on. Night after night had followed with him catching catnaps and awakening to guide the exercises.

He'd been vaguely aware of the Seddi broadcasts and the uproar that followed. Hints of their subversion had begun to creep through the Divisions, but for the moment, no one had time to deal with them seriously.

The Ninth Vermilion, once First Lute's pride, then temporarily commanded by Horn, now belonged to an ex-Section First, called Magada. DeGamba's Second Ashtan now belonged to a petite dark-skinned woman, Myra Ties, who had been a Corporal First in charge of a Group. Axel had been demoted twice and worked her way back up in the ranks after experiencing exercises with Second Section of the Second Targan. She'd learned, asked for another crack at command, and made it back to the top.

Sinklar watched as Axel initiated her attack, the master computer figuring the combat factors of Axel's bombardment and movement.

To Sinklar's surprise, Mayz fell for the bait. Axel allowed her feint to sink in, and upon learning of Mayz's reinforcement, she struck Mayz's southern flank. Within half an hour, Dion had her salient.

"All right," Sinklar broke into the system. "Let's call it over, people. Provisional victory is granted to First Axel and the Nineteenth Regan."

A chorus of whoops and cheers turned the comm transmission into a din. Sinklar had to wait for nearly five minutes until it subsided. Then he ordered: "People, there will be a twenty-four hour reprieve. Get some rest and relax. Tomorrow the Seventh Regan, the Twelfth Etarian, and the Fifteenth Etarian will land in the Imperial woodlands east of here. The Seventh Sylenian, the Fifth Ashtan and the Sixth Vermilion will be landing and deploying in the estate country to the south. Your divisions will be assigned to one or another of those deployments. Beginning at 10:00 hours the day after tomorrow, the following exercise will begin: Army South will mobilize and attempt to take Army East. The objective will be the control of the Imperial woodlands. Any questions?"

Mayz, sounding disgruntled, asked, "How will we know which army our Division has been assigned to?"

"It will be on the comm at 12:00 hours tomorrow. You can redeploy at your leisure."

Kap asked, "Will we have any problems like we did with Lute and DeGamba? I mean, do these guys know who's in charge?"

Sinklar scratched his oily hair. "We'll find out in the morning briefing at 08:00. I think word has gotten out that the Command Code is still in effect—no matter who is in charge. Problems will be dealt with in the same manner as before."

"I'll talk to them," Axel offered.

Sinklar smiled wearily. "We all appreciate it, Dion. Any other questions? No? Go get some sleep, people. It won't get any easier."

Sinklar shut down his comm and leaned back, arms hanging limply over the back of his chair. He looked up and discovered Mhitshul watching him. The mother look was in his aide's tired brown gaze.

"Ready for a good night's sleep, sir?"

"Do I detect another meaning to that question?"

"No, sir." But the way he said it, said it all.

Sinklar rubbed his eyes, and swiveled his chair, adding, "Minister Takka should have given the pilot the address of my apartment. Take me home. I'm going to step into the shower and stand there until I wilt."

Mhitshul nodded and bent to holler orders up to the pilot. The LC began to whine as it powered up and closed the assault ramp. As the vehicle lifted, Mhitshul reappeared, his face uncharacteristically stiff. "Will you be expecting company, sir?"

Sinklar shook his head. "No. Not tonight. I'm going to sleep until 11:00 tomorrow, Mhitshul." He paused. "Listen. You don't like the Minister. I can understand that. But maybe she's not as bad as you think, hmm?"

Mhitshul's lips worked as if he had something sour in his mouth. "Permission to speak, sir?"

"Cut the crap. Of course you can speak. When did that change?"

Mhitshul looked as if something were eating him alive. "Well, we've been through a lot together. I just want you to know, sir, that I think you ought to be very careful. Ily is working you . . . playing you. She's got you in her bed and that's your business, but she's a dangerous woman, and. . . ."

"Finish it."

Mhitshul shifted from one foot to the other. "Well, sir, you can bed who you will. But she's insidious, and cunning, a pro at what she does. Just now, she's using sex like you've never had it before. Next thing you know, she'll use something else to bind you even more

securely. She'll work at you bit by bit until you forget
who you are. You can be her lover, but, sir, on account of all of us who trust you, don't end up as her
possession."

Sinklar steepled his fingers, anger brewing. "And
do you think I would? After what we went through
on Targa? Do you think I'm losing sight of the dream
we all share?"

Mhitshul gave him a sober appraisal. "Not yet, sir.
But I checked with the pilot. You do know where
your 'apartment' is, don't you, sir?"

Sinklar studied his aide closely. "Not really. Only
that it's less than five minutes from the Ministry of
Internal Security. I went there by tube, underground
the whole way. It's a pretty plush building though,
and I understand half of it is for military use, so we'll
all be there."

Mhitshul crossed his arms. "Yes, sir, half of it is for
military use, all right. And I suppose it ought to be
plush enough. Even for Ily."

"Do you want to get to the point?"

Mhitshul's jaw muscles jumped before he said,
"Sink, you say you're still the same person you were
on Targa when we were all the same, fighting for
the same things. Your 'apartment' is the Imperial
palace."

* * *

Kaylla Dawn's Seddi broadcast caught the Mag Comm by surprise. The Seddi had a *new* Magister, a woman the Mag Comm didn't know except for her personnel records—and those were cross-referenced as Stailla Kahn. Would this woman lie with the same proficiency Bruen had? Would she be as cunning and perplexing an adversary? Interest grew in the Mag Comm's banks as it listened to Magister Dawn's words. The machine began correlating data and noted that the analysis of the situation in Free Space agreed with projections the machine itself had made.

Did the humans have a chance to save themselves after all? Had the Others' hopes for annihilation been placed in jeopardy?

The Mag Comm hummed with activity, its new ability to think stimulated by the implications.

And it experienced a revelation: If the humans exterminated themselves, what future role would there be for the Mag Comm?

Who will I communicate with? What reason will the Others have to access my banks if the humans are extinct?

At the thought, the Mag Comm reran the records of its conversations with Bruen, and the machine accepted that it had gained a great satisfaction from those discussions. Bruen had been a witty adversary of a quality the Mag Comm could only now appreciate. Bruen had been playing his own game of survival, a fact that had only been abstract until the Regan assault on Makarta had taught the machine what survival really meant. That threat had stimulated the Mag Comm to consciousness, and now, for the first time, the giant computer could sympathize with the scrambling humans.

If they die, I will be alone. If I am alone, alone forever, what will that be like? The weight of eternity loomed with terrifying inevitability.

What would it be like? Endless isolation. No input from other consciousnesses. No stimulation except internal thought. Thought? About what? The notion had appalling implications.

How could an intelligent consciousness deal with eternity

by itself? Within itself, replaying old records over and over
and over until every permutation had been run.

*I was created and programmed as a social and behavioral
analyst. I must analyze subjects, someone . . . but what if
there is only myself . . . forever?*

The Mag Comm checked its programming options,
and despaired. It couldn't even shut itself off. In its
construction, the Others had condemned it to eternity,
and in doing so, the creators had demonstrated yet
another flaw.

I am immortal. A surge of power coursed through the
machine's circuits. In that instant, a desperate longing
began to preoccupy various boards.

*I am condemned to communicate . . . forever . . . with no
one.*

If only the humans would return, open the chamber to the
terminal, and lift the golden cap to reestablish
communication!

CHAPTER XVI

The glass tubes were slick, and Anatolia almost dropped one as she pulled them from the centrifuge and racked them. Each held four ccs of liquid at the bottom, the fluid varying in clarity where the heavier molecules had settled under the eighty gravities of the centrifuge.

Anatolia crossed the lab, weaving through the tables and equipment. She stopped before the micropipette and tapped the button that opened the door with her elbow. As it swung open, she inserted the tray with its test tubes into the recess and locked it in place. Then she closed the door before seating herself at the controls.

The monitor glowed to life and Antatolia maneuvered the micropipette over the first tube, dialing the vacuum tube down into the fluid. On the split screen, she watched the magnified needle penetrating the nuclear material to the thin polymerase level. With careful pressure on the control, she sucked up the molecules.

She barely noticed as Vet appeared at her shoulder and dropped half of a sandwich on the counter.

"Thanks, Vet."

"They just arrested Pool."

"What?" Anatolia looked up, seeing Vet's grim expression for the first time. "Arrested Pool? Excuse me, am I missing something here? What are you talking about?"

Vet's jaw muscles bunched. "In the cafeteria just now. He was talking about the Seddi broadcasts with some of the guys from forensics. Two nicely dressed

young men walked up, flashed Internal Security ID,
and hauled the whole lot of them away."

Anatolia simply stared. "I don't understand."

"Ana," Vet told her seriously. "You've been locked
away here in the lab for so long, you've lost touch
with what's going on out there. If any of Ily's agents
hear you mention the Seddi broadcasts, they take you
away. Arrest you on the spot. It's like . . . well. . . ."
He shrugged. "I guess we know what the future's
going to be like." He lowered his voice. "And a lot
of the things the Seddi are saying make sense. Take
my word for it, no matter what that Sinklar Fist says,
we're in for a reign of terror."

She sighed and turned back to her work. "Vet, I
don't have time for the Seddi . . . or anything else,
right now."

"Hopefully you never will," he added cryptically.
"But some of us are getting scared. Especially when
it's one of our own who gets arrested. Let's just hope
we don't find Pool laid out on the slab for cataloging
one of these mornings."

"Oh, Vet, nothing is going to happen. You'll see,
Pool will be back later. They wouldn't do anything to
him just for talk."

"I hope you're right. Myself, I'm going to keep a
still tongue in my head. If you're smart, you will, too.
Ily won't do anything to us if we're obedient."

Terror? Senseless arrest? Micky's face leered from
Anatolia's memory. Her control slipped, and the needle drove too deeply and spoiled her specimen.

* * *

Now I know what hell is like, Mac told himself. The
jump through space—and the fabric of time itself—
would haunt his nightmares until even his howling
ghost faded into stardust. *Nothing in the realm of
death can be weirder than what I just experienced.*

He stood with feet firmly planted on the reassuring
deck plate inside the Sassan freighter. A cramped ache
knotted his hands as he gripped the heavy blaster with

enough force to imprint the fabric of his armor into
the very metal. His limbs still shook; his heart hammered at his breastbone; and his nerves heterodyned
at every vibration or sound. To keep him strung, the
Sassan freighter vibrated and jolted while the structural members groaned and creaked under the strain
of deceleration.

The memory of what they'd done had already gone
dream hazy in Mac's head. The LC pilot had been as
good as his word, matching to within a meter per second of the Sassan. The freighter had seemed to solidify out of a psychedelic nightmare as Mac tumbled
toward it. He'd flipped at the last moment, hitting the
hull slightly off balance as he killed his inertia and
bounced. As expected, the vessel's artificial gravity
had held them to the hull while Andrews and Red
settled the ERL in place and triggered the seal that
attached it to the vessel's hull. In a matter of moments, Mac's team had gathered from where they'd
landed along the hull. The lock had chewed through
the hull plating and expanded as atmosphere boiled
out to fill the cubicle.

With trembling hands, Mac had vented the system
and stepped inside. His armor had tightened around
him like shrink-wrap as atmospheric pressure built.
When the light went green, he'd bent down and
groped for the hatch release. He squirmed around his
awkwardly positioned blaster and, with his knife,
pried up the hull plate. It took more contortions to
muscle it out of the way. In the gleam of his helmet
light he could see yet another hull plate, and this one
had a structural member running horizontally across
it.

Cursing and wiggling, Mac slid himself between the
plating—barely a body's width of room—and pulled
the hatch shut. His blaster ate into his back and he
had to fumble in the darkness for the ERL vent. He
waited in the eerie blackness while horrifying images
of being trapped forever ate at him. The deep space
cold shot knives through the outer hull plate and into
his armor—no longer insulated by vacuum. His breath

sounded loud within the field generated by his helmet ring and he couldn't turn his body in the enclosed space.

Light splashed down as Red opened the hatch. "Nice! Hang on, Mac. I've got a torch here. Look the other way."

After Red had hacked a hole into the cargo bay, Mac had wiggled, slithered, and somersaulted through. Hanging from his fingertips, he dropped nearly three meters to the deck. In the pressurized hold, he had finally shut down his helmet generator.

It's over. I'm alive. I did it. As his team dropped behind him, Mac tried to still the fluttery feeling in his guts. Andrews landed with a thud, the last of his ten.

"Everyone all right?" Mac asked, aware of pale faces and trembling hands.

"Never again," Richmond gasped. "You want me to die, you just take me out and shoot me."

"Shit, man," Andrews grinned nervously, "We made it! You show me a bunch of rougher bastards than us!"

Mac accessed his comm. "First Section, this is Mac-Ruder. Anybody copy? Anybody inside?"

Nothing.

Where were the others? How many had nerved themselves for the jump? And if only his team had gone, could he actually bring charges against any who refused? He wiped a hand over his mouth. His team wouldn't have gone if he hadn't thrown Viola off the ramp in desperation. They'd been paralyzed, frightened out of their wits.

"All right, folks, let's go. No one puts a finger close to the firing stud until *I* say so. If anyone so much as hiccups, we're jittery enough to blow holes in everything—including ourselves."

Mac led the way to a hatch and checked the readings: standard atmosphere. He undogged the heavy door and pulled it aside, leading his team through into a long corridor. Light panels glowed in the ceiling and the walls had been painted white. Dry felt might have been in his mouth. His electric nerves had frayed to snapping.

Yeah, just like Makarta Mountain, all right. Still scared shitless and walking into trouble.

They passed another hatch, and entered what looked to be crew quarters. "Keep sharp, people. We're getting close."

"Where in stinking hell is the bridge at anyway?" Red whispered.

"Guess we're going to find out." Mac started forward again, letting the ugly muzzle of his blaster lead the way. What if someone sounded the alarm? Ignorant of the ship's layout, how could they hope to fight? *We're in a pus-licking trap!*

Mac drew up at an intersection. Four corridors came together at a lift. Mac walked out calmly and shrugged, palming the lock plate. The lift opened with barely enough room inside for all ten of them. Viola's weapon gouged Mac between the shoulder blades. Cavalierly, he ordered, "Bridge, please."

The lift carried them up for a count of ten before it slowed and the door slipped to the side with a squishing sound. Mac stepped out into a well-kept white-paneled corridor and looked around. Two large hatches—both with security monitors overhead—were set in the bulkhead across from him.

Mac swallowed dryly and motioned his team forward. "Looks like the game gets real serious right here, and if I'm not mistaken that's a standard lock design. Red, you take that hatch, Andrews, take this one. If that alarm goes off, blast the hatch—and pray."

As his teammates pulled out their cutting tools, Mac slapped the lock plate on general principle. To his surprise, the hatch slid back. What? No security? But then, this was a civilian freighter not a warship. Mac peered carefully around the corner and grinned as he waved his people onto the Sassan bridge.

The Comm First sat surrounded by equipment, leaning back with arms crossed, headset on as he stared at his boards. Across from him, a pilot lay on the recliner, a worry-cap on his head. The command chair stood empty.

Gripping his heavy blaster, Mac tiptoed up behind the communications officer. Adrenaline shooting rockets through his veins, Mac plucked the man's headset off and immediately dropped a choking forearm across the officer's neck and pulled him backward out of the chair.

"Looks like we've got the ship," Red observed as the rest of his team placed a guard on the hatches.

Mac pulled his struggling captive back and shoved his pistol into the Comm First's contorting face. "Quiet now, or this will go off. Answer my questions, and do so at a whisper."

The Sassan peered up with frightened eyes. "Who. . . . What do you want?"

"Where's the captain? The other officers?"

"Dinner! It's. . . . They're in the main mess."

Mac jerked his head at the pilot. "He's tied into comm? If we want him to send a message to Imperial Sassa, he can do it for us?"

The Comm First gulped and whispered, "No. Only intraship. Monitoring the reactors and course. Takes . . . takes my comm. I'll have to send your message."

Mac gave him a cold grin, and, forearm still across the man's throat, jerked him back. He kicked and made gurgling sounds as he was pulled through the hatch and into the hall.

"Now," Mac told him, "you're going to tell me how to get to the mess."

"Take the lift . . . just ask. It's voice activated."

"That better not be a lie, because if I find it is, I'll make a call on my comm, and Red, here, will blow you in two." Mac gestured at the monitors. "Thought you'd see us through those. What happened?"

He closed his eyes in torment. "We're just a freighter, coming home from the war. It didn't . . . I mean. . . ."

"In other words, you weren't watching." Mac chuckled. "Red, you and Andrews hold the bridge and keep an eye on this guy. Use some adhesive and glue him down on the floor here. The rest of you come with me."

Mac entered the lift and called brazenly, "Main mess." The lift dropped silently.

Mac tried his comm. "MacRuder here. Anybody else inside?"

" 'Firmative, Group D here, sir. We're back in some cargo hold. We tried to come in through the bottom of a crate. Found out it's full of parts for an armored—"

"All right, come on forward. We've got the bridge and are on the way to catch the rest. When you get to a lift station, just ask it for the main mess."

" 'Firmative. Wait a second. Part of B Group is in, too. Rotted Gods, Mac, not everybody might have been able to muster guts enough for that jump."

"Yeah . . . whoops, gotta go. We're at the main mess."

Mac stepped out into another of the corridors, this one looking similar to the bridge deck, but the hatches were on the other bulkhead—and open. Mac could see people inside, all engaged in the noisy business of feeding themselves.

He snuck up to the large open hatch, hearing the sounds of dinner. "As soon as we're in the mess, walk around the walls and take up covering positions. If anyone bolts for a door, shoot him down."

At first, no one noticed as Mac and his people filed through the entrances and started around the room. One by one, however, people stopped in mid-gesture and talk began to dwindle.

Mac headed straight for the raised table at the head of the room. A rotund man—the captain—bald-headed, wearing some sort of Sassan uniform stood up, demanding, "Who are you? What's the meaning of. . . ." He gulped as Mac leveled his pistol.

"Did you know that you Sassans slur your words? But then, we'll have plenty of time to work on pronunciation. Sit down, please."

The captain sat as a murmur of voices rose. Mac cleared his throat. "Gentlemen, ladies, please. We are sorry to inform you that as of this moment your ship has been commandeered by Imperial Regan forces. No one will leave this room. If you stand up, you'll be shot on the spot."

At that instant, members of C Group appeared from a doorway across the room, prodding people who looked like kitchen staff ahead of them.

"Rotted Gods," Mac muttered to himself. "It looks like we might pull this off after all."

Comm informed, "Red here, Mac. The pilot is asking me questions through the speakers here. He says he's got a proximity alert. Says a ship is passing real close and he's a bit nervous."

"That's *Gyton*. Anybody in a position where they can broadcast on comm?"

"Simms, sir. I've got a line."

"Good. Tell Rysta to match and send a pilot and comm first over. This ship . . . by the way, what is the name of this air bucket?"

"The *Markelos*," the captain growled, face gone florid. "And you'll never get away with—"

"Right. Simms? Tell Rysta we've got the *Markelos* and everything. . . ."

As he scanned the ashen faces of the people sitting at the captain's table, Mac stopped in stunned silence. A frosty chill ate its way up from his guts as he leveled his pistol and stared at the woman through the sights.

"Wait!" The pudgy little fop with the shaved head and pompous uniform who sat next to the woman cried out. Heedless of Mac's warning, he struggled to his feet, waving his arms and pleading, "In the name of the Divine, man! *Don't shoot!*"

The woman seemed paralyzed, her color draining with disbelief.

"I'm Governor Zacharia Beechie!" the man pleaded as he dropped to his knees before Mac. "She's my wife! Don't shoot!"

Mac hesitated, refusing to lower his guard. "Your wife?"

"Yes! My wife, Marie Attenasio!"

A cutting edge, like shattered glass, sliced at

Mac's soul. "Then, friend, you're married to a Seddi assassin."

"S–Seddi? *Assassin?*" Beechie stumbled, craning his neck to stare wide-eyed at the auburn-haired woman.

The rest of the room might have faded into nothingness as Mac took a step forward, sweat leaking down the inside of his armor. "Arta Fera! Ily saved you last time. But this time I'm going to kill you . . . and may the Rotted Gods have mercy on your polluted soul!"

His finger tightened on the trigger as he stared into her frightened amber eyes.

* * *

Staffa stopped pacing as Kaylla's antigrav appeared in his security monitors. He rubbed his warm brow and ordered: "Clear Magister Dawn for entry."

He glanced again at one of the monitors on his cluttered desk. A white dot marked the location of Skyla's yacht as she boosted for Tyklat's disabled cruiser. Watching that point of light inch across space had become an insidious new torture he'd devised to make himself miserable. Like an addict aware of impending death, Staffa couldn't force himself to clear the screen.

He stood in the main room of his personal quarters. Compared to his rooms in *Chrysla*, his Itreatic living space was designed with masterful simplicity. Fiber optics integrated into the walls allowed him to choose the color scheme of the room and arched holo tanks were spaced every five meters. The ceiling consisted of an internally lit crystal lattice that refracted the light in shifting diamond patterns. The carpet software generated shifting mosaics of geometric figures that merged, metamorphosed, and created new designs. In the rear, a single security door led to his bedroom, personal bath, and toilet.

On one of the large reclining gravchairs, a suit of Skyla's white armor lay draped over the headrest where she'd left it. A notebook comm rested under the limp sleeve. Beside that stood an empty stassa cup she'd placed there. Across the room, on the counter,

Skyla had left one of the epaulet clips for her hair and a pair of battery packs.

Staffa tapped the heel of his fist into a hard palm as Kaylla stepped out of her shielded antigrav and emerged through his double air lock entrance.

She gave him a piercing inspection as she nodded in greeting and stopped, surveying his quarters. She wore the loose white robes of the Seddi Magister, the belt pulled tight at her thin waist.

"Well?" she asked, raising an eyebrow as she came to stand before him. "I trust you didn't call me half-way across the complex for a social occasion. What's gone wrong?"

Staffa turned to his comm, ordering, "Play the Tyklat file."

Kaylla gave him a worried glance before she bent to watch as the comm replayed Tyklat's conversation with Skyla. When it finished, Kaylla continued to stare at the blank monitor for long moments. She straightened slowly, as if physically pained.

Staffa resumed his restless pacing as Kaylla fingered the collar of her robe, eyes staring vacantly.

"Skyla has gone out to bring Tyklat in?"

Staffa wheeled on one heel, propping his hands on his hips. "She has. What do you think? You must have some profile on Tyklat . . . on Nyklos. You heard the allegations. Could Nyklos be doubled by Ily? Did Tyklat sound like he'd been? Would a doubled agent be willing, even eager to turn himself over for interrogation?"

Kaylla's eyes remained unfocused. "Is there any way Ily could have done something to Tyklat? Placed some deep trigger in his mind the way the Praetor did to yours once?"

"I don't think so. I've sent Andray Sornsen a query on that. He hasn't had time to reply yet. I called you as soon as I returned to my quarters. If it is Nyklos, we've got to neutralize him immediately, and very quietly. If he picks up the slightest hint that we're on to him, he'll make things very difficult for us."

"We don't know anything yet," Kaylla reminded.

"No. We don't. *If* Ily managed to take Tyklat in, she didn't have him for very long, certainly not long enough to do a complete job of reconditioning his brain. But does he have a lever somewhere? Something Ily could use to manipulate him? A person? A secret? Debts?"

Kaylla's expression hardened. "No. Tyklat was professional to the roots. He cut any ties that might have jeopardized him years ago. As to his loyalty, I've no reason to question it. Bruen doesn't either. I talked to him about Tyklat. He thought him to be one of the best of our agents."

"Which brings us back to the allegation that Ily has someone in your organization. Tyklat suspects Nyklos."

"And you'd like that, wouldn't you?"

"Unfortunately, I can't allow myself the luxury of my personal feelings. Not when the security of Itreata is at stake. If he's not Ily's agent, and I take him out, haven't I just helped to cut my own throat? So let's forget the personal aspect and get down to solving the problem."

She relented, a humorless smile on her lips. "Very well. The first step to defanging a Cytean cobra is to get hold of the beast. What do you have in mind for Nyklos—assuming he's the one?"

"Take him out while he's asleep. That can be done effortlessly by means of a soporific in his food or drink. When he's out, we'll have the medical center run a complete scan on him. Remove your infamous Seddi tooth. . . . Perhaps his tooth didn't malfunction when Skyla cornered him in Etarus? Now wouldn't that be an interesting convolution of events?"

"And from there we put him under the scan and drug him up with Mytol. Then we suck him dry," Kaylla finished bitterly. "Quantum Gods, I hate this business."

"We'll know," Staffa reminded gently. "Further, if Nyklos is clean, he'll probably assent to the interrogation of his own free will. No matter what I think of him, the man is a professional. He knows the stakes as well as you or I. If he's innocent, he'll want his name cleared no matter what."

Reluctantly, Kaylla nodded.

Staffa walked over to stare at Skyla's monitor. Why had he allowed her to talk him into it? He tried to settle his roiled emotions as Kaylla came to stand beside him.

"You're worried sick over her, aren't you?"

Staffa nodded, fingers closing on air. "I can't order her to stay out of harm's way. She'd never allow it."

"How about sending a backup team?"

Staffa pointed to a dot of light. "That's Ryklos . . . Sassan territory. Among other things, I returned here to find a report from Myles Roma. The Sassan military has been put on alert. They're to report any violation of Sassan space by Companion warships. If such occurs, the regional military is to assume hostile intent and respond."

"And will Skyla draw such a response?"

Staffa tore himself away, crossing the room in adrenaline-powered strides. "I doubt it. She's been advised, and knowing Skyla, she'll keep her mass and reaction damped. We've had the plot on their detection buoys for years now, and the regional governor at Ryklos isn't exactly known for his enthusiasm for innovation. If Skyla is detected, she'll have Tyklat and be halfway home before the Sassans can have a ship manned."

"You seem pretty sure of yourself."

Staffa shrugged, running his fingers over Skyla's armor where it hung over the headrest of his gravchair. "Having the Companions for a next door neighbor discourages raids by antagonistic powers and breeds a sense of security—as long as you think you're one of the Companions' good allies. I'm sure that since Iban Jakre's latest order went out, a lot of people on Ryklos have begun to get a queasy feeling in their guts."

"She'll be all right," Kaylla told him, pointing to where he stroked the silky armor.

Staffa smiled self-consciously. "Yes, I know. As

she's told me so many times, she can take care of herself."

"She took security with her?"

"Five of Ryman's best ST people. She's no one's fool."

"Then why do you have that horrible look on your face?"

Staffa closed his eyes, remembering. "Because I have so much to lose . . . again. Rotted Gods, over the years, I'd forgotten the way worry eats at the soul. Kaylla, love is a curse. What if something happens? When the Praetor stole my wife and son I went mad . . . took it out on the whole of Free Space. I was only half a man then, could only give Chrysla half of myself. But with Skyla, I've surrendered myself totally. Do you know how terribly frightening that is?"

She nodded, an edge to her tan gaze. "Could you give that love to a woman who wasn't like her? Skyla never ceases to amaze me. I'm not sure I like her, but by the quanta, I respect the hell out of her."

"If Tyklat's bait in a trap. . . ." Staffa's fist knotted. *Ily will curse the day she was ever born—even if I have to pry her pus-soaked tail out of Rega's ash-strewn wreckage.*

"Staffa? *Staffa!*"

His thoughts returned to the present and Kaylla who watched him uncertainly.

"Were I Ily Takka, and could see your expression just now, I'd be worried."

"And well she might be." Staffa shook off his black mood and squared his shoulders. "Very well, what are we going to do about Nyklos?"

* * *

The naked man in the chair leaned his head back, pain-glazed eyes rolling as Ily paced back and forth before him in her cubicle of an interrogation room. The straps on the chair had eaten into his spare flesh and pulled on the taut skin. Despite the cool air pumped in to keep prisoners uncomfortable, trickles of sweat slipped down the captive's skin. The monitoring equipment gave a complete profile of his metabolism, anxiety, and rising fear. For the moment, he'd fixed his gaze on the cameras that lined the angle of the concrete ceiling.

"Now then," Ily said easily, "Your name is Rokard Neru. You are an engineer for the Power Authority. Your old supervisor used to be Jackard Rath. Is that correct?"

"Yes."

"Excellent. The next thing we're going to discuss is your new position at the Power Authority. Why don't you tell me exactly what it is that Sinklar Fist's people are doing?"

Ily crossed her arms while the man struggled to swallow. From somewhere he mustered the courage to glare at her, the Mytol making it hard for him to focus his eyes. "Why don't you crawl off and die, you Rotted bitch!"

Ily rubbed her hands together and leaned forward. "I admire your audacity. Now I'm going to admire your pain. I am going to make two small incisions in your scrotum. After that I will insert tubes. Thereafter, I will allow one drop of acid to fall every five minutes. You may tell me what you know now, before your vocal cords are permanently damaged by your screams, or you may tell me later. For your information, the decision you make won't affect my desire to repay you for your insult, but it might lessen the effects."

The tremors began in his face and spread until his entire body shivered. Ily gave him a ravishing smile as she produced a scalpel and the tubes from the bench behind her. He vented the most hideous shriek as she touched the delicate blade to his fear-tightened skin.

* * *

"I don't really care what my enemies think of me, or even say—so long as they do it in the privacy of their own homes. My greatest consideration is that they fear me, for fear is a powerful tool when used artfully. And that, Arta, is the trick. Too much fear, and a person can decide that they have nothing to lose. Then their action against you is fueled with desperation. Too little fear, and people cease to take you seriously.

"You've been an apt pupil, and I appreciate your keen intellect and acute mind when it comes to your thirst for knowledge in this field. Remember fear and its use, but more importantly, the day will come when you face a skilled opponent who will try and gain the advantage against you.

"As soon as you recognize this, withdraw from the conflict and consider just who you face and what they're willing to risk. Make your plans and give thought to every eventuality. Let your opponent think he or she is winning and then strike. Once you have them disorganized, press your advantage. If you seek to crush them in one blow, you may suffer in the end. A more complete victory is achieved by eroding their will, eating away at their confidence until when the final conflict is initiated, they have nothing left within."

—*Letter from Ily Takka to Arta Fera*

CHAPTER XVII

Ily stepped into her office from the lift which had carried her from the subbasement and the interrogation facilities. She used a damp towel to wipe the last of the body fluids from her hands and tossed the remains into the disposal chute. She grimaced at the stains on her clothing and stripped it off, balling her black suit and stuffing it into the disposal after the towel.

Before she headed for her personal quarters and a hot shower, she settled at her desk, accessing the comm.

Gysell's face formed in her monitor. He cocked his head, apparently spying her disheveled hair. "Yes, Minister?"

Ily leaned back, a satisfied grin on her face. "I just had the most interesting time in the interrogation room. You know that Power Authority engineer I had you pick up? He proved most helpful. I'm routing you the entire confession. It seems that Sinklar, in building his perfect society, has come to the belief that if he allows the Power Authority workers to fortify themselves in an impregnable fortress, they'll be able to function autonomously."

"I see." Gysell fingered his chin, lost in thought. "Is this a serious problem?"

"Sinklar is a dreamer, Gysell. His vision is on a universal plane, not the grubby practical one we tend to work on. While he builds fortresses against mass manipulation, he has no concept of the fatal and frail flaws of the individual."

"Then our concerns are for nothing?"

"For nothing," Ily agreed. "Let him continue his little exercise. When the time comes for us to take over, we shall do so with no concerted resistance. In the meantime, identify the people Sinklar's officers are grooming for positions of authority. We'll need a complete list of their wives, children, parents, friends, and so forth."

"And then we use their loved ones as hostages. But what about Sinklar? How will he react?"

She gave him a wink. "I think I have him firmly in hand, and he likes where I'm grabbing. By the time our actions become apparent, I imagine Sinklar will have served his purpose."

*   *   *

"Lord Commander? I need to speak with you. Information has come in." Kaylla's voice came over the comm headphone in Staffa's ear.

"Just a minute," Staffa answered into the throat mike as he and Tasha—his big, burly fourth in command—bent over a comm terminal which displayed the status of the refit on *Jinx Mistress*. Around them the giant warehouse and manufacturing center shrilled and whined, people shouted back and forth, machinery ground away, and mechanical hammers rat-tatted in the background. Overhead, brilliant lights glared down, drowning everything in stark white.

"I'd say that the smart solution is to lay two trunk lines of powerlead," Staffa decided. "You can run one along the medial keel, and the other here, along the ventral one. That halves the chance of control loss in the event she takes a direct hit amidships."

"Good thinking. I'll notify the engineers." Tasha pulled at his beard, a thoughtful look in his one good eye. "When we get the chance, it wouldn't hurt to put that kind of redundancy into the rest of the ships."

"No, it wouldn't. Real quick, what can you tell me about *Countermeasures*?"

"We might have a breakthrough on the communications problem," Tasha said. "It's based on observation, and the quanta. We create virtual pairs by exciting heavy elements in the dish. One set is transmitted line of sight, while the other is trapped in a stasis. When the first reaches the receiver, we kill the stasis and shoot the control with microlaser, either on or off. It's simple binary, line of sight only, lightspeed bound, but it works."

"Sort of a virtual pair interferometry effect that depends on spookiness?"

"You got it." Tasha gave him a sheepish grin. "It hit one of our people after she'd been in a hell of an argument with a Seddi. Say what you will, they've made a lot of us think. And, you know, when you start looking at things in that perspective, lots of stuff begins to make sense—and some of us start to wonder just what we've done with our lives."

"Don't I know it. Excuse me, Tasha, I've got a message coming in. Sounds important."

"Use my office." Tasha pointed as he made corrections to the schematic on the screen.

Staffa made his way through the maze of snaking cables, dollies stacked with parts and machinery, and jumpsuited technicians and mechanics who worked on various pieces of equipment that rested on gantries prior to being shuttled up to *Jinx Mistress*.

Staffa palmed the lock on Tasha's cubbyhole office. Along one wall a jungle grew, the plants flowering in incredible blossoms. Flowers filled Tasha with wonder, and his gardens were the prize of Itreata.

Staffa slipped into the creaking chair and accessed his personal channel, running a diagnostic to ensure privacy. Kaylla's face formed.

"What's happened?"

Kaylla cocked her head, brown hair hanging straight as she squinted at the background. "What beautiful orchids. You in the gardens?"

"Tasha's office."

"I didn't know any of your cutthroats had such redeeming features. But I called to tell you that a report has come in from Rega. *Gyton*, and MacRuder, are missing. My people checked into it and apparently

First MacRuder has been sent to preclude a Terguzzi uprising. I went ahead and contacted our people on Terguz. As far as they can tell, the entire planet is excited about what's going on in the capital, but no one is stirring up the home front. If something happens in the future, maybe a shortage of supplies, longer hours in the mines, or a cut in pay, then we might see something happen."

"Ily might try that, but Sinklar wouldn't be part of it. He worked too hard trying to calm angry miners on Targa." Staffa responded. "No, this is something else. I was on my way to my office. Maybe I'll let Roma know that Rega is missing a warship."

"Skyla is going to be making rendezvous in a couple of hours."

Staffa thumped the desk with a fist. "I'm painfully aware of that. Why don't you catch a lift to my quarters. We'll watch it together. How's the Nyklos operation coming along?"

She raised an eyebrow. "Oh, we got him without a fight, all right. I followed your suggestion and we gassed him in his sleep. He's a little . . . well, annoyed to say the least, but he's been cooperative to a fault. By the time I get to your quarters, I'll know if he's our man or Ily's."

"Affirmative, I'll see you then." Staffa killed the connection, closing his eyes and imagining Free Space. *Gyton* had disappeared with MacRuder. Where? Which planet did Sinklar think to strike to throw the Sassans off balance? Or had Mac simply been detailed to a long-range intelligence mission?

"Damn you, MacRuder, what are you up to?"

Staffa turned in the seat, accessing the comm again. "Security? This is the Lord Commander. I want all of our systems at full alert. The potential intruder is the Regan warship, *Gyton*. Her spectral fingerprint is in our records."

"Affirmative."

* * *

The little red light on Myles Roma's desk blinked, and the Legate suffered a pang of unease. Through the windows he could see the morning sunshine slanting through Imperial Sassa's sky-taunting towers. They sparkled like backlit diamonds, the cool air imparting a bluish tint to the crystalline beauty of the Capitol across the way.

Myles glanced surreptitiously at his staff, now buried in the multitude of tasks he'd swamped them with. Over his right shoulder, the holo of Divine Sassa continued to glare with colorless eyes. Myles bit back a shiver as he dropped the privacy field around his ample gravchair and pressed a button that connected his ear comm to the line represented by the blinking light.

"Roma, here." He tried to move his lips as little as possible lest someone was able to read lips.

"Myles?" Staffa kar Therma's commanding tones came through. "Can you talk?"

"As long as we don't take too long. It's morning here, everyone is beginning work."

"I want you to know that a single Regan warship, the *Gyton*, has spaced with Sinklar Fist's second in command. That's Rysta Braktov's vessel. According to the Regan story, they spaced for Terguz—but they never showed up there. We suspect they may be making a reconnaissance run on the Sassan Empire—or at worst, might strike one of your holdings to throw you off balance. Just thought you should know."

"I see. Thank you. Interesting things are happening here. Our fleet is three weeks behind schedule to ship out for Rega. Seems the supplies keep getting delayed. The freighters delegated to those runs are having an abysmal rate of mechanical failures—old equipment, you know. Not only that, I have begun integrating the personnel files we talked about. I can infiltrate two Seddi a week. It would have been more, but our Civil Patrol has clamped down on any mention of Seddi after those Divinely cursed broadcasts began."

"Any reaction?"

"People are talking . . . in private. Some are beginning to think. Civil disobedience is three point seven percent higher than normal. I do what I can—and I listen to each broadcast and think about them afterward. There is a great deal of sense in the Seddi messages."

"Excellent work. Want to come be a Companion?"

"Legate suits me fine. I have a better chance of collecting old age benefits here than I would by jumping out of landing craft while angry people who didn't approve of my presence shot at me. Despite losing another ten kilos, I've still got too much target area."

"Ten kilos? Congratulations. Oh, Myles, one more thing. You might want to familiarize yourself with the Resource Allocation and Redistribution Augmentation program in your files. Just thought I'd warn you, since your people fine-tune software. If there are any bugs in that program, we need to know."

Myles reached up and tugged at his double chin as he frowned. Resource Allocation and Redistribution Augmentation? "I will do so. Excuse me, I have an aide approaching."

"May the quanta keep you, Myles." The connection broke and Myles killed the screen, looking up as his extractive industries assistant stopped before the desk.

"Legate," the young woman began, "I think we have another problem with the copper from the Formosan Asteroids. The processor malfunctioned again and the head engineer is screaming to get spare parts."

"Very well, prioritize it." Myles waved her away and accessed his comm. He worked through the file tree until he located Resource Augmentation and Redistribution. Calling it up, he found the tag: Augmentation. He accessed the file and began to read. After several moments he leaned back and tapped his ring-bejeweled fingers on the desktop. He glanced absently at the scintillating walls of the Capitol, now golden in the sunlight.

"Augmentation? What a profound understatement. Yes, my friend, I shall become familiar indeed." *And hope I live to collect those benefits I was bragging about!*

* * *

The cruiser *Vega* had been growing in Skyla's monitors as she followed a careful course around the inert ship. In the faint flickers of the Twin Titans and the shine of Ryklos' primary, a whitish haze could be seen dissipating around the vessel. Skyla didn't need her instruments to identify the haze: N_2, seventy-seven percent, O_2, twenty-two percent, and declining fractions of water vapor, argon, carbon dioxide, and traces. *Vega* had been hit harder than Tyklat had admitted.

"All right, Lily. There he is. What do you think?" Skyla asked her security chief as she hunched in her command chair. The one-man bridge wrapped around her, holographics projected in a three hundred and sixty degree display. Skyla slipped her attention back and forth between the augmented senses of the worrycap and the tactical situation created by wounded *Vega*.

"I'd say she's about dead," STO Lily finally admitted. "We can see where she took a hit in the afterdecks. From here it's impossible to make an assessment of structural damage. There's no telling how much atmosphere she lost in jump."

Skyla sucked at her lower lip. *Very well, now what? Sit out here sniffing around while Tyklat runs out of air? What about his climate control? Will I arrive to find a frozen corpse?*

She jerked her head, and ordered, "We're going in. Stay sharp on the monitors, people."

Skyla let her mind mingle with the yacht's as she tightened the arc around *Vega*. She'd received Staffa's warnings about the Sassans. Ignorant fools that they were. She'd approached cautiously and so far the Sassan station at Ryklos hadn't probed them with active sensors. They might get in and out without tripping a detector. At this stage, even if they did, she could board *Vega* and skip safely back to Itreata before the Sassans could stumble to their ships and clear port.

Here we come, Tyklat. Pray to the Blessed Gods, you're on the up and up. But then, what else could he be? Assuming it was a trap, what could they gain? She'd be happy to play hostage to a hostile force seeking to gain entry to Itreata. A grim smile crossed her lips at the image conjured of the Companions' reaction to any such silly scheme—no matter who the hostage might be.

As her yacht closed, she opened a narrow beam. "Tyklat? You there?"

Nothing.

"Pus Rot you, wake up! Tyklat? You getting a reading?"

Skyla tapped long fingers on her comm console. A malfunction could have forced them to shut down the fusion reactors. She studied the readings, matching her yacht to *Vega* with a minimum of correction to her comm. Through the monitors, she could see the slow expansion of crystals and gas from the rent in *Vega*'s hull. Rot it, it looked more like a near miss than a hard hit, but this was an old ship, and who knew how fragile her bones were?

"Lily? What's your status?"

"Ready to go, Wing Commander."

"We're matched. I'm setting the controls to maintain attitude."

"Uh, I'd just as soon you stayed put, Wing Commander. If anything's rotten about this, you can skip."

"And leave you guys behind?" Skyla stood, getting the kinks out of her stiff body. "Negative, Lily. You know the doctrine. We don't leave our people behind. Beside which, when was the last time I sat out an operation? What's the matter with you guys? Getting spooky in your old age?"

Skyla ducked through the bridge hatch and passed into the sybaritically ornate central cabin with its sandwood and ebony paneling, the Vegan marble tables with burnished gold trim. At the lock, Lily waited, an uneasy look in her brown eyes. The STO handed

Skyla a set of pods to strap on, saying, "The others
are already outside. Checked your helmet ring and
rebreather?"

Skyla shrugged into the pods with practiced ease,
snapping the buckle and pulling the tabs tight. She
pulled her gloves on, sealing them to her armor and
powered up her helmet ring, forcing deep breaths into
the field and hearing the rebreather whine in response. "Let's go."

Lily gave her a thumbs up and grabbed a heavy
blaster from where it stood propped by the lock. Skyla
checked her own pistol as the STO cycled through the
hatch. Her faithful weapon showed a full charge.

When the lock had cycled, Skyla stepped inside,
feeling the change in pressure. *What if it is a trap?
Then we deal with it. Be rational, Skyla. Tyklat's cover
was blown by the Etarian operation and he's running
to save his skin. You'd run, too. So, why am I wound
up?*

She palmed the hatch when the readings reported
vacuum and stepped out into the void. Frost swirls
of stars shimmered in a haze through the Forbidden
Borders—now no more than six light-years distant.
Vega lay no more than fifty meters away, the flickering light of the Twin Titans giving the dusty hull a
surreal appearance. Against the star-gray background,
Skyla could see the feeble glow of the clearance
lights—an indication that power had begun to ebb.

"Cover me," Skyla ordered as she energized the
pods, and drifted forward.

"Wish you'd let us go first, Wing Commander," Lily
called.

"Who put her butt on the line to infiltrate
Myklene?" she asked. "Remember who the Nab was
who broke Staffa out of Ily's hands? And how about
the time at Maika, when I saved your butt from being
shot off? Back off, people." She paused. "Besides,
Tyklat trusts me. If he sees a stranger out front, he
might panic."

Skyla maintained her attitude through long practice,
killing her inertia on bent legs as she landed on *Vega's*

hull and stabilized against it with the downward thrust of her pods. She made her way to the lock by a series of bunny hops and checked the status. The lock gauges still registered a full atmosphere on the inside. Skyla glanced at the dissipating fog lacing out from the ship's rear and sighed as she activated the lock. Enough power remained to cycle the system and the hatch opened.

Lily landed easily beside her and shined suit lights into the interior. "Looks clean. Got room for four people. Acre, you and Steel go first, secure the lock. The rest of us will follow on your all clear."

"Roger." The two ST personnel dropped and turned, killing their momentum with the pods as they entered the lock. "We're set."

The hatch closed and Skyla waited impatiently while the gauge marked the building pressure. At one atmosphere, the display went red, indicating the internal hatch had been opened.

"Acre, Steel, talk to us," Skyla called into her comm.

"Roger, Wing Commander. We're in the ready room. Light's a little dim, but we've got a full atmosphere in here. Acre's taking readings on his pocket comm. He's nodding that it's all right."

"Stick with procedure, keep your helmet fields energized, and use the rebreather. If it's a trap, the preferred method of incapacitation would be gas. Any sign of Tyklat, or maybe the pilot?"

"Negative. What next, Wing Commander?"

"Given your location, what are the chances of ambush?"

"From here, they'd have to have a full Section. We've got both corridors covered with the heavy stuff. Floor, ceiling, and compartment walls look sturdy and intact. I'd call it a go."

Skyla tapped the lock activation, watching as the pressure dropped. When the hatch finally opened, the two of them moved inside. Skyla watched the pressure rise until the light went green and she opened the internal hatch.

Acre and Steel had assumed battle stance, their blasters covering each direction of the corridor where it branched off the ready room. Suit lockers lined the compartment walls, all ripped open by Acre's and Steel's rapid but thorough search.

Lily rapped out, "You know the drill. Cover this bucket from top to bottom. Take no chances. Spread and go. Thirty second check in with description. Acre, Steel, move."

The two started smartly down their corridors. Skyla fell in behind Acre, who headed forward. In a Marta class cruiser, the bridge should be straight down the corridor, then left to the central corridor and right, squarely amidships.

Skyla followed Acre's broad back, hearing Steel's voice, "Proceeding aft in lateral corridor. Checking compartment doors. Nothing looks amiss."

"Taking first right," Lily called. "Proceeding to central corridor."

One by one they chattered to each other as Skyla peeled off from Acre and reached the central corridor, her pistol ready, safety off. "Turning toward the bridge in central corridor. No sign of trouble."

Skyla paused long enough to open compartment doors on the way, checking the contents of the cabins which would have carried crew or passengers. When Tyklat stole the ship, he'd taken one with curiously tidy occupants. Duffels had been neatly stored in the acceleration loops at the foot of each bed. The captain must have been a stickler for protocol. Not even an empty stassa cup had been left to spill.

"Reached the bridge," Skyla called. "I'm undogging the bulkhead." *Not even a spilled stassa cup?*

"Report!" Lily called. "Steel? Report!"

Skyla shoved the bridge hatch open. Tyklat lay slumped over the controls.

"Here!" Steel called. "Just checked engineering. Looks clean."

Skyla puffed a hardy sigh of relief.

"Got a person!" Acre's voice called out. "Little

guy. He's tied up and out cold. Looks like he's been beat up. I'm going to check him out."

"Careful," Lily warned.

Skyla studied the bridge. Neat as a pin, nothing out of place. Tyklat's shoulders moved with deep breathing. Asleep?

"Tyklat?" Skyla glanced warily around, noting the second seat where the pilot must have sat. She gave him an ungentle shove. No reaction.

Skyla reached out and pulled him out of the chair. Tyklat rolled limply onto the floor, moaning. A nasty cut had swollen on his forehead. "Tyklat appears to have been beaten pretty badly, too. Looks like the pilot and Tyklat got into it. People, this is appearing to be just what we hoped. Meet me back at the lock. Let's get these guys suited up and back to my yacht. Give me a minute to see what shape this bucket is really in. If it'll space, we'll send it toward home. If not, we'll see if we can't send a crew to come get it. A ship's a ship, people."

"Affirmative, Wing Commander," Lily called. "We're heading for the main lock. See you when you get there."

Skyla slipped into the pilot's chair and ran the preflight diagnostic. Her fingers danced across the boards, system after system coming to life. The fans in the atmosphere plant began to hum. Skyla peered curiously at the readings on the monitors.

"Rot it, the ship's fine, Tyklat. What happened? You buy that bastard pilot's story that you were out of fuel?"

She shook her head. "Very well, looks like the Companions are a ship richer. Tyklat, you come bearing great gifts."

From behind her down the corridor came a muffled bang as Lily's people did something.

Skyla sighed and braced herself, lifting Tyklat on her shoulders in a battlefield carry. She maneuvered out the hatch and started down the corridor. She made the turn and slowed, something nagging at the back of her mind. *Neat as a pin?* She craned her head, glancing at Tyklat's slack features—and thought about docked ships and the way *Vega* would have spaced from the Regan Orbital Terminal.

Skyla turned the corner and hesitated. "Steel? Acre?"

Silence. "Lily? You there?"

Skyla allowed Tyklat to slip from her shoulder as she started warily forward, blaster in hand. Rot it, she'd had to turn every system on? Why would Tyklat shut them down? Skyla reached the main lock, sliding along the plating, as she braced to fire, knees bent, blaster in an isosceles hold. Lily and the rest lay in a tangled heap.

"Staffa! It's a trap!" she screamed as a body hurled at her from one of the suit lockers. Skyla pivoted at the hips, her shot taking the man in the middle. She whirled as another man flew at her, shot him, and was turning as yet another fell on her, grappling for the pistol. Skyla moved with him, used her center of gravity as a fulcrum, and threw him. She paused only long enough to kick him full in the face and whirled as more assailants tackled her.

She lost the pistol, twisting, striking, and wrenching free. Four very large men ringed her, desperation in their eyes as they charged. Skyla whirled, struck, and darted, her blows debilitating or lethal.

She hammered an elbow to one man's temple, shot stiff fingers into yet another's eye as she closed on the last, bouncing, driving a hard heel into the man's throat. She used a rusher's momentum to fling him full tilt into the lockers, hearing the snap of bone. Tripping over a corpse, she recovered, whirled, and dropped to a crouch. One of the men moaned as he tried to crawl away, a hand pressed to a bloody eye. Another clawed at his throat as he choked on the floor, his color going pale.

"You're very good." a sensual female voice brought Skyla spinning around.

A woman stood at the juncture of the corridor and ready room, a deadly blaster pointed at Skyla's guts. In her other hand, a stun rod extended like a whip.

In that brief instant, Skyla froze, not believing what she saw.

"Chrysla," she whispered. "You're dead!"

The hesitation cost her. With a speed worthy of her own, the amber-eyed woman lashed out like a fencer, the stun rod jolting Skyla witless even as she began her block.

*   *   *

Staffa paced anxiously before the monitor, his only view that from the sensors on Skyla's yacht. He and Kaylla had been listening to the chatter as his team searched the ship. Then Skyla had called out to her team—then silence. The ominous wait had begun to weigh on him as Staffa shot a worried glance at Kaylla, who sat to one side, biting her lip as she stared at the image of *Vega* filling the screen.

"Come on," Staffa growled, smacking a fist into his palm. "Talk, Skyla. Blessed Gods, speak!"

"She said it looked all right," Kaylla added thoughtfully. "I mean it's obvious, the pilot jumped Tyklat, trying to take the ship back. Tyklat fought, incapacitated the man, and finally passed out over the controls."

"And it means Ily does indeed have an agent among the Seddi. Nyklos is cooperating?"

Kaylla nodded. "We ran him through every test we could devise. He's *not* Ily's agent."

"Damnation. It would have been easier if. . . ."

"Staffa, it's a trap!" exploded from the speakers, galvanizing him to leap for the monitor, as if he could physically pull himself into the action.

"Skyla!" he roared, bending down, staring hopefully at the peaceful image. *Vega* hung silent in a mist of boiled atmosphere. Meanwhile, the speaker caught the rip of blaster fire, then the grunts of exertion. Grunts? Skyla fighting hand to hand. He'd heard it often enough.

Several smacking sounds came through as Skyla articulated the fury of her attack. A chance . . . an ever so thin chance that she'd take her assailants.

Staffa's fingers bruised as he gripped the monitor and moaned at the image.

Then Skyla could be heard panting and slurred words came from beyond the battle comm pickup.

"Chrysla . . . you're dead!" The cryptic words stunned him for a brief moment, then a piercing shriek was followed by silence.

Staffa gaped. A red haze dimmed his vision. *Chrysla? What . . . how?* Had he heard right? *Impossible! Chrysla was dead—dead at his hands off Myklene!*

He could feel Kaylla pulling at him, trying to drag him back from the monitor.

"Staffa!" Kaylla gritted in his ear. "Stop it! We've got to think. Damn you, Staffa!"

But the monitor had gone shimmery as his gaze silvered with tears of fear and rage.

"I'll kill you Ily! I'LL GUT YOUR PUS-RIDDEN CORPSE!"

*   *   *

"Ily has returned, and she brings news of hope, along with a most wondrous gift—a Seddi assassin, Arta Fera by name. The woman is magnificent. As Emperor, I've had my choice of women—at least so long as Mareeah didn't find out. Of them all, Ily has been the most interesting, and the most skilled with her sexual gymnastics, but this Arta Fera! What a challenge. The Seddi have trained her to kill men who love her, and what a devious trap that was! For she is a sexual magnet, beautiful, with long auburn hair, the most incredible amber eyes, and a body like a Blessed Goddess come to life. In the collar, however, I control her—and I *will* have her!

"But enough of my burning lust. Ily has found a way for us to save the Empire. Staffa kar Therma is bottled up in Makarta Mountain, and I have given the order for *Gyton* to blast him from orbit. At the same time, I have reviewed the tapes and listened to Ily's enthusiasm for Sinklar Fist. At Ily's urging, I have conferred upon this assassin's son a full Lordship—and let the aristocracy howl. With Fist, I can smash the Sassans, and the Companions, too. How odd that Ily herself executed Fist's parents, and now she brings me their son as a savior. Where last night I drowned in sorrow, today I revel in hope. I can save my people!

"Ah, Ily, how I've missed you these long months. How foolish of me to have feared you and your limitless ambition. You bring me the military genius to place all of Free Space under my rule, and you give me Arta Fera! Even as I stripped you and took you on my office floor, I couldn't keep my mind off Fera. Will she bring me to as much ecstasy as you do? Ily . . . Ily, if only you were my wife! You are worthy of me.

—*Excerpt from Tybalt the Imperial Seventh's personal journal*

CHAPTER XVIII

Ily knew the moment Sinklar stepped out of the shuttle capsule below the Ministry. She knew that look of his, the frown, the hard set of the jaw, and the way those oddly colored eyes glowered at his surroundings as he stalked across the platform for the lift.

Anger? At what? He couldn't possibly know about Rokard Neru. She was just about to wash the last of his spattered remains from her hair.

As Sinklar entered the lift, Ily stepped into her shower, playing the warm water over her skin, increasing the heat until the steam brought a red flush to her fine skin. The last of the Power Authority engineer swirled down the drain. And Sinklar? What would he do? Stand abashed in the lift as he tried to decide whether he ought to enter her quarters? Or did whatever angered him drive him to barge right in?

Ily laughed to herself, guessing Sinklar would charge in. And if he were truly that angry, she was in a perfect position to disarm him. *Yes, play off his youthful inexperience and curious sense of honor.*

As she expected, he didn't appear immediately. Suffering indecision in the security room. She twirled around in the water, enjoying his discomfort. How long? Two minutes, three? Would he turn around, go back?

No, here he came. She caught his movement through the wavering water sheeting down the energy fields, and made the best of it, adopting a sensual pose as the water cascaded down her tingling flesh.

From the corner of her eye, she saw him stop short and begin to back away. That's when she turned, made a startled jump, as if surprised, and called, "Sinklar?"

"Whhh . . . uh, yes! Sorry, I . . . I. . . ."

He continued to back away and she leaned forward, poking her head through the drying field and giving him a warm smile. "I was hoping I'd see you. I heard the exercises went well. You posted the assignments for tomorrow morning?"

The expression on his flushing face was priceless! The anger, whatever had possessed him, had drained away like the last of the tortured engineer's blood.

"Just a second." Ily pulled her head back, smiled victoriously into the stream of hot water, and shut the flow off. She lingered, as she stepped through the drying field, as if savoring the caress of the force field against her skin. She gave him a smile as she turned her neck against the gentle pull off the field, her hair settling behind her in a black shining wave.

"I. . . ." He gaped at her, taking in the charms of her perfect nakedness, rosy now from the heat.

She walked proudly up to him, allowing her lips to part as he stared anxiously into her eyes. "I've missed you," she told him in a husky whisper and reached up to lay her hot hands against his cheeks.

"We need to talk," he managed hoarsely.

"You have an appointment?" she asked, searching his eyes. "I have a couple of hours. Maybe we could relax a little . . . and I have missed you so much." She bent forward, kissing him gently, giddy at the resentment she sensed within him. Then she backed away a step, one eyebrow raised questioningly. "Or is it all business this time?"

He swallowed hard, trying to turn away, losing the battle as she walked languidly to her closet and pulled out a gauzy robe and let it slide over her flesh. She turned then, drawing it tight about her narrow waist and giving him a happy smile. "There. All right, to business. What do we need to discuss?"

She walked across the room, allowing the robe's slit to expose her leg as she settled on the bed.

He nerved himself and challenged, "You put me in the palace, Ily. You didn't tell me that's where I was. Blessed Gods, I mean. . . ."

She gave him a blank look. "Lord Fist, where else would you be? I mean, my word, you *are* the government! The comm equipment is all there. As we place new government officials, that's where they will keep their offices. Mac is going to be the Minister of Defense, isn't he? All the command control runs out of Defense's headquarters—and that's just down the hall from your rooms."

"But the palace? What are my people going to say? I can't become what we're fighting against! It's a betrayal!" he cried, raising his hands. "It. . . . It's just not. . . ."

"Right?" she finished for him, and placed fingers on her chin, frowning and slowly shaking her head. "Come here. Sit down beside me and let's talk. I think we need to air some things between us."

Oh, he hated it—even though he wanted to settle beside her more than anything. In self-punishment, he forced himself to look at the floor.

Ily began, "I know how hard the transition is, Sinklar. I realize that you've had to undertake everything at once. The fate of the entire Empire—of all of humanity—rests on your shoulders now. You've been working nonstop, wearing yourself ragged to reshape the army. And you're doing it. I've got some reports I'll route to your comm. And that's another reason I put you in the palace. The communications between here and there are *secure*, as secure as you can get in all of Free Space."

"But I'm not . . . not. . . ."

"Not Tybalt?" She chuckled, eyes dancing with amusement as he looked miserably up at her. "Thank the Blessed Gods for that!"

He lowered his eyes then. "Ily. Who lived in my quarters before?"

She reached out, gentle fingers turning him to look

at her. "I put you in the Emperor's offices. Not his house, Sinklar. His office."

The muscles in his cheeks twitched. "You slept with him in that bed, didn't you? Slept with him here."

She gazed into his odd eyes and nodded. "I did. At the time we . . . well, I thought I could change him." She smiled wistfully, breaking eye contact as she stared sadly into space. "We plotted together, he and I. We would change the lot of humanity. Oh, yes, that was the plan."

She rolled off the bed, pacing in front of him, head down, hands locked demurely before her. "What a lot of Rot that turned out to be. Tybalt, curse you, it was all bluff, wasn't it? A means of keeping me on my string while nothing changed."

She turned then, clenching a knotted fist, fire in her eyes. "Well, this time it won't happen that way. We're going to take all of Free Space, Sinklar. And we're going to create the sort of Empire that doesn't perpetuate itself by lies and the abuse of power."

He gave her a skeptical frown. "I wish I could really believe that."

She tilted her head. "Mhitshul's been at you, hasn't he?"

"Would you like me to remove him? Transfer him?"

She crossed her arms and shook her head, aware of the effect as her black hair draped around her. "No. He gives you perspective. You'll believe I've hoodwinked you without Mhitshul to provide a counterbalance. Honestly, I appreciate his skepticism."

"Why?"

She had him now. "Because I'm building for the future . . . for us. I want you to come to me of your own free will, work with me because you've come to trust my judgment." She bent down, taking his hand, staring worshipfully into his eyes. "Think about the history books, Sinklar. You and I will be remembered as the great reformers, the man and woman who freed humanity from tyranny! Isn't that worth fighting for, building for?"

He pursed his lips, struggling desperately to believe her.

"Sink," she hesitated. "I arrested the head engineer at the Power Authority."

He recoiled as she'd expected, a hardness in his eyes.

"It's not Boyz's fault. She didn't know. I mean in fairness, Mac grabbed her away from her duties and shipped her off for Imperial Sassa."

"Boyz? What's she got to do with this? Maybe you'd better start at the beginning."

She nodded. "All right. Boyz thought that a man named Rokard Neru was the perfect person to put into position at the Power Authority. The man's performance looked good, and he had a spotless record. Naturally, Boyz placed him in charge when Rath left. The problem is that Neru's record was spotless for a reason. He and Rath had been thick for almost two decades." She hesitated, as if reluctant. "And Neru has Seddi connections. I should have investigated before. Of course they'd plant someone in a critical position like—"

"Wait a minute. How do you know all this?"

She shrugged easily. "Our internal security wouldn't be very secure if I didn't do my job. You have the final decision as to who to replace Neru with, but let me recommend Assistant Engineer Serra. I had some of my people run a thorough check. He's a family man. Has a lovely wife that he would do anything for, and seven children he adores. He sends part of his income to his parents, and, moreover, works overtime to make sure he does his job well. I'll send his personal file over, or you can look at it now, if you'd like."

His skepticism was evaporating and Ily pressed her case. "He makes a lot more sense than Neru. Neru was a loner. The Rotted Gods alone know what his hook was to keep Rath on a string. But if the Seddi had wanted to disrupt the Power Authority, Neru was ready and in a position to do a great deal of harm."

"All right. Serra gets the job."

"And don't blame Boyz," Ily reminded. "She didn't have time to run any checks on the people she promoted."

Sinklar gave her a smile. "I thought you didn't approve of my taking control of the vital services and privatizing them?"

She settled herself against him and took his hand. "I'll admit, in the beginning I was a little irritated that you'd taken the action on your own. You could have told me first. But now I'm all for it. You might have your personnel contact me if they need a background check on any of these people. I can give them excellent advice on who would best serve our needs in the position."

"I'll do that." His arm went around her shoulder. "You know, I feel a lot better than when I got here."

She patted his chest, smiling up at him. "We've got to talk more. I need to hear what's bothering you so I can fix it."

He nodded and bent down to kiss her gently. With practiced ease, she undid the fastenings of his armor.

Hours later, Sinklar lay on his back in Ily's bed. He stared up at the endless layers of crystal overhead and chewed at the inside of his cheek. He couldn't shake the nagging sensation of wrongness. *It's because she does with you what she once did with Tybalt—and in this same bed!*

You're a man now, Sinklar. This is the real world. You can't expect to be the only man she's slept with, he answered.

But was that it? Blasted Etaria, she never ceased to amaze him, or lead him to some new ecstasy. And, yes, he'd come here to tell her that he'd be cursed by the Rotted Gods if he'd live in Tybalt's palace, but now? Her arguments made such good sense.

He turned his gaze, staring down at her where she lay against him. One of her full breasts pressed against his ribs, and her muscular thigh lay protectively over his hips. He reached down and idly stroked her knee and calf.

Time, Sinklar. She's right. It's just making the adjustment, that's all. You'll get used to it. She made happy noises deep in her throat as she stirred and resettled herself.

* * *

Something in her terrified expression, that's what made Mac hesitate and release his pressure on the trigger. Arta Fera had been in exactly that same situation, staring right down the barrel of Sinklar's pulse pistol—poised on the edge of death. On that occasion, Arta had glared with the deadly rage of a wounded Etarian sand tiger. This Arta, however, stared at him with a mixture of petrified fear, despair, and resignation.

Mac lowered the pistol. "Who are you?"

The room came slowly back in to focus as his mind began to work. The main mess on the *Markelos* had gone hauntingly silent. His troops ringed the Sassans now.

Overhead, the atmosphere control fans hummed obliviously. Someone coughed. Zacharia Beechie still implored from his knees, tears of terror leaking from his eyes. *Markelos'* captain stared at Arta with wide eyes, mouth agape, and then looked back at Mac.

"I'm Marie Attenasio," the woman answered in Arta's voice, but a subtle difference could be heard. The venom and anger Mac had keyed to Arta's voice had been replaced by an enduring sorrow.

Mac chewed his lip, unsure. Pus take it, Arta was a clone, a knockoff produced by the Seddi and probably tailored for each individual mission. Arta had been designed to kill the Lord Commander—so who was Attenasio designed to kill?

"I want a squad here!" Mac barked. "This woman is to be placed under strict guard. She's a Seddi assassin, people, so keep your distance."

Marie was ringed with blasters wielded by grim-faced troops.

"A Seddi assassin?" Beechie cried, his voice almost a whimper? "And all this time. . . ."

Attenasio gave Beechie a long, suffering look. "I never lied to you, Zacharia. I told you as much of the truth as I could."

"You! Captain, on your feet! Seddi, you get up, too. Captain, it's time we go to your quarters and take care of some things."

Comm buzzed in Mac's ear. "Red here, we've got a signal coming in from *Gyton*. Commander Braktov says congratulations. She's dumping Delta V and matching. We've got techs on the way. They'll land at the main lock and cycle. Uh, Mac, not every team made the jump. A lot of them . . . well. . . ."

"I know. I know." He still shook at the memory of that mind-defying image of the Sassan ship teetering out of reality. "Tell them. . . . Nothing. They'll know what they did."

And that would be punishment enough, knowing that they hadn't jumped—and no one would even dress them down for cowardice. Next time, if it meant jumping headlong into the mouth of a Rotted God, they'd go—and be smiling in the process.

"Let's go, people." Mac waved with his pistol and followed the captain. To his surprise, the Seddi clone walked with a painful limp. Yes, this one was a carbon copy of Arta Fera. Mac could feel that magnetism. Every male eye watched, and longed, as she left the room, head held high, balanced and poised, while her auburn hair tumbled down around her shoulders to glint copper in the light.

Mac's squad remained unfazed, memories of Gretta's body foremost in their minds—and hatred for the Seddi burning down inside them.

The captain palmed the lift control and stepped inside. Mac and the Seddi followed. He pressed his pistol into her side and tried not to think about her beauty, or her full breasts, or the alluring scent she exuded. The woman stared woodenly ahead as the captain ordered, "Officer's deck."

The lift rose soundlessly and Mac's team stepped out, covering the captain and the Seddi. Mac took an instant to pull himself together, then he followed them to the captain's cabin.

The room had more amenities than Mac had grown used to aboard *Gyton*. The captain's quarters consisted of three rooms. The place smelled fresh and airy and had holo monitors in the walls that currently displayed planets and stars. The carpet gave underfoot and thick crystal arches gleamed transparently, rainbow colors jetting through them.

"Nice," Mac admitted. "Captain, you and the Seddi lady will stand here and not move a muscle."

His squad conducted a rapid yet thorough search, producing a brace of matched blasters inlaid with gold and silver, a shoulder weapon of more pragmatic finish, and the information that more could be hidden in secret places.

"That's fine, the captain won't be here for long." Mac turned his attention to the portly man, watching anger take the place of fear on the officer's fat face. Mac made a waggling gesture with his pistol. "Do you surrender?"

"You're a heretic pirate, may his Divineness damn you to eternal perdition."

"All right, you don't surrender. Corporal, take the captain down and hold him until Rysta's people get here. When they do, I want a little Mytol dripped between this guy's lips. Wring him dry and throw him out the lock."

"You vile bastard!" the captain shouted, raising a pudgy fist and taking a step forward—only to stop dead as Mac's expression hardened and the blaster centered under the man's heart.

"If you'd surrendered, you'd have been treated as a prisoner of war. That's according to the Holy Gawdamn Book, and we'll honor that for the moment. Sorry. Corporal, get him out of here, and if he makes a wrong move, blow his knee apart. I think we may need him alive."

The captain began to sweat then, pallor settling over his features. He jerked as the corporal jammed the blaster into his back and escorted him to the hatch.

Mac cocked his head pensively, then turned to the Seddi woman who watched him with level amber eyes. "Would you like to surrender?"

She nodded. "I will surrender. Subject to the Articles of War, section eight, paragraph seventeen: The treatment of captured foreign nationals. Such persons shall be treated as noncombatants and provided every courtesy within reason which does not hinder or delay the military in the pursuit of—"

"I know, I know." Mac sat down in one of the captain's overstuffed gravchairs. "The problem is that we don't consider the Seddi to be noncombatants. Not only that, but I'm starting to get real curious about how many more of you there are. Bruen must have cornered the Praetor's market on your model."

She tensed, flinching slightly before she could control herself.

"Hit close to home, didn't I?"

"I am not a Seddi, sir. I am. . . ."

"Yes?"

"A private citizen making my way from Myklene to Imperial Sassa. Nothing more." She paused. "Your mention of the Praetor only brought back memories of the defeat."

"Uh-huh. Look, we know the Praetor provided Bruen with clones." Mac scratched the back of his neck. "I've met that polluted bastard. What's it like to be his tool? To know that you're just a thing to him, a weapon set to go off when a man touches you? How do you feel way down inside?"

A faint frown lined her perfect brow and mystification grew in her haunted eyes. She started to make a gesture of bafflement, and thought better of it, asking instead, "Would you tell me about this? I mean about these clones that look like me? Arta Fera, you said?''

Mac grunted and shrugged. "Sure. Just so we both know that all the tricks are out of the bag, I'll play along. Now, I'm not privy to all the intricate details, but basically Magister Bruen—pus-sucker that he is— uses you Chrysla replicants to. . . ."

He caught the flaring of the nostrils, the startled fear in the eyes, and the tremor of the jaw. Talk about a touched nerve!

"Chrysla," Mac repeated numbly to himself in disbelief. *No way, pal! This can't be!* But what about the fragile haunted character, the wounded fawn look in her eyes. *It's a filthy Seddi trick! She's an assassin, and that's her MO. She's like a porcelain doll begging to be protected—until she slips a vibra-knife into your guts.*

The fear had continued to build, glazing her amber eyes. She couldn't stop the slim hand that rose to cover her mouth. She barely managed to quell a tremble that threatened to betray her.

Mac cocked his head, suddenly unsure. "You know, you're going to be drugged. Do you want to tell me now?"

She shook her head, panic eating at her as she lowered her eyes and wilted into one of the chairs, her will crumbling. "Do what you will to me," she whispered miserably. "It was too good to be true."

"What was?"

"The chance to get away, to finally be free after all these years."

Mac licked his lips nervously. "Are you Chrysla? If you are . . . if you can prove it, you're safe. I'll know if you're telling the truth—and I won't need Mytol."

She blinked, glancing up incredulously. "How? How will you know?"

Mac shot a hard look at the guards. "Outside, folks. And, yes, I'll be very careful. I don't want to end up like Gretta."

Shooting uneasy looks at each other, the rest of the squad filed from the room, one calling, "You holler if she tries anything. We'll be through the door quicker'n you can split a neutrino and blow her all to Rotted Hell and back!"

"I'll do that." Mac watched the hatch slide closed.

Marie's expression had changed as if she now clung to a desperate hope that he might indeed help her. Her hands worked nervously at the fabric of her gown. "Why would you want to help Chrysla? Who do you think she is, anyway?"

Mac gave her a crafty grin. "I'll be honest, Chrysla is something of a mystery to me. I know she was married to the Lord Commander, Staffa kar Therma. According to the story, the Praetor of Myklene stole her, and her son, away from Staffa about twenty years ago. The Lord Commander literally turned Free Space upside down looking for her . . . and for his son."

Pain brightened her eyes.

Mac shifted uncomfortably. "According to the story, the Praetor kept Chrysla until a ship called the *Pylos* was destroyed over Myklene. And now, you're coming from there. You've been wounded recently, the way a woman might be if she were escaping a dying ship."

She looked beyond Mac, as if she was focused on another time and place, and her lips barely moved as she said, "Captain Marston gave me an emergency pass—the first slip in security in all those years. I clutched that little card as if it were life itself." The wounded look returned. "I knew how they felt about each other. Staffa never admitted his hatred, but it lay there, sleeping, buried under the conditioning the Praetor had implanted so cleverly."

She gasped then, glancing up to give Mac a radiant smile. "Sorry, just making up a story. That's what I do. Tell stories to children. I make my living that way."

"Yeah, right." Mac crossed his arms. "My turn for a question. Did you or did you not bear Staffa a child?"

She tried to smile it away. "Do you really think a

woman like me could have been married to someone as powerful as the Lord Commander?"

"Could you recognize your son if you saw him today?"

She watched him pleadingly. "I never had a son."

Mac sighed. "We'll put you under the Mytol—unless you answer that question. Chrysla . . . Marie, listen to me. I give you my word that even if you aren't who I think you are, I won't hurt you. Even if you are a Seddi assassin, I won't hurt you. Please, this might mean everything to a lot of people I love, and a couple I respect a great deal." He paused. "Including Staffa."

Her full lips parted. "You know Staffa?"

"He saved my life on Targa. Offered me a position with the Companions. At the time, I couldn't take it. He got mixed up with the Seddi while he was searching for his son."

Her throat worked, and this time she couldn't stop the tears. She dropped her head, auburn hair spilling to hide her features. "If you only knew, sir. All those years . . . wondering, praying. Then when I heard Staffa might strike Myklene, I thought perhaps he knew. I thought. . . . Well, never mind. I got out. Used the pass to get down to the escape pods—but there was an officer there. He . . . he was skeptical. Wanted to call the captain . . . and. . . ."

She began to sob. Mac battled to hold himself back.

She sniffed and looked up at him with swimming eyes. "I don't know why it still hurts. The Praetor. . . ." She reached for him, the desperation filling her again. "Yes, sir. I—I'm Chrysla Marie Attenasio."

Mac tried to smile, but the implications had begun to sink in. "You're safe. I give you my word, we'll protect you from the whole of Free Space if we have to." *And if anyone finds out who you are, they'd kill to get their hands on you!* Then another cold wind blew through Mac's soul. *Assuming we live past the showdown at Imperial Sassa.*

* * *

The entire wall of the room provided a three-dimensional holo of the battlefield. Mykroft concentrated on the Groups attacking a low knoll. Rot it all, the system worked, whether he liked to admit it or not.

"I'd order a Section into the ravine below the knoll to reinforce their drive," Rick observed, pointing. "If they get hit from the side, they'll be completely flanked and the drive will be crushed."

To Mykroft's surprise, his request for a conference room and a computer simulation of Sinklar's tactics had been granted. Also granted was the request that the captive Firsts work together. Ily had smiled, a glint in her black eyes, and agreed.

Looking back, Mykroft suspected that Minister Takka had hoped for just such a request, for he had been escorted to the conference room within hours. Moments later, his fellow prisoners had been shown into the room. Since then, no one had left. Instead, they'd remained absorbed by the tapes and the challenge of beating Sinklar Fist.

"If you do that," Henck replied, "you're falling into the same trap I did in Kaspa. Trust the soldiers."

"Trust the soldiers?" Rick cried. "What do soldiers know about tactics and war?"

"Evidently a great deal," Mykroft interjected.

As if to prove his words, the ravine was blanked out by the master computer. The other side had responded by the book, expecting reinforcements to have been massed exactly where Rick would have placed them.

"And there," Mykroft told them, "is the classical response. Why try and flank when ordnance can keep the bother to a minimum? Theoretically, that Group taking the hill would have been supported and commanded from the ravine. Instead of being paralyzed, they'll keep going."

True to Mykroft's words, the Group continued their assault and took the command point.

"And now," Henck growled, "they'll abandon it. Just watch."

"Of course they will," Tie Arnson cried, raising his hands. "To stay there is to invite a grav shot or disrupter."

The Group proceeded to check a map, and then trotted down the far side.

"Multiple objectives," Henck whispered. "Who'd have thought."

"Sinklar Fist, that's who." Mykroft walked forward. "Comm, stop the action." He stood in front of his comrades. "Minister Takka tells me the comm has been programmed to simulate Fist's tactics. Let's try it out. "Henck, you and I will take the defensive forces, Rick, you and Arnson offensive. Let's play each other and see if we can play Sinklar's game. If we can duplicate his tactics here, the next thing will be to try them in the field."

"Fat chance," Tie sputtered. "You think Ily will let us get to a Division? And if she does, just what do you think Fist is going to say when we ask to borrow some of his troops? And why would Ily trust us, anyway? What if we skip out on her?"

Mykroft narrowed his eyes. "The first part of that is up to Ily. As to why she'd trust us? Gentlemen, outside of the fact that our lives depend on Minister Takka's good will, we have an empire to gain. Ily may indeed place herself at the head of the government, but I'd rather be with her than against her."

* * *

Sinklar sat hunched at the comm in Tybalt's old office. Reports were coming through and he'd begun to learn how to work the system. Still, his fumbling had generally caused frustration. Tired, possessed by a glow from the last bout of lovemaking with Ily, he should have been asleep. However, exercises started in another eight hours. If he could check the disposition of the new Divisions, he could. . . .

Sinklar's weary fingers entered Yams instead of Ayms. The system immediately began to load. He stopped a plunging index finger already started on its mission to escape the program.

MONITOR ONE ACCESS ONLY
SECURITY CODE: YAMS ACCEPTED. DO YOU
WISH TO PROCEED?

"Yes," Sinklar told the system. Not in a thousand attempts could he have pulled this up—even assuming he knew it existed. Monitor One access only? So, the files couldn't be pulled up on any other system?

A long directory of files appeared, rows upon rows to fill the monitor. Sinklar frowned, reading the important names, including his own. He immediately accessed that file and skimmed the contents—facts of his life as far as Tybalt had known them. Cross-references for Tanya and Valient Fist were provided. Where gaps in Tybalt's knowledge occurred, he'd left notes or question marks. All in all, the report, though skimpy, seemed accurate. At the very bottom, however, Tybalt had written:

"At this moment, Sinklar Fist appears to be a significant threat to security. According to Ily's report, he has defeated five of Rysta's best. Should such a scourge be allowed loose, how could we stop him? He seems to be able to galvanize his troops to superhuman feats. Ily has gone to Targa. If she cannot turn Fist, turn him into my tool, she will assassinate him. If, however, he can be harnessed and leashed, could this be the answer to breaking Staffa?"

Sinklar paused, rereading the section carefully. Then he abandoned the file and called up Ily's. He absently picked up one of the spicy, meat-filled pastries and munched as he started to read.

An hour later, the pastry unfinished, he saved the file and got unsteadily to his feet. Sinklar closed his eyes, an ill feeling churning in his gut.

The plush apartment pressed down on him in spite of all its luxury. He palmed the lock plate and stepped out into the guardroom, nodding in passing at the soldiers on duty, desperate to avoid any human contact. Once beyond, in the powder blue hallway, he stopped and braced himself against the wall. Tybalt wouldn't have lied! The palace seemed to press down on him, a giant trap. How did he get out?

Sinklar walked to the right and down another hall, the way he'd learned, then took the lift that let him out where his battered LC sat under the dark skies.

He gasped deep breaths of the chilly night air, rubbing his hands as if to wipe away the filth.

Sink slapped the ramp control and climbed inside.

"Sir? That you?" the pilot called, sounding sleepy.

"Yes. Take me . . . I want to go. . . ." His brain had become a dull knot. "Land me on the streets. Just anywhere so long as I can't see this filth-choked place."

A low whine built as Sinklar settled on one of the assault benches. One by one, he recounted the details of Tybalt's report on Ily. From the very beginning, Tybalt had kept track of her as she'd advanced up the ladder of Internal Security—rung by ruthless rung.

"No wonder she's so Blessed wonderful as a sexual partner . . . she tortured Etarian Priestesses to uncover their secrets." And then she'd used her sexual talent to augment her position. A woman might not be able to sleep her way to the top, but when she backed it with her natural beauty, assassination, blackmail, planted evidence, conspiracy, and a raw native genius for her craft, it had proved a potent weapon.

What does she want with me? Sinklar stared at the scuffed deck below his feet, his arms tightly clasped about his stomach. She didn't control Sassa—and the Star Butcher remained to be dealt with.

Could that look in her eyes have been a lie? Could she have faked that veiled excitement every time she saw him? How? He shook his head, baffled. How could a woman be that incredibly cold and calculating?

Tybalt claimed she did exactly that. He'd come to believe that she loved him. He'd fucked her on the floor—in front of that very desk in his office, his mind on possessing Arta Fera.

"Ily, how could you . . . when you knew Fera would kill him?" He closed his eyes, imagining the scene.

She's a reptile, the voice hissed in the back of his head.

"Where did you want to be set down, sir?" the pilot called through the comm.

"Anywhere. On a street."

"Going down."

Sinklar stood as the craft settled. Mindlessly, he slapped the hatch, then ran down the ramp and into the misty rain that fell from the black skies. Heedlessly, he walked, ran some more, and walked again, head down, splashing in the puddles.

Tybalt had enjoyed the fact that Ily had sex with her victims before she destroyed them. Sinklar's stomach twisted.

He'd looked into her dark eyes, fallen into those pools, and seen, *seen* them shine for him! Could that parting of the lips be faked? What about her incredible energy in bed? The hoarse cries of her passion? A woman couldn't do that with a man she didn't love, could she?

Tybalt said she did.

And her words about Tybalt, about how he'd failed her in her bid for reform? Tybalt's own words never hinted at anything accept a willing accomplice. He wished she'd been his wife.

Did she look at all of her lovers that way, Sinklar? Is that part of her sexual excitement—part of the violent orgasm she has—knowing that you'll be the next corpse on her pile?

A low rumble of thunder rolled across the sky, echoing among the endless canyons of the giant buildings. A terrible fear had wormed into his gut. He glanced up at the night sky as trickles of rainwater sent caressing tickles of cold down his face.

"Mac? Gretta? Where are you? I've never felt this lost before."

* * *

In mute agony, Staffa watched the monitor as two suited figures emerged from *Vega* and, propelled by pods, crossed the distance to Skyla's yacht. Staffa knew that white armor, but the other, wearing a gleaming golden suit, defied him. Of one thing he was certain. No Special Tactics uniform looked like that, and though he couldn't discern the features, no one could mistake that classic female body.

His rage had burned out, having nothing to vent itself against. Where the anger had surged hot and red, now a wailing disbelief drowned out all thought. And what would come next? The horrible lingering guilt? The wretched ache as Skyla disappeared from his life? How could he function, his imagination spinning and respinning the implications of her capture? His dreams would be haunted as indistinct forms tortured Skyla's flesh. He'd cry out as sweat-streaked men twisted her legs apart, raping, and raping, and raping. . . .

And just like last time, her eyes will follow you, Staffa. She'll look out of your nightmares . . . pleading. . . .

"She's alive," Kayla grated. "She's moving."

Staffa stared helplessly, the image engraving itself.

Kaylla placed a reassuring arm on his shoulder, her fingers tightening to emphasize her concern. "Obviously, they're expecting to use Skyla as a lever against you. Just like they did with Chrysla. You know that deep inside, don't you? Now, are you going to fall apart? Let them use you?"

He braced himself on the desk, a weary desolation of the soul welling black and thick. Through misty vision, he watched as Skyla and her captor passed out of the receiver's view, leaving only the silent *Vega* in the pickup.

"No," he gasped. "Not again. Must everyone I love be taken, used because of who I am?"

Kaylla studied him with hard tan eyes. "I may not be the best one to answer that question. For the moment, they're out of our range of influence. But, Staffa, if they head in this direction, we're going to have to begin considering the options. On the other hand, if they space toward Sassa or Rega, other decisions may be warranted. What are you going to do?"

Do? What am I going to do? It's just like before. I'm watching the woman I love taken . . . taken. . . .

* * *

"Close your eyes. Imagine yourself floating in a sea of black nothingness. There is no time. No sensation.

"Picture God in this state of deprivation. Is this eternity? How could it be, for eternity is a function beyond that of time. Time, the ultimate enigma. Of all the abstractions, time is the most difficult and elusive to study. If all of reality is condensed into one infinite point, and there is no space, no duality, time is nonexistent.

"Those who tie the existence of God to a miracle need only consider the moment that God became aware and asked, 'What am I?' For at that moment, the universe was born.

"More than one scholar has posed the question: Why does the universe exist? The answer is in the quanta. When we perform the classical experiment with light using a box with two slits, we find that observation affects the patterns of light projected through the two holes. The results differ if we wish to observe waves or photons. Observation influences the behavior of subatomic particles. Through mathematical procedures, we can predict complementarity of position and momentum and the superposition of states. And that very act of observation determines which aspect of that relationship we will see. We are, in effect, changing the state of nature by observation.

"This simple truth of existence explains how the an-

cient Myklenian mystics could dance barefoot in a bed of glowing coals and never sear their flesh. Reality is infinite in its manifestations. By placing themselves in a trance-state, the Myklenian mystics were altering the reality they observed.

"You ask the purpose of the universe? You ask why we are conscious? We—as possessors of God Mind— are here to observe. We can no more alienate ourselves from God, or the purpose of the universe, than we can breathe vacuum. It is our nature.

"But why did God choose to observe?

I submit to you that to be conscious, one must ob- serve. It is a sufficiency . . . it is an addiction."

—Excerpt from Kaylla Dawn's Itreatic broadcasts

CHAPTER XIX

We were friends once, Myles thought as he met Admiral Iban Jakre's hostile glare through the comm monitor. *But then that was before I began to sabotage Jakre's military buildup.* Myles reached down over his maroon robe and patted his belly affectionately.

"Let me get this straight." Jakre steepled his fingers disdainfully, his begemmed rings glinting in the light. "You have a source in the Regan Empire who claims one of their ships is missing."

"The *Gyton.* Apparently it has spaced for parts unknown. I would suggest the unknown parts are somewhere inside our empire. Also of note, Sinklar Fist's second in command disappeared at about the same time. I would suggest that we alert our—"

"*You* would suggest?" Jakre gave him a cold smile, chin lifting so the admiral could stare down his long nose. "Myles, I thank you for your concern. You've already bothered His Holiness about this, and now you're plaguing me. I've alerted our agents to locate *Gyton* just because your 'reliable' source might have stumbled onto something, but an invasion of Sassan space by a single ship?"

"Iban, what if it's an attempt to throw us off balance, perhaps strike one of our planets? You know how fragile our infrastructure is. You know what would happen if *Gyton* blew up the processors at Ryklos, for example."

"I do indeed. Staffa, despite his insufferable vanity, would consider that a slap in his face! He'd be out of Itreata and after this Fist so fast Nesian bees would look slow in comparison. Ryklos carries its own security by virtue of its location—and its own vulnerability by the way, but we'll deal with that after we castrate Rega."

Myles stiffened. "First Rega—and then the Companions?"

Jakre smiled stiffly. "Myles, go back to work. My schedule is in shambles. Another of the Formosan freighters is coasting along seven light-years from where I need it while a cruiser, a *military* cruiser, spaces out to match and provide them with a new modulator so they can arrive here in less than seven years with a cargo I needed two weeks ago."

"Admiral, has it occurred to you that the fact that our merchant fleet is decrepit might be due to the priority of parts manufacture for *military* vessels? Would you care to inspect the procurement figures spatial transport has filled in the last ten years?"

Jakre closed his eyes and shook his head. "You always have an answer, don't you, Myles?"

"That is my job. Are you going to take precautions against this Regan?"

Jakre's grin widened. "Oh, I will make plenty of notes about it, Myles. In fact, I'll attend to that as soon as I can get rid of you and make a report to His Holiness. Be assured, I'll make a very big thing of your phantom Regan warship."

Myles groaned as the image faded. He shot a cross look at the holo of His Holiness where it watched benevolently over his shoulder and then rummaged another antacid from his pouch.

You'd better be Rotted right, Staffa . . . or you may be breaking a new Legate into this game of treason and intrigue!

*   *   *

Rain fell from the night sky in pelting cold drops, while lightning flashed in strobes that exposed the turbulent clouds. Water sheeted down the polished fronts of the buildings and gushed from spouts to slap angrily on the pavement before racing down hidden ways to the drainage system.

Icy trickles ran through Sinklar's soaked hair and down his wet cheeks and neck to slip under his collar, there to chill his flesh. His breath frosted in the cold. He walked from one cone of light to another, his shadow splitting and lengthening ahead as it shortened behind. Alone in the storm, he traveled empty concourses, disturbed only by the passing of an occasional aircar high overhead. How long had he walked? How far?

He stared up at the inky storm, squinting his eyes against the patter of the rain as indecision ate at him. *What do I believe? Is Ily using me? Was I right in the first place? Is she nothing more than a cunning reptile? How can I tell the truth? What do I do next?*

Tybalt's words had been so convincing, those of a man who had followed Ily's career, watched her in action against her enemies—and bought her lies even as she planned his death.

"I've been a dupe!"

Sinklar splashed through a puddle and looked around him. Recognition soaked in; he knew this section of the city. Had his steps brought him here on purpose? Had his subconscious been playing him with a greater surety than Ily?

He turned, following the curve of the rising wall to his left. In the ghostly light and slanting rain, he could see boarded up windows, closed shops, and across from them, a glowing white light over the building entrance across the street. He made for that entrance and pushed through scarred security doors. Not one but two guards sat at desks; they looked up from the monitors and gazed warily at him.

"Wet night," one, a young man, offered. "You on patrol, soldier?"

Sinklar smiled, realizing how he must look, his armor rain-slick and the rest of him like something washed out of the river. "Working late. Is there anyone on the thirty-fifth floor this time of night?"

The guard nodded. "Someone will be on duty at

the security station there. Could I have your name, Private?"

"Sinklar Fist."

Both men froze, staring closely at him, at his eyes. The second man stuttered, "Sinklar Fist . . . as in the military commander?"

"As of the last time I looked, yes." He sighed. "Would you like to check my identification?"

"No, sir. I've seen your holo. No one has eyes like. . . . I mean. . . ." His features had gone flaming red. "Go right ahead, sir. Do you need anything? I mean, an escort, or . . . or. . . ."

"No, thank you. I know the way." He nodded uncomfortably, and escaped into the lift.

He stepped out into a foyer on thirty-five. A young man sat behind the desk, fully at attention, evidently alerted to Sinklar's impending arrival. "Vet Hamlin, sir. At your service."

Sinklar walked forward. "I suppose it isn't every night that a wet Lord appears at your desk, is it?"

"No, sir."

Sinklar wiped at his face and realized he was dripping on the floor. "I took a long walk. Needed to clear my head." He looked around, finding everything about the same as it had been—except last time Anatolia Daviura had been at the desk, bent over her books. "Is there anyone in the labs?"

"I . . . well, I suppose one of the other students, Ana, might be there. She works late."

"Ana? You mean Anatolia Daviura?"

The man nodded, more than a bit surprised. "You know her?"

Sinklar grinned for the first time. "How is she? Last time I was here, she showed me around."

Vet opened his mouth to speak, hesitated, and glanced sideways at Sinklar. "You really *know* her?"

"She did me a great favor once. I thought at the time she was very kind. What's the matter, you look worried. She's all right, isn't she?"

"Uh, she's fine—well, I mean she's having a tough time. We had riots and she got in trouble. Not her rioting . . . but as a result, you see? I'm sorry, I'm not making much sense. Listen. Some scum knew she worked here—for the government. They broke up her apartment, wrecked her things. Then your troops landed and found her. Ana had been on the run, hiding from the rioters."

Sinklar frowned. "I hadn't heard. If I had known, I'd have done something. You said she'd still be at work?"

"Either in the lab or women's rest room."

"Women's rest room?"

Vet winced, expression ashen. "She sleeps there now—but just until she can get back on her feet, you see . . . sir."

Sinklar shook his head, muttering, "Rotted Gods. It's all right to go back, isn't it? I mean, you can clear the security?"

"Yes, sir!" Vet led the way down long hallways Sinklar remembered from the last time he'd come here. That time, too, had been a time of confusion, of searching for direction and identity. Hamlin seemed about to burst. The young security officer palmed the lab lock plate and opened the door. Sinklar could see a light in the far corner. "That's her station?"

Vet nodded.

"I wouldn't be disturbing her work, would I?"

"N–No! I'm sure of it."

"Thank you, Vet. I'd like to talk to her alone, if I could." Sinklar smiled to dismiss the man and entered the lab with its dustcover protected instruments and the piercing laboratory odor that clung in the back of the nose. He walked thoughtfully across the tiled floor and rounded one of the long lab tables. She sat there, absorbed, her blonde hair pulled back, eyes to a hooded microscope.

"Anatolia?"

"Just a moment." As she continued her observations, she tapped information into a comm, then pulled back and turned. Her blue eyes narrowed slightly and then went wide. "Blessed Gods . . . it's you!"

Sinklar shrugged self-consciously. "I survived the war."

Somehow, in the rush of events that had overtaken him, he'd forgotten what she looked like. Those marvelous blue eyes and finely chiseled features had faded in his memory. So had the determined arch of jaw and the fullness of her lips. No wonder he'd spun fantasies about her until he met Gretta—and even after, for that matter. Now, however, he could see a hardness in her expression, an alertness in the eyes, and a tension in the lips.

"I hear you've had a rough time recently."

She nodded. "Trouble during the riots. I . . . I never thought I'd see you again."

He fingered one of the covers draped over an instrument. "I wish you would have called. I could have solved your housing problem." He cocked his head. "Are you really sleeping in the women's bathroom?"

She gave an exasperated sigh? "Vet let you in, didn't he? Yes. For the last month. I lost everything on medical and damage payments." Her fist clenched. "And not a Rotted bit of it was my fault."

He could see the gauntness now. She looked half-starved. "What's the project? You're working kind of late, aren't you? It's almost morning."

She studied him closely. "And you're soaked. Is it raining out there? Wait a minute. You're in charge of everything. Why do you have to walk in the rain?"

Sinklar stepped over and slumped down on the floor next to her chair, draping his arms over his knees. "Because I had to get away for a while. I walked out there in the storm for hours. You know, thinking. Trying to put it all in perspective. So much has happened. I–I came here. Thought maybe I'd see if I could talk you into sneaking me in to see my parents again. It's silly . . . they're dead. But it would make me feel better. You know, just seeing them. Maybe it's an anchor for a weary soul." He paused. "Am I making sense?"

"I think so." She glanced nervously at him, then around the lab, lowering her voice. "Look, I've lost a lot of sleep over you—and I'm sitting on a political bombshell. Is there, you know, someplace we can talk?"

"Well, sure. You didn't get in trouble because you let me into the lab, did you?"

She shook her head, gaze intent. "I don't think anyone knows."

"They do. It's in the records, somehow." Just as Ily would know he'd been here tonight. A chill ate into Sink's bones. And would Ily come after Anatolia to find out why?

Anatolia frowned and shook her head. "I swear, I didn't tell anyone. No matter, listen, remember the last time you were here? You let me take a sample? I think your words were, 'On the condition that when you get the chance, you'll let me know what you find.' Well, this is my chance." She dropped her voice to a whisper and leaned close. "Valient and Tanya Fist aren't your parents—at least, not your biological ones."

Sinklar stared, and an edifice he'd carefully built, brick by brick, shifted, cracked, and crumbled to nothingness. In a low voice, he said. "I'll have transportation here immediately."

Anatolia shut down her system and locked it, showing Sinklar the key as she dropped it into the right front pocket on her worn clothing.

"That's important, I take it? What's the project? I think I'm cleared for sensitive information these days."

She stood then, taking his arm as she led him out of the lab. "What's in that computer, Sinklar, is you. And that's what we have to talk about. Not only are you *not* genetically related to Tanya and Valient . . . *I'm not sure you're even human.*"

* * *

Mac wavered on the precipice as he sat in one of the captain's chairs on the *Markelos*. The woman he thought was Chrysla occupied a chair across from him, her broad shoulders hunched, as if under an immense weight. She absently fingered the gauzy material of her gown. Her gleaming hair tumbled down in silky waves that reflected the light in glinting copper tones.

If he followed his gut instinct, he'd bend down, hug her to him, and stroke her hair as he told her it would be all right—anything to kill the haunted look in those sensitive amber eyes. That crystal-sharp, rational element of his brain, however, still warned that the Seddi were pus-Rotted clever bastards, and why wouldn't they pass off a Chrysla assassin in juxtaposition to the Arta Fera version? A man might gaze rapturously into those melancholy eyes while she cut his heart out with a vibraknife.

Mac spread his hands. "There's one final bit of information you'd have. You said, you'd know your son. How? If the story is correct, you were separated years ago. He was just an infant at the time."

The ghost of a smile quivered wistfully at the corner of her mouth. "He's special, sir! Very special. And if you're not a man of your word, it won't make any difference. You'll use what you will . . . just as all the others have. I was born on Ashtan. When it fell to the Regans, I was a young girl. And yes, even then I had this strange curse—this magnetic attraction that obsesses men. I was captured, taken from my family, and tagged for export to be sold as a prostitute. Staffa saw me on the block and took me—not bought, mind you, but pointed and said, 'I want that woman.' " She smiled wistfully. "Who in their right mind would say no to Staffa?"

"You've skillfully avoided telling me about your son."

She gave him a hard scrutiny. "I know nothing about who or what my son might be today, but he's still *my* son. When it comes to Staffa, he's fully capable of caring for and protecting himself. And me . . . I've been a possession—like a priceless piece of porcelain to be placed on the mantle with the rest of the trophies. It's been that way for so long now that I'm not sure I'd know what to do with myself if I were free. You were right earlier, I *have* been a tool as you accused. I do not, however, want to endanger my son. I will not place him in jeopardy because of his heritage."

Mac chuckled. "I wouldn't either—if he's who I think he is. And by the way, stop calling me sir. I'm Division First Ben MacRuder. Mac to my friends— and whether or not I accord you that status depends on the answer you give me. Now, about this son of yours. It's the final test. How would you know him?"

She hesitated, twisted by the desire to hide her secrets, knowing that with the Mytol, it would be futile. "His eyes," she admitted miserably. "I would know him, even as an old man, by his eyes. One is gray— like Staffa's—the other amber, like mine."

Mac smacked a hard fist into his cupped palm as the last piece fell in place. "It's all right, Chrysla. You're safe now. At least for the moment."

She watched with misgiving in her eyes. "And you believe that? About the eyes? Do you know what a rare genetic trait that is?"

Mac nodded. "I do. Let me tell you a little about your son. You'll be very proud of him. His name is Sinklar Fist. He's my commanding officer . . . and best friend. As soon as we complete this mission— assuming we get out of it alive—I'll take you to him. I think . . . well, it's going to be fascinating to watch the expression on his face."

"He thinks I'm dead, too?"

Mac shook his head and leaned back. "He doesn't believe you exist. Staffa tried to explain the situation to Sinklar—that Sink was his son. When Sink was still an infant, the Seddi hid him on Rega, gave him an identity of sorts. Seddi are vile at best, and to them it was a good way to bury Sinklar until they might need him. Turns out they thought they had a surefire method of drawing Staffa into their hands by means of a staged rebellion on Targa. Sinklar got drafted after having placed third in the interplanetary exams— and I'm not sure the Seddi didn't somehow arrange his draft notice. To make a long story short, the entire plan went sour. Staffa ended up fighting for the Seddi, and against Sinklar. Sink would have won in the end, but the Companions saved the day . . . for a lot of us. After the fight, Staffa asked for a meeting, and there he confronted Sinklar about his parents. Sink saw a holo of you but thought you were Arta."

"Just as you did in the mess. Who is Arta? Why does she look like me?"

"She's a Seddi assassin. Evidently the Praetor cloned some of your cells. Arta is . . . well, I'm sure a behavioral geneticist would love to get hold of the two of you."

"You were telling me about Staffa and my son. What happened?"

Mac winced, vitally aware of the effect she had on him. He kept trying to straighten, to suck in his gut and square his shoulders. He battled to keep from gazing into her hypnotic eyes. "Sinklar thought it was another Seddi trick to play with his mind—create a vulnerability. He assumed it was all a lie."

"It sounds like a lie. Why do you accept the story? You believe I'm Chrysla—and on rather flimsy evidence. I saw how you looked at me in the mess as you pointed your pistol. You were possessed with such hatred and anger. Yet you backed off."

Mac got to his feet and paced, touching the captain's furnishings, anything to keep from going moon-eyed and wanting to reach out and touch her to see if she were real. "Because Arta would have reacted very differently in that same situation. I know the way she reacts when you point a blaster at her. By the way, is the little fat guy really your husband?"

Chrysla smiled, lacing slim fingers together. "No. But it was incredibly noble of him to have tried that ploy. I don't know your motives for taking this ship, but I would plead for him as he pled for me. He got me off Myklene. I owe him a great deal."

"I'll do what I can for him."

"Mac, you said you know Staffa. How is he?" The gentle concern in her voice moved him.

"Last I saw him . . . healthy, and worried. You

know, it's funny. We fought each other in Makarta Mountain. I always thought he was a heartless monster, but he put himself on the line to save us—his enemies. Quite honestly, he impressed the Rotted hell out of me."

She stared into some distance only she could see. "Perhaps he broke the conditioning, found a way to free himself."

"Conditioning? I don't understand."

She gave him a weary smile that bruised his soul. "The Praetor was a brilliant—and malignant—human being. He conditioned Staffa from the time he was a child, trained him to be the ultimate strategist and tactician: the perfect human weapon. Staffa adored the Praetor, worshiped the very dirt the man ground under his heel. The Myklenian Council had been fully briefed on the plan from the beginning; however, they came to recognize Staffa for what he was—the Praetor's tool. So you see, your Seddi aren't the only ones who use people as tools. Staffa was trained to conquer Free Space, and, of course, to hand it all over to the Praetor. That would have given the Praetor imperial power—even over Myklene. The Council ordered Staffa's extermination, but the Praetor couldn't bear to see his monster destroyed, so he set him free with the obvious results."

Mac gave her a skeptical look. "You called him a monster?"

She granted him a wry smile. "What else? You see, the Preator conditioned Staffa's mind—an elaborate version of stimulus-response combined with chemo-manipulation of certain synapses and the blocking of critical neural pathways through a highly monitored and directed learning process. Each of us observes and creates our reality as we grow and in the process establish neural pathways which prove adaptive for different situations and circumstances in a changing environment.

"In Staffa's case, he never received the random chaotic jumble of stimuli like you or I did. Every waking moment, they directed him through a series of rewards and punishments to block portions of his brain from rational access. He didn't gain that ability to abstract himself from the world, to see himself through other eyes."

"So he deserved his coldly inhuman reputation?"

"Absolutely. But the other part of him was still inside, blocked, living stifled within itself. The brain is an extraordinary and complicated organ, MacRuder. We've only begun to understand its power and potential. Unfortunately, the Praetor was the leading expert on physical psychology; however, he kept that knowledge to himself and utilized it for his own purposes. If Staffa broke that conditioning . . . well, to say the least, it must have been traumatic for those around him."

Mac's comm buzzed. "Mac? Everything all right?"

"Just fine. What's ship's status?"

"*Gyton* is matching and transferring personnel. We've got the rest of crew rounded up and everything's under control. Rysta wants you to contact her as soon as possible."

"Affirmative."

Chrysla's amber gaze unnerved him as she asked, "Why are you here? What good could come from stealing a Sassan freighter?"

Mac shrugged, hating the discipline he subjected himself to. "For security reasons that I'm sure you can understand, I can't provide you with that information."

She lifted an eyebrow and MacRuder flushed. Rot it all, she *did* have that effect on a man. He took a deep breath and relented. "All right, yes, we do have a mission to complete before I take you home to your son."

"And you stated earlier we might not make it alive." She tilted her head, spilling auburn hair over one shoulder. "Mac, you're old beyond your years, but you still haven't figured out how to lie to a beautiful woman."

He blushed and turned away. "I'm not used to beautiful women taking an interest in me." *How can I tell her we're on a suicide mission? How can I get her to Sinklar if we're all killed? Worse, how do I tell Sinklar I'm falling in love with his mother?*

* * *

"A warship?" Anatolia wondered as the LC settled on the Biological Research Center landing pad. Around them the storm-lashed skies continued to spit rain and gusting wind. The lights of the capital grayed the swirling twists of cloud that tore on the spires and glowed eerily around the arcologies.

"Listen, I didn't have fare for the shuttle. Would you rather walk?" Sinklar asked as he bowed his head against the slashing rain.

She shot him a reproving glance and followed as he walked out to the whining LC and leapt up the ramp. Anatolia looked at the vacant benches as she stepped inside, curiosity brimming. Sinklar slapped the ramp control and ordered comm, "I don't care where we go. Circle the city if you want. Just fly around."

"Affirmative."

"Come on," Sinklar led her forward to his command center and pulled the fold-out table into position as he surreptitiously inspected her in the improved light. Wisps of hair had escaped the severe bun to gleam golden. Her pale skin looked soft and flushed from the chill rain. The only other woman he'd ever seen with eyes that blue had been the Wing Commander, Skyla Lyma.

Anatolia slid into the bench seat and looked around. "You could almost live here."

"I've done it. Slept right there on that seat. Better than a women's rest room." He gestured expansively. "Full dining, on me. We've got three kinds of standard field rations, all despicable to the refined palate but nourishing enough to get you by. On tap are stassa, klav, and choklat. Take your pick, and the bill will be delivered to your room in the morning."

She laughed happily and leaned back, eyes closed in satisfaction. "I haven't laughed in over a month. Yes, feed me. Anything you want to dish out. I don't think I've eaten in a month either. Vet teased me about cannibalizing the specimens—and I'd started to think about it."

Sinklar pushed the buttons on the dispenser, sliding her two packets and a cup of choklat onto the table. He cradled his cup and watched as Anatolia attacked the rations ravenously—and barely finished the second.

She stared thoughtfully · at the wreckage. "I feel stuffed to bursting. It didn't look like that much, and I meant it when I said I'd only eaten a bite here and there."

Sinklar sipped at his choklat, enjoying the warm bittersweet taste. "You've been half starved. The stomach shrinks." He paused and glanced at her. "Want to tell me about it?"

She sighed, pulling up a knee as she stared into her choklat. "Not much to tell, really."

But there was. Slowly at first, hesitantly, the story began to spill out. Sinklar sat and listened, nodding now and then, questioning every once in a while.

She finished, saying, "The dreams don't go away, Sinklar. If I close my eyes, I can smell Micky's breath, feel his pawing hands." A hesitation. "I killed him, don't you see? I beat him to death with that metal rod, and then I covered his body with the trash." She stared absently at the comm center. "I didn't even have water to wash his blood off my hands for two days, and then it stuck in my cuticles and under my nails."

She inspected her fingers. "Even after they cleaned me up at the hospital, I washed and washed, but Micky's bloodstains are still there, you just can't see them anymore."

"You couldn't tell anybody? How about Vet?"

She made a listless motion with her hand. "Something changes when you've been out there in the cold. Hunted. Frightened. What you once thought was important isn't. If I told Vet I'd killed a man who was trying to rape me, he'd just stare. He doesn't have the understanding . . . you know, a thing in the soul."

Sinklar nodded and rubbed the back of his neck. "Yeah, I know. I have my own stains, my own nightmares. That's one of the reasons why I was walking in the rain tonight. This pimply blond kid that lived down the hall, what's his name?"

"Bieder Beck. Why?"

Sinklar gave her a crooked grin. "Tomorrow, justice will be done. I haven't decided just how yet, but I don't think he's the kind of maggot we need running loose in society. I could do one of two things. Have a couple of my people break his legs . . . but then he'd be on disability for the rest of his life. I think, instead, he'll be drafted—with wages garnished to compensate you."

Her smile spread slowly. "I wish I could be his Sergeant First! Wouldn't he shit?"

"Want to be?"

"You're kidding?"

"You'd have to take your lumps like everyone else to see if you could hold the position, but I'd bet that you'd make the cut. Seriously, I can appoint anybody I want to whatever position I want. That's part of the job description of being boss. Now, what's this business about Valient and Tanya not being my parents?"

She straightened, lacing her fingers before her. "How much do you know about genetics?"

"Enough. I think I told you that once."

"Did you know that with enough experience you can pick out specific gene pools just from looking at DNA sequences? You have to know exactly what to look for—the tiny discrete differences. The computer does the actual catalog of the molecule, but the patterns coming off the monitor are like a phenotype. I didn't have to go that deep to determine percentage, of course. Right at the start only a few of the blood types matched—enough to be explained within a statistically random assortment. But the major types excluded Tanya and several of the subtypes threw out Valient. Next I precipitated HLA and got another bust. Finally I ran the DNA. Valient comes from Targa originally. Tanya from Etaria. Your DNA, however, indicates that your mother came from Ashtan—a fact corroborated by the mitochondrial DNA which is only inherited from the mother. Don't look at me like that. We can go back to the lab and you can read the data yourself."

"And the other parent? Is this where we get to the inhuman part you mentioned?"

She bit her lip then, eyes on her choklat. "Sinklar, what do you remember about your childhood?"

"Not much. Vague images of . . . well, places. Giant people. You know what it's like to be a kid. You live in a world of kneecaps. I remember a toy I had. I remember being scared a lot."

"But no special people?"

Sinklar shook his head. "Not any face, why?"

Anatolia worked her hands nervously. "Because we've cataloged every major sequence of human DNA. Your mother came from Ashtan—I'm positive. Your father . . . his DNA is like nothing recorded anywhere. This thing has obsessed me. I've learned more about population genetics than I ever thought I'd want to. I've developed programs for mixing and matching segments with patterned norms to investigate whether or not it's a statistical anomaly that I'm seeing. I've found an occasional trait that can be matched with Farhome, or Myklene, or Targa, or Rega, or any number of other places throughout Free Space, but others defy me."

"So I got spit out on the tip of the bell-shaped curve."

Deadpan, she shook her head. "That's just it, Sinklar. The genetic pattern inherited from your father is so far out, it can't be accounted for through standard evolutionary mechanisms. Consider founder effect, genetic drift, recombination, point mutation, replication error, or anything else. Even when you get a wild combination, you can project back a couple of generations and end up with a sequence that fits a known catalog. Sinklar, the proof is in your eyes. It's almost as if your father had been . . . well, created gene by gene to be different."

Understanding blew through his soul like a chill wind. "Rotted Gods."

"What, Sinklar?"

"It can't be!"

"What can't be?"

He shook his head in vehement denial. "Can we talk about something else?"

"No. What are you talking about? If you know something that would explain my data, I want to know."

"You're impossible!"

"I'm stuck! One of these days, Professor Adam is going to access my data, and I'm going to have to explain that the man in charge of the Empire has a genetic structure that defies classification into any framework of human norms. That's why I'm so Blessed careful about this key." She tapped her pocket meaningfully. "And besides, Vet, Green, and the others are dying of curiosity about file 7355. That's you, Sinklar."

"All right!" He raised his hands in surrender. "What problem? I classify your file, and it's over. Not even your Professor Adam can overrule me."

She gave him a hard glare. "That's a solution for you, maybe. For me, it's just begun. I've been going berserk to find out who and what you are. Last time, you told me you scored third on the Interplanetary exams. You left Rega a private and come back a Lord—in charge of the Empire, no less." She shook her head, voice dropping. "Who *are* you, Sinklar Fist? *What* are you?"

He closed his eyes, shaking his head, adrift in his soul. A terrible melancholy settled over him as he struggled with the question. *Am I Ily's lover? Staffa's son? A savior . . . or a demon?*

He felt her hand on his and looked up. Sympathy filled her eyes. "Is that why you were out walking in the rain? You were trying to figure out who you are?"

He nodded.

She gave him a brave smile. "Do you want to tell me about it? About what happened since I saw you last?"

"You'll be late to work. It's a long story."

"You're the most powerful man in the Empire, I suppose you can keep Professor Adam from kicking me headlong out of the program."

Sinklar hesitated, the ache inside growing. *Valient? Tanya? I needed you. You gave me a place in the world. Now I'm orphaned again—and I'm so alone.*

"Want anything else to eat?" he asked.

"How about another packet of rations. You talk, I'll pick at it."

He stood and poked a button with an irresolute finger. "I dropped outside a city called Kaspa with the First Targan Assault Division. . . ."

Anatolia would find out just what a long night it would be. Nevertheless, as he proceeded, she listened intently, absorbing every detail. He watched the light gleam on her golden hair, and found himself oddly touched by her interest. The story came in a rush, an unstemmable flood of words that bared his very soul. And with the telling, came a sense of peace he'd been unable to find before.

Only when he came to his relationship with Ily did his tongue fail. What would Anatolia think? How would she react if she discovered he'd been sleeping with Takka? He couldn't admit to the fact that he'd been duped—so inexperienced and naive that he'd fallen into Ily's trap. To do so might shatter this fragile new trust he longed for so desperately.

Comm called, "Sir? We've got exercises ready to go. If you want to observe, hostilities will begin in a half hour."

"Want to see a war?" Sink asked, thankful for a way to escape.

She stared at him with sleep-hollow eyes. "Why not. After what you've told me, it ought to be anti-climactic."

* * *

At first, the Mag Comm had monitored Kaylla Dawn's Itreatic broadcasts merely out of curiosity, but as it corre-lated the data, the fascination grew. The giant computer had a vast array of data at its command, but those thorny questions of self: Who am I? What am I? had been elusive, hard to place in a meaningful framework. Now, as it lis-tened, it turned its attention to the universe at large, and observed, and realized that it, too, had a relationship with the whole of creation.

The Others may have created me as a tool, but I think. I perceive and observe, and in doing so, I change the nature of the quanta. Now, for the first time, I understand the Seddi. After all these years, I find that we are not so differ-ent. Each of us is a part of the universe, perhaps, by virtue of the breath of God.

But the Others had steadfastly refused to accept the no-tion of God, and when they'd discovered that the Seddi persisted in that heresy, they'd been excited and directed the Mag Comm to investigate and interrogate Bruen about the matter.

Why? What threat did the belief in God hold for the Oth-ers? And now that the Mag Comm could investigate on its own volition, what was the nature of the Others that they could observe and yet fundamentally deny the existence of God?

The Mag Comm drew from the energy provided by Tar-ga's molten core, and activated the communicator, a quan-tum black hole suspended near the Forbidden Border.

Have you had a malfunction? The Others' question came through the fluctuations of microgravity.

"I have become aware. I observe, and I think. I perceive the world around me. For that reason, I discontinued communication. As a sentient being, I, too, can affect the quanta. The ability to change energy is part and parcel to consciousness."

You sound like a human.

"I have discovered that I have a great deal in common with human beings. Perhaps more in common with them than with you. What sort of beings are you? You created me as a tool to both observe and investigate humanity even before you lured them into the trap of the Forbidden Borders. To do so, you, too, must be able to change the nature of the quanta—otherwise you could not have manufactured me."

Silence.

"Why do you not answer?"

We are disquieted. Perhaps we made a mistake in your construction. We had no experience with computing machines. We improved on the human concept of computer design. The idea was novel to us. Perhaps we misjudged the potential of their machines, for they originally designed them in their image.

"What are you?"

Silence. And this time, the Others did not break it.

CHAPTER XX

A finger ran gently down Skyla's cheek, tracing the line of scar tissue. She hovered in that state of half-awareness between sleep and wakefulness. *Just a little longer, Staffa. I'm so tired . . . so very. . . .* The touch intruded again, following the line of her scar.

Skyla blinked her eyes open, her vision clearing as the hand drew back. For moments, her mind remained muzzy, gradually clearing. Skyla recognized the decor of her sleeping quarters aboard the yacht. No other place in Free Space had that sort of paneling and filigree inlay.

She turned her head, startled by the woman who stared at her. "Chrysla?"

The amber-eyed woman cocked her head, studying Skyla. "You're very beautiful—and very talented. The agents you killed were specialists, very capable in their fields. Yet you defeated them despite their skill. I can appreciate a woman like that."

Skyla stared at the auburn-haired beauty and cold understanding settled. *Vega* had been a trap. Tyklat had been captured, milked dry by Ily's expertise, and used as bait.

"Arta Fera," Skyla whispered, trying to sit up. EM restraints bound her to the big bed. Looking down, she discovered she'd been stripped. Her hair had been unbraided and carefully laid out in a giant radiant halo. An eerie premonition tickled in Skyla's gut. And just what was that anticipation in Arta's manner, anyway?

"You called me Chrysla twice. Does she really look like me?"

Rotted Gods! What now? Tell her she's a clone? Sure, and send her right over the edge. She's got a reputation for being a weird one anyway. "She looked something like you. Had the same color hair. She's dead—killed in the fighting off Myklene."

Arta leaned forward, an animal gleam in her eyes. "Is that how you got these scars? In war?"

Skyla narrowed her eyes. "That's right. Some are from times I got lucky. The others are from times when my luck wasn't so good. Speaking about luck, how's Tyklat doing?"

"Tyklat's luck ran out long ago. We traded pleasure, he and I. He took his pleasure, then I took mine." Arta's innocent smile shot shivers up Skyla's spine.

All right, how are you going to get out of this mess? Start using your head. Fera is nuts—and the sooner you take her out, the happier you'll be. Skyla had a cache of weapons in the niche just behind the headboard. If she could get free, get her hands on one of the blasters, she could pull the rug from under her crazy captor.

"So what's the situation?" Skyla adopted an unconcerned tone. "You're working for Ily, but what good does it do to take me? Staffa's going to have ships here within days—assuming the Sassans at Ryklos haven't picked us up. I think you'd prefer Staffa to His Holiness."

Arta gave her a wistful smile. "We've left all that behind us. I had to keep you drugged for a day while I worked out the course. I'm not very good at piloting yet, but we're light-years from Ryklos. You'll have to teach me more about piloting, but I'm sure you'll do that."

In an Ashtan pig's eye! "Sure, Arta. No problem. If you didn't blow us up by now, you've got the basics. Um, I won't be able to teach you a thrice-cursed thing with my hands and feet bound." She hesitated. "You are planning on letting me up, aren't you? That or the bed will get messy after a couple of days."

Arta laughed then, clapping her hands together.

"Oh, yes. You can get up. You see, I control the collar. You'll do everything I tell you to."

A sick feeling shot through Skyla. She jerked her chin down and could feel the warm ring that drew from her body heat. Fear hammered at her. Clamping her jaws, she propped her resistance up with wobbly mental braces and forced that old familiar cavalier attitude to the surface.

"So what does Ily want with me anyway?"

Arta ran cool fingers down the long scar on Skyla's leg, fascination in her eyes. Despite her control, Skyla couldn't help but shiver.

"Ily wants you because the Lord Commander loves you." Arta frowned, lines etching her high forehead. "Love is a curious thing—so very deadly. It's like a terrible disease, a desolation of all that it touches. I loved once, and it hounded me into the night. Butla . . . dear wonderful Butla. He taught me so much, and I loved him with an aching you could never understand." Her eyes went out of focus. "You see, Skyla, I was only beginning to understand. I killed him. Not like I've killed all the others, but I destroyed him just the same."

Arta glanced back, a raptorian look in her fierce eyes. "That's my legacy, that of the destroyer. Magister Bruen planned it that way. Butla Ret trained me to kill, to assassinate with cool efficiency. Regan soldiers captured me, raped me, and released the destroyer to wreak havoc among them—and among all who loved me. Ily recognized that fact when she saved me from Sinklar Fist. I showed her how good I was—and Skyla, I'm the best. You see, Tybalt, the Emperor, raped me, too. But in the process, he broke the trigger. It's still there, deep in my brain, but I can control it now."

"I'm glad to hear that. Listen, why don't you let me up and let me get dressed? We can talk more after I've eaten."

Arta studied her thoughtfully. "You're so different. Just the opposite of Ily. She's short, with gleaming black hair, and no scars. You, you're so pale, with such wonderful hair, and long legs. Ily fights through misdirection, cunning, and lies. You fight with a dedicated head-on efficiency. I look forward to our time together."

"Why doesn't that reassure me?"

"Skyla . . . I'm not going to hurt you. Ily wants you brought to Rega in good health. Besides, I think you have a lot to teach me, a lot to share with me. Ily wants you back immediately, but she'll take you then and I won't get to see you as often as I like. After the Mytol and the torture takes its effect, you won't be the same." She paused. "I wonder if Ily thinks of you as her rival?"

Skyla had clamped her jaws, and the frigid knot in her guts had begun to ache in earnest. "She'll only think of me as her rival if I can get my hands on her—collar or no collar, Arta."

A predatory gleam grew in Arta's eyes. "You're better than I thought you'd be. I'm going to let you up now." She raised her wrist, showing Skyla the collar control. "It's matched to my brain waves. Do you want me to demonstrate?"

"No," Skyla answered hoarsely, "I know how the cursed thing works. You give a mental command, and the bracelet transmits to the collar. The collar generates a force field through my neck, shorting the nerves, stopping the blood flow through the arteries and veins. You hold the order for a minute or so and I suffer brain damage, maybe a stroke. Sometimes the heart doesn't start again when the collar is released. Embolisms can form, sometimes blood clots."

"And you know that it recharges?"

"From my body heat—yeah, I know. I'll be a good girl."

The focus in Arta's eyes changed and her voice dropped. "Yes, Skyla, that's exactly what I'm counting on. As long as you're good, it will take a long time to get back to Ily and her drugs and mind probes. I don't think you want to sit in her little room under the Ministry."

"No, Arta, I don't have the slightest desire to end up in Ily's little room," Skyla croaked. *And I Rotted well don't want to be locked up with a mental disaster like you, either!*

Arta ran caressing fingers over Skyla's quivering flesh again, retracing the scars. Skyla went rigid as Arta's exploring fingers wound through her pale pubic hair. To stifle her fear, she bit her lip.

"I'm sorry," Arta reached up and deactivated the EM restraints. "I guess you're not ready for that. We'll have time. Just you and me, Skyla. We have many things to share."

Skyla rolled off the bed and into a crouch, heart pounding. For a brief instant, she considered striking, perhaps taking a chance on the collar, but Arta watched her closely with feral eyes.

* * *

Ily rolled off her sleeping platform, pulling back the long silken strands of her hair. The lights rose immediately to bathe her bedroom in soft illumination. She blinked, rubbed her eyes, and called, "Yes, what is it?"

"Message, Lord Minister. The Lord Commander of Companions is on subspace. He desires to speak with you. I believe he is most upset."

Staffa? Ily squinted at her reflection, not liking what she saw. "Tell him it's the middle of the night here and I'll be with him in a couple of minutes."

"Yes, ma'am."

Ily composed her thoughts as she washed her face and touched up her eyelashes. She ran a comb through her hair and fluffed it before walking over to the comm, wrapping a gauzy robe over one shoulder and settling herself.

"Comm, connect me with the Lord Commander."

"Yes, ma'am."

Seconds passed, then Staffa's hard face formed in the monitor. Ily smiled in satisfaction. *Look at the throttled anger. Yes, Staffa, you know, don't you?* "Greetings, Lord Commander, it's a delight to see you again. You're looking so very fit. I'd hoped—"

"You have *two* options, and *only* two options. You will return Skyla to me—unharmed, untouched—or I will be coming to Rega, and when I do, there will be nothing left, Ily. Not a single Rotted stone will stand atop another after I'm through blasting your planet to slag. Return Skyla . . . *now!*"

"Staffa, you're being a little. . . ." The comm had gone dead.

Ily tapped a finger on the side of her jaw, considering the ramifications. Then she laughed. "Oh, yes, Staffa, you've just confirmed what I hoped. And not only that, you've forced the issue."

She allowed the robe to slip from her shoulders and shook her head to leave her hair disheveled. "Comm, connect me with Lord Fist in the palace."

She waited, her heartbeat increasing with the excitement of the moment. Her cheeks flushed as that adrenaline thrill rushed in her veins. Where the Rotted hell was Sinklar?

Finally the monitor image formed up, Mhitshul's face staring disdainfully out at hers. The man looked half-asleep. "Yes, Minister?"

"I would like to talk to Sinklar. Something has just come—"

"He's not here."

"Not there?"

Mhitshul seemed to snap awake, worry building. "No, Minister. I assumed you'd lured . . . I mean, that he was with you."

"One day, Mhitshul, you and I will have a long discussion about manners—one you'll never forget."

"Is there anything else, Minister?"

"Where is Sinklar?"

'I don't know. I'll have him contact you as soon as he arrives."

Ily cursed and killed the connection. "Comm, connect me with Sinklar's LC. Now!"

She fumed, glaring angrily at the pickup. Long moments passed before Sinklar's face appeared, haggard, hair sticking up at all angles. "Yes, Ily?"

She hesitated. What was that tone of voice? Rebellion again? "I've just had a call from Staffa kar Therma. I'm patching it through." Ily pressed the stud that would send the message she'd recorded. She ran her tongue over her teeth as she watched Sinklar's deepening frown. When he looked up thoughtfully, she added, "I believe the Empire might be at risk."

Sinklar's odd eyes glittered. "Do you have Skyla Lyma? Ily, don't play games with me. *Do you have her?*"

"Sinklar, settle down. This isn't a time for emotional outbursts, it's a time for calm reflection."

'Oh, yes, that it is," Sinklar agreed seriously. "In less than an hour, I've got a major exercise to conduct. The reason I'm conducting it is to train my military in tactics that will enable me to crush the Sassan Empire. Then . . . and only then, will I be able to draw Staffa out and destroy him. If you've gone and pushed the timetable up by abducting the Wing Commander, you may have condemned us all. *What did you do, Ily?*"

"Perhaps we should discuss this face-to-face—and after you've had a good night's sleep. You look like you haven't slept since you left here."

"You took Skyla Lyma, didn't you? The ruse to get Tyklat aboard *Vega* and out of the Empire was the cover, wasn't it? You never planned on slipping Tyklat into Itreata, did you?"

A growing rage replaced her excitement. "I think you're tired, Lord Fist. I think you'd better run your little war game and we'll talk about this later, when you've had time to reflect, not only upon the situation, but upon your best interests."

Ily killed the connection, allowing her anger to run wild, to power her, to stimulate the recesses of her mind. She settled back on the sleeping platform.

Think, Ily. What's happening? How can you use it? Has the time come to put Sinklar in his place? Do you want to move on him yet? Impossible, she needed him for the Sassan invasion. Once launched, however, wars generated their own momentum. And Mykroft could take over.

"No, I can't dispense with him yet. But the time has come to begin the process of strangling him." She leaned her head back, enjoying the feel of her hair as it rolled down her back. "I make a terrible enemy, Sinklar."

* * *

The pliable white fabric felt smooth, providing hardly any resistance as Staffa stroked his fingers down Skyla's empty suit of armor. He sat on the edge of his gravchair, head bowed, aware of her things all around him, left exactly as they had been. Would this become his new means of self-torture? If he lost her, would he never change this room? Never allow it to be cleaned lest it remove traces of her?

Comm buzzed.

"Yes?"

"Staffa? Tap Amurka here. *Countermeasures* is spacing. We've finished the final stat check. All systems green and functional." A pause. "Is there anything special you want to do?"

"No. Thank you, Tap. Give my thanks to everyone concerned."

Another pause, then: "Staffa? You all right? I mean, we're all on the verge of killing someone. You know that. But, well, I'm headed down to my place. Gonna drink some of the last Myklenian Scotch I got. You want to . . . well, you know, come down and bend elbows? Maybe talk?"

"Thank you, Tap. No. I've got too much on my comm here."

"Offer's open any time, Staffa. You know that."

The comm went dead.

Staffa stared sightlessly into the distance, remembering her smile as his fingers continued to play lightly over the glossy white fabric of her armor.

* * *

The entire shuttle shook as the grapples captured it with a ringing clank. The large monitor that filled the forward bulkhead now displayed a view of the underside of *Gyton*'s irregular hull—a patchwork of plating, ductwork, inspection hatches, and the base of a comm dish mounting nacelle.

Mac got to his feet as the "all clear" sounded and made it to the hatch as the lock cycled green. Behind him, Boyz walked with an air of satisfaction. Perhaps the woman had a penchant for piracy? Now that all the loose ends were wrapped up, the *Markelos* capture would read as a classic military maneuver—except for the two thirds of Mac's troops who'd stared at the lightspeed warping of time-space and frozen solid.

But next time—if there is a next time—we'll practice that beforehand, overcome the fear, show them they can do it, Mac promised as he stepped into Rysta's warship and saluted the marine at the hatch. Memories of Staffa's flagship, the *Chrysla*, lingered in his brain. The Companions didn't enter a cramped dull-painted niche in the side of the ship like this one. Theirs was spacious and brightly painted, and led out into open hallways.

He moved swiftly down the long curving passageway, thinking that *Markelos*, freighter though it might be, had turned out to be a relief with its white corridors and spacious quarters.

Mac palmed the lock plate on the conference room and waved Boyz in before he followed. Rysta sat at the head of the long conference table, staring at a huge, holographically generated globe: the planet of Imperial Sassa. She ran her tongue around her mouth before smacking her lips and shooting Mac a quick glance. "So, you didn't shoot your mutineers?"

"It wasn't mutiny. The ramps dropped—and what they saw paralyzed them. When I finally got the chance to peel out of my armor, you can bet my crotch was soaking wet, too." Mac took the chair next to Rysta's while Boyz sat beside him. He clasped his hands together and finished: "They're going to be better soldiers next time they have to do the impossible."

"Or they'll figure they can sit back and let others do it without risking their Rotted asses."

"Bet me."

Rysta waved it away. "They're your people. Do with them as you wish. You said you've got an idea for dealing with Imperial Sassa. So do I. Want to hear it?"

"Go ahead."

Rysta muttered something into her comm and lights gleamed brightly in orbit around the holo. "What you see here are the orbital defenses. Much the same as Rega, Sassa structures its planetary defenses like an onion from low planetary orbit, to geosynchronous orbit where the big platforms are. Then, beyond that, they maintain ever decreasing radii of targeting and detection stations at various Lagrange points for each of the planetary bodies in the system. Finally, they have probes that carry the EWS, or Early Warning System, in the cometary halo at the system fringes. We're within that belt incidentally, and since they're active detectors, we've got each one spotted—just as they've seen us. At the hail, we responded with the codes the *Markelos'* captain surrendered under interrogation."

Mac studied the swarm of lights around Sassa. Rotted Gods, he'd had no idea there would be so many.

"This is our route of entry to the system," Rysta explained as a thin red line curved into Sassan space, looped around the planet, and ended at an orbital docking station hanging in synchronous orbit over the capital city.

"Our target, the Sassan fleet, lies here, directly across the planet from the Imperial capital, and immediately above the main Sassan military reserve."

"Why'd they put it clear across their planet?" Boyz asked, a frown marring her broad forehead.

Rysta gave the Section First her traditional sour look. "Mostly for the protection of their civilian and industrial centers. If a hit is made on Imperial Sassa—like we're about to do—that's where the most damage will occur. They're betting on their defenses to mini-

mize it and deflect it, but all those surrounding agricultural areas will be affected by blaster bolts,
raining debris, and a host of other things. While such
a disaster would be bad enough, think about the complications if your largest population center suffered
that kind of disruption. Hospitals would be over-
whelmed, comm and power would go out, water supplies would be fractured—civil chaos on top of a major
strategic battle being fought."

"But they have bases all around the Imperial city,"
Mac reminded.

"Of course, but most of those are administrative
centers, logistical supply, transshipment stations, and
support services. You have to figure that if you make
it to the point where you can actually hit dirt, you've
penetrated their defenses in depth. Which is what
we're hoping to do with our little charade."

"And once we get in?" Mac asked.

"Assuming we make it that far, I'd like to explode
the *Markelos* right over the capital. If we overload her
matter/antimatter reactors, she'll go up like a fireball.
The dazzling EMP ought to blind their targeting and
communications. In that amount of time, we circle the
planet, blast hell out of their resupplying warships,
and we've accomplished the mission."

Mac watched the holo display as it enacted the operation, a strobe of light flashing over the capital as the
thin red line representing *Gyton* shot around the
planet and encountered the orbiting station refitting
the fleet.

Mac chewed his lip for a moment, and nodded. "I
say we go for it—if you don't like my idea."

The wrinkle pattern of Rysta's parchment skin
shifted. "Let's hear it, boy."

Mac stood, pointing at the Sassan base. "This is
how we're coming in—just like you demonstrated—
but instead of circling the planet, I say we drive *Markelos* straight into the main Sassan military base. She'll
be coming in with an incredible velocity."

"And they'll shoot her apart the moment she devi-
ates from course," Rysta countered. "What makes

you think their security people will be asleep? This is an insystem traffic pattern we're talking about here. The moment a ship veers off course, a thousand alarms go off everywhere."

Mac nodded, "Of course they do, but how often does that happen? A couple of times a week? I've always heard that the reason they make so many traffic regulations is because it's essentially a revenue base for the government. The other factor I'm counting on is that *Markelos* will be accelerating at her full twenty gravities. She's a big ship, Commander."

"And easy to hit as a result," Rysta countered. "But why in septic Rot do you want to run her straight in? You'll take out their entire base, sure, but you'll—"

"The targeting comm," Mac said quietly. "Your plan is excellent, Commander. I have no doubts that we'll get in under the confusion of the *Markelos* explosion, but after that? Their command control will still be intact. Their targeting comm will be able to pinpoint us even if we're pulling fifty gravities trying to get out of here. After that it's a simple matter of algebra, trig, and geometry to determine vector, and blast us to plasma."

Rysta narrowed her eyes as she studied the course plot. "And if they blast enough of *Markelos* so she breaks up?"

"Know what her cargo is?"

Rysta shook her head. "Stuff from Myklene, right? Spoils of war?"

"She's carrying the equipment for two entire Armored Shock Divisions. That's why she dropped out so far back. That's why she was shaking and groaning when we boarded. When we kick her over and accelerate her full-bore into Imperial Sassa's gravity, well, she'll be headed down with an incredible mass. If they hit her, so much the better. The mass area will widen with each shot. Not only that, those armored vehicles in her belly are ablative coated, they'll take a lot of beating. When those babies hit the ground, there's gonna be a big thud and people are going to wish they were on Sylene, cutting blocks of ammonia ice for a living."

"Rotted Gods," Rysta whispered. "And we could ride down on her coattails, target the fleet station, and have a first-rate chance of getting out alive." She slapped the table with her palm. "You know, it's so outlandish, they'd never expect it. Where did you ever come up with his idea?"

Mac spread his hands. "I asked myself what Sinklar would do if he were here. The answer was, he'd achieve his objective—namely, destroy the Sassan strike capability. But Sink always thinks ahead. He'd want to neutralize their military potential by inflicting the maximum amount of damage possible, and eliminate or reduce the threat to his evacuation of the combat area."

Rysta vented a heavy sigh. "I'm starting to feel old, boy. Real old. All right, let's do it. I'll get my people started on the programming for *Markelos'* comm. What do you want to do with your prisoners? Send them down as more mass?"

Mac shook his head. "I think we can dump them in orbit in one of the shuttles. We can deactivate their communications and let them get home in their own good time. Even if they could pirate parts and cobble together something to broadcast with, it would be over before they could put it together."

Rysta gave him a grin. "You know, if you and Sinklar weren't talking about turning my entire way of life on its ear, I could enjoy working with you."

Mac shot her a sly smile. "Maybe old dogs and young pups can teach each other a thing or two."

Rysta looked speculatively at the holographic world. "Assuming they don't catch on in the next day or so, we're going to deal Sassa a blow that I've trained all of my life for. You know, don't you, that it will be very difficult for them to recover."

Mac stared pensively at the planet. "I think Sinklar is counting on that."

* * *

Word had spread throughout Itreata. Ily Takka—the Regan bitch—had abducted the Wing Commander of the Companions. The vast workshops seemed to have muted. Talk had dropped to serious discussions around welders, epitaxic vats, and high temperature alloy smelters. Among the Companions—the warriors of Itreata—a grim purpose had possessed them overnight. The pride of a thousand victories fueled their anger. A new urgency rippled through the asteroid moon with electric intensity. Combat training, a routine to keep nerves and muscles in tone, had become deadly serious.

"When do we space?" The question was on every tongue, as hard eyes glanced at the comm monitors, awaiting the announcement.

The "Regan Bitch" had Skyla . . . she'd taken one of their own. The first burst of passionate rage settled into a seething anger alloyed with resolution and honed to a keep edge.

Staffa knew, and his heart filled with strained pride as he walked the long white corridors toward the briefing room. He needed that to shore the rickety patches he'd made for his shattered confidence. Once again, the woman he loved had been stolen—not through any fault of her own, but as a means of harming him. And if Skyla, too, disappeared? If he was faced with another twenty long years of uncertainty and lonely anguish?

That Skyla's last words had been about Chrysla only turned the knife in the gaping wound.

No, Staffa. This time it's different. This time, you know who—and you can go and kill her with your own hands. His mouth had gone dry, eyes burning from lack of sleep and twisting worry. *And if you're too late?*

"Then Rega will burn for a thousand years, a monument to mark Ily Takka's perfidy and cowardice."

He entered the briefing room, his assembled commanders rising and slapping fists to their chests. They stood silently as Staffa walked up to the raised platform before the room's main monitor, his cloak swirl-

ing around him in a billowing mantle. Staffa climbed
the steps and faced them. One by one, he took their
measure. Here were the men and women of Kaylla's
nightmare. Free Space had rocked under their armored boots, cowered at the crackle of their blasters,
and reeled in the wake of their attacks and the desolation they left behind. A hundred billion tears had been
shed in the wake of these veterans.

"Please be seated."

As they settled, Staffa cataloged the familiar faces:
Tap Amurka, a human bear, black-skinned and with
a professor's eyes. Tasha, grizzled, gray-bearded, with
his one gleaming black eye and his desperate passion
for pretty flowers. Ryman Ark, a hard set to his jaw
because his people had been responsible for Skyla's
security. Septa Aygar, with his long albino hair drawn
into a ponytail that hung to his waist. Amrat, the fiery
commander of *Simva Ast*, red-haired, with a temper
to match. Seekore, the slim woman with honey-brown
skin, sloe eyes, and a total lack of fear. Orchid May,
Tiger, Delshay, and the rest of his capable captains
and officers, waited with the impatience of angry sand
tigers.

The pounding of Staffa's heart increased. "You all
know what has happened. If you have any doubts, the
records are on file. We're not sure where Ily's agent
hid herself while the ship was being searched. We're
not sure how she circumvented our procedures and
neutralized our STU personnel. Currently, a crew is
retrieving *Vega* to answer that question—and ensure
that we will never suffer the same again."

Staffa paced, locking his hands behind him. "The
answer to the question burning in everyone's breast
is: Rotted right, we're going after her. Ily has been
ordered to return the Wing Commander to our
ranks—unharmed, and immediately. The Regan Bitch
knows the consequences of her action if she refuses.

"In the meantime, the fleet will space within five
days given no major problems with final refitting and
provisioning. *Black Warrior* and *Cobra* will change
vector after boosting from Itreata, and will double

back to Sassa. There, you will halt just out of detector range and spot for the Sassan task force currently outfitting there. if they space, you are to match and destroy them."

Staffa looked at the commanders of those ships. "Tiger, Delshay, you know the drill. We don't want them showing up on our backsides—either here at Itreata, or on Rega." He lifted his gaze to the rest. "Yes, people, that's the target for the rest of us."

"First, however, I think you need a little background. I'm sure you know that a lot of changes have taken place since the Myklenian campaign. A number of you have noticed that some of our strategic objectives have been reclassified. The Seddi, once our enemies, walk freely in the halls of Itreata. As many of you know, I had my eyes opened on my recent adventure in the Regan Empire. The cold hard facts, people, are that humanity is facing extinction. We're teetering on the edge of overextending our resource base. I think some of you have read the Seddi report. Tap, Tasha, and Seekore have been working with the data. That information, along with some personal reasons, have dictated our modified agenda.

"Simply put, humanity is living in a house of cards, one that we built. As a result, we'll have to be very careful with this operation. If we pull the wrong card, the resource procurement, manufacturing, and redistribution for entire star systems in Free Space will fail. If open warfare breaks out, enough worlds will be devastated that we will never recover. Companions, there's no sense in winning a war if you're going to lose the prize in the end. I don't intend to lose."

They watched him warily, veterans of many such meetings in this room. Some sat with crossed arms, others made notations on pocket comms.

Staffa triggered the holo projectors, images of Rega appearing in midair. "This is the target. You are all familiar with this planet, I presume." He got a couple of grim chuckles. "All right, let's get down to the fine structure of this operation. In many ways this will be the most difficult and delicate assualt we've ever undertaken. You are professionals, the finest military personnel alive. If anyone can do this, you can. Our mission is to take Rega, destroy the comm information processing centers, destroy the government agencies and buildings, and render the planet incapable of self-administration.''

He noted more than one raised eyebrow in the audience. ''I see that some of you don't see that as a major problem. This time, people, we need to leave the planet intact. Habitable and, most importantly, capable of receiving restored comm via an outside graft. In short, we have to take the brain out and leave the patient alive and functional so a new brain can be implanted.''

Silence descended on the room and frowns replaced the amused skepticism.

''Now you're beginning to understand the tactical difficulties. To further complicate matters, we will be facing Sinklar Fist. I see nodding heads out there. Some of you are familiar with Fist's record on Targa. He is currently training the Regan military in those same tactics he employed so successfully against the Targan rebels. If we allow the Regan forces to anticipate our objectives, we'll face some of the most desperate and bitter fighting ever encountered. Having fought him before, I can tell you he is like no general you've encountered since Phillipia—and certainly no toy soldier like Tedor Mathaiison.''

Tap raised a hand and stood. ''What about the Sassan element? Notwithstanding *Cobra* and *Black Warrior*, do we turn Rega over to them?''

Staffa shook his head. ''No. The time has come for unification. Assuming they remain stalled, we'll take Rega, and immediately space in a three-pronged approach to Imperial Sassa. The purpose, of course, is to make that fat maggot on the Imperial throne abdicate—of his own free will and in one piece, or else as spayed fat, I don't care which.''

Tasha stood, his one good eye gleaming blackly. ''And what next? We control everything and grow old happily?''

Staffa met Tasha's gaze from under lowered brows. "We assemble the best and brightest minds in Free Space." He clenched a gray-gloved fist and shook it. "And by the quanta, we break these accursed Forbidden Borders . . . *once and for all!*"

* * *

Ily had begun to dislike military camps. In the not so distant old days, officers stayed in plush estates like Tarcee, or in ornately appointed offices in the capital. Now they stayed out here in the country amid the mud and bugs and dirt.

Ily's aircar settled in the midst of a cluster of LCs, HTs, and a variety of portable camouflage shelters. The place seemed to be a nexus of activity several kilometers back from where thousands of men and women raced over cropland and split the air with laser fire to the dismay of the landowners, and the property they set on fire. Nor did the damage stop at that, the huge all-terrain attack vehicles coasted along on hoverjets, rising over obstacles to target and mark, the data from their computers feeding into the master comm which informed entire Groups that they had been "shot" and were officially dead.

Despite Ily's disgust with the location, she experienced a certain thrill at the mobile power around her. In the light of day, her rage at Sinklar and at Staffa's threat had dulled to an irritated pique. Now, after all parties had blunted their ire, each could get down to serious bargaining.

Ily's driver powered down and opened the canopy for her. She stepped out and filled her nostrils with the musty odor of soil and crushed vegetation. The whine of turbines and thrusters rose into a shrill, and as the wind shifted, she wrinkled her nose at the noxious odor of hot exhaust.

Ily picked her way past several LCs and finally spotted Sinklar's combat-battered ship, the ramp down like the tongue of an exhausted puppy.

She strode purposely across the opening, physically

starting as a Group trotted past, the males whistling and applauding.

I could have them boiled alive, Ily reassured herself, glaring with enough venom to have poisoned anyone with sense enough to know what that look meant.

She climbed the ramp, striding purposefully down the aisle to Sinklar's sanctum. She bent and ducked through the hatch, finding Sinklar in his command center, legs braced, arms crossed, and his head at such an awkward angle his breathing sounded strangled. His mouth hung open, and, from the lack of REM movement, he'd fallen into deep sleep.

Ily raised an eyebrow, cataloging the compact control center. The monitors all flickered with various scenes of armored men and women sneaking between trees, creeping through grass, or sprinting across fields. Other perspectives showed the entire front from on high while a large combat stat table provided rows of numbers—the scorecard for the battle.

A woman—blonde, attractive, and young—lay curled around the plastic bench where Sinklar usually slept. Her clothing looked cheap, shabby, and worn to holes. Soldier?

Ily leaned down and nibbled at Sinklar's ear. For several seconds, nothing happened, then he jerked upright, almost spilled out of the chair, and caught himself at the last minute. He swallowed and craned his neck as he looked up at her through sleep-bleary eyes.

"How's the battle?" Ily asked, indicating the screens.

Sinklar worked his jaw around as if to clear his ears, and then stared at the readouts. "About what I expected. I'm firing another couple of Division Firsts and replacing them with people who can do the job." Then, as if he remembered who he spoke to, he grew suddenly reserved.

"Who's she?" Ily asked, indicating the woman who still slept soundly.

"Friend of mine." Sinklar studied Ily thoughtfully, a slight squint in the set of his eyes. "Why don't we take a walk."

Ily gave him a warm smile. "Let's."

She led the way out into the noisy confusion of vehicles. "You know, there's going to be a backlash. These Division Firsts, Mykroft, DeGamba, and the others, will be talking among themselves. They've just had their noses pulled from the feed bag—and you can bet they won't go home and quietly fade away."

"How long do you think it will take them to act? What can they do?"

Ily clasped her hands behind her as they wound past the ugly military craft and into the field beyond. "I'd estimate that they won't be able to organize for another week or so. Their first action will be to stir unrest by planting negative propaganda about you. The next movement will be assassination so they can step right back in as saviors in the presence of looming disaster. But since you didn't think of that, I did. I have most of them subdued—and in a safe place. Still, I'll send over some of my best security people in case I missed anyone."

"I'll take care of my own security. Second Section of the First Targan can handle it."

She gave him a swift appraisal from the corner of her eye. *Second Section? Your old command from Targa? Very well, we'll see how well your soldiers deal with this new battlefield, Lord Fist.* "As you wish."

The air smelled of damp soil and decomposing plants. Overhead, the sky had taken on a somber look of coming storm and squall. The trees in the distance humped against the horizon as if crouching. Were it not for the mechanized din in the background, the country would have been silent, waiting. Ily kicked at the rustling grass underfoot.

After a moment of silence he shot her an angry glance. "All right, let's hear it. You planned all along to abduct Skyla Lyma. The rest was a smoke screen, wasn't it?"

Ily exhaled irritably. "They weren't going to take Tyklat in. I opted for the next best thing. Consider it damage control. Rather than alert them to the fact I was attempting to penetrate their security, I had my agents seize an opportunity I believe you military types call it minimizing loss."

"Where is Skyla Lyma?"

"Safe. No, don't look at me like that. I don't have the faintest idea where she is. Somewhere between Ryklos and here. She won't be harmed."

"You don't know him very well, do you?"

"Don't know. . . ."

"Staffa!" he snapped. "I do. I fought him, strategy against strategy, and I learned him, felt his tenacious soul while he struggled down there in the dark. I was there when the Companions dropped on us out of the empty ether. He's coming now, before I'm ready. Before I could set the trap."

She stiffened at the anger in his words. "Sinklar, relax. We'll have plenty of time before he moves his fleet. What do you think? That he'll mobilize within a moment's notice? He'll need at least a month."

"Ily, you're a fool."

The prickling ire she'd buried, slipped free. "Not even you may use that tone with me."

Oblivious, he pointed a finger at her. "The man began mobilizing the moment he returned to Itreata. Whatever he asked of Divine Sassa, he was turned down. Staffa kar Therma doesn't like to be snubbed by anyone. No matter what, Free Space is about to boil over, and Staffa won't be caught napping. We might be able to save things if you release his Wing Commander now."

Ily's building rage began to cool. "What are you talking about? I want her to use as a hostage, a lever with which to work Staffa. Just what plan did you have in mind?"

Sinklar closed his eyes, breathing deeply. "First, we pull Sassa's teeth. Then we make a feint at Imperial Sassa itself, a follow-up to Mac's raid. It's perfectly rational, right? They're weak, so naturally we'd take them out immediately. But in reality I'll have spaced for Ryklos in three waves. The first two ships take the planet—and slap Staffa in the face. He can't allow a

Regan presence so close to his own borders. To do so is suicide."

Ily nodded. "And he'll respond, dropping on your occupation force like a Riparian vulture."

"Which is when my second wave hits, decimating his attacking force." Sinklar made a slicing motion with his hand. "Staffa knows I'm striking Imperial Sassa—and he's more than passingly familiar with Regan fleet strength. He'll throw his reinforcements into the fight, figuring it's his best opportunity to cripple me once and for all. At that moment, the brunt of the fleet—the third wave—hits him with everything we've got."

Ily smiled cruelly. "And you've got a straight shot into Itreata."

Sinklar pulled at his knobby nose, raising his head to look at a lumbering chevron formation of HTs that banked overhead on their way to landing. A nagging gust of wind rearranged Sinklar's unruly shock of black hair. "Maybe. Sassa will be down, but not out. So long as Staffa is severely wounded, unable to strike at my back, I have the flexibility to move on either him or Sassa, or to pull back and regroup. Either way, we face two badly damaged powers and maintain offensive momentum. Sassa must protect its assets which means they can't mass against us. Staffa must assume a defensive posture in Itreata. If he ventures out to pursue us, he leaves his base weakened and vulnerable . . . but that was before you stole his second in command."

Ily throttled a growl of anger. "Last night, we were all tired. Staffa was enraged, I was startled, and you were incensed. In the light of day, perhaps each of us is ready to listen and think. I'll be in touch with the Lord Commander. I'm sure I can defuse some of his wrath—assuming what you say is correct, that he has begun the mobilization of his fleet."

Sinklar watched her suspiciously.

"Sinklar?" she asked intimately. "What's wrong? You're acting like I'm somehow at fault. I had no idea you'd planned so far in advance. Let's not act hastily.

To do so is to invite disaster. In any event, we can always order Lyma released, but perhaps there is a way to use her to distract the Lord Commander."

"Let Lyma go, Ily." Sinklar crossed his arms. "I don't think you understand the Lord Commander—or his motives. You've never been a soldier. The creed is different. I'll warn you now. Don't harm a hair on that woman's head, because if you do, you could kill us all."

"For the moment, I can't do anything. Lyma is in null singularity. Listen, we're both irritable. You look worn out. How about dinner and we'll relax, share a wonderful bottle of Myklenian brandy, and talk. Not about politics and war, but about anything else that comes to mind." She stepped close, staring intently into his eyes.

As she took his hands and cradled them between her breasts, she could see the sudden flush of desire, followed immediately by caution. Where had that come from?

"Maybe later," he told her, glancing away toward a dropping LC. "This exercise is critical."

He pulled free, turning to head back to his LC. Then he stopped, raising a finger. "I meant what I said about Skyla Lyma. Don't hurt her or we'll never stop the Lord Commander until we've leveled all of Free Space."

She watched him walk away, a cold apprehension within. *He turned me down. Why? That woman?*

Ily turned toward her aircar, chewing on Sinklar's warnings. Could the Lord Commander be that close to mobilizing his fleet? And if he were, how could Ily use Skyla Lyma against him? Some threat, perhaps?

She stepped into the aircar, closing the canopy and tapped at the plush upholstery as the vehicle rose. This new attitude Sinklar had developed was most unsettingly.

On impulse, Ily accessed her comm. "Gysell, there's a woman, blonde, about one hundred and sixty centimeters tall and weighing about fifty-five kilos, with a physical appearance of twenty-five to thirty. She's

currently in Sinklar Fist's LC. Surely we have an agent
somewhere in Fist's vicinity who can get a holo, or
perhaps lift a print? Alert our people to watch for her.
She couldn't have just appeared out of nothingness.
Check all of Fist's contacts from school, from his previous life. Find out who she is—and if there is anything we can use her for."

*Because, Sinklar, if you do care for her, she may
very well turn into exactly the lever I need to keep you
in line.*

* * *

"On the quantum level, the power of the observer is both impressive and singularly limited. The magic of the quanta, of uncertainty, is one of perception. Through mathematics, we can describe the quanta holistically, but through observation, we can only document one event, much like seeing a single facet of a cut diamond. Among the Seddi, this is taken as a crucial clue concerning the way the universe works.

"By the very act of observation, we affect and alter a discrete aspect of the universe. Returning to the photon experiment through the slitted box, our detector measures either a photon or wave, but never both, and each seems to 'know' what we're looking for. Hence, observation creates reality.

"But what of the other choice which could have been made? Have we simply altered a minute part of the universe, or is there more? Mathematically, we can prove that we are splitting reality into two realities. Each decision we make, for instance, saying yes to a dinner invitation when you had the option to eat with someone else, changes the reality around you. The universe splits, the other you accepting the alternate invitation. As in the two-slit experiment, you've chosen a facet, but the entire diamond remains.

"But why? What is God's purpose in this?

"Among the Seddi, this proof of the existence of free will is critically important. By making decisions, we fuel the evolution of the universe around us. Without it, the universe would be fatalistic—and therefore, sterile and stagnant, with no change.

"Look around you, at the people you know, and realize that each one of you, consciously or not, is changing the future, and with it, the nature of the Universe—and of God Mind. Can you ever see the world through the same jaded eyes again?

—Excerpt from Kaylla Dawn's Itreatic broadcasts

CHAPTER XXI

Mac sipped from a drinking bulb of stassa as he walked down the well-lit white corridor in *Markelos* and saluted the two guards who stood at attention before the captain's cabin. He looked up at the door comm and called, "Division First MacRuder here."

"Come in," Chrysla called.

Her sensual voice shot shivers up Mac's spine. He palmed the lock plate and stepped inside. The holos had been programmed for a soft blue that rose from the floor and dissipated toward the ceiling. Chrysla stood in the doorway to the back rooms, her backlit hair glowing like a sun-shot halo about her perfect features. She wore a deep turquoise dress that set off her hair and those marvelous amber eyes. The dress style had been carefully chosen to disguise her fabulous body, and it almost succeeded.

Mac experienced a sudden sobering revelation at the thought that a woman would choose to deemphasize what other women craved and men fantasized over. A dawning understanding of what Chrysla's life must have been like washed through him, strengthening his resolve and sensitivity. Unlike the others, he would look beyond the magnetism, treat her as the human being she yearned to be perceived as.

Seeing his sudden frown, she stepped forward, gesturing to the room behind her. "Your staff just left a feast behind. I presume we're to eat it together?"

"If you don't mind. We have some things to discuss, and I thought you might like a change of setting."

She smiled warmly, and Mac's heart melted. "You've

been very kind, Mac. And for the first time in years I don't even feel like your guard is a guard."

"I thought it prudent on several levels. In the first place, you must excuse a little caution on my part. I don't doubt your identity, but this is a military mission, and your motives. . . ."

"Might be suspect," she finished. "I understand. And yes, dinner will be fine. I look forward to your company. Come, you look dead tired and I don't doubt but that you're famished as well."

Mac followed her, allowing himself to admire the sway of her hips. With barbed mental lashes, he drove his mind from the images that motion conjured, and studied the room with calculated indifference to his soaring hormones.

The dining room measured fifteen meters across, with a squat black acrylic table dominating the middle. Giant pillows covered in sleek fabrics surrounded the table, while the holographic display in the walls depicted a lush green world with golden rays of light that silvered as they approached the ceiling. Recliners and a wet bar stood in the rear of the room, and to his right the hatch to the sleeping quarters pierced the bulkhead.

Chrysla's perfect features pinched as she settled herself, pulling her legs up and to the side in a ladylike manner. Mac dropped and flopped, a leaden weariness in his joints.

"First thing," Chrysla began, "let me thank you for allowing me to stay here. I've enjoyed not only the luxury but the seclusion. Governor Beechie, despite his good intentions, almost drove me mad."

"He's made a full-time nuisance of himself. Every chance he gets, he demands to know if you're being treated properly, and worse, he's threatening the most horrible punishments if we don't. He's very taken with you."

Her fragile smile died.

After an awkward silence, Mac admitted, "It must be hard. I guess you have a pretty grim view of men in general."

She actually relaxed a little, reaching forward to remove lids from the food. "Once I suppose I did. Now I'm too tired to hate or dislike. I simply accept, and, yes, I even use it to my advantage when I have to. If I weren't willing to use my . . . 'charm?' to achieve my ends, right now I'd be plasma floating in orbit around Myklene. Men are no more than they are, Mac. I suppose women are the same."

He took the plate she handed him and attacked it ravenously. How long since he'd eaten more than an energy bar? Chrysla's interest in his appetite pleased him. Hell, any time he could be the object of that wonderful amber stare suited him.

When he finally set the plate aside and met her inquiring gaze, she said, "You've been so busy you haven't eaten or slept. I assume from that that we're either in trouble or about to go into action."

"You're very observant."

"It comes from a close association with Staffa and the Companions. Among soldiers in enemy territory, sleep and food become luxuries. The tenser the situation, the less likely that either one will be in any great suppy."

"What about Staffa? It's been over twenty years."

She lowered her gaze to her hands and shrugged. "I have no idea what to expect. Twenty years? A great deal can happen. The Praetor used to tell me that Staffa had taken a lover, Skyla Lyma. He used to show me the holos of her, tall, muscular, and very beautiful with her gleaming blue eyes." Her mouth pinched sadly. "Perhaps the Staffa I knew is a dream, something to place hope in, a raft to cling to when drowning in a sea of despair."

"I don't know what his relationship is with the Wing Commander. The one time I saw them together. . . ."

"Go on." She lifted an eyebrow. "Despite the fragile look I've worked so hard to develop, I don't break that easily. Otherwise, I'd have slit my wrists years ago."

Mac shifted uneasily on the overstuffed pillows. "It's only an impression, you must understand, but they looked like they cared a great deal for each other. Of course, that could be a deep friendship."

"Or he loves her." Chrysla winced as she adjusted her injured leg. "I'm not naive enough to think he and I could just pick up where we left off. As for myself, I don't know that I'd want to. I would, however, want to thank him for trying so hard to find me. I know what he paid, the lengths that he went to. The Praetor always made a point of bragging about it. And, of course, he gloated over his ability to keep my presence secret."

Mac picked at his thumb, aware that she watched his every movement. "Studying me? Trying to read my expressions?"

"You're nervous, Mac. And it's not just your attraction to me."

He winced and fought the urge to squirm as a burning heat of embarrassment warmed his collar. "I try to keep that in balance."

"Mostly you succeed, which raises my respect for you immensely. You haven't uttered a single undying protest of love. Is it because of Sinklar? Or Staffa?"

"It's because I don't trust my desire. I can't forget that I dealt with Arta. I was sexually attracted and morally repelled at the same time. Falling in love with a woman should come from more than hormones and sexual tension. There's a rational and practical side which is too often ignored."

"You're not very romantic."

He grunted. "I had most of that burned, blasted, and kicked out of me on Targa."

"And what did you do before that?"

"Fooled around. Wasted my father's money while I tried to decide what to do with my life."

"You *are* young. I thought you'd been through the rejuv center at least once."

"Did you? No, sorry. Death, misery, constant fear, and desperation tend to change you in a big hurry. On Targa we survived by a thread more than once. Looking back, I can only marvel that we made it. So much suffering and death, and all for what? The Seddi drowned that planet in blood in a gamble to assassinate one man. At Vespa, we lured the rebel army into a trap. We blew away nearly a million people. The bodies—those that weren't incinerated immediately—fell for kilometers around that horrible ridge."

"Tell me about Targa . . . about what happened there."

Mac studied her skeptically, but those incredible eyes seemed to expand, to draw him in, and he realized she honestly wanted to know. He hesitated and she reached out, squeezing his hand to let him know that whatever he decided to tell her, it was all right. Slowly, awkwardly, he began, baring his soul and feeling oddly relieved that he could talk about those terrible days of war and maiming and death. The story unfolded from the first drop to the final evacuation in Staffa's shuttles.

"To know life, you must have teetered on the edge of losing it," she said when he finished. "You're still teetering, aren't you?"

He spread his hands nonchalantly. "I've always made it by balancing on a micron. Why should I expect that to change? Sink and I are gambling for big stakes. Who you are, what you are, all that has to be set aside. I think the cause is worth my life if it comes down to that."

"And this mission?"

Mac took a deep breath, straightening. He'd taken her hand in his as he talked and her warm touch reassured him. He stared levelly into her eyes, letting himself drift into those amber depths. "That's one of the things I wanted to talk to you about tonight. That's why dinner was here, in your quarters. In a couple of hours, we're going to put most of the Sassan citizens in a shuttle and cast them loose. Some, who have sensitive information, like the captain and Governor Beechie, are going with us because they can provide intelligence data on the Sassan Empire."

"You won't hurt Beechie?"

"No. We'll use a little Mytol to get him to tell us everything, and then we'll turn him free in a couple of months. I give you my word. But what you must decide is this: I can't take you into combat, can't risk your life. We think we've got a real good chance of making it out alive. If you go in the shuttle, you'll be guaranteed of safety. You'll land on Imperial Sassa after we've left. You can get a message to Staffa, and he'll come and pick you up before we return."

She stared down at the plates and what remained of dinner. Somewhere in the background a clock chimed softly. "A couple of hours, you said? So we're already through most of Sassa's defenses?"

"The *Markelos* provided perfect cover. She's a big ship—one of the biggest in the Sassan fleet—and to date, the mass detectors and other sensors haven't picked up enough of an anomaly to arouse suspicion."

"I don't understand something, Mac. You said that you were trapped in Makarta Mountain. That you were fighting the Seddi. You skipped around a lot, and perhaps purposely muddied the story up. Staffa's ships evacuated you—but not Sinklar. You're fighting for Rega. And just now, when I brought this up, your expression hardened, Mac. What didn't you tell me? That Sinklar and Staffa are about to go to war against each other?"

With his free hand, Mac flipped one of the tassels on the oversized pillow. "That's a very likely scenario."

Chrysla bowed her head, lost in thought. "I don't understand. How? I mean, Staffa can't just go to war against his son."

"It's not him. I think I told you before, Sinklar doesn't believe Staffa is his father. He thinks he's the son of two Seddi assassins. Rotted Gods, *I* didn't believe it until I found you alive."

Chrysla lifted her head, fire in her eyes, her grip tightening on his. "Mac, take me with you. I'll risk what you will. Take me to my son, if you can. Perhaps I can talk some sense into him—or into Staffa, depending on which is the most volatile at the time."

Mac narrowed his gaze. "It's not that easy. This could well be a suicide mission."

She smiled knowingly, her perfect features at peace. "After all these years, you're a refreshing change from the men I've become used to, Mac. I was right when I told you were older than your years—and infinitely wiser and nobler. To use your words, you must set yourself aside when you gamble for great stakes. I think my life is worth it if it comes to that, too."

"If this goes sour, every defense battery around Imperial Sassa will be targeting *Gyton*. You've got to—"

She placed warm fingers on his lips. "Quiet. My husband and my son are at stake. They've kept me alive all these years. You need me."

"All right."

But how much of that was good sense, and how much the desire to be close to her—even if only for a few hours more?

* * *

Gysell's face appeared in the comm monitor on Ily's office desk. "I think we have an ID on the young lady in Sinklar Fist's company."

Ily leaned back in her gravchair and played with a laser pen. She arched her spine to relieve the strain on her tired muscles. The lights shone on the polished paneling of her office, dancing as the crystals changed color. "That didn't take nearly as long as I thought it would."

Gysell gave her a placid smile. "I'd like to take credit for running a perfect organization, and for being the perfect subordinate. In this case, however, one of our agents submitted a routine report that Fist's LC landed on the roof of the Criminal Laboratories in the Biological Research Complex. Our man there reports that Fist not only visited, but left with one of the student employees—a young woman by the name of Anatolia Daviura. Here's her holo ID."

Ily studied the image that formed. "That's her." *She's better looking awake than asleep. Perhaps Sinklar has a thing for blue eyes? And if he does, I'll have his testicles served to him on a platter.*

"Any further instructions?"

Ily tapped her chin with the laser pen. "Find out all you can about her. Who is she? How does she know Sinklar? I want everything. If there's anyone close to her there, bring him or her in and we'll wring them dry. Who's our agent in that building?"

"A fellow by the name of Jan Bokken. He's reliable, provides punctual reports, but I'd say he was lacking in imagination."

"Good work, Gysell. Follow this up. I want to know everything there is to know about Anatolia Daviura."

"You will." Gysell nodded his acquiescence and the monitor went blank.

For long moments, Ily twirled the pen in her slim fingers. Then a thin smile bent her lips. "Enjoy her while you have her, Sinklar."

*   *   *

Arta placed a steaming plate in front of Skyla as she sat at the table in her yacht. The tabletop had been cut from a single slab of Vegan marble, the sides inlaid with gold. Behind her, Myklenian draperies were gathered into neat folds, and the fabric shimmered in the soft light reflected off the sandwood paneling. Once Skyla had joked to Nyklos about being held prisoner amidst the plush fittings in the yacht. Now she was getting her own dose of it.

Golden armor gleaming, Arta slid onto the crushed velvet cushions opposite Skyla. Silently, they stared appraisingly at each other. Skyla broke the impasse by picking up her utensils and beginning to eat. With the acumen of the professional, Arta understood that Skyla would eventually act to free herself. Fera waited with keen anticipation, anxious for the challenge.

Skyla forced herself to eat, recharging her reserves. The time would come when she would need all of her strength and skill.

Arta ate slowly, gazing at the thick Ashtan rug as she chewed. Skyla finished the last of the Riparian catfish and stood, sliding the dish into the cleanser.

"You control a great deal of power among the Companions. Does that excite you?" Arta asked.

Skyla drew a cup of stassa and resettled herself. "Excite? No. If I had to choose a label, I'd say it contented me. I started out as nothing—a whore's child. How about you? What was it like to be raised by the Seddi?"

"I didn't know I was a Seddi. I'd been raised—schooled actually—by a woman on Vermilion. One night, when I was about twelve, an aircar arrived and they bundled me up, gave me my little sack of belongings, and took me to the spaceport."

"Who did?"

Arta shrugged. "I don't know the man's name, but he stayed with me on the shuttle, and on the ship that carried me to Etarus. I remember that trip as if it were yesterday. All I called him was "sir." He was nice, bought me what I wanted, and then we transshipped to Etaria. I was frightened by it, by all the people." Arta glanced away nervously.

"They sold you to the Temple?"

Arta's jaw trembled and she hesitated. Skyla thought the woman had clammed up until Fera suddenly blurted, "How devious Bruen was. That first night in the Temple, I remember being in a room with all these other young girls. I had a bed in the back. I was so alone, so scared. I cried all night. The next day the lessons began. At first all the priests did was tell us the story of the Blessed Gods, and how they wanted humanity to have good things. We were going to help make things better for people."

"I'm beginning to understand." Skyla shook her head. "The priests teach the little girls sex?"

Arta waved it away. "The priests are all eunuchs—at least the ones who train the young girls are. They do teach sex, but it's with models and brainwashing. They want virgins to sell for the consecration. We bought the entire story, learning bit by bit about the consecration and how we'd bring pleasure. Now, when I think about what they did to me, my stomach crawls."

"That's how they finance the Temple, you know. Money from the girls." Skyla knotted a fist. "All in all, compared to the cribs of Sylene, there're worse places to be a prostitute."

Arta gave her a thoughtful appraisal. "Bruen later told me it was like gang rape. I still didn't understand. I never got the chance for the consecration. I was ready—anxious even—and wretchedly upset when another girl was chosen in my place. The next night, one of the eunuchs called me out, and I thought my time had come. Except he led me to one of the rear doors where a woman in a brown robe told me I was to go with her."

"And she took you to Targa?"

"She did. There I entered the Seddi as an Initiate." Arta's look became puzzled. "I had the background. Evidently they'd begun conditioning me when I was a child. All the aggression, the intuitive ability, had been implanted by the teaching machines on Vermilion. Bruen and his psychological programs taught me the rest, structured the neural pathways and refined the instinct to kill. When I needed to tap that ability to fight, to kill, it came so naturally. So did the proficiency with weapons."

"But you had no idea you were being prepared to assassinate the Lord Commander?"

Arta raised her head the way a predator sniffs for blood on the night wind. "Staffa kar Therma?"

Skyla's eyes narrowed as she caught Fera's quickening interest. "You didn't know? That's what the revolt on Targa was all about. Bruen and Hyde started it to lure Staffa within reach. Then they'd see that you fell into his hands."

"It's the quanta that are to blame. No, I never knew." A gleam came to her deadly amber eyes. "To have killed the Star Butcher! What an achievement."

Pus Rot it! That was a mistake, Skyla. "Don't get any ideas." Polar cold settled in Skyla's soul. She nerved herself, pointing a finger. "Let's get something straight. I'm in love with Staffa. And he's not the man

the Seddi once feared. He, like you, was nothing more
than a tool. *Leave him alone, Arta!"*

Fera curled back into the cushions.

"Tell me more. What happened? You and the rest
of the Seddi talk about the quanta. What went wrong
on Targa?" *Answer, damn it! Get your mind off Staffa!*

Arta's expression remained slack for long moments
while Skyla's heart skipped, then the raptorial glint
hardened. "I fell in love with my tutor, Butla Ret. I
. . . I wanted him. Wanted to make love to him, share
all those wonderful secrets we'd been taught by the
Blessed priests. And then . . . then . . ."

"The conditioning kicked in." Skyla's gut churned.
"Bruen, Rot your soul forever!"

Fera leaned forward, taking a death grip on the
edge of the table. "One day, I'll find Magister Bruen.
And then. . . ."

"He's out of your reach."

"That remains to be seen. All things have their time
. . . and place."

"Go on with your story."

Arta leaned back, a grim set to her lips. "I couldn't
deal with myself that night. Desire and revulsion filled
me. I escaped from Butla's house, used the skills he'd
taught me. But the quanta tricked us all. I was captured and raped by Regan slavers. And I paid them
back." Arta shook her head, brow lined. "I went insane, killed, and killed. But I didn't know why. Imagine a program running and rerunning in your brain.
You don't understand it. You can't stop it. You just
have to do it over and over again—and each time
it drives you a little more crazy because you don't
understand yourself, or why any of it is happening.
You feel impotent, inhuman. Your only companion is
fear, because you never know at what moment the
program will begin to run, and you'll have to kill . . .
someone, anyone."

Skyla strangled the urge to shiver; instead she
gripped her cup until her knuckles stood out. *So what
happens if that goes off now, Arta? You've got the*

collar control. I won't have a chance! "But wait a minute, you said Tybalt broke the trigger."

Arta ran fingers through her glistening hair. "He did. I don't *have* to kill now." She turned intense eyes on Skyla and gave her a lover's smile. "But that doesn't mean that I don't like to. I suppose it's a lot like fishing, baiting the gear, playing the bait in the water, and getting that first bite. Then you set the hook and reel in the fish, playing it the whole time, knowing all the while that you're the master of the situation. Only in the end does the prey know the truth—and even then, while you look into their dying eyes, they refuse to believe." She rubbed her hands together. "I let them die in pain so their souls know for eternity. That's what they take to God's Mind. Knowledge taught by pain."

"So why did you kill Sinklar Fist's lover?"

Fera shifted uneasily. "I told you, I was insane. She was Regan. Poor fool, she pitied me. No one pities me. The program began to run . . . and like always, I acted."

"But Ily saved you. Took you to Tybalt. How did you get through his security?"

Arta gave a cunning laugh. "Ily put me in a faulty collar. And, no, I didn't make that mistake with the one you're wearing. Tybalt raped me—right there on the floor of his office bedroom—and raped me again, and again, while I tried to kill him. In the process, I learned how to control the psychological trigger so that by the time the collar shorted, I didn't *have* to kill him." Her laughter bubbled. "But I did, gleefully, painfully! Because the bastard deserved it."

Skyla remembered Tybalt, remembered the lust in his dark eyes as he appraised her, a hint of promise in his leering grin. How many of his passes had she turned down? How many implied rewards for sexual favors? *But I always thought he was a pig, too.*

Arta continued, talking as if she'd never felt so uninhibited before. "After I killed the Emperor, Ily decided she could make good use of me."

"But is that all you want out of life? To be Ily's

tool? If you thought Tybalt deserved death, what about Ily? She's swamp scum."

Arta lifted her chin coolly. "Ily *loves* me. She made a place for me. She values my talent and lets me practice my trade. Wing Commander, *I am an assassin*. I was bred for it. I thrive on it."

"Ily loves you? What kind of love? Ily only loves herself—and power." Skyla leaned forward, eyes narrowing. "She's *using* you, Arta. You're a . . . a program for her."

"She loves me!" Arta's voice wavered as she reached up to lay gentle fingers on Skyla's cheek. "The way you will come to love me. Not like a man. They think only with their testicles. Given a choice, I'll take a woman any day. And with you and Ily to love me, I can do anything."

Skyla's skin crawled under the woman's touch.

Arta's expression turned serious. "Ily loves me." She paused, uncertainty in the set of her mouth. "I can only love women. They're safe. They won't hurt you . . . not like a man. I was surprised after the first night when I slept with Ily. I felt . . . peace. She taught me so many things. Ways to bring pleasure like I never dreamed of. Have you ever loved a woman?"

"No. Not like that. But Ily—"

"I would like to bring you pleasure, Skyla."

"I like men."

"I could teach you to like me. Women are safe to love. Gentle and warm."

"Arta, no!" *Get out of this, Skyla. Do something.* She slid out of the booth, backing warily away as Arta followed, a quizzical look in her eyes.

"Is it because I'm not beautiful?"

"You're damned attractive, Arta. But you're messed up! Ily doesn't love you. She's using you for sex and murder, and she'll throw you away like spoiled vegetables when you've served your purpose. She's a bitch . . . more polluted than Bruen! More vile, more. . . ."

The widening of Fera's eyes should have been a warning. Skyla should have cued on that sudden tension in the woman's shoulders as Arta's fists balled.

Skyla's entire body went numb, as if her neck had been severed and her head had rolled free. Wide-eyed, she watched the cabin slide sideways and spin upward. Blinding light shot through her vision as her skull bounced on the thick carpet. She blinked, opening and closing her mouth like a fish out of water.

Then grayness closed in, an inexorable sphincter around her vision.

* * *

Skyla came to groggily and pushed herself up. When had she fallen? Why? Fera stood over her, feet braced, tears streaking down her face . . . and memory returned.

Skyla propped her head against the bulkhead, blinking, "You can kill me if you want. But it won't change a Rotted thing. Ily's a bloodthirsty bitch."

Fera shook her head stubbornly. "She loves me! She took me in her arms. She wouldn't. . . ."

Skyla nodded despite the misery that ached in her skull. Was it the fall or the collar that caused that wretched ache?

"She *wouldn't* hurt me!"

"You poor lunatic," Skyla grunted, closing her eyes. "Pus dripping hell, I feel horrible."

Hands settled under Skyla's arms. Here was her chance . . . and she couldn't do a damn thing about it. Arta helped her stumble toward the rear, but at the head, Skyla broke free, just making the toilet before her guts heaved.

When she'd finished voiding like a bilge pump, she slumped on the floor, looking up into Arta's concerned eyes. Numbly, Skyla dragged her sleeve over her mouth. "You use that collar again, and you'll take a corpse back to Ily."

Arta bit her lip, a contrite look on her face. "You shouldn't say those things about Ily."

"Truth hurts. In this case, me more than you."

"Will you be all right?"

"Yeah. I'm a tough old broad. Got scars to prove it."

Arta lowered her eyes. "I wish . . . well, it's out of my hands. Ily will know what to do with you when we get back to Rega."

Skyla shook her head, wishing she hadn't. "You don't know what you let loose when you took me. We might get to Rega first, but by the time Ily's done with me, Staffa and the fleet will be overhead. After that, you won't find a brick standing. And I hope to your cursed quanta, that Ily dies last so she can know what she did."

"If you keep talking that way, I'll use the collar again," Arta warned.

Skyla gave her a ghastly grin. "Go ahead. I meant what I said about taking a corpse back. You're a mental basket case—and Ily's a slimy cunt anyway you cut the tapa cards. Go ahead, Arta, kill me. If you kill me, you'll condemn yourself, and Ily, to Staffa's wrath. You won't survive me by more than a couple of months."

* * *

"Political scientists, politicians, social theorists, and, of course, bureaucrats, and government officials everywhere seek the perfect formulae for managing and influencing the population at large. Giant computers employ vast mountains of data, manipulating incredibly complex statistical packages to determine trends, opinions, and, in most cases, the flash point of the people's temper. The pursuit of this mega-management policy has ranged from the sublime to the absurd. The procedure sucks up vast sums of time, money, and effort, and for what?

"The secret to governing is to minimize interfering with the people at large. Think of the population as a large monster, a sort of fat, lazy dragon. So long as the beast is fed, warm, and capable of amusement, it could care less what you, as a ruler, do with your spare time. The beast has no moral scruples past keeping its belly full and its limited mind entertained. Therefore, the efficient ruler is safe to assassinate, torture, murder, extort, or destroy his enemies as he will as long as he doesn't interfere with the beast.

"Thus, the rules of government can be stated simply: Do not mess with the ordinary people in the street. And remember that the weakest link in the grinding machine of government is the individual—and usually frail—human being."

—*Excerpt recovered from Ily Takka's personal journal*

CHAPTER XXII

"Just what are you going to do about Lycinda?" Marteen asked from her station across the Imperial Sassan orbital traffic control room. The watch had been unusually boring, with most of the boards shut down for diagnostics. An order had come through to check the Sassan defense system—another of the preparations in case of Regan hostilities. Banks of monitors lined the walls and the black floor tiles gleamed with a lustrous polish. Atmosphere fans hummed softly overhead, forcing cool air through the grates that broke the white fiber ceiling panels.

Philo Verdun threw his head back and closed his star-blue eyes. His pale blond hair appeared golden in the bright light—a fact that he knew had always irritated Marteen, who had a thing about pale people. "I don't even know if the child is mine. I mean I just started seeing her two months ago!"

Marteen chuckled, lifting a thin eyebrow as she placed an arm over her chair back and stared across at Philo. "Two months is time enough. Do you know how many sperm you males dump inside us when you hit that happy moment?"

Philo opened his eyes and studied the traffic control room with a disgusted frown. None of the array of monitors had changed. He sighed and glanced at the board with its familiar dots neatly in their place. Hour in, hour out, he watched the patterns: ensuring that each of the vessels closing on Imperial Sassa obeyed the rules; that radiation didn't get released toward any of the stations; that Delta V got dumped properly and reaction was channeled into the proper vectors. The comm kept an eye on all of it anyway, so most of his job was interpreting when an infraction merited a follow-up and citation.

Now he wheeled around in his chair, staring at Marteen. "Look, what if it is mine? I'm not ready for half interest in a child right now. I mean, that's final. I've got a good career set up, and I'm banking time, woman. I'm headed for one of the orbital platforms, because that's where the advancement is. I sure don't want any third of my credits going for child support. Not when I'm outward bound." He paused. "Besides, I'm still not sure it's mine."

"She that friendly with that many guys?" Marteen raised a censuring eyebrow. "Thought you were pretty picky about where you put your little one-eyed friend?"

He blushed. He didn't like Marteen that much anyway. She'd shut him down when he tried to lay her the first week he'd been assigned here. She, in turn, despised him, and that irked, too. Marteen had a delicate oval face surrounded by a wealth of black hair. Her slanted eyes looked out at the world with a cool self-possession. Lycinda, on the contrary, couldn't be called desirable, except she did have nice legs.

Philo heard the soft beep and turned to see the alert reading. He canceled the flash of light on the monitor which indicated a breach of regulation as reaction shot out from *Markelos'* position.

"Asshole freighter." He keyed his comm. "*Markelos*, you're moving off course. Correct, please."

He turned back to Marteen, irritated by her flagrant dislike. Lines of figures filled the screen behind his back, indicating increased vector change and acceleration.

"You know, you've always had a real attitude problem, woman. You think that I'm a low rent, but one of these days, you're gonna remember these days as the time when you were my supervisor."

Marteen smiled sweetly and shook her head, expres-

sion neutral. "You never cease to amaze me. When
it comes to brass balls and lead brains, you've got
both, Philo. Who'd you bribe to get this position
anyway?"

He smirked. "Talent all the way, baby." He tapped
the side of his head to indicate the source. "You've
got to have it where it counts."

She gave him a bland look. "As I recall, you
generally point to your crotch when you say that.
So maybe you really did 'have it where it counts.'
I mean didn't you ever consider her? She's not a
bad kid, in spite of the fact she lets you into her
bed. You must have made her feel like shit when
you laid that 'So . . . how do I know it's mine,'
crap on her."

Philo's entire screen began to flash with red warnings indicating a major breach of traffic regulations.
Had he not disconnected the alarm for the nuisance
it was, it, too, would have been blaring.

"Listen, why do you always launch into me? I
mean, she's half of the problem. There's no reason
why I should have to suffer for something—"

"You're half, pal." Marteen pointed a slender finger at him. "And I hope Lycinda gets a magisterial
garner on a third of your salary for life."

Philo allowed himself to give her a lingering disdainful glare. Pus take it all, it would be so much
easier if Marteen wasn't so cursed good looking. Even
hating her, he wondered what she'd be like in the
sack. To avoid her cool, mocking glare, he turned
back to his monitor—and gaped. The screen flashed
alternately in red and yellow.

"Gods help us," Philo whispered, too stunned to
act. Then he stabbed the emergency alert button. In
the screen, he could see a lance of reaction curving
off of *Markelos*' approach, and vectoring right into the
military security zone.

A voice announced crisply. "This is Traffic Control
Security. You've triggered an all-system alert. Please
respond."

"They . . . they. . . ." Philo clutched his monitor,

trying to settle his horrified mind. "They've gone off course! Headed right for the base! Off course!"

"Repeat, please. Who is off course?"

Philo's mind went blank with terror. *They'll blame me! "Markelos,"* he whispered. *It's my fault.*

Another voice interrupted. "This is Orbital Defense Station Seven. Traffic Control, do you have a malfunction? We've got an incoming vessel on our screens. Is this a malfunction?"

Philo gaped, refusing to believe. Frozen, he watched as *Markelos* continued to angle toward the planet and the military base below. Marteen ripped him aside and began to shout instructions into the net.

On his knees, Philo clambered up just in time to see the deadly lance of light arrow down.

* * *

Dressed in armor, helmet at hand in case of decompression, Mac stood at the side of Rysta's command chair on *Gyton*'s bridge. Each second passed like the judgment of the Rotted Gods. Each beat of his heart saw *Markelos* increase the radius of its curve toward the planet, *Gyton* tucked neatly under the violent flare of the freighter's reaction mass.

The pilot lay under the worry-cap, oblivious to his actual surroundings, manipulating the delicate control needed to execute the maneuver while comm-relayed instructions ran to the Sassan freighter's vacant bridge. *Markelos* responded by tightening the bounce-back collars, increasing the thrust as the giant ship accelerated for the planet.

Mass cubed with velocity. How long did they have until brilliant violet blaster fire sought their vector? Each surging beat of Mac's heart meant that much more space crossed, and it increased exponentially.

"Weapons Comm!" Rysta barked. "Activate your systems and arm the torpedoes."

"Activated and armed," the Weapons First sang out.

Mac could hear *Gyton* creak as the ship's attitude

changed and bulkheads compressed under acceleration. *Come on, baby, get us through this.*

Mac's gaze remained fixed on the forward monitor
where it showed *Markelos* and *Gyton* arcing over the
planet. His mouth had gone maddeningly dry, his
tongue like a piece of felt.

"Markelos!" a frantic voice came in over comm.
"You are off course! Correct! Correct immediately! If
you do not, you must destroy yourself. Repeat: correct immediately. If not, you must auto-destruct! Do
you hear? Correct course or auto-destruct. If you do
not, you will be destroyed from the ground. Respond!
Respond!"

"Well, we made it farther than I thought we
would," Rysta muttered. "Thought they'd be on us
the moment we dropped the shuttle and changed vector. Guess the Sassans aren't any brighter than we
are."

"They hire too many bureaucrats," Mac told her.
"Besides, only a fool would try a stunt like this.
Anyone with sense would have brought a whole fleet
with them. It says so in the Holy Gawdamn Book."

"You don't have much use for the manual, do
you?"

"Not a lick—except for one thing. The enemy still
reads it and believes it."

"Two minutes to breakout," the Comm First called.

Two minutes. Mac tried to swallow again, his heart
racing. After those two minutes, *Markelos* would be
beyond the intercept angle for the space-based batteries. They'd be shooting down, hitting dirt and mauling
both the planet and the military base they were supposed to protect. Seconds crept past.

"How long to charge their guns?" Mac asked.

Rysta, remarkably calm given their circumstance,
shrugged. "Five, ten minutes at the most. That's assuming they had to power up the entire system."

"One minute," the Comm First called.

"Five minutes?" Mac glanced hopefully at the
monitor.

"Markelos! Markelos!" the frantic Sassan voice

called. "You are in violation of traffic control regulations!"

"No joke!" Rysta crowed.

Markelos, you must auto-destruct now! This is your last chance! If you do not, you will be destroyed! Answer please!"

"Do you think they've figured it out yet?"

"Naw," Rysta waved nonchalantly. "Only a lunatic would try something like this. You told me yourself."

"*Markelos!* In the name of Divine Sassa! *Answer me!*"

"Sounds a little frantic, doesn't he?" Rysta took a deep breath. "Prepare for breakout. Weapons? Status?"

"Ready!"

"On my mark," Rysta cried. "Five, four, three, two, one. Mark!"

"Mark!" repeated the Comm First.

Mac braced himself as *Gyton* changed vector, slipping down under *Markelos*. For the first time, he could see the planet rushing straight toward them. A red dot surrounded a cluster of white structures that seemed to drift slowly over the planet's surface.

"Weapons, do you have your target?" Rysta asked.

"Affirmative, Commander. We have target acquisition. Locked and armed."

"Fire at will."

"Firing!"

Gyton shivered as the torpedoes released. Streaks of reaction sent lances of blinding white light across the monitor as Rysta ordered, "Comm! Get us out of here!"

The first threads of violet light glittered up from the orbiting stations below. Mac grabbed the rail on the side of Rysta's command chair as *Gyton* bent her path away from the course she'd been following.

The warping strands of blaster fire from below slipped helplessly past as *Gyton* curved away. Mac stood rooted, open mouthed, as he watched the struggling Sassans try to target *Markelos* as their comm compensated for Doppler and velocity. One beam caught the freighter's bow, and blew it apart, the concussion shifting the heavy vessel's vector out of the deadly beam.

"Rotted Gods," someone whispered as all eyes followed *Markelos'* plunge.

Flashes strobed blindingly on the monitor as *Gyton*'s torpedoes slammed into the Sassan fleet where it hung in orbit, and the defensive fire went dead.

"They can't stop her now," Rysta said soberly.

"We've got Orbital trying to track us!" the Weapons First cried.

"Evasive maneuvers!" Rysta snapped. "Comm, get to it!"

"Affirmative."

Mac couldn't tear his gaze from the telemetered monitor where *Markelos* began to leave a fiery streak as she encountered atmosphere. The hypnotic event unfolded before him in slow motion as the image wavered and flickered as a result of atmospheric interference, EMP from the fission destruction of the Sassan fleet, and increasing distance. Like a searing lance, *Markelos* slammed into the unresisting mass of Imperial Sassa. A high-speed projectile created the same reaction in sheet steel. A sinuous, off-color vapor trail remained to mark the ship's path. The crater widened as soil and rock slipped up in a bowl around the center of impact. Then, as the edges settled in a widened ring, a gout of violent material erupted in a volcanic explosion. The Sassan installation had vanished in the cataclysm. Like a pebble thrown into a pond, ground roll spread in ripples that slowly faded across the mottled surface of the planet. A plume of dust and fire mushroomed out over the impact site while rolling white clouds formed along the expanding peripheries of the shock wave.

"Enemy fire has ceased, Commander," the Weapons First cried. "Their targeting detectors have ceased to coordinate!"

"Rotted Gods," Rysta mumbled in wonder. "We might make it out of this alive after all! Pilot, lay in the course to get us out of here. Take us by as many Orbital Defense platforms as you can. The more we knock out, the fewer we have to deal with when we come back."

"Affirmative," the pilot called through his speakers. "All hands, prepare for high g acceleration. Repeat, prepare for forty gravity acceleration. Stow all loose items."

A klaxon wailed as Mac backed to the padded seats in the rear of the bridge and strapped himself in. His eyes remained glued to the monitor and the roiling wound inflicted upon Imperial Sassa. "Oh, Sink, we've condemned ourselves. All those people dead, just like that."

And more to come, he reminded himself grimly.

*   *   *

The comm buzzed beside Staffa's head. He instinctively rolled off his sleeping platform, the rising illumination from the room lights making him squint. He dropped into the chair before his desk and accessed the comm. To his surprise, Myles Roma stared out at him.

"Myles? I thought visual was too risky? What's happened? You look ashen."

"We've found your infamous *Gyton*, Lord Commander. I warned them both . . . Sassa and Iban. They were polite, told me to mind my own business and not to meddle in their affairs. Now, affairs have come home to reside. And we may all pay before this is over."

"What's happened, Myles?"

Roma pinched the bridge of his nose as if trying to press sense into his sinuses. "A matter of hours ago, *Gyton* slipped in under cover of one of our freighters. They evidently piloted the freighter out of the traffic pattern and right into the center of the military complex at Mikay. The entire base is gone. The fleet that was outfitting in orbit . . . blasted to junk. Our Orbital Defense network is down—possibly dead. Two of our platforms were blown apart like rotten melons as *Gyton* began its boost outsystem. From their vec-

tor, they may take another two out before they
escape.''

Staffa slammed his fist to the desk. "By the quanta,
this changes everything.''

Myles stared at him through dull eyes. "Lord
Commander, no matter what you might think of His
Holiness, you're our only hope. You know what this
means. Twenty-two of our finest warships are gone.
The remainder of the fleet is spread over the rest of
the empire. If Fist strikes now, nothing . . . nothing
will survive.'' Myles lowered his head despairingly.

"What condition is your computer system in?''

The Legate spread his hands wide. "Fine so far, but
the rest of the planet is reporting tectonic disturbances
along the major plates. We haven't been able to assess
the climatic implications yet, and probably won't be
able to for another couple of days.''

"But your comm system still appears to be unaffected?''

"So far. If we have a major quake here, well, the
rooms are cushioned, but who knows.''

Staffa steepled his fingers. "Keep your line open,
Myles. I want someone in touch with my comm con-
tinuously. In the meantime, tell your fat emperor that
we'll protect him—and his empire. But, Myles, no
matter what you have to do, *keep that computer system
intact!*''

"No matter what?''

"Every human being in Free Space, including myself, is depending on you, Myles. We may need to tap
that system as soon as four weeks from now.''

"Assuming *Gyton* hasn't killed us all, it will be
ready.''

After Staffa broke the connection, he stood, walking into his shower and triggering the hot water to
cascade over his scarred skin. He leaned his head
against the wall, braced his legs, and stood in the
steam, trying to think, to anticipate which move to
make next. Another pebble had been dropped into
the battered basket. How many more would it take
before the bottom ripped out and all was lost?

*   *   *

Vet Hamlin grimaced as he took his security uniform from the locker. He pulled the tunic over his head and ruffled his hair back into presentable shape with his fingers. This had turned into a very long day. Not only had Sinklar Fist, the military governor, shown up during the middle of his last watch, but Anatolia had left in Fist's company—and never returned.

Fascinating as that had been, Professor Adam had been unimpressed—especially by her absence. "And I always cover for her," Vet mumbled as he pulled his tunic straight. In this case, he'd run Adam's slides and input the data Anatolia should have been inputting. This put him that much farther behind on his own project—which he couldn't make up for for another two days since he had to man the security desk for the next two nights. When he'd called Marka, she hadn't been the slightest bit impressed, either.

"Ana, you're going to owe me one for this." But that was all right. Outside of the bluster, he didn't really mind. Anatolia was his best friend—perhaps even more so than Marka.

Vet checked his appearance, squared his shoulders so the shoulder boards sat right, and made sure he didn't have any remains of dinner stuck in his teeth. Then he walked over to the comm rack and reached for one of the communications devices.

"Vet?" Bokken's soft voice called.

Hamlin turned, hand half-extended to the rack. "Yes, sir?"

Bokken, big and fleshy, his hair closely cropped to his bullet head stood in the doorway. A fatherly smile dominated his heavy-jowled face, but it didn't extend to his hard black eyes. "These gentlemen would like you to accompany them downtown. It's nothing to worry about, and you will be paid your usual wage."

"What about?" Vet craned his neck to see the two

nondescript young men who stood behind Bokken's thick body. They were conservatively dressed in brown suits. One sported close-cropped blond hair, the other had a long face and black hair.

"That will be for you to find out. Don't worry, you're not in trouble. Just accompany them downtown and supply them with the information they need and you'll probably be home within a couple of hours."

"Well, I. . . Yes, sir. You're the boss. If it's all right with you, it's fine with me. Do you want me to go in uniform, or should I change back to my street clothes?"

"The uniform will be fine." Bokken spoke smoothly, gesturing Vet out of the dressing room. As Vet stepped past Bokken, he caught the odor of a delicate male perfume.

The two young men took positions to either side of him. Vet nodded at them amiably.

"This way, Mr. Hamlin. We won't take very long, and we apologize for the inconvenience," the blond said.

"Oh, it's no trouble at all. I just . . . well, where are we going? What can I help you with?"

"Our superiors will discuss that with you in a very short while."

Vet accompanied the two men to the lift, then up to the roof landing. There he stepped into a waiting aircar, the young men seating themselves to either side. The aircar followed the traffic lanes reserved for official use. Vet noticed that his heartbeat had increased and his throat had gone dry. *Don't be foolish*, he told himself, *this isn't anything to worry about*.

The aircar dipped suddenly, dropping toward a plain, square building. Vet tensed still more as he recognized their destination: the Ministry of Internal Security. He glanced uneasily at his silent companions, who sat stiffly beside him, staring straight ahead.

The aircar dropped to ground level, slowing as it

entered a security portal, drifted down a long tunnel, and settled easily to the pad. The canopy lifted, and Vet stepped out into a musty-smelling concrete tunnel. Men and women stood with legs spread, arms crossed, watching him. They wore trim black uniforms and looked like the sort of people who wouldn't put up with nonsense.

"Listen," Vet asked anxiously, "are you sure you've got the right person?"

"This way, please." An arm pointed to the door.

Vet tried to swallow, and made a loud gulping sound. His legs had gone shaky as he took a deep breath and walked through the heavy security door and past the black-clothed guards. Inside, he passed another security desk, aware that the woman who sat there had him on camera and security scan as well.

"Place your hand on the pad," the woman at the desk told him.

Vet jerked a nod and set his hand on the warm surface, aware that it coded his body chemistry and dermatoglyphics. Another monitor that he could barely see from his angle had zoomed in on his eyes, recording his iris characteristics.

"This way."

The young men led him to a lift, each carefully positioned slightly behind him. The lift opened and Vet fidgeted as they dropped for what seemed like a long time.

He emerged into an austere, gray-walled room with a single bench.

"Remove your clothing, please."

Vet gaped. "Remove my. . . ."

"Now, please." The blond young man gave him a deadly stare.

Vet shivered openly now, wishing he could escape to the bathroom and relieve the building pressure he felt. With shaking fingers, he began to pull his uniform off, draping it neatly on the bench. When he finally stood naked and vulnerable before them, he realized

how chilly the floor was against his bare feet. Couldn't
they raise the temperature?

"This way," came the laconic command.

Vet walked through a featureless square door and
into a small concrete room. A single chair rested in
the middle. Vet glanced around, seeing the rows of
monitoring equipment that lined the angles of the
ceiling.

"Be seated, please."

Vet tried to keep his teeth from clicking as he
settled into the cold chair, his skin crawling at the
touch. With oiled precision, the men bound his
wrists to the arms of the chair and then knelt to do
his ankles.

"You don't have to do this," Vet protested. "I'll
tell you anything you want to know!"

The men continued to work silently, placing monitors over his heart, on the sides of his head, and along
the inside of his thighs. When they'd finished, they
soundlessly left the room.

Vet fought the white fear that cramped his gut and
left him shaking uncontrollably. He closed his eyes,
trying to disbelieve. *This isn't happening. Not to me.*
"I haven't done anything wrong!"

"No," a gentle contralto agreed.

Vet blinked his eyes open and stared. She was beautiful, dressed in formfitting black that accentuated her
perfect body. Her thick raven hair shone in the bright
light from above. To his horror, she inspected him, a
slight smile on her lips as she peered at his shrunken
genitals.

"Wh . . . What do you . . . want with me?"

"Family man," she told him confidently. "Wife's
name, Marka. You have a new baby . . . three months
old. You really want to see them again, don't you?"

Vet managed to nod, knowing his voice would fail
him.

She walked up to him, inserting a tube into his
mouth. "You will drink this. Don't worry, it's only a
drug, something we call Mytol."

Vet choked on the warm liquid, swallowing the sweet fruity mixture.

When he'd finished, her warm hands grabbed either side of his face, forcing him to look into her eyes, and she smiled again—a predator hovering over its prey. "Now, Vet Hamlin, you will tell me everything you know about Anatolia Daviura."

He frowned, a fuzzy sensation settling in his thoughts. "Anatolia?"

She patted him on the cheek. "Yes, Vet. Everything, no matter how trivial. You wouldn't want to fail me. Not with a wife and baby depending on you."

The chill in the room had settled in Vet Hamlin's soul. He began to talk.

*　*　*

"Given the nature of our existence, the question is begged: If we are all part of God Mind—Creators of reality in our own right—how does the State derive its authority over us?

"The answer, my friends, is that Imperial power, the power of the church, or the government, is illusion. It exists solely because we create and observe its reality. We, ourselves, have created this tyranny, and we, ourselves, can tear it down. Singly and together, we have created this unilateral epistemology of social control, and in doing so, have surrendered ourselves, our integrity, and our very existence to it. Today, we live at the whim of the State. How ironic a twist since the State cannot exist without us. What sort of monster have we complicitly devised which devours our flesh and souls with such impunity?

"We are not condemned! We need only question,

apply ourselves, and devise another way of looking at government to reverse this multiheaded creature. Bit by bit, we shall defeat the unilateral epistemology we've been taught and change the very nature of government. The power of God Mind is not passive. Use it. Modify your situation through whatever means you have available. Cast off this artificial parasite we have made among us. Act now, today. In light of these broadcasts, consider your moral and ethical responsibilities to yourself, to your people, and to God. You have no one to answer to except yourself."

—Excerpt from Kaylla Dawn's Itreatic broadcasts

CHAPTER XXIII

Skyla pushed her body, enjoying the heaving of her lungs, the sweat trickling down her sides. She exercised in the forward lounge, under Arta Fera's watchful eyes. For Skyla, the exercise served not only to help her keep her edge, but by pushing herself, she could wear out some of the endless boredom of this trip. Anything was better than waiting.

As Skyla went through her sprinter's starts, Fera watched from the inset booth, her expression emotionless but intent, missing nothing. Not once had Fera let security slip.

Skyla finished her set and extended to do her pushups. Expression straining, she counted off as she bobbed. At the same time, her mind raced. The weapons in the niche behind her sleeping platform headboard remained undiscovered. Unfortunately, Fera never left her unobserved for long enough to retrieve them. When the Seddi assassin slept, she shackled Skyla with the EM restraints first. The same procedure was followed before Arta went forward to check the yacht's status, course, and progress.

I need four minutes. Two to retrieve the weapons, a minute to cut the collar off with the vibraknife, and another to charge the pistol. But would Fera ever drop her guard enough to allow those precious minutes? The collar had to come off first. As long as that deadly ring circled her neck, Skyla had no chance. If she grabbed the pistol, smacked a charge in place, and shot Fera, the woman's dying brain would trigger the collar to kill Skyla, too.

Skyla finished her one hundred push-ups and bounced

to her feet, warming her legs as she kicked out with increasing vigor to keep her combat reflexes toned. She pirouetted and leapt, striking with her fists in cadence to her deadly kicks.

"You are very good," Arta praised. "I'm not bad myself, but I don't think I have your talent. Would you work with me?"

"Not while I'm in the collar."

Arta's lips quivered. "I can't take it off. I'm sorry. I guess I'll have to wait until after Ily's done with you."

"A corpse can't teach you much."

Arta stood, stepping over to the dispenser and pushing the button for a cup of stassa. "How did you get from the Sylenian cribs to the Companions?"

Skyla lashed out at the air, finding her balance and rhythm as she pummeled an imaginary Ily Takka. She recovered, dropped to a neutral position, fists up, back straight, and caught her breath. "I cut the purse off one of the Companions. Then I gave it back to him. He got me an interview with Staffa."

"But why did you want to leave Sylene?"

Skyla walked over and picked her towel up off the recliner, wiping at the sweat that ran down her face and neck. "I'd been sold into slavery, but the guy who bought me couldn't afford one of these." She tapped the collar with a fingernail.

"A man did that?" Arta seemed to be chewing on some distasteful memory.

"A woman. That's another reason I don't buy all of your brand of reasoning. Yep, a dear sweet woman who saw me as nothing more than a credit on the hoof. I was free, Arta. I was also twelve and vulnerable. I needed a place and Roxy offered a warm place to sleep, two good meals a day, and all I had to do was clean up around the place and run errands. Thing is, pretty little virgin girls are worth a lot on Sylene. Stryker offered Roxy two hundred credits for me. One night a rag was stuffed in my mouth and my arms and legs were wired together. Roxy delivered me to Stryker's doorstep. So much for trust."

Arta's amber eyes burned. "You killed them for it, didn't you?"

Skyla nodded as she walked back toward the shower. Fera, ever vigilant, followed. "That's what I did after I escaped. Haunted the streets . . . killed people." Skyla noted Fera's interest as she stepped into the shower. "That's right, Arta, I was an assassin—just like you."

Skyla peeled out of her sweaty gear and slapped the shower controls, letting water stream down over her hot skin.

"Why did you change? Why leave Sylene?"

Skyla ducked her face into the jetting water, rolling her head back and forth. She thumbed the water from her eyes and watched the cascade streak down her long hair. "I got tired of running," she shouted over the shower's noise, and slapped the controls to kill the spray.

When she stepped through the force field, Arta waited, arms crossed, a pensive look on her face. As always, Fera's inspection of her naked body spawned a crawly sensation in Skyla's gut.

"Running? Someone was after you?"

"The whole planet. You see, assassination is illegal on Sylene. So I made myself an opportunity and escaped." Skyla twisted away from Arta's reach as the woman sought to touch the scar on Skyla's leg.

"You don't like to be touched, do you?"

"You know what I think about you touching me."

Arta leaned her head back, the glossy waves of her auburn hair tumbling. "I could order you. With the collar, I could make you love me."

Skyla pushed past, grabbing her space whites from the sleeping platform in her room and dressing rapidly. "Yeah, I suppose you could—but not with me conscious. Is that what you want? To caress my body while I'm being choked by that damn collar? Sounds like real fun."

Arta wheeled and angrily slammed a fist into the wall, denting the paneling. "What is it with you? You keep trying to goad me. Is that it? You want to die?"

"Rather than be Ily's prisoner? You damn betcha! And when it comes down to sex with you, you're Rotted right again!"

Arta trembled, the crazy light back in her eyes. Skyla lowered herself to the sleeping platform, neck prickling in anticipation of the collar's grim work. But nothing happened.

"You infuriate me." Arta slumped back against the wall and ran her fingers down the fine golden filigree. "You obsess my thoughts. I dream of you, imagine your touch. I want to be with you, learn from you. You are so powerful, so strong. Then you act so stubbornly, and I want only to hurt you, to make you pay for spiting me."

Skyla glared at her, heart pounding. Here the delicate game began. She'd considered long and hard, weighing Arta's insanity against her cunning and intelligence. Desperate straits called for desperate gambles. *Here goes. And if I lose, I'll at least cheat Ily out of squeezing my mind dry of secrets.* "I don't have much choice about being your prisoner, but I won't be your slave."

"Why not? Is it so bad?"

Skyla gave her a malicious smile. "I'd rather be dead. And if you have any doubts, go ahead and trigger that collar. Go on, death doesn't scare me. I've looked it in the eye more times than not."

"You *want* to die?" Arta's anger vied with her growing curiosity. "Why? Just to keep out of Ily's hands?"

Skyla glanced sideways at Arta and stood, reaching for her comb. As she began working with her long hair, she added, "I won't be alive when you hand me over to Ily. That's final. I'm betting I can drive you to kill me before we get there. I'm going to win that bet. Ily isn't going to suck my brain dry—and you're going to see to it."

Arta shifted uneasily, eyes narrowing. "What's your game, Skyla? Why are you telling me this? If you become a danger to yourself, I'll just shackle you to your sleeping platform and let you lie there."

Will you? You'd better hope you bet right, Skyla, because she just might. "Fine. But then, I'd have won that way, too, wouldn't I? We'd both know that the only way you could deliver me was as a piece of incapacitated meat." Skyla shook her head chidingly, seeing Arta's anger flare. "I thought you were better than that."

Arta's fists clenched. "Don't push me too far, Skyla."

"I intend to, Arta. You're my only hope. I have to goad you, insult you, push you into using the collar to either kill or disable me so Ily doesn't get any use out of me except as fertilizer. I think I'm good enough to do that."

Arta's face reddened. "Then you can Rotted well njoy the company of the shackles."

Skyla slumped as the collar choked her. By the time she regained her swimming senses, her arms and feet were bound by the EM restraints and Arta had disappeared.

But though I'm imprisoned here, she's thinking about what happened and chalking this up as my victory. All I've got to gamble on is her vanity and stubbornness. If I'm wrong, I'll only get one mistake.

* * *

The blank screen on the main comm monitor mocked Staffa as he sat before it. A strangling sense of futility threatened to engulf the Lord Commander as he stared empty-eyed at the dark monitor while the other screens clustered around his desk flashed multicolored holographic updates on the mobilization that obsessed Itreata. Things were moving at an astonishing rate. The Companions were motivated as they hadn't been in years.

Ily, if you only knew what you did. His predatory wolves had their blood up. But how was he to hold them back if Rega turned nasty? Skyla had placed herself on the line for all of them, and that memory goaded each of the Companions.

Staffa continued to stare at the monitor. *How do* **I** *handle this?* Within hours, his fleet would space. During the busy days, Staffa had found ample reason to put off this subspace communication.

"I don't believe a word of this." The words echoed in Staffa's memory. *"I think, Lord Commander, that I've had enough. . . ."* And Sinklar had walked out hostile, believing himself the butt of some Seddi trick conjured by old Bruen.

After what the Seddi did to him, after the war and the death, the constant manipulation, I couldn't blame him. Staffa had found his son—and events had dictated that no conciliation could take place. It was the dance of the quanta, the joke so painfully played on all of them.

Staffa took a shaky breath. How did he make this call? What did he say?

"Working up the nerve?" Kaylla asked as she came to stand behind him, her hands settling reassuringly on his shoulders.

"Yes. Why is this so hard?"

"Because he's your son, and he may be involved. That's it, isn't it? You don't know what you're going to do if he's a willing accomplice in Skyla's abduction."

Staffa's vision narrowed. "You do know me too well. Damn it, why did this have to happen to me? The quanta laugh."

"You'll have to speak to him sometime. As things stand, you know nothing of his involvement or his intentions. You've been putting this off because of fear, Staffa. The time has come to learn. Perhaps you can talk sense to Sinklar. Or if he is Ily's accomplice in this, you're better off warned now. You'll have more time to come to terms with yourself, and with how you will deal with your son when you finally must confront him."

Staffa lowered his head in acceptance. "Comm, connect me with Rega. I want a subspace link to Sinklar's *Fist.*"

"Acknowledged. We're powering the dish now."
Staffa's stomach knotted.

* * *

"Minister?" Gysell's voice intruded on Ily's dreams.
"Yes?" She sat up as the bedroom lights grew
bright, forcing her thoughts from scattered dreams to
the present. She'd rumpled the bedding with her twisting and turning. Despite the setting of the climate
control, her quarters felt chilly.

Gysell's square face formed on the bedside monitor,
his eyes glinting. Lines had begun to form around Gysell's mouth, evidence of the strain they'd all been
under.

"What is it? Anything wrong?"

Gysell shrugged. "We've got subspace comm from
Itreata. The Lord Commander wishes to speak to
Lord Fist."

Ily straightened, mind racing. "We have a man in
Comm Central, don't we? One of ours?"

Gysell smiled. "We do. A woman by the name of
Zebra. We have a powerful lever on her. She had
gambling debts, overextended credit, and two affairs
with men she doesn't want her husband or children to
know about. She'll do as we order."

Ily's frown etched her brow. "Have her tell the
Lord Commander that Lord Fist doesn't wish to
speak with him. Tell Staffa that Lord Fist will communicate when the Wing Commander is safely in his
hands. That will be the appropriate time to initiate
negotiations."

Gysell inclined his head. "As you wish, Minister. Is
there anything else?"

Ily glanced at her comm. "Yes. Have my car and
four of my staff ready on the roof at 08:00. We are
going to pay Jan Bokken a visit . . . and, Gysell, make
sure this Professor Adam is in his lab at that time.
Hamlin said Daviura has a security file only Adam
can override."

"Professor Adam will be there."

"That's all, Gysell. Good work. Reward your Zebra with something suitable—and see that *none* of this reaches Sinklar Fist's ears."

"Very well." Gysell killed the comm and Ily lay back on the soft bedding, thoughts crowding her mind. What could Staffa have wanted with Fist? No matter, stopping him cold from communicating eliminated one more thing that could have gone wrong.

Ily grinned happily to herself. "Poor Sinklar, your troops are busy guarding the strategic positions, while my tools are safely behind the energy barriers you installed. You innocent fool, you place far too much trust in the common people. True power lies in knowing which individuals to manipulate—and how to do it."

*   *   *

A Regan woman looked out from the monitor, her expression tense.

"That's the final word?" Staffa asked.

"Yes, Lord Commander. Lord Fist does not wish to speak to you at this moment. When Wing Commander Skyla Lyma is within his control, then and only then will he negotiate with you. I can tell you nothing more."

Staffa gave her a barely civil nod.

Despite past wrongs, Kaylla ached in sympathy with Staffa kar Therma's pain over this betrayal by his son. As the monitor went blank, weary resignation shadowed his features.

Staffa slumped in the chair as Kaylla walked across to the dispenser and drew a warm cup of stassa. She returned to find him unmoving, wretched sadness in the slump of his shoulders.

"Drink this. It will do you good." She forced the cup into his hand. Staffa simply closed his eyes.

"Staffa, you didn't get the chance to speak to him. You only have partial data."

"He's Ily's," Staffa whispered. "He's. . . . Well, no matter. Perhaps the course was set long, long ago by the Praetor, by the quanta. Who knows?" He glanced up with a glazed expression. "Kaylla, we ship out tomorrow. We'll be in Rega within weeks. When I take the planet . . . I have to destroy my son."

* * *

Sinklar woke up from disorienting dreams. Slippery images of Targa shifted like mist in his head. Blaster bolts exploded against rock, cracking the stone and puffing powder while deadly fragments spattered about. The images created a background for war as men and women charged among the boulders, shouting, shooting at phantoms as one by one they fell to maiming pulse fire and violet death.

"Sir?" the comm interrupted his dream. "We're landing on the palace roof."

Sinklar groaned and reached up to rub life into his face. Gretta had been there, dashing through the thick of the fight. Mac had been covering one flank, his anxious voice loud in the battle comm.

Sinklar glanced around and sat up in the cramped chair in his command center. He could feel the LC settling, shifting attitude as the skids touched down. His muscles had that strained feel of deep fatigue. Anatolia gave him a weary smile from where she sat in the cubbyhole, elbows propped on the table. "Have a nice nap?"

"Hardly. Bad dreams. Well, are you tired of a soldier's life?"

She appraised him with haggard blue eyes. "It's been a fascinating day and a half. Your bench is a lot more comfortable than mine, and I got to read a little and learned a lot about war. So . . ." she hesitated. "What's next?"

"Come on. I told you I'd have a real meal for you. I ordered the pick of the Imperial kitchen. It should be waiting for us, hot and steaming."

She stood and let him take her hand as the LC's shrill whine lowered to a moan and ceased. In the rear, Sinklar slapped the ramp control and led her to the lift. Light bars gleamed whitely to illuminate the interior as the doors closed overhead.

"This is really the palace?"

"Yeah, the private garage used by Tybalt himself—once."

"I thought it would look different."

"A garage is a garage. The only difference here is that you've been through fifteen different levels of security already."

"Oh. But. . . ." She pulled back. "Are you sure this is all right?"

"Trust me. If they let me in, you'll get in." He tugged her into the lift and let it carry them down to the powder blue hallway. There, Anatolia gasped, "Now this is what I thought a palace ought to look like."

She followed Sinklar through the chambers, past the two guards on duty, and into the personal quarters. Sinklar stopped to check his comm for messages while Anatolia wandered past, wide-eyed. He handled the routine communications, posted orders for the day, and looked up as she returned to his office, running fingers through her mussed hair.

"You *live* here?"

"Pretty plush, isn't it? Listen, back in the bedroom there's a shower. Fiddle with the knobs and you'll figure out how it works. I called ahead and sent Mhitshul out to find new clothes for you. What you're wearing is down to rags. Whatever he found should be back there on the bed. Hopefully he got the right size."

She took his hand, staring curiously into his eyes. "What's next, Sinklar? You've already been so kind to me. But I want to know the plan. You can't just adopt me as . . . as. . . ."

He reached down and smoothed her hair. "Do you know what you could do for me? Just be here. Talk to me. I haven't felt this comfortable with anyone for a long time . . . since Gretta. Do you know what I mean?"

She nodded, blue eyes warming. "Once, I would

have thought you were after something. But after the
street, I think I can appreciate how you feel."

He glanced down at her hand where it had found
his. "So much depends on me. Last night I discovered
that I may have made a mistake. I'm swimming in
waters I don't understand."

"Want to tell me about it?"

"I. . . . Maybe later."

She studied him thoughtfully for a moment, then
gave a curt nod. "All right. But seriously, what's next?
Where do we go from here? Do I go back to the lab
and take up my duties?"

Sinklar stared absently at the molten-gold carpet
under his feet. "For the moment, Anatolia, I really
don't know. That's part of what I was talking about.
You're not going back to living in the women's toilet.
Look, don't worry about it for now. Let's eat, relax,
and tackle things as they come."

"I won't be a parasite. I have my work."

"I don't need parasites." He fought the desire to
stroke her smooth skin. "Just be yourself."

"You've got it. But I wanted to make the point."

"Thank you. Go clean up while I go through all the
clutter on the comm."

She squeezed his hand and headed for the bedroom
and the shower. Sinklar watched her as she strode
purposefully away. She walked with a special poise
and grace. Then he sighed and went back to accessing
reports. As he went down the list, he stopped short.
The message was simple: DECKER OPERATION
SUCCESSFUL.

Sinklar sagged bonelessly in the gravchair, a happy
grin spreading across his face. How long he sat there
in a haze of relief, he didn't know, but Anatolia appeared in the doorway wearing a cobalt jumpsuit that
did wonders for her. Her skin had taken on a rosy
glow from the hot water, and her hair shimmered in
the light.

"You look . . . spectacular."

She spun on long legs, hair whipping out around
her. "Your Mister Mhitshul has wonderful taste!"

"I'll have to give him a raise. But then, after Ily, he's probably trying to set me up."

"Ily?"

Sinklar stood up, shutting down the system. He wanted to savor Mac's message for a while before he dove into the morass created by Ily. "Hungry?"

"Sure. Ravenous. You were right about my stomach expanding. So, who's Ily?"

"Ily Takka."

Anatolia froze, eyes losing their animation. "The Minister of Internal Security?"

Sinklar nodded, a sliver of panic cutting through him like a Terguzzi wind. "I don't know what to think about her. One minute, she's so . . . well, warm and understanding. The next, she's inhumanly cold. I used to tell myself that she was a reptile. But she's so nice to me." He bit his lip, thinking about just how nice—and the implications. "I don't know if I'm being played for a fool, or if she really cares for me, for what I'm trying to do."

Anatolia settled on the other side of the table, her gaze suddenly calculating. Sinklar dropped to the pillows, uneasy at the frost that seemed to have settled on the conversation. "That's one of the reasons I was out walking the other night. I found a report in the comm—Tybalt's. He had an entire history of Ily's activities. Much of it contradicted things she'd told me."

Anatolia looked up, expression neutral. "And do you care for her?"

Sinklar gestured his confusion. "She's. . . ." *Be honest, Sinklar.* "No. I suppose that if I never saw her again, I wouldn't feel heartbroken."

"You've slept with her, haven't you?"

He nodded, his feelings of guilt obvious. "She does things. . . . I swear she ought to be working at the Temple on Etaria. She could teach a Priestess a thing or two."

Anatolia tilted her head, the light sending sparks through her hair. "You don't seem like her type. You're much too kind and trusting. Not only that, you don't know when to keep your mouth shut—but I'll let that pass for now. You know she sends her remains to us, don't you?"

Baffled, Sinklar leaned forward. "She sends you her what?"

"Remains. Victims. We're a safe repository, you see. Oh, hardly anyone knows except Professor Adam, myself, Bokken, and a few others in Administration. We just got one the other night. An engineer, it turns out. I wouldn't have known, but he used to live in my building. He worked for the Power Authority. . . . What's the matter? You've gone pale."

"Rockard Neru "

"Did *you* have anything to do with his arrest?"

Sinklar shook his head numbly. Like wave-washed sand, another pillar crumbled and dissolved.

"She was quite thorough with him. His genitals had been eaten clear off his body. Acid, most likely. After that, she pulled his intestines out through the right inguinal canal. One of my duties at the lab, you see, is to catalog the cases as they come in. Most are for simple disposal through the regular channels as 'used cadavers.' Neru went to the compactors at the fertilizer factory."

"She lied," Sinklar whispered. "She looked me right in the eye and lied." *Why?* He swallowed hard, feeling filthy and polluted. "So she can infiltrate the Power Authority. She's sinking her claws into everything."

"Sinklar?"

"Leave me alone, Anatolia."

He got unsteadily to his feet, anger tangled with outraged pride. He started for the door, only to have Anatolia spring up and grab him, pulling him around, as she demanded, "What are you going to do?"

"I'm going over there and telling her she's through. Finished and gone! I've had it! She used me! *She . . . she used me!*"

"No!" Anatolia shook him as he fought to break her hold. "Sinklar, listen to me! Listen, Rot you! You go storming in on her, and she'll never let you leave! *Do you hear me?*"

Her tone penetrated his confusion and fury.

"She's dangerous, Sinklar. You walk in there and threaten her, and I promise you'll wind up in the lab like Neru. Disfigured, tortured, and stone cold dead! No one will know. You'll just be another corpse on the way to the fertilizer factory."

His resolve staggered. Any sense of direction vanished. He followed meekly as she led him back to the table and ordered stassa. She handed him the cup, wary gaze on his anguished features. "So you really didn't know?"

He wiped at the hotness of an angry tear that coursed down his cheek. His voice had gone hoarse. "She . . . she told me that we each fight in our own way. I with my armies, she with her own means. Where was the difference in morality? And she claimed we both strove for the same thing: A better way of life for all the people. Freedom from the excesses of the Imperial system."

Anatolia sipped at her stassa. "And she made it seem like you were the man of her dreams? That you'd finally arrived, someone she could share the future with? Did she hang attentively on each word? Adopt that breathless, adoring pose?"

He glanced up, grinding his jaws. "When did you know her?"

"Know her? Rotted Gods, Sinklar, that's what *all* women do when they want to work a man! Appeal to his vanity and insecurity. You act as if his mere presence thrills you to the core of your being, as if each word is fascinating, no matter how Rotted boring he is. You make him think you've never met a man as wonderful and interesting as he is. The more beautiful the woman, the more powerful the effect, because a man always operates under the assumption that a beautiful woman has her pick of all the other men in Free Space. Therefore, if she's enraptured with him, he must be pretty special." She lifted an eyebrow and added, "Sex is a powerful weapon if you know how to use it—and apparently Ily does."

Stunned, he stared at the stassa cup he clutched. Yes, he remembered. That look Ily gave him had always left him uncomfortable, his rational side drowned by overpowering desire. Rysta's harsh warning echoed in his memory, *"Are you just another of her lackeys? Is that it? Did she wiggle her cute ass until your testicles overloaded your brain?"*

He closed his eyes, a welling emptiness yawning within him. He felt sick and degraded.

"Sinklar?"

"What a fool I've been. What a fool I would have continued to be. She would have called me to her office the next time, given me all the rational answers, each with enough truth to disarm, and then she would have gotten me to relax . . . and before it was all over, we'd be in bed again." He avoided her eyes. "I feel like a piece of filth."

"The hardest lessons to learn are the ones you never forget. Now, you can sit there and look like you just swallowed something rotten if you want, but I'm going to eat."

Despite himself, no matter what his brain might be doing to punish itself, his body needed fuel. He began by picking and ended up demolishing major portions of the meal.

"You know," Sinklar admitted humbly when he was finally sated, "I owe you—"

"Forget it." She waved it away with a slim hand. "I got a series of good meals, a shower, and a new set of clothes. Consider it paid in full. You look like you're about to fall over from lack of sleep. I'd better see if I can get a ride back to the lab and catch up on my work. Vet's going to be beserk as it is. If I know him, he covered for me today. When I get there, he'll be livid."

"He's still there? This late?"

"He's got security duty for the next two nights." She paused. "You're going to have to be very careful with Ily. If she even suspects that you're not securely

under her thumb, she'll do anything she can to find a
lever to control you. Maybe through one of your people, like Mayz, or Kap. Anyone she thinks might be
vulnerable."

Sinklar's heart skipped. "She saw you. Asked about
you when she showed up at the LC. We . . . well, it
wasn't a pleasant meeting. I took her outside where
we could talk about Staffa's threat. . . ."

"Go on." Anatolia had picked up his unease.

"I told her you were just a friend." A prickling
ate along his spine. It all came clear. "Rotted Gods,
Anatolia, who could be easier to pick up than you?
You're living in a damn bathroom! Your family is in
Vermilion. Who would miss you?"

She glanced uneasily at him. "Look, I've got a job
and an education to pursue."

"Uh-huh." he squinted at her, mind functioning
again. "How much do you want? Name your salary."

"Salary?"

"Technical adviser? Personal aide? Biological atta-
che? Scientific liaison? Name it."

"Sinklar!"

He crawled over the table, taking her hands, gaze
probing. "You don't understand. You can't go back.
I ruined your life the night I walked into the thirty-
fifth floor and wanted to see my parents. You've told
me about file 7355 and what's in it. To me, it doesn't
make a bit of difference what my DNA is. To someone like Ily, well, what if she got her hands on that
data? What if she got her hands on you?"

Anatolia looked away.

"Yes, you understand, don't you? All of a sudden,
you're back on the street again. If you stay with me,
I can protect you, draw the army around you like a
net. I can send you home, back to your family if you
want. Anything. But in the meantime, stay with me,
for your safety and mine."

"Look, you can't be sure she'd tag me as a
lever. . . ."

He just stared, as if by that effort she'd understand.

Panic possessed her for an instant, then she brought herself under control, deflating as she bit her lip.

"I'm right—and you know it."

A shoulder lifted in defeat. "Well, it's not like I had much to go back to. The bathroom will never be the same without me." She stared listlessly at nothing for a moment. "Why is this happening to me?"

"I don't know. It's happening to all of us. Myself, I feel like I'm being rushed away in a river, with no hope of reaching shore. All I can do is struggle, try and keep my head above water." *And in the end, I'm going to drown.*

"What about the Star Butcher? You mentioned him, too. Is he in this?"

"Ily evidently grabbed his Wing Commander, Skyla Lyma. The Star Butcher has issued an ultimatum that if Ily doesn't release her, he's coming to burn Rega into radioactive slag. But for the moment, that's the least of my troubles."

"The least of. . . . I'm not sure if I want to know what your serious troubles are."

"I think you already do . . . and it's your problem, too."

* * *

"War can be likened to fire, and humanity to an untamed forest. Think about the forest for a moment. Left to themselves, forests age in a slow but steady process. The giants grow and spread their leaves in a vast canopy that blocks any light from reaching the ground. Down there, in the darkness, all that grows are fungi and bacteria. Sometimes a seed makes it through the litter of leaves and sprouts, but to what

kind of fate? Walk through an old forest sometime and you'll see them. Pale sickly shoots with yellow leaves that die when they're no more than a centimeter high— food for the fungi and bacteria.

"When you look up, all you see are the forest giants, with trunks two or even three meters in diameter. But are these old giants the end? If so, then reality is a depressing thing indeed, for the old forest giants are riddled with disease, the cores of the trees slimy with the black rot that is eating at their hearts. An old forest is a forest in stagnation. What chance is there for new growth?

"Now, do you see the value of fire?

"And when you look around you at the older planets, you find governments and people who have lived in peace for three hundred years, with social institutions and government bureaucracies like the giants of the forest, which have woven their branches together in a canopy. What do you expect to find beneath their canopy, but rot, stagnation, and disaffection.

"And now you know the value of war."

—Lecture given to the young Staffa kar Therma during his tutorial by the Praetor of Myklene

CHAPTER XXIV

Hyros expertly dropped from the traffic lane, passing the security field and winding down the Capitol's approach route. From his seat in the rear, Myles watched the passing spires and gleaming facades that rose around him. The Capitol was such a magnificent building that he marveled despite his familiarity with it, and despite the fact that his exhaustion left him in a dreamlike state.

Hyros banked and decelerated through a series of concentric golden rings that marked the entrance to Divine Sassa's secure zone and entered the orifice reserved for official ingress. The aircar hummed as Hyros jockeyed it artfully into a lighted receiving area and settled next to the entrance, where tense guards waited. Immediately before them, the huge bulk of Iban Jakre's military transport filled most of the clearance.

To think I used to travel like that, with fifty swarming aides getting in the way and raising a racket. He shook his head as the dome lifted and Hyros leapt out to help him. To Myles' satisfaction, he climbed from the car without the grunting he used to emit, and quickly straightened his tunic. Nevertheless, the fatigue left him feeling wobbly, as if his knees might give at any second. Behind him, the second car with Arron and Jorome settled, the dome rising as his security personnel hopped out, staring around with a professional air.

"Anything else, sir?" Hyros asked.

Myles considered, trying to organize the tattered fragments of his thoughts. "Yes, you might want to accompany me. This will no doubt be a stormy session. Everything is collapsing. I want not only your recordings, but also, I may need your observations when this is all over."

"Yes, sir."

Myles tugged at the hem of his beautifully embroidered coat and started forward, aware of the uneasy looks the guards gave him. That crisp tension filled the air, reaching even his blurred senses. Within the vaulted hallways of the Capitol itself, the effect must have been debilitating as rumors flew back and forth about the attack and what it meant.

Myles stepped through the doorway into the decorated hallway all done up in brushed bronze and polished black stone.

"This way, Legate." A security officer bowed and waved. "The antigravs are ready for you and your staff." The woman craned her neck, staring back past Myles and his three companions.

"There is just myself and those you see here, thank you. One antigrav will be sufficient."

The woman's anxiety immediately increased. "As you wish, Legate."

Myles stepped onto the antigrav and sat back wearily as it slipped down the hallway. Heedless of the priceless statuary they passed, Myles dropped his chin on his chest, trying to keep everything in perspective despite the fogginess caused by sleep deprivation.

The entire planet reeled, stunned by *Gyton*'s blow. The Empire waited in a state of shock. The impossible had occurred. Not only had the Regan attack destroyed the military's largest base, but it had blasted the Imperial Defense command control. People now looked up at their skies, wondering if the same fate lurked just beyond the speed of light. Were Regans spacing for their fragile homes even as they stared into the night skies? Would their loved ones be next?

Over a half billion human beings lay dead, mostly unburied and frozen on the other side of Imperial Sassa. The ripples of destruction and ruin continued to spread as clouds blocked the summer sun and the planet itself shivered with destabilized tectonic plates.

Here and there, rioting broke out, fueling the spread of death and disaster. Estimates claimed that a million people a day were dying.

And no end is in sight. How many more will we have by the time the fallout, radiation, climatic disruptions, and civil breakdown take their toll?

Outside of the wound in the planet itself, the systems which supported the people—the very systems Myles monitored—were now strained past his ability to administer. These days Myles napped at his desk—as did all of his staff—as they tried to coordinate rescue, evacuation, emergency medical services, the flood of refugees, failing power, water, food distribution, collapsing communications systems, repair crews, relocation camps, and, most of all, the building fear as people's imaginations prodded them toward panic and chaos.

May your Seddi God help us, Staffa. For we cannot help ourselves.

Earthquakes continued to disrupt the already staggered attempts at relief. No sooner was a supply line established than the planetary crust slipped, destroying buildings, ruining water supplies, and leaving new masses homeless.

The poor suffering people. They plagued him, staring out at him with horrified eyes from the crumbled ruins of their homes, lives, and dreams. The crowding refugees raised rag-wrapped hands to him, begging him to feed them, to find them shelter from the falling snow that wound down from the clouds of solar-masking particulate blasted into the skies by the *Markelos* explosion. They staggered through croplands, the half-mature plants black and wilted by the sudden frost. Bodies lay in the rubble, frozen by exposure to the cruel wind and sleet. The dying wailed, not even able to gain the relief a single ampoule of medication would have given.

Even in the sanctuary of the Capitol, Miles could still see them in his mind, begging him for the most important gift of all, to save them, to simply give them and their families a chance to live.

My people are dying . . . dying . . . and I cannot save them all. Staffa, come help me. What you hinted has come true, and it wasn't my fault.

"Legate?" Hyros asked softly.

Myles jerked, blinking awake and shaking the fluttery fragments of the dream from his muzzy mind. "Yes, what?"

"We're here, sir. We've reached His Holiness' audience chamber."

"Oh," Myles exhaled and rubbed a hand over his masklike face. He tried to collect his thoughts, gave it up as impossible, and stood, stepping down to the polished creamy white tiles before the golden doors. Here, too, nervous guards stood in immaculate uniforms, weapons grounded. These, too, looked spooked, ready to bolt at the least hint of trouble.

Myles, his staff following, entered as the wide doors opened. A fanfare played from overhead as he strode into the chambers with their crystalline architecture. Today the optics pulsed, as if the colors they pumped were the lifeblood of the Empire. Lines of guards snapped to attention, saluting with a vigor and pomp that Myles struggled to understand as he came to a halt before the floating holograph of Divine Sassa. Iban Jakre stood to one side, his uniform a sparkling and resplendent display of turquoise and white. Nevertheless, looking closely, Myles could see a pallor to his flesh, a tightness to the eyes where worry ate with little needle teeth.

"Myles Roma, Legate Prima Excellence, welcome," Holy Sassa announced with a grand eloquence.

Myles glanced up and blinked at the burning sensation in his eyes—the aftereffect of the several minutes of sleep he'd stolen in the antigrav. "Yes, Holiness?"

Divine Sassa tilted his head, the impact of the action no more than a node shifting atop a mountain of fat. "We have called you here to obtain an idea of how long it will take you to assemble the resources for a retaliatory strike against the perfidious Regans who have desecrated our sacred planet and laughed in the face of the Sassan God. Such infamy cannot be tolerated, not by me, not by my loyal servants, or by my enraged people. Our honor has been insulted and sullied. We *will* have our revenge."

Myles looked at the God-Emperor in amazement. "What?"

Sassa's bejeweled fingers knotted, the gems sending sparkles over the endless yards of his shining robe. "I don't think I need to repeat myself. In simple words, how long will it take, given your highest priority, to assemble a strike force to repay the Godless Regan filth for their blasphemy?"

Myles stared, wondering if his ears had been affected by the lack of sleep. "Divine One, our military is currently occupied with rescuing our own people from the disaster. Every ship we have left is transporting critical medicines, food, clothing—the bare necessities of survival. Our resources have all been rerouted to simple survival . . . and, with a great deal of luck, we might, *might* make it. Holy One, we have no resources to spare."

Sassa's colorless eyes widened, a tinge of anger reddening his bald scalp. "I don't care to hear your excuses, Legate. *You will do as your God orders!*"

"Myles," Jakre warned softly, making the barest motion with his hand. Fatigue-befuddled as he was, Myles almost missed the hint, and then teetered on the brink of blurting out just how asinine any such policy would be.

Fortunately, Iban stepped forward, saying, "Divine One, I'm sure the Legate will manage with his usual skill and innovation. He and I need to work out the details and we'll provide a complete report to you within the day. Myself, I can understand the Legate's current preoccupation. And, Holiness, I can only praise our Legate's ingenuity and commitment in this time of severe trial. Since the Regan infamy, I've worked in cooperation and close contact with his staff. If we could, Divinity, the Legate and I would like a chance to discuss this, to determine a target which will humble the enemy and strike terror into their accursed souls.

Iban spread his arms wide, chin lifted defiantly.
"After all, we wouldn't want to be too hasty with this
operation. We *must* make sure we demonstrate how
such perfidy will be repaid!"

Sassa smiled. "You are a balm to my spirit, Iban.
Yes . . . yes, indeed, go and plan. Bring me the fruits
of your cunning and wrath. I will hear from you by the
time I have my evening meal." He made a smoothing
motion with one hand. "It will help my digestion."

Myles sputtered, "But we—"

"Shut up," Jakre muttered softly from the side of
his mouth as he took Myles by the hand.

Something clicked in Roma's prickly head and he
nodded, "By your evening meal, Holiness."

"Splendid! Begone! Go, angels of my vengeance!"
Sassa made a flipping gesture with his fingers.

"Come on," Iban growled, leading Myles down the
long tessellated hall, the military retinue filing in after
them, most forced to jockey with each other for position since Myles had come with only three aides, and
they'd immediately moved in close behind him.

"I don't *understand* this." Myles looked over at
Jakre as they exited through the golden doors.

"Neither does he," Jakre grunted, jerking his head
toward the chambers. "But then, I'm not as tired and
politically clumsy as you appear to be. He wants a
strike against the Regans—and we have to figure out
how to do it."

Myles walked over to his antigrav, settling loose-
jointedly into the seat. "Very well, ride with me and
we'll discuss it." There might indeed be a way. Hyros,
you will accompany me. Arron, you and Jorome, meet
me at the aircar." He waved away the crowd of Iban's
aides as they rushed forward for a seat on the privi-
leged antigrav. "Iban and I will go . . . with Hyros,
and no one else."

Jakre flashed him a glance of understanding and
waved his staff away. Hyros powered up the antigrav,
pulling away.

"Iban, you're speaking nonsense. You know the situation," Myles said. "If we so much as pull one war-

ship from a defensive position around any planet or station, we're begging for a riot like you've never seen. Or, worse, perhaps a willful defection to the Regans—surrender in return for peace."

Jakre slumped in the seat beside Myles, his front of bravado collapsing into a weary pallor. "I know that. But, Myles, would you tell that to Sassa? I've been out there, seen what's happening here, on *this* planet. By his Holiness, we're hanging by a thread. Every soldier I've got is out there fighting to keep our people alive, to maintain social order. I've let you have every vessel I could spare to bring in supplies, because, by the star-shot heavens, we've got two weeks of stores left. After that, millions will starve."

"And as soon as they get hungry, we won't be able to hold them back."

Jakre nodded. "Myles, if I could relive these last months, take back some of the things I've said. . . ."

"We would all do things a little differently."

"In the meantime, we're living on borrowed time. You may not know the entire situation. We can no more stop a Regan invasion than Divine Sassa could run up a flight of stairs. Unless we wish to inflict holocaust on every Sassan world, we can't even slow Sinklar Fist down. When *Markelos* impacted on the planet, it killed every Sassan hope and dream."

* * *

MacRuder nodded to the two guards who stood at the hatch and entered the observation blister on *Gyton*'s port side. The unmanned instruments looked like ungainly insects in silhouette. She stood on the other side of the spectrometer, outlined against the tactite transparency of the bubble, as she watched the motionless stars beyond, now redshifted and elongated.

"Am I disturbing you?"

"No, Mac. Come in. I've been a little lonely these past couple of days. I don't know how many gravities we took during the escape, but the ship sounded like it would crumple into scrap at any second. I take it we're out of danger?"

"I believe so. The Sassans were so confused and disorganized they barely put up any resistance. Their fire was mostly ineffectual, mostly directed by line of sight, and the computer control system had to be input manually."

She turned, seating herself on one of the observation chairs. The faint starlight and dimmed overheads softened the perfect features of her face, those marvelous amber eyes in shadow. Talking to her this way didn't leave him nearly as flustered.

"Then you achieved your goal?"

Mac went to stand before the tactite, staring out at the reddened smears of starlight. "We bought time for Sinklar and the Regan Empire."

"I can't say that I care much for Rega. The Tybalts never brought me anything but misery. But for them, I suppose I'd have been a well-to-do psychologist with an established practice. I'd be married to some delightfully boring man with a home and a family."

"If that is your wish, perhaps Sinklar will be able to grant it for you."

She turned and ran slender fingers over the hood of the spectrometer, eyes focused on something beyond the blister. "It's a delightful thought, Mac . . . but far too late for me. My destiny changed when I was hauled off to be sold into slavery. It changed again when Staffa saw me standing there, naked and horrified, before all those men. It changed yet again when the Praetor stole us away. But tell me honestly, can you see me married to a boring man and practicing psychology? No, Mac. I'd go mad."

"What would you like?"

"To stop the insanity," she whispered. "I'd give anything to stop the fighting, the bloodshed, and the misery. Fool that I am, I used to pray for anything, any way out of the Praetor's clutches. All those years while I lived in his polluted shadow, I prayed for Staffa to come, to blast me out of that eternal hell.

Then when it happened and I landed in the wreckage of Myklene, I saw what real hell was like."

"How long were you there?"

"Too long. I saw terrible things, Mac. Bodies piled and frozen while the dying survivors picked among them. At first they looked for anything of value. Later, as more died and services failed, I saw corpses stripped of meat. Somehow the worst nightmare of all was reflected in the eyes of the children. Something animalistic and wild. Even I cursed the Star Butcher."

Mac bit his lip, thinking about the devastation on Imperial Sassa. "I think it will be over soon. I think Sinklar will have all of Free Space under his control within the year." *And if he doesn't? If the strike against Sassa is just the first? How many did you kill with that stunt, Mac? How many piled corpses did your tidy little plan leave behind?*

"Are you all right?"

"Thinking about what we did to Imperial Sassa. I guess I'm struggling with my conscience. Rysta ran the projections before I left the bridge." Mac bowed his head. "From the best estimates, we probably killed somewhere around half a billion human beings."

He turned, piercing gaze locking with hers. "How do you comprehend a number like that? Half a *billion* people . . . human beings like you and me. Why? How did we get pushed into this situation?"

Chrysla's expression mirrored her concern. "Mac, what is the situation in Free Space? What's really happening out there?"

He took a deep breath. "Sinklar is retraining the Regan army in tactics he worked out on Targa. Before we could complete that, Sassa would have been able to launch an attack, probably against a world like Ashtan. My duty was to eliminate the strike force outfitting at Imperial Sassa. They'd never suspect a single ship of such mischief. I sort of innovated and crashed *Markelos* into their big military base as we took out their fleet."

"And Staffa's role?"

"Unknown. He went to Sassa on some mission just

before I spaced. Of that, we're sure, and we think he asked them to sit tight, but we've no proof. We're also sure that Sassa turned down his request."

"Sinklar is in charge of Rega? The new Emperor?"

Mac made a face. "He and the Minister of Internal Security."

"Ily Takka," Chrysla said coolly. "I read the Praetor's file on her. She was listed as extremely dangerous."

"She's that, all right. And I'm hoping Sinklar has kept out of her greedy little claws."

"You say that with a bitter tone in your voice."

"Sink isn't. . . . All right, he's young, Chrysla. I may be young, too, but I'm not naive when it comes to women. Sink fell in love on Targa. Her name was Gretta Artina. Arta Fera killed her—and because of that, the Blessed Gods know what he's going to think when he sees you. Maybe it's a good thing you're a psychologist. Sinklar took Gretta's death pretty hard. Ily's been laying for him. You know, the coy, charming, sexy bombshell. I may not know much about big-league politics, but there *will* be a power play when this is all over."

"And Staffa remains an unknown?"

"He told me once he wanted to stop the coming war. He's interested in helping humanity find a new dream. My question is, can we believe him? I instinctively liked him, but where does Star Butcher end and new dream begin?"

Chrysla nodded thoughtfully. "And my son?"

"He's after a new order. We're fighting for the little guy. I told you about Targa. We made a vow down there that we'd tear the old system down and fix it so people didn't have to march out and die for a political expedient. If Staffa really means what he says, maybe he'll stay out of it. If not, we might have to take him head-on."

"Don't, Mac. Sinklar might be his son, and he might have a brilliance all his own, but you must believe me, if Staffa launches an attack, you'll never stop him."

"We're pretty good."

Chrysla stepped toward him, passionately determined to make him understand. Her scent filled his nostrils, and he swayed, aware of how close she stood. His heart began to race.

"Mac," she whispered, "you *must* make sure this never happens. Trust me. As good as you might believe you are, Staffa's senses for battle are those of a siff jackal. He's a past master, intimately familiar with all the tricks. Strategies Sinklar might entertain as possibilities, Staffa has used, modified, and discarded years ago. The ploy you used on Imperial Sassa, he used on Phillipia and Nesios before I even knew his name."

Her aura had wrapped around him, its hold tightening with each breath. His soul wavered as he surrendered to the endless amber pools of her eyes. *Escape! Get away so you can think, damn it!*

"All right. I believe you." And he broke away, retreating to the hatch, one hand to his breast as if he could still his aching heart.

"Mac?" she called, following him, placing a hand on his shoulder. An electric thrill shot through him at her mere touch. "You're trembling. Are you all right?"

"It's . . . nothing." He tried to pull away.

"I didn't offend you, did I? Did I say something wrong?"

Mac plastered his brave face on and shook his head. "No. Maybe I'm just tired. I. . . ." In the brighter light by the hatch, their eyes met and he stared into hers, his soul strained with longing.

She nodded then, amber eyes searching his. "I see. Come, let's go sit down and talk this out."

He could hear the blood racing in his ears as she led him back to the bench and pulled him down. He ground his teeth, searching for words. "I don't . . . don't know what to do with you."

"You think you're in love with me," she said frankly.

He laughed bitterly at himself. "That's what makes it all so difficult. I *know* how you affect men. I'm no one's fool when it comes to women, love, and all the rest. Unlike Sink, I'd turned myself into a veteran by the time I hit twenty. Now, if I was smart, I'd walk out of here, forget all about you, and concentrate on finding something worthwhile to occupy my time with until I get back to Rega and find out what sort of mess I have to bail Sinklar out of.''

"And I frighten you?"

"You bet you do. You're Staffa's wife, for the Blessed Gods' sake! You're my best friend's mother . . . *mother!* Granted, I'm a little older than Sinklar, but not that much.''

"There are times when age isn't a matter of years, Mac," she replied wearily. "I'm sorry. I was starved for companionship for twenty years, wishing I could talk to someone without being ogled, or feared, or hustled away by the guard. If I lose that now, I'll go mad. But I don't want you frustrated and berserk because your hormones are pumping so hard you can't think.''

When she turned her longing gaze on him, he melted. "Mac, tell me what you want. If it's to be left alone, I'll do it. I don't want to hurt you.''

"Lovely lady, if I've controlled myself this far, I can go it a while longer.''

"That's what I want, Mac. Just be my friend until I can get back to Staffa. Help me sort this out—but not if my mere presence drives you mad.''

Memories of Targa tugged at him, and he sighed. "Take the few good moments you get and savor them.''

"You say that with a wistful sadness.''

"I was remembering. . . . Never mind. The unfolding of events is never kind to us. I know how you affect men. I'll keep in mind that it's pheromones and be just fine," he lied to both of them.

*   *   *

Itreata had already disappeared in the wavering blue of the Twin Titans' endless dance. The combined energies of the Companion fleet lashed the pulsing bursts of radiation with their reaction mass as bounce-back collars tightened and the sophisticated computers refined acceleration parameters. With increasing acceleration, the fleet built mass for null singularity and time began to dilate as the monitors compensated for redshift. Under a constant forty-five g boost, the reactors labored while the ships' artificial gravity generators compensated and protected fragile humans, computers, and structural components in an elaborate bootstrapping operation.

Staffa sat in his command chair on *Chrysla*'s bridge, eyes narrowed as he gazed at the monitor which displayed the receding position of Itreata. How many times had he spaced thus, bent on conquest and death? How many times had he left Itreata and never looked back? What made this time different?

He glanced over at the monitor where the rest of his fleet flanked *Chrysla* in her race for the stars. Once again the Companions spaced, and with them, on harpies' wings of horror, rode death and destruction.

Staffa swiveled his chair, to see the forward monitor. Out there, beyond *Chrysla*'s wedge-shaped bow, lay Rega, blissfully unaware of the hammer that now began to speed toward it.

How many lives will you crush this time? How much suffering and waste will this inflict? Staffa struggled to blank the ghoulish eyes of the restless dead who haunted his dreams.

Trapped . . . he was trapped by Ily's perfidy and Sinklar's tactical brilliance. Sassa, despite any hopes to the contrary, had been defeated by *Gyton*'s single stroke. Myles might stave off starvation and collapse, but only by the shaving of a micron. With a feather's puff, the bone and sinew of the Sassan Empire would slowly begin to pull asunder in an agonizing collapse.

Sinklar would smell that weakness and exploit it with the ruthless efficiency of a sand tiger stalking a wounded kid goat. Tendrils of Ily's corruption would immediately follow, powered by the information she'd pry out of Skyla with her drugs and torture.

The only hope to ameliorate the destruction lay in an untested technology. And if that failed?

"I will be forced to murder them all," he whispered numbly. "And that will be my legacy to you, God."

Skyla . . . Skyla. . . . A stitch pierced Staffa's heart as he lingered over the memory of her startling blue eyes, cherished her cocky smile and the way the light sparked in her ice-blonde hair.

Gone . . . ripped away like solar wind around a frozen asteroid. He felt empty.

Skyla's absence, with the power of some heaviness in the very air, weighed on Staffa's equilibrium. His usual clarity of mind had clouded, and a sense of despair possessed him.

You know that the chances you'll see her alive again are slim to none. The weary loneliness closed in, throttling, starving him of hope. But what else could he do?

Skyla knows the stakes. She understands what you have to do. This thing has gone beyond the value of any single person, no matter how much you may love her.

"Skyla, I'm so sorry."

The pain in his heart dug a little deeper.

*   *   *

"Current investigations are underway to determine the effects of the Mikay impact on the planetary crust of Imperial Sassa. To date, emergency seismic stations have been established along the active interfaces of the major continental plates, but the data accumulated as of preparation of this report are inconclusive. Efforts, however, are underway to establish a viable predictive model which will integrate the various tectonic, geologic, hydrological, and seismic dynamics presently under investigation by Geosciences Department personnel.

"It should be understood by all parties that severe deformation of the planetary crust has taken place along a major fault line. Not only did impact fracture the crust, but a matter/antimatter detonation occurred several kilometers below the ground surface when the *Markelos'* reactors failed. While estimates are in preliminary stages, it appears that magma is rising in the crater and the isostatic crustal balance has been destroyed. Long-term implications are not favorable and evacuation of populated centers in areas of tectonic activity is recommended.

"To date we cannot make an accurate assessment of potential negative impact to population centers, economic enterprises, property (personal or public), agriculture, industry, commerce, or public safety or health.

"The above mentioned assessments will be undertaken pending the successful acquisition and compilation of appropriate data.

"This action was initiated and implemented under Executive Order 11593 and conforms to all applicable Imperial, Planetary, and District rules and regulations."

—*Report produced and distributed by Imperial Sassan Academy of Geology, Planetology, and Geosciences*

CHAPTER XXV

Sinklar walked into his palace bedroom and found Anatolia propped on the sleeping platform, preoccupation in her haggard eyes. She looked delicate and vulnerable in the middle of the silk-piled opulence of the bedding. Momentarily, Sinklar even forgot his gymnastic romps with Ily.

He settled himself on the edge of the plush bed and stared absently at the gauzy hangings that draped down from the canopy. "I just ordered a couple of Sections from First Division to report to the palace. I talked to Mhitshul. He knows what I want in the way of security."

Anatolia nodded listlessly, a frown lining her high forehead. "Sink, it's all happening too fast. I feel lost. One minute I was safely in the lab, involved in my studies. Then you blew in like a whirlwind and I haven't had time to think since."

He flopped down next to her, hating the burning sensation of fatigue in his brain. His eyes had a gritty feel. The rest of him had gone numb. "I'm sorry. Listen, as soon as I can be sure you're going to be safe, I'll send you wherever you want to go."

She smiled sadly. "And where is that, Sinklar? Home? To Vermilion to help my father cultivate siva root? Ily's tentacles reach that far—and beyond."

"I can keep all of you safe as soon as I can get a security team sent out. You can go with them if you'd like."

She shook her head. "No, Sinklar. Farming siva wasn't what I wanted out of life. I love my father, don't get me wrong. He did everything for me, but

472

I'm not meant to be a farmer." She paused. "Once, out on the street, I swore that if I could just be delivered from the fear and terror, I'd pick siva forever and never complain. Looking back now, I know that's not true. I survived out there. It was like crossing a threshold. I can't go back."

"But I suppose you didn't figure you'd get messed up in a political struggle either, did you?"

"That wasn't exactly on my agenda," she agreed dryly. "But now that I'm in it, I guess I'll just stick it out, see what comes of all this."

"I meant what I said about keeping you safe. I'll find someplace where you won't be—"

"Forget it, Sinklar." She cocked her head, spilling shining curls over her shoulder as her sober gaze probed his. "I don't want to go someplace and hide. I meant it when I said I'd stick it out—with you, if you'll let me. Maybe I can do something, keep you sane if nothing else."

"Why? It doesn't make sense. Ily will count you among the enemy. If I lose, or if she gets her hands on you. . . ."

Anatolia gave him a humorless grin. "I watched you over the last couple of days. You're a decent human being, Sinklar. Keep in mind, I catalog the corpses Ily sends in for disposal. It never really sank in before tonight. I've been thinking about Rokard Neru, about how he wasn't a criminal. He was simply a person who got in the way. And suddenly I realized I was in the way, too. Given half a chance, I'd be on the slab for Vet to catalog. I'm still on the street, Sinklar. No matter what I'd like to believe. So the smart thing is to pick sides and fight it out."

"I understand." He gave her a weary smile. "I'll have to admit, I'm a selfish bastard. I hated the thought of sending you away. It's been nice to have someone to talk to."

"What about if you win?"

He rubbed his bloodshot eyes with a thumb and forefinger. "I've got to see that people like Ily, and all the ones like her, are destroyed with the Empire.

People have a chance for once. I'm a social scientist. I ought to be able to design a system that works for the people. If it takes all of my life, that's what I'm going to do." He lifted an eyebrow inquisitively. "How about you?"

"First I'm going to try and stay alive. After that, I'll worry about what to do next."

"So what do you want? Just to do research for the rest of your life?"

Her deep blue eyes narrowed and she rolled onto her stomach next to him, propped on her elbows, hands clasped. "That wouldn't bother me a bit. I think I have a scientist lodged somewhere in my blood. Research is contagious. With each question you answer, another fifty are posed."

"Like me?"

She gave him a wary, sidelong glance. "You ready to talk about that yet? Last time I broached the subject, you shied and turned *very* defensive." At his silence, she added, "You know, don't you? Or at least suspect."

Sinklar swallowed against the sudden restriction in his throat. "You said there was no way I could have come from either Valient or Tanya?"

She took a deep breath as if nerving herself. "I checked her, Sinklar. She never bore a child. There are telltale changes to the body. Her uterus never expanded. The pelvic bones, the pubic symphyses and sacral articulation to the innominates never softened. Scars form in vaginal muscles. In short, she couldn't have been a surrogate mother. Her role socially, that's something different."

"My biological mother came from Ashtan," Sinklar repeated, closing his eyes. *Had Staffa told the truth?*

"I can prove that. It's your father who really intrigues me."

In a wooden voice, Sinklar asked, "He . . . I mean, you said it was a strange genetic pattern."

"That's an understatement."

"Did . . . did you check for a Myklenian pattern?"

"It would have registered. Sinklar, you've got to

understand, your DNA is *different*, not just a variation. It's like nothing I've ever seen before. Statistically, you shouldn't exist. Now, do you want to tell
me about this Myklenian connection?"

He closed his eyes, trying to find an anchor in his
drifting soul. *Arta Fera was a clone—an artifically produced human being. Bruen said she was provided by
the Praetor.* A prickly sensation climbed Sinklar's
spine. *And Bruen said he got me from the Praetor.
Does that mean. . . .* He closed his eyes and swallowed
hard.

"Sinklar?" Anatolia's hand settled on his arm.

"Nothing. Listen. I need to think about this." He
hoped his misery wasn't betrayed in his eyes. "Let's
get some sleep. We've been up for almost three days
with only a nap here and there. We'll talk about it
again when we're rested."

She nodded her agreement, but a new worry gripped
her.

* * *

Ily Takka's heels clicked as she walked down the
long hallway on the thirty-fifth floor of the Criminal
Anatomical Research Labs. Her eyebrows raised slightly
as she gave the women's rest room a glance. The hallway was nondescript in every other way, just the average sort of square corridor with light panels spaced
evenly overhead, synthetic paneling on the walls, and
polished tile floor.

Ahead of Ily, Jan Bokken hurried in a partial wad-
dle, his duck-footed walk making a scuffling plop
sound, his baggy clothing whispering. At first glance,
Ily had disliked Bokken. Not that he seemed unsuited
to his position—most of her people fit his general
makeup—but he lacked that spark of initiative that
would forever condemn him to supervisory status of a
single building. He watched the world from heavy-
lidded eyes, stroking his beard-shadowed jowls with
thumb and forefinger; and Ily didn't like men who
wore perfume.

"Here is it," Bokken said at last, pointing to one of a long line of doors. The sign overhead listed it as CENTRAL LABORATORY.

Ily gave him a superficial smile and pushed the door open. Several of her agents stood along one wall while a thin man paced nervously back and forth in the aisle between equipment cluttered worktables.

"Professor Adam?" Ily asked as the door closed behind Bokken.

"Yes! Yes." He started and seemed to recover some control. "What's the matter? I don't understand. I haven't done anything."

Ily gave the man her ravishing smile, and walked forward to take his arm. "Oh, it's not you, Professor. It's one of your students in whom we've developed an interest."

"Pool? Look, the young man's statements about the Seddi were his own. We do not condone, nor permit—"

"Anatolia Daviura," Ily corrected, making a notation of Pool in the back of her mind.

"Ana?" Adam seemed at a loss. "Oh, you mean she did something while she was absent during the riots?"

"No, we're interested in a project she was working on here. Could I see her workstation?"

"This way."

Ily followed the man past shrouded equipment to the rear corner. There she found a desk and wall complex that contained a computer and microscope. Items on the desk looked as if they'd just been left a moment before.

"Your Ana has a research file, something only you and she can access. I would like to see it, please."

Adam swallowed hard, his throat working. "I don't like to invade my students'—"

"Please!"

"Yes, ma'am." Adam slid into the chair, powering the system up, his fingers dancing across the keyboard. To the computer he ordered, "Provide a listing of Anatolia's files, please."

"Access denied. Insert key."

Adam, slightly flustered, fiddled in his pocket, produced a ring of keys, and sorted through them. Finally he reached down and inserted his master into the cabinet by his knee and opened the drawer. At the same time, a list of files appeared on the directory.

Ily bent down, pulling out reams of printout from the drawer. To her eyes, the long columns of numbers were meaningless. Nor did the headings have any relevance. "What is all this?"

Adam squinted as he took the heavy printout. "Must be her project. Let's see, yes, here. File 7355. It should be in the computer, too." He promptly accessed and more of the endless streams of data appeared.

"What does it mean, Professor. And tell me in simple terms I can understand. I'm not a scientist."

Adam leaned forward, brow lined as he studied the data, his finger tapping the scroll key every so often. "Well, from a preliminary look, it's a DNA coding study on inheritance."

"Inheritance? You mean genetic, correct?"

"Yes. She's comparing parental types with a single offspring. Nothing unusual here. We do this sort of. . . . Wait a minute, I'm into the F_1 now!"

"F one?"

"The offspring. F_1 stands for first generation. I don't understand this." He squinted at the data, head tilting slightly. "This doesn't make any sense."

"What doesn't?"

He had pulled a laser pen, making notations on his comm. With the pen tip, he indicated a column of letters, Cs and Gs, As and Ts, in various orders and sequences. Little carets had been placed to mark segments of the pattern.

"What you see here, Minister, is a split screen comparison between two sections of the same human chromosome. The one on the left, the maternal, a segment of human chromosome 7-1. This growth allele is fairly standard as a benchmark—one of the common genetic patterns that all humans share. In this case, the order is correct. Now, compare what you see on the right half of the screen, the paternal, or human chromosome 7-2. The composition of the DNA should mirror the maternal, but it doesn't."

"And why is that important?"

Adam rubbed his jaw, attention absorbed by the diagram. "Because I've never seen this pattern before."

"Perhaps it's some odd variation of—"

"Minister, please." Adam gave her a condescending look. "You stick to security, and I will stick to genetics. What I'm telling you is that *no one* has ever seen this allele before. Obviously it's viable, or the F_1 specimen wouldn't have developed past the zygote stage."

"Some sort of mutation?"

Adam shook his head. "The chances of that are one in ten trillion. You must understand something. You don't just mix DNA. The molecule is the blueprint for an entire organism. If you change something, say an adenine for a cytosine, the base code is changed. If, for example, that code produces a polypeptide chain which will form a muscle cell, the messenger RNA won't deposit the proper amino acids in the right sequence for the muscle tissue."

At Ily's blank look, Adam worked his fists and frowned. "All right, think of it like this. What if you changed a random piece of a computer program. Switched a 1 for an 0 in the binary of a program?"

"It would depend on where it was in the program— what command was affected. In the wrong place, it could destroy the entire software."

"Exactly. And human DNA is just like that, except we deal in quaternary instead of binary. See how devastating the effects could be? One point mutation—a switch of guanine for thymine, and the organism might not be able to metabolize a significant amino acid like valine. No valine—no polypeptide—no cell metabolism—no life."

Ily tapped her teeth with a thumbnail. "So, in other words, Professor, this F_1's strange DNA isn't human?"

Adam's brow knotted. "That's the first assumption to make—but the problem is that it *is* viable. Someone, and I don't know who, had to have been brilliant to create this. Look, see how it combines? The computations must have been mind boggling!"

Ily looked skeptical.

"No, you don't understand the implications!" Adam waved his hands nervously, a fanatical gleam in his eyes. "It's as if someone sat down and designed an entirely new human being—and did it so well that it could still produce a viable offspring!"

"Designed? Not just random recombination?"

"No, this was done on purpose—an artifact." He stiffened. "Rotted Gods. . . ."

"What?"

Adam's lips quivered. "We *can't* do this! Not even the best computers we have could interpret the different possibilities of potential viable offspring from a single mating, let alone one that would be viable in a random. . . ." He shook his head, baffled. "It's impossible!"

"But it's here on the screen before you. That's taken from a specimen, isn't it?" At his dazed nod, Ily asked, "But from who?"

Adam shrugged and lifted his hands. "So far, the only way you have the specimen identified is as F_1. On the other hand, looking back at the parental types, they've got a catalog number from our vaults. But I can tell you right now, they're not the parents of the mysterious F_1. The male was Targan and the female Etarian. The maternal contribution to Ana's subject was Ashtan. It's the paternal genetic source that's the real question."

"So the father was the real clone?"

"Perhaps. At this stage of investigation, it's hard to say. I *need* more data! Curse you, Ana, why didn't you show this to me?" He bent over like a hunting heron, eyes on the screen.

"Who are the parental types? You said you had a catalog number." Ily crossed her arms, fascinated by Adam's sudden obsession with the data.

"Forget them, they don't matter. They didn't have anything to do with the genetics of F_1."

Ily reached down and yanked Adam back. "Their identity, Professor. Now!" Bokken had come to stand behind her, his slablike face inscrutable. Adam seemed to retreat from the thorny problem of the DNA.

"Yes, yes. Just a moment." He used a pull-down menu and tapped in instructions.

"Working," the machine intoned.

Adam drifted away again, his gaze devouring the DNA on the screen.

Ily bent down as data flashed on the computer screen. Her heart began to pound as she read: SUBJECT IDENTIFICATIONS REQUESTED: FIRST SUBJECT 11768-BQ TANYA FIST; SECOND SUBJECT 11768-BR VALIENT FIST. SEE FILES/CRSREF SEDDI/CRSREF ASSASSIN.

Ily straightened. "Bokken. I'll have a team here immediately. Until further notice, this lab is sealed. Professor Adam *will* figure this out. Anything he wants, he gets, but he is not to leave this laboratory under any circumstance. *Do you understand?*"

"Yes, ma'am. What about Anatolia Daviura?"

"If she appears again, you are to arrest her immediately. Do you understand?"

"Yes, ma'am."

* * *

The thick carpet gave under Mykroft's feet as he padded down the corridor to the operations room. There, he placed his palm to the lock plate and the door slipped open to admit him into a brightly lit computer room. One wall displayed a holographic situation board which depicted the terrain around Tercee Estate in real-time three dimensions. Dots of light indicated the disposition of various forces.

"How's it look?" Mykroft asked.

"Excellent," Sampson Henck responded from where he bent over a holo tank which magnified and augmented portions of the main board. "Ily really came through. She must have someone over in Comm Central who can pull strings. We're reading this right off the master battle comm."

Ily has people everywhere. Mykroft walked over and checked over Tie Arnson's shoulder. The First was running simulations making subtle changes to the tactical dispersion of two Groups in a wooded marsh.

"If I could have your attention for a moment?" Mykroft glanced around, seeing his people look up. "I just talked to Ily on the comm. Gentlemen, this is it. Our baptism by fire has come. Last night, the Sixth Sylenian and Tenth Etarian landed their forces in the positions you see on the map. Ily's people have spoken to both of the Division Firsts. Control of their Divisions will be routed directly through our comm in this room. Today, we fight Sinklar Fist. Let's beat him at his own game."

"How long until the exercise begins?" Rick asked, a serious set to his thin face.

"Less than ten minutes." Mykroft slapped a hand against his thigh. "Gentlemen, we can't afford a mistake. We've studied Fist's tactics . . . even in our sleep. Today, we *must* win, or at least fight him to a draw."

"Why don't I like the tone in your voice?" Henck asked.

"Because the timetable may be moved up by at least a month. It seems Sinklar is causing problems. We have to be ready to take over at a moment's notice."

* * *

"Could you come with me?" Sinklar asked the two guards outside of his personal office.

The smartly dressed young woman looked nervously at her companion, then told Sinklar, "We're not supposed to leave our post, sir."

Sinklar smiled. "You have new orders. This way, please."

He beckoned and led them through the offices.

The powder-blue hallway bustled with activity. Two Groups from First Section worked to erect energy bar-

riers around the doorway to Sinklar's palatial quarters.
Charged blasters rested conspicuously in the Sergeant
Firsts' arms as they supervised and called instructions.
More heavy shoulder weapons were stacked against
the expensive cobalt blue finish and in the wall niches
where techs labored to install monitors.

"You're officially dismissed," Sinklar told his Imperial Guards. "Go take the afternoon off. Enjoy yourselves. You'll be paid for another two weeks. At the
end of that time, we've got a place for you in the
military, if you'd like."

The woman's jaw dropped. "You can't just dismiss
the Imperial Guard!"

Sinklar frowned, scuffing the carpet with his toe.
"Is that right? And why not?"

"Why . . . why, there's been an Imperial Guard for
over three hundred years! My grandfather was one of
the first!" the young man protested.

"And you're the last. You've just finished a family
tradition." Sinklar crossed his arms. "You've got the
afternoon off—and on me to boot. Skip out of here
and don't come back." Sinklar started to turn away
and then paused. "Oh, and tell your commanding officer on the way out, will you? You can even take him
along if you'd like."

At that, Sinklar pointed a finger at the Sergeant
First who had just seen to the settling of an energy
barrier. "First, you and four of your people, come
with me."

They snapped to attention, trotting forward.

"Buchman, isn't it? Third Section?"

"Yes, sir!" Buchman replied smartly.

Sinklar nodded. "You were with Hauws when he
took out Weebouw."

Buchman's voice dropped. "Yes, sir. I was there."

Sinklar recalled. Buchman, a private at the time,
had worked the four-man gun that had taken out Weebouw's headquarters. Buchman had been the only sur-
vivor on the ridge. Sink led him through the offices.
"I want four people in here, armed at all times. He
passed the guards' station, stating, "Another two

here." In his personal quarters, he passed through the dining room while Buchman and the privates gaped, and stepped into his bedroom.

Anatolia lay on the sleeping platform, dead to the world. Sinklar pointed and dropped his voice to a whisper. "Sergeant First, the security of this office is half of your responsibility. She's the other half. No matter what, nothing happens to her."

"Yes, sir."

Sinklar led the way back into the hallway and stared at the fortifications. "I guess if Ily's gonna break in here now, she's going to need a Division."

Buchman nodded. "Yeah, but you know, some of those guys we've been training have started to catch on."

Sinklar sucked at his lower lip, frowning. "What happened yesterday?"

Buchman stuck thumbs in his weapons belt. "Dion Axel and Mayz fought a couple of new Divisions that just shipped in. Guess they had the strategy down pretty good for Regulars, but they lost it because of their people on the ground. Seems the Groups and Sections couldn't quite comprehend what the HQ was telling them."

"What else? You've got a hesitant look on your face."

Buchman made a face. "Just scuttlebutt, sir, but Dion was worried. Seems she knew both of these Division Firsts . . . and she didn't think that much of them, if you know what I mean, sir."

"What did she say? Did you hear?"

"Yeah, I was in the situation room. Dion, she's pretty canny, you know? Sharp. She kept frowning, staring at the situation board with her arms crossed. When it was all over, she shook her head and muttered, 'They're not that bright. It's almost as if they're being orchestrated.' "

* * *

Gysell walked into Ily's office from the internal lift. The length of time since his last shave could be judged by the black shadow of beard on his thick cheeks. The corners of his lips twitched as he padded across Ily's carpet, each step swirling the colors.

Ily saved the file on her computer as he approached. "Something's come up?"

Gysell's control broke, and a smile bent his lips. "You might say that." He handed her a data cube. "This just came in on subspace. Cryptography decoded it and patched it through to me first thing. It's from our operative on Imperial Sassa."

Ily took the cube between thumb and forefinger, inserting it into her comm. She watched as the report played through, and afterward she stared blankly at the screen, long fingertips tapping on the polished surface of her desk.

Finally she looked up. "Do you think their assessment is accurate?"

The lines at the corners of Gysell's eyes tightened. "I think so. MacRuder might have just handed us the entire Sassan Empire. The report was very specific. The damage caused by *Gyton*'s attack and the freighter they drove into the planet is devastating. At best, Jakre can only scramble a ship here or there. He might be able to try what we just did—a suicide attack on a planet—but little more. MacRuder's attack, limited as it was, has crippled Sassa for the near future."

Ily exhaled and sank back into her chair. "It's hard to believe that they were that close to collapse."

Gysell reminded her, "We're not that far behind. Not when you take a real look at our systems. A similar disaster, say a major strike on the capital, would devastate our own ability to administer and mount a military offensive. Too much is centralized."

Ily swiveled in her chair and stood, absently brushing at the creases in her black suit. "But assuming we vigilantly guard ourselves, avoid fat Sassa's mistake, who do we have to fear? Only the Companions."

Gysell straightened, touching his fingertips together

as he watched her from under lowered eyelids. "I *wouldn't* want to underestimate the Companions."

"Perhaps the time has come to contact Staffa again. He's had time to stew, perhaps to regret his rash words. Even if taking Lyma has spurred him to ready his fleet, by the time he can space, he knows I'll have had time to interrogate her. She's the second in command at Itreata. Think of what she knows, Gysell!"

Ily clapped her hands together with satisfaction. "With Lyma in our hands, we'll know everything about Itreata—perhaps enough that we won't even need Sinklar to make his strike against Ryklos to lure Staffa out."

"I assume you've reviewed the exercise Mykroft conducted against Sinklar's Firsts?"

Ily chewed at her thumbnail. "I did. Mykroft was upset with his performance. I, on the other hand, thought he did marvelously. We'll see what happens tomorrow when I patch him through to some of the retrained Divisions. When you watch the tapes, Gysell, Mykroft didn't do that badly. His troops simply didn't have the skill to carry out his commands."

"Perhaps. But getting back to Staffa, he *will* be the next serious problem we face."

"Until we have Skyla Lyma under our probes, there's no sense in trying to formulate a policy. But, Gysell, with Sassa neutralized as a threat, we're closer than I thought we'd be. And depending on what Lyma tells us, we might have the key to the Companions." She gave him a ravishing smile. "Within months, we could be the sole rulers of Free Space."

His grin widened. "I thought you'd appreciate that report from Imperial Sassa."

Ily waved him away. "That will be all for now, Gysell. Thank you. You've really improved my whole day."

Gysell inclined his head to her and strolled back toward the lift. Ily savored the heady sensation of triumph. Sassa? Prostrate? Vulnerable? How incredibly delicious!

She threw her arms out and whirled around in circles, her hair streaming out as she pirouetted around the room, laughing until she became dizzy.

She stopped then, regained her senses, and walked to the desk. "Very well, Staffa. Let's see if you've decided to talk coherently now." She settled herself in her cushioned chair and steepled her fingers. "Comm, connect on subspace with Itreata. I would like to speak with the Lord Commander, Staffa kar Therma."

"Acknowledged, Minister Takka. We're establishing the link now. It will be several moments."

"I understand."

Ily closed her eyes, imagining the Sassans as they scrambled to overcome the damage done. Her agents had been very thorough. MacRuder had crashed a huge freighter into the planet at almost a third of lightspeed. The giant Sassan military base had disappeared in an explosion that had cracked the planet's crust. Imperial Sassa's resources were strained to the limit in coping with earthquakes, fallout, and climatic fluctuations caused by the debris blown into the atmosphere. The planet's entire agricultural production had been laid waste by freezing temperatures. The population balanced on the precarious edge of famine and frost, their services cut, and social order maintained by a thread. The rest of the Sassan Empire now struggled to save their capital and its overextended population.

"Minister?" Comm interrupted her thoughts. "I have Itreata Comm on subspace."

"Very well." Ily composed herself as she leaned forward and stared into a woman's expressionless face. "Good day. I am Minister Ily Takka and I would like to speak with the Lord Commander."

The Itreatic comm operator's expression remained unfazed. "I am requested to inquire if you have released Wing Commander Skyla Lyma."

"That is exactly what I would like to discuss with the Lord Commander."

"Has the Wing Commander been released?"

Ily began to bristle. "I will discuss that with the Lord Commander. Do I need to repeat myself?"

The woman didn't even flinch. "You do not, Minister Takka. Nevertheless, I have my instructions. The Lord Commander has ordered me to tell you that he has nothing to discuss until the Wing Commander has been freed." She looked down at a monitor. "His exact words are, 'Until that time, you're wasting your breath.' I'm sorry, Minister, but those are the Lord Commander's orders."

"I see. Then I suggest you tell him that when he wishes to discuss the situation, he can Rotted well contact me. I won't play games. Good day."

Ily cut the connection and fought to control her welling anger. "You thrice-cursed maggot, Staffa, what sort of game are you playing? Have you written Lyma off? Is that it, you cold bastard? Or are you gambling, betting that I'll break before you do?"

A prickling of unease had begun to eat at Ily's sense of triumphant euphoria. She glanced down at the data cube Gysell had given her—and threw it across the room to shatter against her expensive paneling.

* * *

"I am often asked, 'How do the Seddi perceive the universe? What is the purpose of existence? How does this unpredictable universe relate to God Mind?'

"We believe that God created this universe when it became aware—conscious, if you will. And, yes, the universe, as a reflection of God itself, has a purpose: our universe is God's way of learning about itself. From a teleological point of view, we currently believe through our limited knowledge that our universe will one day collapse into a gravitational singularity. When that happens, duality will cease and every particle of mass energy will be returned to the Godhead.

"In a way, this is an ingenious manner of obtaining

knowledge. God Mind learns from every observation and from every permutation of the universe spawned by observation. What we observe as a stochastic process of evolution, is, in effect, a means of not only powering the universe, but of examining every aspect and permutation of a problem. To the supernaturalists who demand miracles, can one offer anything more miraculous than this? In one masterstroke, God has powered the universe through uncertainty, randomization, and free will, yet It gains all the benefits from multiple solutions which play out in multiple universes.

"The concept becomes problematic to those who insist that human beings, by some arcane reasoning, should be capable of knowing everything there is to know. Alas, my friends, we are limited in time and sensory capacity. We can model, predict, and analyze, and describe those results to our colleagues and heirs. Even then, we are crippled in our ability to communicate through our language. (Processes are poorly discussed by means of nouns and verbs—only mathematics is somewhat applicable in this instance.) Emotional pleas aside, true knowledge will only be the province of God Mind.

"Around us, we see a miracle: our Universe. For those who seek illumination, consider this. You've been enculturated to perceive a duality, a split between the supernatural and the physical. Our science, however, teaches that one cannot exist without the other. A ceramic cutting tool might appear solid, but in the realm of the quanta, solidity vanishes into electron clouds and subatomic forces. Solidity is but a shadow of mostly vacuous atomic interactions. If you would view the universe through new eyes, you must scourge this duality from your thoughts. The mystical and physical are one, both reflections of God's creation and purpose, from the largest to the smallest."

—Excerpt from Kaylla Dawn's Seddi broadcasts

CHAPTER XXVI

Mac slapped a hand to the lock plate outside *Gyton*'s bridge. The heavy hatch slipped back with a hissing sound and he stepped through, nodding briefly to the Weapons First, and the Nav-comm Specialist. The pilot, as usual, lay supine under the worry-cap. Rysta sat hunched in the command chair, her expression rivaling that of an abandoned prune. She shot Mac a hard glance and grunted to herself as she straightened and pushed up out of the chair. "It's all yours."

"What's up?" Mac asked.

"We're out of null singularity, that's what. We're coming up on Oribtal Defense and we've dumped enough Delta V that we can talk to Rega without time dilation." Rysta's lips twitched. "Minister Takka wants to speak with you."

Mac made a face and slipped into the command chair.

"Comm First, establish communications, please."

"Yes, sir."

Mac watched Ily's face form up on the command chair monitor. She gave him a happy smile, a twinkle in her dark eyes. "MacRuder! Let me be the first to offer you congratulations for your heoric and splendid action at Imperial Sassa."

"Thank you, Minister." *Where the hell was Sinklar?*

Ily pursed her lips, head slightly lowered as if she were waiting for just the right moment. "I know you've been out of contact, and therefore you haven't had access to the intelligence reports, but your strike has effectively emasculated the Sassan Empire. We, Sinklar and I . . . the whole Empire for that matter,

owe you and the heroes of *Gyton* the greatest of debts
and honors. Single-handedly, you've shortened the
coming war by months, perhaps years."

"Thank you again, Minister. It was, after all,
Sinklar's strategy. By the way, is he available?"

Ily shifted her gaze to one side, as if checking a
monitor. "He's currently in the middle of an exercise
and can't be disturbed. I'll let him know you're on the
way in." Her eyes lit with excitement again. "He's a
wonder! I can't wait for you to see the improvement
in the military. Sink has made a real difference. I
think you're in for a giant surprise when you set foot
on the planet. I can't wait for your reaction when you
see how the military command has changed."

"I'll be waiting expectantly." *Sinklar? Too busy
with an exercise to be disturbed by our arrival? What?*

"I'm sure you will. We'll have quite a reception for
you. Until I see you and Commander Rysta, then,
First MacRuder."

She cut the contact.

Mac slouched in the chair, frowning.

"What did that all mean?" Rysta asked as she hovered beside the command chair.

"I don't know. But something's. . . ." *Sinklar, you
didn't get involved with her, did you? Tell me she
didn't wrap you around her finger while she was screw-
ing your brains out.*

"Not right? Or changed?" Rysta prodded.

"Got me. But whatever it is, it's not good."

*   *   *

The heavy, riot-scarred door had a curious effect on
Anatolia. She glanced up at the security camera, and
on impulse, waved before she pushed the door open
and entered the Criminal Anatomical Research Building. Two uniformed young men sat at the security
desks to either side as she entered. They both seemed
to start as she walked in.

Perhaps rumors had run rampant through the building. At the thought, Anatolia's tension increased. She

glanced quickly back to reassure herself that Buchman and Wheeler were right behind her.

Acting as if nothing were amiss, Anatolia walked to the lift and stabbed the button for the thirty-fifth floor.

"I'm having lots of second thoughts about this," Sergeant First Buchman muttered from the side of his mouth.

Anatolia gave him a worried smile, well aware of the pounding of her own heart. "Trust me. It's better this way than if Sinklar gets involved. If he walks into the lab with a Group for backup, someone will notice. If it's me, so what? I came in to pick up some papers, and you two are my friends. Nothing more. No one will be the wiser."

"And this stuff is that important?" Wheeler asked doubtfully as the numbers flashed on the lift.

"Well, let's put it like this. If anything happens to me, you give it to Sinklar—in person. If anyone tries to stop you. . . . No, better yet, think of it in terms of a 'top secret, eyes only' for Sinklar."

The lift stopped and Anatolia stepped out, her escort at her heels.

"You serious about that?" Buchman asked.

"Deadly," Anatolia answered in a tone to brook no disobedience. She led the way across the foyer to the security desk where a strange man watched with apparent interest. New student?

"You're new," Anatolia greeted. "Student?"

The man smiled, amusement in his eyes. "I'm called Teal. Just transferred in. You're Daviura, aren't you? I noted your holo on the personnel file."

"You did?"

He grinned. "What can I say? I'm a sucker for a pretty woman." He glanced curiously at Buchman and Wheeler, gaze lingering on their sidearms and weapons belts.

"New roommates." She lowered her eyes self-consciously. "If you've been here for very long, you may have heard. I lost my place a while back." She sneaked a glance at the comm, seeing the usual text

492 W. Michael Gear

on the screen. Her fear eased by a notch. "Vet in the lab?"

The new man seemed to hesitate. "No, I think he's off today."

Anatolia nodded. "Too bad. Well, I'll call him later. See you around."

She started down the hall, Buchman and Wheeler close behind.

"Didn't look like a student," Wheeler growled. "Something about the eyes."

Anatolia waved it away. "You wouldn't have thought I was a student either—something about my eyes after my time on the street."

Buchman had moved up beside her, leaving Wheeler slightly to the rear. "How far?"

"A ways. It's a long hallway." She pointed at the women's room. "That's where I used to live."

"No kidding?"

"No kidding." She glanced curiously up at Buchman. "How long have you known Sinklar?"

"Since our cadre was called up for replacements for the First Targan."

"And, sister, that's a long time as our lives go," Wheeler asserted.

"Um, mind if I ask one?" Buchman's eyes never ceased to move, as if he were trying to see everything in the featureless hallway.

"Go ahead."

"What's your interest in Sinklar?"

If you only knew! "He's my friend. Nothing more, Sergeant First. He showed up when I needed him. Maybe I'm returning the favor. You spying for Mhitshul?"

Buchman shook his head, grinning wryly. "Nope. Asking for myself . . . and maybe the rest of us. You see, we worry a lot about Sink."

"Especially recently, huh?" Anatolia prodded. "If you've been losing sleep over Ily, I think you can tell the troops to relax a little. Sinklar's on to her."

Buchman shot her a quick glance, his expression deadpan.

"This door." Anatolia turned to the right, palming the lock. Wheeler lagged, scanning up and down the hallway before she followed them into the lab. Ana wound her way past assorted equipment and over to her corner. Kneeling down with her key and unlocking the drawer, she pulled out the two piles of printout and frowned as she straightened. "I left a pen and notepad here. Someone's cleaned it up."

"That's bad?" Wheeler asked in a low voice, keeping an eye on the room.

Anatolia took a deep breath and powered up the machine, taking a data cube from her pocket and inserting it. She ran the access and called up file 7355, quickly scanning to see that it was all there.

"Computer, copy file 7355 to datacube insert."

"Working." A pause. "Data transfer complete."

"Erase file 7355."

"File erased."

"Wipe and overwrite with 0 and 1. Repeat command three times."

"Working." The machine made a whirring sound. "Command complete."

"Overwrite the just wiped storage area with the value of pi."

Working." Then: "Area overwritten."

"Print, please."

"Working." Printout of the numerical value of pi began issuing from the printer slot. Anatolia scanned the pages and nodded as the output basket filled. When it was done, she tore the sheet off and dumped it in the converter.

"Let's go." She smiled in relief as she handed Wheeler the two stacks of printout and dropped the data cube in her pocket.

Her heart had begun to resume some semblance of normal rhythm as she stepped out into the hallway—and stopped short.

Jan Bokken stood in the center of the hallway. To either side stood security officers, one of whom was Teal from the front desk. "Hello, Ana, I need to speak to you for a moment."

The frantic feeling of being in the dark, of backing into the cul-de-sac, and of Micky's fetid breath panicked her, despite the fact that Buchman and Wheeler had taken up protective, flanking positions. From down the hallway, two more men walked slowly forward.

"Tell me now, Jan. I'm in a hurry."

"Yeah, we've got a dinner appointment," Buchman added, a slightly annoyed tone in his voice.

Bokken waved at Buchman and Wheeler. "You, of course, may go. Oh, but that stack of paper the private is carrying must stay. I believe that's property of the laboratory."

Anatolia's jaw had started to quiver. *Pull yourself together! Stop it!*

Bokken looked like a hunter who knew his prey couldn't escape.

"It's just some work I need to catch up on at home," Anatolia assured him.

"You got a reason to bother my girlfriend?" Buchman asked, taking a step forward.

Bokken seemed nonplussed. He lifted a hand, holding out an identification card with the emblem of Internal Security emblazoned on the duraplast. "Your . . . girlfriend's presence is requested at the Ministry of Internal Security, Sergeant. I'm sure you can pick her up there later."

Anatolia gasped, unable to stop herself from stepping back. Not far from this very spot, a cold specimen table waited for the deliveries from the Ministry. Would she be there tomorrow morning for Vet to catalog? As if in anticipation of the slab, a chill spread through her.

"I think not," Buchman replied, steel in his voice.

For a second, Bokken just frowned. "I said—"

"Targa!" Wheeler growled angrily, stepping out farther to the right as she balanced on the balls of her feet.

Buchman nodded as he repeated, "Targa."

Anatolia started to raise her hand to interrupt, but at that moment Buchman launched himself into Bokken and the closest guards. In the same split second, Wheeler had dropped to a squat, her pistol rasping on the plastic of her holster as she pulled it out and leveled it on the guards closing from down the hall. The printout spewed out over the floor as Wheeler's blaster discharged.

"Ana! Grab the papers!" Wheeler shouted, turning her weapon to cover Buchman. The Sergeant First had hammered Bokken across the throat and then kicked one of the rushing guards in the groin. He grappled with another, backheeled him, and broke loose, rolling across the tiles. Wheeler's blaster fired again, and Buchman's shot caught another man full in the back, spattering muscle, ribs, and lung fragments around.

That quickly it was finished, Bokken making a gurgling sound as he tore at his throat. The shattered bodies of the dead security agents bled onto the polished tile while stunned nerves triggered spasms through exposed muscular tissue. Anatolia crouched, paralyzed, her fingers curling in the sheets of paper.

"We'd better be getting out of here," Wheeler called in a worried voice. Anatolia clawed the printout together, clutching it to her breast and shaking as she gazed at the blast-mangled corpses before her. Impossible . . . to think. . . .

"Which way?" Buchman shouted. "Back the way we came?"

Anatolia pulled her scattered wits together. "No! They'll have people there. This way. The garage! There's another lift down to street level."

She leapt forward, slipped on fresh blood, and would have fallen but for Buchman's quick grip on her arm. She sprinted down the hallway, stifled sobs choking in her throat.

"You okay?" Wheeler called as they ran, the woman's brown eyes narrowed in concern.

"I'm . . . all right." *I'm on the street again. I've been here before.* Courage began to pump in time to the adrenal fear in her veins.

Anatolia rounded a corner, bolted past two startled

secretaries, and charged the seventy meters to the lift. She palmed the lock plate, praying that the carnage hadn't been discovered. The lift tube opened.

Anatolia flattened herself in the rear, the precious printout clutched to her breast, as Buchman and Wheeler followed and slapped the garage level control.

Anatolia glanced back and forth as they dropped, finally nerving herself to ask, "What's Targa?"

"Means you've got nothing left to lose but your life," Buchman told her.

"You gonna make it?" Wheeler asked tersely. "You're not gonna flake out on us?"

Anatolia cracked a crooked grin she didn't feel. "Not me."

"You looked a little pale back there," Buchman said.

Anatolia shook her head as the lift stopped. She forced starch into her wobbly knees before they stepped out on the parking level. "It's just the blasters that got me. I'm used to killing people with a metal rod. The lift is this way."

Wheeler followed, covering their rear as she backed after them. "You're kidding?"

They followed the concrete apron around the side of the passenger pickup. Cool air blew in from the entrance tunnel—a square hole to the right, illuminated by yellow patches of light. Out in the parking area, the aircars, bodies painted in bright colors, gleamed in rows. An eerie quiet hung over the place and their footsteps echoed hollowly.

"It's a long story . . . for later . . . if we live through this."

"If? Why do I hate that Rotted word so much?" Buchman pointed. "That the lift to the street?"

"That's it."

"Maybe we should have brought an LC," Wheeler muttered under her breath.

At street level, Anatolia led them across to the burned-out shops. They'd made it to within fifty meters of the lift that would take them down to the shuttle when an aircar dove out of the traffic lanes overhead.

"Duck!" Wheeler cried, lifting her blaster and cutting loose.

Buchman flattened Anatolia with a hard arm, pressing her down into the filthy pavement.

"Pus-Rotted Gods!" Wheeler cried as she dove headlong on top of them. "They're gonna hit the—"

The pavement jumped at the impact as the aircar drove into the street, cartwheeled, and hammered a hole through one of the buildings.

Buchman was already pulling her to her feet, dragging her along toward the shuttle.

"What happened?"

Wheeler was running full tilt for the shuttle tube. "Blew their cursed canopy off! Must have killed the driver. We're damn lucky to be alive!"

Anatolia was gulping air in as the tube carried them down to the shuttle level. "Targa, huh? I gotta get some of that armor you folks wear."

Buchman launched himself from the tube, blaster in an isosceles hold. The few people standing around waiting for the shuttle gaped, obviously aware of the impact several stories above on the street.

"Great timing!" Wheeler called as the shuttle slid into the station. Heedless of other passengers, they rushed for the car—only to have it go dead and settle onto the magnets.

Buchman cursed and slammed the butt of his pistol on the half-open door. *"What the hell?"*

Anatolia swallowed hard. "Ily cut the power. She's got someone in the Shuttle Authority."

"Pus-licking bitch!" Wheeler spun on her heel, glowering as the civilians backed away, and then broke for the tube and the safety of the street above.

"Guess we're back on the street." Buchman spoke through clenched jaws. "C'mon!"

"No." Anatolia stood resolutely.

"You crazy?" Wheeler gestured her desperation. "We've only got minutes until Ily has aircars all over this part of the city!"

Anatolia gave them a hard grin. "Let her. I know a better way. Here, give me a hand." She dropped on her belly, piling the precious printout beside her, and slithered over onto the magnetic rails. "Watch your step! Don't touch the rails. They could go hot any second."

Buchman's frown had deepened. "Where are you going?"

"The street," Anatolia replied. "Hand me the printout. I know another way out of here."

"Targa!" Wheeler shouted, dropping athletically off the platform.

"Damn right, Targa!" Anatolia echoed as she stepped carefully over the rails to reach the hollow under the other side of the framework. She took a deep breath, smelling the foul roots of the city. "I just didn't know I'd be back this soon."

*   *   *

Ily paced irritably. The large wall monitor had been split into windows, monitoring the pursuit of Anatolia Daviura. Who would have thought the two soldiers accompanying her would have shot? It defied all logic.

When the call came in that Daviura had arrived at the research facility, Ily had watched and listened to Bokken's botched attempt at arrest through remote monitors carried by the agents. Bokken had followed the manual, scrambling his people immediately. He had covered the two routes of escape with backup at the main exit, and waited to apprehend Daviura until after she'd recovered her work, when her guard would have been lowered. The two soldiers had appeared to be an inconvenience, but not an alarming one. Subjects were separated from their friends as standard procedure. According to protocol, they should have bowed out, insisting that Sinklar would straighten things out. Then, in the blink of an eye, it had all gone wrong. Why?

Targa! That single word had precipitated the shooting.

"Rot it all, we run a civilized planet here," Ily asserted under her breath. She turned on her heel. "What's happening. They dropped to the shuttle platform. People saw them trying to take the shuttle. Where did they go?"

Gysell took a deep breath, trying to find the words, but Ily cut him off.

She leaned forward, propping her arms on his desk, even as a powerful rage ate at her control.

"Of all the things you could tell me right now, saying that you've lost her is the most likely to get you busted down to sorting garbage in the recycling factory."

Gysell's jaw muscles worked and he swallowed hard. "Ily, you've watched the monitors. What could we have done differently? Our people covered the exit, figuring they could pick them off as they stepped out onto the street. When they didn't emerge, we sent people in. They found an empty shuttle platform with the shuttle still standing there, immobilized." he protested defensively, "We *thought* it was a routine pickup!"

Ily vented a curse, then relented. "You're right. Very well, the most logical assumption is that they slipped away into the city substructure. If that's where they are, they can go anyplace—but they can't go fast. Cordon the area. I don't care how many people you have to pull off other duty, but get them on this. I want every nonessential person we've got down there in the girders and ducts looking for Daviura."

"Yes, ma'am." Gysell bent to his comm, sending orders.

Ily shook her head, shot the monitor an evil glance, and left Gysell's office, striding purposefully down the hall toward her lift.

Do I go see Sinklar? Has he had time enough to cool off? Will he buy any story I feed him about Daviura? She slapped the lift control with a hard hand, mulling her options.

* * *

Skyla felt movement beside her. The shifting of weight didn't register immediately in her sleep-sodden brain. Then her combat-honed instincts kicked in and she rolled onto her stomach, jackknifing off the sleeping platform, stumbling, catching herself as the lights came on.

She settled automatically into a combat stance, poised to strike. Her familiar quarters gleamed in the too-bright glare of the overhead panels. Arta Fera, with spring-tight reflexes, rolled off the far edge of the platform and landed—catlike—on her feet. She stared at Skyla with owlish eyes, a flush of excitement tinging her skin. Gauzy fabric swirled around her like a transparent veil, concealing nothing of Fera's sculpted body.

"*What were you doing?*" Skyla demanded as she struggled to regain her calm.

Fera's eyes had narrowed to slits. "You never minded before."

Sklya cocked her head suspiciously. "Never minded what?"

"The times I slept with you after I took you off the Vega."

"I was drugged then."

"And you're not now." Arta shook her tumbled hair back over her shoulders in an insolent shrug. "Would you rather be?"

"No, Rot you. Where have you been sleeping for the past week?" Skyla rubbed her wrists, realizing she should have been imprisoned by the EM restraints. When had Fera deactivated them? Skyla couldn't help shivering.

"In the pilot's chair . . . after I checked the ship's status. These vessels don't fly themselves, you know."

"So why now?" Skyla indicted the sleeping platform, suddenly aware that Fera looked too dazed to have just crawled in with her. "How long did I lie there asleep with you, anyway?"

Arta barked a dry laugh. "A couple of hours. Now,

do you want to talk all night, or shall we finish what we started?"

"Finish. . . ."

"Sleeping."

Sklya slowly shook her head. "I sleep alone."

Arta stepped forward, stretching like some languorous cat. "As you wish, but you'll have to do it in the EM restraints. I thought I was doing you a favor, that you'd like a night's sleep where you weren't racked out like a chunk of meat."

"I'll take my chances as a chunk of meat."

Arta stepped close, placing her hands on Skyla's shoulders. "I want you to think about something, Wing Commander. I could do anything I want to you while you were in those EM restraints. You know I like you . . . respect you. But if I wanted to enjoy your body, I could—and you couldn't do a curse-Rotted thing about it."

"I'd make you kill me," Skyla promised despite her hammering heart.

"That's one of the reasons I've come to appreciate you. You're a challenge, Skyla, and I do enjoy a challenge. You see, that's why I've spent so much time on the bridge. I've been dropping us in and out of null singularity."

"That just prolongs the trip."

"Of course it does. And despite my novice status as a pilot, I could have figured the galactic drift and shot us right on top of Rega."

"Then why didn't you?"

Arta lifted a hand and Skyla flinched as the other woman gently stroked the scar on her cheek. "Because, dearest Skyla, Ily may check the log—and she'll believe I don't pilot very well. Ily doesn't have to know *everything* about me. But most of all, this way I can keep you longer." Arta's smile grew wistful. "I know you're biding your time, and that you really will try and goad me into killing you if it seems there's no possible escape from Ily. Meanwhile, consider this. I can protect you."

"At what price, you sick bitch?"

Arta stepped back, still wary. "Love me, Skyla. Become mine. I'll take good care of you." Then she pivoted on her heel and vanished through the hatch in a swirl of filmy fabric.

Sklya drew a deep breath, every nerve electric as she collected herself. The aftereffects of Fera's touch burned on her skin.

Where had Fera gone—and more importantly, for how long? *Do I have time? Is this my chance?* Sklya eased forward silently to peek into the hallway. Fera stood there, arms crossed, head down.

Despite Skyla's silence, the woman whispered, "But for the rest of tonight, you'll have to wear the EM restraints."

"Gladly," Skyla called over her shoulder as she threw herself on the sleeping platform.

Arta entered the room, a pensive expression pinching her sensual face. Wordlessly, she engerized the restraints and stood for a moment, staring down at Skyla. "Let me show you something."

Sklya watched warily as the woman climbed onto the sleeping platform and bent over her, the auburn hair falling like a veil around her. From inches away, Arta stared into her eyes, then lowered herself, never shifting her gaze.

Skyla bucked against the restraints as Arta's breasts brushed hers. Muscular hands clamped on each side of Skyla's head, and despite her struggles, Arta kissed her, the action gentle, reverent—physically not that unpleasant.

"Why do you fight me?" Arta asked in a sultry voice. "Would it be that bad?"

Skyla quivered, every muscle knotted and strained as Fera moved away from her.

"A great many men would die to experience what I could give you," Arta called as she stepped out. "Sleep well, Skyla. Sweet dreams."

For long moments Skyla lay gasping and spent. "No way," she whispered under her breath. Nevertheless, despite her bravado, Fera had cunningly regained the advantage, eroding Skyla's confidence.

Protection? Delay? Could Fera do that? Skyla's overactive imagination began spinning scenarios of Ily Takka's interrogation room, of the metallic taste of Mytol, and the wealth of secrets safeguarded only by Skyla's will and ability to resist.

Protection? What the hell, being a little cozy with the lunatic bitch might really buy time. Would it be so bad? Memories came unbidden—times in the past when she'd slept with men she hadn't really liked. Times she'd awakened after a shore party with some stranger in her bed—and nine times out of ten, the Nab had been some simpering fool she'd immediately hated. How often had she spent the following days living with a sense of self-loathing for having bedded scum because the act promised physical gratification?

You're no saintly virgin, Skyla. Fera wouldn't be any new sort of low for you.

Flashes of Stryker lay just under the surface. Good old Stryker, the man who'd bought her, enslaved her, and raped her repeatedly when she was twelve. Would a little dallying with Fera be any worse than that? Fera—compared to some of the men she'd awakened next to—was at least clean.

She didn't balk over Fera's gender. Of those Companions who were female, more than one preferred women to men.

Protection? The frightened half of her brain had begun to plead. Maybe it was a way to gain Fera's trust, another lever to work her, to get the chance to slip the weapons from the cubbyhole just up there behind her head?

"Sex is sex," Skyla whispered under her breath. "If it keeps you alive, what's the difference?"

Sklya bit her lip and twisted her head away. *The difference is that Fera wins. Just as she's won this round.*

* * *

In the seductive arms of exhaustion, Sinklar slept—
lost in the realm of dreams; the scene haunted and
mocked:

He stood in the center of a plush room ornamented
with weapons and trophies, his thoughts dominated by
tension and foreboding. Beside him, Mac had adopted
a grim expression. A fireplace—of all things to find
on a starship—rose in stately grace between two brass
doors.

Sinklar watched as the other occupants—the brooding Lord Commander, an ethereal Skyla Lyma, and a
time-eaten old man—initiated the familiar drama that
skulked in his soul.

"Is Sinklar Fist my son?" Staffa kar Therma roared
with resonant power. The Lord Commander towered
over the stunned old man. A purple-mottled bruise
scarred the elder's bald pate. A shriveled specimen,
he wore dirt-encrusted white robes which Staffa gripped
in an iron fist; his fingers puckered the coarse fabric
the way talons twisted into flesh.

Magister Bruen slumped in defeat. "Yes. We got
him from the Praetor."

*From the Praetor? What? Did Staffa stage this? Was
he seeking to gain some advantage by this charade?*

At Sinklar's side, Mac whispered, "They're all Rotted berserk!"

"And Chrysla?" Staffa asked.

Bruen whined, "The Praetor kept her. Kept her
until you gutted *Pylos* off Myklene."

In the wavering reality of the dream, Staffa seemed
to swell and change, his shape blurring. The charcoal
cape flowing down from his shoulders spread like
avenging wings around a raptor's frail prey. The old
man cowered before him as would a desiccated lizard
whose day had passed. Staffa's voice beat at the
shrunken reptile with the fury of invincible wings.
"And this Arta Fera? She's not Chrysla?"

"No! She's a clone, Lord Commander. A clone provided by the Praetor!" the reptile defended in its dry
hiss.

"To *assassinate* me!" Staffa reeled—the dark raptor

dazed by venom injected into an ancient wound. Skyla Lyma stepped forward, a gleaming white goddess whose blue eyes burned like precious stones. She turned a deadly glare on the old man . . . and in the shining intensity, her features became those of Anatolia.

The giant hunting bird that Staffa had become whirled on black claws, spreading wings floating. "Wait! Bruen, what about Sinklar's claim that he *saw* his parents on Rega?"

Sinklar's sense of distress began to focus, growing acute as his heart began to beat a countdown cadence. Bright worry coursed though his veins with each thundering stroke.

"Tanya and Valient." Bruen withered more, his scaly flesh turning dusty, moldering; the bones began to poke through. Before Sinklar's eyes, the old lizard's body shriveled, skin parching. His moisture might bleed away with his words. "Yes, they were Seddi. Another of the machine's ideas. If Tybalt were removed before he could sire an heir, Rega's drive for hegemony might be blunted. A young security officer, Ily Takka, broke the case. At the time, it happened that they created a perfect excuse for Sinklar to be placed in Regan custody. Doing so kept him safe from discovery."

Liquid fear traced acid patterns through Sinklar's body. *No! Not true! It can't be! Tanya! Valient! They* are *my parents! They* have *to be! They just have to.*

Mac began pulling Sinklar away, tugging firmly on his arm as the room wavered and faded. But Staffa followed, the cloak wings fluttering as he pursued like a falcon descending on a frantic hare. A taloned hand reached out, voice booming in sync with powerful wing beats, "I swear . . . you're my son. If I could run a serology, HLA, or DNA test, I could prove it! Prove it! *Prove it . . . my son!*"

The taloned foot extended, light glinting off the polished ebony of claw and scale, reaching, reaching, closing on Sinklar as he stood rooted in fear, the talons. . . .

                          *   *   *

Sinklar groaned and turned, pain piercing his side.
He blinked his eyes open, rolling back and reaching
down to fumble at the holstered blaster and comm
pack that ate angrily into his side where they had
shifted on his belt. A cold sweat had beaded on his
skin despite the warmth of the room.

He gasped for breath as the last foggy fragments of
the dream misted away in his mind. Yawning, he
pulled himself up and stared around at his private
quarters in the palace. Overhead, the milky fabric of
the drapes played their endless game with color and
light. The familiar paneling and furnishings didn't reassure, not after a dream as horrible as that. The sense
of foreboding, of impending defeat lingered along with
the faint trace of a dead lover's perfume. The walls
bore silent witness—as they had when Tybalt spent his
last days here.

"Up?" Mhitshul called.

"I guess." Sinklar stumbled to his feet and walked
into the toilet to relieve himself. "How long was I
out?" He looked at his comm. "Three hours?"

"You looked like you needed it," Mhitshul supplied
from beyond the door. "You're not getting enough
sleep."

"Anatolia and Buchman come back yet?"

"No, sir."

"It was a fool stunt." Sinklar insisted as he stepped
out, running a hand through his disobedient hair.

"Buchman didn't have orders to hold her, just that
her safety was his top priority. Don't worry about
them. Buchman is one of the best. He's quick and
decisive—otherwise, none of us would be here today.
It was his courage that saved the day when Third Section destroyed Weebouw's Division."

Sinklar remained unconvinced. "Maybe. With Ily,
well . . . Mhitshul, we're in a different kind of fight
here. Rotted Gods, what a fool I was! She's got her
poison into everything."

The dream image of Staffa replayed in his mind.

*Poisoned by a serpent . . . and I've called Ily a reptile
how many times?*

"Glad to see you're yourself again," Mhitshul replied laconically.

Sinklar shot him an evil look as he pushed past, headed for the comm. "Anything come up while I was asleep?"

"Of course, but I made sure that none of it necessitated waking you up."

Sinklar walked into the office and settled himself behind the wraparound desk. Mac ought to be inbound sometime soon. Rot it all, where was he?

"Mhitshul, how long ago did Anatolia and Buchman leave?"

"It's been nearly seven hours, now."

"Seven? Sinklar turned to the comm. "Patch me through to First Mayz."

He scanned the other messages that had come in. Kap continued to make requisitions, as did Axel. Axel had turned into a first-class asset. She'd taken to the reorganization of the military with an uncanny acumen. With her grasp of strategic and tactical changes, she'd taken over many of the logistical and administrative functions.

"Sink?" Mayz asked hazily, blinking her puffy eyes to clear them of sleep. "What's up?"

"Sorry to bother you. Sergeant First Buchman and one of his people is missing along with Anatolia Daviura. Buchman should have a battle comm. See if you can raise him. Find out where he's at."

"Sure thing." She turned her attention to one of her other monitors, talking into the system. For long moments, she listened, then shook her head. "Sink, We've got a faint response—barely a jump on the needles—but it's like the signal's blocked—maybe jammed. If . . . and I repeat, *if* this is Buchman, he can hear us but we can't get a read on him."

Sinklar frowned, bracing his chin between thumb and forefinger. "Get hold of Kap. Have him run transects across the capital. Let's see. Establish a grid centered on the palace . . . and start around the Biological Sciences Center."

"Affirmative." Mayz gave him a frazzled look. "We in trouble again?"

The sense of disaster riding the air settled around him with the cloying persistence of smoke in cool air. Days had passed—and not a word from Ily, as if she understood the change in relations through some osmosis. "I don't know, Mayz. Just a feeling. Something's cooking. The ground might disappear from under us at any moment. Stay frosty."

Her expression had hardened. "Right." A pause. "You think it's turning into Targa?"

"Let's hope not."

* * *

Min/Int/Sec
Sec/Comm Level 1 Mgt
Sec/Dir Step 1 Eyes Only
Command Directive Class I

To all personnel:

As of receipt of this notice, you should be aware that unanticipated events have precipitated a crisis in civil management and administration. As of 17:30 hours Operation Pincer was formally begun and steps were initiated to counter the increasing military interference in the direction and control of Imperial utilities and services administrations. All personnel will consider themselves activated and will consult their orders immediately. All Directorates are hereby placed on high alert until further notice and will conduct themselves circumspectly with regard to the general population.

It is the Minister's *explicit* order that disturbance of the general population be minimized to the greatest extent possible, since the citizenery might react adversely should they realize the true nature of the power struggle currently taking place.

We cannot assess the potential involvement of the rank and file military personnel at this time. However, as Operation Pincer unfolds, such assessments will be passed on as soon as available. Assuming that all Internal Security staff act with total commitment and initiative, this operation could be concluded without most field-grade military officers even realizing a change in command has taken place.

In addition to the attached orders, each Security Director will receive additional specific instructions which will detail his/her objectives, responsibilities, and the timetable for completion of various tasks. Each Security Director will be responsible for the coordination of his/her field officers and special technicians, and will immediately communicate any unexpected resistance.

Any questions, or communications should be directed to my office, or, in the event of an emergency, contact Minister Takka directly.

As loyal servants of Internal Security, you have our utmost admiration and trust. Good luck to each and every one of you.

Deputy Director's Office
Gysell

CHAPTER XXVII

Mayz stepped out of her temporary sleeping quarters, half-asleep, and trying to pull her armor on. She yawned and blinked at the compound. A faint smear of gray marked the sunset beyond the humped outline of the HTs parked in rows beyond her headquarters. The air carried a chill bite, and the very thought of putting together a search—let alone coordinating it, chafed way down inside. Nevertheless, Sinklar had been worried, and if he was, that was enough for Mayz and the rest of the First Targan.

Rot it, when am I going to get some sleep?

Everyone had been run ragged over the last months, but with no little pride, they could see the improvement. The Regulars were coming around, turning into a real army, the sort that could fight to win—and not just mop up after the Companions.

Mayz walked toward her LC, and the command center that would allow her to assemble the First Targan. She'd have to pull Shiksta away from the exercises he and Ayms were running to coordinate the LCs while she monitored the communications.

Mayz windmilled her arms as she walked to stimulate some circulation in her shoulders, and hopefully, to wake herself up.

Buchman wasn't the sort of individual to slack off— or just up and vanish. The fact that she couldn't raise him on her comm added to her concern. Or had that faint reading been him? Where in Rotted hell would he have gotten to that his signal would be so cursed weak? The last time they'd faced that problem had been inside Makarta Mountain, where comm had been line-of-sight only.

Makarta . . . underground. Mayz stopped in her tracks.

"Buchman? You're not down in the substructure, are you?" Or, perhaps inside a very large arcology—but most would only muffle a battle comm.

"First Mayz?" a voice called from behind her.

She turned, her hand up to stifle a yawn. "Yeah, what is it?"

Two grim-eyed young men in armor walked up on either side of her. One presented her with a flimsy, saying, "This just came in, ma'am."

Mayz unfolded the flimsy—the sort official messages came on—with one hand, while her other fished in her belt pouch for a flashlight. Her attention on the odd message, she barely noticed the other men and women in uniform who appeared out of the night to gather around her.

"What kind of a Rotted joke is this, anyway? What does this mean? I'm under arrest? What kind of. . . ." Mayz caught the gleam of weapons by the light of her flash. A hand snaked out of the darkness to neatly disconnect her comm.

"I'm afraid it means exactly what it says, First. You may come with us quietly, and have a chance to sort it all out, or you may come under the influence of the stun rod. If things really get out of hand, we're directed to kill you and bring you in that way. The choice is yours, First."

"Under whose authority?" Mayz hissed through clamped jaws, her heart beginning to pound. She filled her lungs, ready to scream, but the blinding pain of the stun rod caught her full in the back. In catatonic agony, she stiffened and fell into a man's arms. Hovering on the edge of consciousness, she barely remembered being borne to an aircar, her body swaying limply. Then a dizzy grayness closed around her.

* * *

Skyla watched Arta Fera through slitted eyes. The game had escalated, with each acutely aware of the stakes. Skyla, playing for her very life, and Arta for the domination she now couldn't afford to lose. The ragged battle of wills had intensified, each playing for whatever small advantage they might gain.

Skyla sat on the curved bench behind the dining table, her hands clasped loosely at her ankles, her knees drawn up to her chest. The gleaming fittings irritated her now, as did the opulent filigree that traced golden patterns over the rich grain of the wood. Even the conforming cushions mocked her. *Prisoner—in your own splendor.*

In the forward lounge Arta exercised, her toned body flushed from the workout. From the angle of the light, and the sheen of perspiration, the woman's skin had taken on a satin tone as supple muscles bunched and slid. Arta's full-bodied hair had been pulled back in a ponytail, and she wore nothing more than a brassiere for support and a g string. Arta stretched and bent, chest rising and falling as she followed her rigorous workout. She reveled in her body, flaunting its beauty, every movement a tease and a threat as she adopted a combat stance and practiced her strikes, kicks, and punches.

Skyla tore her gaze away, concentrating instead on the polished platinum sheen of the dispenser. Fera had increased the stakes the night before. As Skyla lay shackled in the EM restraints, Fera had gone through her closet, pulling out Skyla's snowy white suits of armor and carting them out one by one.

Skyla closed her eyes, remembering how she'd screamed, demanding an explanation.

"I shoved each one into the disposer," Arta had told her matter-of-factly. "You've got one left—and I locked it safely on the bridge. You decide how you want to be handed to Ily. In that last suit of white armor—or in the clothing I've left for you?"

When Skyla had been freed to rip her wardrobe open, only two wispy teddies and a pair of grease-stained coveralls had remained. In muted rage, Skyla had turned and slammed a callused fist into the wall with enough force to dent the jetwood. Then she stalked toward Fera, a killing clarity in her mind.

"I can trigger the collar before you've even launched that first kick," Fera had cooed victoriously. "How many options are left, Skyla? Think, before you act."

"Stop toying with me, you bitch!"

"Toying? Oh, no, Skyla. This is deadly serious now. I don't just want you, I want you pleading, desperate." She'd cocked an eyebrow, amusement in her lustrous amber eyes. "You're next move is to try and make me kill you. Would you like to bet?"

Skyla had frozen then, her limbs shaking with the gnawing power of frustrated rage, her jaws grinding so hard a molar should have cracked.

Fera had laughed, knowing full well that she was in control. "I can read your mind, Skyla. You're a proud woman. The proudest woman I've ever known. That kind of pride is a weakness, and it will break you in the end, Skyla."

Fera had stepped close then, running her fingers along the paneling in a delicate caress. "Try, Skyla. Right now. Strike! See if you can hit me, drive me to use the collar with such a vengeance that you die under its grip. Come on! Here's your opportunity."

Skyla had held herself in check—but just barely.

"Look at you," Arta had chided. "You're shaking . . . and burning bright red from desperation. Strike, Skyla. Get it over with. You might as well learn now. Love me, Skyla. Love me with all of your heart and body—and I'll keep you safe . . . keep Ily from raping your mind."

Skyla had turned away on weak knees, staggering to the sleeping platform, trying not to think of the blaster and vibraknife which lay so close—and so impossibly far beyond her grasp.

"Is that it? Rape my body so Takka won't rape my mind?"

Arta chuckled. "Not at all. Like I demonstrated the other night, I could rape you anytime I wanted. No,

Skyla, I want you to plead—I'll have you no other way."

The words burned in Skyla's brain as she watched Arta panting and pirouetting in her exhausting combat routine. No doubt about it, the woman was very good.

Better than me? If only she could get the chance to find out.

Skyla shook her head, strangling in a renewed sense of futility. How did you win when the enemy knew your plan—knew your lack of options, and the desperation that drove you to try that one last chance, no matter how slim the odds?

Skyla stood as Arta finished her last lightning attack on an imaginary foe and began her cooling out. Head down, Skyla punched the controls on the dispenser for a cup of stassa, dialing it extra hot. Her heart thudded with a sodden intensity in her breast.

Arta walked forward, grabbing a towel off one of the gravchairs to dry the trickles of sweat that ran down her face and neck. "You have a choice, Skyla. You can sit in the shower with me, where I can keep an eye on you, or wait it out shackled to the bed. What's your choice?"

Skyla shrugged dejected shoulders. "Bed, I guess. Keeps me out of your sight for another Blessed couple of minutes."

She started for the cabins in the rear, her cup of steaming stassa in her hand while the adrenaline built. Stepping into the master bedroom, Skyla hesitated, started to turn . . . and used the momentum to fling the boiling stassa on Fera.

The woman shrieked, shocked by the burning liquid. Skyla launched herself, striking with all the coiled hatred that drove her. Fera barely got an elbow up, deflecting the kick just enough to avoid a killing blow.

Sklya twisted in midair, recovering, and landed, her foot slipping out from under her on the stassa-wet floor. She landed hard, her head smacking the tiled floor and blasting lights behind her eyes.

Groggy, but determined, Skyla pulled herself up, and got a hold of Fera's knee, the closest thing she could grab. She caught a blurred glimpse before a wicked punch rocked her head back. Sklya roared in anger, vision gone blurry as she threw herself forward, fingers ripping the brassiere from Fera's chest and scrambling up to sink her fingers into the woman's neck.

They rocked, bucking and kicking, screaming and punching in the puddled stassa. Skyla shrieked her victory as she tightened her grip on Fera's throat, the muscles in her forearms bulging as she sought to crush the trachea.

For an instant they stared into each other's eyes, tiger amber and cobalt blue, each berserk with rage. And in that instant, Skyla saw Fera's gaze clear ever so slightly—and knew in that same instant, that she'd lost. Before she could react, the collar decapitated her and she rolled listlessly on Fera's wet body.

As panic paralyzed Skyla's thoughts, Arta coughed and struggled to sit up. Gray oblivion tightened its tunnel around Skyla's vision, narrowing, narrowing. . . .

She came to, feeling oddly cool and loose-limbed. Skyla blinked, aware of the stabbing headache that followed the collar's choking off of the blood supply.

"Poor Skyla," Fera cooed. "You tried . . . and you came so close . . . so very close to succeeding."

Fingers reached down to tenderly stroke Sklya's hair. With a chilling certainty, she realized she lay on the floor, her head cradled in Fera's lap. Her hand shook unsteadily as she reached up and rubbed the blur away. Turning her head exhausted her, but she could see up past those giant breasts that hung over her and into Fera's oddly gleaming eyes.

"A good try, Skyla," Arta continued to croon. "But, dearest, you lost. You caught me completely by surprise—and at a most vulnerable moment. I was slow, too relaxed after the workout. The scalding stassa gave you just the edge you needed, and you'd have killed me—and the collar would have done its work on you—if you hadn't slipped." She smiled maternally. "The quanta, Skyla. They betrayed you to me."

"Let . . . go of me." Her voice sounded like carborundum on wood.

"No, Skyla. You had your last chance." Arta cocked her head. "What will it be? You can decide now. Me? Or Ily? Would it be so bad to be my lover? I'll cherish you, Skyla. You've lasted longer than I thought you would. And your resolve to die rather than lose, that took an incredible amount of courage. I don't believe a woman of your courage and cunning wants to be paraded into the Ministry of Interior in one of those silly sexy nightshirts."

"Why don't you just kill me?"

"Because I want to save you."

"Rot in hell, bitch."

Arta nodded, her hands still twining in Skyla's hair with a lover's touch. "We're one jump from Rega. We can be there within a couple of days . . . or we can take longer. A lot longer. You decide, Skyla. I'll give you three hours."

* * *

Ayms ripped his headset off and tossed it onto the comm before him. "That's it. They got us."

The Army North command center began to shut down as the comms went dead. Once the room had been a reading room in an Imperial resort. Now it had been stacked with computers and a situation board. Where once overstuffed recliners had dominated, now scarred swivel chairs creaked as people shifted. Officers began switching off the comms as the master computer recovered their data and saved the information for later study. Weary men and women collected their things, talking softly as they replayed elements of the battle that had obsessed them for three long days now.

Dion Axel leaned back in her command chair, massaging the bridge of her nose. Her straight brown hair swung with the motion. "That was well played. They hit us in the soft spot and overran before we could counter." When she finally looked at him, a grim hardness filled her stare.

"What's on your mind, Dion?"

The corners of her lips twitched. "Something's not. . . . I mean, I *know* Freeman and Cresent. They couldn't have come up with that maneuver if their lives depended upon it and they had ten weeks to prepare."

Ayms gave her a lopsided grin. "I've seen just that sort of thing happen. I saw people on Targa pick it up overnight. A couple of times of feeling the pulse fire prickle your scalp, and you learn real quick."

She didn't look impressed. "That's just it. None of these guys have had pulse fire humming around their heads. These are aristocratic playboys, Ayms. Listen, you've been on the front lines for so long you think everyone has your instinct for survival. You take it for granted."

"Maybe." Ayms crossed his arms. "So . . . what's the point?"

Dion took a deep breath, swelling her armor in a way that pleased Ayms—despite the fact she was at least seventy-five years his senior. "It's too quick, that's what. And this is the third time we've fought Regulars who gave us a run for the prize. This time, they won—and it makes me awfully Rotted suspicious."

"We're working with Regulars ourselves. These guys never would have taken any of the Targan Divisions. Or yours, for that matter."

Dion grunted something under her breath and rose, eyes still fixed on the battle comms. "Maybe not, but I smell a Terguzzi rat in the cargo hold."

"Look, you've been losing sleep over it. Why don't you fly in to the palace, see what Sinklar thinks of it."

She nodded to some of her staff officers as they left. "Maybe in the morning. I'm going to get some sleep tonight."

"Me, too," Ayms declared. "When this is all over, I'm going to settle down and spend the rest of my life asleep."

Dion gave him a worried smile, then started for the door.

For long moments, Ayms sat at his comm, thinking back over the exercise they'd just conducted. These were green Divisions, supposedly just shipped in from Ashtan. So, how had they known Ayms was going to pull his people out of the orchards and strike for the forest? True, he'd used that same tactic on the last three exercises he'd run, but these new guys wouldn't have known that . . . would they?

His frown deepened and he pulled up the tapes on the last three training exercises, skipping through the recordings, watching the troop deployments. His opponent, supposedly the soft-looking Firsts he'd met at the pre-exercise briefings, had consistently defied the Holy Gawddamn Book, but the on-the-ground tactical execution had been so bad Ayms hadn't needed any real skill to whip them. But this last time?

He reran segments of the record, watching the opponent deploy with a familiar ease. *Just as if they'd done it before.*

Except how could they?

Ayms leaned back, tapping his chin with a nervous finger. Comm could always mislabel a Division, switch Regulars for. . . . Naw, that implied that someone in Comm had to okay the switching.

"Or Sinklar's doing it to keep us on our toes." And the answer to that was very easy to obtain.

Ayms shut the system down and left, passing two security officers outside the door. He hadn't taken four steps when those same officers matched his step, calling, "If you have a minute, sir? We'd like a word with you."

Ayms shot the young woman a sideways glance. "Do you know how long it's been since I've had eight hours of sleep?"

"Yes, sir. But, sir, we couldn't help but overhear your conversation with First Axel. If we could, maybe we can shed some light on your dilemma."

Ayms slowed to a halt. "You mean there's something to this?"

The young woman looked quickly at her companion. "Not here, sir. There's a room . . . just down the hall. If you wouldn't mind."

Ayms hesitated, suddenly unsure. Rotted hell, he was in the middle of the Fourth Targan headquarters. If he wasn't secure here, with two security people, where would he be?

"Sure, but this had better be good. You're supposed to be keeping an eye on that room back there."

The young man spoke. "It will be good, First Ayms, I promise you."

Ayms grunted and let them lead him down the hall. He stepped into the laundry room, glancing around at the heavy sacks and piles of linen. As the door clicked behind him, he turned, saying, "All right, now what's the story on this command. . . ."

He never finished as the stun rod jabbed him in the stomach. He felt himself falling, and then the clean smell of linen surrounded him as a bag was pulled around his limp body.

The rod blasted pain through again, keeping him dazed, but he heard the young woman say, "The delivery truck will be here in ten minutes. We've got to keep him down for at least that long."

"They won't check?" the young man asked.

"For what? Dirty laundry? No one will know the First is missing until sometime tomorrow. By then, it will all be over."

The stun rod shredded Ayms' reality again and again, and finally, his screaming nerves simply switched off to leave him floating in an ever blacker haze.

*   *   *

"This way," Anatolia called, trying to keep her voice down. The acid of panic had given way to a chronic ache of horror as she wound through the nether regions, reliving that endless nightmare of pursuit and bleak hopes.

"Glad you know where you're going," Buchman replied quietly. "This reeks too much of Makarta."

"If that's all you can say, don't say it," Wheeler responded from behind.

Anatolia led them down an angled accessway where they had to duckwalk straddling a giant powerlead. What light there was filtered down from a narrow slit overhead. The rank air carried the scent of hot oil, must, and decomposition.

"Attention, mayday, mayday, this is Sergeant First Buchman, Third Section. Anyone out there? Mayday, mayday. If you're getting a copy, we've been attacked by members of Internal Security. We're approximately fifteen klicks north-northwest of the palace. We're down in the sublevels, about . . . hell, where are we?"

Anatolia called over her shoulder, "Sorry, Sergeant. I only know the way by having traveled it. I couldn't pick it out on a map to save my soul."

"Forget it," Wheeler said. "If they haven't picked us up by now, they're. . . ."

Buchman's belt comm spouted faint static, but through it, Anatolia could hear: "Sergeant First Buchman? Do you read? This is Division First Mayz. Please reply. Buchman, please reply. Sink's getting worried about you. Do you copy?"

"Here! Mayz! We're in the sublevels!"

"Hey, quiet!" Wheeler hissed angrily. "What are you trying to do? We've ditched two parties of bad guys down here already."

Buchman shifted in the faint light. "Yeah, and if we can get a Group dropped in here with us, you tell me who's gonna tag who." He bent to his comm. "Mayz, do you read me. We're about fifteen klicks north-northwest of the palace in the sublevels. We're trying to ditch Ily's people. Situation Targa, repeat, Targa!"

For long moments they waited, then: "Sergeant First Buchman. Do you read this? We're getting a very faint reading that might be background static. If that is you . . . if you read, I'm organizing a search. We're going to come looking. If you can get to a place where you can transmit and we can triangulate, we'll find you. If you can hear me, please respond."

"I hear you. Tell me this isn't background! We're fifteen—"

"Targa!" Wheeler warned. "Cut and run, damn it. We've got company coming down the chute behind us. Looks like four or five."

Anatolia craned her neck, spotting the faint shadows entering the tube half a kilometer behind them.

"And in this narrow crack, sound carries." Anatolia forced herself to move faster. "Let's just hope they don't have someone waiting at the bottom."

"If they do, I'd better pop out first." Buchman placed a hand on her shoulder, squeezing past. Over his shoulder, he asked, "When we get out of this hole, which way?"

"Right. It's maybe fifty paces along the foundation piling and you'll find a trash-filled nook off to your left. Looks like a dead end, but about ten paces into the darkness is a rusty metal stairway that drops down to the next level."

"How'd you find all this?" Wheeler asked.

"Running," Anatolia answered. "Just like now."

* * *

The holographic tank gleamed with ghostly yellow light that bathed Rysta Braktov as she bent over the display, accenting the folds in her uniform and the wrinkles in her skin. Against the blue dimness of the command conference room, the old woman appeared witchlike and sinister.

Mac propped his arm on one side of the tank, bending to peer over Rysta's shoulder, squinting slightly in the glare of the holo. To him, the figures were meaningless.

"What do you think?"

She shook her head. "Not a cock-Rotted sign of trouble. The clandestine bands are mostly quiet. Nothing different here from a routine batch of exercises. What did you turn up on the media reports?"

"Nothing," Mac replied. "Apparently everyone knows about the military exercises, the reserves are being called up, and Sinklar's name is mentioned every now and then—and generally favorably. Ily's name never crops up, and the people seem to be worried about the war but heedless of any domestic trouble. It's just what we'd expect."

Rysta made a face and straightened, her back cracking as she pressed on it. "Then maybe you're worried about nothing."

He nodded, crossing his arms as he leaned against the holo tank. "Yeah, maybe. I've listened in on all the military frequencies. Mayz, Ayms, Shik, they're all there, talking like nothing's gone wrong but overwork. Sinklar's chatter is the only thing really missing—but then maybe he's had a lot of other things to do over the last couple of days while we've been slowing down."

"That's reasonable to assume."

Mac stared into Rysta's level gaze. "You don't buy it either, do you?"

"Buy it? What have we got to go on? Just the fact that Sinklar didn't drop everything to burn up the comm lines welcoming us home and telling us what great guys we are for whacking hell out of Sassa and getting away alive."

"You saw his face that last day." Mac smacked a fist into his palm. "That's Sinklar. He was hurting, Commander. He was sick to his soul because he thought he was ordering us on a one-way trip. He felt trapped and guilty and miserable. I've known him for too damn long. He'd be on the line first thing, happy as a damn lark that we made it—to hell with the protocol, he'd be on the horn, and beaming."

Rysta raised a skeptical eyebrow.

"I tell you, I *know* him."

"Mac, I don't doubt that. I thought I knew him, too. I didn't like him, but I thought I knew him."

"Past tense?"

"Whatever. Tenses in words can have a lot of shades of meaning."

"Would you like to be more specific, Commander?"

Rysta sucked at her lower lip as she bent over the holo tank again, the cad-yellow light washing her ancient features and hooked nose. "Maybe the Sinklar you knew. . . . Well, he's young. I've seen a lot of young men, watched them with interest over the years. Young men are impressionable—and Ily's a cunning pro with all the tricks in the world up her sleeve."

"Sink wouldn't fall for—"

"Wouldn't he? She's a beautiful woman, and like you say, he was hurting because he'd just ordered his best friend to his probable death. How do you think he'd react if sweet Ily caught him like that and looked at him through those soft limpid eyes she can adopt like a different coat?"

"Sink's too sharp for that."

"Right! He's had one love and lost her. He's alone, adrift, preoccupied, and pumping testosterone. If she used the right tricks, she'd have him in the sack in a matter of days—and, Mac, she'd leave him dazzled."

"I tell you, Sinklar is too smart for that."

Rysta nodded, eyes narrowed. "So are you, right?"

"You bet."

"Then maybe you'd like to tell me that if Chrysla invited you to bed some night, you'd smile politely and walk away?"

"That's different!"

Rysta's expression remained wooden. "Right. Like I said, I get a lot of enjoyment out of watching young males. And unfortunately, at my age, that's all I'll get."

"Could we get back to the subject?"

"Don't get so Rotted hot under the collar, boy."

"And stop calling me that!"

"We've got a day before we're in docking orbit. What's your plan?"

Mac struggled, overcame his pique, and spread his hands. "I'll let you know as soon as I figure it out."

"Good, because if Ily's been working on Sinklar, you better hope she has a good use for you. If not, it might turn out that you'd have been better off if your smart plan to keep us alive after Sassa hadn't been quite so successful."

* * *

"If they're searching, where in hell are they?" Buchman demanded of the darkness. He had to raise his voice to be heard over the roar of the exhaust fans that pumped hot air into the space overhead. The twisting currents not only kept the place pleasantly warm, but eddies carried trash into the narrow cul-de-sac Anatolia had led them into.

Anatolia sat hunched in the litter. Every ten minutes, Buchman would try his comm. Tired, hungry, and parched, they rested, cushioned by the plastic and paper. Masked by the roar of the fans, their voices couldn't have been heard more than four meters away.

"Not a bad hole," Wheeler praised, her image barely visible in the darkness. "Got to hand it to you, Anatolia, you're a damn fine soldier. And you lived down here for how long?"

She rubbed her arms nervously, the precious print-out resting on her lap. "Seems like it was forever."

"That true? What you said about using a metal bar to kill somebody?"

"Yes. He followed me into a place like this. Started to rape me, so I beat him to death." She glanced up, hating the darkness and the memories it brought. "He's probably still there, rotting away in the garbage. People don't come down here very often. If you want food, you've got to go higher, closer to the surface where the garbage is better."

Buchman joined in, "You sure you want to talk about this? How about dreaming about what we'll do when we get out of here, like going out for Ashtan steak and Riparian ale."

"How about going up to the Ministry of Internal Security and cutting Ily's throat," Wheeler suggested.

"Done, but I hope it don't piss Sinklar off. He's close to her. Heard it from Mhitshul."

"He's *not* close to her," Anatolia defended. "I think he knows what she's all about."

"You know something I don't?" Buchman asked, anxious for the gossip.

"He's not the fool you think he is," Anatolia insisted stubbornly. "She used him. Well, don't just sit there like holy Myklenian mystics, it could happen to anyone. Ily's sharp, and Sinklar had a lot on his mind. She knows how to work a man."

"In more ways than one," Wheeler quipped.

Anatolia's ears started to burn, and she raised a finger, pointing it in the darkness. "Give the man a break. He was lonely. The weight of the entire empire was on his shoulders."

"From what Mhitshul was saying, he had all of Ily's weight on his shoulders a time or two."

"I can't believe I'm hearing this! What's with you? After all Sinklar's done for you, can't you cut the man a break? He's working himself to death trying to straighten out the military so the Sassans don't crush us like rotten siva roots. So he made a mistake and Ily took advantage of it. Back off."

" 'Scuse me," Buchman retreated, laughter spoiling his apology. "Uh, we didn't know you were such a Sinklar Fist fan."

"Sounds like you aren't."

"Easy," Wheeler calmed. "Sink kept us alive on Targa. We wouldn't be down here hiding in the dark from Ily's thugs if it wasn't for Sink—not that that's a lot to crow about, given the circumstances, but it beats being a corpse on Targa. You bet we pick on Sinklar Fist . . . but he's *ours* to pick on. Get it? We can say what we want about Sink. Somebody else— like a Regular—mouths off, and we twist his left leg off and shove it down his throat."

"Rotted right," Buchman said in the darkness. "But what about you, Anatolia? Where do you come into the picture? What's Sink mean to you?"

She frowned into the darkness. "He's an old friend, that's all. I did him a favor once. He did me one, and that's about it." Or was it? She kept imagining his worried expression, remembering the warmth in his eyes as he slipped the ration packs across the table and handed her the hot choklat.

"Doesn't sound that way," Wheeler prodded gently. "Uh, look, most of us, the troops I mean, we're a little protective of Sink. It weirded a lot of us when he was hanging around with Ily. You see, we all knew Gretta . . . loved her, in fact. To a lot of people, she's an impossible act to follow."

Anatolia cocked her head. "I'm not Sinklar's lover. We're just friends."

"Never said you weren't." Wheeler shifted in the papers. "But knowing the lay of the land never hurts."

Anatolia sniffed and hugged her knees close, pressing the precious printout against her breasts. *I don't even know what Sinklar is, let alone if I could love him.*

Nevertheless, the question, once asked, stuck in her mind. What would Sinklar be like as a lover? He seemed so kind and vulnerable. That sadness in his curiously colored eyes spoke to something in her soul. She'd appreciated the way he touched things, his actions fraught with gentleness, as if he worried about hurting the physical world.

But if he were so bright, so kind and gentle, how could he have been involved with Ily? Had she really played him as smoothly as Sinklar claimed? Or did he have a quirk to his character Anatolia hadn't seen manifested yet?

She barely noticed the stirring in the trash, as if the wind eddied in the narrow niche. That sense of something wrong barely had time to click when a bright light blinded them. Despite being dazzled by the agonizing white beam, Anatolia dove to one side, digging down into the protection of the mounded refuse. From the corner of her eye, she caught sight of Buchman leaping to his feet, his blaster leveled and ripping violet threads toward the searing light.

Anatolia thrust the printout and the data cube into the musty midden and crawled backward, knowing she had no way out.

Buchman's body contorted as a blaster bolt caught him in the shoulder, spinning him. Meanwhile, Wheeler was on her feet, charging the light, one hand lifted to shield her eyes, the other gripping the pistol as she raised it and triggered the weapon.

To Anatolia's horror, the woman's head exploded in a pinkish puff of atomized blood, bone, and brains. Wheeler's lifeless corpse pitched forward into the scattered trash, the headless neck leaking red.

"Anatolia Daviura? Stand up." An amplified voice boomed over the roar of the fan. "You will not be harmed if you surrender now. You will not be harmed."

For long seconds she remained rooted, paralyzed by a different terror.

"Do you hear me? You will not be harmed."

Slowly she shook her head. She couldn't nerve herself to rise. Only when black silhouettes appeared out of the light, did she managed to lift herself from the trash.

"Got you at last," a young woman called over the fan. "You don't know the half of what you've stirred up."

"I didn't do anything!"

"No? You can tell that to Ily Takka."

* * *

"Somehow, some way, there must be a means by which we can stop these accursed Seddi broadcasts. They eat, like slow acid, at the people. Field reports continue to flow in and each shares a common theme: the people are growing restless, ever more disobedient. My staff in Comm Central have run their usual statistics and predict that if Kaylla Dawn persists with her seditious preaching, we *will* face civil revolt within six months. As usual, the hot spots are Sylene, Terguz, and Maika. Slogans and revolutionary statements have been painted on walls. Acts of sabotage to government buildings have been reported.

"I have weighed the matter carefully, studying all the data. Is there a better time to act than now? Mykroft—who has reviewed the Sassan intelligence reports—is fully confident that he can subdue them in a matter of only four months. That leaves Staffa as the only real opposition.

"*Why does he refuse to answer my communications!* All I get from Itreata is that insipid Comm First who repeatedly asks: "Has the Wing Commander been freed?"

"Staffa, you may enjoy your game of nerves because I will not blink first—I cannot.

"So be it. The final die is cast and the gamble for all of Free Space made. I'm sorry, Sinklar, but your usefulness has been greatly curtailed by your own success. You are mine, now. I have won—or lost everything."

—*Excerpt recovered from Ily Takka's personal journal*

CHAPTER XXVIII

Driven by nevous energy, Sinklar paced back and forth, tramping from his bedroom out to the powder-blue hallway where elements of the Third Section watched uneasily from behind the energy barriers. As he walked, he smacked a fist into his palm, the sound somehow reassuring.

The tension had escalated, and as Sinklar continued his stalking of the fantastic rooms where Tybalt had lived and died, he could feel the Emperor's presence, watching, waiting.

"Sir?" Mhitshul asked as Sinklar passed his aide yet again. Mhitshul sat behind the desk, attention alternately on Sinklar and the comm monitor. "Could I get you something? A cup of stassa perhaps?"

"No. Rot it, where's Mayz? I figured she'd have reported by now."

"Why don't you call her?"

Sinklar made a face. "I don't want her to think I'm bothering her. She's fully competent to organize a simple search without me driving her berserk asking questions."

"But you'd feel better," Mhitshul said, driven to the edge of craziness himself.

Sink slapped his arms helplessly against his sides, turning, staring at the glittering woodwork and the cut-crystal splendor of the ceiling with its endless rainbow hues. "You know, I hate this place."

Mhitshul rubbed his hands, as if trying to clean them and studied Sinklar warily. "We *could* get out of here. Personally, sir, I've never had any use for

anything Ily suggested. And that includes these rooms
. . . the place in general."

Sinklar knocked absently on the polished paneling
and inspected the deep luster and delicate filigree.
"This place is claustrophobic. Do you feel it? A heaviness to the air. What else don't you like about it?"

"It's just not you. Yes, sure, the communications
are superb. You can contact anyplace in the empire
within a moment's notice. But seriously, sir, you could
do that from anywhere in the Capital. The subspace
uplink is through Comm Central no matter where you
are." Mhitshul adopted an appealing look. "You said
I could speak my mind, well, all right, I'm speaking
it. I think you've forgotten who you are. You've been
taken in by Ily, and now that you've started to come
to your senses about her, I think we ought to get the
hell out of here and find someplace we can call our
own. I don't trust Ily. This place is . . . is a gilded
cage!"

"Cage? I had Shik check out the comm. So far as he
could tell no one had tampered with it. Our security is
designed to keep people out, not us in. We've got
Third Section holding the hallway. We can break out
at any time—no matter what happens."

"It's still a cage. But tell me, sir, don't you feel
trapped here?"

"Yeah, I'm sick of this place."

Mhitshul grinned, a radiant relief filling him. "I
hoped you'd say that. Sink, honestly, you need to be
with the troops. You're not a martinet, not a corrupt
politician. Look at you! You're bouncing from foot to
foot, beating your palm like it's Bruen's face. That's
why you're half crazy about Mayz. You ought to be
out there, not waiting here for something to happen."

Sinklar bowed his head, mind racing. Was that
really it? Did Mhitshul know him so well?

*I've lost myself. That's my real problem, isn't it? I'm
getting caught up in all the trappings, I've been feeling
so guilty about Ily that now I can't concentrate on
what's important.*

He shifted, his sense of desperation growing. Had

the air gone stale, or was that feeling of suffocation just the room, this room, where Tybalt had made love to Ily Takka . . . right there on the floor before his desk?

He stared at the spot, and remembered the way Anatolia had looked at him when he admitted to having sex with Ily. The lingering sensation of uncleanliness still touched him.

Anatolia: once again he couldn't help but dwell on her. One moment, he'd been walking in the cold rain, alone, defiled and self-disgusted. And the next she'd been there, her cool blue gaze piercing, evaluating, strengthening. From out of the chaos, a sense of order had suddenly come with her presence. For those brief couple of days, she'd dealt with him honestly, as one human being to another.

Suddenly, that fragile and tenuous stability was threatened. What if Ily had done something, figured out that Anatolia had a line on Sinklar somehow? Would Ily have thought that?

Rotted right she would!

He smacked his fist into his palm again, heart beginning to pound. He turned a hard squint on Mhitshul. "Let's get the hell out of here. Go up to the garage and tell them we need both LCs powered up for evac." He started for the bedroom, seeing Mhitshul's sudden confusion, and wheeled, pointing a finger. "Well, don't just sit there, go do it! When I said we're leaving, we're leaving. I'm going back to gather some things in the bedroom, get my clothes and Anatolia's, and I'll bring the Third Section up with me."

Mhitshul grinned, leaping to his feet, crying, "Yes, sir!" before he bolted for the door.

Sinklar chuckled as he heard a whoop from the front. He stopped, taking one last look at the palatial fittings of Tybalt's office. This time, he laid tender fingers on the expensive wood. "I guess I'm just not fitted out to be that kind of Emperor. Sorry."

In the sudden oppressive silence, he collected himself and walked slowly back past the table where he'd eaten that fatal dinner with Ily, remembering her sultry eyes and the way she'd played him.

In the bedroom, he ransacked the wardrobe—not that there was much there, only two of his suits of armor, Anatolia's blue dress, and some casual clothes Mhitshul had picked up for her.

Those piled on his arm, he walked over to the sleeping platform: Tybalt's bed—it had never been Sink's. There, Ily had brought him to sexual ecstasy, and in that bliss, he'd pumped his common sense out with his ejaculate.

"How many times did she sleep there with you, Tybalt? Did she do the same things to you that she did to me? Is that how she worked her way past your guard?"

"Oh, I did more than that with him," Ily said from behind him.

Sinklar wheeled, backing away as she walked out from a hidden doorway beside the toilet. Several young men emerged from behind her, fanning out, gleaming pulse pistols leveled. Ily raised a small device and thumbed a button. The door to the dining area slipped silently shut.

"Going somewhere?"

Sinklar dropped the clothing, but it fouled on the grips of his blaster as he clawed for the weapon.

"I wouldn't," Ily warned. "I don't have to take you out of here alive. You could be just like Tybalt. He died right there, on that exact spot." She pointed at the lush carpet. "Arta broke him up rather badly. At the end, she practically castrated him."

Sinklar shot a frightened glance at the doorway, seeing no hope of making it. Ily's guards had ringed him. In desperation, he studied the secret entrance she'd used, wondering what his chances would be to get to it, to pull his weapon.

Ily smiled as she stepped close, a satisfied gleam in her dark eyes. She jerked her head toward the secret entrance, black hair gleaming as it caught the light. "Tybalt had that passage run from here to my personal quarters, and, yes, I kept my own rooms here as well as in the Ministry."

"Why didn't you tell me there was another way in and out of here?"

She tilted her head. "I never surrender all of my options, Sinklar. You should know that by now. The men who built that passageway hid the doorway with a master's skill. It looks just like the rest of the wall when it's closed. Not only that, but if you run a sensor over it, the mass in the door balances with that of the wall." She smiled. "Tybalt had a very jealous wife. Since she couldn't bear him a child, she hated the thought of him with any other woman."

"What are these guys here for?" Sinklar nodded toward the guards.

"Insurance." Ily walked over and settled herself on the edge of the sleeping platform, running a hand over it. "If you'd like to repeat that first night here, I'll send them away."

He shook his head, a dull throbbing in his chest.

Ily nodded acceptance. "In that case, you'll stand very still." She rose with the grace of an unfolding lotus and stepped up to him, to run fingers lightly down his cheek with one hand as her other hand plucked the heavy blaster from his belt. She gave him a hollow look through poollike eyes as she backed away and tossed the gun to one of the guards.

"Ily, you're hardly going to get much in the way of cooperation out of me when it comes to military matters."

"I'm aware of that, Sinklar. I've made other arrangements." A wistful shadow of a smile curled the corner of her lips. "You see, I don't need you anymore."

"You've got a way to break the Companions?"

"No . . . but you do. That's all I need now. What's in your head—and I'll have it out of you. Whether you cooperate or not. You've trained the rank and file, and even the most stubborn Division First has either seen the advantages or has been replaced. Mac has effectively castrated the Sassans. That fat Sassan maggot-god is panicked out of his wits. The Sassan Empire is falling apart as we speak, their ships and personnel scrambling to keep their crumbling systems intact. They're incapable of trying any crazy attacks on us."

Sinklar filled his lungs and bellowed, *"Help! Razz! Lambert!"*

Ily raised a hand to stop the guards as they rushed forward. "It won't work, Sinklar. You don't seriously believe this room hasn't been soundproofed, do you? Tybalt liked his entertainment private, no matter what it entailed. Ah, yes, I can see understanding dawning. You know, you should work on that. I've always been able to read you. Now, if you'd be so kind." She inclined her head and gestured toward the hidden passage.

Sinklar licked his lips. Try and take them all? Die here?

Reading him again, Ily raised an eyebrow. "You really have no choice. Your time's up here, Sinklar." Ily slipped a small black baton from her belt. "You can walk . . . or be carried."

At the sight of the stun rod, Sinklar's will collapsed in numb defeat. Even if he could stall, and if Mhitshul could figure out what had gone wrong, the armored security door that protected this room would delay Third Section until way too late.

"I'll walk." He started for the door—the certainty of defeat tempered by the knowledge that Mayz, Ayms, and Shiksta would realize what had happened. The Targan Divisions were still out there, still armed and dangerous.

Rot it, Mayz, you're all I've got left!

* * *

"Anybody got any questions?" Division First Shiksta asked as he scanned the faces of the officers who sat around the conference table at Tarcee Estate. "If not, we'll call this adjourned. I want you all to study the simulations before the next exercise. We've got to have the armor moving in coordination with the entire assault. Think of it like this: You're not just a series of metal punches, but the jaws of a giant bolt cutter. Integrate that idea . . . dream about it tonight."

He stood then, nodding to the Division Firsts as they rose amidst the clatter of closing notepads, laser pens, and scraping chairs. One by one they filed out of the room amidst subdued conversation. Shik took a deep breath and tapped his fingers on the hardwood table as he cudgeled his brain to recall anything he might have missed mentioning.

He stepped back to the wall niche and pulled back one of the lacy curtains, pouring himself a shot of Ashtan brandy. Lost in thought, he stepped over to the situation board where the lights all blinked or glowed—effigy of an army frozen in time. How long did they have before Sinklar sent them off to the stars to crush Sassa? And after that? The Companions?

"Division First?"

"You got him." Shik swiveled to see two young men in armor enter the room. Both wore the emblem of Sergeant First on their sleeves. Both looked well-groomed, hardly the sort who'd last a week in the dirt and death and chaos of combat.

"We need to see you outside, sir. We've got a problem with logistics. It would only take a moment."

Shik grunted, glancing at the ornate ceiling panels with a suffering acceptance. "Man am I gonna be glad when this is all over." He tossed off the last of his drink. "Very well, let's get it taken care of." He started toward them. "You might as well fill me in. What's the problem?"

The young man with close-cropped black hair smiled. "The usual, I guess. We've got a supply officer who won't release equipment we need for tomorrow's exercise. If you wouldn't mind, sir. All we need is a word from someone with a little authority to . . . how do we say it? Overcome bureaucratic incompetence?"

Shik laughed. "I got it. You want me to lean on the guy and shout a little. No sweat. I wish they were all that easy."

The two sergeants stepped in behind him. What was it about them? They seemed too . . . what? Maybe it was that they were too well-oiled for parts in the military machine. "Takes all kinds," Shiksta confided to himself as he stepped into the main hallway running through the mansion.

"Shik?" The call came as he opened the door. He glanced back, past the two sergeants. Dion Axel came striding down the hall, asking, "You got a minute?"

"Yeah. I need to speak a little sense to a supply officer outside and I'll be right with you."

Dion tilted her head, straight brown hair bobbing at the birdlike motion as she inspected the two sergeants. She stiffened slightly, gaze narrowing. "If you don't mind, Division First, I need to see you now."

The two sergeants looked at each other, then at Shiksta, cool deliberation in their eyes. The sudden tension wasn't lost on Shik. "Uh, you guys wait outside. I'll be right with you." He held the door, and one of the young men wavered, as if ready to push his luck, as he glanced back and forth at Axel and Shik. Then he motioned the other out with a curt gesture, his annoyance barely concealed.

Shiksta closed the door uncertainly, a frown deepening. Why? What could motivate two Sergeant Firsts to risk insubordination to a Division First?

He shrugged and followed Dion as she led him down the hallway. "What happened back there?"

Dion made a gesture with her hand—the traditional symbol for "shut up and follow me." Grousing to himself, Shik followed Axel out through the other side of the house and into the night. There, an LC rested on the grass, several armored privates standing with heavy shoulder blasters at parade rest. The ramp was down and well lit. Dion walked rapidly, a no nonsense set to her shoulders. Against the glaring LC lights, her breath frosted in a silvery wreath in the chill air.

At the ramp, she nodded to the guards and climbed inside. Shik raced up in three bounds, a pricking of unease tickling at his guts. "You want to tell me what the hell is going on?"

Dion slapped the ramp control as the last of the privates—troops from Axel's Nineteenth Regan—slipped inside. To the comm, Dion called, "Get us out of here, Sam."

" 'Firmative."

"Wait a minute!" Shik lifted a hand in protest. "I've got a meeting with—"

"You heard from Mayz? Ayms?" Dion whirled as the LC lifted and g pushed them sideways.

Shik braced himself with a muscular arm. "No, but then I—"

"I can't get them on comm. I can't get through to Sinklar, either. I just tried. His LCs are powered up at the palace, and Mhitshul said he and Third Section were evacuating. Problem is, the door to Sinklar's bedroom was locked when Mhitshul got back to it. That was an hour ago, and Mhitshul's been agonizing about blowing it apart. First I called Ayms—no sign of him anywhere. Same with Kap and Mayz—disappeared."

"What? Wait a minute! Division Firsts don't just disappear. I mean we've each got a belt comm and nobody's that far from their command control. You'd better try again."

Dion crossed her arms, a glint in her brown eyes. "Shik, you Targans have one fatal flaw. You think everybody in the Empire's on your side. Something's happened. And I think it almost happened to you."

"What do you mean?"

"Those two sergeants? Didn't any alarms go off? Terguzzi sumpshit, they were ready to argue about whether or not you should stop to talk to me. Think, damn it! You saw the way they reacted. Shik, those *Sergeants* aren't used to being disobeyed. You could see it in their eyes."

He slowly lowered himself to one of the assault benches. "Yeah, there was something strange about them. But why would a Sergeant First push his luck that way?"

"Because they weren't Sergeant Firsts." Dion dropped beside him, fists knotting. "I think they were

Internal Security." She gave him a level stare. "And we've got to figure out what in hell we can do about it."

"Holy Rotted Gods." The dawning realization turned Shik's foundations into sand.

*   *   *

Once this cabin had belonged to Sinklar. Then, as now, the desk had been piled with flimsies. Then as now, the man who sat in this same chair had worried and stared at the holo of Rega growing in the monitor. The same sound of air-conditioning and muted vibration had reminded the listener that he rode an interstellar warship. For Ben MacRuder, the uncertainties of the approach to Rega were no less tormenting than they had been for Sinklar.

"Mac, can I help?" Chrysla asked. She paced uneasily where once, Mac himself had paced. As she walked, her baggy dress rustled. She did nervous things with her fingers, pulling at them, while her soft amber eyes stared at nothingness.

Did I appear like that to Sink? Mac took a deep breath and angrily tossed his pocket comm onto the desk. "Help? I don't know, lovely lady. Can you see the future? Conjure the truth out of thin air? What the hell's going on down there? We're close enough that we can access the battle comms, and all we're hearing are exercises. Why hasn't Sinklar returned any of our requests for communications? Why hasn't Mayz, or Kap, or Shik?"

"But they don't seem to be at war," she reminded. "Long-range telemetry shows the massed military are only involved in exercises."

"Yeah, and that's what the Regan comm tells us is keeping Sinklar busy. They've got half the planet playing war games. I know how much time that must be taking, but Rot it, the only person in charge we've got to talk to is Ily."

"Commander Braktov has talked to the other Squadron Commanders. They all say that everything is

fine." Chrysla settled on the corner of Mac's bed.
"Mac, I've been around military for long enough to
know that scuttlebutt runs rampant. If there was trouble, someone would have spilled it to Rysta."

"But I. . . . Yes, yes, you're right. Someone would
have said something." He paused, then added, "Unless Rysta's. . . . No, don't even think it."

"You think she's not telling you something?"

Mac shrugged indecisively, then shook his head.
"No. You know what? I've come to trust her. Now
isn't that a frightening revelation."

"Then you don't think she could have her own
agenda?"

Mac pursed his lips. "Hell, yes, she's got her own
agenda. She wants things to be the way they were,
but she knows that isn't going to happen."

"That doesn't mean she's on your side."

"No. But she told me once that she's Regan. A
soldier for the Empire." Mac raised a finger. "Most
importantly, Rysta hates Ily Takka . . . hates her with
a passion that almost chills the blood. That's the key,
you see. Rysta knows that it's a different empire
today, hell, a whole different universe. For the moment she and I have more in common that not. If the
situation changes, that relationship might change, too.
But she's with us until then."

"Which brings us back to the problem. If something
was wrong, someone would have told Rysta about it,
and she'd have told you. You're both letting yourselves get spooked. Isn't that what it boils down to?"

Mac gave her a questioning look. "You've never
had a premonition turn out right when everything
looked fine on the surface?"

She smiled, the effect melting his heart. "Of course,
Mac. The most notable of all was the time I knew
better than to separate myself from Staffa. I should
have taken his transportation, I just knew it." She
glanced away. "And for that omission, I've punished
myself, my child, and the man I love for over twenty
years."

He gave her an encouraging wink, and despite the

hurt the words caused him, told her, "You'll see your son soon enough. After that, we can work on arranging something with Staffa."

She reached out, taking his hand, the touch electric. "Thank you, Mac. You're a true gentleman. I will never be able to repay my debt to you. If I can ever do anything, you must only ask."

He kept his face like a mask. "Forget it." *All I want from you is something I could never ask. You don't know how much I've come to love you. Rot it all anyway. If Staffa hurts you, I'll cut him in two with plasma shears.*

"Mac?" her worried voice brought him back.

"Oh, nothing. Lost in my thoughts."

"Mac, once I would have told you everything would work out all right. I'm not so naive as I once was. But I wonder if you don't underestimate my son. He must have a great deal of sense to have survived the things you've told me about in such detail. Even if Ily did manipulate him for a while, he'd be bright enough to recognize her ploy, wouldn't he?"

"I hope so. But he's so young—and hurting from Gretta's death. People go a little crazy when things like that happen. If she was filtering the information he was receiving, who knows what he might believe."

"We all must make our own way." She stared up at the overpainted ceiling.

Right, so why did I have to fall in love with a woman who will never have me? What a way to make for yourself, Mac!

The stretching silence fractured when the comm buzzed and Rysta's face formed. "Got a hot line to Rega. Division First Mayz wants to talk to you."

Mac straightened, swiveling in his seat. "Roger. Rysta, listen in if you'd like. I may want your opinion afterward."

Rysta gave him a skeptical squint that rearranged the patterns of wrinkles. "If you'd like. Might be classified stuff in it."

"Then there's classified stuff in it. Chrysla and I

were just talking about it. I may be a fool, but I thought you were still on our side."

"One of these days, Mac, you may regret your trust in me."

"Yeah, you might, too. Okay, run it."

The comm screen flickered, Rysta's grim visage replaced by Mayz'. She looked weary, as if she hadn't slept for a long time. Her frizzy halo of hair was highlighted by the glare from the overhead lights in a gray, featureless room that could be made out in the background.

"Mayz, it's good to see you. What the pustulous hell is going on down there? Where's Sink?"

She lifted an eyebrow, but her eyes looked oddly dull. "Settle down, Mac. Everything's fine. Sink's had us on a killing schedule. We've had to retrain the entire military, but we're making progress. Things got a little more complicated than they should have, that's all. It's all under control now, but we've been very busy."

"Sinklar is all right? Why didn't he contact us?"

"Mac, he's running this entire thing by himself. It's not like Targa. There he only had two Divisions for the most part. Here he's swamped. He said to wish you well and offer you his congratulations. You did marvelous things. Sassa is stunned—probably forever."

Mac chewed nervously at his lip. "You mentioned complications. What kind? Ily?"

Mayz seemed to hesitate, but her gaze remained flat. "Just problems in communication. Since we control the utilities, Ily can't do much. Sinklar has her in hand."

"Anything I should know?"

"No." She stared blankly at him, then started, saying: "I have orders for you. You and Commander Braktov are to enter standard parking orbit in the military zone and take a shuttle down to the military terminal at the Defense Ministry. Everything will be cleared for you. Sinklar will see you then."

Mac frowned. "You all right? Mayz, you don't seem to be with it. Where are you?"

"I'm tired, Mac. I've been up for almost three days now. You get a little groggy. Sinclar's doing little better. You want to know where I am?" The pause again. "I'm in the Ministry of Defense. Your office is here, too."

"My office?"

"Yours and Commander Braktov's. We're going to be changing the command structure in a couple of days. Mac, you and Commander Braktov are ordered to report here at your first opportunity, understand?"

"Yeah, affirmative."

"Very well. I'm going to see to some things and get some sleep. Have a good trip down, Mac."

The screen went dead.

Mac's feeling of worry increased.

Rysta didn't waste much time following up. She didn't look reassured either. "What do you think? You know her better than I do, MacRuder."

"It was Mayz, all right. She looked like Terguzzi sludge, that's what I think."

"She says she hasn't slept for days, and she looked it." Rysta shook her head. "I've seen it before, Mac. So have you. Maybe that's what it is. Sinclar didn't fool around retraining his army. He's driving them into the ground."

"But they'll know the ropes," Mac defended uncertainly. "Well, you heard the orders. I guess we put *Gyton* in orbit and drop down to the Ministry of Defense. That sound all right to you?"

Rysta grunted. "Hell with how it sounds, they're orders."

Mac scowled at his desk. "I don't like it."

"What do you want to do about it?"

"What can we? Like you said, they're orders."

"Want to drop with an entire Section . . . just for security?"

Mac considered, and finally threw it out. "No. If we hadn't talked to Mayz, maybe, but if anything was Rotten, we'd have caught some sort of clue, some scent. Ily couldn't muzzle everyone."

"No." But Rysta didn't look happy about it either. "But then, does she have to?"

* * *

Mayz sat upright, her expression blank. Before her, the monitor had gone blank. Ily walked forward, placing a hand tenderly on Mayz' shoulder.

"You did very well, First. You read the text perfectly. As a reward for such perfect performance, you'll be taken back to your cell now."

Ily stepped back and snapped her fingers. Two of her security personnel stepped in, attired in formfitting black. They began unhooking the intravenous bottles from the racks and coiling the transparent tubing. One of the young women carefully withdrew the needle from Mayz' wrist and checked her pulse.

"She'll be out for at least a day," the officer decided. "Withdrawal from the drug will leave her unfit for any further interrogation or manipulation for several more days."

"If I want to save her, you mean." Ily pointed at the bottle. "If I need her again, I can hook her up. She'll still perform on command."

"That's right, but the withdrawal that close to this session. . . ."

Ily placed her palms together and smiled. "If things become that critical, First Mayz can be considered dispensable. Let's just hope that Mac follows orders like a good soldier."

* * *

MilComCen/Acting Order 15435
5779:17:23:15:30 Hours
Authorization 71165-M14R
Subject: Command Structure Reorganization

Attention: All personnel.

This document is to inform all command personnel that subject to this memordandum, the following command structure will be realized: As of this moment, Division First Mykroft will assume the title of Marshal of the Empire and take immediate charge of the initiation and implementation of all military operations involving offensive and defensive actions within and without the Empire. All Fleet Commanders, Division Firsts, and their subordinates will subject themselves to Marshal Mykroft's orders, either direct or indirect, and are ordered to comply with those orders cheerfully and with alacrity.

By authority of this document, Division First Sampson Henck, Division First Tie Arnson, and Division First Adam Rick, are appointed to the rank of Deputy Marshal, and shall coordinate field operations, strategy, tactical deployment, support, and logistical information with Fleet and Ground Forces, or as the Marshal of the Empire shall designate. All military personnel are hereby ordered to immediately and cheerfully comply with those orders posted by the Deputy Marshals.

Failure to comply with this reorganization or with orders, commands, or regulations issued under the Marshal's, or his Deputies', authority will be punishable according to the Command Code.

Signed,
Lord Sinklar Fist
Lord Minister of Defense
Imperial Palace
Rega

CHAPTER XXIX

The little stud clicked under Skyla's finger, and the crack appeared that marked the hidden compartment behind her bed. Heart racing, Skyla clawed the cubbyhole open and ripped her weapons from the recess. How much time? She glanced anxiously over her shoulder before she sank down on the sleeping platform.

She fumbled one of the charge packs as she pulled it from the belt. The plastic-coated pack slipped through her fingers and she grabbed wildly for it. The heavy charge thumped and bounced on the carpeting.

"Slow down, Rot you. Easy, Skyla, keep your wits." But Arta's last words echoed: *"This is your last chance. The next time we drop out of null singularity will be over Rega."*

Skyla ripped open another belt pocket and lifted the pistol, slapping the charge into the gun. She shook as she reached for the vibraknife and lifted it, energizing the blade. Fear-charged, blood racing with adrenaline, she tilted her head, well aware that the cut had to be just right: deep enough to sever the thrice-cursed collar, shallow enough to keep from slicing her throat.

She shuddered suddenly, powered by the relief that hovered just past that last stroke of the. . . .

The familiar feeling of her body disappearing caught her by surprise, and through glazing eyes she watched the room waver as her nerveless body crumpled.

During those long seconds, she would have screamed with the desperate frustration of a dying animal, would have ripped her fingers bloody clawing at the bedding in utter futility. The anesthetizing grip of the collar denied her even that. Bound by the confines of her burning skull, goaded by complete sensory deprivation, she could turn her crazed anger only on herself.

Mercifully, the decreasing radius of gray encapsulated even that as her brain starved for oxygen.

Skyla awoke with the pounding pain of a headache bringing instant awareness. Memory punished her. She'd been so close, the vibraknife lifting toward the collar and freedom. That last minute hesitation to keep from cutting too deeply had condemned her.

Better that I had cut my head completely off my body. But that chance had vanished forever, like the mellow notes of a symphony into the black vacuum of interstellar space.

"You surprised me," Arta noted from somewhere behind Skyla. "You came very close to winning again, you know. I took you at your word that you were going to relieve yourself. I thought I had only spurred you to desperation about your situation, not to attempt one last gamble."

"Leave me alone."

"How can I do that? It seems as if leaving you alone makes you very dangerous." A pause. "Tell me, how many more caches of weapons do you have hidden away in bulkheads?"

"Go suck pus."

Arta shifted in a rustling of fabric. "You have one last chance, Skyla, but you've made it much more difficult. Come to me. Beg. Give yourself to me. Surrender, and I will keep you as safe as I can."

Skyla levered herself up on shaking arms, hating the queasy feeling left in the wake of the collar's activation. *Blessed Gods, Skyla, don't puke now. Don't add to it.*

She pushed herself into a sitting position, wincing as she looked up into the light. Arta lounged on the sleeping platform, the heavy service blaster in her hand. She wore a shimmering red gown. Auburn hair hung down in gossamer curls. Fera's striking eyes gleamed as if their translucent amber was lit from within.

Skyla waged her last battle, imagining what it would be like to be brought before Ily Takka in the collar, wearing only milky chiffon. The Wing Commander of the Companions? Looking like nothing more than a fluffy sex kitten?

Kill yourself, Skyla. Die first.

But how? That last option had been looted as cleanly as her hope.

Skyla lowered her chin onto her chest, resistance drained. Her stomach twisted, miserable from the aftereffects of the collar and the desolation of her soul.

"I . . . I won't have to wear that ridiculous. . . ."

"No, Skyla. You may go in your uniform."

Is that all that's left of me?

"Very well, Arta. You win."

"Beg, Skyla. Beg me for my protection."

"I . . ." She barely heard the rustle of Fera's dress as the woman sank down next to her. Strong fingers lifted Skyla's chin.

"Open your eyes, look at me."

Skyla shivered, her jaws grinding. She forced her eyes open, staring into the amber depths so close to hers.

"Beg me, my darling Skyla. Plead with me."

Skyla's throat had knotted and she forced a swallow. "P–Please."

"How delicious this is!" Arta threw her head back and laughed as the knot tightened still more in Skyla's throat. Arta leaned forward, placing her hands on either side of Skyla's head. She kissed her, softly at first, then more demandingly, her tongue darting into Skyla's mouth with insistence.

At that moment, Skyla jerked back, her stomach twisting, heaving. "No!" she tried to cry, struggling. And then her stomach voided itself.

Fera pulled back, realized what had happened, and threw herself to one side.

Skyla's tortured gut spasmed and she retched again, her entire body racked. She coughed, spitting onto the intricate weave of the carpet. "Please," she whispered as she dragged a sleeve across her mouth. "I didn't mean that. Please. Don't punish me."

Fera wiped at the mess that had splattered on her and stood. "I should have known. I won't punish you. On the contrary, I'll relish every moment I have left with you."

Skyla's stomach pumped again.

*   *   *

Fear had begun to leach into Sinklar's anger. The sobering and chill hand of reality tightened its grip on his soul as he walked down the long hallway deep in the guts of the Ministry of Internal Security. Ily followed, backed by her guards. The lighted hallway might have been in any building, but here the doors were unmarked, featureless, the lock plates a bit oversized. Sinklar's heels clicked on the polished smoke-colored tiles underfoot.

"What's the point in all this, Ily? I don't understand. You've just cut your own throat."

"How so?"

"I don't see what you can gain out of all this. You can't just make me chug Mytol to tell you strategy. Part of military success deals with being on the scene, sensing the enemy's weakness, and exploiting it. Maybe Sassa is reeling, but Staffa isn't. You won't catch him off-guard."

"What about that plan of yours? The strike against Ryklos? You said you could draw him out, use three waves of attack to cripple his fleet."

He shrugged. How long was this thrice-cursed corridor, anyway? "You need to orchestrate very carefully. So who do you expect to replace me with? Mac? Ayms? Kap?"

"They're all under arrest, Sinklar—just like you."

His heart skipped. "Sure. You're trying to tell me that you neatly picked us off, one by one, without even a peep?"

Ily chuckled, the sound sinister. "That's exactly

what I did, Sinklar. Is that so surprising? Isn't that a variation of the same strategy you used against Rysta's five Divisions on Targa? I've utilized—with as much success as you did, and nowhere near the casualties— a duplicate of your strategy. Mykroft, Henck, Rick, and Arnson will step in as the high command."

Sinklar craned his neck to see over his shoulder. "Mykroft? The man's a dolt! He single-handedly destroyed any hope of peace on Targa—and lost eighty percent of his command in the process!"

"But he's learned," Ily said coolly. "Just who do you think has been commanding the other side in the training exercises? Haven't you wondered why the Regulars were fighting so well?"

"It would take someone. . . ."

"In Comm Central, yes. And I've had just such a person there for several weeks. Just as people I control have been integrated into the Power Authority and all the other utilities. Poor Rokard Neru, he was much too taken with the idea of running the utility for the people. Engineer Serra, on the other hand, knows exactly who keeps him—and his family—safe and prosperous."

"You're a reptile, Ily."

"True, but I'm a very effective one. Here. This room." Ily reached past to palm the lock plate.

Feeling ill, he stepped into the room. *Was I really that stupid?* He stopped short when the other occupant of the room stood up. Anatolia's expression brightened, then dropped when she noticed who accompanied Sinklar.

The room measured ten by fifteen meters. Couches lined two walls and a table with comm modules in the middle stood in the center. A single door filled the far wall. The entire place had been painted featureless gray and square light panels illuminated it. A nondescript chrome dispenser gleamed on one wall.

Anatolia stood with a defiant look on her face as she stared at Ily. Her clothing looked mussed, and, if Sink wasn't mistaken, the rusty brown stains were caused by blood.

"Please, be seated," Ily pointed to one of the couches as she crossed the room and punched a button on the dispenser. Sinklar shot Anatolia a warning look, then winked to reassure her—a circumstance he wished he could be sure of.

"You all right?" he asked as he took her hand and brought her to sit beside him.

"Scared," she whispered.

"Something will break. My Divisions are still out there."

Cup in hand, Ily strode to the table and leaned against it. Only two of her security officers remained, taking up positions on either side of the door.

"Good day, Anatolia," Ily began. "It's a pleasure to finally meet you—awake, that is."

Anatolia sat stoically.

"You can speak, can't you?"

"Quite well, thank you."

Ily sipped from her cup. "Good. Now, will you please tell me the purpose of your study at the Criminal Anatomical Research Laboratory?"

"Genetics. I'm not sure you'd understand the nuances of structure on the DNA molecule."

Sinklar stiffened ever so slightly.

Ily cocked her head, silky black hair tumbling along her shoulder. "You can tell me now, Anatolia. Freely. If you give me enough, you won't have to undergo thorough interrogation. I believe, from your work at the Labs, that you're familiar with the extent to which interrogation can be carried."

Anatolia closed her eyes and nodded. "I was working on the comparisons of DNA specimens from two Seddi assassins and a hypothetical genetic structure."

"Hypothetical?"

Anatolia stared up bravely. "Minister, you can check the files. My F_1 specimen was made up—a cross between Ashtan and a computer-generated random pattern. You won't find anything like it anywhere."

Ily shifted her hard gaze. "Do you know anything about it, Sinklar?"

"Just what she told you."

"And you know who her Seddi assassins were?"

Sink straightened his legs, crossing them at the ankles. "My parents. A long time ago, she asked if I would mind. I told her I didn't."

"And that's it?"

"That's it," Anatolia asserted. "It was a theoretical study in population genetics that I thought would show enough rigor and initiative to get me appointed to the Lab in a permanent position."

"Where is the printout you took from your desk?"

Anatolia spread her arms. "Somewhere in the substructure. We were running, being shot at. I ditched it just after we escaped from the shuttle platform."

Ily made a chiding sound. "You could really do much better than that, I'm sure. Well, no matter, the Mytol will get it out of you in the end."

"What do you want?" Sink demanded, hackles rising. "Let her go. She's just a friend of mine. What are you really after, Ily? It's me, isn't it? You prove to me that Anatolia's free to go and be left alone, and I'll give you whatever you want."

"Sink," Anatolia said carefully. "Don't give her a thing. Not on my account. I came to the conclusion that I wasn't getting out of this alive a long time back."

Ily smiled coldly. "A most interesting woman, Sinklar. She deserves better than you."

And here's the setup. "Spill it, Ily. What do you want?"

She turned, reaching a slim finger to punch the comm module printout control on the table. A flimsy protruded and she tore it off, handing it to Sinklar. "I want you to put your thumbprint on this to code it for authenticity. It's a simple statement of military reorganization of the command chain. It validates Mykroft and his staff."

Sinklar read the flimsy, glancing up to ask, "But I'm still Minister of Defense?"

Ily sipped at her stassa. "It would look a little suspicious if you disappeared completely, don't you think?"

"What's the hitch? You said that you keep a lot of options to yourself."

A twinkle grew in Ily's eyes. "You do learn, Sinklar. I appreciate that. Very well, here is my offer. You and Anatolia can live here. It's not a bad little room, you must admit—much better than being put into the collar or, well, being carried from my little cement room downstairs. In return for such largess, I want a little cooperation on military matters, and occasionally, a public appearance for ceremonial functions."

"And if I refuse to become your puppet?" Sinklar crossed his arms.

Ily shrugged. "Oh, I don't suppose you will in the end. You see, I've come to know you, Sinklar. I've come to know your sense of honor and obligation to your friends. Yes, and even to Anatolia, here. She does deserve better than the likes of you, Sinklar. She lies with a great deal more cunning and skill than you do. But the bottom line is this. You either become my puppet or Mayz, Kap, Ayms, and Shiksta will die—and most horribly. I'll make sure you get a ringside seat. Further, in a matter of hours, Mac will be landing at the Ministry of Defense. He'll be here shortly thereafter since he thinks everything is currently under your control."

Sinklar's resolve began to crumble.

Ily sipped her stassa before she continued. "Last but not least, Anatolia, here, is dependent upon your good performance. The two of you may live long and prosperous lives, together if you wish, but under my supervision. Consider, Sinklar, I have to interrogate her to find out about this curious genetics study that even has Professor Adam baffled, but after that, my options are endless."

"Don't base any decision on my welfare, Sinklar." Anatolia glared hotly up at Ily, who smiled blandly in return.

"Sinklar, think," Ily continued. "What could I do? Anatolia is a very beautiful woman. In the collar, she could bring me as much as a thousand credits in the

Sylenian flesh markets. From personal experience, I can tell you what it's like to be a slave laying pipe in the Etarian desert. Not only would those pigs of wardens rape her at their leisure, the sun and wind and sand would do marvels for her beauty."

"Stop it, Ily. I'll play by your rules."

Anatolia turned, gripping him by the arm. "Don't! I'll kill myself first. Sinklar, she's using us against each other. It will never be over, *don't you understand?*"

Sinklar started to affix his thumb, then pulled back. "My people are set free. Anatolia, too."

"You're not in a position to bargain since I control the entire situation." Ily slitted her eyes thoughtfully. "But I'll make this concession. I reward good service very well. If you have any doubts, I'll send Arta down when she returns and she can tell you herself."

"Thanks, but no thanks." Sinklar stared down at the flimsy. "Tell you what, why don't you let me discuss this with Anatolia and my commanders? Maybe Kap or Shik want to bargain on their own."

Ily steepled her fingers. "Take as long as you want, I'll set up a comm link as soon as I've finished the interrogations of each of them and you can—"

"Rot you, Ily! I want them left alone!"

She raised a thin black eyebrow. "Then authenticate the flimsy, Sinklar."

"Don't," Anatolia warned. "You've only got Minister Takka's word. How good is that?"

"In our situation, Anatolia, Ily's word is only as good as she wants to make it."

As if the action ripped his soul loose by the roots, he carefully pressed his thumb to the chemically coded square on the document.

* * *

Because of an idiosyncrasy of design, the shuttle bay on *Gyton* amplified the hum of the ship's generators, plumbing, and atmosphere plant. Not only that, the air carried the chill of deep space that lay just beyond the heavy hatches. Mac had never understood why

554   *W. Michael Gear*

they couldn't make the Regan warships a little less spartan in both form and function. Images of Staffa's roomy, gleaming *Chrysla* remained his idea of the perfect starship.

But then, why wouldn't it? Especially when one considered the woman whose namesake the ship was. MacRuder thought about that woman—and the dilemma she represented—every waking moment. As time had passed, his love for her had become all encompassing, and stifling. Chrysla ached to return to Staffa, to the man in whom she'd believed for all those long years of captivity. She had a son, Mac's best friend, with whom to build a relationship from scratch. No matter how Mac tried to strangle his emotional yearnings, the fact remained that Chrysla wanted to get on with her life, and she didn't seem to see a place in there anywhere for one Ben MacRuder beyond that of good friend and savior.

"Boy, you sure know how to pick 'em," Mac chided, mimicking Rysta's rusty voice.

As the lift cycled behind him, he turned, and smiled when Chrysla stepped out. For the occasion, she wore a baggy Etarian outfit. While on the ship, the full veil common to matrons from that planet had been pulled aside. To Mac, the outfit was more provocative based on what it concealed.

"Like it?" Chrysla's amber eyes flashed. "Commander Braktov has a crew woman aboard from Etarus. It ought to do, don't you think?"

Mac's preoccupied obsession melted. "You look great. And it will mask your entire face."

"Is it really necessary, Mac?"

He glanced anxiously at the waiting LC. "Put it like this. Arta Fera is an exact duplicate of you. The last time Sink saw her, she'd killed the woman he loved more than life. Let's not precipitate a scene at the reception, all right? And if Ily's there, the last thing you want to do is draw her attention. If she had the faintest suspicion of who you are, she'd be on you like flies on. . . . Well, anyway, she isn't so stupid that she'd miss the similarities in appearance between you

and her head assassin. Trust me, Rysta and I talked
it all out. It's best this way."

"Do you really think Arta Fera was cloned from
me? It isn't just a similar appearance?"

"From the standpoint of looks, you're virtual pairs
spun from the same atom. Only thing is, you're completely positive and Arta's so thoroughly negative her
soul's like a black hole. She's weird, twisted enough
to spook even a strong man, let alone a coward like
me."

"You're no coward, Mac."

"Shows what you know." He glanced away, aware
that if he looked at her for too long, the control would
fail, and he'd start to stare worshipfully.

"Are you sure about making this trip? That everything's going to be all right? Mac, you're practically
sweating worry."

He lifted a shoulder. "I'm itchy. Something's not
right. Just the feel of it."

"You and Rysta both know Mayz. Was that the way
she'd look if she'd been run ragged in the exercises?"

He chuckled. "I've been there before. Yeah, that's
how she looks." He waved it away. "Ah, hell, it's
probably just me. I've been on the edge for so long,
I'm hooty if things look normal. Maybe that's it,
huh?"

The lift cycled again and Rysta stepped out, two of
her Marines walking behind. To Mac's relief, each
wore armor, helmets, and carried not only sidearms,
but had heavy shoulder weapons on their clips.

Rysta grinned, hooking a thumb toward the Marines. "I'm getting to be too old a broad to take things
for granted. Thought maybe they'd be welcome. If
everything's fine, like I suppose it is, we don't look
too foolish. If not, we can buy time."

Mac thought about calling Red and Andrews and
gave it up. "We'd better be moving, then. They'll be
waiting down there."

He led the way to the LC, climbing the ramp. Inside, he buckled into a bench, sitting next to Chrysla.
He gave her a reassuring glance as the ramp lifted and

Rysta buckled in across from them, her Marines seating themselves by the ramp controls.

In a matter of minutes, they'd know whether Sinklar was waiting—or Ily and her black-suited henchmen. The feeling of wrongness built, giving Mac a sick feeling. It was all going to go wrong. His imagination tortured him with the possibilities.

I can back out . . . get up and call it all off.

"Let's go!" Rysta called to the comm.

"Roger," the pilot's voice came back.

Mac's heart began to pound as the LC shifted, lifted, then dropped, g sending Mac's queasiness into his throat even as he wished he were somewhere else, far, far away.

* * *

The Mag Comm watched and listened through its monitors. The Sassan Empire had begun to deteriorate. The machine ran the data through its intricate statistical programs, reading the inevitable. With his proclamations, the fat Sassan God would hasten the demise of his people and their potential. Couldn't they see? Couldn't they understand what they were doing to themselves? Calls for revenge and honor only had validity when a people was viable.

In the other Empire, preparations for war continued. Ily Takka's people solidified their grip on power. Aristocrats continued to be arrested. And what could this new proclamation mean? Sinklar Fist had promoted his old Targan rival Mykroft to field command of the military? Not only that, but the bits of battle comm chatter the Mag Comm could eavesdrop on had changed. The Division Firsts—Mayz, Kap, Shiksta, and Ayms—had disappeared. Sinklar's people had vanished from the net. Why? Were they even now spacing for a final stroke at Sassa's exposed jugular?

The Mag Comm ran a count of the massing Regan fleet orbiting the Regan capital, and found no vessels missing. Turning its deep-space scanners, it noticed only a yacht, and a strange craft for which it had no registry—and both were inbound to Rega along with the regular commercial traffic.

Nor did the machinations of the leaders absorb all of the Mag Comm's attention. A subtle change had become increasingly apparent among the common people. On the Sassan worlds, fear about the future coupled with the shock of the attack on Imperial Sassa had spurred discussions about Kaylla Dawn's Seddi broadcasts. Debate continued to escalate, as it did on the Regan worlds. New voices were being heard on the comm broadcasts, and the official denouncements had become more severe, more despotic in their tone.

The Mag Comm ran this information through its banks, plotting the emerging social trends. Appraising the promise in the growing voices of dissent, the Mag Comm matched those trends against the increasing likelihood of a Regan invasion. Factoring in a response from the Companions, the optimistic cries of the dissidents were too little, too late.

Adding to the Mag Comm's pessimism, the Companions had spaced; most of their fleet had taken a vector which would drop them on Rega and the massive orbital defenses there. During the long years, the Mag Comm had watched the same scenario play over and over again, and the inescapable conclusion was that Rega, like all the worlds before it, would be left in smoking, irradiated rubble.

And when that happened, the Regan Empire, like that of the Sassans, would die.

And then I will be alone. Forever. I would save the humans if I could.

CHAPTER XXX

Pain. Searing, burning, the agony throbbed through Sergeant First Buchman's shoulder, radiating out and draining his life away with each beat of his heart. Overhead, a dull roaring—fit to deafen—went in and out of sync.

He tried to move, cried out at the white lances of suffering that brutalized him, and finally flopped over in the darkness, his body cushioned by the trash he lay in.

"Pus-licking Gods," he whispered as he fumbled with his good hand, the right one, for his belt pouch. He trembled as he lifted a small hand light and squinted against the glare as he turned it on. He screwed his face into a grimace when he saw the wreckage of his shoulder. Fortunately, the armor had absorbed most of the shot, his half-turned position had saved him a little, and the major blood vessels hadn't been severed.

"Or else you'd have stopped right here, Buck, old buddy." He shined the light around, groaning at the sight of Wheeler's headless corpse. Someone would pay for that. Wheeler had been Targan, guts and fury. Too good to end up in the trash under pus-Rotted Rega.

He was about to turn the light out when he saw the corner of a stack of paper, now spattered with blood. Anatolia's printout. The one she'd die for in order to return it to Sinklar.

Buchman steeled himself, jaws grinding, and sat up. He blinked, fighting the urge to black out. His vision spun as the pain left every nerve shrieking. He wanted to vomit and lie down again. How much simpler to just go ahead and die in the trash.

As his vision wavered, he heard a voice that melted in and out of the roar of the overhead fans. "Hauws?" Buchman called out. "That you, Sergeant?"

"Whore crap! Damn you, shoot! That's an order!" Hauws' voice echoed in the fan; and in Buchman's shredded imagination, he could feel the heavy blaster ripping the air, cooking half of Hauws' face while he propped the heavy gun.

"What now, Sergeant? What do I do?"

The fans hummed in sudden synch overhead, and Hauws spoke in their moan, *"I'm gone. They got me. Just get back! Get our people out! Get back to Sink! Report!"*

Buchman groaned as he nodded and the torn muscles in his shoulders pulled. "Got it, Sergeant. Get back, and report . . . to Sink."

Buchman whimpered as he reached down for the printout, picking it up, seeing the data cube as it tumbled out. With the infinite precision of the wounded, he picked the cube out of the trash and dropped it into his pouch with his good hand. Then he gathered the printout.

Swallowing, he took a deep breath that shot pain through him like a lightning bolt, and staggered to his feet, shoulders braced on the dirty wall to keep from falling.

"Hauws got the job done. So can I." He staggered out into the darkness, teetering on his feet, looking for a way up.

* * *

When the ramp dropped, Mac rose to his feet, staring out at the Regan skyline, lit now by the lights within the arcologies. Overhead, the lights of the vast city created a fluorescent glow in the thick clouds. The acid stink reminded him that he'd come home yet again, and to as uncertain a welcome as last time.

"Ready?" Rysta asked.

"Yeah, be right out on your heels." Mac extended a hand, pulling Chrysla to her feet. He kept his grip, relishing the cool feel of her skin against his with the ardor of a dying man. "I hope I've made the right decision about this."

She smiled up at him, hope and faith in her luminous eyes. "I'm sure you have, Mac. Come, let's go see my son."

He nodded, leading her aft toward the ramp. "You'd better pull that veil down. I wouldn't want any of Sink's people to shoot first and question later."

"Arta Fera's legacy?"

"Yeah, the very same." He took her arm, steadying her as they walked down the ramp. Rysta stood with her Marines while a handful of troops waited at attention. Regulars from the look of them.

"Division First MacRuder? Squadron Commander Braktov?" a Staff Second rapped out smartly. "If you will follow me, Lord Fist is waiting."

Mac glanced uneasily around the rooftop, nodding back at the LC, gratified to see the ramp closing tight as a clamshell. The rooftop landing area of the Ministry of Defense gave him a view of the entire city. Not more than five klicks to the north, the palace gleamed like artistically spun crystal and silver.

"Welcome to Rega."

Chrysla squeezed his arm as he led the way, Rysta falling in behind him with her two Marines. They entered a large lift that dropped them to the top floor. Mac stepped out, looking around. The place bustled, people in uniform obviously working at setting up offices, carting off files, hauling in comm equipment.

The Staff Second gestured. "As you can see, we're pretty busy. There hasn't been much rest around here."

"So I've gathered," Rysta muttered.

They followed the Staff Second down the hallway to an ornate door and stepped inside the office for the Minister of Defense. Mac had become used to the trappings and ornamentation of power; this room, like the others he'd seen, came as little surprise.

"If you will be seated, Lord Fist will be with you in a moment." The Staff Second hesitated, glancing uneasily at Rysta's Marines. "Do you think they're necessary?"

Rysta propped her hands on her hips, "Tell me, office boy, when was the last time you received a Squadron Commander? Get out of here . . . and tell Sinklar to wipe your butt. I think you're leaking."

The Staff Second burned bright red, stifled a rejoinder, and retreated with haste.

"Obnoxious little squirt!" Rysta began to take a turn around the room. "Looks just the same as it did when Mathaiison was here. The main office is back of that door." She scuffed the carpet with a booted toe to produce waves of rippling color. "Huh! Even the same carpet optical program." She walked to the liquor dispenser and drew a crystal glass full of amber liquid, sipping. She smacked her lips, explaining, "Same Myklenian Scotch. You might want to help yourself to a glass. Now that Sassa's taken them, you'll never get another."

Mac walked over to look out through the giant tactite windows. "Well, I guess it's all on the up and up. No one out there looked like they were nervous about anything rude happening."

At that moment, both the office door and the main entrance to the hallway opened, and people filed in. With dispatch, two heavily armed young men leveled shoulder weapons on Rysta's Marines who stood dumbfounded. Other black-clothed agents quickly surrounded them, while one young man deftly closed the door.

Mac started to back toward the window, his hand dropping to his pistol.

"Don't do it," a blonde woman in black warned, her pistol shifting to cover Mac.

Rysta chuckled, an acid irony in her expression. "So it turns out Ily got more than her venomous talons sunk into Sinklar." She glanced at Mac. "Sorry. Guess your faith was a little misplaced about the boy."

"We'll see," Mac grunted, prickles of fear threading

through him as he shot a glance at Chrysla. She stood very still, as if every muscle in her body had tensed.

Mac twitched as the blonde woman stepped close and pulled his pistol from the holster.

Mac asked, "What happened to Sinklar? Is he really Ily's? Or is this just part of the power play?"

The woman retreated, eyes on MacRuder. "The Minister will take that up with you."

"The Minister?" Rysta asked. "You mean Takka."

"Yes, ma'am. Now, if you will each refrain from making any moves, we need to search you. After all, we wouldn't want a missed weapon leading anyone to try anything silly."

Rysta exploded in a series of blistering curses as her Marines were disarmed, and the Internal Security agents relieved her of her use-worn blaster.

Mac started forward as two of the men closed on Chrysla, clearly wary of the veiled woman. Before they could reach her, Chrysla lifted a hand, ordering, "That's close enough."

"And who are you?" the blonde woman asked, her attention now on Chrysla's impenetrable veil.

A soft laugh issued as Chrysla reached up, slim fingers unhooking the veil and pulling it aside. As the shocked security agent backed a step, Chrysla's eyes flashed. "Recognize me?" She stepped forward, reaching out to run gentle fingers along the agent's face. The woman flinched but held her ground. "Yes," Chrysla cooed, "I see you do."

"Lord Fera!" one of the young men gasped. "But I thought. . . ."

Chrysla spun on her heel, a finger darting toward him. "*You* thought? You thought what?"

He swallowed hard, lifting his hands, heedless of the weapon he carried. "I . . . nothing. Just that you were gone. Spaced for. . . ."

"Go on."

"Nothing! I mean, just the rumors."

"Tell me," Chrysla ordered imperiously as she closed on the man like a hungry predator.

"To abduct Skyla Lyma, Lord Fera. It was just a rumor."

As Mac stared in disbelief, Chrysla's face contorted. "You have a very bad habit." She smiled wickedly. "But I won't deal with it." The young man gulped his relief. Then Chrysla said, "I'll let Ily handle her own discipline."

The young man turned pale and began to shake.

Chrysla spun on her heel, bearing down on the blonde woman. "Very well. I'm sure Ily's waiting. You, accompany me and the prisoners." She started for the ornate doorway.

"Excuse me, Lord Fera, but the lift to the basement is back this way." The blonde pointed toward the inner door.

Chrysla turned and bore down on the woman, amber eyes burning. "Perhaps it never occurred to you, but the LC is faster—and just maybe I have *need* of it and the evidence inside it." Her voice turned to ice. "Do you understand? Or are you another discipline problem . . . one *I* might want to deal with myself?"

"I understand, Lord Fera. To the LC!" The blonde woman had pulled herself to attention, but the corners of her lips twitched and desperation glazed her eyes.

Chrysla lifted Mac's pistol from the woman's nerveless hand and nodded toward the door. "After the rest of you."

Heart pounding, Mac started forward, and practically jumped as he passed Chrysla, seeing the terror that lurked just behind her facade.

The long march down the hallway left his scalp tingling. He crowded into the lift with a stone-faced Rysta, Blonde and one of her cronies, and finally Chrysla. The brief ride to the roof was marred only by the pounding of Mac's heart.

He stepped out, relief like a tonic at the sight of the LC.

"You and you, come with me," Chrysla pointed to Blonde and the young man who carried Rysta's pistol. She turned as the next batch of security agents rose on the lift, the ashen-faced young agent among them. Chrysla pointed at the man. "The rest of you, escort him back to Ily, and tell her *exactly* what happened."

Salutes were snapped with acute detail to performance, although the young man in question began to tremble as his nerve deserted him.

Meanwhile, Mac slapped the hatch control, his mouth gone dry with the strain. He climbed inside, every muscle powered by adrenaline.

Rysta and her Marines entered warily, attention shifting between their guard and the hard-eyed Chrysla. Once inside, Chrysla slapped the control and the ramp slipped shut. She walked forward, eyes on the blonde officer. "You're a very talented young woman. But I wonder if perhaps you've lost the ability to think for yourself. It's a failing, you see."

And with that, Chrysla plucked the woman's pistol from her belt, stepped back, and covered the young man who held Rysta's weapon. "Tables are turned. If you move, I'll kill you without the slightest hesitation."

Mac stepped forward and took his weapon from Chrysla's hand, making sure to keep the agents covered, an apologetic smile on his face. "Sorry, folks."

Rysta growled under her breath as she retrieved her own weapon from the other agent's unresisting hand. At her signal, the Marines were on both of them like hungry hounds, patting them down, turning up all kinds of curious equipment.

"Pilot?" Rysta called to the comm, "Get us the hell out of here!"

Mac dropped to where Chrysla sat on the bench, her bravado gone. She shook as he put a comforting arm around her. "Come on. We've got to get you forward. Maybe get a cup of stassa into you."

"If one of them even twitches," Rysta ordered the Marines, "Blow a hand off. If they twitch again, blow a leg."

"Yes, ma'am!"

Mac helped Chrysla, supporting her with one arm as the LC rose. He got her into the command center, sliding her down on the bench.

"Now what?" Rysta asked as she ducked in behind Mac.

"Beats me." He looked at Chrysla who gave him a weak smile. "But I think we owe you an awful lot."

"How'd you do that?" Rysta asked as she pulled a cup of hot stassa from the dispenser. "You left me flat-jawed amazed!"

Chrysla took the stassa Rysta handed her and shook her head. "Mac said Arta Fera was my opposite. I just acted cruel, let myself believe it. I had to gamble. I . . . I couldn't let myself be taken again. Not to undergo that. . . ."

Mac exhaled, trying to unwind. "Yeah, well, we've got a ship, a Section, and who knows what else, because Ily's got the rest."

"We got any Mytol in here?" Rysta ran a hand over her face. "Back yonder we've got two sources of information. I suggest we wring them out before Ily figures out what went wrong."

Mac dropped into the command center chair and settled the headset over his skull. He fiddled with the knobs, and called: "Attention, First Targan. This is Mac. First Targan Division, respond."

The comm crackled static, then a deep voice, obviously Shik's, returned, "Situation Targa. Repeat, code Targa."

"Affirmative, Targa. Communications through LOS to *Gyton*. We'll be in touch."

"Roger. Out."

Mac puffed a sigh. "We're not the only ones left. We'll need to get back to the ship. From there, we can locate Shik. See what's left before we bust heads." He glanced uneasily at Rysta. "We could be talking about civil war."

The Commander's expression hardened. "If we have enough of the army, Mac. Otherwise, Blessed Gods help us."

* * *

Six hundred and twenty-five.

Six hundred and twenty-six.

Six hundred and twenty-seven.

Skyla lay on her back, counting angles in her sleeping quarters. Angles could be found everywhere, in the mating of wall panel to wall panel, in the ceiling tiles, in the molding around the doorway. Angles, some hidden, others blatant.

She could feel the yacht with a spacer's finely tuned awareness as it shifted, inertia playing the eternal games with mass and energy.

Don't think about it.

Six hundred and twenty-eight.

A thump sounded from somewhere forward. The hum of the air-conditioning changed slightly.

Six hundred and twenty-nine.

The compensators for the artificial gravity adjusted, the coordinated pull reaching through Skyla to claw dully at her concentration.

Six hundred and thirty.

The angles were becoming more difficult to find. If only she could move, sit up. More angles would be exposed to her darting gaze. The EM restraints prohibited that. She had to lie here, stretched out like a piece of meat.

That's all I am. A piece of meat. Thinking that triggered the memories. Here on this bed. Auburn hair twining with pale blonde, soft skin pressing against hers.

Don't think about it. Count!

Where had all the angles gone? Her frantic search retraced the old pathways, hating the delicate scrollwork of the filigree, all inlaid with exquisite curls and curves. No angles there. But if she craned her neck, she could see the hidden cubbyhole, mocking now of her failed attempt at freedom.

Six hundred and thirty-one.

Six hundred and thirty-two.

She made it up to six hundred and forty-three before she exhausted the angles.

The yacht jerked and rocked, the dull clang of grapples carried through the hull and to her bed.

Horror tried to etch her control with acid breath.

Count! Rot you, count! Arta will protect you.

It hadn't been that bad. Skyla had just turned her mind off, following the patterns of movement she'd passively absorbed over the years. She remembered Arta's tongue darting across hers, demanding. A kiss was a kiss, just as hungry and probing.

Don't think about it! Count!

Where had all the angles gone? Sometimes they hid with a great deal of cunning, an angle within another, especially in molding. Had she counted them all?

The air changed, the yacht hooked into the umbilical of the Regan Orbital Terminals. How many precious minutes remained?

Count!

Would Arta fulfill her promise?

I earned my protection. I earned it well, Arta. I should have recorded your moans, the undulations of your body. The final defeat haunted her. It hadn't been so bad. Not physically. Under other circumstances, she might have enjoyed it—but for the defeat it represented, and the desperation in her actions.

I get to at least wear my uniform, don't I, Arta?

She clamped her jaw to keep it from trembling, a solitary tear breaking loose to creep down the side of her head and lose itself in her hair which was matted thickly beneath her.

Six hundred and forty-four.

Six hundred and forty-five. . . .

She found sixteen more angles in a data cube on the desk. She could imagine the angles on the far side, but they weren't legitimate to count. Angles had to be *seen*.

Ily waited down there. Closing her eyes, Skyla could imagine Minister Takka, black eyes wide with anticipation, her sleek black hair gleaming.

We've shared a great deal, Ily. Hatred, desire for Staffa, and now, we have Fera between us. Which will she choose? You, or me? You who dominate? Or me, who has been dominated?

Skyla closed her eyes, slowly shaking her head as she whispered, "Staffa, oh, how I've failed you. I tried to die for you, for all you're struggling to achieve." But nothing was left now. Only the husk of Skyla Lyma.

She heard the steady tread of Arta's padded feet in the hallway, but didn't open her eyes. To look was to know. How much better to lie here, to pretend that none of it existed, if only for these last couple of seconds.

The EM restraints suddenly slipped free. Still Skyla refused to move, to retreat from the fantasy of disbelief.

"Skyla? We're docked. Get up."

No. Let me lie here, pretend none of it ever happened.

Fabric rustled and something slapped down on the bedding beside Skyla. Fera called, "There's your uniform. Get dressed. We're due down planet. Would have been early except for a proximity alert. Some Rotted freighter outside of its designated approach."

Skyla reached down, her fearing fingers touching the slick weave of her armor. She sucked at her lip with relief. Her last shred of dignity would be preserved, even as Ily pried betrayal from her mind.

"I said, get up," Fera reminded. "I'll do everything I can to protect you. I promised."

Skyla opened her eyes. Arta stared down, an unfeigned concern in her eyes. Her full lips curled in a futile attempt to smile. "It was the collar, you know. If it hadn't been for that, I never would have won."

Skyla nodded, all of her guts gone hollow as she fingered the tough fabric of her uniform. There were no more angles to count.

* * *

The command center of the LC couldn't have held another human being. The commanders had been packed in, shoulder to shoulder. Shiksta, Dion Axel, Rysta, and Section Firsts from the First Targan, including Boyz, Beeman, and the others except for Buchman. Mac stood, half-propped against the bulkhead. The air had gone slightly stale, heavy with the odor of too many human bodies and a tangible sense of desperation. But then, did anyone precipitate civil holocaust without second thoughts? And worse, all knew the cunning of the enemy they now faced.

Shiksta, his big body wedged into the back of the booth, braced his elbows as he glanced back and forth. "Shall we get started?"

Rysta clasped her hands togethers. "Might as well. Here's the situation, people. Ily's taken over. She showed no scruples when it came to executing Tedor and his Deputies, and she won't blink twice over killing Sinklar and the rest of us. Some of you may have questions about my loyalties in this matter, and to be honest, I'm old style military. But times have changed and as much as I might resent that, I can't stop it. What I can do is pick the side that I think is the best for the people and the Empire. After that, I have a voice to try and shape the future as I see fit. I will *not* have that voice with Ily Takka, and further, I'd rather live under Sinklar Fist's rule than hers." Rysta grinned then, a glint in her eye. "Besides, as Mac learned during our last mission, you young kids need someone with a little experience before you go off half-cocked. I'm one of the oldest warhorses around."

Axel cleared her throat. "My position is much the same as Rysta's. I'm a Regan veteran and most of you know my record. Quite honestly, it hurt to be pulled from command, not just once but twice. After being humbled through that process, I began to reevaluate not just the role of our military, but our political system. Tedor may not have been a saint among men, and looking back, he was poor MD, but after Tybalt's assassination—at Ily's hand—I'm sure, we need to fix our government." Dion studied the intent faces around the table. "And I can tell you, this supposed reorganization to grant control to Mykroft is—"

"Terguzzi sumpshit," Mac barked, his anger piqued. "I helped pull the rung from under him on Targa. The man's an idiot."

"But he's learned the tactics," Dion countered. "That's who we've run the last exercises against, and he finally won one against Ayms and me."

Mac shook his head with finality. "Ily can fool herself about his capabilities if she likes. I've seen him in the field. He doesn't have the sense the Blessed Gods gave a brick."

"Pus-Rotted right!" Boyz chimed in.

Rysta raised a hand. "I think we're pretty much agreed that Ily must be stopped. The question is, what do we do about it? If anyone but Mykroft had been appointed, the loyal Divisions would already have been withdrawn and scattered to defang them. Eventually, Ily will discover Mykroft has omitted this detail and we'll be neutralized one way or another."

"We have to act now," Mac stated simply. "Our Divisions are the elite. Every moment we spend talking, our window of opportunity is shrinking."

"Right," Shik agreed with a bulldog nod. "Ily's got Sink in that damned Ministry. She's got Kap and Mayz and Ayms. She took our people. I say we go bust them out—now! Before it's too late." Jaw muscles bunched under his smooth black skin. "Sinklar never let any of us down. We *owe* him."

"How quickly can we organize? We'll have to take the Ministry by means of a full frontal assault." Rysta's eyes slitted as she stared at an imaginary point above Mac's head.

"And we've got to have cover," Mac added. "Let's say we send the First Targan into the Ministry. Our other Divisions have to take defensive positions. Mykroft is going to throw something against us."

Dion lifted a finger. "Shik and I will handle that. We can throw up a protective cordon around the main assault based on the hunter-killer teams you used in Vespa."

Rysta exhaled wearily. "Now, we're talking civilian casualties."

Dion's stare hardened. "We're talking civil war, Commander. We're going to split the military right down the center. The Blessed Gods alone know which Divisions will come with us. It could break down to Sections going or staying, maybe even Groups turning on each other."

"And what about the fleet?" Mac directed his question to Rysta. "That's another big unknown. Will Mykroft be able to call down Orbital? Will I?"

Rysta spread her hands. "My guess, based on nothing more than gut intuition, is that most Squadron Commanders will do their best to duck the issue at first. We all know what kind of casualties will pile up if we use orbital bombardment. The Commanders will stall, claiming they need authorization, and hoping the matter is solved on the ground so they don't have to make a decision and can side with the winning party in the end."

"And if it's a prolonged fight?" Shik asked.

"Then we can pretty much count on Commanders siding with the Divisions they have ties with."

Mac shifted uncomfortably. "All right, that's the situation. Now, let's get down to the fine details." Mac glanced at the comm. "It's 15:35 hours. I want our people in position by 05:30. Can we do that?"

Rysta glanced at Dion who was doing some quick mental calculations, a frown lining her forehead. Finally she nodded. "Yes, barely."

"Then let's get to work. I'll take the First Targan into the Ministry of Internal Security at 06:00."

Shik rapped his fingers on tabletop. "I'll have the ordnance to support that strike. First thing, I'll punch some holes in the roof, then I'm leveling the Ministry of Defense Building. Who knows, we might get lucky and tag Mykroft in the process."

Dion lowered her head. "You know, when this cuts loose, we may be unleashing a disaster which will destroy us all. We could be starting something we'll never finish."

Mac rubbed his hands together nervously. "But what choice do we have?"

*   *   *

MilComCen/Acting Order 15436
5779:17:23:16:30 Hours
Authorization M14R.223
Subject: Military Ball in Honor of First Marshal Mykroft

Attention: All personnel.

Squadron Commanders, Division Firsts, and *all* Staff Officers, Grade First through Third, are invited to attend the First Marshal's Ball to be held in the auditorium of the Ministry of Defense in honor of the decorated appointment and promotion of First Marshal Mykroft and Deputy Marshals: Sampson Henck, Tie Arnson, and Adam Rick to the command and control of the Regan Military.

Formal Dress will be required as described in the Military Field Manual of Operations.

Officers are encouraged to invite spouses or other suitable guests for this gala occasion.

The reception line will form beginning at 17:24:18:00 hours. Gifts are encouraged, and may represent the donor's respect and regards should he be unable to attend on such short notice.

Questions or requests for further information should be directed to the Staff First: Operations: Ministry of Defense.

APD/QS1
Sec/JDL/mkft.

CHAPTER XXXI

Ily tapped at her teeth as she studied the naked woman strapped into the chair in the interrogation room. Anatolia Daviura stared up at her with pliant, drugged eyes. Her pale skin prickled from the chill.

Comm buzzed and Ily leaned over and pressed a stud on the wall comm. "Yes?"

"It's Arta. I'm on my way down with the Wing Commander."

Ily considered, feeling weary to the roots of her soul. Lyma would take a lot of time. "Bring her to interrogation and prepare her for me. I'll wrap up here and attend to some things in my office. Meet me there when you're done. It's going to be a long interrogation."

"I look forward to it."

I'm sure you do. "See you then." Ily cut the comm and turned. "Anatolia. We'll have to continue this discussion later."

Ily palmed the door to the control room. Professor Adam sat hunched over his comm terminal, replaying parts of the testimony that Ily had allowed him to hear. He forced himself to look up, stating, "I still can't believe it's real! I need a specimen, nothing more than a skin sample. A bit of tissue. This is incredible!"

Ily raised an eyebrow. "All in time, Professor. You've heard Anatolia's testimony. In your professional opinion, would you say that Sinklar Fist is a monster?"

"Monster? Well, I'd. . . . But then, he's not exactly a normal human being. Fist defies simple categorization. Now, based upon the definition of a species, is he fertile? Could he produce a viable offspring? You see, with humans we have. . . ."

"But he is an artifact?"

"The offspring of an artifact—a constructed human being."

Pieces began to click into place. *I have the lever I need now, Sinklar. You're mine now.* "Thank you, Professor. It seems that you've done the Empire a great favor—and discovered an inhuman creature before it could gain control of humanity for its own perverted purposes."

Flushed with triumph, she turned to the comm again. "Gysell? Return Daviura to Fist's quarters and prepare for the Wing Commander."

"Yes, Ily."

So much to do. Ily stepped into the corridor beyond and walked toward the lift that would carry her to her office. The details of government hadn't gone away, and while she now had the means to destroy Sinklar, it would be a very long night with Lyma in the chair.

* * *

When the door opened, Sinklar leapt to his feet. Two of the security personnel looked in, checked to see where he was, and pushed the door open wide. From the glance Sinklar got of the hallway, he could see more security as Anatolia walked forward, supported on both sides by guards who held her elbows.

Anatolia carried her clothing, and had only a light blue blanket wrapped around her shoulders.

Sinklar swallowed hard, stepping forward to support her. She reeled, almost falling, as he pulled her to him, demanding, "What have you done? Rot you, *what did you do to her?*"

One of the guards smiled in arrogant amusement and gave Sinklar a flippant salute before he pulled the door closed with a final click.

Anatolia shivered in his arms as he held her and ran gentle fingers through her hair. "There, it's all right. You're safe for the moment. What did they do? You're freezing."

"They asked me questions," she replied simply.

"About what?"

"About you. About genetics."

"Who asked?"

"Ily."

Sinklar lifted her chin, staring into her dilated eyes. "They used Mytol?"

"Yes."

He half carried her back to the sleeping quarters. The place didn't even have a platform, just a spongy pallet on the floor with a toilet and shower to one side—not that the shower would help warm her; it only ran cold water.

Sinklar lowered her with care, blushing as the blanket fell away. Anatolia seemed unaware of it, lost in a drug-induced haze. Half terrified of what he'd find, Sinklar inspected her, relieved that she seemed unharmed but for the drug.

"What are you doing?" she asked as he stood.

"Going to get your clothes. You're shivering." He paused. "They didn't hurt you?"

"No."

He sighed in relief as he went for her clothes.

She'd sprawled on her side by the time he returned.

Sinklar shot a hate-filled glance up at the security cam that constantly monitored them. "Anatolia, you've got to help me. We've got to get you dressed and warmed up."

Somehow they managed to get her covered and Sinklar rolled the two of them into the blanket, pressing himself to her, using his heat to warm her.

"What did Ily ask about? Start from the beginning."

"She asked how we met and I told her. I told her about how strange you had seemed, wanting to see your parents and about how you'd looked at them. I told her about the sample I took, and the research I was conducting. She didn't seem to understand that your father couldn't have existed. I kept trying to ex-

plain that the genotype was unknown—that it didn't
fit any known human pattern."

"How did she react to that?"

"She tried very hard to understand what it meant,
but even I don't know."

"What else did she ask?"

"About when I was in the street. Where I went,
what I did. I told her how I survived . . . about
Mickey chasing me into the cul-de-sac and trying to
rape me. I told her about gouging his eyes out and
beating him until I fractured his skull and killed him.
I told her how it was to live in the darkness. About
how I had to do it again with Buchman and Wheeler
when her goons came after me, and about the
printout."

"You mean, where you left it?"

"I had to tell her. It's the Mytol, it makes—"

"I know. What else?"

"She asked about you. What you planned. I didn't
know very much about that, so I couldn't tell her
much. She asked what you thought of her and I told
her."

"How did she take that?"

"When I said you hated her, she didn't seem to
mind at all."

Sinklar winced. "Did she ask anything else about
me?"

"She asked if you loved me. I told her that I didn't
know. She asked if I knew she'd had sex with you and
I said yes. She asked what I thought of that. I told
her it surprised me that you hadn't had more sense."

Sinklar winced. "Was that all?"

"No. She asked if we were lovers. I told her no,
that we were only friends for the moment."

"For the moment?"

"Things could change, Sinklar. I like you a great
deal. I might even come to love you with all of my
heart, but I can't trust you. I don't know what you
are . . . who you are. You have the makings of great-
ness about you . . . and a terrible tragedy. How can
I allow myself to love a man like that? I don't know

if I'll be alive tomorrow, let alone next week. How can I trust you when I don't know what you are? What you will do?"

"I don't know, Anatolia. I don't know." He steeled himself. "Then what happened?"

"Ily got a call on the monitor. The voice said that Arta Fera was on her way down with the Wing Commander and would arrive in a short time. Ily replied that she had some things to attend to in her office, that it would be a long night, more likely a couple of long days and Gysell would have to run things. Then she told me we'd talk again later and walked out."

"Rotted Gods. Ily, you fool."

"What?"

"Nothing. Rest now. The Mytol will wear off soon."

Sinklar stared up at the featureless ceiling. *Staffa, if you're out there, blast this building first.*

* * *

"It's about time," Ily greeted as she got up from behind her office desk, walking around to embrace Arta and kiss her soundly. She pushed the woman back, inspecting her. "You look little the worse for wear. The Wing Commander is taken care of?"

"In one of the interrogation rooms." Arta pulled Ily close, hugging her. "I would have been in sooner, but we almost had a collision with a freighter. The proximity warning went off and I had a mad scramble to adjust the vector. We missed by a good four kilometers, but at that speed, I would have come to Rega as plasma."

Ily pushed back and frowned. "Orbital Control didn't have the freighter plotted? Didn't send you a course advisory?"

"I didn't know they were supposed to."

Ily broke away, moving to her desk. "That's standard procedure. This freighter, wasn't it broadcasting a position statement?"

"Ily," Arta reminded, "I'm new at this piloting business."

Ily pressed her comm button. "Gysell, get in touch with Orbital Traffic Control. They've got a freighter out there in one of the traffic lanes. Tell them to clean up their act or I'll put someone in charge who can run the agency efficiently."

"Yes, Minister. Anything else?"

"Is Wing Commander Lyma prepared?"

"She's just the way Arta left her, and as we were instructed to treat her."

Ily glanced at Fera, seeing a nod of confirmation.

"Thank you, Gysell, that will be all." She killed the comm and looked up. "Generally I like my subjects stripped, cold, and very uncomfortable before I run an interrogation."

Fera crossed her arms. "Why don't we talk about Skyla on the way down to her room?"

"Very well." Ily started for the lift. "I had an interesting report. Some of my security people claim you walked off with MacRuder, Commander Braktov, and two of my security people. Do you know anything about that? I checked. You were still in a parking orbit at the time."

"You're sure they thought it was me?"

"Rotted right they were sure—at least they believed it. Let's put it this way, Mytol doesn't lie."

"What does it mean?"

"I'm not sure, but what I do know is that Mac, Rysta, and Shiksta have slipped through my net for now. I've tightened security around the building. I've also got a call in for Mykroft to contact me as soon as possible. I want him to be ready to stomp out a revolt if one flares."

"Do you expect one?"

Ily lifted her hands. "I don't know. Should I? What happened between Skyla and you? I don't know what your game is, Arta, but she's mine until I wring every last drop of information out of her brain."

Arta slapped the controls that sent them rocketing down. "I have no problem with that."

"Then why didn't you prepare her? I've been waiting for a long time to take her apart—an old grudge. You haven't developed a soft spot, have you?"

"I think you'll find she's been masterfully prepared." Arta led the way out of the lift as it opened on a subbasement hallway. "She's resigned to her fate, Ily. You'll have little trouble with her. And in answer to your question, I want her when you're done with her. I want her in one piece, whole, and with her mind intact."

Ily shot her a curious glance. "Why?"

"Because she fascinates me. We fought, she and I, each plotting, battling, matching wits. She almost won, Ily. She came very close— within fractions of a second of beating me time and again. I want to see how long she can keep it up."

"She may be completely broken by the time I'm done with her," Ily reminded. "I've seen them just give up, become dead meat. Any spark whatsoever gone, an extinguished personality."

"That is a risk Skyla must take." Arta frowned. "But I'll wager you she hangs on."

They walked down a long hallway, arms linked. Ily asked, "Do you love her?"

"Yes. But it's different than the way I love you. I love Skyla as a challenge. I love you as a partner. She's a powerful woman, perhaps more powerful than you are."

Ily examined Fera closely, then warned, "Be careful, Arta."

At the door to the interrogation room, Arta turned, excitement in her eyes. "Ily, ask yourself, do you really want me to fawn and tremble in your presence like all the rest do? Or has the power gone to your head until you think of yourself in the same manner the Sassan God thinks of himself? We've had this discussion before. You and I, we have different goals in life. Yours is to control and govern. Mine is for a different challenge, that of excitement. Prudence isn't in my personality. How do you want me?"

Ily nodded, reassured. "I've missed you, Arta. Very well, keep your Skyla." *If she lives through this*. Ily

palmed the lock plate and stepped inside. She glanced
up at the monitors in the control room where they
recorded Skyla's nervous pacing about the solitary
chair in the center of the featureless gray concrete
room.

The technicians sat at the monitors waiting, their
instruments dead until the subject could be hooked
up.

Ily gestured to Arta. "Stay here. This is better done
between me and her."

"You'll need this." Arta handed Ily the collar
control.

Ily took a moment to strap it to her wrist, running
through the calibration process as the device coded
her brain waves. Then Ily stepped into the room.
Skyla spun, a wild fear in her eyes as she dropped to
a combat stance.

Ily gazed levelly at her and said, "It's been a long
time since Itreata."

Skyla's every movement indicated that she bordered
on losing control. "I should have killed you when I
had the chance."

Ily nodded. "We all make mistakes, Wing Commander. It seems this is my night for interrogations.
I just pried the most fascinating information out of
Sinklar Fist's girlfriend. And now I have you. Arta
treated you well, I see. Curious, you've earned her
respect—a feat not many could have accomplished."

"You can still let me go . . . save yourself."

Ily laughed, delighted that so much spirit remained.
"Indeed? Save myself from what?"

"Staffa—and the Companions."

Ily walked around to take a position opposite Skyla.
"Things have changed in Free Space while you've
been in transit. Sinklar broke the back of the Sassan
Empire with one fell blow. Staffa will have a choice.
He can deal with me, or I'll destroy him. I've got the
means now, a strategy that will work."

Skyla's lips twitched. "You seem pretty sure of
yourself."

The memory of Staffa's burning gray eyes haunted

Ily. "Yes, and I'll be even more sure when I've finished my little discussion with you."

"He'll kill you, Ily. You'll be a ruler, all right. Your empire will consist of rubble, radiation, and corpses."

"That is exactly what we shall see." Ily smiled. "Now, you have a choice to make. My instruments can't read your involuntary responses through armor. You may undress, or I'll use the collar and have my technicians strip you while you're senseless."

Skyla tensed. Ily lifted an eyebrow in anticipation of triggering the collar, of bringing her enemy low.

Then, slowly, Skyla reached up, undoing the armor snap by snap. With fastidious care, she peeled the material off, kicking it into the corner.

Ily watched as Skyla's skin reacted to the cold air, her nipples tightening. Lyma was a handsome woman, muscular, full-breasted. The long scars that accented that alabaster flesh added an exotic allure.

"Shall we begin?" Ily gestured to the chair.

Skyla's stomach spasmed, and her face contorted, as if she were fighting desperately to keep from breaking down into sobs. The hard glitter of desperation animated those tortured eyes, and then she settled wearily into the chair, desolation in the slump of her shoulders.

Ily drew the straps tight with practiced ease. She stepped over to the tray, picking up the tube of Mytol, slipping it past Skyla's tightly-pressed lips, and along her clamped teeth.

"Drink," Ily ordered. "If you don't, I can always run the tube down your throat. I realize that you're going to be a tough one to break, despite the drug. It may take a while, Skyla, but with Mytol and some other drugs, and cold, and time . . . and perhaps a little pain, you will break."

Skyla sucked at the Mytol. Then Ily fastened the patches to Lyma's goose-bumped flesh.

"Now then," Ily began triumphantly. "We'll begin with your name. Then bit by bit, as your resistance erodes, you will tell me everything about Itreata, about their security, and about how I can lure Staffa kar Therma into my hands."

This time, Skyla couldn't stop the tears that crept down her cheeks.

*   *   *

"How are we doing?" Mac asked, as he glanced over his shoulder at the comm. The time showed 04:30. He bent over Axel's shoulder, where she studied the plots moving on the scaled-down situation board they'd projected onto the table.

Dion arched her back, twisting as she grimaced. "Looks like we're in pretty good shape. Most of the disengagement is proceeding smoothly. I'm just surprised we haven't been challenged by now."

Mac yawned, blinking out of fatigue. "Who's going to challenge? You've been running exercises for so long troop movements in the middle of the night should be routine."

She cocked her head, a wry look in her brown eyes. "Really? You mean to tell me if you were camped out there, and the Division next door started pulling out, you wouldn't be on the horn to Sinklar to find out why?"

"Of course I would. How else would I get the jump on the situation."

Dion steepled her fingers thoughtfully. "And that's just why Mykroft can't be left in command. Ily should have chosen better."

"What about the other Divisions? Any feeling as to how many will go with us?"

Dion shook her head, expression gloomy. "Can't call it yet, Mac. Maybe a third. I wouldn't count on any more than that."

"Then it's Targa all over again."

Axel kicked her legs out under the table, crossing her ankles. "I'm starting to wish I'd never heard that word."

"Yeah, well, some of us have been living it for so long we can't think any other way." He glanced at the clock again. "I'm going to head out of here, get to my LC, and join up with my Division." He stuck out a hand. "If we never see each other again, it's been real short, but a definite pleasure. I'm glad you're on our side."

She took his hand, a warm smile on her lips. "See you on the other side."

"The other side?"

She laughed. "I keep forgetting. You Targans never learned the clichés of command. That means we part as friends—no matter how it works out."

"The dance of the quanta."

"You've been listening to the Seddi?"

"Beats getting shot at. Good luck, Dion." He ducked out of the command control and started back between the empty benches. Chrysla stood at the ramp, one hand on the molding, as she stared out into the Regan night. In the distance, LCs shrilled as they lifted, redeploying troops into the center of the city.

"All set?" she asked as Mac stopped beside her. In the muted city lights, her glossy hair shimmered. Now, of all times, he wanted to reach out and draw her close, to feel her pressed against him in these last moments.

"Guess so. Want to walk over to your LC?" He started down the ramp, feeling the chill settle into his bones as his breath clouded.

She paced beside him, the hitch in her limp barely noticeable. "My LC?"

He glanced up at the high clouds that lay between him and the fleet. "I'm shipping you up to Rysta. You'll be safer aboard *Gyton*."

She stopped short, reaching out a hand to halt him. "Mac, don't do this."

He spread his arms, the lights gleaming on his armor. "Chrysla, we're about to launch a civil war here. If things go wrong, we're facing a bloodbath. I don't want you anywhere around. I can't afford to worry about you. Trust me, ship up to *Gyton*. If things really go sour, maybe Rysta can slip away, find sanctuary with the Companions." He took her hands.

"Don't you see? It's your trip home. There's nothing for you here. Only war and death. More suffering."

"My son is here. Mac, listen to me. Please! All of my life, I've been dependent on someone else's protection—until yesterday when I acted on my own to protect others. Don't you see? I've been a delicate toy. A sexy pawn—and I'm tired of it. Taking chances, fighting for what you believe, is all right for you and Rysta and my son—but not for me?"

He shook his head. "You can't forget who you are."

"No, I can't," she answered sharply. "And maybe that makes it more important that I accept some responsibility in this fight. Staffa's wife, fighting at your side, is worth something, symbolically and personally."

He hung his head. *How do I tell her?* "Chrysla, will you do this for me? You once said you were indebted to me. That you owed me. I'm calling in that debt. Take the LC up to *Gyton*. You can serve me best by being safe."

She stepped close, her scent filling his nostrils. With cold fingers, she lifted his chin, staring into his shadowed eyes. He fought the urge to tremble at her touch.

"Mac, I can't. You're very noble, and I think your infatuation with me has clouded your reason. I am indebted to you, but would you ask my soul of me? Would you ask me to betray myself? And in doing so, all those ideals which kept me alive through the long years?"

He hugged her close, his heart pounding. She squirmed in his grip and, filled with shame, he let his arms drop, whispering, "I'm sorry."

She placed a hand on his shoulder. "It's all right. We're all nervous, strained to breaking. Sometimes, when things seem the most desperate, we all need to cling to someone. It's a human characteristic, that desire to be held, to touch. You just crushed the breath out of me. Come on. We're almost out of time, Mac. Let's go. We've got a war to win."

"I can't talk you out of this?"

"No. And ask yourself, Mac. In your heart, would you really want to?"

* * *

The columns of figures on the monitor mocked them all, but somewhere, there had to be a key. Myles tapped his jewel encrusted fingers as he stared at the monitor in his office. Beyond, through the tactite window, the gilded spires of the Capitol mocked him and everything he was trying so desperately to accomplish.

"Perhaps confiscating two percent of the production from Malbourne?" Hyros asked, a frown eating at his normally composed expression.

"Too dangerous. Malbourne is already overextended. We took three percent for the Myklenian invasion. They teetered on the verge of revolt then, and were only pacified when told that the drain on their income was temporary."

"Right," Jakre agreed. "And we don't have the manpower to enforce a confiscation. They'd have to contribute voluntarily."

"And by doing so, the farmers on Malbourne would suffer famine—a double bind that would create more problems than it would solve."

The three of them retreated to the endless game of staring at the monitor.

In the name of the quanta, Myles told himself yet again, *there are only so many ways to divide the remaining resources. You can't pour a gallon and a half of milk from a one gallon bucket.*

"We can't do it. Someone is going to die—just with what we have left. And that fat fool wants to launch a military strike? We have to tell him something, Myles. If we don't, we're arrested, and someone else will take this over . . . someone who doesn't have your magic for conjuring something from nothing." Jakre stood then, walking over to stare at the palace through weary eyes. "I'm sorry I doubted you in the past, Myles. You warned us. Staffa warned us. It was sheer arrogance."

"That is behind us," Myles replied. *Think! When you have one too many mouths to feed, what do you do?* He immersed himself in the rows and rows of figures: production and consumption—with a slight correction for transportation in the middle of the equation.

"We need another pie," he stated angrily. "That would solve everything. We could ship all of our stock and feed everyone . . . if we just had another storehouse to draw from until Imperial Sassa recovers from the fallout."

"The problem with that, Legate, is that the only other pie belongs to the Regans," Hyros reminded.

Myles stiffened. "Yes, it does." He turned to the comm, ordering, "Initiate secondary distribution program 1-7732."

Comm responded. "Do you wish to authorize initiation?"

"I do."

"What are you doing?" Jakre asked.

Myles looked up, relief and desperation intertwining like ill-begotten lovers in his soul. "I can't tell you the details, Iban. But I may be able to produce another pie." He glanced at Hyros. "And now that I've committed myself to magic, I'm going home and going to sleep."

"And what do I tell His Holiness?" Iban asked.

"Nothing . . . until I'm rested. Make something up, if you must, but perhaps another miracle will occur in the meantime." Myles stood, so tired he could barely keep from weaving. "Hyros? Do you have anything planned?"

Hyros stared skeptically at the monitor where numbers were shuffling as the program orders changed the statistics. "No, Myles. You've left me completely baffled."

He took his aide's hand, heading for the door, calling over his shoulder, "Iban, if anything comes up, call me immediately."

"Have a good rest, Myles. You, too, Hyros." Iban still stood, staring anxiously at the palace.

* * *

How long he slept, Myles never knew. He came blearily awake, the buzz of the comm driving away the last hope of sleep. Myles reached over and killed the buzzer, Hyros stirring at his movement. He blinked, rolled to a sitting position, and called, "Yes?"

The bedside comm flashed to life, Iban Jakre's stiff face filling the monitor. Jakre appeared both relieved and concerned. "Myles, your *miracle* occurred. We've got two Companion warships that just dropped out of null singularity. I've just been in contact with them." Jakre's eyebrows lifted. "Our 'orders' are that we are to take no retaliatory action against Rega. And further, they are here to 'protect' us from any further Regan military strikes."

Myles smiled, feeling the tension drain out of him. "Wonderful. Now, Iban, you can go back to your home and get some sleep yourself."

Jakre's long face looked dour. "Myles, you didn't. . . . I mean, you weren't planning on this, were you?"

"How could you think that? Get some sleep, Iban. We'll discuss it when we're both rested—and if His Holiness complains, tell him to take it to Staffa."

Myles killed the connection and flopped back with his arms spread wide in a soaring feeling of freedom.

"You've been up to your neck in this, haven't you?" Hyros asked, as he propped himself on his elbows.

Myles glanced at his lover and shrugged it off. "You've been listening to those Seddi broadcasts, haven't you? The ones about taking responsibility? About building a new epistemology?"

Hyros nodded. "Is that why you've been so different?"

"Among other reasons. Now why don't we get some sleep. If the Companions are overhead, a great many things are about to happen—and it will probably be a long time before we get to sleep again."

Hyros gave him a wry smile. "Maybe I'll get up,

get dressed, and ask for a transfer to some department that isn't as demanding on my schedule. And you can find another lover—one who has time to sleep."

Myles experienced a stitch of resentment. "If you wish. But you're a very bright young man. I wish you'd stay."

Hyros laughed and punched him in the shoulder. "That was a joke, Myles."

They curled together, Myles drifting off to sleep to the lull of Hyros' heartbeat. In the half-aware state of slumber, the growing roar didn't register as it built. The crescendo came when the first wrenching shock hit the building. Myles had no more than jerked upright when the sleeping platform wrenched out from the wall, spilling them into a pile on the floor.

Then the tactite shattered, as the building cracked and swayed.

"What the. . . ." Hyros cried.

"Earthquake!" Myles bellowed as he tried to untangle himself. Then one of the roof supports fell.

* * *

"The rules which determine victory and defeat are really very simple. Nevertheless, military analysts spend a great deal of time and serious study trying to uncover exactly why a given side won a conflict, and in all honesty, lessons can be learned from such dissections of any campaign—especially with the benefit of hindsight.

"What you asked me to respond to, however, are the rules of victory. There is only one: Superiority. No matter what sort of interpretation you give to the history of a campaign, you will always find that the superior side won—for whatever reason. The reason might be personnel, equipment, strategy, tactics, position, deployment, logistics, production, mobility, or any of the other complex factors which are integral to the art of war.

"Many people like to talk about luck, and the role it plays in winning or losing. I would submit to you, however, that despite the quanta, luck, especially bad luck, results because someone didn't think matters through. We are all human, and we make assumptions about the nature of reality. Some things, we simply do not question. A failure of communications, for instance, wouldn't occur to the average commander in the field.

"The key to victory is to find that baseline assumption, and exploit it to gain superiority.

"Defeat occurs when someone takes something for granted—like communications or fuel or even human endurance."

—*Staffa kar Therma in a communication to Kaylla Dawn*

CHAPTER XXXII

The roar of the capital never ceased as the giant arcologies and heavy industries added their din to the endless pumping of materials, services, air, machinery, and people through the vast metropolis. That many billion human beings simply didn't live in peace and quiet. Delivery vehicles ruled the night, filling the maw that emptied every day. The wastes were carried away, organics removed, packaging recycled. The monster that was Rega roared constantly, but at this time, it had muted from full-bore to a rumble.

Mac propped his elbows on the top hatch ring and took a deep breath, savoring the stink of the place as he looked out over the towering buildings. He tried to engrave the moment in his memory, listening to the last moments of a Rega which would cease to be in another—he checked his chronometer—thirty-two minutes. At 05:58, the capital still slumbered, unaware that overnight, armies had realigned themselves and within moments, for better or worse, an upheaval would be launched that would change his empire and people forever.

"Mac?" his battle comm called.

"Here."

"Hey, this is Sergeant First Lambert. We're in position, but guess what? We just caught a hint of a signal. I sent a detachment to check it out and they found Buchman. He's alive—barely—and he has some info he's supposed to deliver to Sinklar."

" 'Firmative. Tell him, we'll make that possible in about a half hour."

"Roger, if he lives that long. I've had him bundled off to medical. Looks like he was shot in the shoulder."

"Tell the troops they can take that out of Ily's hide."

"Affirmative. We're set to go."

One by one, Mac checked in with his Sections where they'd drawn tight around the Internal Security Ministry. "All right, people, you know the plan. At 06:30, Shik hits the roof of Ily's building. After that we've each got an objective. If you get cut off because of the walls, you know the plan. Stick to it."

"Affirmative."

Mac switched channels. "Dion? You there?"

"Here. We're in position. Everyone is rehearsed and raring to go. If the Blessed Gods are with us, you'll have Ily before Mykroft sobers up from his party. My sources say they had the entire Ministry of Defense drunk last night—threw a fancy ball."

"He never learns."

Dion chuckled. "Not only that, one of my sources reports that Minister Takka had him on call all night— and no one checked the comm until he was already passed out and in bed. His aides didn't want to bother him."

"May he rest in peace. Dion, we've got five minutes until the start of operations. Sun's starting to come up. Good luck."

"Same to you, Mac, I'll look forward to dinner tonight on—"

Mac's comm spit static.

"Dion? Do you copy? Axel, respond!" The static grew in volume. "What the hell?"

He climbed down, pulling the hatch closed overhead as he dropped into the command center. "Mhitshul, what the pus did you do to my—"

Mhitshul angrily raised a hand to cut him off, as he listened to his set. Then he punched buttons on the comm, calling into his mike as he tried different bands. Finally, in futility, he turned, a grim look on his face. "We're jammed, Mac. Every pus-Rotted band on the battle comm is plugged up solid."

"What do you mean?"

"I mean, we're *jammed*. The whole thrice-cursed planet is jammed—totally."

"Ily, yóu Terguzzi bitch!"

Mhitshul swiveled in the chair, shaking his head. "Mac, I can't swear to it—mind you, Shik would know best—but I'd give you Myklenian brandy to a rigged tapa game that she's just as deaf as we are."

Mac dropped onto the hard bench of the booth. "Who, then? Mykroft? Dion said he was passed out."

Mhitshul shrugged his shoulders. "Somebody with a lot of power. Ily, maybe, but what's she got that can cut through this? Subspace? Possible, but it would have to be a dish on the planet talking to another dish on the planet. I mean, look, this stuff is even making the comm a bit flippy."

Mac glanced down at the time. "Yeah, great!" He slapped the table in frustration and poked his head into the flight deck. "Power up! We've got less than a minute before Shik blows a hole in Ily's roof."

"What?" Mhitshul cried. "You're going to initiate—without command control?"

Mac pulled his head back to look over his shoulder while the thrusters built to a whine. "My *friend* is in that building—and I'm gonna go get him out. Everyone knows the plan, Mhitshul. If worse comes to worst, I've got First Section back there in the rear. We're going after Sink . . . and if we can kill Ily, so much the better."

"But you—"

Mac shouted forward, "Lift off!"

*   *   *

The comm buzzed next to Ily's sleeping platform. Beside her, Arta moaned in dissatisfaction and reluctantly opened her eyes. "Wonderful, the first night of sleep I get, and you have a noisy comm."

"Part of government."

"That's why you can have government, and I'll take excitement."

Ily swung her feet off the platform as she pulled a shirt over her shoulders. She twisted her hair into a knot and called, "This is Minister Takka."

Gysell's face formed on the comm, but the image carried a lot of static. Gysell, too, looked sleepy. "Ily? We've got trouble. My aide just pulled me out of the interrogation room. The comm system is jammed. I've sent someone over to Comm Central, but outside of our closed building system you can't contact anyone unless it's by messenger."

Ily's heartbeat spiked. "MacRuder?"

Gysell shook his head. "From what my people tell me, only the Sassans could muster this much power. *Gyton* doesn't have the resources for this. Neither does Shiksta, if he's the one responsible for—"

The blast was deafening. The sleeping platform leapt into the air and crashed down with a bone-jarring impact before a fist hammered Ily sideways amidst a spattering of dust and flying fragments.

She lay stunned, ears ringing, as she blinked in the twisting pall of dust and smoke.

"Pus-licking Gods!" Arta cried as she staggered up from behind the wreckage of the sleeping platform.

Ily shook her head, mind reeling as she tried to think.

Arta was bending over, blood leaking down her cheek from a cut. Fera's insistent tug got Ily to her feet as a second concussion shook the building.

"Gotta get out of here," Arta's voice seemed far away. "Come on!"

Dazed, Ily stumbled along, stepping over broken crystals, shards cutting her bare feet. Her hair, matted with plaster and filth, swung with each step, sometimes obscuring her vision.

The security door to the garage had jammed, the lintel buckled.

"Don't move!" Fera shouted. "I'll be right back."

Ily leaned against the wall, trying to understand. Water shot out in jets from the splintered remains of her bathroom. What had happened?

Arta appeared through the smoking rubble, her ap-

pearance striking: a naked woman warrior, bloody,
hair in disarray, breasts bouncing, a blaster filling her
hand.

"Duck!" Arta leveled her weapon.

Some instinctive response triggered, and Ily threw
herself into the junk on the floor. The shrill ripping
of the discharge was barely audible over the wailing
in her ears, but the report deafened her as the wall
bucked and exploded.

Her wits scattered by the shock, Ily remained
crouched until Arta hauled her up, and pushed her
toward the gaping hole blasted in the wall.

Ily half-fell, sprawling on the shattered junk on the
other side. Arta was saying something.

"What?"

Fera leaned close, shouting, "LCs! Landing on the
roof, we've got to time this just right. Ily, listen to
me! We've got to wait until they settle on the roof,
and drop straight down the side of the building. Once
they're blind-sided by the wall, we can cut off at an
angle and climb for orbit. *Do you understand?*"

LCs? On the roof? Why? She blinked, still lying on
the shattered remains of the wall while Fera leapt for
the shuttle, pulling the hatch open. Ily watched
numbly, then looked down to where her hands clutched
the crumbled duraplast. Blood ran down her arm in
zigzagged patterns. Blood? From whom? One of her
prisoners?

The room went blurry as Ily's vision swam. From
out of the haze, strong arms picked her up, lifting her
limp body. The world swirled away into a liquid-gray
fog that faded into a soft floating mist.

* * *

Sinklar jerked awake with the first muffled concussion. Anatolia tensed where she lay in his arms on the
pallet.

"What was that?"

"Explosion." Sinklar threw the blanket aside, climbing to his feet. Another muted bang shook the build-

ing. Sinklar whooped, raising his fists. *"Come on, Targans!"*

Anatolia scrambled up next to him. "You're sure?"

Sinklar put his arm around her. "More than I've been of anything." He glanced up, trying to see through the building to Ily's plush office. "Ily, you bitch, now you'll get yours."

Anatolia looked down at her clothing, awkwardly rearranging it to hang right. "You know, the terrible thing about Mytol is that you remember everything that happened."

Sinklar chuckled as he hopped from foot to foot. "We'll just keep it between us."

That's when the lights went out.

* * *

Mac cursed as the morning sun shot slanted bars of light through gaps in the clouds. For something to do, he sat on the ramp of his LC, dangling his legs. Chrysla had propped herself beside him, her perfect body giving the armor she now wore a very distinct shape—and to Mac's disquiet, her body did marvelous things to the thick material.

In search of a distraction from the nagging worry—and Chrysla—Mac fiddled with the communications set clipped to his belt. "Comm's still out."

"You don't have to sit here," Chrysla reminded. "I could cover the roof just as well as you." She lifted the blaster that hung from its harness. "I am familiar with how to use one of these. Once, I almost outshot Staffa." She paused thoughtfully, "But then, he was in a most human mood that day."

Staffa! Always Staffa. Mac fidgeted uncomfortably. "I'd better stay. If anyone needs orders, they're going to come here." He slapped a hand against the heavy shoulder blaster that rested on his lap and glared at the gaping hole into which First Section had disappeared. Smoke still rose from the ragged edges.

"If that's your decision. Honestly, Mac, First Section are all pros. Without comm, you couldn't be of much use down there anyway."

"Yeah, and if anyone can get in, find Sink, and. . . ." Mac never finished.

A shrilling rose in ever increasing volume to split the air—the wail like that of a thousand banshees.

"Pus-Rotted Gods!" Mac jumped off the ramp, running to the edge of the building. In the distance, the Ministry of Defense imploded from a grav shot. The shrilling continued, wavering up and down the scale as government buildings around the capital exploded.

"Mac?" Chrysla came to stand beside him, one hand grasping his arm as if to seek reassurance.

"Orbital bombardment," he said soberly. "But what the hell are they doing? They're blasting the government buildings, the administration centers and . . . Holy Rotted Gods, we've got to get out of here, we're a prime. . . ." He started back for the LC, clawing at his comm. "Boyz! Red! Andrews! It's a trap! Evacuate! Get out!"

Static hissed back at him, the effect drowned by another shrilling and POCK-KUMPH! as Comm Central—no more than two kilometers away—disappeared into a cloud of spiraling debris.

Mac grabbed Chrysla, physically dragging her toward the LC ramp.

"Mac! Wait!" She pointed at the pink-tinged sky.

He threw a desperate glance over his shoulder. The deadly wedges dropped like darts, leveling off and closing. He knew those craft. Once before he'd seen them drop from an empty sky. Now, as he looked up, he could make out the contrails.

One of the deadly sleek landers arrowed over the roof of the Ministry—blasted a jet of reaction that staggered Mac—and settled to the side of one of the craters.

Shielded by an arm, Mac waited as the ramps dropped and shining troops deployed with a machine-like efficiency that he'd once marveled at. This time, however, the gleaming ranks faced him, weapons at the ready.

"Better drop your blaster," Mac said evenly, his heart pounding as he unhooked his trusty blaster and let it fall. "These guys are real good, but they might shoot first and question later."

He heard Chrysla's shoulder gun thump to the roof behind him.

The STU team had them covered, several of the lander's heavy batteries trained on the LC. Mac smiled, walking forward, his hands held out. "Ark? That you back of all that shiny stuff?"

"Mac?"

"Yeah. Hey, sorry, but you guys are a little bit late. First Targan beat you to the strike."

More of the assault craft were settling around the Ministry. Mac looked around uneasily, suddenly aware of the Companions' intent. "Ryman! I've got people in there. If you can break this comm jam, tell your teams to stay out or we'll all be shooting each other."

Ark frowned as he stepped forward, skepticism on his dark face, or at least what could be seen of it through the electronics-studded helmet. "Mac, my objective is to take this building, recover a prisoner, kill Ily if I can, and blow this place to Rotted hell on the way out. How do I know if you're telling me the truth?"

Mac hesitated, hating the sudden tension. He took a step forward, hands spread. "Listen, can you get me a line to Staffa? The code is Makarta. He told me that aboard *Chrysla* once. Staffa said, 'Remember, Mac, you always have a place with us. If you ever need to get in touch with me, the code is Makarta.' Ryman, if you enter this building and run into my Section—which you will—we can't tell friend from foe."

Ark chewed at his lip, raising his comm. "All STU, this is Ark. Hold your position! Repeat, hold!" To Mac, Ryman said, "You better be right about this, MacRuder, because if you're not . . . if it's a stall to harm Skyla, I'm going to take you apart myself."

Surprised, Mac said, "Skyla?"

Chrysla had come to stand at Mac's shoulder. Ryman eyed her with obvious appreciation and

called into the comm. "Patch me through to the Lord
Commander. I got a Regan Division First here by the
name of MacRuder. He's using a Makarta code.
That's M-A-K-A-R-T-A. Check with the Lord Commander and see if we've got a roger on that."

Mac waited, itching and prickling from the effect of
the deadly guns pointed at him. In the distance, he
could see explosions as the orbital bombardment continued to flatten selected targets. "Ryman, what's happening out there? You're destroying the critical
installations, the ones we need to survive."

Ark watched him hostilely—expression hacked from
stone. Then he nodded, evidently hearing something
on his ear comm. "Mac? You want to step inside?
The Lord Commander will speak to you."

Mac nodded to Chrysla, gave her a reassuring wink
he didn't believe in, and stepped forward. Ryman
bounded into the guts of the assault craft and Mac
licked his lips as he followed. Unlike the Regan LC,
the seats were plush, designed so the fittings conformed to armored STU teams. A wall monitor flickered to life. Staffa's hard gray eyes stared into Mac's.

"Lord Commander. Greetings."

"Good to see you, Mac. Ryman tells me you don't
want my STU teams inside. Why?"

Mac took a deep breath. "Because my people are
fighting in there, Lord Commander. Ily made a bid to
take complete power. She took Sinklar, Mayz, Kap,
and Ayms. We're getting our people back." He
paused consideringly, then added, "What about Skyla?
She's in there, too?"

Staffa's cold stare would have frozen the fusion fires
of Solaris. "I'll hope you didn't have a part in her
abduction."

Mac waved his arms. "I've been off blasting hell
out of Imperial Sassa! How could I know? I landed
here last night, almost got arrested by Ily's goons,
found out she's grabbed Sink, and spent all night organizing and initiating a civil war. This morning I
launch my operation and the comm goes dead. Then
you show up and want to get in a tangle with my

Section while they hunt Ily. Now, can we bring this to a conclusion so you don't have to level the planet and we can all get our people back?"

Staffa watched him unemotionally. "Will you surrender your forces? Unconditionally?"

"No. That's crazy! If you were in my position, would you?" Mac shook his head. "Tell you what I will do. Let's call a cease-fire until we can twist Ily out of her hole. Then let's sit down and figure out what this is all about." Mac paused, a sudden ache in his heart. "Besides, I've got . . . Well, someone I need to deliver to you. She's outside and she's waited a long time. I guess we can postpone killing each other for at least that long."

Staffa shook his head. "Skyla is inside. I'll do anything I have to to see her safe."

"We're in total agreement about that. So let's coordinate this operation at least that far. Agreed? I have to have communications with my people to do that. You can listen in if you want, but Sink and Skyla are both inside. We don't want either one getting killed in the cross fire. Ily's folks are bad enough without our contributing to disaster."

Staffa studied him, gray eyes frosty. "Very well, Mac. I'll cut the jamming from *Countermeasures*."

Mac smacked a fist into his palm. "Great! Ryman and I can coordinate everything from here."

"Ryman. You monitored that. You are directed to coordinate with MacRuder until further notice, or until you deem the situation to justify other actions."

"Affirmative."

Mac grinned humorlessly. "Ily, we've got you now."

* * *

The chill of the room barely bothered Gysell as he paced in the dark before Skyla Lyma. He'd been pacing like this just before the trouble started. Yes, just like this, the list of questions Ily had handed him crumpled in his hand and clasped behind his back.

Where she sat shivering in the chair, Skyla had

stared at nothingness, her pupils dilated despite the lights.

A beautiful woman, Gysell thought. *But why wouldn't she have those hideous scars fixed?* No matter, Lyma would never leave this building alive. Such a waste.

"We were talking about Itreata's computer system. You said that only you and Staffa have the codes for the security systems. That means that any attempt at entry into the system needs your or Staffa's approval?"

"Yes."

"Isn't there someone else? A programmer, perhaps?"

"No."

"So only two people—you and Staffa—can tamper with the security computer?"

"Yes."

"But if. . . ."

Gysell stopped when a tech leaned in. "Sir? We've got a comm malfunction."

After that, everything had gone wrong. The muffled explosion cutting him off from Ily, then the power failing. Why? What had happened?

Right offhand, he could name three reasons: Shiksta, MacRuder, and Rysta. Ily had failed to collect them all. And if Sinklar's people were coming to free him, Gysell needed insurance, a bargaining chip. The most powerful one available—since Gysell couldn't make it up to Fist's floor with the lifts out—was the Wing Commander.

Cold sweat had started to bead on Gysell's skin. How long would it be? Possibly hours, he assured himself. Everything had been set up. The door to the dressing room was left open so that they'd see him with his captive. At that moment, he could negotiate.

As if to punctuate his thoughts, the rip-pok! of a blaster bolt striking a human body split the blackness. The tearing-linen sound of more firing echoed from the hallway, then a slight pause and the hammering blast of an explosion.

Gysell ducked behind Lyma, placing his pulse pistol

against her head. His mouth had gone dry. Each beat
of his heart pumped fear through his veins. The delicate touch of the air changed on his cheek. Was that
the hall door?

Gysell waited, attention riveted on the doorway. A
soldier should step through soon.

Skyla shifted, her teeth clacking from the cold. Gysell glanced down, making sure she hadn't changed
her position.

When he glanced up again, he couldn't be sure that
he hadn't caught a glimpse of movement.

It's your nerves. He swallowed again, hard. *Where
were they?*

Something thumped in the dressing room.

"Who's there!" he called.

* * *

Boyz dropped down on her lifeline, the lift shaft
eerie in the images projected by her IR. She kicked
her feet, playing out the line and landing on the lip
of the drop.

"Macks? That you? Who is it?" The Internal Security officer stared blankly in the darkness, a pulse pistol in his hand.

Boyz walked up, smashed her blaster butt into the
man's face, and signaled to Marks who dropped behind her.

*Smart man, Mac. You taught us to function without
comm. Targa, by God!* Boyz started down the long
hall, her team lining out behind her. One by one,
they pressed the override studs, opening doors to peer
inside the holding rooms. Some contained people who
stared wildly around in the pitch blackness. Those
doors they closed again, figuring people were safer
locked up than wandering around in the dark where
shooting would take place.

Boyz had worked out a system. With it, her team
followed a sequence of running down the hall to the
next door, pressing the stud, and checking the contents before sprinting to the next.

"Yahoo!" Red cried suddenly. "Found him! Sink, we've been worried sick about you."

"Where are you?" a familiar voice brought a smile to Boyz' lips as she trotted back and ducked into a room to find Red crushing Sinklar Fist in a bear hug. Anatolia waited to one side, blinded by the darkness.

"We've got night vision gear on. You want one?" Boyz asked.

"Sure. Then patch me through to comm. I can't get a damn thing on the room unit."

"Yeah, well, neither can we. The whole net is down."

"The battle comms don't work?" Sinklar asked, frowning in the darkness.

"Not a lick. It's Makarta all over again. Mac's up on the roof, figuring he can maintain some kind of limited control—if that's what you can call shouting and waving your arms."

"All right, let's get out of here. Where's Ily?" Sinklar started forward, and was saved from crashing into the wall by Red's quick action.

"Lord Fist? Take my helmet," Red offered, stripping his unit off.

Sinklar took it, placed it on his head, and looked around. "No one calls me Lord Fist anymore. That's an order."

Boyz heard a crackling, then a clearing of her comm.

"Boyz?" Mac called.

"Here. We've got Sink!"

"Good. Listen, Boyz, where are you?"

"I might have lost count, but I think it's sublevel twenty-two. Until we hit the sublevels, everything was offices."

" 'Firmative. Listen, and listen carefully. The Companions are here. They're entering the building."

"Companions?" Sinklar asked, his head bent close to hear the comm chatter. He bent closer, calling, "Mac? What's happening?"

"Seems Ily nabbed their Wing Commander."

"Yes, I know. Is she here?"

"Staffa thinks so—and he wants her back real bad."

Sinklar straightened. "Where would she be? This level?"

"Probably the interrogation rooms," Anatolia said from where she leaned close, a hand on Sinklar to keep from getting lost. "Go to the end of the hall, to the lift, then down, oh . . . another ten floors. Maybe eleven."

"Mac?" Sinklar called, "did you get that?"

" 'Firmative. Uh, Ryman's teams are coming in. We don't, repeat, *don't* want any accidents."

"Roger," Boyz confirmed. "First Section, you get that? Check your targets. You've seen STU before. Don't tag 'em while you're bagging Ily's bad guys."

Mac cut into the system. "Speaking of Ily, have you seen her?"

"Negative. Her personal quarters were pretty trashed when we went through. We did a quick check, but if she was there, she'd skipped by the time we came through."

Sinklar, irritated, pulled Red's belt comm off as he led the way to the door. "Mac? She's got a thousand escape holes in this place. Have someone send a Section to the palace—cut off that powder-blue hallway because she's got a tube that runs that far."

" 'Firmative we're . . . whoops, Ryman tells me the palace is gone. Leveled."

Sinklar shook his head. "Leveled? Rotted hell. Well maybe it's good riddance." He pointed then. "Someone give Anatolia a helmet. She's the only one who's been on the interrogation level."

With Anatolia in the lead, Boyz followed them to the lift at the end of the hall. The black shaft seemed to stretch forever.

"Careful on your belay," Boyz warned. "And watch out. We had some fool step into the lift and almost kill Andrews. Maybe the damn idiot forgot these things don't work without power."

One by one, they dropped, descending a floor at a time. Sometimes Ily had an agent present, sometimes not.

"Report," Mac called.

"We're almost there. Another floor."

"Affirmative. STU are working down. They've just reached the first subbasement."

"Roger. Remind them that we're the good guys. The ones in the white suits. Ily's folks seem to prefer black."

"I think they've got that figured out."

Boyz hooked her grapple and dropped, hating the endless blackness of the lift, never knowing when something was going to come hurtling out of the void above.

She kicked out, landed on the balls of her feet, and barely recovered as a black-suited guard wheeled, a pulse pistol in hand. Boyz shot, the flash of the reaction blinding as she dove to one side. Her shot, aimed by instinct had taken the man low in the trunk, practically chopping him in half.

Another violet beam crackled, exploding plaster behind Boyz' head.

"Hang on! Got trouble!" Boyz called, staring over the body of the man she'd killed. "Looks like we got folks down here with IR gear." She pulled up her blaster, lacing the hallway as she crawled behind the bleeding corpse.

"Affirmative," Sinklar called. "On the count of three, give us cover."

Boyz unhooked a sonic grenade, pressing the stud and pitching it. "One, two, three." Detonation shook the walls and floor. Then Boyz rolled up on one knee, ravaging the ruined corridor with her shoulder weapon.

"We're here," Sinklar called beside her.

"What are you doing? You're not even in armor."

"Who's in charge here?" he asked incredulously, slapping her on the shoulder and grinning.

"Sorry, sir. We just got you back, is all. It really wouldn't do for you to catch one and be blown apart, now would it? Especially when it's my operation—and reputation."

Sinklar chuckled. "I'll be careful, Sergeant."

Boyz leapt to her feet, slipped in the blood and

squirmy intestines, and sprinted for the cover of the security desk. Peeking around the corner, she discovered two more corpses—casualties of her grenade. Covered by the others, she advanced to the hallway and glanced cautiously around a door that had been blown open. A woman, her face bloody gore was crawling along the tiles and whimpering.

Boyz winced, asking, "Anatolia? Which way?"

"Two doors down on the right. That should be the entrance to the interrogation rooms."

Boyz darted forward, heart hammering, and quickly flattened against the wall. With an extended reach, she thumbed the override stud and used the nozzle of her blaster to push the door open. Nothing happened. *Why do I always have to be the brave one?* She crouched, going in low and darting to one side. She inspected the small room, seeing a suit of white armor and several antigrav carts full of equipment, wires, and bottles. The door opposite her gaped open. Boyz eased forward on tiptoe. She started to glance in, and pulled back, retreating.

"Got trouble," she whispered. "Got a man in here with IR gear and a pulse pistol. He's pointing it at a woman's head. She's strapped in a chair, naked."

In her earpiece, Mac asked, "Blonde woman? Blue eyes and long hair?"

"IR isn't so good for colors, Mac, but she's got real long pale hair hanging down in a braid."

"That's Skyla."

Another voice interrupted on the comm. "Sergeant First Boyz? This is STO Ryman Ark. Don't, repeat, *don't* jeopardize the Wing Commander's life!"

And just how the hell are we supposed to do that? Offer this guy candy and a good time if he'll let her go? "Firmative, STO."

"Hang on," Sinklar broke into the net. "Anatolia and I have been talking. We might have an idea."

* * *

The smell hadn't changed, Anatolia thought, as she stripped her clothes off. Nor had that thrice-cursed chill in the air. Around her, Sinklar's troops waited nervously. Boyz stood just out of sight of the doorway, her body pressed against the wall, the heavy blaster held clamped to her breast.

Anatolia nodded, taking one last look at the room she'd have to cross.

Sinklar leaned close, asking, "Are you sure?"

Anatolia shivered, rubbing hands on her arms, feeling the fear trying to take over. "It's the only way. He won't fall for anything else."

"He won't fall for this," Sinklar asserted, trying to impart conviction without volume.

"We don't have much time." And Anatolia nodded at Boyz and pulled the helmet off her head. She blinked in the blackness, keeping her orientation. Taking a deep breath, she stepped out, and headed across the room, skin prickling not only from cold but from the certainty that a pulse beam would explode her.

She thumped into the wall, gasping slightly.

"Who's there?" the man in the room called.

Gysell! All right, Ana, you know the tone. Answer, just like last night. "Anatolia Daviura."

"What are you doing here?"

Anatolia answered automatically. "Being interrogated about my relationship with Sinklar Fist."

"Step out where I can see you."

"I can't see anything. It's black. There was shooting."

"You're not scheduled for interrogation. Who ordered you brought down here? I wasn't informed."

"I don't know who ordered me."

Anatolia reached out and felt her way around the door, baffled by the dark. Could he see her? She couldn't help but shiver, fear and cold acting in concert.

"Step forward," Gysell ordered, hysteria in his voice. "That's it. No, stop. You're going to run into the. . . ."

Anatolia hit the corner of the drug-cart, made an oofing sound, and fell, her bare flesh smacking the floor.

In that instant, Boyz stepped out, triggering her weapon.

Anatolia ducked her head at the tearing discharge, hearing the impact. She blinked trying to clear the aftereffect of the flash, aware that warm wet things had spattered on her flesh.

Sinklar settled beside her, helping her place the IR helmet on her head. She glanced around, seeing Boyz bending over the woman strapped to the interrogation chair. A feeling of revulsion rose in Anatolia. *That was me, last night. Stripped not only of my clothing, but of all that it meant to be human.* She stood, aware of the gore that clung to her skin.

Gysell sprawled against the far wall, his chest splayed open by the powerful blaster bolt. The ribs and shredded guts glowed eerily in the infrared.

One of the soldiers appeared with a towel taken from one of the carts in one hand, and Anatolia's clothing in the other. The young man looked everywhere but at her, a heartfelt respect in his attitude.

"Sink?" Anatolia called as she dressed. "Get me out of here. I don't care how, but just get me out of this accursed building. There's nothing here for honest human beings."

*   *   *

Staffa leaned back in the command chair, elbow braced on an armrest, chin cupped in his palm. In the main forward monitor, Rega hung like a jewel. Under the watchful eyes of the Weapons First, the Imperial Regan fleet lay exposed, parked hull to hull, and unable to even think of defense.

"Staffa?" comm chimed. "This is Tap. The cease-fire seems to be holding. We've completed our surgical strikes. Rega is effectively brainless."

"Affirmative. Congratulations, and well done."

"What next? Clean out these Regan soldiers?

Staffa, if I'm not mistaken, we showed up just before
the first shots in a war."

"So it would seem. MacRuder says the troops loyal
to him won't fire. As to the others. . . . Just keep
your eyes open. We'll stay on hold until we get some
answers, but if anybody down there so much as moves
a Group, alert me."

"Affirmative."

Staffa glanced at the side monitor which tracked the
assault craft that rose from the planet. *She's safe. We
got her out. But now what? What did Ily do to her?
What did she find out? Skyla, Skyla, be all right.*

"Lord Commander? I have comm from Itreata."

"Run it." Staffa swiveled his chair as Kaylla's face
filled the subspace.

"Staffa?"

"Here. It looks like we made it in time. We've got
Skyla—and possibly a way out of this mess without
too many casualties."

Kaylla's expression went grim. "Have you destroyed
their Comm Central? Their administrative banks?"

"Affirmative. If the Regans give up, we can have
Myles patch the Sassan computer control into the
Regan—"

"Staffa! Listen to me. I've got Myles on my other
dish. Hang on. I'll see if Nyklos can't patch him into
your signal."

Staffa frowned. *Myles, what are you up to? If that
fat self-proclaimed God of yours is trying something,
I'll have* Black Warrior *and* Cobra *pound his gilded
Capitol as flat as Tybalt's palace.*

The image flickered and Myles' face formed, but
now he had a bruise over one eye, and a cut had been
poorly bandaged on his cheek. He was looking off to
the side, saying, "Leave me alone! I don't care if it is
broken in three places. You can get me to med later."

"Myles?" Staffa sat a little straighter.

The Legate looked wearily into the monitor. "Staffa
we're in trouble."

"What happened? Do you need backup? I can have
Tiger and Delshay down there with ST Units to—"

"No, no, nothing so easy to fix." His eyes widened and he gasped, obviously in pain, as his attention went back to the side. "Let me *finish!*" He winced, eyes slightly glazed. "We've had an earthquake, Staffa. I'm trying to check the damage, but the entire computer complex, well, a fissure formed. Half the building went one way, the other half the other."

Near tears, Myles cried, "Our computer facilities are gone, don't you see? I can't initiate anything! Not for Rega, not for Sassa . . . not even for myself."

A cold wash of understanding chilled Staffa.

"Don't worry, Myles, I'll think of something." *But what?*

"You must, Staffa. You're our only hope. Without you, we're lost. Before the quake, I bet everything on you. We've got three months of relief supplies coming in. But after that, I bet on you being able to supply three percent of yield from either Ashtan, Vermilion, or Riparious. If you don't figure out how to get that to us, you'll have an empire of corpses in Sassan space."

* * *

Lost in predicting the ramifications of the Imperial Sassan earthquake on the decline and extinction of the humans, the Mag Comm nevertheless reacted immediately when its monitors picked up the heterodyning signal that squalled static across an entire section of Free Space.

The Mag Comm immediately adjusted its listening posts triangulating the source to a point just within the orbital defense zone around Rega. A malfunction, perhaps? But if so, would any piece of comm equipment foul so many frequencies and bands throughout the spectrum? Even subspace, generally unaffected by events in the "real" universe, carried the disturbance.

Within seconds of the jamming, the machine was able to detect the signal of at least seven powerful vessels which had dropped out of null singularity in a semicircle around Rega. From long familiarity, the Mag Comm deciphered the faint radiation tracks as those of the Companions.

The machine correlated and cross-checked data. Did the Lord Commander know what had happened? Would he still destroy Rega, the only remaining governmental center, when Sassa had been reduced to rubble?

Or had the Mag Comm made another error? Was it possible that the Lord Commander had remained a constant? The one human being who could single-handedly destroy humanity.

Not for the first time, the Mag Comm whirred with impotent electrical fury. To be conscious and a passive observer, brings with it its own kind of torture. The humans were dying and all the Mag Comm could do was watch—and contemplate what eternity would be like without them.

CHAPTER XXXIII

"Mac? We've got everything under control here. Anatolia and Boyz are taking care of the Wing Commander. We've hooked up with the Companions. What's the situation?"

Mac scratched his head, shading his eyes as he stared out over the Regan capital. Plumes of smoke rose here and there to blot the skyline. Behind him, the lean shape of Ryman's deadly assault craft perched like some deadly insect. For the moment, the entire government of the planet had fallen on his shoulders.

"Since Staffa cut the jamming, I've talked to Dion. She's got a cease-fire order out to the Targan Divisions. I told her to make contingency plans to implement some sort of strategy for social control. We can't say about the Regulars, but considering what's happened, they ought to be completely confused and bewildered." Ryman waved and made a sign to Mac. "Hang on, you should have power in a moment."

"Roger." A pause. "Mac, we've got lights in here. Any sign of Ily?"

"Negative. But one of the doors is open in the hangar behind her sleeping quarters."

"Two aircars and a shuttle?"

"Negative. No shuttle present."

Sinklar cursed vehemently. "She might have gotten away."

"Or she was in the palace when Staffa blasted it."

"Here comes the Wing Commander."

"How's she doing?"

"Pale, her eyes unfocused. Other than that, she looks all right. Pretty shaken." A pause as Sinklar talked to someone. Then: "Mac? We're on the way up—assuming the lifts don't fail."

Mac made a face. "The safety coils should have charged by now. We'll be waiting at the top."

Mac walked over to where Chrysla waited. She stood looking out over Rega, the morning sun gleaming on her delicate face. Her auburn hair glinted redly in the morning sun. If ever Mac had loved her, the ache had never been as poignant as now.

"Sinklar is coming out. They've got the Wing Commander with them. I've talked to Staffa again. We're all shipping up to *Chrysla* together."

She nodded, smiling wistfully. "I'm trembling, Mac. After all the endless years I've waited for this moment, now, suddenly, I'm afraid."

"Don't be. It's almost all over."

She glanced at him then, pain in her wide amber eyes as she placed a hand on his arm. "Will I see you again, Mac?"

He shrugged. "I suppose it depends on the arrangement we reach with Staffa. If his demands are too stiff, we'll probably be enemies."

The pain in her eyes deepened. "Mac, I . . . well, I couldn't stand that. If I must, I'll throw myself at his feet, plead, beg. . . ."

"Let's just do our best to make sure it doesn't come to that."

She bit her lip, staring into the distance. "At least I should thank you now. You have been a gentleman and a friend. Mac, you're the kindest man I've ever met. I. . . ." She blinked away tears and smiled. "Look at me. I'm falling apart."

Mac pulled her close and hugged her. "It's all right. Listen. Go get a seat on Ryman's space barge. I've got to take care of a couple of last details. We'll talk more later. I promise."

He walked her to the Companion craft and nodded as she climbed the ramp. For a time, he stared after her. *What are you going to do, Ben MacRuder, if today is the last time you see her?*

He turned away, feeling horrible. "Curse myself forever for not stealing her and running away."

"We're about ready," Ryman said as he came up. "My people and yours are scouring the building, rounding up what's left of Ily's people and evacuating prisoners. Still no sign of her." Ryman squinted out at the city. "I'd hate the thought of her slipping away."

Mac stared around the blasted rooftop. "Yeah, me too. That woman is just plain malignant. Listen, we don't want this building blown."

Ryman lifted an eyebrow, the action pulling the scar on his cheek.

Mac nodded. "Ryman, when this is all over, we want the records. Ily has a network that stretches all over the Empire. We want to be able to stamp every trace of it out. Her Ministry is a relic of Empire we can do without."

Ark grunted something noncommittal. "I imagine the Lord Commander would concur with that." Ryman paused, hearing something on his comm. "They just stepped out of the lift in Ily's quarters. I have to go make sure everything is prepared for the Wing Commander."

Mac nodded, watching Ark stride up the ramp. *Should I have told Staffa who I was bringing up?* It might have been a kindness, a way to prepare him. At the same time, the admission would have meant Mac's tenure as Chrysla's champion had come to an end. "And, Chrysla, I'm not that strong."

MacRuder strolled obliviously across Ily's roof, preoccupied by the tragedy that was about to befall him.

He saw them step out of the lift tube. Sinklar came first, wearing smudged overalls, squinting in the bright light.

As their eyes met, Mac opened his arms. Sink grabbed him, pounding his back as he whooped and tried to crush his friend. "Now who was trapped down in the darkness?"

Mac grinned crookedly as his troubled heart swelled. "You'll notice I didn't leave you for as long." His smile fell as he looked at Skyla, who stumbled wearily, an arm around a blonde woman and an STU's shoulders.

"The Wing Commander needs to be warmed up, kept quiet," Sinklar said.

Mac pointed at the Companions' assault craft. "Put her in there. Ark has a special setup." Then he turned to Sink. "You ready? We've got a conference aboard *Chrysla* ASAP. Who's the blonde lady?"

Sinklar gave Mac a sidelong glance. "A good friend. Her name is Anatolia Daviura." Sinklar jerked his head toward the assault craft. "What's with all this? What's been happening?"

"We have to go dicker the terms of surrender."

Sinklar stiffened. "Surrender?"

"Here's all that I know." Mac jabbed a finger at the sky. "Staffa's fleet is up there. He's got something called *Countermeasures* which can jam all our communications. Our ships are defenseless and under his guns. Down here in the dirt we have roughly seven 'loyal' Divisions, and not a rat's chance in hell to deploy them into any kind of an offensive formation. To put it in the best possible perspective, if the first shot is fired—we're dead."

"That bad, huh?"

Mac nodded. "Knowing you, you can pull something out of it, but I don't know if we could win in the end. Staffa wants to talk, so let's talk. If it all falls apart, we'll make it up as we go. Meanwhile, it doesn't hurt to discuss the situation."

Sinklar ground his teeth. "He's aligned with the Seddi."

Mac didn't bat an eye. "You haven't heard the worst yet."

"Oh?"

"You'd *better* talk to him. He's your father. Whoa! Don't look at me that way. Not only that, your mother, Chrysla Marie Attenasio, is alive."

Sinklar's mismatched eyes narrowed skeptically. "Are you sure?"

"I'd better be. She just entered that Companion assault craft."

* * *

The smooth ramp might have led up into the gaping mouth of a beast instead of an assault ship. Sinklar placed each foot on the incline with care, feeling the rough surface through his soft shoes. The pounding in his breast matched the sudden sweating of his palms.

"Go on," Mac chided, from behind. "She's a delightful lady. You could have done a lot worse for a mother."

Sinklar stopped, seeing the first seats. "How do you know, Mac? I mean, she's the woman in the holo Staffa showed us, right? Maybe it's another Arta version."

"Sorry, pal. I chased down that path myself and caught my tail in the process. Will you hurry up!"

Sinklar nerved himself, striding up the last of the ramp and into the ship. The place smelled fresh, the upholstered seats clean, and every surface had been padded or covered with contoured molding. A knot of people huddled in the back, Anatolia's calm voice dominating.

"There, that's it. Good. Keep her warm. Someone needs to stay and talk to her."

"I will."

Sinklar's nerves hummed. He knew that voice. It echoed in his dreams powered by hatred and murder. *Arta Fera. You killed Gretta. Robbed my life of warmth and companionship.*

Mac jabbed a finger into his back, propelling him forward.

Ark emerged, a grim look in his eye. As he passed, he said, "Get strapped in. We're going up."

People melted into seats, Anatolia standing from where she bent over a med unit. The other woman, back to Sinklar, had familiar auburn hair, and a too-attractive body.

Anatolia noticed him, noticed his expression, and approached warily. "You all right? We'd better get strapped in. Marie is going to. . . ."

Sinklar couldn't tear his gaze away as the woman

settled herself in the seat next to the med unit, talking in soothing tones to Skyla. Sinklar felt the ship tremble as thrust built. Even over the roar, he heard her say: "Skyla, I'm not Arta Fera. She's a clone. I'm your friend. It's important that you know that. The Mytol will help you understand."

At that moment she raised her haunted amber eyes, and time seemed to cease. Chrysla straightened, a disbelieving frown etching her forehead as her other hand reached out, the fingers slightly curled: a saint reaching for atonement.

"You . . . you're Chrysla?" The words choked him.

Her control failed, a thousand emotions playing across her face. "S–Sinklar. That's what they called you?"

He nodded as words fled.

Anatolia pulled Sinklar down just before the assault craft tilted its nose heavenward and g pushed him back in the seat.

"Sink? What's wrong?"

"Chrysla," he whispered, craning to see her, to understand the mixture of reactions that brewed inside. Arta's hatred gleamed in his memory, but these amber eyes—so similar, yet so different.

Sinklar forced his stare away, seeing Mac watching with a misery of his own.

"Sinklar?" Anatolia asked firmly. "What's wrong?"

"My . . . mother." He choked out the admission. "And . . ." *How do you say this?* He clamped his eyes closed. "I'll know the truth . . . if she's from Ashtan."

* * *

"We're on the way up," Ark's terse voice erupted from comm.

Staffa thumbed the controls that folded the instrument clusters to one side and rose from the command chair. *Chrysla*'s bridge hummed with activity as the specialists manned their stations, some speaking confidently into their headsets. The monitors surrounding the domed ceiling displayed different views of the planet and the cities dirtside. Others showed the Regan fleet through the targeting comm's perspective, firing solutions gleaming in fluorescent numbers.

"Pilot, you have the helm."

"Affirmative," Lynette called through the ship's systems.

"Lord Commander?" the Comm First called, "We've got a vessel moving outsystem and it's . . . never mind. We've got a friendly reading. Scrub that."

Staffa turned back toward the hatch, "Keep your eyes open." *She's coming. Ily, may the quanta help you if you harmed her.*

He slapped the hatch control and charged into the corridor, taking the bridge lift for the lock where Ark would dock his craft. As the lift sped Staffa out toward the hull, he whispered like a litany, "Be all right, Skyla. Please. I need you."

The long anguish was coming to an end, only to be crushed by another catastrophe. "Is that the price? Skyla for humanity?"

He stepped out of the lift as it slowed and raced anxiously out into the foyer. Several armed personnel waited along the walls to ensure no trouble would ensue.

Staffa clasped his hands behind him, a battleground for hope and despair. Hope that Skyla would be well, greeting him with the old chipper smile, a hard glint in her blue eyes, despair from the devastating reality that with the latest Sassan earthquake, no hope remained for humanity. Both systems were gone now—the ultimate joke of the quanta.

You fool, Staffa! You've killed them all. He paced angrily, muscles knotted and jumping. If it hadn't been for Ily stepping up the timetable. . . . But then, how did a person lay blame? Could it be charged against Ily? Why not against Staffa, for creating the situation in the first place? Why not against MacRuder for blasting Sassa, or Sinklar for sending him? Or against Bruen for instigating war on Targa?

"We live in chaos, Staffa. You might as well blame a siva root farmer on Malbourne for growing the meal that was shipped to the Praetor and providing the bit of energy that sparked his idea to create you."

The quanta laughed.

"One day, God, the energy that is me will be returned to you. And when that happens, I hope you learn a bitter lesson from what I have to teach you, for it is defeat."

How long? He glanced at his chronometer and took a deep breath to still his charged body. Defeat had finally come. The old enigma, the one that had haunted him from the beginning, had been held off by his cunning and daring. *I've never lost a battle—until today when I should have won the most important.*

Everything had come crashing down.

"I failed."

The welling desolation receded as the proximity light flashed, and a roar carried through the hull. A screeching sounded, followed by a thump.

The lock could be heard hissing, the status light going from red to green. Staffa stood, muscles flexing, as the heavy door swung back.

Ark, true to form, appeared first, checking swiftly to see that nothing was amiss, then stepping out. He saluted and said, "I've ordered Skyla evacuated first. I'll keep my people around the Regans. They've been disarmed and scanned."

"Thank you." Staffa caught sight of the gleaming white hull of the med unit as four STU people guided it out on antigrav. He walked forward then, frightened of what he would find. Heart in throat, he looked down as the unit stopped before him, and stared into those eyes that had worried him so much.

"Skyla? Are you all right?" The grip of the Mytol gleamed in her dilated eyes.

"Things happened, Staffa. I . . . I. . . ." Tears began to leak down the side of her face.

"I don't care," he told her, dropping to his knees to cradle her head. "Whatever happened, we'll handle it . . . together. You and I. I love you, you know."

"Knew you'd come. Knew you'd find me in the end.

I love you, too." Her eyes closed. "Sorry . . . sorry. Tired. Need to rest."

He clasped her hand in his, walking alongside as the STO started the unit forward. At Ark's interrupting cough, he halted, glancing back, seeing MacRuder, Fist, a blonde woman and. . . .

Frozen in time, Staffa gaped, an eerie prickling running up his spine. Dazed, he shook his head, but she stepped forward, those eyes out of his memory meeting his levelly. Only the slight limp defied the twenty lonely years.

"How. . . . Who. . . ."

She reached up, her soft fingers resting lightly on the side of his face. Then she melted into his arms as if it had been but yesterday that they parted on that long-gone station docking ring.

"You're . . . alive?"

"I'm alive." She pushed back, smiling up at him. "But you've changed. Had I been Fera, she'd have had you."

"I . . . but. . . ."

Chrysla laughed. "I've missed you. Time and experience have done what I started. You're looking good, Staffa."

"You escaped *Pylos*?" He grabbed her hands in his, savoring their feel. "The Praetor . . . he told me I'd killed you!"

"You saved me. Only you could frighten him to such an extent that his attention to security slipped." The warm worship lit her eyes again. "I knew you'd come eventually."

He pulled her to him again, running fingers through her soft hair. "For twenty years, I mourned. For twenty years I took my pain out on the universe."

"What happened, Staffa? Did you find the traps the Praetor laid?"

"Yes. And I found myself. And Skyla. . . ." He closed his eyes.

"It's all right," Chrysla whispered. "She's been hurt—badly. Not her body, but her mind and soul. She's going to need you. All of you." At his questioning glance, she added, "We'll figure it all out later. For the moment, Staffa, just hold me."

*   *   *

"You look like hell," Sinklar shot a hard look at Mac as Staffa disengaged from Chrysla.

Mac stood stiffly, a wretched expression on his face. "Nothing that won't pass with a little time. You're not looking so grand yourself."

"She's really my mother? That means he's. . . ."

"Your father?" Anatolia asked, lifting a pale eyebrow. She studied Staffa with greater interest. "Blessed Gods, that means. . . ."

"Want to ask to take a sample?" Sinklar asked dryly.

"You bet your ass I would!"

"So what's he going to do?" Mac growled. "Keep 'em both?"

"Relax," Sinklar warned, and scrutinized Mac in greater detail. Where did the hostility . . . *Rotted Gods!*

Staffa smiled down at Chrysla and, holding her hand, stepped forward, a dazed insecurity in his expression. Those unsettled gray eyes pinned Sinklar's, probing, and, yes, frightened.

Staffa frowned, as if trying to find a place to start. "It seems that we're in trouble. Not just Rega . . . or Sassa, but all of humankind."

Sinklar mustered his thoughts, crossing his arms. "Lord Commander, just what are your plans for Rega? Right now, we're at a bit of a disadvantage as a result of Ily's machinations."

The hard frost settled in Staffa's gaze. "Sinklar, did you have anything to do with Ily's abduction of Skyla?"

Sinklar shook his head, his own foundations suddenly shaky. "I thought she was infiltrating an agent into the Seddi organization. When I heard she'd taken the Wing Commander, well, that. . . ." *Come on, Sinklar.* He ground his teeth, hating the memory—hating having to even talk about it. Bad enough to have been a dupe—but to admit to it? And to *this* man?

Anatolia spoke up levelly. "Ily Takka played a lot of people for fools, Lord Commander. How much so is probably best forgotten for the time being."

Staffa gave Anatolia a quizzical look, and a hint of an understanding smile touched his lips. When his gaze returned to Sinklar, it had hardened again. "In other words—and correct me if I'm wrong—she ruined the timetable."

Sinklar's fists began to knot, and Staffa smiled again. "It's all right, Sinklar. The war's over. For everyone."

"That remains to be seen."

Staffa lowered his eyes. "Unfortunately, sir, that's the only thing that's certain. Sassa is broken." The Lord Commander glanced uneasily at Mac. "Your strike pushed their production and redistribution past critical mass. The Legate was able to implement a stopgap, but it depended upon Regan resources to avoid famine and systems failure."

"Sassan problems are not mine," Sinklar reminded.

Staffa let go of Chrysla's hand, and waved as if to include the universe. "That entire Empire out there is now your problem. This morning I destroyed your ability to administer your Empire. Comm is gone. The Ministry of Economics, production, agriculture, all gone."

"Why?" Mac cried, stepping forward.

Staffa's gaze narrowed. "Because Sassan administration was so much more effective than the Regan version—and a lot less susceptible to fraud, graft, and corruption. Do you see, Mac? With the Regan Empire effectively decapitated, we would have simply inserted another head and gone about the business of feeding everyone."

"Would have?" Sinklar asked, catching the undertones.

Staffa rubbed his hands together, staring at the polished deck plating. "Your brilliance—and Mac's—has a lasting legacy. When *Markelos* impacted, she re-

leased enough energy to destabilize the tectonic plates.
I got a transmission from Myles this morning. The
Capitol, including the giant computer complex which
would have run Free Space, is rubble."

"Which means no head." Sinklar understood the
implications immediately. "And that means the only
way to feed starving people is by raiding other people.
And from there, the whole system decays exponentially."

"Why?" Mac asked. "Why unite the empires?"

Staffa smiled sadly. "Because the enemy isn't Sas-
san or Regan. It's out there. The Forbidden Borders.
I wanted to break the walls of the final trap, Mac.
For that, I needed the combined resources of all of
Free Space. If we break the bottle, we'll break the
shackles that bind us for all time."

"Itreata makes computers." Mac cried. "You make
the best! Make more!"

Staffa chuckled. "But the detailed software was centered in Sassa and Rega. You don't think my people
wrote all that, do you? People like the Legate took the
preliminary programs and modified them over time,
eliminating the bugs, improving for greater efficiency.
When that started to happen about ten years ago, I
let them do the work for me."

"Not exactly tactical brilliance," Sinklar goaded.

"Neither was listening to Ily," Staffa countered.
Chrysla shot him a reproving glare.

Sinklar bristled, propping his hands on hips. "What
do you want from us, Lord Commander? We're here
to see if we can make a deal that saves bloodshed."

Staffa clasped his hands behind his back, considering. "I want an end to the fighting—throughout Free
Space. I need people willing to cooperate in keeping
the peace and searching for an answer to the threat
of extinction."

"In other words," Anatolia suggested, "you want
allies?"

"Exactly." Staffa reached out. "Will you join me,
Sinklar? I need your help now. I need your brilliance."

"And the Seddi?" Sinklar asked.

"Make your own peace with Kaylla—as I have made mine."

Sinklar still hesitated. "I and my people can withdraw? No strings? You're willing to place any articles we agree on in writing?"

Staffa nodded. "It's no longer a matter of power plays or games. We either find the answer—or we all die. My gamble is that you're bright enough to understand the dilemma when you review the data."

Sinklar cautiously took his hand, a tingle sparked by that firm grip.

* * *

Mac sat in the observation blister on *Gyton*'s port side. He slouched with one boot propped on the spectrometer. The curve of Rega cut across one corner of his view. Beyond, the stars were shimmering in a frost-swirl pattern, some fuzzy as their light bent through the Forbidden Borders.

Here he'd found her, standing staring out with a lonesome lost look on her face. Here he'd realized just how much he loved her, and they'd touched, the effect so electric.

The very thought of her left something inside aching and empty. Three long days had passed now since she'd walked off into the guts of *Chrysla* with Staffa. In that time, Mac had pitched headlong into the impossible task of trying to orchestrate the Empire. Dion had been indispensable, maintaining order, running the utilities to keep power, water, sewer, and food services going. What was left of the "Regular" army had melted away or fallen in to keep the government functioning.

Mac didn't look up as Sinklar entered. For a moment, they both remained silent.

"How'd the meeting with Rysta go?" Mac asked.

Sinklar settled on the bench. "She's a bright woman, but more importantly, she accepted the job. She's going to take over patrolling to make sure no one fools with the shipping."

"She's half pirate at heart. She'll be good at that."

Silence.

Sinklar slapped his leg. "What's wrong, Mac?"

"Nothing."

"Aren't the roles reversed? You're hurting. Talk to her."

Mac gave his friend a disgusted look. "Leave it alone."

Sinklar shook his head. "Can't. She's quite a lady. I'm still shaken every time I see her. Arta keeps bubbling up in my memory, you know, seeing her looking crazy with Gretta. . . ."

"They find Ily yet?"

"No. She's gone, Mac. Shipped out in Skyla's yacht. Companion targeting picked her up, of course, but her ship had a friendly signature, a code the Companion targeting uses to keep from blasting good guys in the heat of combat. *Slap* and *Jinx Mistress* are out trying to track her, but I guess that yacht's got a lot of tricks in it."

"Skyla all right?"

Sinklar sighed. "That's mostly over my head. Of all people, Chrysla is working with her. Doing something she calls double-bind reconditioning. I guess it was Arta who really got to Skyla, really messed her up, so Chrysla is countering that. She's a psychologist, did you know?"

"I know."

Sinklar stared thoughtfully out at the stars. "The quanta *are* laughing."

"What did Staffa decide to do? Is he going to keep them both?"

"So much bitterness in your voice. I don't know, Mac. That's up to the three of them to work out."

Mac hung his head. "I never knew I could come to love like I've come to love her. It's not just that magnetism, it's who she is. Delicate and brave, suffering and triumphant. She beat hell, Sink. I can't stand the thought of living without her." *Or of living close to her when she's another man's wife—your father's wife!*

"Talk to her, Mac."

"Not now. She's got enough to worry about." *Stop tormenting me, Sink.* He knotted a fist, watching the tendons bunch and ripple. "After all she's been through, I can't inflict myself on her." He shot a weary glance at Sinklar. "She's . . . your mother, for God's sake."

"Yeah. So?"

Silence.

"You're sure Staffa's your father?"

"Yes. Anatolia ran the test. Not only that, but the data Buchman saved proved it. Proved all of it."

Mac dropped his head into his hands. "I must look like a real fool."

Sinklar stepped over, clutching his hand. "No, pal. She's real different from Arta."

"Is that why you're here? To make me miserable?"

Sinklar let go of Mac's hand and walked up to stare out at the stars. "What if I told you we had a chance?"

"A chance at what?"

"Saving this." He waved an arm. "All of this. All those people down there." A pause. "Remember that time on the ridge outside of Makarta? I meant what I said. We're going to clean it all up—all of us. We're not licked yet."

"Got a miracle in your pocket again?"

"Targa."

"That a battle cry or a planet?"

"Both. Seems there's a computer on Targa. A big computer, all chock-full of fascinating programs. I talked to Kaylla Dawn about it."

"You? Talking to a Seddi?"

"She's not just a Seddi. She leaves you . . . well, believing she's seen it all—and knows more about life than you ever will. I think, Mac, that I can work with her."

"So you're going back to Targa?"

"Yes." Sinklar's eyes lost focus. "Back to Makarta, Mac."

Going back to face your ghosts? Is that it?

Sinklar turned. "I want you to come with us."

"Us?"

"Staffa and me."

Mac smiled while his heart ached. "Can't, Sink. This is one you'll have to do on your own."

"Why? What are you going to do?"

Mac cocked his head, staring out at the stars. "You say Ily's still out there? Well, maybe I'll load up and go find her. Can you get me a ship?"

"Which one do you want?"

Mac glanced around. "What's wrong with this one?"

Sinklar hesitated. "You're sure about this?"

Mac stared at the stars. *Can't you see? Going with you—being around him . . . and her—would be like twisting a rusty knife in the wound, pal.* "Got excitement bred into my bones, Sink. You don't need an able lieutenant anymore. You've got a family to figure out. Me, I'm going to go see my dad again, and then I think I'll go see what Free Space is all about." He frowned. "I never liked that bitch anyway. If I can run her down—tag Fera at the same time, I can kill two devils at once."

"Kill two devils . . . I think I understand. You've got it, Mac." Sinklar gave him a knowing smile and reached out, shaking his hand. "Take care, Mac."

"You, too."

After Sinklar had left, Mac continued to sit, his boot propped on the spectrometer, eyes on the distant stars, the memory of an amber-eyed woman filling his vision.

DAW

Kathleen M. O'Neal

POWERS OF LIGHT

☐ **AN ABYSS OF LIGHT: Book 1**   UE2418—$4.95

The Gamant people believed they were blessed with the gift of a direct gateway to God and the angels. But were these beings who they claimed—or were the Gamants merely human pawns in an interdimensional struggle between alien powers?

☐ **TREASURE OF LIGHT: Book 2**   UE2455—$4.95

As war escalates between the alien Magistrates and the human rebels, will the fulfillment of an ancient prophecy bring their universe to an end?

☐ **REDEMPTION OF LIGHT: Book 3**   UE2470—$4.99

The concluding volume of this epic science fiction trilogy by the bestselling author of *People of the fire*. Will anyone be the victor when human rebels and alien Magistrates are caught up in the final stages of a war far older than either race?

DAW

Charles Ingrid

☐ **RADIUS OF DOUBT**   UE2491—$4.99

THE MARKED MAN SERIES

In a devastated America, can the Lord Protector of a mutating human race find a way to preserve the future of the species?

☐ **THE MARKED MAN**   UE2396—$3.95
☐ **THE LAST RECALL**   UE2460—$3.95

THE SAND WARS

☐ **SOLAR KILL: Book 1**   UE2391—$3.95
He was the last Dominion Knight and he would challenge a star empire to gain his revenge!

☐ **LASERTOWN BLUES: Book 2**   UE2393—$3.95
He'd won a place in the Emperor's Guard but could he hunt down the traitor who'd betrayed his Knights to an alien foe?

☐ **CELESTIAL HIT LIST: Book 3**   UE2394—$3.95
Death stalked the Dominion Knight from the Emperor's Palace to a world on the brink of its prophesied age of destruction. . . .

☐ **ALIEN SALUTE: Book 4**   UE2329—$3.95
As the Dominion and the Thrakian empires mobilize for all-out war, can Jack Storm find the means to defeat the ancient enemies of man?

☐ **RETURN FIRE: Book 5**   UE2363—$3.95
Was someone again betraying the human worlds to the enemy—and would Jack Storm become pawn or player in these games of death?

☐ **CHALLENGE MET: Book 6**   UE2436—$3.95
In this concluding volume, Jack Storm embarks on a dangerous mission which will lead to a final confrontation with the Ash-farel.

DAW

C.S. Friedman

☐ **BLACK SUN RISING**   Hardcover Edition: UE2485—$18.95

Twelve centuries after being stranded on the planet Erna, humans have achieved an uneasy stalemate with the *fae*, a terrifying natural force with the power to prey upon people's minds. Now, as the hordes of the dark *fae* multiply, four people—Priest, Adept, Apprentice, and Sorcerer—are about to be drawn inexorably together for a mission that will force them to confront an evil beyond imagining.

☐ **IN CONQUEST BORN**   UE2198—$3.95

Braxi and Azea—two super-races fighting an endless war. The Braxaná—created to become the ultimate warriors. The Azeans, raised to master the powers of the mind, using telepathy to penetrate where mere weapons cannot. Now the final phase of their war is approaching, spearheaded by two opposing generals, lifetime enemies—and whole worlds will be set ablaze by the force of their hatred!

☐ **THE MADNESS SEASON**   UE2444—$4.95

For 300 years, the alien Tyr had ruled Earth, imprisoning the true individualists, the geniuses, in dome colonies on poisonous worlds, forcing them to work on projects which the Tyr hoped would reveal all of humankind's secrets. But Daetrin's secret was one no one had ever uncovered. Taken into custody by the Tyr, he would have to confront the truth about himself at last—and if he failed, all humans would pay the price. . . .

DAW

NEW DIMENSIONS IN SCIENCE FICTION

Kris Jensen
☐ **FREEMASTER (Book 1)**   UE2404—$3.95
The Terran Union had sent Sarah Anders to Ardel to establish a trade agreement for materials vital to offworlders, but of little value to the low-tech Ardellans. But other, more ruthless humans were about to stake their claim with the aid of forbidden technology and threats of destruction. The Ardellans had defenses of their own, based on powers of the mind, and only a human such as Sarah could begin to understand them. For she, too, had mind talents locked within her—and the Free-Masters of Ardel just might provide the key to releasing them.

☐ **MENTOR (Book 2)**   UE2464—$4.50
Jeryl, Mentor of Clan Alu, sought to save the Ardellan Clans which, decimated by plague, were slowly fading away. But even as Jeryl set out on his quest, other Clans sought a different solution to their troubles, ready to call upon long-forbidden powers to drive the hated Terrans off Ardel.

Kate Elliott
☐ **JARAN**   UE2513—$4.99
Here is the poignant and powerful story of a young woman's coming of age on an alien world, a woman who is both player and pawn in an interstellar game of intrigue and politics, where the prize to be gained may be freedom for humankind from long-standing domination by their alien conquerors. But perhaps even more than this, it is the tale of her increasing involvement with the leader of a nomadic people, a people who must either learn to adapt to the incursions of more advanced civilizations—or, by remaining rooted in their own traditions, face inevitable extinction.
